WRIGHT MORRIS:

A Reader

WRIGHT MORRIS:

A Reader

Introduction by Granville Hicks

EQUINOX BOOKS / PUBLISHED BY AVON

AVON BOOKS
A division of
The Hearst Corporation
959 Eighth Avenue
New York, New York 10019

First Equinox Printing, March, 1974.

EQUINOX TRADEMARK REG. U.S. PAT. OFF. AND IN
OTHER COUNTRIES
MARCA REGISTRADA, HECHO EN U.S.A.

Printed in the U.S.A.

WRIGHT MORRIS:

A Reader

Contents

Contents

PART III
IN THE SUBURBS

PART IV
AND ELSEWHERE

Introduction

THOSE of us who strongly admire the work of Wright Morris—a not altogether inconsiderable number of not altogether inconsiderable people—are always wondering why everybody doesn't see his writings as we see them, as one of the most imposing edifices on the contemporary literary horizon. We, who look forward to each book of his as it is announced, and talk about it with excitement when it appears, cannot understand why so many pulses remain calm. Morris has been read, has been praised, has been honored. When anyone sets out to list the best living novelists, his name is usually mentioned. But not always, not automatically, as it ought to be. There is a new aristocracy of men and women of letters—admired by the discriminating and read by the many and therefore, in this affluent age, freed from economic pressures and limitations. That Morris is not yet among them indicates that both he and the reading public are getting less than they deserve.

Morris has written nineteen books: three excursions with camera and typewriter, two collections of essays, fourteen novels. What the French would call *un oeuvre*. We have here the results of more than twenty-five years of disciplined productivity, to be read and enjoyed and meditated upon. As the books appeared, critics were sometimes puzzled because each was different from what had gone before it. This variety is one of his great qualities, and yet I can say, as one who has read them all, that all his books hang together. And it is as a whole that we should look at his books at this time.

Places

In 1955, in *Twentieth Century Authors*, Morris wrote: "I was born in Central City, Nebraska, and the first ten years of my life were spent in the whistle stops along the Platte Valley to the West. The books I have written, and hope to write, are apt to bear, on close examination, the stamp of an object made on the plains."

The years in the whistle stops, 1910–1919, were followed by five years in Omaha and then three in Chicago. But there were summers spent on farms in Nebraska and Texas and cross-country trips with his father. In 1930 Morris entered Pomona College, which he left after three years for a *Wanderjahre* in Europe. (He had been on his own economically for quite a while by then.) From 1938 to 1958 he lived mostly in the East, although he spent some time in Mexico and made several continental crossings. In the past decade he has traveled a good bit in Europe, but his base has been on the West Coast.

In his most recent book, *God's Country and My People*, which is one of the three containing photographs as well as text, we find on the first page a photograph of an abandoned house—just a door and a window on the first floor and another window under the eaves. The text on the facing page reads: "Is it a house or an ark? A scud seems to blow on the sea of grass and the land falls away like the sea from a swell. On the receding horizon waves of plain break like a surf. The colors run where the grain stirs, or bleed where the blacktop smokes like an oil slick, or evaporate into a shimmering blur of heat and light. The color scheme is sun-dried denim and kiln-dried earth. Like the sea there is no shade. There is no place to hide. A mindless wind fills the void, but nobody hears it: it's the thunderclap of silence that wakes the sleeper. The mast of a dead tree, its spar shattered, tilts to the leeward its tattered rigging; in the winter it is locked in a sea of dry ice. The man who built the house had a whaleman's eyes in a plainsman's face. He brought the clapboards in by ox cart over the rolling cattle trail up from Salinas. A windy crossing. Little wonder this house resembles an ark. The porch is gone from the front, shingles from the roof, and the last tenants went thataway with the Okies—except for those who stand, immaterial, at the windows, or move about with the creak of hinges. The land has tired of the house but it will not soon be free of the inhabitants."

In the first chapter of *Ceremony in Lone Tree* we read: "At a child's level in the pane there is a flaw that is round, like an eye in the glass. An eye to that eye, a scud seems to blow on a sea of grass. Waves of plain seem to roll up, then break like a surf. Is it a flaw in the eye, or in the window, that transforms a dry place into a wet one? Above it towers a sky, like the sky at sea, a wind blows like the wind at sea, and like the sea it has no shade: there is no place to hide."

The comparison of the plains with the sea is not merely a vivid figure of speech; it is one of Morris's ways of telling us what the plains mean to him. They mean, that is, all that the sea meant to Melville or to Conrad—a symbol, if you will, of the universe.

Of the three picture books, one, *The Home Place*, is entirely devoted to the plains, and the plains are prominent in the other two. The plains figure indirectly in the first two novels, *My Uncle Dudley* and *The Man Who Was There*, and directly in *The World in the Attic* and *The Works of Love*. Much of what happens in Mexico in *The Field of Vision* grows out of what has already happened on the plains, and in *Ceremony in Lone Tree* various characters from the earlier book are brought together in Nebraska.

Although Morris has emphasized the importance of the plains in the shaping of his career as a writer, he has lived in other places and written about other places. Two suburban novels, *Man and Boy* and *The Deep Sleep*, are laid near Philadelphia. There are the two novels set in Europe, *What a Way to Go* and *Cause for Wonder*. The action in *The Huge Season* takes place on the West Coast and the East and in Paris. *Love Among the Cannibals* moves from Los Angeles to Acapulco.

Morris's debt to the plains is great. "I am not a regional writer," he said in 1955, "but the characteristics of this region have conditioned what I see, what I look for, and what I find in the world to write about. So I believe in shearing off, in working and in traveling light. I like a minimum of words arranged for a maximum effect. . . . As the writer of the South inclines toward the baroque, and strives for the symbolic ornamental cluster, the writer on the plains is powerfully inclined to sheer the ornament off. If he does not, it is no longer an ornament." What he learned on the plains, especially his feeling for the importance of place, has served him well wherever he found himself.

People

There are no villains in Morris's work. Unlike certain of his contemporaries, he finds it no easier to believe in absolute evil than in absolute good, and he has little use for the doctrine of original sin, even as a metaphor. His people are always mixtures of traits that may seem either good or bad according to the circumstances in which one encounters them. In *One Day*, when she is depressed, Chickpea has a spell of going to inferior movies. "An indescribably bad movie, with the horses shyly nuzzling one another, what was it but the waxworks museum of life *brought* to life? All crazy. All indescribably marvelous. There it all was, the loony bin of life, so desperately sad, so intolerably touching, that her eyes filmed over. . . ." The mind of another character in *One Day* moves in the same way: "Except among those creatures referred to as beasts it seemed to Cowie that life showed two eternal aspects, an infinite capacity for corruption, a finite capacity for perfection. For this libretto love provided the music, some good, some bad." Morris finds people frequently pathetic, often terribly exasperating, and endlessly fascinating.

There are no villains and no heroes of the romantic sort, but Morris does have heroes of his own variety. That is, there are characters who are set apart from the mass of men by virtue of special qualities. We find examples in his first novel, *My Uncle Dudley*, and in his most recent, *In Orbit*. The distinguishing characteristic of a Morris hero is audacity; he is a man who refuses to accept the limitations by which most men are held prisoner. Dudley is no model citizen; on the contrary, he is, when occasion requires, an unscrupulous con man. But he has a boldness that attracts other men to him, and he gets his little bunch of misfit refugees two-thirds of the way across the continent. As Morris sees it, audacity reveals itself in appropriate gestures, and the book ends with a foolish but magnificent gesture on Dudley's part.

In the recent novel, Jubal Gainer, a high school dropout,

in the course of a day engages in a fist fight, steals a motor-cycle, is accused of rape (of which he is at least guilty in intention), beats one man, and stabs another. Although Jubal is unaware of it, each violent act he performs is a symbolic gesture. He is a kind of natural force, like the tornado that simultaneously visits the town. Some of the more thoughtful of the townspeople who are involved in Jubal's escapades feel the significance of his deeds. One is Hodler, editor of the local newspaper: "Hodler is a sober man, but for this boy on the loose, free to indulge in his whims, he feels a twinge of envy. There is something to be said for impulsive behavior, although Hodler is perhaps not the man to say it. Visiting spacemen are free to act in a way he is not." Later, when Jubal has vanished, Hodler listens to the unhelpful replies that bystanders give to the sheriff. "Did they all dream of being a man on the loose? Envied by inhibited, red-blooded men, pursued by comical galoots like the Sheriff. He went that-a-way. With the thoughts, fantasies, and envious good wishes of them all."

In *The Huge Season* we have an apparently more conven-tional hero, Charles Lawrence, who tries to make the auda-cious gesture a way of life. He makes such an impression on his associates that, more than twenty years after his death, his example is the central fact in their lives.

One of the most interesting specimens is Gordon Boyd, the "successful failure" of *The Field of Vision* and *Cere-mony in Lone Tree*. The former occupies a key position in the Morris canon, for it examines several recurrent themes: the relativity of all knowledge, nostalgia and the general problem of the past, the possibilities of human transforma-tion, and the role of heroism. As a boy and young man, Boyd made a series of gestures that evoked the astonished admiration of his companion, Walter McKee: he tried to walk on the water, made off with the pocket of a famous baseball player, and kissed McKee's girl, Lois Scanlon. Although he has never forgotten that there was something special about Boyd, McKee knows that, by conventional standards, he has been a success and Boyd a failure. When they meet by accident in Mexico City and, with their various friends and relations, attend a bullfight, Boyd contrives a gesture, though a ridiculous one. He also lures McKee's grandson, who is named for him, into making a gesture that separates him from his grandparents.

At the end of *The Field of Vision* Boyd seems to have won a victory of sorts, but in *Ceremony in Lone Tree* the situation is not so clear. After his encounter with the McKees, we learn, Boyd went to Acapulco in a deep depression. Unaccountably, as it seems to him, he decides to accept McKee's invitation to attend a family reunion. Near Las Vegas, on the eve of an atom bomb test, he picks up a young woman with a brassy manner, considerable courage, and some wisdom, whom he takes with him to Lone Tree. He talks to her about the McKees, telling her that Lois is the only real woman in his life. We now learn that Lois engaged herself to McKee so soon after Boyd kissed her because she was afraid of being roused as Boyd had roused her. Although she has managed to seem as much "on the ice side" as her husband, her passions have been inhibited but not destroyed. McKee remains as stolid as ever, but, though he is willing to bear witness to Boyd's past heroism, he does not want him in his present. Boyd, "a completely self-unmade man," has at last come to terms with his past; what he will do with the present is another matter.

If certain of Morris's characters are audaciously active, others are disturbingly passive, none more so than Will Brady in *The Works of Love*. Morris defines him in negative terms: "In time he grew to be a man who neither smoked, drank, gambled, nor swore. A man who headed no cause, fought in no wars, and passed his life unaware of the great public issues—it might be asked: why trouble with such a man at all? What is there left to say of a man with so much of his life left out? Well, there are women for one thing—men of such caliber leave a lot up to the women— but in the long run Will Jennings Brady is there by himself."

Brady is a man alone, not always in the flesh but always in the spirit. He establishes a profitable egg business, but money gives him little pleasure. He builds expensive houses, but doesn't know how to live in them. There are women in his life, but they do not stay there long. He has a son, or a boy who passes as his son, and loves him dearly but cannot come close to him. "Why are you so different?" the boy asks him, and he can't answer. In time his life dwindles away until his only human contacts are with his landlady, waitresses in the cheap restaurants in which he eats, and other casual acquaintances who will listen to the tales he makes up about his son.

Morris dedicated the book to his friend Loren Eiseley and "to the memory of Sherwood Anderson, pioneer in the works of love." Anderson would have understood Will Brady, a misfit like so many of his own characters, but because of his virtues not his shortcomings. One of his women observes that he knows how to give, "but what he didn't know was how to receive anything." He is a giving man in a getting society, and the most suitable role that society can offer him is that of department store Santa Claus.

It is a moving book and nowhere more moving than in the pathos of the ending. Brady periodically writes a post-card to his son, but then he doesn't mail it, because he wants to wait until he has moved into less disreputable quarters.

Such a card is found on his body when it is drawn out of a stinking Chicago canal:

DEAR SON—

Have moved. Have nice little place of our own now, two-plate gas. Warm sun in windows every morning, nice view of park. Plan to get new Console radio soon now, let you pick it out. Plan to pick up car so we can drive out in country, get out in air. Turning over in my mind plan to send you to Harvard, send you to Yale. Saw robin in park this morning. Saw him catch worm.

If some of Morris's men are passive, several of his women are active enough to take your breath away. The earliest appearance of the species was in a short story called "The Ram in the Thicket," published in *Harper's Bazaar* in 1948. In 1951 the story grew into a short novel, *Man and Boy*. The first part covers the same ground as the story: the rising of Mr. Ormsby, the emergence of Mrs. Ormsby, and their preparations for a trip to Brooklyn, where she is to christen a ship named after their son, Virgil Ormsby, killed at Guadalcanal. In the second part, devoted to the trip, Mrs. Ormsby talks with a young soldier, Private Lipido, and the boy's questions and comments illuminate the relationship of the Ormsbys one to another and the relationship of each to the son. In the end, after winning a skirmish with the Navy, Mrs. Ormsby grandly performs her duty.

In the short story Mrs. Ormsby is a disagreeable character, not only domineering but self-indulgent, not merely bossing Ormsby but enslaving him. This effect is somewhat softened in the novel, and as the story proceeds we are forced to recognize her virtues, as is Private Lipido, at first a scoffer. It is a funny book, with page after page of amusing dialogue, but the intent, of course, is serious. When David Madden asked him about the position of women in his work, Morris replied: "Betrayed by man (deprived of him, that is), woman is taking her abiding revenge on him—unconscious in such figures as Mrs. Ormsby and Mrs. Porter, where she inherits, by default, the world man should be running. Since only Man will deeply gratify her, the Vote and the Station Wagon leave something to be desired. One either sees this, or one doesn't. As of now both men and women are tragically duped: the Victor has no way of digesting the spoils."

This thesis has been set forth by D. H. Lawrence and Sherwood Anderson, both writers whose work Morris admires. The novels, however, are not intended to illustrate the thesis; they simply take literary advantage of a situation that exists. Mrs. Porter in *The Deep Sleep* is in essentials like Mrs. Ormsby, though superficially different. Mrs. Porter is married to a judge, and they have an ample house on the Main Line. The story occupies something less than twenty-four hours the day after Judge Porter's death. The Porters' daughter—their only living child, for a son died in the war—has come home with her husband, Paul Webb, an artist. The judge's mother, in her ninety-ninth year, is still an occupant of the house. The only other important character—and he is very important as a key to all the others—is Parsons, the Porters' handyman and the judge's confidant. The daughter, Katherine, realizes that neither she nor her father has been able to live in the house: "They had worked out a way of doing their living somewhere else." Parsons, who tells Webb that Mrs. Porter is a woman of principle and has no human failings, is aware of and sympathetic to the judge's occasional exasperation and frequent escapes. To Webb his mother-in-law is a holy terror and cause for wonder, but, as Private Lipido in *Man and Boy* ended by cheering for Mrs. Ormsby, so Webb pays a final tribute to Mrs. Porter. "Webb's act," Morris wrote to Madden, "reflects his respect for the forces that both salvage human life and destroy it: the pitiless compulsion that testifies, in its appalling way, to the spirit's devious ways of survival."

When, in *The Field of Vision,* Gordon Boyd encounters McKee in Mexico City and asks him how he is, he is told, "Mrs. McKee and me couldn't be happier." The appalling thing is that, most of the time, McKee believes it. And it seems altogether probable that Mr. Ormsby and Judge Porter would make the same affirmation. Since, as we have seen, Lois Scanlon married McKee because she did not want passion in her life, it scarcely seems fair that she should blame him for being dull and matter-of-fact, but she does, and she punishes him. Her revenge is less unconscious than Mrs. Ormsby's and Mrs. Porter's, for she has some idea what it is she has missed.

There are women in Morris's work who are not at all like Lois McKee. The first example, perhaps, is Lou Baker in *The Huge Season*—"Montana born *aus* Bryn Mawr chick," who has "the ring of gold in an age of brass"—but the best specimen is the girl in *Love Among the Cannibals* who is known as "the Greek." The narrator of the story is Earl Horter, who writes words for the popular songs for which Irvin K. Macgregor, Mac, provides the music. Horter has to work hard to get the phony touch that he knows is essential to success in the business; to Mac it comes natural.

In Hollywood to work on a movie, they spend most of the time on the beach, and it is there that Mac meets Billie Harcum, a would-be singer from the South. Horter sees Eva Baum at a party, and immediately falls for her. In the place that probably has the highest concentration of phonies in the world, she is perfectly genuine. Instead of running away from passion, as Mrs. Ormsby, Mrs. Porter, and Mrs. McKee do, she welcomes it. Unlike Billie Harcum, who has a price and collects it, the Greek gives herself freely. Perhaps because she nearly died in childbirth when she was fifteen, she lives altogether in the present. ("This life I have is a gift," she tells Horter. "Why should I hoard it?") She makes no pledge of fidelity and demands none. When she leaves Horter, as inevitably she does, he believes that he will see her again, but he knows that he has and can have no hold upon her.

Since he created the Greek, Morris has portrayed a number of young women who might be regarded as daughters of Eva. In *Ceremony in Lone Tree* Etoile Momeyer, niece of Lois Scanlon McKee, has her aunt's beauty and none of her inhibitions: she wants her cousin Calvin and gets him. The girl Boyd picks up and calls Daughter is a more sophisticated example of the species. Seventeen-year-old Cynthia in *What a Way to Go* represents a variety of goddesses to a variety of men, but she chooses middle-aged Professor Soby as the man most likely to help her discover what she really is. The most appealing of the seekers for the new freedom is Chickpea in *One Day*. Almost as young and just as eager for life as Cynthia and Etoile, she is exposed to more kinds of experience than they are, for she belongs to the generation that has ideas about changing the world.

In a discussion of *One Day* contributed to Thomas Mc-Cormack's *Afterwords*, Morris writes: "The characters in my novels—now that I can appraise them after more than twenty years of screening—prove to emerge from abiding pre-occupations. Archetypal figures (reasonably clear in a montage of fourteen novels) have the final say as to *who* will appear as a character in my fiction. They may bear a close resemblance to an actual person (as such persons resemble archetypal humors) or they may be assembled, whole cloth, from my imaginings and the needs of the novel. *One Day* has both. Harold Cowie, for example, is a contemporary mask on a personality I consider unchanging—the decent, sympathetic, reflective dropout who does not have (or does not *choose* to have) what it takes to make the scene. He is both the square and the square peg, sympathetic to his own predictable failure. He keeps in touch with life, and what he values, through children, eccentrics, dogs and cats. He relates to Will Brady in *The Works of Love* and to Peter Foley in *The Huge Season*. He receives something of a trial run as William Bryan Jennings in *Ceremony in Lone Tree*. But something still remained to be said, and in *One Day* he says it."

We know some of the other archetypes: the man of audacity, such as Uncle Dudley, Charles Lawrence, and Gordon Boyd; the domineering wife and mother, Mrs. Ormsby and Mrs. Porter; the young woman who scoffs at conventions, such as the Greek, Etoile, and Chickpea; the young men whose rebellion takes criminal forms—Lee Roy Momeyer, Charlie Munger, Jubal Gainer, and in a sense Lee Oswald. All the characters in a particular category are sufficiently alike so that we can define what Morris calls his "abiding preoccupations," but the differences are equally important. Peter Foley may resemble Will Brady, but in many ways he is more like Professor Soby in *What a Way to Go* and Warren Howe in *Cause for Wonder*. Gordon Boyd and Charles Lawrence have more differences than resemblances. Etoile has a lot to learn before she can measure up to the Greek.

"If I judge myself a novelist," Morris says in the essay already mentioned, "if I accept it as a calling, if I might, like James, refer to it privately as 'my dear genius,' it is because my talent, such as it is, finds its realization in the creation of *characters*." Although his talent is many-sided, as we shall see, we cannot disagree with him about his primary virtue. No talent is more important for a novelist. No matter how his characters may be categorized, they are never predictable, and that is why they are so much like the people we know.

Things

In the late Thirties and early Forties, Morris spent much of his time in photography. In *Twentieth Century Authors* he said: "Objects, what few there are on the plains, acquire a dense symbolical significance, and certain simple artifacts have a functional and classic purity. The windmill, the single plow, the grain elevator, the receding horizon, are both signs and symbols at the same time. They speak for themselves. The man who loves these things, whether he knows it or not, is a photographer. Such books as *The Inhabitants* and *The Home Place* grew out of the plains just as I did, and they are experimental in the way I am an experiment." The photographs in a third collection, *God's Country and My People*, were taken at the same time as the others, but the text was written in 1968, the year in which the book appeared.

A word should be said about these books with pictures. *The Inhabitants*, though it contains some superb photographs, is rather scattered in effect. *The Home Place*, better unified, makes a stronger impression. The photographs show some of the artifacts that had a part in the author's life as a boy, and the text gives an account, partly fact and partly fiction, of the author's return as a young man. In *God's Country and My People* most of the photographs again reflect the plains, and the text is frankly autobiographical and reflective. All three books frequently remind the reader of places, people, and ideas that appear in the novels.

As epigraph for *The Inhabitants*, Morris has a fine passage by Thoreau: "What of architectural beauty I now see, I know has gradually grown from within outward, out of the necessities and character of the indweller, who is the only builder—out of some unconscious truthfulness and nobleness, without ever a thought for the appearance, and whatever additional beauty of this kind is destined to be produced will be preceded by a like unconscious beauty of life. . . . It is the life of the inhabitants whose shells they are."

Because people may be known by the shells they have formed, Morris regards artifacts as means of revelation. In his first novel, for instance, *My Uncle Dudley*, he describes with affection the old Marmon in which the adventure took place. It is no wonder that he once wrote an article called "The Cars in My Life," for these particular artifacts have meant much to him. Cars figure in many novels: Lawrence's Bugatti in *The Huge Season*, Will Brady's Overland roadster, the jazzy number that disintegrates on the beach at Acapulco in *Love Among the Cannibals*, "the low-cut foreign-type car" in which Larkspur made her newsworthy continental crossing.

The part that things play in Morris's novels is almost incalculable: the contents of the boys' rooms in *The Huge Season*, the view from the Lone Tree Hotel in *Ceremony*, the motorcycles outside the One-Stop Diner in *In Orbit*. Yet there are never the tedious catalogs one so often finds in the novels and tales of John O'Hara. Morris never calls attention to an artifact simply because it happens to be occupying space; it must have done something to his imagination.

In a lecture that he delivered at Amherst College in 1958 Morris spoke of a specific artifact, Babe Ruth's Pocket. (In *The Field of Vision* it belonged to Ty Cobb, but it was Babe Ruth's to begin with.) "It is this pocket," he said, "that gives birth to the character of Boyd rather than the character producing the pocket." What we need to notice here is the relationship between the artifact and the imagination—Morris's imagination at any rate. Things are important when they speak for men.

Shapes

In *The Territory Ahead* Morris has written: "The history of fiction, its pursuit of that chimera we describe as reality, is a series of imaginative triumphs made possible through technique." None of his contemporaries has a more brilliant record of technical experimentation than Morris. His innovations are not showy, nor does he waste much time talking about them. He is not interested in experiment for its own sake; he is simply trying to find the right way of getting at reality. Technique is not only a way of expression but also a means of discovery.

Morris's first novel, *My Uncle Dudley*, is a straightforward first-person narrative, the narrator being a participant in the action but not the central figure. Even here, however, the telling of the story from the Kid's point of view shows a good deal of technical sophistication. The second novel, *The Man Who Was There*, attempts a more difficult problem, for the man of the title isn't there; he is missing in action in the Pacific. Agee Ward is given to us by the reports of certain individuals who were influenced by him and through descriptions of a series of photographs of him and of artifacts associated with him. The persons who bear witness are humble souls, but they make it clear that Agee Ward was there and therefore, in a significant way, still is.

With *Man and Boy* Morris introduced two narrative methods that he has used, with variations, a number of times. In the first place, the action is concentrated into a short space of time, a matter of hours. This is also true of *The Deep Sleep, The Field of Vision, Ceremony in Lone*

Tree, One Day, and *In Orbit*. In the second place, the story is told from several specified points of view, each chapter bearing the name of the person through whose eyes we are looking. The general method is used in *The Deep Sleep, The Field of Vision, Ceremony in Lone Tree*, and *One Day*.

The Field of Vision is the most tightly woven of all Morris's novels. The action takes place in the two hours or so occupied by a bullfight. During most of this time the seven characters are sitting together on the shady side of the ring, and the sections are presented from the points of view of five of the seven. Each of the five is living in his own world, and no two, as Morris specifies, see the same bullfight. Indeed, there are two persons—Paula Kahler and Scanlon—who don't see the bullfight at all. The reader not only has to try to make out what is going on in the present; he has to reconstruct the strange relationship of Boyd and the McKees, the mysterious past of Dr. Lehmann and Paula, and the mythic past of Scanlon.

Brilliant as the construction of *The Field of Vision* is, *The Huge Season* is an even better example of Morris's skill in the solution of problems of form. Morris set out to contrast a group of persons as they were in the late Twenties and as they were in the early Fifties and also to contrast the two periods. The problem, of course, was time, and, although Morris could probably have solved it by the use of flashbacks, at which he is adept, he found a better way, a way calculated to give life to both parts of the story and emphasis to the contrast. There are two narratives in alternating chapters, one with "The Captivity" as its running title and the other with "Peter Foley." The former, written in the first person, is Foley's account of what happened to him and his friends in college. The latter tells in the third person about Foley's experiences on May 5, 1952, when he is moved to seek out some of these former comrades. Each story is wonderfully dramatic, and they perfectly balance and support one another.

After succeeding so well with the tight construction of these two novels, Morris deliberately relaxed his hold in order to get a different sort of effect. Like *My Uncle Dudley*, *Love Among the Cannibals* is told in the first person, and its movement is largely shaped by external events. *Ceremony in Lone Tree*, though it follows the same pattern as *The Field of Vision*, to which it is a sequel, is not so tautly held and has an air, deceptive of course, of improvisation. *What a Way to Go* is pleasantly playful in both content and form. *Cause for Wonder*, returning to the problem of past and present, resembles *The Huge Season* in form. *One Day* is given a firm structure by the limited period of time imposed on the action, but it is one of the most varied of Morris's novels and the longest. *In Orbit*, on the other hand, is the shortest, but in its free-swinging way it covers a lot of ground. To analyze it is to recognize that under the appearance of artlessness lies an art that has matured through a quarter of a century.

Words

"I like a minimum of words arranged for a maximum effect," Morris has said. From the beginning he has written in the vernacular; seldom does one find in his novels a word that cannot be heard in the day-to-day speech of moderately well-educated Americans. The rhythms of his prose, moreover, are basically the rhythms of ordinary talk. "When it was cold we walked around," *My Uncle Dudley* begins. "When it was morning the pigeons came and looked but when nothing happened walked away. When it was warm we sat in the sun."

This is the Kid speaking, since he tells the story, and of

course he talks as a sixteen year old would. But *In Orbit,*
written twenty-five years later and in the third person, has
the same tone: "This boy comes riding with his arms high
and wide, his head dipped low, his ass light in the saddle, as
if about to be shot into orbit from a forked sling. He wears
a white crash helmet, a plastic visor of the color they tint
car windshields, half-boots with stirrup heels, a black horse-
hide jacket with zippers on the pockets and tassels on the
zippers, Levi's so tight in the crotch the zipper on the fly is
often snagged with hair. Wind puffs his sleeves, plucks the
strings of his arms, fills the back of his jacket like a wine-
skin, ripples the soot-smeared portrait of J. S. Bach on his
chest. His face is black as the bottom-side of a stove lid,
except for his nose, which is pewter-colored. He has the
sniffles, and often gives it a buff with his sleeve. He is like a
diver just before he hits the water, he is like a Moslem
prayer-borne toward Mecca, he is like a cowpoke hanging
to the steer's horns, like a high school dropout fleeing the
draft. If he resembles this the least it is understandable: it is
what he is."

This flexible, conversational, amusing, unpretentious
style, which is in fact extremely artful, can serve many
purposes. Here, for example, is a serious statement of the
philosophy underlying *The Field of Vision:* ". . . gathered
at a bullfight. The sanded navel of the world. Gazing at this
fleshy button each man had the eyes to see only himself.
This crisp sabbath afternoon forty thousand pairs of eyes
would gaze down on forty thousand separate bullfights,
seeing it all very clearly, missing only the one that was said
to take place. Forty thousand latent heroes, as many gorings, so many artful dodges it beggared description, two
hundred thousand bulls, horses, mules and monsters half
man, half beast. In all this zoo, this bloody constellation,
only two men and six bulls would be missing. Those in the

bullring. Those they would see with their very own eyes. This golden eye would reflect, like a mirror, every gaze that was directed toward it—like the hub caps, Boyd thought, displayed on their racks along the boulevards."

The style, only slightly modulated, will serve for the sorrowful ending of *The Works of Love:* "Beyond this, as if a fire was raging, there was a bright glow over the street, and from these flames there arose, along with the din, a penetrating smell. The old man let his eyes close, as this was not something he needed to see. He could breathe it, like the carbon, he could taste it on his lips. It was like the grating sound of steel, a blend of the sour air and the track sound, of the gas from the traffic, and the sweetish smell of powdered Christmas balloons. All of the juices of the city were there on the fire, and brought to a boil. All the damp air of the chill rooms that were empty, the warm soiled air of the rooms that were lived in, blown to him, so it seemed, by the bellows of hell."

If the style can be somber, it is more often humorous in a wry and teasing way. Morris likes to bring himself and the reader up short. For instance, at the end of the paragraph from *In Orbit* I have quoted, we have a series of apt and amusing similes; but suddenly Morris puts the brake on by telling us that what the boy least looks like is what he is. Like many of his fellow-countrymen, especially those on the farms and in the small towns, Morris is likely to use a deadpan irony when he is most serious. In *The Works of Love*, for instance, we read such passages as this: "It might be going too far to say that Will Brady lived in this house, as he spent his time elsewhere and usually had other things on his mind. But he came back there every night, went away from there every morning, and something like that, if you keep at it, gets to mean something." Always he relies on indirection: "When a man has lost something he would like to get back, say a wife, a boy, or an old set of habits, he can walk around the streets of the city looking for it. Or he can stand on a corner, nearly anywhere, and let it look for him." Many of his characters coin epigrams: Warren Howe, in *Cause for Wonder*, remarks, "My uncle, Fremont Osborn, came too late for God and too early for the Farm Security Administration."

Clichés are an essential part of Morris's style. Whereas most writers think about clichés, only in the hope of avoiding them, he uses them for his own purposes. Horter and Mac in *Love Among the Cannibals* specialize in clichés, Mac by nature, Horter by intent. "Every cliché in the world," Horter reflects, "once had its moment of truth. At some point, if you traced it back, it expressed the inexpressible." In time, of course, the cliché becomes a poor substitute for thought and feeling and imagination. Morris, by twisting a cliché so that you have to look at it, shocks you out of your insensitivity. *God's Country and My People* he has named his latest book: "The men called it God's country —but the women asked, who else wants it?" "The plow that broke the plains lies buried in the yard," he observes, "and it is clear that the plains won the return engagement." Of his Uncle Harry he writes: "He was strong as a horse, stubborn as a mule, slow as molasses, smart as a whip, but what there was that was human in his nature was slow to emerge." "It is a custom of the people to look you in the eye, but not through it. To look you in the face but not behind it."

Morris's way of manipulating clichés is effective in a polemic such as *A Bill of Rites, A Bill of Wrongs, A Bill of Goods*. In his discussion of advertising, for instance, we find: "If the image is good it pays to advertise. If the image is bad you need a new press agent. People are made by fools like you and me, but only prime time can make an image." "What are the hippies coming to?" he asks, and replies,

"The old American pay-off: success. You start with something *echt* and *kitsch* takes over." In a chapter called "Face Value" he makes a political observation: "The crisis of the nation is not in Vietnam, or in Watts or in Selma, or the fire next time, but in the profound and disquieting realization of the people that their face value of Lyndon Johnson was wrong. His face value is *out*. We have no idea what is in." Often he piles one cliché upon another: "There is no accounting for tastes, but how many of us are enchanted by the poetry of the space program? Is it the gorge or the heart that rises from the pad at Cape Kennedy?—is it the 'coverage' or the program that has sold this moonshine to the public? Our words fly up, but our thoughts remain below."

Morris's figures of speech, which are numerous, are usually derived from familiar artifacts or commonplace experiences, from the stuff of ordinary life. In *The Field of Vision*, as we have seen, the bullring reminds Gordon Boyd of a hub cap. In *Cause for Wonder* Warren Howe sees M. Dulac in bed as "a small fox waiting for the appearance of Little Red Riding Hood." In *The Huge Season* the watch that had belonged to Foley's father serves to indicate Foley's relationship to the past and hints at the differences between the generations: "Time, for my father, seemed to be contained in the watch. It did not skip a beat, fly away, or merely vanish, as it does for me. So long as he remembered to wind the watch Time would not run out." In *Man and Boy* we read: "Carrying his shoes, Mr. Ormsby followed the throw rugs to the closet, like a man crossing a swift stream on blocks of ice." The son in *Works of Love* "wasn't much bigger than a rabbit, and he had the dark unblinking eyes of a bird." Once he has seen the Greek, Horter in *Love Among the Cannibals*, explains: "I didn't *know* how she looked—I would only recognize her by how I felt. How did I feel? The way I often feel in elevators."

In *A Bill of Rites* Morris's similes and metaphors are likely to be paradoxical and to have a touch of the absurd. For instance, after describing the costume of a hippie, he sums up: "The effect is that of Lawrence in Taos, passing as Buffalo Bill." Of the way literature is taught in many colleges he observes: "The idea that books are safes with secret combinations, and poems are ingenious double crostics, is not new, but only recently has reached the status of a doctrine." Worrying the subject of images, he comments: "An image currently in need of much improvement is the image of war. I was recently watching war with Huntley and Brinkley, on prime time. . . . I was properly amazed to see the war slipped off on a siding in western Kansas to let the Capote *Cold Blood* express roar through to Holcomb. For two or three minutes, that is, Capote had higher billing than Vietnam. On the exchange, *Cold Blood* went up as war went down. Both were news, and at that precise moment both were advertising on prime time. That is stranger, in its way, than the murders he reported, or what the author referred to as new fiction. No fiction is so strange as what we see nightly on prime time."

Some people are puzzled or distracted or even offended by Morris's style. It seems to many of us, however, that he has forged an almost perfect instrument for the expression of his understanding of life and feeling about it. That it is so close to the vernacular is one source of its vitality; it echoes the voices of living people. Like most speech, it calls for response. Although it flows so unpretentiously, it constantly challenges the reader to take his part in the activity of a creative imagination. That is one reason why Morris so often interrupts himself with a paradox, an apparent non sequitur, or a wisecrack; he demands a more than perfunctory participation. Although he is not a difficult writer in the *avant-garde* sense of the adjective, there is always much more in his books than immediately meets the eye or the ear.

Ideas

Being an intelligent and responsive human being, Morris is a man of ideas. Ideas are important to him; he respects his own and pays courteous attention to others'. His ideas, it ought to be unnecessary to say, are never present in the fiction as ideas; they are implicit, never explicit. But Morris has published two books that are expository by intent: one a discussion of, for the most part, literary matters, the other a critique of contemporary culture.

In *The Territory Ahead* he talks about certain American writers, past and present: Thoreau, Whitman, Melville, Mark Twain, Henry James, Hemingway, Wolfe, Fitzgerald, Faulkner. A careful reader and uncommonly well informed, he talks impressively about all these men. At the moment, however, we are concerned with his general ideas, two in particular. First he emphasizes the danger of the artist's relying on raw material, and cites Thomas Wolfe as the horrible example. Art is created by the transforming— the processing, as he would say—of raw material. He points to Henry James, "one on whom nothing was lost," as the antithesis of Wolfe. It will be observed, however, that Morris chose as an example of the transforming power of the imagination not one of James's novels but *The American Scene*. Here, more than in any of the novels, James accepted the challenge of an appalling mass of raw material and triumphed over it.

His second thesis is that nostalgia has been the curse of American literature, and he illustrates this theory by examining the successes and failures of the writers mentioned above. What seems to be more important than the general idea itself is the light it sheds on Morris's work. At the start and for a long time thereafter he was concerned with his own past and the conditions that shaped it. All of the plains books, including *The Inhabitants* and *The Home Place,* grew out of this concern, and it has served him well; he has not repudiated his earlier books, nor is there any reason why he should. In time, however, he was troubled by his enslavement to the past, and *The Territory Ahead* expresses his rebellion. The characters in his following novel, *Love Among the Cannibals,* live wholly in the present, and the same thing is true of *What a Way to Go* and *In Orbit. Cause for Wonder* is a new and in large measure successful attempt to make imaginative use of the past in the present. From this point of view, the text of *God's Country and My People* is important. The pictures, taken more than twenty years ago, were part of Morris's attempt to get at the past by means of a camera. But the text is proof that at last he has exorcised nostalgia.

A Bill of Rites, A Bill of Wrongs, A Bill of Goods is a book about the crazy world we live in. Reading it, one alternates between laughter and outrage. Ours is a shoddy culture, Morris says, built on greed, ruthlessness, and hypocrisy. The evidence is everywhere and he produces enough of it to give us all the jitters.

Many American writers have done their best work when they were comparatively young and thereafter have declined. Henry James is the conspicuous exception—a man who not only went on writing through decade after decade but also went on growing as a writer. As Morris approaches his sixtieth birthday, he is still going strong, full of energy, full of plans, and, to play Morris's game with clichés, full of promise.

GRANVILLE HICKS

Grafton, New York

PART I

ON
THE
PLAINS

THE
SCENE

From *Ceremony in Lone Tree*

COME to the window. The one at the rear of the Lone Tree Hotel. The view is to the west. There is no obstruction but the sky. Although there is no one outside to look in, the yellow blind is drawn low at the window, and between it and the pane a fly is trapped. He has stopped buzzing. Only the crawling shadow can be seen. Before the whistle of the train is heard the loose pane rattles like a simmering pot, then stops, as if pressed by a hand, as the train goes past. The blind sucks inward and the dangling cord drags in the dust on the sill.

At a child's level in the pane there is a flaw that is round, like an eye in the glass. An eye to that eye, a scud seems to blow on a sea of grass. Waves of plain seem to roll up, then break like a surf. Is it a flaw in the eye, or in the window, that transforms a dry place into a wet one? Above it towers a sky, like the sky at sea, a wind blows like the wind at sea, and like the sea it has no shade: there is no place to hide. One thing it is that the sea is not: it is dry, not wet.

Drawn up to the window is a horsehair sofa covered with a quilt. On the floor at its side, garlanded with flowers, is a

3

nightpot full of cigar butts and ashes. Around it, scattered like seed, are the stubs of half-burned kitchen matches, the charcoal tips honed to a point for picking the teeth. They also serve to aid the digestion and sweeten the breath. The man who smokes the cigars and chews on the matches spends most of the day on the sofa; he is not there now, but the sagging springs hold his shape. He has passed his life, if it can be said he has lived one, in the rooms of the Lone Tree Hotel. His coat hangs in the lobby, his shoes are under the stove, and a runner of ashes marks his trail up and down the halls. His hat, however, never leaves his head. It is the hat, with its wicker sides, the drayman's license at the front, that comes to mind when his children think of him. He has never run a dray, but never mind. The badge is what they see, through the hole where his sleeve has smudged the window, on those rare occasions when they visit him. If the hat is not there, they look for him in the lobby, dozing in one of the hardwood rockers or in one of the beds drawn to a window facing the west. There is little to see, but plenty of room to look.

Scanlon's eyes, a cloudy phlegm color, let in more light than they give out. What he sees are the scenic props of his own mind. His eye to the window, the flaw in the pane, such light as there is illuminates Scanlon, his face like that of a gobbler in the drayman's hat. What he sees is his own business, but the stranger might find the view familiar. A man accustomed to the ruins of war might even feel at home. In the blowouts on the rise are flint arrowheads, and pieces of farm machinery, half buried in sand, resemble nothing so much as artillery equipment, abandoned when the dust began to blow. The tidal shift of the sand reveals one ruin in order to conceal another. It is all there to be seen, but little evidence that Tom Scanlon sees it. Not through the clouded eye he puts to the glass. The emptiness of the plain generates illusions that require little moisture, and grow better, like tall stories, where the mind is dry. The tall corn may flower or burn in the wind, but the plain is a metaphysical landscape and the bumper crop is the one Scanlon sees through the flaw in the glass.

Nothing irked him more than to hear from his children that the place was empty, the town deserted, and that there was nothing to see. He saw plenty. No matter where he looked. Down the tracks to the east, like a headless bird, the bloody neck still raw and dripping, a tub-shaped water tank sits high on stilts. Scanlon once saw a coon crawl out the chute and drink from the spout. Bunches of long-stemmed grass, in this short-grass country, grow where the water drips between the rails, and Scanlon will tell you he has seen a buffalo crop it up. A big bull, of course, high in the shoulders, his short tail like the knot in a whip, walking on the ties like a woman with her skirts tucked up. Another time a wolf, half crazed by the drought, licked the moisture from the rails like ice and chewed on the grass like a dog out of sorts. On occasion stray geese circle the tank like a water hole. All common sights, according to Scanlon, where other men squinted and saw nothing but the waves of heat, as if the cinders of the railbed were still on fire.

It seldom rains in Lone Tree, but he has often seen it raining somewhere else. A blue veil of it will hang like the half-drawn curtain at Scanlon's window. Pillars of cloud loom on the horizon, at night there is much lightning and claps of thunder, and from one window or another rain may be seen falling somewhere. Wind from that direction will smell wet, and Scanlon will complain, if there is someone to listen, about the rheumatic pains in his knees. He suffered greater pains, however, back when he had neighbors who complained, of all things, about the lack of rain.

In the heat of the day, when there is no shadow, the plain

seems to be drawn up into the sky, and through the hole in the window it is hard to be sure if the town is still there. It takes on, like a sunning lizard, the colors of the plain. The lines drawn around the weathered buildings smoke and blur. At this time of day Scanlon takes his nap, and by the time he awakes the town is back in its place. The lone tree, a dead cottonwood, can be seen by the shadow it leans to the east, a zigzag line with a fishhook curve at the end. According to Scanlon, Indians once asked permission to bury their dead in the crotch of the tree, and while the body was there the tree had been full of crows. A small boy at the time, Scanlon had shot at them with his father's squirrel gun, using soft lead pellets that he dug out of the trunk of the tree and used over again.

From the highway a half mile to the north, the town sits on the plain as if delivered on a flatcar—as though it were a movie set thrown up during the night. Dry as it is, something about it resembles an ark from which the waters have receded. In the winter it appears to be locked in a sea of ice. In the summer, like the plain around it, the town seems to float on a watery surface, stray cattle stand kneedeep in a blur of reflections, and waves of light and heat flow across the highway like schools of fish. Everywhere the tongue is dry, but the mind is wet. According to his daughters, who should know, the dirt caked around Tom Scanlon's teeth settled there in the thirties when the dust began to blow. More of it can be seen, fine as talcum, on the linoleum floor in the lobby, where the mice raised in the basement move to their winter quarters in the cobs behind the stove.

To the east, relatively speaking, there is much to see, a lone tree, a water tank, sheets of rain and heat lightning: to the west a strip of torn screen blurs the view. The effect is that of now-you-see-it, now-you-don't. As a rule, there is nothing to see, and if there is, one doubts it. The pane is smeared where Scanlon's nose has rubbed the glass. The fact that there is little to see seems to be what he likes about it. He can see what he pleases. It need not please anybody else. Trains come from both directions, but from the east they come without warning, the whistle blown away by the wind. From the west, thin and wild or strumming like a wire fastened to the building, the sound wakes Scanlon from his sleep before the building rocks. It gives him time, that is, to prepare himself. The upgrade freights rock the building and leave nothing but the noise in his head, but the downgrade trains leave a vacuum he sometimes raises the window to look at. A hole? He often thought he might see one there. A cloud of dust would veil the caboose, on the stove one of the pots or the lids would rattle, and if the lamp was lit, the flame would blow as if in a draft.

One day as the dust settled he saw a team of mares, the traces dragging, cantering down the bank where the train had just passed. On the wires above the tracks, dangling like a scarecrow, he saw the body of Emil Bickel, in whose vest pocket the keywound watch had stopped. At 7:34, proving the train that hit him had been right on time.

To the west the towns are thin and sparse, like the grass, and in a place called Indian Bow the white faces of cattle peer out of the soddies on the slope across the dry bed of the river. They belong to one of Scanlon's grandchildren who married well. On the rise behind the soddies are sunken graves, one of the headstones bearing the name of Will Brady, a railroad man who occasionally stopped off at Lone Tree. Until he married and went east, Scanlon thought him a sensible man.

Down the grade to the east the towns are greener and thicker, like the grass. The town of Polk, the home of

7

Walter McKee, who married Scanlon's eldest daughter, Lois, has elm-shaded streets and a sign on the highway telling you to slow down. There is also a park with a Civil War cannon, the name of Walter McKee carved on the breech and that of his friend, Gordon Boyd, on one of the cannon balls. In the house where Walter McKee was born grass still grows between the slats on the porch, and the neighbor's chickens still lay their eggs under the stoop. At the corner of the porch a tar barrel catches and stores the rain from the roof. At the turn of the century, when McKee was a boy, he buried the white hairs from a mare's tail in the rain barrel, confident they would turn up next as garter snakes. In the middle of the century that isn't done, and a TV aerial, like a giant Martian insect, crouches on the roof as if about to fly off with the house. That is a change, but on its side in the yard is a man's bicycle with the seat missing. The small boy who rides it straddles it through the bars: he never sits down. He mounts it slantwise, like a bareback rider, grease from the chain rubbing off on one leg and soiling the cuff of the pants leg rolled to the knee. Gordon Boyd still bears the scar where the teeth of the sprocket dug into his calf. Bolder than McKee, he liked to ride on the gravel around the patch of grass in the railroad station, leaning forward to hold a strip of berry-box wood against the twirling spokes.

The short cut in the yard, worn there by McKee, still points across the street to a wide vacant lot and to the tree where McKee, taunted by Boyd, climbed to where the sway and the height made him dizzy. He fell on a milk-can lid, breaking his arm. Mrs. Boyd, a white-haired woman, had put his arm to soak in a cold tub of water while Gordon went for the doctor on McKee's new bike. Over that summer Boyd had grown so fast he could pump it from the seat.

The Boyd house, having no basement, had a storm cave at

the back of the yard where McKee smoked corn silk and Boyd smoked Fourth of July punk. The white frame house still has no basement, and the upstairs bedroom, looking out on the porch, is still heated by a pipe that comes up from the stove below. When McKee spent the night with Boyd, Mrs. Boyd would rap a spoon on the pipe to make them quiet, or turn down the damper so the room would get cold. The old coke burner, with the isinglass windows through which Boyd and McKee liked to watch the coke settle, now sits in the woodshed, crowned with the horn of the Victrola. The stove board, however, the floral design worn away where Boyd liked to dress on winter mornings, is now in the corner where the floor boards have sagged, under the new TV. Since the house has no porch high enough to crawl under, Boyd kept his sled and Irish Mail under the porch of a neighbor. Along with Hershey bar tinfoil, several pop bottles, a knife with a woman's leg for a handle, and a tin for condoms, thought to be balloons and blown up till they popped on the Fourth of July, the sled is still there. The boys don't use the ones with wooden runners any more. The chain swing no longer creaks on the porch or spends the winter, cocoonlike, drawn to the ceiling, but the paint still peels where it grazed the clapboards and thumped on the railing warm summer nights. Long after it was gone Mrs. Boyd was kept awake by its creak.

The people change—according to a survey conducted by a new supermarket—but the life in Polk remains much the same. The new trailer park on the east edge of town boasts the latest and best in portable living, but the small fry still fish, like McKee, for crawdads with hunks of liver, and bring them home to mothers who hastily dump them back in the creek. The men live in Polk, where there is plenty of

room, and commute to those places where the schools are
overcrowded, the rents inflated, but where there is work.
At the western edge of town an air-conditioned motel with
a stainless-steel diner blinks at night like an airport, just
across the street from where McKee chipped his front teeth
on the drinking fountain. Once or twice a year on his way
to Lone Tree, McKee stops off in Polk for what he calls a
real shave, in the shop where he got his haircuts as a boy.
The price for a shave and a haircut has changed, but the
mirror on the wall is the same. In it, somewhere, is the face
McKee had as a boy. Stretched out horizontal, his eyes on
the tin ceiling, his lips frothy with the scented lather, he
sometimes fancies he hears the mocking voice of Boyd:

> "*Walter McKee,*
> *Button your fly.*
> *Pee in the road*
> *And you'll get a sty.*"

Although he comes from the south, McKee goes out of
his way to enter town from the west, passing the water
stack with the word P O L K like a shadow under the new
paint. Just beyond the water stack is the grain elevator, the
roof flashing like a mirror in the sun, the name T. P. CRETE in
black on the fresh coat of aluminum. The same letters were
stamped like a legend on McKee's mind. The great man
himself was seldom seen in the streets of Polk, or in the
rooms of his mansion, but his name, in paint or gold leaf,
stared at McKee from walls and windows and the high
board fence that went along the lumberyard. T. P. Crete's
wife, like a bird in a cage, sometimes went by in her electric
car, making no more noise than the strum of the wires on
the telephone poles. It was this creature who deprived
McKee of his friend Boyd. She sent him, when he proved to
be smart, to those high-toned schools in the East that indirectly led to the ruin he made of his life. Destiny manifested

itself through the Cretes, and the sight of the name affected McKee like a choir marching in or the sound of his mother humming hymns.

Beyond the grain elevator is the railroad station, the iron wheels of the baggage truck sunk in the gravel, an OUT OF ORDER sign pasted on the face of the penny scales in the lobby. On the east side of the station is a patch of grass. Around it is a fence of heavy wrought iron, the top rail studded to discourage loafers, pigeons and small fry like McKee and Boyd. Polk is full of wide lawns and freshly cropped grass healthy enough for a boy to walk on, but for McKee the greenest grass in the world is the patch inside the wrought-iron fence. He never enters town without a glance at it. If it looks greener than other grass it might be due to the cinder-blackened earth, and the relative sparseness and tenderness of the shoots. But the secret lies in McKee, not in the grass. No man raised on the plains, in the short-grass country, takes a patch of grass for granted, and it is not for nothing they protect it with a fence or iron bars. When McKee thinks of spring, or of his boyhood, or of what the world would be like if men came to their senses, in his mind's eye he sees the patch of green in the cage at Polk. Tall grass now grows between the Burlington tracks that lead south of town to the bottomless sand pit where Boyd, before the eyes of McKee, attempted to walk on water for the first time. But not the last. Nothing seemed to teach him anything.

Southeast of Polk is Lincoln, capital of the state, the present home of McKee and his wife, Lois, as well as of Lois's sister Maxine and her family. Tom Scanlon's youngest girl, Edna, married Clyde Ewing, an Oklahoma horse breeder, who found oil on his farm in the Panhandle. The view from their modern air-conditioned house is so much like that around Lone Tree, Edna Ewing felt sure her

father would feel right at home in it. Tom Scanlon, however, didn't like the place. For one thing, there were no
windows, only those gleaming walls of glass. He had walked
from room to room as he did outside, with his head drawn
in. Although the floor and walls radiated heat, Scanlon felt
cold, since it lacked a stove with an oven door or a rail
where he could put his feet. Only in the back door was
there something like a window, an opening about the size of
a porthole framing the view, with a flaw in the glass to
which he could put his eye. Through it he saw, three hundred miles to the north, the forked branches of the lone tree
like bleached cattle horns on the railroad embankment that
half concealed the town, the false fronts of the buildings
like battered remnants of a board fence. Even the hotel,
with its MAIL POUCH sign peeling like a circus poster, might
be taken for a signboard along an abandoned road. That is
how it is, but not how it looks to Scanlon. He stands as if at
the screen, gazing down the track to where the long-
stemmed grass spurts from the cinders like leaks in a garden
hose. The mindless wind in his face seems damp with the
prospect of rain.

Three stories high, made of the rough-faced brick
brought out from Omaha on a flatcar, the Lone Tree Hotel
sits where the coaches on the westbound caboose once came
to a stop. Eastbound, there were few who troubled to stop.
In the westbound caboose were the men who helped Lone
Tree to believe in itself. The hotel faces south, the
empty pits that were dug for homes never erected and the
shadowy trails, like Inca roads, indicating what were meant
to be streets. The door at the front, set in slantwise on the
corner, with a floral design in the frosted glass, opens on the
prospect of the town. Slabs of imported Italian marble face
what was once the bank, the windows boarded like a looted

tomb, the vault at the rear once having served as a jail. A sign:

$5. FINE FOR TALKING

TO

PRISONERS

once hung over one of the barred windows, but a brakeman who was something of a card made off with it.

The lobby of the hotel, level with the hitching bar, affords a view of the barbershop interior, the mirror on the wall and whoever might be sitting in the one chair. Only the lower half of the window is curtained, screening off the man who is being shaved but offering him a view of the street and the plain when he sits erect, just his hair being cut. Tucked into the frame of the mirror are the post cards sent back by citizens who left or went traveling to those who were crazy enough to stay on in Lone Tree. The incumbent barber usually doubled as the postmaster. In the glass razor case, laid out on a towel still peppered with his day-old beard, is the razor that shaved William Jennings Bryan. In Lone Tree, at the turn of the century, he pleaded the lost cause of silver, then descended from the platform of the caboose for a shampoo and a shave. On that day a balloon, brought out on a flatcar, reached the altitude of two hundred forty-five feet with Edna Scanlon, who was something of a tomboy, visible in the basket that hung beneath. The century turned that memorable summer, and most of the men in Lone Tree turned with it; like the engines on the roundhouse platform they wheeled from west to east. But neither Scanlon, anchored in the lobby, nor the town of Lone Tree turned with it. The century went its own way after that, and Scanlon went his.

From a rocker in the lobby Scanlon can see the gap between the barbershop and the building on the west, the yellow blind shadowed with the remaining letters of the word MIL NE Y. On the floor above the millinery is the office of Dr. Twomey, where a cigar-store Indian with human teeth guards the door. He stands grimacing, toma-hawk upraised, with what are left of the molars known to drop out when the building is shaken by a downgrade freight. When Twomey set up his practice, the barber chair served very nicely as an operating table, a place for lancing boils, removing adenoids or pulling teeth. A flight of wooden steps without a railing mounted to his office on the second floor, but they collapsed within a week or so after he died. He was a huge man, weighing some three hundred pounds, and it took four men to lower his body to the casket on the wagon in the street. The stairs survived the strain, then collapsed under their own weight.

A hand-cranked gas pump, the crank in a sling, sits several yards in front of the livery stable, as if to disassoci-ate itself from the horses once stabled inside. At the back of the stable, inhabited by bats, is the covered wagon Scanlon was born in, the bottom sloped up at both ends like a river boat. Strips of faded canvas, awning remnants, partially cover the ribs. Until the hotel was built in the eighties, the Scanlon family lived in the rear of the millinery, and the covered wagon, like a gypsy encampment, sat under the lone tree. Before the railroad went through, the pony ex-press stopped in the shade of the tree for water. Scanlon remembers the sweat on the horses, and once being lifted to the pommel of the saddle, but most of the things he remem-bers took place long before he was born.

In the weeds behind the stable are a rubber-tired fire-hose cart without the hose, two short lengths of ladder and the iron frame for the fire bell. When the water-pressure system proved too expensive, the order for the hose and the fire bell was canceled. On the east side of the stable, the wheels sunk in the sand, a water sprinkler is garlanded with morning glories and painted with the legend VISIT THE LYRIC TONITE. The Lyric, a wooden frame building, has a front of galvanized tin weathered to the leaden color of the drain-pipes on the hotel. It stands like a souvenir book end at the east end of the town, holding up the row of false-front stores between it and the bank. Most of the year these shops face the sun, the light glaring on the curtained windows, like a row of blindfolded Confederate soldiers lined up to be shot. A boardwalk, like a fence blown on its side, is half concealed by the tidal drift of the sand—nothing could be drier, but the look of the place is wet. The wash of the sand is rippled as if by the movement of water, and stretches of the walk have the look of a battered pier. The town itself seems to face what is left of a vanished lake. Even the lone tree, stripped of its foliage, rises from the deck of the plain like a mast, and from the highway or the bluffs along the river, the crows'-nest at the top might be that on a ship. The bowl of the sky seems higher, the plain wider, because of it.

A street light still swings at the crossing corner but in the summer it casts no shadow, glowing like a bolthole in a stove until after nine o'clock. The plain is dark, but the bowl of the sky is full of light. On his horsehair sofa, drawn up to the window, Scanlon can see the hands on his watch until ten o'clock. The light is there after the sun has set and will be there in the morning before it rises, as if a property of the sky itself. The moon, rather than the sun, might be the source of it. In the summer the bats wing in and out of the stable as if it were dark, their radar clicking, wheel on the sky, then wing into the stable again. At this time of the evening coins come out to be found. The rails gleam like ice in the cinders, and the drayman's badge on Scanlon's hat, bright as a buckle, can be seen through the hole he has rubbed in the glass.

If a grass fire has been smoldering during the day you will see it flicker on the plain at night, and smoke from these fires, like Scanlon himself, has seldom left the rooms of the Lone Tree Hotel. It is there in the curtains like the smell of his cigars. His daughter Lois, the moment she arrives, goes up and down the halls opening the windows, and leaves a bottle of Air Wick in the room where she plans to spend the night. For better or worse—as she often tells McKee—she was born and raised in it.

The last time Lois spent a night in Lone Tree was after her father had been found wrapped up like a mummy, his cold feet in a colder oven, and paraded big as life on the front page of the Omaha *Bee*. The caption of the story read:

MAN WHO KNEW BUFFALO BILL
SPENDS LONELY XMAS

although both his daughter and McKee were out there in time to spend part of Christmas with him. The story brought him many letters and made him famous, and put an end to his Lone Tree hibernation. To keep him entertained, as well as out of mischief, his daughter and her husband took him along the following winter on their trip to Mexico. There he saw a bullfight and met McKee's old friend, Gordon Boyd.

In Claremore, Oklahoma, on their way back, they stopped to see Edna and Clyde Ewing. Clyde claimed to be one fifth Cherokee Indian and an old friend of Will Rogers, whoever that might be. Although they had this new modern home, the Ewings spent most of their time going up and down the country in a house trailer just a few feet shorter than a flatcar. It had two bedrooms, a shower and a bath, with a rumpus room said to be soundproof. In the rumpus room, since they had no children, they kept an English bulldog named Shiloh, whose daddy had been sold for thirty thousand dollars. Scanlon never cared for dogs, and being too old to ride any of the Ewings' prize horses he was put in a buggy, between Ewing and McKee, and allowed to hold the reins while a white mare cantered. It made him hmmmphh. The Ewings were having a family reunion, but Scanlon saw no Cherokees present.

While they were there, they got on the Ewings' TV the report of a tragedy in Lincoln: a high-school boy with a hot-rod had run down and killed two of his classmates. An accident? No, he had run them down as they stood in the street, taunting him. On the TV screen they showed the boy's car, the muffler sticking up beside the windshield like a funnel, the fenders dented where he had smashed into the boys. Then they showed the killer, a boy with glasses, looking like a spaceman in his crash helmet. His name was Lee Roy Momeyer—pronounced *Lee* Roy by his family— the son of a Calloway machineshop mechanic, and related to Scanlon by marriage. At the time he ran down and killed his classmates, he was working in a grease pit at the gasoline station where Walter McKee had used his influence to get him the job. Eighteen years of age, serious-minded, studious-looking in his thick-lensed glasses, Lee Roy was well intentioned to the point that it hurt—but a little slow. Talking to him, McKee fell into the habit of repeating himself.

"Mr. McKee," Lee Roy would say, "what can I do you for?" and McKee never quite got accustomed to it. And there he was, famous, with his picture on TV. In the morning they had a telegram from Lois's sister, Maxine Momeyer, asking if McKee would go his bail, which he did. Two days later, as they drove into Lincoln, coming in the back way so nobody would see them, there was no mention of Lee Roy Momeyer on the radio. A man and his wife had just been found murdered, but it couldn't have been Lee Roy. They had *him*, as the reporter said, in custody. Before that week was out there had been eight more, shot down like ducks by the mad-dog killer, and then he was captured out in the sand hills not far from Lone Tree. His name was Charlie Munger, and he was well known to Lee Roy Momeyer, who often greased his car. Between them they had killed twelve people in ten days.

Why did they do it?

When they asked Lee Roy Momeyer he replied that he just got tired of being pushed around. Who was pushing *who?* Never mind, that was what he said. The other one, Charlie Munger, said that he wanted to be somebody. Didn't everybody? Almost anybody, that is, but who he happened to be? McKee's little grandson thought he was Davy Crockett, and wore a coonskin hat with a squirrel's tail dangling, and Tom Scanlon, the great-grandfather, seemed to think he was Buffalo Bill. But when McKee read that statement in the paper there was just one person he thought of. His old boyhood chum, Gordon Boyd. Anybody could run over people or shoot them, but so far as McKee knew there was only one man in history who had tried to walk on water—and He had got away with it.

McKee filed his clippings on these matters in a book entitled THE WALK ON THE WATER, written by Boyd after he had tried it himself. When it came to wanting to be somebody, and wanting, that is, to be it the hard way, there was no one in the same class as Boyd.

TOM
SCANLON

From *The World in the Attic*

I WALKED in the cinders, trying to think what it was that walking in cinders made me think of—something connected with walking the rails, or walking the ties. The weedy spur curved in behind the station, the semaphore shadow lying on the tracks, and I stopped in the shadow to look through the door into the Waiting Room. The great pot-bellied stove, the VOLCANO, was still there. Above the stove was the arrangement for trapping the heat—as my father said—generally used for drying wet shoes, coats and gloves. Underneath, on the stove board, the long poker and the crank for shaking down the ashes. The drafts were open, the damper in the elbow-joint half closed. On the wall behind the stove, thumb-tacked above the bench, was a facsimile War Bond made out to John Doe, the word "boy" carefully added to the Doe. On the side wall the wooden slat grill was still the cage around the ticket office, but the ticket window, where my father stood, was closed. I walked from the back of the station to the front. In the old stations the agent's desk sat at the front, in a bay of windows, so that he could sit there and look in either direction, up and down the tracks. The big window at the front would usually be closed, against the noise and blast of the Mail train, but my father liked to keep the small windows at the side halfway up. That was for him to see out, and for me to see in. From a block down the tracks I could see his face, light green from the visor shadow, and hear the click as he worked the telegraph key. There would be a lamp over his desk, with a glass shade the color of his visor, and the metal freight tags on a wire near the wall. I could see them, glinting in the light, and the rack that held the dozen rubber stamps, some of them with labels, some of them that had to be stamped to be read. I could see through one window and out the other, far down the tracks to the cattle loader, where at 9:17 the semaphore would switch from red to green. And my father would rise from his desk and with the length of bamboo, with the loop in the end, stand out in front for the pick-up from the Fast Mail.

That window was down, but when I shaded my face, pressed my nose to the glass, I could see my father, the dark ridge along his forehead, sitting there. His right hand, with the "indelible" fingers, relaxed beside the small black key, and a purple stain, like a birthmark, where he moistened the pencils with his lips.

My father was not a man who could turn boys into lads by putting his hand on their heads, but he had known such men, and he had passed the faith on to me. Men like that, he gave me to understand, were a passing thing. They are tied up in my mind with the old Harvey Houses, where my father liked to eat, and where men of that stamp would sit at the counter, smoking their cigars. Their heavy cowhide luggage on the floor beside them, with the colored labels of faraway hotels, and a way of saying— "Will, is that your boy?" that made a man of me. Such men, standing out on the platform of an east-bound caboose, or an observation car, was the way we made heroes, out here, before Babe

Ruth came along. We made our dream of fair-women through the Diner windows where such a man, seated across from this woman, poured water from a crystal goblet into a crystal glass. We made our dream of the future night after night as the Flyer passed, trailing the wild whistle, and the stream of coaches, full of such men and women, made a band of light across the wide plain. But the times have changed. We try to make things differently now.

We've given up, I know, trying to make men of small boys that way. I think we've also given up the notion that it can be done. I used to laugh at my father when he said that he voted for William Jennings Bryan because he wanted a man, as well as a monkey, for President. Back then it was men out of monkeys, now it's monkeys out of men. Men are born and raised, my father said, other people are educated—and by that he meant to dismiss my notions, as well as himself. In his opinion we had both lost an essential thing. Men of that caliber produced, it would seem, everything in the world but men of that caliber—out of a silk purse it is also hard to make a good sow's ear.

Now when my father sat here a good many men walked the ties. Not far, perhaps, but they set off walking on them. The man who knew about that was a friend of my father's, and at some time or other he must have told him his story, as my father began it, I know, time after time. He called it Tom Scanlon's story—but he never finished it.

"Tom Scanlon—" my father would say, then, as he was a man who never smoked, take a match from his vest and put it in the corner of his mouth. If you were standing at that point, you would sit down. My father would swing his chair around and point through the window, toward the cattle loader, but just to the left—at the rear of the New Western Hotel. Tom Scanlon had a room on the top floor, facing the west.

The Western Hotel was built at a time when men were saying, "Go west, young man, go west—" but the town of Junction, as well as all the young men, was going east. No house or store, no building of any kind, lay to the west. The windows on the west side of the hotel looked out on a spur of the main line tracks, several piles of tarred ties, and a mile or so of burned ditch grass. In the winter and early spring this grass was green, a fresh, winter-wheat color, but people in the hotel always had the burned smell in their noses. As there was a prevailing western wind the smell of the grass hung over the town, and never left the rooms, Tom Scanlon said, of the Western Hotel. In the middle of the winter a man could smell it in the hall. City women would sometimes wake their husbands, sure that there was a fire in the building, or throw up the windows and look out in the street, or the empty side yard. In the early summer a Carnival might be there. And in the early morning, a little after sunrise, a man might see as far as Chapman, where the sun would be bright on the tin roof of the grain elevator. The wide plain would be green, like a sea of grass, winter wheat, or whatever you want to call it, with a house here and there at the end of a sand-colored road. One could see by the tracks, crossing and recrossing, tangled on themselves like so many mop strings, that neither the traffic, nor the road, were going anywhere. What traffic there was went to the east. As the afternoon sun was hot on the windows, fading the bedspreads and the rug on the floor, the woman who made the beds made it a point to draw the blinds. Very few men ever troubled to let them up. They were all traveling men, and they knew well enough what the view was. Newcomers, however, Omaha people who didn't know grass from winter wheat, would sometimes raise the blind and stand there and look out. They would see the plain, the dark tracks in the road, and if the last snow had melted they would see the charred fence posts from last summer's fires. The chances are they would not raise the blind on that side again.

The front of the Hotel was on Main street, where there were wide steps, and a hitching bar, but men like Tom Scanlon hardly ever came in that way. At some time or other some traveling man—very likely just one man to start with—got into the habit of coming in the rear. The back door was right there, facing the tracks, with a night lantern above it, and saved a tired man the walk around to the front. They were traveling men, and anxious to get to bed. Over a period of time what one man started—Tom Scanlon, in my father's opinion—became the general rule for traveling men. They came in through the back, two or three at a time, stopped long enough to see what was cooking, then dropped their bags in the lobby and went upstairs. They gave up, more or less, signing the ledger, and some of the more regular men kept their keys in their pocket, not troubling to turn them in. It saved everybody quite a bit of needless work. There was no fuss and bother, everybody knew where everything was. The old timers paid their bills when they thought of it. They left their sample bags in the lobby, their hats on the back of the chairs, and fell into the habit of treating the place like home.

This fellow Tom Scanlon, for instance, was known to have slept in his clothes. He smoked a good deal, lying in bed, and left his cigars in a pile in the nightpot, which he kept on the chair at the side of his bed. When he got sleepy he would pull the quilt over his legs. Even in winter he seldom got between the sheets. An odd man, in many ways, he liked the small room at the back where the only window opened on the west. Right straight down the tracks, the telephone poles, and the semaphores. Sometimes Mrs. Riddlemosher would find him sitting there. There was no excuse for this as there were comfortable chairs in the lobby, a brass rail for your feet, and a big window on the street. But in the winter, when it got dark early, Tom Scanlon was known to pull his bed, lazy as he was, over to the window so he could look out. Men walking down the tracks would see the glow of his cigar.

Over the years Tom Scanlon saw a good many things, where, as a rule, there was nothing to see, the next crossing being clear out of town. Just for that reason men would use it now and then. Maybe to go around a freight, that had stopped on the siding, or to do away with the nuisance of the railway gates. Waiting for those poles to go up or down irritated some men. They would drive their teams west, to the open crossing, and every now and then, two or three times a year, number 7, with the eastbound mail, would meet them there. Sometimes, it was said, the wind was strong, blowing from the east against the whistle, and sometimes, so it seemed, the man just didn't give a damn. Anyhow, that was what my father said. Around the turn of the century a good many men seemed to feel that way. Sometimes Tom Scanlon would see the team standing there, their traces dragging, as if they had walked off and left the buggy on the farm. Or he might see the buggy, and have to look around for the team. Now and then he saw a horse tossed up in the air, like a bale of hay, with the driver left sitting, or standing, with the reins in his hands. Or his hands there, firmly clasped, but the reins gone. And for reasons of their own all kinds of men, with a bottle in their hand and one in their stomach, figured there was no finer place in the world to walk than the ties. Right down the center, right down the middle, to Kingdom Come. Men who didn't seem to give—as my father said—a good goddam.

Try to explain what it was they liked about the tracks? What it was they saw, far down at the end, while walking the ties. Men in their teens, with a soft red beard, or men in their forties, with everything to live for, or men without it, but for the moment with a bottle in their hand. Anyhow, they saw something. Tom Scanlon insisted on that. And he would have been the man to know as he saw these men, wandering out in the evening, stopping now and then to lift the bottle, or hold it to the light. Seeing in the bottle, as the saying goes, what they seemed to see on the horizon, where the tracks pointed toward the red and green lights, the swinging semaphores. Tom Scanlon was the only man in town who knew that the place to look for Emil Bickel was not in Omaha, or Kansas City, but on the telephone wires. There he swung, like a sack of grain, his arms dangling like the sleeves of a scarecrow, and every last button gone from his vest. Popped, so my father said, by the force of it. A good man, with an honest wife, three sturdy kids. There was a freight parked on the siding and some men said that Emil Bickel, a man with everything to live for, had stepped out from behind it, died that way. Other men said that was just a way of leaving town. Of getting away, so to speak, from what you had on your mind. The only man who might have known was Tom Scanlon, but all he ever said, at that time or later, was where they should look for him. Emil Bickel had been dressed for church, and the watch in his pocket, the crystal unbroken, had stopped at exactly eleven-seventeen. The night mail, rolling down the grade, had been ninety seconds late.

No, no doubt about it, Tom Scanlon had seen a good many things. Sitting there at the window, leaving burns on the sill with his cigars. No one would have said, however, that was why he was lying there. A man named Muncy once suggested that Tom Scanlon, as everybody knew, spent his time in bed because he was just too damn lazy to walk. Or he would have been killed, like a lot of other men, along the tracks himself. Not that he was a drinker, but he certainly didn't give a hoot. When he died in bed, a cigar in his mouth, a good many men would have felt cheated— except for the fact that he sat the nightpot on his head. Very likely he knew it, when it came, but as he didn't have the time to walk out on the tracks, and to die like a man, he did what he could. He took the nightpot and sat it on his head. It had been full of his stubbed cigars, and they lay all around him, spilled into his lap, and left a grey, hoarfrost ash in his dark beard. And yet not a ghoulish sight at all, as the woman who had found him said, but very much like him, another one of his pranks so to speak. So much so, so exactly like him, that she stood in the door, wagging her finger, thinking that he was making another prank for her. She wasn't really sure until she saw that his cigar, a King Edward, was out.

FREMONT
OSBORN

From *Cause for Wonder*

MY uncle, Fremont Osborn, came too late for God and too early for the Farm Security Administration. They might have fruitlessly advised him that where he planted wheat in Texas it seldom rained. Not that it would have helped. He was not a man to take advice. He was a farmer, but he never noticed, with his eyes on the horizon, the color of the sky. Fremont Osborn was born a few miles west of the line that divides the long grass from the short grass country—or it did, that is, until he came along. For thirty years the line has been concealed by drifting sand. With a small assist from me, Fremont Osborn invented what we now refer to as the dustbowl, staking out his claim near Hereford in the panhandle of Texas. Virgin soil. Never turned by a plow. In the winter of 1923 he turned up fifteen hundred acres of it. That winter it rained. He had to go to Tulsa to get help to harvest the crop. In the winter that followed the soil began to blow. Even the Indians had a word for it—wrong side up.

When I showed up, five years later, it had not rained for seven years, and there were large raw blowouts on his land that looked like shell holes from a plane. He cursed the wind for that, pulling off his mitten to shake his chapped clenched fist at it, his mouth almost closed, the roots of his teeth caked with dirt. But what he didn't eat or swallow blew away. As you may remember reading, some of it darkened the sun over New York. He was a pioneer, my uncle, one of that fearless breed of land pirates who took possession of, and broke, as they say, the plains. He was now living in Quartzite, Arizona, at the La Golondrina tourist court. A handyman. That he had always been. I see him now, something more than lifesize, the crack of dawn like a bow between his legs, crossing the yard toward his tractor with a milk can in each hand. Full of milk? No, kerosene. He was about to break the soil with a gangplow on a new piece of unbroken land.

I haven't set eyes on him for thirty years, but I hear about him at Christmas. My Aunt Winona encloses one of his letters with her Christmas card. She's in her seventies, he is now eighty-one. For approximately seventy years he has shocked and pleased her with his agnostic opinions. Her faith remains unshaken. His opinions unchanged. The last letter from Quartzite was dated November, '61.

Nona Dear:

Took a run up to Oakland a few weeks ago, looked in on Myron's family. His big-ankled Frau tells me she contacts his spirit daily. Know what he told her? That I come just to borrow money. Can you beat that? She comes down to these parts now and then to attend a big spiritualist conclave. She really thinks she communicates with all her loved ones' spirits, whatever that is.

Seems now that Violet's got a little money she feels it burning a hole in her pocket. Al still looks good. Tells me he hasn't changed a bit, in spite of thirty-four years with that woman. You speak of Donna. I recall her as a very sweet kid. Damsite more sense than her mother. I got so interested in your letter I came near forgetting the afternoon dance. Still like to swing the girls, some of 'em half my age. Old Abe Lincoln, God bless him, said, "God surely must have loved the common people he made so many of them." And so it is with the ladies. Which reminds me:

> *King David and King Solomon*
> *Led merry merry lives*
> *With many many lady friends*
> *And many many wives.*
>
> *But when old age crept up on them*
> *With many many qualms*
> *King Solomon wrote the proverbs*
> *And King David wrote the psalms.*

I suppose I'll carry on till I'm carried off, but I better get this over to the P.O. first.

Love,
FREMONT

When I was in college, a sophomore, my Uncle Fremont appeared on the campus and asked the first student he met to be directed to his nephew, Warren Howe. They used the campus, in those days, for movies, and my uncle resembled one of the extras. He wore stirrup boots, a string tie, and a suit like those of Alfalfa Bill Murray. That afternoon I was in a seminar devoted to the poetry of Keats. We sat in a room with the windows open, and through one of them I saw my uncle approaching. His hands were free, but he walked, or rather cantered, as if he held a milk pail in each hand. His escort trotted at his side. Shown to the room, he took an empty seat as if it had been for him the class had been waiting. He sat attentive, squint-eyed, with his broad-brimmed hat in his lap. Perhaps I had never looked at him before. A plainsman, a seaman's colorless eyes in his weathered face. In the dim light of the room he seemed to grin with his customary squint. His hat removed, he appeared to be freshly scalped. About him, however, was the perceptible aura of something unique, an uncaged but exotic bird, or more accurately, a hawk or falcon perched without its hood. Serenely detached. Disturbingly self-sufficient.

What did I *feel?* I hardly knew, never before having felt anything like it. Pride in my kin. An unheard-of sentiment. He listened attentively to the teacher read aloud passages from "Endymion," and when he had finished courteously asked if he might have the name of the poet. With a borrowed pencil he jotted it down on the back of a card he took from his pocket. On the front of it was a snapshot. Of whom? My uncle, Fremont Osborn. Bound together with a piece of elastic, he had perhaps two, or three dozen of them. He asked Percy's permission, as the class broke up, if he might offer the cards to some of the young ladies, who might in turn pass them on to a possibly interested party. Interested in what? In holy matrimony with my Uncle Fremont. His name, age, and Texas address were stamped on the card. I was the last to leave the room, too late, happily, to receive one of the pictures of my Uncle Fremont, his hat off, his brow scalped, his seaman's eyes fastened on the horizon. Together we walked silently to the station, where I saw him off. Five weeks later he wrote me he had found the woman he wanted, a Pasadena widow of comfortable means. I never met her. A few weeks in the dustbowl changed her mind. He had more cards printed, and sent me a packet of them. Two years later, back in Kansas, he found the ideal mate he wanted, and it was with her he came to Europe and Schloss Riva on his honeymoon. A Gladys Bekin. The honeymoon ended the spring they returned to Texas. A soft woman? Let me tell you what it was like.

The town of Hereford is in the panhandle, about forty miles west of Amarillo. Quite a big town now, but thirty

years ago you went in by bus, only cattle trains stopped. I
remember two, maybe three buildings, set on the plain as if
the water had receded. Nothing else. A dead sea, a luminous
sky. I was born on the plains myself, but it is *this* plain I
remember. Empty. Offering no place to hide. Only now, of
course, would I put it like that.

I came in at dusk, and a clerk in the store came out and
pointed in a westerly direction. No road. A few wagon
tracks in the grass. Off there—he said, wagging his finger—
about two hours' walk was my uncle. I should follow the
fence on my left, keep my eyes on the tracks. As soon as the
plain was dark I would see the lights. Of his house? No, of
the sweeping beam of his tractor. They would come and go,
of course, as he circled his section of land. Twenty-three
hundred and forty acres the day I arrived.

On the clerk's suggestion I left with him the brown fiber
suitcase I was carrying. It was heavy. I had before me a
twelve-mile walk. I got off about a quarter mile when he
whistled me back to deliver a letter. One for Fremont
Osborn. I had written it a week before, myself. It contained
the happy news that I was coming, and hour of my arrival.

About ten o'clock, and ten miles later, I saw the glow of
the lights of the tractor, and maybe forty minutes later the
wind blew me the *cough-cough*. A lamp no brighter than a
candle marked the house. Sometime around midnight I delivered the letter to a man filling milk cans by the light of a
lantern. Preoccupied. Unaware that I was walking up. The
man turned out to be my Aunt Agnes, getting ready to take
her turn on the tractor. Her husband, Fremont, had just
come off it and gone to bed. He would sleep six hours, then
take it again at dawn. That is, I would. To do just that was
why I had come. We stood there together while she read
the letter, announcing in eager terms my arrival, the tractor
coughing like a dragon, the lights flickering as the motor

idled. Together, silently, we returned to the house. In a dark, windowless room, my uncle raised on his elbow to greet me. Had I no bag? Oh yes, I had left it in town. Without raising his voice he cursed me, fluently, impersonally. Did I realize if I had brought it along, it would not be necessary to drive in and get it? I was slow to realize it, other things being on my mind. In the lantern light I saw my uncle's face, his colorless eyes. Dust caked his lips, dirt caked the roots of his teeth. Rabbit hair from the earmuffs of the cap he wore stuck to his ears. He said he had no time to sit up talking, nor did I since I would take the tractor in the morning. His wife Agnes would show me to my bed, which she did. How did I sleep? I slept fine.

I slept fine the twelve weeks, five days, and nine hours I was there. Every hour counted, I counted every hour. For my sixteen-hour day I received twenty-five dollars a month. And my keep. I've always loved that word *keep*.

In the morning I saw nothing but the food on my plate, the slit of light at the window. It was on the horizon, but it might have been attached to the blind. Dawn. Sunrise would not come for another hour. The wind blowing under the house puffed dust between the floor boards, like smoke. There was never any talk. My uncle would slip off his coveralls, like a flight suit, and eat in his two suits of underwear: one of fine, snug-fitting wool, flecked with gray, like a pigeon; the other of heavy nubby cotton flannel with the elbows patched with quilting, the fly-seat yawning. The outer suit came off in the spring, but the fine inner suit was part of my uncle. In the three months I was there it came off just once. I saw him, like a plucked chicken, standing in a small washbasin of water while my Aunt Agnes wiped him off with a damp towel. Dust. He was dusted rather than washed. I learned to leave a film of it on my face and wrists to prevent chapping and windburn. Under the suit of underwear I seldom took off my skin was talcum'd like a baby. The layers of wool filtered out the coarse stuff, left a powdery ash.

Where did it come from? The prevailing wind was reasonably clean until it reached the rise where my uncle and I were making history. From the blowouts dust blew off like smoke from a grass fire. Some of the natives thought it was. They reported the matter in Hereford. No matter from what angle the wind blew, it blew the dust in my face as I plowed around the section. Sometimes I had to stop the tractor till the air cleared. One day I crawled beneath it and bawled. At the mercy of the elements, the element I feared the most was my Uncle Fremont. What God was he fighting? In his opinion all Gods were dead. What did he want of a flunky like me?

In that respect he resembled Monsieur Etienne Dulac, of Schloss Riva, who liked to put his guests, me in particular, to the test. To prove what? God only knows. In my case it merely proved that the flesh was weak. A great believer in progress, and one of the soldiers in Colonel Ingersoll's agnostic army, it had not occurred to me that my Uncle Fremont had something in common with the Meister of Riva. Temperament? Something more than temperament. They had disliked each other on sight—less than sight. A Texas Yankee in King Arthur's court, my Uncle had hardly arrived at Riva—he handed me the two bags he was carrying—when he stopped to inspect the medieval machine we used to raise buckets of rocks from the deep dry moat. A primitive winch. You can see them in the drawings of Bosch. At the sight of this object he almost died laughing. Was I crazy *too*, he wanted to know. He decided to extend his visit at Riva until he had introduced certain improvements in the way we pumped water, raised rocks, sawed wood, and cleaned snow from the roofs. He had seen idle men in the streets of Muhldorf: he would put them to work. If the idea was to rehabilitate Riva, then get on with it. He was not able to get on with it, himself, due to something unforeseen the following morning. Snow fell on him. A ton or more of it from the roof. It didn't kill him, but it did leave him impressed. I tried to explain that it was not unusual, that it happened frequently. Just a week or two before it had fallen on me. The slam of a door might set it off—among other things. Allowing for a day and a half to recover, my uncle and his bride cut their visit from the week they planned, to the weekend. I rode down with them as far as Stein, and walked back. He advised me to leave before—as he said—I was nutty as Dulac.

The castle in the Wachau and the shack on the panhandle had certain things in common. A place to hide? Some might put it like that. I'm thinking of the way one thing seemed to prevail: the snow and the wind. At Riva the snow sealed the place off like that castle in the glass ball. On the panhandle we were sealed off by the wind. Impersonal, impartial, mindless, inexhaustible prevailing wind. In three months there must have been one windless day, but what I remember is one windless night. Like a clap of thunder it woke me up. As if a supporting hand had been removed from the wall, the house shuddered. Silence? How describe it as louder than noise? I raised on my elbow in order to breathe. The silence of planetary spaces broken only by the music of the spheres is now an abstraction I find easy to grasp. A lull—that's all it would be—in the prevailing winds.

That morning I heard the crack of dawn like a whip. Just as, less than an hour later, I could peer out and see the wind where there was neither dust, lines of wash, nor even grass to blow. The yard was like a table, with a dull, flat gloss where the shoes buffed it toward the privy. Scoured by the wind, the cracks had been picked clean by the chickens. Out there, as nowhere else, I could see the wind. The five minutes in the morning I lay in a stupor listening to Agnes build the fire, I would face the window, dawn like a slit at the base of a door. In the kitchen Agnes would put fresh cobs on the banked fire. Was it the sparks in the chimney, the crackle in the stove? The cats would hear it, five or six of them. With the first draw of the fire they would start from the grain sheds toward the house, a distance of about one hundred yards. Was that so far? It can be if you crawl. In the dawn light I would see only the white cats, or those that were spotted, moving toward the house like primitive or crippled reptiles. How explain it? The invisible thrust of the wind. The hard peltless yard gave them no hold. Even the chickens, a witless bird, had learned never to leave the shelter of the house at the risk of blowing away, like paper bags. A strip of chicken wire, like a net, had been stretched to the windward of the yard to catch them. They would stick like rags, or wads of cotton, till my aunt would go out and pick them off. The cats and the hens were quick to learn about the wind. That it would prevail. My Aunt Agnes knew, but preferred not to admit it. The last to learn was Fremont Osborn. He hung on for two more wives, and ten more years. When the last of his money was gone with the wind he went back to his homestead on the Pecos—and from there to Quartzite, where he was known as a handyman.

In the early thirties I doubt if the town of Quartzite was on the map. One of those gas pumps where cigarettes, aspirin, coffee, and water were sold. In the late forties the new gold diggers, armed with walkie-talkies and Geiger counters, found deposits of uranium in the nearby hills. The town is now the home, as the sign says, of 38,000 friendly people, all of whom will greet you with *howdy, stranger* at

the drop of a hat. Most of the friendly inhabitants still live
on wheels. They sit hub to hub, in trailers, on the man-
made mesas at the edge of the freeway. In the desert light it
is often hard to tell if they are putting up a town, or tearing
one down. I came in from the west, past a sign that warned
me to keep an eye out for children, and another that advised
me it was 2740 miles to New York.

Due to certain accidents of my boyhood I feel that time
exists in space, not unlike the graphic charts that hang on
the walls of up-to-date schoolrooms. On these charts the
past lies below, in marble-like stratifications: this sort of
time can be seen better at the Grand Canyon than on the
face of a clock. A young man born where the 98th meridian
intersects the 42nd parallel might also feel that time, like
space, has a point of departure and a direction. I'm sure that
Fremont Osborn did. The past lay to the east—from where
one had come. The future lay to the west, where one was
going. In *my* time, these directions were reversed. The
past—the mythic past—lay to the west; the beckoning,
looming future lay to the east. A sense of direction does not
come easy to Americans.

At the west side of town the trailers merged with what we
describe as mobile homes. My uncle's court, the La Golondrina, featured a sign on which a bird had been painted. It
set back on what was left of the old gravel road. It had once
been a campground—a sign reading FREE WATER was still
nailed to the trunk of a sycamore. Parking space was now
renting for $20.00 a month and up.

In the mid-afternoon a light burned at a trailer with a
strip of aluminum awning, a snatch of picket fence orna-
menting the steps of the porch. A placard with the word
OFFICE was wired to the screen, to the right of it a notice
advising late arrivals to ring the bell. Before I buzzed it a

hoarse voice cried, "Yankee, go home! Yankee, go home!"
A molting parrot, chained to a perch, eyed me from where
he dangled head down. Just beyond him, undisturbed, a
woman crouched in an armless rocker. White-haired. She
sat leaning forward as if about to rise. Hard of hearing?
Neither the bell nor the parrot disturbed her. The window
toward which she leaned forward to peer was a TV screen.
On it, a man stood alone, hatless, half bowed as if in prayer.
A hushed voice enjoined quiet. A dignitary visiting a shrine,
perhaps? A religious service? My nose pressed to the screen,
I could see that the hatless gentleman held a stick. After a
moment of concentration he made the putt. With her I
watched the ball arc toward the hole—but I did not see it
drop. She had leaned forward so that her head blocked my
view. A shout from the crowd seemed to lift her, then the
fall set her to rocking. In the general excitement the parrot
croaked, "Yankee, go home!"

"We're full up!" she said without turning. I watched her
adjust one of the knobs for sharpness.

"I'm looking for a Mr. Fremont Osborn," I called. "I
understand he lives here."

"Who?" she barked, then, "Oh him." She got up from
the rocker to unhook the screen. Without glancing at my
face she wagged a finger in the direction of a tree. "He's
under it. If he's not there he's fussin' somewhere. You just
wait."

To get to the tree I followed the lane used by the trailers.
License plates were used to ornament the doors, seal up the
cracks. A dog my uncle would have called a little fice
trailed along. Several trailers occupied the leaky shade of
the tree, but one sat back so that it leaned against it. Both
the trailer and the car sat up on blocks. The car, a Ford V-8
coupe, had the weathered coloring of a desert reptile. The

hood was honed down to the metal, the upper third of the windshield like frosted glass.

The dust did not blow like that in Quartzite, but during the war, and the late forties, my uncle lived in the car on his homestead along the Pecos. It had become a piece of the landscape, an armor-plated fossil with a single frosted eye. Cans for gas, oil, and water were now in a rack on the running board. A patch of grass, a little larger than a doormat, grew between a frame of white-washed rocks, a slab of petrified wood placed in the exact center, like a petrified eye. My uncle was a great one for natural wonders, excluding man. His temple of worship was the Carlsbad Caverns—caves appealing to him more than canyons—where the architecture was known to be thirty or forty million years old. To free my mind of certain crass superstitions he took me to the bottom of the caverns, where the tourists, holding candles, assembled to sing the hymn "Rock of Ages." This spectacle brought tears of laughter to his eyes. Smaller in scale, but of the same order, were small bits of crystal known as Pecos diamonds, found around the holes of small desert rodents. They were like tiny stubs of pencils, made of rock. Six-sided, sharpened at both ends. To my Uncle Fremont they testified to the subtle craftsmanship of the Devil, gems from his workshop, to stupefy the crude craftsmen of the Lord. If they defied Aunt Winona's explanation, it pleased my uncle to think they defied all others. When I left the dustbowl for college he presented me with a Bull Durham sack of his Pecos diamonds, with which I would stupefy the men of learning as well as those of the Lord. Soon enough I found they were a type of crystal. Did I think, he asked, *that* was an explanation? He wanted miracles, but he wanted his own kind. The Pecos diamonds were pieces of his own miraculous cross.

I stood gazing at the petrified eye he had planted in his

small garden. Several leaves of long-stemmed grass sheltered it like lashes.

"That is wood," said the voice. "Would you believe it?"

An old man with a stubble of beard, smiling, removed his glasses to see me better. He held them out before him to see what it was that blocked his view. Dust? They were fly-specked. He drew them back to sigh a breath on each lens, but without moisture. The air was too dry. He returned them, unpolished, to his eyes.

"Is that so?"

"Yes it is. I polished it myself."

Stooped, I could see the sweat-stained crown of his hat. In the band there were several blue-tipped kitchen matches. Another cornered his mouth. He wore hook-and-eye work shoes, with box toes, khaki pants pressed with an iron, gal-luses that left their shadowy trace on the back of his shirt. A watch weighted the pocket of his shirt, a leather thong looped to the gallus. He removed the match from his mouth, and used the chewed frayed end as a pointer.

"They estimate such wood to be eighty thousand years of age."

"Is that so?"

"Yes, indeedy."

Glancing at him, sidelong, I saw an elderly hired hand, employed. Nothing in the way of a shock of recognition in what I saw, only in what I heard. The voice? No, the speech. The uncultivated cultivation. I had been wrong about the smile. With the match out of his mouth the expression was one made by the weather, the eye-protecting squint lifting the corners of the mouth.

"You want space? I'm afraid we don't have it. Full up. We've been full up for months."

Over the crown of his hat I saw the familiar wasteland of

a used-car lot. What he saw seemed to please him. "Full up for months," he repeated. He spoke with pride.

"I wasn't looking for space. I was looking for you."

"For me?" He removed his glasses, put his head forward as he did at dawn, in the flickering lights of the tractor, to shout directions and curses above the cough of the motor. His eyes slits in the mask of dust. In them, however, I saw nothing of the apprehension I would have felt if a stranger had found *me* out. Nothing but puzzlement. "Now why would that be? You from Mrs. Wylie? I'm afraid I've had to give up the haying. I have not recovered from an operation as readily as I had hoped."

"You don't remember me? That's funny. I have your letter here somewhere. You wrote me to ask if I wouldn't come to Hereford and help with the tractor. Good job. Board and twenty-five bucks a month. Well, here I am."

For a moment, blinking, he searched his mind for the letter, unaccustomed to that sort of horseplay.

"I'm sorry—" I interrupted, feeling like a fool, but he put his hand on my sleeve to stop me. As if he might sneeze, he turned away and drew a kerchief from his rear pocket. But he did not sneeze. He blew his nose, daubed at the corners of his eyes. Still faced away he said, "Don't josh me, boy. I just don't see quite as sharp as I once did."

"Neither do I." He took that for granted. The frailty of others never surprised him.

"You got the letter? Winona gave me your address. You move around so much I can't track you."

"I got it." I felt around in my pocket thinking I might show it to him. "It's from Riva. You remember Riva?"

"Let me get a chair—" he said, turning away, and dipped his head as he stepped through the door of his trailer. One he had made? Birds were nesting in the small peep window at the front, unopened. "Here, boy," he said, and reached me a chair with a freshly patched cane bottom. The legs wired. He took a stool from under the sink for himself. "No, no—" he said when I tried to swap with him—"what would Nona think if I sat you on a stool?" The urban softness of my life had always been a subject of amusement. Before I could comment he was back in the trailer. "Grape-ade or root beer. Do I recall you like root beer?"

I had liked root beer until the winter in Hereford when I had to rinse the dust out of my mouth with it. It had always seemed a little gritty to me since. "Make it grape," I replied, and he made it grape, dissolving the mixture from an envelope into a tall glass of water. He stirred it with the handle of a spoon. With a pick he broke a little ice from the cake in his icebox, a cooling sound I hadn't heard for many years.

"I'm thinking of wiring the trailer, Warren. It would help with my reading. Help my eyes." The confession was intended to make me more his equal, as it did. He had never needed glasses to read, nor pain-killers when he went to the dentist.

"You're looking fine," I said, and looked at him. Did he look fine? It had not occurred to me that Fremont Osborn would age like normal people. Die he would have to, but somehow without aging. Was it correct to say that he had? He offered me the grape-ade—having root beer himself— then sat erect on the backless stool. The remnant of color in his eyes matched the faded denim in his shirt. His tucked-up pant leg, the seam sharp, exposed the fold of underwear in his gartered sock. In the creases of his shoes, and his body, there would still be Texas dust.

"I had an operation, Warren. Prostatic. Clean you out with a piece of wire. Very painful. I passed a good deal of pus and blood. It seems to me my recovery is slow."

"These things take time."

"Five hundred dollars. Dr. Goodnight said, if you can't pay it, Osborn, fill these forms out. Dr. Goodnight, I said, if I could not pay for it I would not have the operation. I paid it. I believe he thought me a plain damn fool."

"Things have changed even in my time."

"Warren, what would you say your time was?" He was not ironic, merely curious.

"My time?" I looked around as if I might see it. Cars. Cars flashing by on the thruway. "At least part of it is your time. Between us, you know, we invented the dustbowl. Just last month or so I heard it was still blowing. Like the good old days."

He put a hand to his forehead, the thumb resting on his cheekbone. Between the fingers I could see the pale veined lids of his eyes. Was he recalling? Did it seem near to him or far? He had been in his late forties—about my age—when I went to work for him in Texas. Perhaps that was not his past at all, but my past. To jog his memory I said, "You remember the trip to the Carlsbad Caverns?" He seemed to.

"I hope you've learned to drive a car, Warren, better than you did then." On the way back from Carlsbad, driving at night, I had run over the curbing of a street divider in Rosswell, denting both front rims. I remembered, but it was not the sort of thing that popped into my mind.

He had bought a radio the size of a piano that operated on storage batteries. They had run down before I got there. The names of foreign stations were printed on the dial. The battery space was used to store cartons of the Haldeman-Julius Little Blue Books. "The Little Blue Books?" I said. "You still have them?" I carried one on the tractor with me. *How to Improve Your Vocabulary.* I memorized lists of words, one of them being vertiginous. His head was wagging slowly, as if it hurt him. "You don't remember what happened to the Blue Books?"

"I guess Howard took them, Warren. He was a fine boy, Howard."

"Howard?"

"He come from Wichita, Warren. Nephew of Agnes. Came right along when he heard you left us. He was about your size—" he looked at me—"size you were then. But not afraid of work."

"I was probably not enthusiastic about getting up at four-twenty in the morning. But I got up. I wouldn't say I was afraid of it."

"He wore the clothes you left, so he wasn't any bigger. Might have been a little smaller. But he could work."

"How long did Howard stay?"

"Till Agnes died, Warren. Maybe two, three years."

"He must have really liked to work, but I wouldn't go so far as to say he was smart."

"Howard was smart enough to finish his schooling, Warren. He was smart enough to finish what he started."

That I hadn't finished my schooling had been a sore point with Fremont Osborn. I had left him to go to college, then left college to go to Europe. He shook his head slowly. "Howard was a country boy, Warren. He knew how to work. You had a city boy's ways."

To have survived three months on my uncle's dust farm, sixteen hours a day, thirty days a month, with a rash on my body from the diet of pork and eggs, had been a point of pride with me for more than thirty years. From the seat of the same tractor the past looked a good deal different. The boy who was proving himself to be a man was a beardless kid with soft city boy's ways, subject to a rash from the diet of pork and eggs.

My uncle's head began to wag. "You were a funny kid,

Warren. You wouldn't eat. You'd eat one egg and a biscuit and leave your meat. Agnes used to say no wonder you couldn't work since you didn't eat."

The mention of the food brought its taste to my mouth. Pork. Pork fried in its own fat, then stored in an oil barrel at the back of the house till Agnes fished it out to fry with the morning eggs. If I didn't bolt an egg down fast the smell of the pork would make me sick. I let the biscuits dry in my pocket and ate them on the tractor like hardtack. Had I complained? I took it—I thought—like a man. My uncle uncrossed his legs to place his hands on his knees, rocking forward. His silent laughter brought tears to his eyes. "You're old enough to tell now, boy, but I don't think Agnes ever got used to it. You wet your bed. Boy your age a little too old for that."

A wheeze escaped him as he thought of it, he slapped a thigh. I let it pass. Better to ignore it than touch on the subject of a boy's wet dreams. My uncle shared the hog we butchered with a family of tenant farmers named Gudgers. The oldest of their nine children was a girl named Georgia. She liked to wrestle with boys. I was known to be a boy and a wrestler. The smell and taste of Georgia had stayed with me like that of the pork. My dreams had been a boy's dreams, up until then, but they began to give me trouble after Georgia. No one had ever told her to stop doing what she found to be fun. My uncle was a great believer in girls and boys, in preference to birds and bees, but his Blue Book library had come a little early for Freud.

To change the topic I said, "You remember the ducks? I was a pretty good shot if it was dark enough."

"You mean geese, Warren?"

I suppose I meant geese. I had shot at them without knowing what they were. Or seeing them. Two hours before dawn we had left the dark house to shoot at what I thought might be cattle rustlers. In the windless pause before my uncle ran forward hooting like an Indian, I prepared myself to shoot it out with Billy the Kid. When he ran forward, hooting, I shot into the sky over his head. A great flapping of wings, but very little honking. I think I managed to fire two or three rounds. Still dark, we came back to the house where Agnes had coffee perking and a fire going. When the sky was light we went out to see if we had bagged any birds. Just shooting blind into the flock we had bagged nine. So we had fresh gamy meat for two weeks and there were scraps of lead shot on my plate in the evening, some of which I kept and used over in my bee-bee gun.

My uncle put a hand to his eyes, then removed it without speaking. What he saw, or remembered, seemed to be of little interest.

"One cannot live in the past, Warren. I'm glad to say I never wanted to."

Did I look at Fremont Osborn as he had looked at the boy who had wet his bed? My legendary uncle, inventor of the dustbowl, the man who sought his new brides with mail-order snapshots—where, if not the past, did he think he was living? Root beer, ice picks, hook-and-eye shoes, the white heel-and-toe worksox with the mottled tops that came in bundles of one and two dozen, tied up in strong twine that I would find around a spool in his kitchen drawer.

"I'm not suggesting living in the past," I said, "but since you brought it up, I'm not sure I wouldn't want to."

"I'm glad your mother isn't here to hear you say that, Warren."

My mother? It took me a moment to remember she was Fremont Osborn's sister. His younger sister, and favorite. I had learned that from Winona. In the four months I had lived with him in Texas he had never once mentioned her name.

"My mother—" I began, but he interrupted.

"If there was one thing she hated it was the past. She hated all of it. If she thought you were fool enough to want to go live there, don't think she would have had you. As it was, it killed her."

The irony of it did not escape him. His head wagged. "What you think the Lord Almighty would make of that?"

I didn't want to open up his favorite topic, the crazy ways of the Lord. "You sure she would feel that way today?" The question did not surprise him. No, I had the feeling he had given it some thought.

"You see that, boy?" He pointed a finger where a piece of frazzled rope dangled from a limb. What was left of a swing. The earth beneath it had been scooped to a trough. "She was a crackerjack, I tell you. Why, you should have seen her. I'd tie bottles to swing from a branch of the catalpa. Fifty yards. She'd be the first between us to hit it. We did that on Sundays when father and the girls would be off to church."

The *girls?* He did not classify my mother as one of the girls. A crackerjack. Time had not blurred the image before his eyes. He seemed to see her as he squinted down an invisible barrel. "Look there!" I looked to where telephone wires dipped between the poles. I looked for birds, sparrows. I had managed to hit a sparrow or two myself. "There, there!" he corrected, "the insulators!" and half rose to wag his finger at the glass knobs on the crossbar. Two were gone. In the desert light the two remaining glittered like ice. "Why, boy, you should have seen her. From the seat of the buggy. Never the need to rein in the horses. From the seat of the buggy she would crack them like bottles!" Two, three times he snapped his fingers. I seemed to see them shatter like light bulbs before my eyes. "See the glass in the ditches when the snow melted. Think the line

crew thought it was the cold that did it!" One of his brown
hands rose from his lap and slapped smartly on his thigh,
like a country fiddler. It set the leg to wagging. "Why,
boy—" he repeated, but paused there when words failed
him. To see what he lacked the words to describe he closed
his eyes.

I had been told my mother was something of a beauty,
but not that she had been a rival of Annie Oakley. I tried to
see her, as my uncle did, on the lids of his eyes. Was this my
mother—my pioneer mother—or Fremont Osborn's dream
of a woman, one of the many that escaped him once his
wife, Agnes, died. One who could shoot a Winchester,
curse God, and skillfully wring the neck of a chicken. My
father, however, would not have wooed a woman who was
quicker on the trigger than the heartstrings, and found little
more to do in the seat of a buggy than load and fire a bolt-
action rifle. Not my father. No, nor his son. What past
were we reporting on? For my uncle the past ended when
my mother stopped shooting at bottles. For my father, with
the birth of his son. For me, it did not end at these points,
but began.

"What would she shoot at today?" I ventured. "The
telphone people might be a little touchy."

He opened his eyes, wide, as if he might see. The windshields of cars flashed on the highway; overhead, somewhere, a plane circled for a landing. He followed its slow
wheeling. Did he think my mother would have sniped at
planes? "The kids played with dolls and toys, Warren. Not
her. She liked the newest and the best. She liked a good
saddle. You know what she would be shooting at today?
She would be shooting at the moon!"

The thought had just come to him. It left him unsettled,
as it did me. In his excitement at my mother's future he
stood up, moved his stool, then sat down. What astonished

me most? Hearing such a remark from Fremont Osborn, her brother, or the thought of my mother bloatedly encased in a helmeted spacesuit, the world's first female astronaut?

"Your mother, boy, had no truck with the past. She turned her back on it. That was the trouble with the girls and father. All of them but Grace believed in his religious nonsense. It ruined their lives. Grace scorned it. She wanted to live—" he brought his hand down on his knee—"right here and now."

Did I seem to question that?

"What are you thinking, Warren?" When we sat around the kitchen range in Texas he would sometimes say, "Boy, what are you thinking?" I never seemed to know. "No, no," he would say, "you are thinking of *something*. The mind never thinks of nothing." So I thought of something.

"I was just thinking that I never before heard you mention my mother."

It set him back. He screwed one finger in his ear as if to clear it of the question.

"What's that? No, no. You have forgotten. I have never for one moment forgotten Grace."

"I didn't say forgotten. I said mention. I don't recall your ever mentioning her name."

"You were young, boy. Same age she was. She didn't moon about the past and she wouldn't want you to. You couldn't do more for her than live right here and now—the way she would have." He blew his nose, then pushed up his glasses to dab his eyes. "You're no more a match for her than Will, boy. That's your father. He was smart but he couldn't match her. If she lived his life would have turned out different, I can tell you."

It was known that my father's life turned out badly. How about mine?

"I don't say better, Warren, just different. So would yours."

"If my mother had lived, her life might have been of interest, but not mine."

"All I know about your life, Warren, is what Winona writes me."

Did that seem to be more than enough? It did. The odd thing about Fremont Osborn was that he believed himself very much like other people. Not quite so stupid, or superstitious, but of the same clay. In what *here and now* did he think he lived? This hired hand with the ballad voice, the careful speech, the buried past, the snapshots for a new mail-order bride, still an active minuteman in Colonel Ingersoll's war to free men of ancient and modern superstitions. A self-made man, a fossil intact as the leaf and the fish found in the rock face, unaware that the land had replaced the sea, and the tree petrified. On what branch of it did he think he belonged? He had washed his own socks, repaired his own heels, paid for and suffered his own operation, and he would die, in due time, his own death. He sat with lean brown hands quiet in his lap, the foot of his crossed leg nodding to a strong pulse. A reasonably fearless man, he feared the phantom past. It was the past, not the freeway, nor hepatitis, nor strontium, nor polio shots, nor fallout that he warned me against. Why? Out of it he had sprung, and my mother, on a spring too fine for rewinding, and in time such distempered metal as myself. My uncle, Fremont Osborn, had been the first of the Osborns to fly in the teeth of custom, to plow up the dust, to buy a car worth more than the shack he lived in, a radio to bring the world to his feet, a library to ventilate superstition—but he was not the first to seek a mail-order bride. The usable past was the here and now. Twenty years after he had put the past behind him he circulated photographs for mail-order brides, none of whom were hog butchers, like Agnes, sharp-shooters like my mother, nor long the wife of Fremont Osborn, man of his time.

What time was *that?* I suddenly remembered why I had come.

"You remember Riva? That old castle you came to?"

He made no sign, then said, "Boy, we seen nothing but old castles. Too many of them."

"I was there. The one near Vienna. I remember you went rabbit hunting."

His hand raised, came down with a slap on his thigh. "Rabbit hunting? You recall it? Ten of us out there all night, not one seen a rabbit. Why, boy, they were all as crazy as that old man. Crazy as a coot."

"He wasn't so old, at the time." My Uncle Fremont had been a good ten years older.

"Looked old to me. Why, he could hardly walk. Think Gladys thought he'd die before we got away from there. One of the things that scared her. Thought she'd freeze to death herself."

"He just died. What I came to ask you is if you'd like to go along to his funeral."

"You in your right mind, Warren? Why'd I do a crazy thing like that?"

"He sent me a notice. Two of them. He wants somebody there. Somebody who knew him." I paused, then added, "Somebody's got to be there."

"I'm glad your mother isn't here to hear you."

"Look—"

"You can't live in the past, boy. Can't even die in it. Take this old fool you mention. If he's dead, he died in the present. Same as you and me will." He grinned, then added, "Besides, Mrs. Wylie's grown accustomed to rely on me, Warren. Something always needs fixin'." He stood up, remembering something. "Shriveled-up little fellow, wasn't he? Way he looked I didn't think he'd last the winter."

On the highway the cars blurred the hills like a flagging

windshield wiper. A pneumatic drill tore something down, or put something up. The polished surface of the petrified wood reflected a foreshortened view of Fremont Osborn. Inside his trailer a buzzer sounded like a door alarm.

"That's Mrs. Wylie, Warren. Guess she needs me." He rubbed his hands briskly together, eager to be useful. "I've got a spare cot, Warren, if you'd like to stay over."

"I've got to get back," I replied. "It's a long drive."

"I remember when it took me three days to get to Hereford." He wagged his head. "Don't they plan to get to the moon sooner than that?" The prospect stirred him. He stepped to where he had a better view of the sky. "I'll tell Nona you were here, boy. She's fond of you. Thinks of you as her boy. You can tell her if there was more women like her maybe your Uncle Fremont wouldn't be a bachelor."

He brought his hand down on my shoulder as he had once brought it down on the haunch of a horse. I led off, but his gait took him past me, crunching the raked gravel in the footpath. From the door of her trailer Mrs. Wylie called, with the handle of a spoon pointed out another trailer. Head down from his perch the parrot croaked, "Yankee, go home! Yankee, go home!" until Mrs. Wylie slapped him silent with a folded magazine.

"How is Mr. Castro?" my uncle inquired, and paused to let the bird gnaw on one of his fingers. With his free hand he waved me a good-by. "If you go to that funeral—" he began, but the parrot, Castro, outsquawked him. Mrs. Wylie threatened him with her spoon, but he paid her no heed.

THE
WORKS
OF
LOVE

A novel

In the Wilderness

1

IN the dry places, men begin to dream. Where the rivers run sand, there is something in man that begins to flow. West of the 98th Meridian—where it sometimes rains and it sometimes doesn't—towns, like weeds, spring up when it rains, dry up when it stops. But in a dry climate the husk of the plant remains. The stranger might find, as if preserved in amber, something of the green life that was once lived there, and the ghosts of men who have gone on to a better place. The withered towns are empty, but not uninhabited. Faces sometimes peer out from the broken windows, or whisper from the sagging balconies, as if this place—now that it is dead—had come to life. As if empty it is forever occupied. One of these towns, so the story would have it, was Indian Bow.

According to the record, a man named Will Brady was born on a river without water, in a sod house, near the trading post of Indian Bow. In time he grew to be a man who neither smoked, drank, gambled, nor swore. A man who headed no cause, fought in no wars, and passed his life unaware of the great public issues—it might be asked: why trouble with such a man at all? What is there left to say of a man with so much of his life left out? Well, there are women, for one thing—men of such caliber leave a lot up to the women—but in the long run Will Jennings Brady is there by himself. That might be his story. The man who was more or less by himself.

His father, Adam Brady, a lonely man, living in the sod house without a dog or a woman, spoke of the waste land around Indian Bow as God's country. It was empty. That was what he meant. If a man came in, he soon left on the next caboose. As a pastime, from the roof of his house, Adam Brady took potshots at the cupola, or at the rear platform, where the brakeman's lantern hung. He never hit anything. In his opinion, God's country should be like that.

Adam Brady's sod house was like a mound, or a storm cave, and after the first big snow of the winter just the snout, like a reluctant ground hog, could be seen peering out. The rest of the year it looked like the entrance to an abandoned mine. On the long winter nights the coyotes would gather to howl on the roof, or scratch their backs on the longhorns put up there to frighten them off. In the spring their tracks could be seen around the door, where the earth was soft.

Adam Brady spent several winters in this house alone. But one windy fall, with the winter looming, he put on his dark suit, his wide-brimmed hat, his military boots from the Confederate army, and rode eighty miles east in search of a photographer. He found one in the up-and-coming town of Calloway. The picture shows Brady standing, hat in hand, with a virgin forest painted in behind him, and emerging from this forest a coyote and a one-eyed buffalo. The great humped head is there, but the rest of the beast is behind the screen.

This picture might have given any woman pause, but

there was no indication, anywhere in it, of the landscape through the window that Adam Brady faced. There was not an inkling of the desolation of the empty plain. No hint of the sky, immense and faded, such as one might see in a landscape of China—but without the monuments that indicated men had passed, and might still be there. In that place, remote as it was, men at least had found time to carve a few idols, and others had passed either in order to worship, or to mutilate them. But in this place—this desolation out the window—what was there? Nothing but the sky that pressed on the earth with the dead weight of the sea, and here and there a house such as a prairie dog might have made.

Adam Brady had ten prints made of this picture, and six of them he mailed to old friends in Ohio; four he passed out to strangers, traveling men, that is, on their way east. A man who wanted a woman had to advertise for her, as he did for a cow. And a woman who wanted a man might be led to forget—for the time being—that great virgin forests are not, strictly speaking, part of the plains. That one-eyed buffaloes are seldom seen peering out of them. For there was some indication that the man in this picture lived in a real house, had friends and good neighbors, and perhaps a bay mare to draw a red-wheeled, green-tasseled gig. And that on Sunday afternoons he would drive his new wife down tree-lined roads. There was no indication that the man in the picture had on nearly everything that he owned, including a key-wind watch with a bent minute-hand. On the back of this picture, in a good hand, it was written that the man to be seen on the front, Adam Brady by name, was seeking a helpmate and a wife. And there was every indication that this man meant what he said.

What became of nine pictures there is no record, but the tenth, well thumbed and faded, with a handlebar mustache added, finally got around to Caroline Clayton, an Indiana girl. She was neither a widow nor, strictly speaking, a girl any more. Her independent cast of mind had not appealed to the returning Civil War boys. What she saw in this picture it is hard to say, as both the forest and the buffalo had faded, the coyote was gone, and someone had punched holes in Adam Brady's eyes. But whatever she saw, or thought she saw, she wrote to him. In her letter, sealed with red wax, she enclosed a picture of herself taken at a time when she had been, almost, engaged. A touch of color had been added to the cheeks. She gazed into a wicker cage from which the happy bird had flown. We see her facing this cage, her eyes on the empty perch, a startled look of pleasure on her face, and though she is plain, very plain, there is something about the eyes—

> *I can see very clearly* [Adam Brady replied] *your lovely eyes, with the hidden smile, but I am not sure that I, nor any man, might plumb their depths and tell you what they mean. I fix my own eyes upon you without shame, and I see your face avert for my very boldness, and I can only compare the warm blush at your throat with the morning sky.*

Another place he spoke of the illicit sweetness of the flesh.

> *—I can say I know the passions of the men about me, and the heated anguish of the blood, but I have never tasted the illicit sweetness of the flesh.*

There was hardly room, in letters such as this, to speak of grasshopper plagues like swirling clouds in the sky, or of the wooden shapes of cattle frozen stiffly upright out on the range. No, it was hardly the place, and when she arrived, the last day of November, Adam Brady had to carry her through drifts of snow while leading his horse. There was no time for her to think, no place to reflect, there was nothing but the fact that a tall bearded man, smelling like a saddle blanket, carried her half a mile, then put her down on the ground *inside* of his house. There it was, right there beneath her, instead of a floor. Had there been something like a road, or a neighboring house, or a passing stranger that she might have called to, Will Jennings Brady, as we know him, might not have been born. But as it was, he came along soon enough. In September, when the grass had turned yellow on the sun-baked roof.

In this sod house, the cracked walls papered with calendar pictures of southern Indiana, Will Jennings Brady, according to the record, was born. The grasshoppers ate the harness off a team of mares that year. That was how Adam Brady, his father, remembered it. Just four years later, in the month of October, Adam Brady put a roll of baling wire around his waist and went up the ladder on the windmill to make a repair. That was all that was known, and the story would have it that Emil Barton, the station agent, found him swinging like a bell clapper between the windmill posts. Adam Brady's boots were given to Emil Barton, as they still had, as was said, life in them, but his ticking watch was put aside for Will Brady, his son.

In the town of Indian Bow there was a dog named Shep, who was brown and white and had a long tail, and a boy named Gerald, about the same dirty color, but no tail. There was also a depot, a cattle loader, several square frame houses with clapboard privies; and later there were stores with pressed tin ceilings along the tracks. In the barber shop were a gum machine and a living rubber plant. Over this shop was a girl named Stella, who ate the boogers out of her nose, and her little brother Roger, who was inclined to eat everything else. Over the long dry summer it added up to quite a bit. But in Willy Brady's opinion it was still not enough.

From the roof of the soddy he could see the white valley

road, the dry bed of the river, and the westbound freights slowly pulling up the grade. These trains might be there, winding up the valley, for an hour or more. Sometimes a gig or a tassel-fringed buggy that had left Indian Bow in the morning would still be there—that is, the dust would be there—in the afternoon. Like everything else, it didn't seem to know just where to go. The empty world in the valley seemed to be the only world there was. A boy on the roof of the soddy, or seated on the small drafty hole in the privy, might get the notion, now and then, that he was the last man in the world. That neither the freight trains, the buggy tracks, nor the dust was going anywhere. But if at times this empty world seemed unreal, or if he felt he was the last real man in it, he didn't let this feeling keep him awake at night, or warp his character. He grew up. He went to work for Emil Barton, the stationmaster.

Emil Barton passed most of the day near the stove where he could tip forward and spit in the woodbox, or open the stove door and make a quick frying sound on the hot coals. Then he would twist his lips between his first finger and his thumb. That always left a brown stain on his thumb, and he would sit there, rubbing the stain between his fingers, and when it seemed to be gone he would hold these fingers to his nose. The smell never rubbed off. It always seemed to be there when he sniffed for it.

Will Brady remembered that, as he did the deep scar on Emil Barton's forehead, which turned bluish white in winter as if the bone was showing through. It was said that this had happened over a woman, in a fight. It was said that Emil Barton had lost the woman, but the other man had lost his right eye, which Emil Barton kept in a whisky bottle at the back of his house.

As Emil Barton's assistant, Will Brady wore a cracked green visor with a soft leather band, black sateen dusters, and an indelible pencil behind one ear. During the long afternoons he sat at the window looking down the curving tracks to the semaphore, the switch near the cattle loader, and the bend in the river called Indian Bow. Now and then the Overland Express roared through, blowing on the windows like a winter gale, rocking the lamps in the station, and leaving a fine ashy grit on his teeth. Once or twice a year the express might stop, to pick up some cattleman or let one off, and when this happened the dining-car windows would throw their light on the tracks. Through the wide diner windows Will Brady would see the men and women from another world. They seemed to think Will Brady was as strange a sight as themselves. They would stare at him, he would stare at them, and then the train would take them off with just the blinking red lights, like a comet's tail, showing down the tracks.

Otherwise he might have stayed there, seated at the wide desk, listening to what the chirping ticker said, married Stella Bickel, and watered the rubber plant in her father's shop. But Stella Bickel married a brakeman on the C., B. & Q., and Indian Bow being on the Union Pacific, she moved east to Grand Island, where she could keep an eye on him. And just six months later, early in March, having made up her mind to go home to Indiana, Caroline Clayton Brady went to bed and died. The decision, Emil Barton said, was too much for her. He didn't say, in so many words, that it would soon be too much for Will Brady, but he let it be known that there were more things opening up down the line. East that is, down the grade toward Calloway. There was a roundhouse there, and a man could go to Omaha on week ends.

And Emil Barton was there, his hat in his hand, the sleeting rain cold on his bald head, when they stood on the raw pine board at the edge of his mother's grave. Over the wide

valley spread a dim rain, the slopes of the hills grained like a
privy clapboard, and the wind blowing a cloud of mist, like
smoke, along the tracks. There was no woman at the station
to see a man off—or ask him to hurry back. There was no
dust to follow the dead wagon back into town. This desolate place, this rim of the world, had been God's country to
Adam Brady, but to his wife, Caroline Clayton, a godforsaken hole. Perhaps only Will Brady could combine these
two points of view. He could leave it, that is, but he would
never get over it.

2

When the eastbound freight pulled over on the siding,
about half a mile west of the town of Calloway, Will Brady
put on his shoes and came out on the platform of the
caboose. Just north of the siding was a lumberyard where
several men were working, piling new lumber, and beyond
the yard was a long frame building with a flat roof. Eight or
ten young women were out on the roof, drying their hair.
When they saw Will Brady two of the girls jeered at him.
They were very young, with loud voices, and this may have
had something to do with the fact that Will Brady took a
great interest in the lumberyard. One of the men in the
yard wore a carpenter's apron, with deep nail pockets at the
front, but another seemed to carry all the nails he needed in
his mouth. He fed them out, one at a time, as he hammered
them.

Now, these goings on seemed to interest Will Brady very
much. He had never seen so much wood before—perhaps
that was it. Nor so many women—though he preferred one
woman at a time. And there was one, oddly enough, seated

on the porch. This woman had also washed her hair, and one man might have judged it golden, like corn silk, while another might have found it somewhat brittle, more the color of straw. But there it was, anyhow, drying on her head. She wore a green kimono with faded red dragons on the loose sleeves. In her hand she held a magazine, but so great was her interest in the lumberyard, and in what the men were doing, that it was placed face-down in her lap. When the men dropped the timber she watched the yellow sawdust rise in the air. She saw it collect in the dark beard of the man who ran the saw. Perhaps it was the smell, like one out of a garden, or the noon sun beating down on the yellow timber, or the white arms of the men now that it was spring and their sleeves were rolled, but whatever it was, it seemed to her a marvelous sight. Not once did she raise her eyes to the young man in the wide-brimmed hat, his face in shadow, standing on the platform of the caboose. Would that explain what came over him? Why, as the express roared past, he took the wide-brimmed hat from his head and sailed it out on the air, as if the wind had sucked it off? There it sailed through the air, the woman looking at it, and as the freight began to move, the young man threw his wicker bag into the ditch, jumped after it. After all, that had been his father's hat. There would be another train, but perhaps in all the world just one hat like that. So he went after the hat, and it would be hard to say whether the woman with the yellow hair saw or did not see what a fine young man he was. A little narrow in the shoulders, but with his father's long legs. And now that his hat was off, there was his mother's wavy hair. Whether she saw these things or not there is no telling, as his hat was on, his face was in shadow, when he walked past her toward the town. No telling what she thought, but every indication that she sized him up.

Through the window of the Merchant's Hotel he could see the potted palms at the front of the lobby, and the row of oak rockers, with leather seats, facing the tracks. In one of the rockers sat a man with a black linen vest. He wore elastic bands on his sleeves, and in one pocket of the linen vest were several indelible pencils with bright red caps. The man was large, but he didn't look too well. His face was about the same color as his light tan button shoes, and when he got out of the rocker he took his time, as if he needed help. But he was friendly enough. As they walked back to the desk he rested one hand on Will Brady's shoulder and with the other slipped a chew of tobacco into his mouth.

"Young man," he said, "I take it you missed your train?"

"I got off," Will Brady said, "I was getting off."

"My name is Bassett," the big man said, "two esses and two tees." He smiled, then he said: "There's nothing in Omaha we haven't got right here." He let that sink in, then he said: "You know what I mean?" Will Brady nodded his head. The man laughed, then went on: "Hotel on the European plan, girls on the American plan—you know what I mean?"

"Yes sir," said Will Brady, as his mother had brought him up right.

"Young man," said Mr. Bassett, and took from the case a box of cigars, placed it on the counter, "I could use a man like you right here if he wasn't afraid of work." He let that sink in, then he said: "Have a cigar?"

"No, thank you, sir," Will Brady said, "I don't smoke."

"You don't smoke?" said Mr. Bassett.

"I just never started," said Will Brady.

"You like a drink?" said Mr. Bassett.

"Thank you very much," Will Brady said, "but I don't drink."

"What is your name, son?" Mr. Bassett said, and put his hands on the counter as if for support. His mouth stood open, and Will Brady saw the purple pencil stain on his lip.

"Brady, sir," he said, "Will Jennings Brady."

"You don't drink an' you don't smoke," Mr. Bassett said. "Tell me, boy—you anything against the ladies?"

"No, sir," said Will Brady, and took off his hat as his face felt hot. From the pocket of his coat he took a clean handkerchief and blew his nose into it.

3

As the night clerk in the Merchant's Hotel, Will Brady wore a green visor, quite a bit like the old one, and a vest that Mr. Bassett ordered for him from Omaha. There were pockets in the vest for indelible pencils, a new stem-wind Dueber-Hampden, and the cigars that traveling men might offer him. "Just because you don't smoke, son," Mr. Bassett had said, "don't think you're any better than the man who does." By that he meant to accept the cigar and keep his mouth shut. Give it back to the man the next time he came around. In the last pocket, pinned there, was the key to the coin drawer. In the coin drawer were stamps, fifty dollars in silver, and a Colt revolver with five deep notches in the mother-of-pearl handle. During the night the Colt was slung in the holster strapped to the leg of the desk.

Most of the day Will Brady slept in a room with several copper fire extinguishers, a stack of galvanized buckets, and about sixty feet of cracked canvas hose. A good many traveling men fell asleep while smoking their cigars. Others were apt to doze off in the lobby, a coat pocket or a vest burning, and the smell in some cases was not much different from that of the cigar. He would have to leave the desk and walk up front for a look at them. On the back of each room door he nailed a sign bearing the signature of Ralph O. Bassett:

PUT OUT CIGAR
Before
PUTTING OUT LIGHTS

Twelve hours a night he sat in the lobby facing the map of the state of Nebraska, or the Seth Thomas clock which he wound once a week. On the wall with the clock were five or six railroad calendars. A man with time on his hands might imagine himself in the Royal Gorge, crossing the Great Divide, or with the honeymoon couple as they motored through the Garden of the Gods. There were no pictures of Indiana, nor of holy men feeding the birds, but, thanks to his mother, he was at home with calendars. They were alike, in that the scenes were all far away.

Nearer at home was the map of Nebraska, with the chicken-track railroad lines, and the dark-ringed holes that the traveling men had burned with their cigars. One at Calloway, Grand Island, Columbus, and Omaha. Every now and then a town was added, the name printed in by the man who had found it, with the help of other men who had been there or had some notion where it was. The country was booming, as one man said. This man could prove it to you, pointing at the map, but the truth was that Will Brady, who seemed bright enough in some ways, had a hard time visualizing such things. He could stare for hours at the hole in the map without seeing very much. Eyes open, all he saw was the map; and eyes closed, all that came to mind was the smell of the floor mop and the ticking of the Seth Thomas clock.

He had arranged with Ralph Bassett to take the night off once a week. What was there to do with it in a place like

Calloway? A married man, of course, didn't face the same problem, but when Will Brady took the night off he walked down the tracks to the building where the girls washed their hair on the roof. At the side of this building was a sagging flight of stairs with a lantern at the top. If this lantern happened to be burning, it was Will Brady's night off. The wire handle on the lantern would be hot from the flame, and he would have to wrap his handkerchief around it before he took it down from the hook and opened the door. With the smoking lantern in his hand, he would step inside. He had learned to set it on the floor, not the rug, but he had still not learned how to take off his shoes, or his socks, without sitting down on the side of the bed. He would tap the cinders in the heels of his shoes into the palm of his hand. If it was summer and warm, he might even take off his socks.

What was he up to? Well, the woman in the bed had a word for it. He was a lover. That was her way of putting it. Her name was Opal Mason and she talked pretty frankly about some things. That might seem an odd way to describe a man who brought nothing along, said nothing loving, and left a good deal up to the woman, to say the least. A lover in some ways perhaps, but not too bright. He went about his business and then he rolled over and went to sleep.

He also slept very well, while she seemed to sleep indifferently; sleeping was something she could do, as she put it, at another time. It was not something she did when she had other things on her mind. The lover lay on his side, his heavy head on her arm, his breath blowing wisps of yellow hair in her face, and she lay on her back listening to the engines switch around in the yard. A big woman, with straw-colored hair, Opal Mason usually cried when somebody died, when babies were born, or when certain men slept with her. Like the lover, for instance. Something about it struck her as sad. In her opinion, a woman's opinion, there was something very lonely about a lantern, the tooting of switch engines, and the way men were inclined to fall asleep. Something strange, that is, about lying awake with a man sound asleep. Perhaps this struck her as the loneliest thing of all. The town of Calloway struck her as lonely since she had the smoking lanterns, the tooting engines, and the sleeping lover all at one time. It made her strangely melancholy. It was a pleasure for her to cry.

Every lover took time as well as patience; and lying awake, Opal Mason had come to have the notion that men did not come, the lovers did not come, merely to sleep with her. No, they came into the room, the lantern in their hand, for something else. In her opinion, all of these strong silent men were scared to death. Of what? Perhaps they were scared of themselves. They were all such strong, silent men, and they all seemed to think they would live forever, make love forever, and then drop off to sleep as they always did. They were like children, and if they came to her—more, that is, than to the younger women—perhaps she reminded them of what the situation really was. There were all sorts of men, of course, there were those who seemed to know this and those who didn't, and then there was this lover, Will Brady, who didn't seem to know anything. That might be what she liked about him. Lying awake she often wondered if that was what he liked about her.

"You men!" she would say, wagging her head, and as this sometimes woke him up, he would rise on his elbow and ask her what the trouble was. For all that, she never seemed to know. She would tell him to please shut up and go back to sleep. From the pocket of the green kimono that she wore she would take the package of Sen-Sen, put some in her mouth, and then lie there whiffling through her nose and sucking on it. It was not the kind of thing a man like Will

Brady could appreciate. If the weather was bad, or the room was cold, he would lie there and try to ignore it, but on the warm summer nights he would get up and put on his shoes. On his way out he would blow out the lantern before he hung it back on the wall, and if the night was clear he might remember to look at his watch. He didn't like to get caught along the tracks when number 9 went through, at three in the morning, so he might stand there till he heard the whistle far down the line. He would still be there, later, watching the receding lights on the caboose.

Sen-Sen, of course, was a small matter, but there was nothing small about her old friends, several dozens of them, who might pop up at any time. Men from as far away as Salt Lake City and Cheyenne. Busy men who found the time, somehow or other, to stop off. And from June through September, four pretty long months, Opal Mason met all of her old friends in Denver, where she liked the climate better, as she said, for a woman in her work. Also, why did she have to mention it? These things were not small, they were serious, and they had led better men than himself to see the weakness in the American plan. It wasn't women he wanted—what he wanted was a woman for himself.

Ralph Bassett, for example, had one, and Will Brady saw quite a bit of her as she spent most of the day on the wire-legged stool in the Hotel Café. She kept Ralph Bassett's books, and once a week typed out a new menu. As there wasn't too much for her to do she spent a good deal of time peering into the pie case, where there was a mirror, and adjusting the hairpins in her heavy black hair. With her arms raised, the bone pins in her mouth, she would arch her broad back and turn on the stool to look at her face, and her hair, in the pie case. Part of Will Brady's trouble over the summer was certainly due to the fact that the long summer days, and the heat, were hard on Ethel Bassett's hair. She spent a good deal of time with her arms raised, fixing it. On the wall behind her was a mirror, so that Will Brady saw her both front and back, in the round so to speak, while she looked him straight in the face. Which was odd, as she never seemed to see anything. A wall might as well have been there, but none was. Ethel Bassett had large dark eyes, and a face that any man would call handsome, but it would be hard to say what she had on her mind. The phases of the moon? Well, she sometimes spoke of that. He had once seen a book with pictures of the stars open in her lap. There was also her son, a boy named Orville, who liked to hug his mother most of the time, and there was some indication, Will Brady thought, that she egged him on. Anyhow, it didn't help a young man settle his mind. Over a long hot summer, while Opal Mason was cooling in Denver, he had nothing to do but watch Ethel Bassett put up her long black hair.

Suitable women, as Ralph Bassett liked to say, were pretty damn scarce. They were safe at home in one of the tree-shaded houses some man like Ralph Bassett had built for them, or they wore sunbonnets and walked about among the flowers with watering cans. Or they were very young, their hair in long braids as in the album pictures of his mother, or they were too old, peering at him over a line of wash, clothespins in their mouths and another woman's baby at their feet. He saw the arms of these women, from time to time, drooping from some hammock like a strand of rope, and other times he heard them at the back of a lawn, in a creaking lawn swing. Their age was uncertain, but it was known they were spoken for. They were as near and as far as the women he saw in the dining cars.

"And now what is it?" Opal Mason would say, as she couldn't stand a man thinking. A man lying *there* and thinking, that is.

"Can't a man just lie here?" he would say.

"You're not just lying there—you're thinking!" she'd say, and there was no use asking such a woman what was wrong with that. He could lie somewhere else, she would tell him, if he wanted to think. But he didn't. It was just that he thought while lying there with her. Trying to think what a suitable woman would be like.

For the important thing about Opal Mason, a "very unsuitable woman," was that he knew what he knew, and she knew, and that suited him. The only unsuitable thing was some ten or twenty other men. The only way to settle a thing like that was to make her a suitable woman, to buy a ring with a stone and make this woman his wife. With the summer coming on he made up his mind, ordered a ring with a stone from a house in Grand Island, and near the middle of May, a warm spring night, he shaved and rinsed with bay rum. He wore the vest to his suit so that he could take the ring along. He walked down the tracks, on the ties this time, to keep the cinders out of his shoes, and with the smoking lantern he stepped into the room, softly closed the door. For reasons of her own, Opal Mason was awake, playing solitaire. Not many women look good sitting up in bed, whether they're playing solitaire or not, and the idea crossed his mind that maybe the time was not right. But he had waited too long, and what he had come to say came out. Still holding the lantern, he said: "Opal—I want you for my wife."

It was some time before she said anything. Before she moved, or anything like a thought crossed her broad face. In that amount of time he saw the board in her lap, a packing-case board with the name RORTY on it, and fanned out on the board her very soiled deck of cards. At the moment he spoke, her right hand had been raised, the thumb ready to flick the tip of her tongue, and the tip of that thumb was white as a blister, the dirt licked off. He saw all of that, then he realized that where he hurt—for he hurt somewhere—was the wire handle of the lantern burning his right hand. "Ouch," he said, but not so much in pain as in what you might call recognition. Then he bent over to lower the lantern to the floor. He was still bent over when he heard Opal Mason begin to laugh.

Now, the thing is that Opal Mason never laughed. In order to account for what he did later you have to keep in mind that Opal Mason, a big sad-eyed woman, often cried a good deal but she never laughed. She grinned now and then, but nearly always covered her mouth, as if her teeth hurt her if she felt a smile on it. A laugh was such an odd sound, coming from her, that the man with the lantern doubted his senses, bending nearer as if to make sure for himself. But the woman was laughing, there was no doubt of it. Perhaps it was the *ouch* that struck her as funny, coming right at the time it did, rather than the sober, simple statement she had heard. Perhaps. Or the fact that he didn't find it funny himself. There's a pretty good chance that if he had laughed she would have married him. But he was an odd one, no doubt about that, and while Opal Mason laughed herself sick he picked up his lantern and went out on the porch. He hung it back on the hook and made his way to the foot of the stairs. There he found a light in the front hall as it was still early, around midnight, and four or five girls had come out on the porch to see what was wrong. Nobody had ever heard Opal Mason laugh before. To these girls, standing there together, one of them in a shawl she had wrapped around her, Will Brady said: "Is there one of you girls that would like to get married?" That did it. They began to laugh, they saw the joke. "I'm not joking," Will Brady said. "Is there one of you girls that would like to get married?"

One girl stopped laughing and said: "Mickey. I guess Mickey would."

"Who is Mickey?" he said, and stepped up on the porch. He was shy of young girls who were bold and named everything freely, but right at the moment he was not shy. He was bold himself. "Where is Mickey?" he said, and for some reason took off his hat.

"My God!" said one girl. "Go get him Mickey!" and they held on to him, holding his arms, while they ran down the long hall to the rear, then came running back. "Here's Mickey," they said, and brought the girl out. She was a kid, maybe fifteen, sixteen years old. She was a thin, flat girl with her hair in braids looped up like stirrups, and there were scratched mosquito bites on her arms and skinny legs. A girl not so thin wouldn't have looked so pregnant, so swelled up.

"I understand you would like a good man," he said, in a friendly way, and smiling at her, but this kid stepped forward and slapped him full in the face. It left his cheek numb, and one eye seeing double, but she stood right before him, her fists clenched, and in the quiet he could hear her gritting her small pointed teeth. He just looked at her, he didn't raise his hand and give her a cuff. After all, just an hour before, he had shaved himself, rinsed with sweet-smelling water, and come down the tracks to ask a woman to be his wife. In the right-hand pocket of his vest was a ring, with an eighty-dollar stone. It makes a difference, something like that, and perhaps even this kid felt it as her teeth stopped gritting and she began to snuffle through her nose. She didn't want to let on that she had started to bawl. There were freckles straddling her nose, and tangled in with her braids were strips of colored ribbon, but looking at her Will Brady didn't feel very much. He was thinking of himself, and what he was doing, and what a fine thing it was for a man like himself to behave so well with a kid like that. No, he didn't feel much of anything till she slapped him again. With her left hand, across the other side of his face.

You have to give it to a kid like that, a kid with that kind of spunk. Until that occurred you might even say that Will Brady hadn't really thought about her, but as a boy he had always taken his hat off to spunk. He didn't have a whole lot of it, put it like that. Before she slapped him again—and he saw it coming—he bent over and scooped her off her feet, and she beat on his head with her fists doubled up, smashing down his hat. Then she suddenly stopped, hugged him tight, and began to bawl.

He carried her down from the porch and along the fence that went around the sawmill, down through the ditch, then up the steep gravel bank to the tracks. He walked on the ties toward the red and green lights in the semaphore. Although she was a skinny girl, she was a little heavier than she ought to be, and not the right shape for carrying more than a quarter mile. Near the water tank he had to stop and put her down. His arms were asleep, his hands were prickly, and he stood there holding her hand and listening to the waterspout drip on the tracks.

"How much further are we going?" she said.

He hadn't thought. He hadn't thought about that part of it.

"Before we go any further," she said, "I think I better tell you we can't get married."

"We can't?"

"I'm already married," she said. "I'm as good as married, that is."

As he was still holding her hand he put it down and said: "I've got a ring here—now why don't you use it?" He took the ring from the pocket in his vest, put it in her hand. "As I won't need it now, you use it," he said. There was a moon behind her, and she turned so that the light fell on the stone.

"Is that the real McCoy?" she said.

"That's the real McCoy," he said. She closed her hand on it and put that hand behind her back.

"What's your name?"

"Brady," he said, "Will Brady."

"My name is Mickey Ahearn right now," she said.

"I'm down here in the hotel," he said, and pointed down the tracks past the semaphore. "The Merchant's Hotel. I'm in the lobby most of the time."

"I'll remember," she said, "I always remember everything."

"Well," he said, rubbing his hands, "it's getting pretty cool, you better run along." She ran off like a kid for about thirty yards, then she stopped. She stood there between the tracks, looking back at him. "You shouldn't run like that any more," he said. "You're not a kid any more, you're a lady."

"That's what I just remembered."

"Well, now you go along," he said. He turned and walked a little ways himself, but when he turned back she was still there. "Now you go along," he said, and shooed his hand at her, like a friendly dog, but she didn't move, so he turned and walked away. When he looked back from the station platform, she was gone.

4

In November Will Brady was sitting in the lobby, waiting for the local to come down from North Platte, when he saw Mickey Ahearn on the platform of the eastbound caboose. She was standing there, her hands on the brake wheel, beside a boy by the name of Popkov, one of the section hands on the C., B. & Q. One of those foreign kids with curly hair that seemed to grow right out of his eyes. He had one hand on her arm, and with the other he held a large duffel bag. Mickey Ahearn looked straight down the tracks toward the sawmill until the caboose passed the hotel, when she turned her head sharply as if she had thought of him. But the sun was on the window, and besides he was behind a potted plant. This kid Popkov might have seen him but there was no reason for him to look, and he kept his eyes, like those of a bird, right down the tracks. So did Will Brady, until the eastbound freight had pulled out of sight.

Early in the spring, about the first week of March, Fred Blake, the Calloway station agent, called Will Brady up and said that he would like to speak to him. "Right away, Brady," he said. "Got something over here with your name on it."

That was a Sunday morning, the one he liked to sleep, but Will Brady got out of bed as it wasn't often anybody sent him anything. As he crossed the tracks he could see that Mrs. Blake, a big, motherly woman, was sitting there in the office with a wicker basket in her lap. The basket was covered with a cloth, like a lunch, but a red American Express tag, fastened on with a wire, dangled from the handle on one end.

As he opened the door Will Brady said: "Somebody put me up a good picnic lunch?" as Fred Blake himself was quite a kidder and liked a good joke.

"This ain't exactly a picnic," Fred Blake said, and though it was too early for flies in the office, he waved his hand over the basket as if there were. Then he raised one corner of the towel, peeked in. "No, this ain't no picnic, Will," he said, and still holding the corner of the towel, he stepped aside so Will Brady could see for himself. No, it was no picnic. A sausage-colored baby lay asleep on its face. A soiled nightshirt, or whatever it is that babies wear that leave their bottoms uncovered, was in a wadded roll around his neck. On the baby's left leg, tied there with a string, was another American Express tag, and Will Brady turned this one over to see what it said.

My name is Willy Brady

and that was all.

"It's a boy?" Will Brady said.

"He's a boy," said Mrs. Blake, and rolled him over on his back, and he was a boy, all right. Around his neck was a strand of black hair with a gold ring braided to it. The ring had what looked to be about an eighty-dollar stone.

"How old you reckon he is, Mrs. Blake?" he said.

"He's about five weeks," Mrs. Blake said, and then she put the knuckle of her little finger in the boy's mouth. She let him suck on it for a bit, then she took it out, sniffed the knuckle, and said: "The poor little tyke—a bottle baby." She shook her head sadly, put the knuckle back again.

"There's an orphanage in Kearney," Fred Blake said. "Think they call it Sister something or other. They say it's not a bad place, don't they, Kate?"

"It's not bad," she said, "as them places go."

"Unless you was thinking," Fred Blake said, "of something yourself."

Had Will Brady been thinking? No. But now he would.

"If it was a girl," Mrs. Blake said, "now I wouldn't know what to think. But there's nearly always someone, it seems to me, who wants a fine boy."

"Don't get in a hurry now, Kate," said Fred. "After all, this boy's got Will's name on him. Maybe Will here would like a husky boy himself."

Mrs. Blake smelled the knuckle of her little finger again. "The poor little tyke," she said, "the poor little tyke."

"Mrs. Blake," Will Brady said, "what would you say he'd need besides a good bottle?"

Mrs. Blake opened her mouth, wide, then she seemed to change her mind.

"What'd you say he'd need, Kate?" said Fred.

"He could use a good woman," Kate Blake said, and scooped the baby up. "You mind I take him home and feed him, Will?" she said.

"Why, no," Will Brady said.

"Kate," Fred Blake said, "what do you say we just keep him till Will here picks up what he needs?"

"Won't that take him some time?" Kate Blake said, and they stood there, looking at her. "You men!" she said, and with the boy hugged tight she went through the door. Then she put her head back in and said: "Now I'll tell you when to come around. I don't want you, either of you, moping around the house." With that she let the door slam, and through the wide window they watched her cross the tracks.

"That's the way they get," Fred Blake said. "Just let a kid come along and that's the way they get." He turned to the basket and said: "What'll we do with this—you won't be needing it."

This Willy Brady was an odd one for a boy, as he wasn't much bigger than a rabbit, and he had the dark unblinking eyes of a bird. They were neither friendly nor unfriendly, nor were they blue like Will Brady's, the watery blue of the faded summer sky. They were more like the knobs on a hatpin than eyes. They seemed to pick up, Will Brady thought, right where his mother's eyes had left off, staring at him from the top step of the porch.

It also seemed to be clear that somebody had made a mistake. If Will Brady has fathered this boy—as Fred Blake liked to say—then Prince Albert was the son of Daniel Boone. The little fellow was also, as Mrs. Blake said, pretty bright. He seemed to have taken after his mother in most respects.

If Will Brady took exception to this he never let on, nor troubled to deny it, but just went about the business of being a father to the boy. That is to say that once or twice a week he bounced the boy on his knee in a horsey manner, and let him play with the elastic arm bands on his sleeves. Mrs. Blake referred to him as Daddy, to herself as Grandma, but she might call the boy any number of things. Sometimes she called him Cookie because of his black currant eyes.

"Now give Cookie to his grandma," she would say, and swing the boy in the air by his heels; but let Will Brady try that and there would be hell to pay. The boy would scrounge around, grunt like a pig, or hold his breath till his black eyes popped. He would turn a grape color and scare Will Brady half to death. "Here, give him to his granny," she would say, and of course he would.

Other times the boy would just sit in his lap like a big cat, watching his face, and making Will Brady so self-conscious he couldn't move his lips. He never said a word about it, naturally, but he knew long before the boy had said a word, any more than da-da, that talking was going to be something of a problem for both of them. Fred Blake could make a fine assortment of faces, barnyard noises, and the like, but as for Will Brady he couldn't even whistle properly. Nor was the one face he had strictly his own. He knew that whenever the boy stared at him. It was just something that he wore that people like the boy saw right through. About all that he could do was wear arm bands with bright metal clips, or gay ribbons, wind his watch with the key, and keep penny candy in the pockets of his vest. Once a month he would bring the boy something special from Omaha. Something he could eat, ride, put together, or take apart.

Will Brady went to Omaha with the idea that almost any day, any warm Sunday morning, he might find Mickey Ahearn out walking on Douglas Street. He might see her in one of the doorways, or leaning out of one of the upstairs windows, with that boy Popkov, or somebody just like him, right at her back. He would be a foreigner, and the hair would be growing right out of his eyes. He also looked in jewelry stores, or better-class pawnshops, thinking he might find her choosing a ring, one with a stone that would be the real McCoy. All he wanted to do was to tell her what a fine healthy boy she had, but that it wouldn't hurt him any if he had his own mother one of these days. That was all. He wasn't going to force anything on her. In his wallet he had a picture of the boy seated on a wire chair, like those they have in drugstores, holding a wicker bird-cage and a Bible in his lap. The boy's mouth was open and you could see his three front teeth.

He would find her and show her this picture, and while she looked at the picture he would study her face, trying to make up his mind if she would be a good mother or not. If he thought she would, he would repeat what he once said. Let bygones be bygones, he would say. If she didn't look healthy, or didn't seem to care, or if she was still married to this Popkov—if that was how it was, why then he would have to think of something else.

He didn't have to think, as it turned out, very long. He never saw nor heard of Mickey Ahearn again, but the spring the boy was three years old, by Mrs. Blake's reckoning, he brought him a birthday present from Omaha. An Irish Mail, with a bright red seat—one of the many things the boy would have to grow into—Will Brady brought it back with him on the train. As he got off, down the tracks from the station, he saw a large funeral passing through town, and he stood there wondering whose funeral it was. In the lead buggy was Reverend Wadlow, and there at his side, wrapped up in a robe, was the widow—a woman who didn't look any too old. She was dressed in black, with a veil, and as the buggy rocked on the tracks she lifted this veil, deliberately, and looked at him. The same kind of look, whatever it was, that Ethel Bassett usually gave him in the pie-case mirror, she now gave him directly, then lowered the veil. In the buggy behind her was her son Orville, with members of her family, who were said to be Bohemians, and who had driven down from their farm near Bruno to be with her. Will Brady stood there, watching, until Fred Blake came along and picked him up.

That same evening, driving the team that Ralph Bassett reserved for Sundays, he drove the widow to the evening service at the church. From there he drove her home, put the team in the barn, and seeing that the spring grass needed cutting, he came back the following day and cut it for her. It was no more than Ralph Bassett's widow had the right to expect. She brought him a cool glass of grape juice, and while he stood there in the yard, sipping it, she sat in the chain swing behind the wire baskets of ferns.

The place needed a man, she said—needed a man to keep it up.

He agreed with that, and when he finished with the grape juice he said that the place needed a man, the way a man with a boy needed a home.

He didn't wait to see if she agreed with that or not. He put the glass on the porch and walked the mower through the grass to the back of the house.

5

The house Ralph Bassett had built for his wife was full of furniture made in Grand Rapids, and in the gables were diamond-shaped pieces of colored glass. When the sun shone through the glass it reminded a railroad man, like Will Brady, of the red and green lights in the semaphores. Inside of the house, it was one of the things that made him at home. In the summer these colors might be on the floor, or cast on the goldfish bowl near the table, but in the winter they made a bright pattern on the wall. Or on the man who now sat at the head of the table, whoever he was. The food on the table was sometimes red, but the man at the table was usually green owing to the way he liked to lean forward, his head cocked to the side. The green light could be seen on his forehead, his wavy dark hair. Out of habit, perhaps, Will Brady—the man who now sat at the head of the table—liked to cock his head and keep one eye on the green light. That was what he liked to see down the spur of tracks, where the switch was open, and in the brakeman's lantern at the top of Opal Mason's stairs. Green. There was something friendly about it.

When the green light was not on his face Will Brady might see, through the rippling bay window, the shrubs that were cut to look like giant birds, or little girls holding hands. Men who thought the house looked like a caboose might not see them curtsy in the wind, or the rambling rose vine that crawled up their arms to put flowers in their hair. But on Sunday, beyond the arbor, any man with eyes could see the tasseled buggies that scoffers drove by, very slowly, to see the house for themselves. Or to remark that Will

Brady, seated in the chain swing, or mowing the lawn, had the look of a man who felt at home about the place.

Another man might smoke, or take it easy, but getting up from the table Will Brady would say: "Well, this isn't getting the grass cut," and hang his coat and vest on the back of his chair. He was not much of a hand with shrubs, but he could mow a lawn. As it happened to be quite a piece of lawn, maybe half an acre if you counted in the barn, by the time he was through in the back it was long in the front again. Not that he minded. Maybe he needed the exercise. As a matter of fact he liked a big lawn, with a few big shady elms around it, and a house with a swing and a wire basket of ferns on the front porch. He had a taste for the good things. Maybe it came natural to him.

When Ethel Bassett had to go and visit her people he slept in the house, in the guest room, as she felt better with a man in the house, as she said. Her maiden name was Czerny, and this helped to explain some of the things he felt about her, as foreigners were apt to be different in funny ways. When her father drove over for her he first spoke of his horses, wanting feed and water for them, then he spoke of his family, the weather, or whatever might come to mind. Ethel Bassett would go home with him, over Sunday, helping her mother with the Sunday meal, and then visiting the cemetery, where the stones were marked with foreign names. Some of them like her own, others hardly pronounceable. Ethel Bassett's feelings about these things was what Will Brady would call religious, as distinct from what he was apt to feel himself. He liked it. It was a thing to respect in her. There was something there, something to go back to, that he didn't seem to have, and he saw that it gave her an advantage over himself. It was part of the finer things she had around the house. It was his own suggestion that he stay in the house—look after these things, as he put it—so she wouldn't have something like that on her mind.

He slept in the guest room, which was on the south side of the house, facing the tracks, but a different air seemed to blow in the window from that in the hotel. It smelled of the grass he had cut himself. The bed seemed to be softer, and even his sleep seemed sounder, though he was a sound enough sleeper, normally. Something about the idea of a place of his own. The keys in his pocket to the cellar door, the lock on the barn. In the morning he served himself a good breakfast, eating his bacon and eggs in the kitchen, but putting off the coffee until he stood in the dining-room. Later he would walk from room to room, his feet quiet on the Axminster rugs.

No, it doesn't take long to get used to the finer things. All you need are the things, and a man with the taste for them. A woman with bird's-eye maple in her room, and small cut-glass bottles, with large stoppers, and an ivory box with long strands of her combed-out hair. Dark and soft as corn silk, not at all wiry like her red-haired boy. Somehow, he didn't care for the boy—his own boy struck him as a good deal finer, and the only thing in Calloway that went with the house. An imported look, like the glass chimes on the front porch. But there was nothing wrong with Ethel Bassett, nothing that he could see. A quiet woman, not given to talk, with something of a religious nature, she seemed to rely on him now that Ralph Bassett was gone. She left it up to him to shovel the snow from in front of the house. And when the snow was gone, it was up to him to cut the grass. He used a grass-catcher on the mower, but when the grass was damp, or he walked a little fast, it would miss the catcher entirely and stick to his pants, so he would need a broom from the kitchen to sweep himself off, and if it was summer he would need a cooling drink—grape juice, with a lump of ice in it, or fresh lemonade. And after putting away the mower he would walk around to the side of house where there was a faucet, and rinse off his hands. It was her own suggestion that he do that in the house. One thing like that leads to another, so he got in the habit of using the kitchen, and she got in the habit of standing there with him, holding the towel. Now, he didn't need a towel— that was what he always said. But she would wag her head, as women do when they find something like that in a man, and he would take the towel but only use the corner of it. And when he rolled down his sleeves, she would hold his coat for him. That was all. There was no need to say anything. Perhaps this was why the night that she spoke he was not at all sure that he had heard her, or that she had said what he thought he had heard.

"Yes—?" he said, and stood there, holding his hat.

What did he think of all the talk, she had said. So he had heard it all right. That was what she had said.

"Talk?" he said. "What talk?" and put his right hand into his pocket, as he did when the boy put a hard question to him. With the boy all he had to do was give him something.

There was talk of their getting married, she said, and he stood there, his hand in his pocket, then he took the hand out and looked at the rusty tenpenny nail. He used the nail to clean his thumbnail, then he said that if there was talk of that kind, he hadn't heard it, but if he had heard it he wouldn't have done much of anything. What he meant to say was that talk like that didn't bother him. That was what he said, then he put the head of the tenpenny nail in his mouth and saw that she was looking at him as she did in the pie case, her eyes wide. He saw that this blank expression, this look she gave him, was meant to be an open one. He was meant to look in, and he tried, but he didn't see anything.

There was talk of their getting married, she repeated, so he raised his voice and said that if that was the talk, why he had no objection. That was all right with him. If that was the talk, he said, his voice ringing, why, let them talk.

Would he be able to wait, she said, another three months?

Would he be able? Why, yes. He nodded his head. Yes, he repeated, he would be able to wait three months. Then he followed her out on the porch, full of wonder about what he had been saying, and picked up the paper, the Omaha Sunday paper, he had left on the swing. He put his paper in his pocket, then he took it out and waved to a man in a passing buggy, then he went down the seven steps and crossed the lawn. There was a brick sidewalk, but he stepped across it, waded into the road. From the park across the street a boy ran out, circled him twice, then ran off crying:

> *"Strawberry shortcake,*
> *Huckleberry pie,*
> *Pee in the road*
> *An' you'll get a sty."*

Somehow it made him feel better, and without looking back he walked off through the park.

In the Clearing

1

They were married in Bruno, a Bohemian town in the rolling country just south of the Platte, four or five miles' drive from where her father had a big farm. They were married in the church where Ralph Bassett had married her. It sat on the rise, overlooking the town, and as it was June the door stood open and Will Brady could see the buggies drawn up beneath the shade trees out in front. An elderly man was combing sandburs from a dark mare's tail. It was quiet on the rise, without a leaf stirring, but in the sunny hollow along the tracks a westerly breeze was turning the wheel of a giant windmill. It looked softly blurred, quite a bit the way the heat made everything look in Indian Bow, with the air, like a clear stream of water, flowing up from the hot earth. Near the windmill a man was sinking a post, and the sound of the blows, like jug corks popping, came up in the pause that his mallet hung in the air. Fred Blake had to remind him—nudging him sharply—to kiss the bride.

They went to Colorado Springs, where he sat in the lobby, reading the latest Denver papers, and giving her time, as he said to himself, to compose herself. A little after ten o'clock he went up, and as he opened the door he saw her, seated at her dressing-table, her face in the mirror. The eyes were wide and blank, just as they were in the pie case. She did not smile, nor make any sign that she recognized him. Could he bring her something, he asked, but when she neither moved nor seemed to hear him, he closed the door and walked to the end of the hall. There was a balcony there, facing the mountains, and maybe he stood there for some time, for when he came back to the room, the lights were off. He did not turn them on, but quietly undressed in the dark.

As he had never been married before, or spent a night in bed with a married woman, there were many things, perhaps, that he didn't know much about. That was why he was able to lie there, all night, and think about it. The woman beside him, his wife, was rolled up tight in the sheet. She had used the sheet on top for this purpose so that he was lying next to the blanket, a woolly one, and perhaps that helped keep him awake. She seemed to be wrapped from head to foot, as mummies are wrapped. It occurred to him that something like that takes a good deal of practice, just as it took practice to lie, wrapped up like a mummy, all night. It took practice, and it also took something else. It took fear. This woman he had married was scared to death.

When a person is scared that bad, what can you do? You can lie awake, for one thing, in case this person might be lonely, or, like Opal Mason, in case she didn't like men who fell asleep. But it was hard to picture Opal Mason rolled up in a sheet. Or what it was now in this room that frightened this woman. As he had never been married before, he was not as upset as he might have been, for it occurred to him that there might be something he hadn't been told. In the marriage of widows, perhaps, a ceremony. A ritual that called for spending one night rolled up in a sheet. He had heard of such things. It was something he could think about. There was also the fact that this woman was a Bohemian, a foreigner, and perhaps she had foreign ways. But nobody had told him. And while he wondered, she fell asleep.

In time he fell asleep himself, but not too well beneath the woolly blanket, which may have been why he dreamed as he did, and remembered it. He saw before him Ralph Bassett, standing behind the desk. He had a large paunch, larger than he remembered, and the front of his vest, between the lower buttons, was worn threadbare where he rubbed against the handle of the coin drawer. A strange dream, but Will Brady fathomed it. All these years—and it seemed very long—Ralph Bassett had rubbed the coin drawer during the day, then he had gone home to rub against his mummy-wrapped wife at night. It didn't strike him as funny. Nor did it strike him as out of this world. If a woman has lived twelve years with a man, and the nights of those years rolled up in a sheet, and this woman was now your wife, it deserved serious thought. And while he thought, this woman, his wife, snored heavily.

Their honeymoon room had a view of the mountains, with Pike's Peak, and a cloud of snow on it, and as it was warm these windows were open on the sky. The glass doors stood open on their balcony. Through these doors he could see the light on the mountains, which were barren and known as the Rockies, and toward morning the eastern slopes were pink with light. He got out of bed and stood for a while on the balcony. There was a good deal to see and to hear, as the city below him was rising, and in the blue morning light the woman on the bed seemed out of this world. Still wrapped in the sheet, she looked prepared for burial. He dressed in the bathroom, and when he came out her white arm lay over her face, shutting out the light, so he closed the doors to the balcony. What did he feel? What he seemed to feel was concern for her. Neither anger nor dislike, nor the emotions of a man who had been a fool. No, he felt a certain wonder, what you might call pity, for this man once her husband, now dead, and for this woman, his wife, who was still scared to death. He felt it, that is, for both of them. They were out of this world, certainly—but in what world were they living? Greater than his anger, and his disappointment, was the wonder that he felt that there were such people, and that they seemed to live, as he did, in the same world. Their days in the open, but their nights wrapped up in a sheet.

Practically speaking, a honeymoon is where you adjust yourself to something, and Will Brady managed this adjustment in two weeks. He worked at it. He gave it everything he had. He learned to sleep, or to lie awake, indifferent to her. And when he learned these things this woman, his wife, gave up her sheet. There it was, back where it belonged, between Will Brady and the woolly blanket, and let it be said for him that he recognized it for what it was. A compliment. Perhaps the highest he had ever been paid.

The truth was that he was flattered, and it was her own suggestion, plainly made, that he learn to do the things her red-haired boy had done. Draw up her corset, and fasten the hooks at the side of her gowns. In the lobby this woman walked at his side, her hip brushing his own, and coming down from carriages she seemed loose in his arms. Another compliment? Well, he could take that too. He had taken something out of this world, learned to live with it. He had discovered, in this strange way, something about loving, about pity, and a good deal about hooks and eyes and corset strings.

He had this concern for her, and she seemed to be proud of him. Her handsome face was blank, with the pleasant vacant look again. They ate a good deal, in rooms overlooking the city, or in cool gardens with flowering plants, or they rode in buses to look with others at prominent views. It was not necessary, eating or looking, to say anything. Everything necessary had already been said.

If in three weeks' time two strangers can manage something like that, working together, who is to say what a year or two, or a summer, might bring? Who is to say what they might have made of something like that? But in three weeks' time he had to help her into her suit, with the hooks at both sides, and kneel on the floor and button her high traveling shoes. Then he held the ladder for her while she climbed into the upper berth. She was wearing a veil, the car was dark, and it might be said that the last he saw of the woman he knew was her high button shoes and the dusty hem of her petticoats. Whatever they had managed, between them, whatever they had made in the long three weeks, went up the ladder and never came down again. It remained, whatever it was, there in the berth. When she started down the next morning, calling for him to steady the ladder, the woman who spoke his name was a stranger again, his wife.

"Ethel," he said, taking her hand, "you're home again."

2

Over the summer he liked to sleep in the spare room, with the window open, as he could see down the tracks to the semaphore. When the signals changed, this semaphore made a clicking sound. On quiet summer nights he would hear that sound and then roll on his side, rising on his elbow, to watch the coaches make a band of light on the plains. The rails would click, and when the train had passed, there would be little whirlwinds of dust and leaves, and a stranger might think that a storm was blowing up.

Beyond the semaphore was the cattle loader, the smell strong over the summer, and down the spur to the west, past the sawmill, the house of a man named Schultz. This man lived alone on a ten-acre farm. In his bedroom, along toward morning, a yellow lamp would be burning, and now and then the shadow of this man Schultz would move on the blind. A hard man, a bear for work, it was known that he had married a city girl, but that the caboose that had brought her to town also took her away. He kept the lamp burning, it was said, in case she came back.

An hour or so after the Flyer went by, the westbound local came along from North Platte, and Will Brady had got into the habit of meeting it. Now and then important men stopped in Calloway. Once a month, for example, the local came along with T. P. Luckett, the man who had charge of the U.P. commissary in Omaha. A big man in every way, around two hundred sixty pounds, Mr. Luckett had his breakfast in the hotel, and while sitting in the lobby, smoking his cigar, he seemed to feel like talking with someone. At that time in the morning Will Brady was the only man there. In T. P. Luckett's opinion, that of a man who spoke frankly, Calloway was dead and didn't know it—a one-horse town with the horse ready for pasture, as he put it. Nebraska had spread itself too thin, he said, the western land was not particularly good, and what future there was, in anything but cattle, lay in the east. Within a day's ride from Omaha, that is. The whole state was tipped, T. P. Luckett said, low in the east, high in the west, and the best of everything had pretty well run off of it, like a roof. The good land was along the Missouri, near Omaha. The good men, as well, and in T. P. Luckett's opinion it was high time a young fellow like Will Brady gave it serious thought. Saw which way the wind was blowing, that is, and got off the dime. Calloway might always need a jerkwater hotel to meet the local, but a jerkwater man could take care of it. This fellow Luckett made it clear that a man like Will Brady, with his oversize head, was doing little more than wasting his time.

Will Brady had never thought of himself in such terms. Whether he was an up-and-coming man, and ought to be up-and-coming with the east, or whether what he was doing or not doing was wasting his time. He simply did it. That was the end of it. But it doesn't take a man long to acquire a taste for the better things. All he needs are these things. The taste comes naturally.

No, he had never given it a thought—but he did now. Running a hotel was little more than sitting in the lobby, between the potted palms, and facing the large railroad map of the state on the wall. There on the map any man could see for himself. There were ten towns in the east for every one in the west. Did it matter? Well, it did when you thought about it. When you're married, in a way, and have settled down, and have stopped, in a way, thinking about women, you find you have time now and then to sit and think about something else. Your future, for instance, and whether you're currently wasting your time.

T. P. Luckett, for example, was a man who had given up thinking about women in order to spend all of his time thinking about eggs. He thought about eggs because fresh eggs was one of the big dining-car problems, and T. P. Luckett was the top dining-car man. This problem kept a big man like Luckett awake half the night. Wondering how he could just put his hands on an honest-to-God fresh egg. Eggs were always on this man's mind, and perhaps it was natural that Will Brady, with nothing much on his mind, would get around to thinking about them. He made T. P. Luckett's problem something of his own. Take those eggs he had for breakfast, for instance; at one time he would have eaten them, that was all, but now he examined the shell, and marked the weight of each egg in his hand. He broke them into a saucer to peer at the yolk, examine it for small rings. He considered the color of the eggs, and one morning he made the observation that the whites of some eggs, perhaps fresh ones, held their shape in the pan. Other eggs, perhaps older ones, had whites like milky water, the yolk poorly centered and slipping off to one side. T. P. Luckett thought this very interesting. *His* particular problem, T. P. Luckett said, looking at him in a friendly manner, was to determine something like that with the egg in the shell. Then he laughed, but he went on to say that any man who could study like that, his own eggs, that is, might well discover anything. He put his hand on Will Brady's shoulder, looking him straight in the eye, and forgot himself to the extent of offering him a good cigar.

A week or two later, toward morning, a time that Will Brady did most of his thinking, the solution to T. P. Luckett's problem occurred to him. The way to get grade-A fresh eggs was to lay them, on the spot. Get the chickens, the spot, and let the eggs be laid right there. Day-old eggs, which was about as fresh as an egg might be. All T. P. Luckett needed was a man to raise as many chickens as it took to lay the required number of eggs. That might be quite a few. But that's all he would need. This egg would be white, as the white egg, by and large, looked best in the carton, just as the rich yellow yolk looked best in the pan. And what chicken laid an egg like that? White Leghorns. It just so happened that a white chicken laid the whitest eggs.

T. P. Luckett listened to all of this without a word. A bald-headed man, he took off his straw and wiped the sweat off the top of his head, peered at the handkerchief, then stuffed it back in the pocket of his coat.

"All right, Will," he said, "you're the man."

"I'm what man?" he said.

"I've got five thousand dollars," T. P. Luckett said, "five thousand simoleons that says you're the man. That'll buy a lot of chickens, that'll even buy you some nice hens." Will Brady didn't have an answer to that. "Tell you what I'll do," T. P. Luckett said, "I'll throw in ten acres I've got near Murdock. Murdock is a lot better chicken country anyhow."

Will Brady had an answer to that. He said: "Mr. Luckett, I've got a wife and kids to think of. My wife has a home, several pieces of property right here."

"You think it over," T. P. Luckett said, and wiped his head again, put on his hat. "You think it over—right now you could sell all this stuff for what you got in it. Twenty years from now you won't be able to give it away."

"In a way," Will Brady said, "I like it here."

"Tell you what you do," T. P. Luckett said; "you put the little woman in the buggy and some fine day you drive her over to Murdock, show her around. Leave it up to her if she wouldn't rather live in the east."

"I'll see what she says," Will Brady said.

"I'm not thinking of eggs. I'm thinking," T. P. Luckett said, "of a man of your caliber sitting around in the lobby of a jerkwater hotel."

"I'll think it over, Mr. Luckett," he said, and T. P. Luckett took off his hat, wiped his head with the sleeve of his shirt, put his hat on, and went out.

As a man could marry only one woman, Will Brady had once brooded over such matters as the several thousand women he would have to do without. As no one woman had everything, in the widest sense of the term, neither did any egg have everything. But he came to the conclusion, after months of consideration, that the Leghorn egg had the most for the "carriage trade." This was how T. P. Luckett referred to those people who were something. What we've got to keep in mind, he always said, is how the carriage trade will like it. A very neat way of putting things, once you thought about it. Will Brady had seen a good many of such people through the wide windows of the diners, and on occasion he had spoken to some of them. Offering a match, or the time of day, as the case might be. It was very easy to tell such men from those who dipped their napkins in their water glasses, then used the napkin to clean their celluloid collars, their false cuffs. With a little experience a man could tell the real carriage trade from that sort of people, as easily as the real carriage trade could tell a good egg. Nine out of ten times it would be a Leghorn.

Well, that was the egg, but what about the chicken laying it? Did it take two, maybe three of them, to lay one egg? Did they quit after a while, die over the winter, or get the croup? To determine these and like matters, he bought three dozen Leghorn hens, kept them in sheds behind the barn, and bought a ledger to keep their record in. This ledger he kept in the basement, and every evening he entered the number of eggs, the amount of grain eaten, and the proportion of large eggs to the case. He compared this with the figures at the local creamery. Every morning he cracked two eggs, peered at the yolks, then fried them, slowly, in butter, or he boiled them and served them in an official dining-car cup. He had never been of much use with his hands, he hurt himself with hammers, cut himself with knives, but it seemed that he could handle an egg with the best of them. He could take five in each hand, right out of the case, and hold them gently, not a shell cracking, or he could take two eggs, crack them, and fry them with one hand. There were people who would like to have seen that, his wife perhaps, and certainly T. P. Luckett, but he did it alone, just as a matter of course, every morning. He studied eggs, just as a matter of course, every night. As all of his own eggs were fresh and didn't need to be candled, he had a case of cold-storage eggs sent out from Omaha. He mixed them up with his own eggs, then sorted them out. It took him several weeks, but he learned—without anyone around to tell him—how a fresh egg *looked*, and about how old a storage egg was.

In April he took a Sunday off to drive his wife over to Murdock, a town of several thousand people and some big shady trees. Just east of town was a two-way drive with a strip of grass right down the middle, lamps on concrete posts, and a sign welcoming visitors to town. There was nothing to compare with it in Calloway. T. P. Luckett's ten acres were just a half mile north of town. A nice flat piece of ground, it lay between the new road and the curve of the railroad, and there was plenty of room for several thousand laying hens, maybe more. Along the north side of the land was a fine windbreak of young cottonwood trees.

They had their dinner in town, at a Japanese restaurant where there were paintings on the walls, and violin music played throughout the meal. They sat in a booth, with a dim light on the table, and though his wife had once been in St. Louis, and seen many fine things, it was clear she had seen nothing like this. At the front of the restaurant was a glass case, with a slot at one side for a coin, and on dropping a coin the violin in the case would begin to play. One hand held the bow, the other plucked the strings. As she was very fond of music he walked forward twice and played it for her.

At the end of this meal he told her what he had in mind.

He described, pretty much in detail, what T. P. Luckett had told him, and how Calloway, inside of twenty years, would be a dead town. A man of his caliber, he said, quoting T. P. Luckett, had no business wasting his life in a jerkwater hotel. He had meant to say small, not jerkwater, but when he got there the word came out, and he saw that it made quite an impression on her. She had never seen the hotel, or the town, in quite that light before. Perhaps she hadn't thought of him, her husband, as a man of caliber. It made a lasting impression on her, and while they sat there a Mr. Tyler, the man who owned the restaurant, presented her, absolutely free, with a souvenir. This was a booklet describing the town of Murdock. There were thirty-two pages, every page with a picture, and at the back of the booklet was a table showing how all the real-estate values were shooting up. On the cover was the greeting:

WELCOME TO
MURDOCK
THE
BIGGEST
LITTLE TOWN IN THE WORLD

and while she glanced through it he walked back to play the magic violin again.

3

In the town of Murdock Will Brady bought a house with a room at the front, which he used to sleep in, and a room at the back where he ate his meals. Once a week, however, he would take his family to the Japanese restaurant, sit them in a booth, and give the boys coins to play for their mother the magic violin. His wife, Ethel, liked to sit where she could see the wax hand move the real bow. Will Brady took the seat facing the window where the yokels that stood along the curb would walk back and press their noses to the glass and peer in at them. He had never really thought much about these people, the kids off the farms and the old men still on them, until he sat there in the booth and saw their corn-fed faces grinning at him. Then he knew that they were yokels, corn-fed hicks from the ground up.

That's what they were, but with the war coming on, things were looking up. Sometimes a farmer with six or seven kids would bring them into town, herd them into the restaurant, but leave his wife in the buggy until she had finished nursing the little one. Will Brady could see that buggy through the window, and it would be new, the spokes would be red, and there might be a new creaking set of harness on the old horse. The horse would toss his head to get the feed at the bottom of his new feed bag. And the woman in the buggy might have a new hat, a Sears Roebuck print dress, or the high button shoes that he could see when she lifted her skirts from the buggy wheel.

And at the edge of town, where there had once been weeds, or maybe nothing at all to speak of, there was now a field of grain or a new crop of beans. Every acre that would grow weeds had been plowed up. And it was no passing thing, people had to eat—hadn't Will Brady himself just read somewhere that the rich Missouri Valley was going to be the bread basket of the world? The world had to eat something, so it might as well be eggs. Fresh, day-old eggs if possible. Somewhere else he had read, or heard a man say, that there were more than four hundred million Chinamen who had never had a really square meal in their lives. Well, an up-and-coming man like Will Brady would give it to them. All that had to be done was to stop them eating rice, start them eating eggs.

In the old country this Kaiser fellow had done a lot of

damage and killed a lot of people, but in the new country he seemed to be doing a lot of good. Will Brady could see it on the faces of the men who came into town. This war boom was about the finest thing that had happened to them. Some of the women might feel a little different, but it was hard to complain about a new buggy, a roof for the barn, and a machine that would separate the milk from the cream. And now and then a tired farm woman liked to eat out. She liked to see her new baby in the red high chairs that came along with the meal, like the cups and plates, and sit there at the table with her own two hands free to eat. Nothing in her lap but the folded napkin and the bones for the dog. Just a year or two before, this same woman came to town in the wagon, with the tailboard down, but now she rode in a tassel-fringed buggy with a spring seat. And having tasted the finer things in life, like Will Brady, she would go on wanting them.

4

The house Will Brady bought had five other rooms besides those he ate and slept in, but he didn't have much to do with them. The house was usually dark in the morning when he left it, and again in the evening when he got home, and rather than fool around with the lamp, he undressed in the dark. The wick of the lamp was charred and left an oily smell in the air.

Was he all right? Once a week his wife, Ethel, asked him that. She spoke to him through the bedroom door, the lamp shadow at her feet. Yes, he was all right—just a little preoccupied. That was it, he was just a little preoccupied.

There was a window at the foot of his bed, but he kept the blind drawn because the street light, swinging over the corner, sometimes kept him awake. As the chairs were hard to see in the dark, he kept one of them in the corner, and the other at the side of the bed for his watch and coat. Sometimes he put his pants there too if he happened to think of it. Otherwise he dropped them on the floor, or folded them over the rail at the foot of the bed, with his collar and tie looped around the brass post. He slept in his socks, but that was not something new—he had always done that. It helped keep his feet warm and also saved quite a bit of time.

The room was always dark, but if he lay awake he could make out the calendar over the stovepipe hole, the white face of the clock, and the knobs on the dresser from Calloway. But the grain of the bird's-eye maple was lost on him. On the dresser was a bottle of cherry cough syrup, which he took when he had an upset stomach, a comb and a brush, and a very large Leghorn egg. This egg had three yolks, but he couldn't decide what to do with it. As it was ten days old, he would soon have to make up his mind. At the foot of the bed, in the cream-colored wall, he could see the door that he used twice a day, and on hot summer nights he left it open to start a cool draft. The rest of the time he kept it closed, with the key in the lock.

It might be going too far to say that Will Brady lived in this house, as he spent his time elsewhere and usually had other things on his mind. But he came back there every night, went away from there every morning, and something like that, if you keep at it, gets to mean something. There were always, for instance, clean shirts in the dresser drawer. There were always socks with the holes mended, and if they had just been washed this woman, his wife, first ran her hand into each one of them. There were always collar studs in the cracked saucer beside the clock. When he was sick, or coughed in the night, or was found there in bed the following morning, the woman of the house came to the door of his room and knocked. She would give him hot lemonade and sound advice. The blinds would be raised to let in the sunshine, his coat and pants would be hung on the door, and she would ask him—after looking for them—for his socks. She always found it hard to believe that they were still on his feet.

The woman of the house lived at the back, in a large sunny room full of plants and flowers, but the children of the house seemed to live with the neighbors, or under the front porch. They went there to eat candy, drink strawberry pop, and divide up the money they took from his pockets on Sundays, holidays, and any other time he had to change his pants. In the evening Will Brady sometimes stopped to peer under the porch, and wonder about it, as nothing ever seemed to be there but the soft hot dust. The lawnmower and the wooden-runner sled were pushed far to the back.

Other evenings Will Brady might stop in the alley and look at the yard, the three white birch trees, and the house that had now been paid for, every cent of it. It looked quite a bit like the neighboring houses in most respects. It had a porch at the front, lightning rods, a peaked roof, panes of colored glass; and in the rooms where the lights were on, the blinds were always drawn. Homelike? Well, that was said to be the word for it. And after a certain hour all of the lights in the house would be out. The people in the house would do what they could to go to sleep. By some common agreement, since there was no law saying that they had to, they would turn out the lights, go to bed, and try to sleep. Or they would lie there making out the shape of things on the wall. Why did they do it? Well, it was simply how things were done. It was one of those habits that turned out to be pretty hard to break.

Will Brady often wondered—when he didn't sleep—what the man in the neighboring house was doing, if he slept well himself, or if he came home and undressed in the dark. This man was a prominent citizen. He had just installed a new marble fountain in his store. Revolving stools, on white enamel posts, sat in front of it. During the evening his daughter, a large pasty girl, would wipe off the counter and the marble-topped tables, and Mr. Kirby himself would walk around and push the wire-legged chairs back into place. A little stout, in his forties somewhere, Clyde Kirby always spoke to you by name, asked about the missus, and sent you one of his New Year calendars. Hard to say, offhand, whether he undressed in the dark or not. He had raised five sons and was old enough to have learned a thing or two.

Will Brady sometimes stood in the alley adjoining Clyde Kirby's house. The blinds were usually drawn, as they were in his own, but one evening the windows were up and he saw Clyde Kirby, with his sleeves rolled up, standing in the pantry door. He was crumbling hunks of cornbread into a tall drinking glass. He filled this glass to the top with cornbread, then he took a can of milk, punched two holes, and poured the heavy cream over the cornbread, filling the glass. With the handle of his spoon, like a soda boy, he slushed it up and down. He seemed to be in a hurry, for some reason, but before he could lift the spoon to his mouth he heard a noise in the house, a door at the front had opened and closed. And like a kid who had got into the jam pot, this Clyde Kirby, a leading citizen, took the glass of cornbread he was holding and hid it behind his back. He just stood there, as if he was thinking, while the woman of the house came out of the hallway and carefully drew the blinds clear around the living-room. One by one she drew down all of the blinds on that side of the house. Then she entered the kitchen, walking past Mr. Kirby like a propped-up ironing board, and drew the blinds around the kitchen, hooked the screen, then went back the way she had come. All of this without making a gesture, without saying a word. And Clyde Kirby stood there, the glass at his back, until he heard the door at the front snap closed, then he crossed the dark kitchen and stood at the sink. He poured more canned milk over the cornbread, slushed it up and down with the spoon, then stood there gulping it down as though he was starved to death.

If it was the man's business to eat in the kitchen, it seemed to be the woman's business to keep the blinds drawn, and to make out of what went on in the house a home. For good or bad, a man seemed to need a woman around the house. And if Will Brady was a father, then this woman he had married was a mother of sorts.

Concerning his fatherhood, Will Brady sometimes walked from the front of the house to the back, tapped on the door, and with a serious face then put in his head. This woman he had married would be sitting there, mending clothes. Will Brady would say what he had to say—something about the poisons in penny candy—and she would agree with him, this woman, that the poisons were there. But the pimples, if that's what he meant, didn't mean anything. All boys had them. And that was what he wanted to hear. The poisons in penny candy were a man's business, and when he spoke she respected him for it; but the pimples on the chin were a woman's business, and he respected her. And it was up to her to make, out of all of this business, something called a home.

Well, that was the woman's business, but what about his own? If you want to get the feel of the egg business you take an egg in your hand—that is, you take thousands of them—and from each egg you slowly chip off the hen spots with your thumb. It isn't really necessary to candle the egg or peer around inside. The necessary thing is to get the feel of an egg in your hand.

That's how it is with eggs, but chickens are something else. A few old hens in the yard are one thing, but when you take a thousand pullets, say several thousand Leghorn pullets, what you have on your hands is something else. To get the feel of something like that troubled a lot of men. No man would rein in his horse to look at one chicken, but there were sometimes four or five buggies, or a wagonful of kids, drawn off the road just east of the Brady chicken farm. On Sunday afternoons even the women would be there. Five thousand Leghorn pullets was something no man had been able to describe. There was nothing to do but put the family in the buggy, let them see it for themselves.

They were usually farm people for the most part, people who ought to be sick to death of chickens, but they would get in their buggies and ride for half a day just to look at them. Some of these families brought their lunches and made a picnic out of it. Monday morning the ditch grass would be short where the grazing horses had clipped it, and the road would be scarred where the buggy weights had dragged in the dust. As these people didn't know Will Brady from Adam, he was free to drive his own team right in among them, let his mares graze, and look on with the rest of them. Five thousand Leghorns, five acres of white feathers, if a man could speak in terms like that. And why not? Somehow he had to describe this thing. Or perhaps a sea of feathers, a lake of whitecaps, when the wind caught them from the back, fanning out their tails and blowing loose feathers along with the dust. Will Brady used the word, though of course he had never seen the sea. Nor had he ever seen a larger body of water than Carter Lake. It was simply that the word came to mind, and Will Brady often spoke of his sea of chickens the way other men would refer to a field of corn. If and when he saw the sea, very likely he would think it looked like that. He would gaze out on the water and see five thousand pullets that would soon be hens.

There were also some sheds, which seemed to float like so many small boats in the sea of feathers, and there was a bare clearing where he planned to erect a fine city house. But from the buggies men saw just the chickens, the high unpainted cable fence, and the green bank of the railroad like a dam to hold it all in. Different men, of course, saw different things, but perhaps the best way to describe it was a remark that T. P. Luckett let drop one day.

"How's your empire, Brady?" he said, and most people let it go at that.

5

Once a month he went to Omaha on business, what you might call a business investment, as he found he worked better if he got away from Murdock now and then. The life in the city seemed to stimulate him. He always took a room at the Wellington Hotel, where there were fine potted palms in the lobby, a large map on the wall, and where altogether he felt more or less at home. He would sit between the palms, facing the street, or he would swing the chair around and face the lobby, the elevator cage, and the cigar-counter girl. She would usually be rattling the dice in the leather cup, or kidding with the old men. Summer evenings he might walk out on the new bridge and look at the bluffs across the river, or at the swirling brown water, more like mud than water, that he saw below. T. P. Luckett had said that part of the state was washing away. Standing there on the bridge Will Brady could see the truth of that. On his walk back to the hotel he would pick up a jar of hard candy for the boys, and make arrangements for the flowers, the roses, he would take to his wife.

"Would the gentleman like to include a card?" the flower girl always said.

"No," he would say, "no, thank you—it's just for my wife."

If the weather was bad he would sit in the lobby facing the girl behind the cigar counter and observing the way she had learned to handle the men. These men were all older, by and large, being traveling men with a sharp sense of humor, but she had learned to talk right back to them without batting an eye. Most of the men played dice with her for cigars. The dice were held in a leather cup, where they made a hollow rattle like peas in a gourd, and after the rattle she would roll them out on a small green pad. The older men liked to do it, it seemed, whether they won or not. The girl would slide back the glass top to the case and the man would reach in, helping himself to a La Paloma or whatever brand he liked. At the side of the counter was a small lamp, in a hood to keep the flame from blowing, and on a chain was a knife with a blade for snipping off the tip of your cigar. They would then purse their lips like a fat hen's bottom as they moistened the tip. It seemed to give these men a great deal of satisfaction just to rattle the dice, win or lose, and to help themselves to a cigar from the glass case. The hollow sound of the dice could be heard in the lobby, and in his room on the second floor, if the transom was down, Will Brady could hear the game being played.

The men usually laughed, a booming manly laugh, if the girl won.

Although he neither smoked nor gambled Will Brady seemed to like the sound of the dice, and something or other about the game seemed to interest him. Perhaps he had a yen to take the leather cup in his hand, shake it himself. To see if he could roll a seven, an eleven, or whatever it was. When the girl won, as she usually did, she would often wink at somebody in the lobby—at Will Brady if he happened to be sitting there. Although he didn't gamble, he would wink back at her. It was something she did with all the old men: it didn't mean anything. The day she spoke to him, for example, she was just playing the game with herself, she didn't trouble to wink, she just spoke to him right out of the blue.

"Come and have a game on me," she said.

"I don't play," he replied, but in a friendly manner.

"Come and play for a good cigar," she said, and rattled the dice. "Three," she said, "you can surely beat a three."

"Maybe," he said, "but I don't smoke."

"You don't what?" she said.

"I don't smoke," he replied.

The girl put down the leather cup she was holding and looked at him. "You're just kidding," she said, "what's your brand? I'll bet it's La Paloma for a man like you."

"Thank you very much," he said, "but I don't smoke." She looked at him for a while, and he looked back at her. She winked at him, but of course it didn't mean anything.

"You don't play either?" she said.

"No," he said, "I don't play."

She rattled the dice in the cup, then said: "You don't play, you don't smoke—what do you do?"

"I work," Will Brady replied, as if that explained everything, and maybe it did. He had never put it just that way before. "I work," he repeated, and smiled at the girl, but this time she didn't wink.

"If you don't smoke, why don't you smoke?" she said.

"I suppose I never started," he said; "if you don't start, maybe you don't want to."

"You really think so?"

"Well, I don't smoke," he said.

"I thought maybe you didn't smoke for your wife," she said. As he didn't get the point of that right away, Will Brady turned and looked at the lobby. When he got it, he said:

"I don't think my wife cares very much."

"I would," she said, "I would if I had any choice." Before he could think of an answer to that another man, about his own age, stepped up to the counter and pushed back the glass top to the case. He helped himself to a cigar, moistened the tip, then went off chewing on it. "You see what I mean?" the girl said, and made a face. When Will Brady didn't answer, she said: "Just imagine kissing something like that."

Turning to face the lobby Will Brady replied: "Well, I hear that some of them do."

"They don't if they have any choice," said the girl, and rattled the dice. He didn't have an answer to that, so she said: "—but I guess they don't have much choice. What choice do you have when some men never take a day off?"

"What would a man want to take a day off for?" he said.

"It's a good thing I don't take you men seriously," she replied.

As he wanted to be taken seriously, he said: "I've never had a day off in my life."

"You men!" she said, and made a clucking sound with her tongue.

"A day off—" he said, "what for?"

"I like men who wear red ties," she said.

He looked down at his new red tie, then he replied: "Not every man can take a day off, but there's some men who can if they want to. Men of a certain caliber are more or less free to do as they like."

"If they don't smoke," she said, "I suppose they've got to do something." She winked at him, and this time he winked back. "That's why I wish I was a man," she said; "a man can do as he likes, but a woman only has one day a week."

"What day is that?" he said, and looked her right in the eye.

"Friday," she said, looking right back at him, "I'm off every Friday at five o'clock." She rolled the dice out on the pad, and when it turned up a four and a three she said: "That means it's lucky for me. What kind of car does a man like you drive?"

Several years before, listening to T. P. Luckett, something of this sort had come over Will Brady, and he had become, overnight almost, a man of caliber. Now he became the owner of a car. An Overland roadster—one of the kind that a man like himself might drive.

He bought this car in Columbus, where he had to change trains, and the new Willys-Overland dealer had a fine big showroom facing the station and the tracks. In the window was the Overland roadster with the sporty wire wheels. They were red, and about the same color as his tie.

As he stood there listening to the powerful motor he let the owner of the shop persuade him that he might as well get into the car and drive it home. On west of Columbus it was wide-open country, there was nothing but horses to worry about, and the only way to learn to drive a car was to get in and drive. Once he got in, and got the car moving, he would find that the Overland drove itself, leaving nothing for the driver to do but sit there and shift the gears. At the railroad crossings he would get a lot of practice in.

He got in a lot of practice, all right, but some of it was lost owing to the fact that he drove along, thirty miles or so, in second gear. The road was so bad that he didn't seem to notice it. Ten miles an hour was pretty good time over most of it. It was just getting dark when he came into Murdock, at the edge of the Chautauqua grounds, where he saw that several boys had built a bonfire near the tracks. One of them, a very spry little fellow, was hopping around. Now, boys often behave like that and he might not have thought anything of it if he hadn't noticed, in the light from the fire, that he had on no pants. He was hopping up and down, hollering and yelling, without his pants. When Will Brady saw who this spry boy was, and what it was they all seemed to be doing, his hand went forward, in spite of himself, and honked the horn. They jumped up like rabbits, every one of them, and ran for the trees. But not a single boy, and there were maybe ten of them, had on his pants. They ran off like madmen, hooting like Indians, through the scrubby willows along the tracks, and bringing up the rear, his bottom bright in the car lights, was Will Brady's son. Farther down the tracks they picked up their pants and ran along waving them, like banners, but there was no time, of course, to stop and put them on. Will Brady just sat there till he heard the motor running, and the hooting had passed.

Perhaps that was why he went to Omaha again the following week. He had it in mind to walk down lower Douglas, where he knew there were doctors "for men," and speak to one of these doctors about the strange behavior of the boys. He had often seen the signs that were painted on the windows on the second floor. So he walked along this street, he read the signs, but he couldn't seem to make up his mind how to describe what had happened, or whether Willy Brady, aged nine, was a man or not. These doctors for men might think that Will Brady was kidding them. He went back and took a seat in the lobby of the Wellington Hotel. It happened to be Saturday, not Friday, but the girl behind the counter had been thinking it over, and she wondered if Sunday wouldn't be a better time for him. Now that he had a car, and in case he really wanted to take the day off.

If there were people in Murdock who had picked up the notion that Will Brady liked other chickens as well as Leghorns, talk like that somehow never got around to him. It couldn't, as he seldom talked to anyone. Not that Will Brady wasn't friendly—everybody remarked how friendly he was—but he didn't have the time, or whatever it took, to make friends. Will Brady was what they called a go-getter, a man who not only was up and coming, but in a lot of things, the important things, had already arrived. Just north of town, for example, he had a chicken farm with five thousand Leghorns, and on a cold windy day some of the feathers even blew into town. And work had begun on his modern thirteen-room house. As illustrated in *Radnor's Ideal Homes*, Will Brady's house would have a three-story tower, and was listed under "Mansions," the finest section of the book. Not listed, but to be part of the house, were the diamond-shaped panes of colored glass, imported from Chicago like the marble in Clyde Kirby's new drugstore. As there were thirty-six windows in this house, including those in the basement and the tower, there would be nothing like it in either Murdock or Calloway. If there was light, it came through a panel of colored glass. If there was no light, as sometimes couldn't be helped, a lantern would be burning in the top of the tower, shining through a green porthole like the semaphore far down the tracks. A man out on the plains could get his bearings just by looking at it.

This fellow Brady was a comer, as everybody said, but not many people would have recognized him, or the girl along with him, on certain warm summer nights. Out in the Krug Amusement Park he would sit on a bench, holding her cone of spun sugar candy, while she rode the roller coaster and other up-and-down rides that made him sick. Early in the evening she would first go swimming, leaving him on the beach with her comb and her lipstick, or in the wicker chairs for parents on the balcony behind the diving board. Before diving, she would turn and wave to him. Chased by boys, she liked to swim under water, and in his anxiety Will Brady would rise out of the chair and somebody would ask him to please sit down. There were other people who had children to account for, this man would say.

Elderly folks, both men and women, often drew up their chairs to speak to Will Brady, ask about his girl, and tell him what a fine-looking child she was. When he agreed, they would point out youngsters of their own. Most of them were plump, good-looking girls, squealing like pigs when the boys edged near them, and Will Brady could see that nearly all parents had the same concern. To be there to wave when the children dived, to tell them when they turned the soft blue color, and to shoo off the boys, like flies, when they sprawled out on the sand. Later would come the Ferris wheel, the Spook House, the balls thrown at something, and if it was hit he would carry the Kewpie doll. He would spend five dollars to win a fifty-cent Ouija board. In the ballroom, with these things in his lap, he would sit on a folding chair in the corner watching her dance with some young buck who had asked her to. A youngster who thought *he* was her father, naturally. And they would bring him a hot dog, a bottle of red pop, and stand there before him, trying to be friendly, looking over their shoulders at the young people who danced.

"Now, why don't you kids go and dance," he would say, and while they did he would eat the hot dog and look at the Ouija board, as the boy would be hugging her. But not too much, as he *was* her father, and after a while the boy would bring her back, shake Will Brady's hand, and try to leave a good impression with him.

"I'm very glad to have met you, sir," these boys would say.

But after the swimming, the riding, and the dancing, she would play with him. She would take him for several long rides on the Swanee River, that is. Will Brady found it spooky and unpleasant, the rocking of the boat troubled him, but on the whole he got along without getting sick. And in the dark part of the river, in the mossy wood, where the water splashed over the mill wheel, she would take his hands in her own and put them around her waist. There she would hold them, tight, until they reached the pier where the ride had ended, and everybody on the pier could see how it was with the pair in the boat. That this man with the straw hat was a good deal more than a father to her. He was her lover. A man to be pitied and envied, that is.

To make it perfectly clear who Will Brady was, she needed help with her clothes in lobbies and restaurants, and out on the street dust was always blowing into her eyes. She would have to press against him while he saw what the trouble was. In the aisles of big stores she liked to swoon, as the high-class ladies swooned in the movies, and to have him come with her while she shopped for stockings and under-clothes. Nobody had taught her how to wear clothes so that she looked covered when she had them on, but she had learned from her mother how to go without them and look all right. Like swimming under water, it astonished and troubled him. Her mother was an actress on the vaudeville circuit, and her father was one of five men, in a ten-minute act, who entered the room and hid under the bed. Will Brady had once seen her mother, on a poster, on lower Douglas Street. Her daughter looked a good deal like her in most respects.

There was little resemblance, certainly, between this girl and sad-eyed Opal Mason, but at night he had the feeling Opal Mason would approve of her. Like Opal Mason, the girl liked to talk. Will Brady often had the feeling that he was there in bed for reasons he hadn't really looked into and were not at all the reasons that an outsider might think. He never said much himself, as he was too sleepy and felt he was there for fairly obvious reasons, but toward morning, without her saying anything, he would wake up. Why was that? It seemed to be because she wanted him to. He couldn't really do much for her, somehow, but one thing he could do was wake up in the morning, roll on his back, and lie there listening to her. Sometimes he wondered if this might be another form of loving, one that women needed, just as men seemed to need the more obvious kind. But he didn't really know, and the talking never cleared it up. As a matter of fact, the more she talked, the less he understood.

Sometimes this girl would begin with the morning and describe everything that had happened; she would describe, that is, every man who had troubled to follow her. She remembered and described these men so well that Will Brady, who saw very little, would recognize these men as the familiar fops he passed in the street. Every one of them useless, whore-chasing men, with a gold-toothed smile, light-tan button shoes, and a pin in his tie he could buy for fifteen cents. And they were all, she insisted, very fine gentlemen. When he scoffed at this she wanted to know what he would know about men like that, not knowing anybody, let alone classy people like that. Then she would go on—she always went on—to tell him that a lady knew a gentleman by the oil in his hair and the fancy silk socks that he wore. And the way that he would stand, in the better-class lobbies, shooting his cuffs.

Well, there were things that he might have said, but he would have to lie there, his mouth tight shut, as right there on the floor, at the side of the bed, were his own dirty socks. Or worse yet, they might still be on his feet, right there in the bed. What could he say—a man like that— about fine gentlemen? Nor could he even ask her where she had picked up such notions. He knew, for one thing—he knew she had smelled this hair at close quarters, snapped the cuff links herself, and praised the gentlemen's taste in socks. He knew, and it was the last thing in the world he cared to hear about.

If she liked these dandies, he had said, and he liked the word *dandy*, what in the world did she see in a man like him?

"Your hair," she had replied. Just like that. That had made him so mad he said what he had on his mind.

"And how are these dandies to sleep with?" he said.

"Oh," she said, "like anybody." But as he lay back she added: "But what's that to do with what I like?"

As he drove into Omaha every Friday and home again on Sunday evening, he may have picked up the notion that it might go on indefinitely. Now and then he did wonder about the girl, and the five days a week he wasn't there to watch her, but he neither wondered nor worried about his wife. She lived in the sunny room at the back of the house, and when she heard him come in, on Sunday evening, she would call out: "Is that you, Will?" and he would answer:

"Yes, Ethel," and hook the screen, turn out the light. Then he would walk through the dark house to his room at the front.

The night she didn't call out, his first thought was that she might be asleep. He didn't worry about it until he got into bed, when the quiet of the house, something or other about it, and the creaking street light seemed to keep him awake. The night, he thought, seemed quieter than usual. That might have been because of the noise of the city, where a street car passed right below the window, but it kept him awake like the lull that follows a wind. He sat up in bed at one point and looked out. He could see the gnats and hear the big fat June bugs strike the street light. Turning from the window he noticed the door that led from his room into the boy's, and on the chair in front of the door were his pants. On holidays, when he might sleep late, the boy would open the door and take some of the small change from his pants. Was that stealing? Neither of them had mentioned it.

It occurred to Will Brady that it had been some time since the boy had come in to swipe a little money, or since his father had opened the door to question the boy. Not since the week the boy had taken to drinking vinegar. He would take the big vinegar jug to his room, hiding it beneath the bed or inside of his pillow, and when the lights were out he would pull out the cork and take a swig. Later he would be sick and vomit over his Teddy bears. It had been a very strange thing to do—like the hooting and howling with his pants off—but Dr. Finley had said some boys would surprise you. And they certainly would.

At that time Will Brady had suggested that the door between their rooms might be left open, but the boy said his father's snoring kept him awake. Perhaps it did. So the door was closed again. But there was no more vinegar trouble and for a while everything seemed all right, until Will Brady came home one night and found the entire house lit up. The boy was propped up in bed with his bears, but his hair was shaved off. He had dipped his head, with all of his lovely curls, in a barrel of hot tar. Several men had been repairing the roof of the church, and while they were up there working on it, the boy had sneaked over and dipped his head in their barrel of tar. God knows how he had ever thought of something like that. A crazy thing to do, but he had done it, and the long silken curls that hung below his shoulders were thrown away with the stiff chunks of tar. The top of his small, narrow head had to be shaved. He looked like a bird that had just been hatched, and it upset Ethel, who was not his real mother, a good deal more than it did the boy. She took to bed for several days herself. It might be that Ethel, who already had a boy, had wanted a small pretty girl for a change, as she let his hair grow and liked to dress him in rompers and Fauntleroys. But the tar had put an end to that.

With his small head shaved Willy Brady was neither a boy nor a girl. In the evening his father would sometimes open the door and look into the room, where the lamp sat on the table, and the boy would be sitting there in bed with his three brown bears. One of them, the papa bear, almost as big as he was. And always reading, as *they* had just learned to read. As Will Brady didn't want to disturb them—the three bears had staring glass eyes—he would close the door without saying anything. Standing there in the dark, he would head the boy whisper to one of them.

Although he had never done it before, he got out of bed, lit his lamp, and opened the door to the boy's room. He first thought the figure propped up in bed was the boy, with his eyes wide open, but it turned out to be the papa bear. The boy was not there in the bed at all. But pinned to the bear's woolly chest was a piece of note paper, torn from a pad, that seemed to be blank until he came forward with the lamp. It was not signed, nor did it say to whom it was addressed, but Will Brady recognized the writing well enough. His wife, Ethel, wrote a fine Spencerian hand.

Willy is with Mrs. Riddlemosher

it said, and that was all. That was all he ever heard from Ethel Czerny Bassett, his wife.

6

With a small pail of sand containing horsetail hairs that would turn to garter snakes when it rained on them, Will Brady and his son moved from the town of Murdock to the city of Omaha. They took a room on the mezzanine floor of the Wellington Hotel. The pail of sand was kept at the front of the lobby, behind the tub with the potted palm, so that Willy Brady, in case it rained, could run outside with it. Sometimes he did, other times he just let it rain.

In the morning the boy would be there in the lobby, sitting near one of the brass spittoons, where he was told he could whittle or spit the black licorice juice. Most of the time he just sat there, with his legs straight out. The women who worked in the hotel restaurant would stop and speak to him.

After lunch, with his friend Mr. Wherry, he would play four or five games of checkers, or a game of parcheesi with the cigar-counter girl. It might be that Mr. Wherry, who was fond of children, thought the girl behind the counter was the boy's sister, as he seemed to think they were both Will Brady's kids. He bought them bags of candy and took them down the street to the matinee. He was a fine old man, but a little hard of hearing; and something like that, a problem like that, was better left alone, as it might prove hard to explain.

If the boy wasn't there in the lobby he might be on the mezzanine, in the phone booth, having long conversations with the telephone girl. He would leave word with her to have his father call him when he came in.

"This is Willy Brady Jr." the voice would say, with the confident tone of a Singer's midget, and somehow his father, Will Brady, was never prepared for it. He would stand there, and the boy would say: "Who is this speaking?"

"This is your father, son," Will Brady would say, in the sober voice of a father, but he never had the feeling that the boy was impressed. He didn't believe it any more than Willy Brady did himself.

Once a week, as a father should, he would borrow the boy from Mr. Wherry and take him to the places a boy would like to go. This was usually to see a man named Eddie Polo, whom they left in some pit, every week, as good as dead, only to come back the next week and find him big as life. The boy was also crazy about Charlie Chaplin, but he had seen everything a good many times, and made a nuisance of himself as he always got the hiccups when he laughed. He would have to be led back to the lobby, many times, for a drink. As Will Brady didn't care for Eddie Polo himself, any more than he did for the roller coaster, he would pass the time eating the popcorn or peanuts he bought for the boy. As he couldn't get his hand in the small-size bag, he had to buy the large-size ones, and near the middle of the movie he usually wanted a drink himself. They would both have a phosphate, usually cherry, at the drugstore when they got out.

Summer evenings, if it was still light after they had got

out of the movie, he might walk the boy down Farnam Street to the Market Place. Will Brady's place of business faced the west, and if it wasn't too late in the evening some light from the sky might be on the new sign he had at the front. This sign cost him three hundred dollars, and featured two roosters, drawn by hand, crowing over a large Leghorn egg. Through a misunderstanding both of the birds were Plymouth Rocks, as well as roosters—a point that troubled Will Brady, but the boy never noticed it. He didn't seem to care what color the eggs, or the chickens, were. On the wide glass window, lettered in gold, were the words:

WILL BRADY
EGGS

but the boy never seemed to realize that name was his own. That one day it would read WILL BRADY & SON. Any number of times, as they came around the corner, Will Brady meant to bring it up, but when they got there and stood facing the building, nothing was said. There seemed to be no connection. Perhaps that was it. There they were, Father & Son, looking through the window of their future—but it seemed to be Will Brady's, not the boy's. He never walked up and pressed his nose to the window, as most boys would do, and he didn't seem to care what went on behind the glass. If Will Brady said: "Now just a minute, son," and felt around in his pocket for the keys, the boy would stand out on the curbing while he went in. Sometimes he made quite a racket to attract attention, or stood in the candling-room, holding some eggs, but the boy never came back to see what was delaying him.

No, the only person that seemed to care, or wonder what it was he was doing, was the old man who sometimes slept in the back of the shop. A drifter, a wreck of a man with a dark bearded face, and one hand missing, he would sometimes get up from where he was lying and come peer at him. He would open the flap to the candling-room and put in his head. There he would be, a strange smile on his face, and perhaps a nail in one corner of his mouth, looking in on Will Brady as if he had called for him. Wagging his head, this old man would say: "Mr. Brady, how's that boy of yours?"

And it had turned out the old man had a boy of his own. Older, of course. Gone off somewhere, that is. A boy who had a mother who had also gone off somewhere. This old man probably didn't understand some of the words Will Brady fell to using, but he had been a father, and seemed to know the way of boys. He would wag his head as if it was all familiar to him. His own name he never mentioned, but a boy named Gregor, and a girl named Pearl, were very much like their mother, a woman named Belle. At the thought of her he would reach for the nail keg, put more nails in his mouth.

The old man kept the stub of his arm in his pocket, but speaking of war, which he knew at first hand, he would draw it out, like a sword, and point with it. The missing hand seemed to be something, like a glove, that he had left in his coat. He kept a small tin of water on top of the stove, to which he added, when he thought of it, coffee, drinking his own from the can but serving Will Brady in a green tin cup. When he stood near the stove the smell of wet gunny sacks steamed out from his clothes. By himself, he spit into the fire, cocking his head like a robin to hear the juice sizzle, but with Will Brady he would walk to the door, spit into the street. The blue knob of his wrist would wipe the brown stain from his lips. Coming back to the stove, he would take off his hat, look carefully into the crown, then use the stub of his arm to hone, tenderly, the soiled brim.

One evening in March, nearly the middle of March, Will

Brady stopped the old man at the door to tell him that he could have the next day off. A holiday? Well yes, in a way it was. He, Will Brady, was taking himself another wife. Taking her, he added, before some other lucky fellow did. The old man seemed to think that was pretty sharp, pressing on his mouth to keep his chew in, and Will Brady pressed a crisp new ten-dollar bill into his one hand. "Have yourself a good time," he said, but perhaps a man who had never had one, never bought one, anyhow, wasn't the man to bring the matter up. The old man stood there with the money, looking at it. Somehow it made Will Brady think of the boy, as when he didn't know what else to do he would give the boy money and say: "Go buy yourself something." The old man stood there, strangely preoccupied. Will Brady left him, but when he looked back he saw that the old man was still in the doorway, but his good arm was stretched across his front to his left side. He was trying to put the money in the pocket where he couldn't take it out. To get it out of that pocket, as he had once said, he had to take his coat off his back, which was not an easy thing for a one-armed man to do. Money put there was usually still there when he needed it.

Will Brady thought of that, oddly enough, when he reached across his front for the girl's small hand, and it may have been why he had a little trouble with the ring. They were married on the second floor of the City Hall. They stood in the anteroom of the Judge's office, facing the Judge himself and the green water-cooler, and the four or five people who were waiting to speak to him. A man who is married for the second time will probably look out the window, if one is handy, and think of the first time that such a thing had happened to him. It seemed, it all seemed, a good while ago. Thinking of that he turned from the window, where a ratty-tailed pigeon was strutting, and looked at the boy—a Western Union boy—who stood in the door. On his way somewhere, the boy had stopped to look in. Perhaps he had never seen a man married before. When he saw Will Brady, and Will Brady saw him, the boy took off his uniform cap, held it at his side, and ran his dirty fingers through his mussy hair. His eyes were wide, his lips were parted, and though there were other people in the room, what you call witnesses, it was only the boy who saw something. It was the boy that reminded Will Brady of what was happening to him. That taking a wife, as he had put it, was a serious affair.

He wanted to go out and speak to the boy, perhaps shake his hand, or give him some money, but all he did, of course, was stand there shaking hands with the Judge. The Judge turned from him to the water-cooler, tipping it forward as it was nearly empty, and had several long drinks from a soiled paper cup. Michael Long, his wife's father, crossed the room to shake Will Brady's hand and give him a wink, showing the gold caps on his teeth. Mr. Long was a dark-haired, rosy-cheeked man who had once been quite an actor, one of the five men, wearing spats, who tried to hide under a bed on the stage. A little old for that now, he had given it up, and come by bus from Kansas City to see the little girl finally hitched—as he said. Mrs. Long herself, a well-preserved woman, was still in considerable demand as the actress who lay in the bed with the men beneath it. This was why she had not been able to come. She was under contract to do three matinees a day.

Michael Long told Will Brady this as they stood in the lobby, but he left the impression with Will Brady that something else, of far greater importance, was on his mind. In the men's room, where they went to think it over, he explained himself. He wanted Will Brady to know, he said—holding his wig flat while he combed it—that he was making no mistake, no sireee, with this little girl. She was just like her mother, he said, who was as good now as she ever was, and by that he meant something better than thirty-five years. Every bit as good, Michael Long said, and put out his hands on something he saw before him, which might have been a stove, a radiator, or a woman's hips.

Mr. Long had told him that before the ceremony, in case he thought he might change his mind, but his hand was still sticky and smelled of hair oil when he shook Will Brady's hand. Will Brady dropped it and wiped his own on the side of his pants. He kissed an Aunt Lucille, who offered a cheek like a piece of saddle leather; then he led his wife down the wrought-iron stairway to the street. They had left the boy with Mr. Wherry, as he was a great stickler for details, knew all about weddings, and might object to one in the City Hall. As they entered the hotel and the smoke-filled lobby, the girl led him forward to meet the boy as if they had been lovers, *her* lovers, and now had to patch up their quarrel.

7

As his bride had never been west before, and as Will Brady wanted her to get the feel of the country, they left Omaha early in the morning on a fine spring day. Just west of Fremont he took the flapping side curtains off the car. In the West, as he told her—that is, he told them, as the boy had got to be quite a city kid—there were no wooded hills as there were along the river around Council Bluffs. It was not hilly country, and the rivers were apt to be wide, shallow affairs, as most of the water was somewhere underground. It was what men called open country, where you could see a good ways. When the sun was right—that is to say, behind you—a man could see from town to town, and his bride, Gertrude Long, seemed to think that this was wonderful. She was so tired of being cooped up in the dirty city, she said. But when the sun was wrong—as it was when you were driving west, along toward evening—everything that you saw, if you cared to look at it, looked quite a bit alike. Pretty much like the same town, usually, with the same grain elevator along the tracks, and the same gas pump out in front of the same hay and feed store. Through the vibrating windshield, as the roads were pretty bad, the wide empty plain seemed to shimmer, and the telephone poles that slowly crawled past appeared to tremble and blur. The evening sun was like a locomotive headlight in their eyes. To get away from this sun the girl dozed off with her head bumping on Will Brady's shoulder, her mouth open, and her tongue black with the licorice she liked to eat. The boy sprawled with his feet on the seat, his head in her lap. A wad of Black Jack chewing gum was being saved on the bridge of his nose.

Will Brady drove mechanically, his fingers thick like those of the boy when he roller-skated, his hands gripping the wheel, his tired eyes fixed on the road. Once he stopped the car, as he had come to feel that one more mile would rattle him to pieces, but as he sat there, brooding, neither the boy nor the girl woke up. A cow tethered in the field near by turned to gaze at him. Her dung-heavy tail made a flapping sound like that of a loose board, wind-rattled, when it thumped, like a bell clapper, on her hollow frame. He returned her solemn gaze until she started to moo, when he drove on.

A little after sundown he drove into Murdock, an abandoned town on a Sunday evening, with no sign of life anywhere but the revolving barber pole. He drove on through the town, past the piles of cases that were stamped WILL BRADY—EGGS—MURDOCK, and that had been stacked under the shelter, ready for loading, on the station platform. He drove down the road that led, as they said, to the Brady Egg Empire. He had planned it that way, to arrive about sunset, so that the last rays of the sun, no longer touching the plains, might be seen on the tower of the new house. But from the bridge over the creek, which was just a mile or so from the farm, he saw the tower to the house and it struck him as higher than he thought it would be. And the house itself, the bulk of it, struck him as even larger than he had remembered, and a good deal stranger than it had appeared in *Ideal Homes*. Something was missing, but hard to say what it was. It was both larger than he had thought, the tower was higher than he had thought, and somehow or other he had expected a few trees. Perhaps he thought the trees came with the house. There had been a small grove around the house he had seen in the catalogue.

Still it was his own place, all right, as there in the fields were thousands of chickens, and on the new shingled roof were the lightning rods with the polished blue balls. He had asked for them, picked that color out himself. It was their place, but he drove on by, neither slowing down nor honking the horn nor doing anything that he figured might wake his family up.

What if they should ask him who in the world lived in a place like that? What if they should want to know, as they would, who in the world had been such a fool as to build, out here in the country, a fine city house. One that needed a green lawn, many fine big trees with a hammock or two swinging between them, and a birthday party going on clear around the run-around porch. What good was such a house without the city along with it? That's what they would ask him, laughing and hooting when they saw that he had no answer, so he drove on by, neither speaking to them nor shifting the gears. He followed one of the quiet, grass-covered roads back into town. When he drew up at the Cornland Hotel he just sat there for a while, with the motor running, reading the sign that asked guests with horses to leave them in the rear. Then he shut off the motor, and the sudden quiet woke them up.

He left them there in the car, the girl rubbing her eyes, while he stepped up to the counter of the hotel, where a Mr. Riddlemosher, once a neighbor, shook his hand. He asked about the boy as he handed Will Brady the counter pen. He watched Will Brady sign his name, then he twirled the ledger around to read for himself, over his glasses, just what it said. *Will Brady, wife & son.* That was what it said.

"Well," Mr. Riddlemosher said, "well, well—" then he looked up from the ledger to see the boy, his hands full of tinfoil, run into the lobby of the hotel. It was Mr. Riddle-mosher who used to buy it from him at ten cents a pound.

8

Ten or twelve hours a day—when he wasn't eating, arguing with his family, or sleeping—Will Brady uncrated the furniture and drove it out to the farm. He had a freight car on the siding, full of it. While he did this he hired a man from Chapman, a farmer with two husky boys, to dig up some small shade trees and plant them in the yard. He wanted *something* to be there in the yard when he drove them out. Something besides chickens, that is, as even the full-grown Leghorn hens looked like so many pillow feathers blowing around a big empty house. They were fine big birds, but they looked awfully small. Everything did.

Now and then he would wake up at night with the notion that his strange house, like a caboose left on a siding, had somehow drifted away during the night. That he would drive out of town in the morning and find it gone. It was a wonderfully hopeful feeling—without it he might not have got up in the morning—but it made it that much worse when he saw that it was still there. Bigger than life. That was the hell of it.

With still half a car of furniture to unload, he had enough sofas for four or five houses, as they would not fit inside of the rooms he had bought them for. The doors opened wrong, or a window proved to be in the way. Some of the beds wouldn't fit in the rooms and he asked Mr. Sykes, his hired hand, if his wife might not care for one of them. What Mrs. Sykes didn't want they stored in the loft of the Sykes barn. It was Mrs. Sykes, of course, who asked him, when he came to the door of the kitchen, when he was going to get around to the kitchen stove. An honest man, Will Brady simply said he hadn't thought of it.

It seemed hard to believe, a little weird in fact, that a man like Will Brady, born and raised in a soddy, had spent three thousand dollars without buying himself a kitchen stove. Had he come up too fast? Mrs. Sykes implied as much. She stood there looking at him, then said: "Well, it's up to the woman to think of the stove," and maybe it was. But not every woman. Not one like his wife.

He tried to explain, as they drove into town, that the reason his wife hadn't thought of the stove was that city-born girls, of a certain type, never cooked anything. They ate in restaurants. The food they ate was brought to them.

And who, Mrs. Sykes said, was going to bring her food to her in the country?

Well, that was one more thing he hadn't got around to thinking about. There had been too many things. There had also been restaurants where they could eat.

But he thought of that, among other things, as he watched Mrs. Sykes build a fire in the stove, breaking the stiff pine kindling between her strong hands and over her knee. Tough pieces she leaned on the leg of the stove, then stepped on them. She set the drafts on the pipes, then dipped a corncob into a pail of kerosene, lit it with a match, and used it like a torch to start the fire. As it roared up the chimney she said: "Well, I guess it draws all right."

Mrs. Sykes was an angular woman, a little blunt in her ways, and Will Brady felt right at home with her, as his own family treated him the same way. As a man, that is, who didn't seem to know anything. Not only in the woman's place, in the kitchen, but if Mrs. Sykes saw him out in the yard she would call to him, put a pail or a shovel into his hand. On a farm, she told him, something always needed to be done.

Would she happen to know a woman, he said, who would like a nice home in the country? A woman like herself, who would like to do the cooking, look after the house.

Mrs. Sykes wiped her hands and stiffened her back at the same time. She held her right hand to her face and picked at a splinter in the palm.

Did he know what it was like, she said, to keep a thirteen-room house?

Suppose they just closed off some of the upstairs rooms, he said. Would a woman like herself mind keeping a five- or six-room house?

Did he think, she replied, a woman would call that *keeping house*? That was what she said, leaving him there in the empty kitchen, with the fire burning, and the smell of the paint rising from the new stove. Then she was back—her head in the door but her face turned away from him. She said that she did know a woman, and if she happened to see her she might bring it up. But she wouldn't recommend it to any woman—not something like that. Then the door slammed behind her in a way that made it clear what she thought.

Four or five days later, a Saturday morning, Will Brady thought he saw Mrs. Sykes in the kitchen, but the woman who turned to face him had white hair. She was panning water from the bin on the range, the handle of the pan wrapped in her apron, and he had the feeling that she might be a little deaf. She didn't seem to be surprised to see him standing there. A tall heavy-bodied woman, with dark skin, she didn't look any too well around the eyes, but to see her working, it was clear that she was strong enough.

"You're from Mrs. Sykes?" he said to her, raising his voice as she didn't seem to hear him. She stooped for some cobs, then settled the kettle over the plate hole.

"Mrs. Sykes said you could use a woman," she said.

"My wife is a city-bred girl," he said, which was true enough, but strange to hear him say it. "And city girls," he went on, "aren't really used to country ways."

That was strange kind of talk for him, but the woman seemed to follow it. It didn't seem to strike her, as it did Mrs. Sykes, that a city-bred girl was out of place in the country.

"To tell you the simple truth," he said, as he felt an urge to speak on this topic, "I suppose what I've tried to do is to bring the city out here." He gestured with his arm at the house, then added, "I wanted her to feel at home out here." Nor did this woman seem to see anything strange in that. "My name is Will Brady," he said, "and I'm very glad you've come to help us out. If the house is too big—" he waved his hand at the house, "we can shut some of it off."

"I'm getting on now," this woman said, "but I can still keep a house."

She didn't seem to feel it necessary to say any more than that. He stood there, and after a moment he realized that the sound that he heard, like a pole humming, was one that she made in her throat. A familiar hymn. She was humming it.

"If there's anything I can do," he said, "I want you to feel free to call on me." Then he coughed, took a drink of water, and hurried out. Where had he picked up such a fancy way of putting things? He turned back to the door and said: "If you want anything, let me know," but she seemed to be busy again and had her back to him. He crossed the yard to Mr. Sykes, who was mixing up a barrel of laying mash, but he stopped when Will Brady walked up to him.

"You happen to know this old lady's name?" he asked.

"Mason," Mr. Sykes said. "Anna Mason—she's a good sort."

"She strikes me as a pretty fine woman," Will Brady said.

"She's a good sort," Sykes said again.

But there was something about the woman that Will Brady felt needed some comment. "I'd say she was a woman a man could depend on," he said.

"Kept house for her brother," Sykes said, "going on about forty years. He died last year. Guess she misses him."

"She never married?" Will Brady asked.

"No, she never married," Sykes said; then he looked up and said: "She had her brother, one of her own people, to think of."

In April it was spring out in the yard, where the fat hens made nests in the dust heaps, but the winter still seemed to be trapped in the house. Mrs. Sykes had finally told him about the stove, but nobody had told him about the furnace, which was supposed to have been in the basement of the house. Now that the house was up, there was no longer any way of getting it there. The basement was a big white-washed room, clean-smelling from the earth, and sometimes even sunny, so he put his desk in the basement and lived down there himself. It was handy to the yard, and getting in and out he didn't trouble anyone.

The boy and girl—that was what he called them—lived, with an oil stove, in the master bedroom on the second floor, where they had their meals unless he drove them into town to eat. During the day they played phonograph records on the machine he had ordered from Omaha, and when the windows were up he could often hear the music himself. The kind of music that they liked sounded very strange in the chicken yard.

Although there was always work to do, and not enough help on the place to do it, he sometimes found himself at the narrow basement windows, peering out. The window on the yard was about chest-high, with a deep sill that he could lean on, and he found that he could see out without Mrs. Sykes being able to see in. Twice a day the local train came down from the north, and even before the bell was ringing, Will Brady would be there at the window, peering out. He liked to watch the smoke pouring from the wide funnel stack. As she came around the curve, the bell wagging, the fireman would climb out of the cab and crawl back over the coal car to the water bin. She took water in Murdock, and he had to be there to pull the stack down. Will Brady would look on while all of this happened, seeing very little from where he stood, but knowing, as an old railroad man, what was taking place. He could hear, on certain days, the water pouring through the chute. He might be able to see a passenger or two get on or off. And all this time the bell would be ringing as there were no guard gates on the

Burlington crossing, nothing but kids who would be standing on the cowcatcher, waiting for the brakeman to run up front and shoo them off.

Will Brady would stand there, maybe five or ten minutes, until the caboose finally disappeared, and he could hear the whistle, thin and wild, as if the train was calling for help. Was something wrong with him? Or was it just spring fever, or something like that. A tendency to let the team idle on the bridge, so that he could see, through the cracks, the clear water, or to let them graze in the sweet grass at the side of the road. Only flipping the reins now and then to keep the flies off their spanky rumps.

After several years of working day and night, perhaps Will Brady had begun to stop working, to stand as if thinking, as if great thoughts were troubling his mind. Mr. Sykes often had to repeat everything he said. It was not the proper state of mind for a man who had around five thousand laying hens to think of, and who had often been asked what he intended to do when one hen took sick. Well, he didn't know. No, he didn't even know that. Standing at the basement window he sometimes marveled at this strange fellow, Will Jennings Brady, known all over the state as an up and coming man of caliber. A man who lived in the basement of his fine new thirteen-room house.

On a Sunday morning, on his way into town, he found this woman Anna Mason walking down the road, her skirts pinned up, and her long underwear tucked into her high laced shoes. When he stopped and spoke to her she said she was on her way to church. A woman nearly seventy years of age, heavy on her feet and not any too well, on her way to a church that was a good three-mile walk.

"Now look here," he said, but she wouldn't listen to him. Nor would she get into the car and ride in with him. She would go to church, she let him know, just so long as she could get there; when she couldn't get there any more, why, then she wouldn't go. She would be dead then, she said, and looked at him.

All right, he replied, but he would be there to bring her home.

If he just happened to be there in the church, she said, if he happened to be there, and she happened to see him, why, then she supposed he might as well bring her home.

He wondered if that was how it happened that most men went to church. There would be a woman there, too old to walk, who would like a ride home. A woman with white or gray hair, her long underwear tucked into her shoe tops, and spectacles that had got to be the color of flecked isinglass. She would be there in the pew, her hands in her lap, or pushing up to share with somebody her hymnbook, then singing, or humming, in a voice that made little boys wet their pants. He had done just that, anyway, many times. His mother had had such a voice, throbbing like an organ on the chorus, and this throb passed down through her arm into his hand, the one she was holding, and made the small hairs rise on his neck, and his knees rub. And when the hymn was over he usually found that his pants were wet.

Now he came late and took a seat near the door, where he had sat that Sunday that the boy had won a Bible, with his name stamped on it, and brought it up the aisle to him. Where, come to think of it, was that Bible now? He had driven them all—it was Ethel then—out to Nolan's Lake for the barbecue, the motorboat ride, and the hymn-singing after dark. The choir in their long white robes on the platform, the hissing red flares very good on the women, and in the dark like that, out in the open, he could sing himself. It was said that he had a fine baritone voice. Well, that night he had sung many hymns, the fires had made it seem like a gypsy encampment, and the boy, who had eaten too much, fell asleep in his lap. The new Bible, with the cover sticky, had dropped from his hand. Will Brady had picked it up and said: "Ethel, maybe you better take that Bible," and she had said yes, and that was the last he saw of it. Moving around, as they did, it was hard to keep track of things.

From where he sat at the back, beneath the limp flags, and with the stack of collection plates beside him, he thought he could pick out Anna Mason's voice. Anna Mason would have his mother's voice, and with it his mother's kind of religion, and a man with his voice, and his kind of religion, was not in her class. He didn't belong, if the truth were known, in the same church. But he was there now, he was sure, for a good Christian reason, and he had something like a religious feeling about the choir. They wore black gowns and sat under the golden organ pipes. They rose as one, the women at the front and the men, who were taller, lined up in back, and the sound of their robes was like the clearing of one great throat. They sang, and he closed his eyes and waited for the moment when they would stop and there would be nothing, nothing—till the first hymnbook closed. That moment always struck him as something like a prayer. He observed it, that is, as he did Memorial Day, and in that sense of the word he considered himself a religious man.

Then he would stand by the aisle, his hat in his hand, until Anna Mason came up and walked by him, and he would not step to her side until she reached the street. She was not a woman to stand out in front and talk with some-one. But she did think it was pleasant to take a short buggy ride. Not in the car, which made her nervous—as she liked the horses out in front, where she could see them, not bottled up, like some sort of genie, under the hood. She liked it off the paving, along the streets where the buggy wheels ran quiet in the dust, and the reins made a soft, lapping sound on the rumps of the mares. As it just happened to be on their way, they usually passed the house where the blinds were drawn, and there were still three birches, a little larger now, there in the yard. He admitted to her that he had owned that house. He said owned advisedly, as the words *lived in* struck him as strange, and did not describe, as he remembered, what he had done in the house. But for several years he had come back and gone to bed there. It was in that house he had had erysipelas, a painful, contagious disease, and a woman, his wife at the time, had taken care of him. Lovingly, as the doctor had said. A very strange word, he thought, and he had marveled at it. She had made him well, she had kept him clean, and when he was fit to be seen again, he had made love to a plump cigar-counter girl. How was that? Time passed. Perhaps that was it. Every morning it was there on his hands, and had to be passed.

But if it was Anna Mason that got him to church, and kept him there while the choir was singing, it was a chicken—a sick chicken—that made him a religious man. It made a man wonder, and wonder makes a religious man. Some people might say that it was the girl, or the city house he had built out in the country, but he knew in his heart it was neither the house nor his family. It was the chicken. Nobody needed to tell him that.

Now, a sick chicken is always a problem, but when you put that chicken with five thousand others, all of them Leghorns, your problem is out of hand. The people in Murdock, you might say, had figured on that. They had all looked forward to it, and some men put their families into buggies and drove them out in the country so they could watch Will Brady's chickens die. All day long he could hear the buggy weights plop in the dust. Just by turning and looking at the buggies he could tell which way the wind was blowing, as they were always careful to park away from the smell. Others claimed they could smell it clear in town. He never knew, personally, as he never got out of the yard, and he slept in the basement where Anna Mason brought him his food. He couldn't have smelled very much anyhow, as he was covered with smells from head to foot, and dirty Leghorn feathers were said to be tangled in his hair. Even Anna Mason, a pioneer woman, kept out of his draft.

In the second week the big hens were dead before he picked them up. It was not necessary to cut their throats or to wring their necks. They were stiff, and yet they seemed very light when he scooped them up on the shovel, as if dying had taken a load off of them. During the third week three experts arrived, at his expense, from Chicago, and took most of one day to tell him there was nothing to be done. Then they went off, after carefully washing their hands.

Sometimes he stopped long enough to look out at the road, and the rows of buggies, where the women and the kids sat breathing through their handkerchiefs. That was something they had picked up during the war. When the flu came along, everyone had run around breathing through a handerchief. In spite of the smell, they all liked to sit where they could keep their eyes on the house, and the upstairs room where the boy and girl were in quarantine. He had more or less ordered them to stay inside. Now and then he caught sight of the boy with his head at the window, peering at him, and one evening he thought he heard, blown to him, the music of their phonograph. Something about a lover who went away and did not come back.

Nothing that he did, or paid to have done, seemed to

help. The hens he shipped off died on the railroad platform overnight. They were left in their crates and shipped back to him for burial. He was advised to keep his sick chickens to himself. Other men had chickens, and what he had started might sweep across the state, across the nation, right at the time that the state and the nation were doing pretty well.

And then it stopped—for no more apparent reason than it had begun. It left him with one hundred and twenty-seven pullets still alive. He sat around waiting for them to die, but somehow they went on living, they even grew fatter, and early every morning the three young roosters crowed. It was something like the first, and the last, sound that he had ever heard. When he heard them crow he would come to the window, facing the cold morning sky, and look at the young trees that he had planted at the edge of the yard. They were wired to the ground, which kept them, it was said, from blowing away.

It would soon be summer out in the yard, but when he went up the spiraling stairs to their room, he could smell the oil burner that they kept going day and night. They liked the smell of it better than the one out in the yard. There was music playing, and when he opened the door a man's clear voice, as if right there before him, came out of the horn that had the picture of the white dog stamped on it. The boy, the girl, and the dog were all listening to him. The man was singing of the time when the girl was a tulip, and he was a rose. This had been, he seemed to remember, her favorite song. As the man went on singing, the girl took hold of his hand, looking toward the horn where the needle was scratching, and he saw that she had no idea of what had happened to him. Not an inkling. Nor had the boy, who was sniffling through his adenoids. They had lived in this private world together, playing their records, caroms, and dominoes, and sometimes marveling at the strange things they saw in the yard. It seemed hard to believe, but somehow it didn't trouble him. When the music stopped he heard her say: "Will, you remember?"

"Why, yes," he said, his head nodding, and put a warm smile on his face. And when they both looked at him, waiting, he knew what he would say. He had come into the room not knowing, not having the vaguest idea, but now he knew, and he looked through the window as he spoke to them.

"How would you two like to go to Omaha?" he said.

In the Moonlight

1

In the middle of life Will Brady bought a house with the roof on sideways, as the boy said, and a yard without grass that he could pay the boy to mow. Under the fenced-in porch were a lawnmower and a cracked garden hose. On the porch were a swing, a hammock rope, and between the stone pillars at the front two wire baskets of dead ferns. In the house were a new player piano and a large box of music rolls.

From the swing on the porch, since the ferns were dead, Will Brady could look down the street to the park, the end of the car line, and the health-giving mineral spring. At night, when the motorman changed the trolley, there would be a hot sizzling sound, and flashes of white light, like heat lightning, would fill the air. From where he sat on the porch Will Brady could see that the ferns were dead.

Beyond the mineral spring, said to be good for you, the green hills were trimmed by mowing machines, and men could be seen playing the new game of golf. They wore breeches quite a bit like those worn by the boy. The hitting of the ball took place near the spring, where the men would stop for a drink of the water while the boys went off with the bags of sticks to hunt for the ball. Will Brady bought the boy a set of the sticks, which he found around the front yard every evening, and a box of the balls, which he often heard rolling around the house. He couldn't seem to interest either the boy or the girl in the park. It was too big, too open, and too much like Murdock, they said.

Sunday afternoons, to be with his family, he would sit in the parlor with the player piano while the boy played some of the rolls backwards, others too fast. The girl would sit on the floor playing card games with herself. On the table at his side were the magazines, the *Youth's Companion* and *Boys' Life,* that came through the mail once a month for the boy to read. He read them himself, and ordered through the mail such things as the watch with the compass in the winder, and the Official Scout knife, with which a clever boy could do so many things. One of the watches he bought for the boy, the other for himself. In the dark candling-room he liked to take it from his pocket and watch the tiny needle waver toward the north, telling him, as nothing else would, about where he was.

On top of the magazines, perhaps to keep them from blowing, was a heavy glass ball with a castle inside, and when he took this ball and shook it, the castle would disappear. Quite a bit the way a farmhouse on the plains would disappear in a storm. He liked to sit there, holding this ball, until the storm had passed, the sky would clear, and he would see that the fairy castle with the waving red flags was still there.

Every morning, with the exception of Sunday, Will Brady would get out of bed at six thirty, fry himself two eggs, and eat them while standing on the fenced-in back porch, facing the yard. At that time in the morning a rabbit might be there. He would then leave some money on the kitchen table and drive through the town to his place of work, a long narrow building with a wooden awning out in front. As the owner of this business he wore a soiled jacket, with blue flaps on the pockets, and when he stood in the door there was usually a clipboard on his arm. On it he kept a record of the eggs that came in, the chickens that went out. He also wore a green visor and a sober preoccupied air. In the middle of life, with his best years before him, he seemed to have a firm grip on all serious matters, and a pretty young wife who called him once a day on the telephone. She called to let her husband know what movie his wife and son were at.

In the morning there was usually ice on the pail where the dung-spotted eggs were floating, and he could see his breath, as if he were smoking, in the candling-room. If he seemed to spend a good deal of time every day looking at one egg and scratching another, perhaps it was the price one had to pay for being a successful man. One whose life was still before him, but so much of it already behind him that it seemed that several lives—if that was the word for it—had already been lived. Had already gone into the limbo, as some men said.

He had his noon meal across the street, usually chicken-fried steak and hash-brown potatoes, or stuffed baked heart with a piece of banana cream pie. After eating this meal he would stand on the curbing out in front. As he neither smoked anything nor chewed, he would usually stand there chewing on a toothpick, and he seemed to have the time to listen to what you had to say. He seldom interrupted to say anything himself. He neither heard anything worth recounting nor said anything worth repeating, but he gave strangers the feeling that one of these days he might. He was highly respected and said to be wise in the ways of the world.

There were evenings that he sat at the desk in the office, with the Dun & Bradstreet open before him, and there were other evenings that he spent in the candling-room. He would take a seat on one of his egg cases, using the thick excelsior pad as a cushion, and the light from the candler would fall on the book he held in his hands. Dun & Bradstreet? No, this book was called a *Journey to the Moon*. Written by a foreigner who seemed to have been there. Will Brady's son had read this book, and then he had given it to his father, as he did all of his books, to return to the library. One day Will Brady wondered what it was the boy liked to read. So he had opened the book, read four or five pages himself. He had been standing there, at his candler, but after reading a few more pages he had seated himself on an egg case, adjusted the light. He had gone without his lunch, without food or drink, till he had finished it. The candling-room had turned cold, and when he stepped into the office it was dark outside.

That night Will Brady had tried to sleep—that is to say, he went to bed as usual—but something about having been to the moon kept him awake. He got out of the bed and stepped out on the porch for a look at it. The moon that he saw looked larger than usual, and nearer at hand. And the light from this moon cast a different light on the neighborhood. There before him lay the city—growing, it was said, by leaps and bounds since the last census—where many thousands of men, with no thought of the moon, lay asleep. He could cope with the moon, but somehow he couldn't cope with a thought like that. It seemed a curious arrangement, he felt, for God to make. By some foolish agreement, made long ago, men and women went into their houses and slept, or tried to sleep, right when there was the most to see.

Over the sleeping city the moon was rising, and there in

the street were the shady elms, the flowering shrubs, and the sidewalks slippery with maple pods. On the porches were swings, limp, sagging hammocks, roller skates, and wire baskets of ferns, and in the houses the men and women lay asleep. It all seemed to Will Brady, there in the moonlight, a very strange thing. A warm summer night, the windows and the doors of most of the houses were open, and the air that he breathed went in and out of all of them. In and out of the lungs, and the lives, of the people who were asleep. They inhaled it deeply, snoring perhaps; then they blew it on its way again, and he seemed to feel himself sucked into the rooms, blown out again. Without carrying things too far, he felt himself made part of the lives of these people, even part of the dreams that they were having, lying there. Was that a very strange thing? Well, perhaps it was. Perhaps it was stranger, even, than a Journey to the Moon.

And the thought came to him—to Will Jennings Brady, a prominent dealer in eggs—that he was a traveler, something of an explorer, himself. That he did even stranger things than the men in books. It was one thing to go to the moon, like this foreigner, a writer of books, but did this man know the man or the woman across the street? Had he ever traveled into the neighbor's house? Did he know the woman who was there by the lamp, or the man sitting there in the shadow, a hat on his head as if at any moment he might go out? Could he explain why there were grass stains on the man's pants? That might be stranger, that might be harder to see, than the dark side of the moon.

Perhaps it was farther across the street, into that room where the lamp was burning, than it was to the moon, around the moon, and back to the earth. Where was there a traveler to take a voyage like that? Perhaps it was even farther than twenty thousand leagues under the sea. Men had been there, it was said, and made a thorough report of the matter, but where was the man who had traveled the length of his own house? Who knew the woman at the back—or the boy at the front who lay asleep? How many moons away, how many worlds away, was a boy like that? On the moon a man might jump many feet, which might be interesting if you went there; but it was no mystery, a man could explain something like that. But what about the man who stood in the dark eating cornbread and milk? What about the rooms where the blinds were always drawn? If there were men who had been there and knew the answers, he would like to know them; if they had written about these things he would read the book. If they hadn't, perhaps he would write such a book himself.

What writer, what traveler, could explain the woman who rolled herself up in the sheet, like a mummy, or the man who came home every night and undressed in the dark? All one could say was that whatever it was it was there in the house, like a vapor, and it had drawn the blinds, like an invisible hand, when the lights came on. As a writer of books he would have to say that this vapor made the people yellow in color, gave them flabby bodies, and made their minds inert. As if they were poisoned, all of them, by the air they breathed. And such a writer would have to explain why this same air, so fresh and pure in the street, seemed to be poisoned by the people breathing it. So that in a way even stranger than the moon, they poisoned themselves.

Was it any wonder that men wrote books about other things? That they traveled to the moon, so to speak, to get away from themselves? Were they all nearer to the moon, the bottom of the sea, and such strange places than they were to their neighbors, or the woman there in the house? What the world needed, it seemed, was a traveler who would stay right there in the bedroom, or open the door and walk slowly about his own house. Who would sound a note, perhaps, on the piano, raise the blinds on the front-room windows, and walk with a candle into the room where the woman sleeps. A man who would recognize this woman, this stranger, as his wife.

But if books would put a man in touch with the moon, perhaps they would put him in touch with a boy—a very strange thing, but a lot of people owned up to them. Mothers and fathers alike seemed to be familiar with them. When he returned the *Journey to the Moon,* he spoke to Mrs. Giles, the librarian, and tried to phrase, for her, some of the thoughts that were troubling him. Had any man taken, he said, a journey around his own house?

Not for public perusal, Mrs. Giles said.

That would be a journey, he said, that he would like to take, or, for that matter, a journey around his own son.

That had been done, Mrs. Giles said, so he could just save himself the trouble. All kinds of men had already done just that.

Was that a fact? he said.

Hadn't he read *Tom Sawyer?* she said.

And who was Tom Sawyer? he said, so she brought him the book. She also brought him *Penrod,* by another man, and several books by Ralph Henry Barbour, that would give him a good idea, she said, of what was on a boy's mind. That was just what he wanted to know, he said, and went off with the books.

He read *Tom Sawyer,* in one sitting, in the candling-room. He took the tin bottom off the candler, so that it cast more light for him, and he used two of the excelsior egg pads to soften the seat. There was a much better light in the office, with a comfortable chair to sit in, but he had hired a girl to sit there at the desk and answer telephone calls. She might not understand a man of his age reading children's books.

He read *Tom Sawyer* during the morning, and reflected on it while he had his lunch; then he came back and read the book by Tarkington. By supper time a great load had been lifted from his mind. If he could believe what he read—which he found hard, but not too hard if he put his mind to it—boys were not at all as complicated as he had been led to believe. When all was said and done, so to speak, they were just boys. Full of boyish devilment and good clean fun. If neither this Penrod nor Tom Sawyer reminded him very much of Willy Brady, that might be explained in terms of how they lived. Penrod had brothers and sisters, many freckles and friends, and a very loving father and mother. Willy Brady didn't have all of these things. But if his father could believe what he read, all Willy Brady had on his mind was baseball, football, Honor, and something called track. In Ralph Henry Barbour's opinion, that of a man who really seemed to know, these were the things at the front and the back of a boy's mind. If he could believe what he read, and Will Brady did, it was coming from behind in the great mile race that made the difference between a boy and a man. But to lead all the way was to court disaster, as the book made clear.

One began with a fine healthy boy like Penrod, who had a real home, a loving father and mother, and perhaps an older sister who brought out the best in him. Then one day, overnight almost, his voice would change. Fuzz would grow on his lip, and his father would send him off to a boarding school. There he would live with other clean-cut boys like himself, eating good food, reading fine books, and talking over the problems of the coming Oglethorpe game. The walls of the room would be covered with banners from big Eastern schools. The window would open out on the field where he would throw the javelin, run the race, and pitch the last three innings with a pain in his arm. In the winter he would sit at his desk and study, or go home with his roommate over Christmas, whose father was a big corporation lawyer of some kind. His roommate's sister, a dark-haired girl who attended some private school in the East, would ask her brother, in a roundabout way, all about him. After that one thing would lead to another until he struck off somewhere on his own, or accepted a position with a promising future in her father's firm. The only problem would be how long he would have to wait for her.

Will Brady hoped it wouldn't be too long, thinking over his own experience, as once out of school, like that, life seemed harder to organize. There were many pressures, and not nearly so many lovely girls. Nor were there many things that a father could do to make sure that the boy picked the right one, when the boy still had neither fuzz on his lip nor a voice that had changed. He was twelve, but he looked more like nine or ten. The only hair on his body was there on the top of his head. But with this boy he did what he could—that is to say, on Sunday afternoons he would walk him through the park to the baseball diamond, and sit with him in the bleachers behind the sagging fence of chicken wire. Thanks to Ralph Henry Barbour, Will Brady knew the names of the players and the places, and he pointed out to the boy the pitcher's mound, and the batteries. In his own mind, of course, he saw the boy as a pitcher, pitching the last three innings with his arm sore, but the boy took an interest in the catcher as he wanted the mask. Nobody else on the field seemed to interest him. He wanted to wear what the catcher wore, and peer out through the mask. So he bought the boy a glove, a ball, and a mask, but he put off buying the rest of it until he had a long talk with the man in the Spalding store. This man, a

Mr. Lockwood, seemed to take a personal interest in Will Brady's boy.

Mr. Lockwood had been a great athlete himself. As a student at the University of Nebraska he had run the mile in record time, the last thing you would think of, so to speak, when you looked at him. He didn't look any too well, as a matter of fact, and he had grown a little heavy for a man his age. In a separate compartment of his wallet, however, Mr. Lockwood had a bundle of press clippings, some of them with faded pictures showing how he looked at the time. The clippings were now yellow, and hard to read, but Will Brady could make out that the man who stood before him had once run the mile, all the way, in 4:23. A mile, as Mr. Lockwood reminded him, was fourteen city blocks.

With Mr. Lockwood's expert help, Will Brady bought the boy shoes for running and jumping, shoes for baseball, special shoes for football, and rubber-soled shoes for doing things inside. He also bought him the shirts, pants, and socks to go along with all of these things. He might grow out of them at any time, but he would know the smell and the feel of a sweatshirt, and the smell was an important thing. As Mr. Lockwood said, it was a smell that he would never get out of his nose.

If there was something about Mr. Lockwood that had gone unmentioned in all of the books, perhaps it was because the author had had no need to bring it up. As a writer of books, Ralph Henry Barbour described what he saw in the newspaper clippings, and the young man that he saw, with his muscles bulging, breasting the tape. He was not concerned with the middle-aged man in the sporting-goods store. Everything Mr. Lockwood said about himself, and his wonderful college life at Nebraska, would lead one to believe that Ralph Henry Barbour was absolutely right.

Everything that had happened to him, back then, had been wonderful. If he had been a writer, he would have written those books himself. Listening to Mr. Lockwood, and he liked to talk, Will Brady often came away with the feeling that Ralph Henry Barbour had given a modest picture of college life. Everything in the world, it seemed clear, had happened to Mr. Lockwood, the great mile runner, but nothing much had happened to the man in the sporting-goods store. Nothing much had happened since then, that is. He still had the smell of it all in his nose, and some people might say there was something like it, if not worse, on his breath. He reminded Will Brady, at times, of a man very much like himself. A man who might live in one of those houses across the street. He would probably have a wife named Gladys, who slept alone in the bedroom at the back, and a daughter named Mabel, or Eileen, who slept in the room at the front. And perhaps at this point people were saying how much the mother looked like the daughter, and talk like that would be scaring the girl to death. Or maybe it wouldn't. That would be hard to say. Perhaps it was her father she took after, having his light-brown hair, his pale-blue eyes, and perhaps the smile that he once had in the photographs. Before he began to die, that is. Before something began to poison him.

It was no help, of course, to say so, but the man in the sporting-goods store, the celebrated athlete, looked like a man who was being poisoned to death. He smoked too much. Perhaps that was it. The man who was pictured in the press clippings did not smoke. Whatever this thing was, it seemed to be something that he had picked up later; it was not in the air on the college campus, nor what he breathed on the track. It was not something that Ralph Henry Barbour felt he had to describe. But something had happened. What had it been? The great mile runner, the baseball star, had accepted an offer from Spalding & Brothers to go out on the road and sell their guaranteed baseballs, their autographed bats. After a while he had married his childhood sweetheart, settled down. For a year or two he had kept his paper clippings just loose in his desk, where he could find them; then one day, one spring day more than likely, he took them out. After mulling them over he put them in his wallet—began to carry them around. Some time later maybe he noticed how dry and brittle they were getting, or maybe he didn't—maybe it was just a chance remark by his wife. Whatever it was, he made a little pile of the best of them. He put the best picture in the back of his watch, the best clipping in his vest. They were always with him, as if he couldn't part with them. Some writer of books might even say that these clippings poisoned him. That they were old, brittle, and fading, like the man himself. People will believe anything that they read, and if they happened to read, in a book somewhere, that a man was poisoned by some newspaper clippings, why they would swallow it. And a writer of books might even say that these people were right.

But what would this man say of Will Brady's son? One that happened to be, as Will Brady seemed to think, the complicated type. A boy that once a week, while his father was shaving, would come to the door of the bathroom and wait for his father to turn from the mirror and look at him. The boy would be wearing his Official Boy Scout uniform. He seemed to wear the shirt more than the pants, as the shirt had faded to a washed-out color, and on his feet were the Official green, chrome leather shoes. They hurt his feet, badly, but he never complained. From his belt hung a flashlight, a compass, a metal canteen in a soft flannel cooler, a key ring with some keys, a medal for swimming, another medal for walking, one for not smoking, and a waterproof kit containing materials for building a fire. This was in case his waterproof matchbox got wet. On his back was a knapsack containing maps, a snake-bite cure, a day's balanced rations, and Dentyne gum, which he chewed for his teeth and to allay the thirst.

"Off for the woods, son?" Will Brady would say, but sometimes the boy wasn't. No, strange to say, he might not be off for anywhere. He would just be prepared, in case he felt like being off. He would follow his father back to the bedroom and sit on the bed. He would sit there and watch his father dress, as if there was something very strange about it, or he would take out his maps and spread them on the bed.

"Where is the exact center of the U.S.A.?" the boy might ask. At one time Will Brady thought such a question was put to him. He didn't answer for the simple reason that he didn't know. But the boy was just talking to himself, as first he would put the question, then he would answer: "The geographical center of the United States is in Osborne County, Kansas." It was never necessary for Will Brady to say anything. Looking at Omaha the boy would say: "The metal smokestack at the smelting works is the highest metal smokestack in the world," or "Omaha spaghetti is now sold in Italy."

It was something of an education for Will Brady to listen to him. They seemed to be educating young people better nowadays. As for himself, he had eight years' schooling, but in so far as he could remember, no one had ever mentioned that Omaha spaghetti was sold in Italy. The boy said it was. And he always seemed to have the Gospel truth.

Right out of the blue, without any warning, the boy once asked: "Why are you so different?" Will Brady had been facing the mirror in the men's room of the Paxton Hotel.

He had taken the boy down there before they went to the show.

"Kid—" he had said, then hearing what he had said he turned the water on, let it run. After a bit he turned it off and said: "Yes, son?"

"I don't mind kid," the boy said, "if you want to call me kid that's all right with me."

"That was a slip, son," he said. "That was just a slip."

"The name I really like is Spud," the boy said. "I always say call me Spud but nobody does it."

"What's wrong with Willy, son?" he said.

"I've been Willy for a long time," the boy said, and Will Brady bent over, turned the hot water back on. What in God's name did the boy mean by that? With a paper towel Will Brady wiped the steaming mirror so that he could see the boy's sober face. His eyes, his mother's eyes, that is, were watching him. What did Will Brady feel? Not much of anything.

"All right, kid," he said, and that was just about that.

He would take them out to eat, where music was playing, and they would sit there together, in league against him, looking at him from a long way off. Very much as if he were an imposter. A father, one who didn't know what being a father was like, and a lover, one who didn't know much about love. More or less hopeless. For different reasons they both pitied him.

2

So he would give them money, put them in a show, and drive downtown to his office, where he would take off his coat and sit at his new roll-top desk.

Some nights he did that, other nights he might walk around the streets, or out over the river, and on Saturday evenings he often stopped in at Browning King. It was Fred Conlen who had got him to wear the soft-collar shirt. In Fred Conlen's private fitting-room he would see himself in the three-way mirror, and it was there that he saw the new expression on his face. While he was talking—at no other time. While he talked this man in the mirror had a strange smile on his lips. This smile on his lips and a sly, knowing look about the eyes. Something shrewd he had said? Well, he never really seemed to say much. Just a good deal implied, so to speak, in what he did say.

"What about a pair of pants," he would say, "that a man never has to take off?" That was all. What did he mean by a remark like that? Whatever he meant, Fred Conlen often thought it was pretty good.

"Brady," he would say, "you ought to be on the platform. You got a head."

"When I was a boy," Will Brady had said, "I had the biggest hat on the lowest peg. Seems to me the peg's lower every time I look at it."

"Bygod, Brady," Fred Conlen had said, "there you said something."

Had he? Well, nothing you could put your finger on. You needed mirrors, so to speak, to see a trick like that. To see a man with a big head, narrow shoulders, the new soft-collared shirt, and along with the toothpick that sly smile in the corner of his mouth. About to say something. And when he did, it would be pretty good.

"I notice these new twin beds are pretty popular now," he would say, and Fred Conlen, with the pins in his mouth, would turn to look at him.

Will Brady bought his clothes from Fred Conlen—Hart Schaffner & Marx, direct from Chicago—and his shoes from

Lyman Bryce, who ran the Florsheim store. If he stopped by in the evening Lyman Bryce would take him to the back of the shop, pull up a stool, and show him what they were wearing in Palm Beach. Will Brady would sit there, his shoes off, and this fellow Bryce, a gray-haired man, would lace him into the latest thing in Palm Beach shoes. He would ask him to stand up and walk around in them. People in the street would come to the door and peer in. Bryce had a fine new home in Dundee, and a prominent place in the Ak-Sar-Ben parade, but what he really liked to do was sit there on a shoe stool and talk. He was a big fellow, like T. P. Luckett, but he was quite a bit different from Luckett in that he hinted that a good egg business was not the last word. Nor was the shoe business. Nor anything of that stripe. Lyman Bryce seemed to think that Will Brady was meant for more than that. "Forget about the money," Bryce would say, "I'll take care of the money." What he seemed to be looking for, as he said himself, was the right man.

What was being done, Bryce wanted to know, down in the deep South, or out in Texas? Wouldn't a little loose money start something really rolling out there? Couldn't a man with a few big tractors start plowing it up? Instead of fiddling with eggs—as Bryce called it—why didn't Will Brady take thirty thousand dollars, or fifty if he liked it, and go out there and start something? "God Almighty, Brady," he would say, "stop fiddling with eggs." He seemed to think the country was still wide open for a man with some cash.

When he talked with Lyman Bryce, Will Brady always had a smile on his face. Was he amused? No, there was more to his smile than that. It was more like the smile he had when he faced three mirrors with just one face. Or when he sat there with Bryce, and Bryce would say: "Now bygod, Brady, I'd like to have you home for dinner. But you know the little woman—the little woman is fussy as hell."

Did he know *the little woman?* From that smile on his face, you would think that he did. You might be led to think that some of these little women were pretty big.

Clark Lee, for example, had one of them. Lee ran the Gaiety, and he was one of the big show men in the state. He used *the little woman* to explain a good many things. "Geez, Brady," he would say, "I wouldn't want the little woman to get wind of this," or "Well, I'd better get along, Brady, if I'm going to keep the little woman in line." Now, both Lee and Bryce were pretty big men, Lee a notch or two above six feet, but the way they talked about these little women made them seem pretty small. You got the idea that *the little women* were all bigger than the men.

For example, the big thing in Clark Lee's life, besides the little woman, that is, was something that he called the *chalk line*. He often drew this line, with his finger, across his desk. Or if he was standing he would draw this line on the air. The little woman expected him to walk that line, he said. Perhaps he did, as this line always seemed to be with him, either there on his desk, drawn on the thin air, or like a pattern in the rug. A line drawn between Clark Lee and everything else. "With the little woman," Lee would say, "I got to toe that line!" and he would tap on it, putting out his feet to where he saw something on the rug. It would be wrong to say that this line was imaginary. It was there in the lobby, in his office, in the sidewalk when he stepped in the street, and it hung like an invisible clothesline in the air. Ready to trip him or support him, as the case might be. Big man though he was, Clark Lee often seemed to lean on it.

Perhaps *the little woman* was sometimes on Will Brady's mind, those long summer evenings, when he stopped in at the Paxton to see if Evelyn Fry was there. She sold cigars, but she was no cigar-counter girl. She knew the one Will Brady had married—she was a married woman herself—and she always asked him how his *kids* were getting along. Sometimes Evelyn Fry liked to go for a ride where they could just sit and look at the river; other times she would make him a cooling drink of something in her rooms. The fellow she had married had left her a lot of furniture. There were tasseled lamps, a grand piano with a shawl and some photographs, and sometimes there was a smell stronger than the incense she liked to burn. A cigar, but that was all right too. That was something they had both come to understand. These things didn't matter so much any more, and perhaps the thing they had in common was the knowledge of what things seemed to matter and what things did not. A cigar or two didn't. Which was why he was often there.

Sometimes he would sit there with the glass of beer she was sure he would like if he would just drink it—until the foam was gone, the beer was warm, and she would drink it herself. Other times he had grape juice with lumps of ice in it. He would suck on the ice while she played him records on the gramophone. Perhaps she thought he was homesick, lonely, or something like that. It probably meant she was sometimes lonely herself.

He liked to be with Evelyn Fry just to be with her, to sit there in the room, and to stir the ice in what he was drinking with one of her spoons. While the music played, nobody had to talk. He would sit facing the piano with the hanging shawl, the vase with the red paper flowers, and the picture of a gaunt-looking man in his underwear, rowing a boat. Her husband. He had left her, naturally. He had a stiff black beard and it had probably tickled her face.

"That song," she would say, putting on the record that he seemed to like, but never knew the name of, "what is it you like about it so much?" Did he ever answer? No, he never had to say. He had ice in his mouth, and perhaps he didn't know, anyhow.

That was how he liked to put in an evening—not too often, just now and then—when he had the need of a little woman for himself. Someone to pour him a drink, and ask him simple questions about his kids. And around ten o'clock he would leave, as he had to and pick them up. If they were at the Empress, but not in the lobby, he would ask the manager, Mr. Youngblood, to run the slide advertising "Will Brady's Chickens and Eggs." This would let them know that he was in the lobby waiting for them. But if they were at the World, or the Orpheum, where slides like that had gone out of fashion, he would just sit there in the lobby until they came out. People like Tom Mix, Hoot Gibson, and Wallace Reid they liked to see twice, which took a good deal of time if six acts of vaudeville came in between. In that case he would buy a bag of popcorn, and the usher would let him sit in the lobby as they had all got to know him and knew pretty well what his problem was.

But in August he found the boy in the lobby alone. As that usually meant that the girl was in the ladies' room for a moment, he sat down and waited while the boy finished eating a peanut bar. When the girl didn't come, he said: "Son, where is your mother?"

"She left," said the boy, "she left before the vaudeville."

"Your mother,left?" he said.

"She went off with the Hawayan," said the boy. "He liked her and she's going to work for him."

"A Hawayan?" he repeated.

"She's going to dance for him," the boy said. "If I could dance I'd have gone to work for him, too."

In the Lobby

1

In the suburbs Will Brady owned a fine house with a chain swing on the porch, a playroom in the basement, and a table in the kitchen where he left pocket money for the boy. But both the boy and the man did their living somewhere else. The boy did all of his living next door—that is to say, he added one more plate to the table that already numbered three on each side and one at the end. So it was the boy's plate that evened it up, as Mrs. Ward said.

When Will Brady walked over to discuss the matter, there was really nothing that remained to be said, as the boy had been living—Mrs. Ward said *living*—with them for some time. If he passed the night at home it was merely to make his father feel all right. Nobody liked to sleep in a big empty house alone. All Will Brady could do, speaking up when he did, was recognize what had already happened and offer to pay, as he did, for the boy's board. It was agreed that he ate around five dollars' worth of food a week. He was small, but a small growing boy could somehow stow it away. It was also agreed that his father should continue to buy his clothes. These matters taken care of, Mrs. Ward agreed to let him see the boy, once or twice a week, and give him pocket money so long as it wasn't too much. She took away from him sums that she didn't think it wise for a boy to have. In case the boy got sick, or really needed something, or might, for some reason, just want to see his father, Mrs. Ward would leave a message for him at the Paxton Hotel. That was where Will Brady, for the time being, had taken a room.

When a man has lost something he would like to get back, say a wife, a boy, or an old set of habits, he can walk around the streets of the city looking for it. Or he can stand on a corner, nearly anywhere, and let it look for him. The boys and girls Will Brady found under the street lights, or playing around the posters in the theater lobbies, didn't know what he had lost but they had learned what he had to give. They could hear the coins that jingled in the pocket of his coat. If he stood on the corner, a well-lighted corner, sooner or later they would gather around him—just as the pigeons would gather around him when he sat in the park. They didn't know what he wanted, but they were willing to settle for what he had to give.

"Hello there, Harry," Will Brady would say, as he liked to call all of them Harry. As it was never their name, it gave them something to talk about.

"My name ain't Harry," they would reply, then: "Gimme three cents."

"What you going to do with three cents, Harry?"

"My name *isn't* Harry!" they would say; then, getting back: "if I had three cents I could go to a show."

"So you think you'd like to take in a show, Harry?" he would say.

"You gimme three cents an' I'll have ten."

They were smart, these kids, and so they would talk for quite a while. Sometimes it took quite a bit of handling—

knowing when to stop calling them Harry—but with a pocket full of pennies a man like Will Brady could talk for an hour.

"Don't tell me, Harry," he would say, "I've got a grown-up boy of my own. I can tell you a thing or two about boys."

"What can you tell?" they would ask, and of course he couldn't tell them much of anything. Nothing but what he had read about this Tom Sawyer, or this Penrod. They were the only boys, it seemed, that he knew very much about.

And as for girls, he knew even less—no, he didn't know a thing about girls until the one called Libby—Libby something—spoke to him. On 18th and Farnam, near the *Omaha Bee*, somebody ran out from the shadows toward him, and he assumed it was one of the boys, some skinny kid.

"Well, Harry," he had said, "is this a holdup?" and put his right hand into his pocket before he really knew—before he looked, that is—at the sharp freckled face. The girl was tall and thin, and the dress she had on was too small for her.

"Well, well," he repeated, "is this a holdup?"

"No, sir," she said, "it's not holdup," but he couldn't see her face as she stood between him and the light. He stepped to one side to look at his hand—in the palm of his hand were coins, most of them pennies—and she came around to lean over his arm, look at them too. She put her small head between him and the light. It was narrow, and the long black hair was in braids. The braids were hooked over her ears, like pulleys, and as she peered into his hand she tugged on them, slowly, tolling her head like a bell.

"That ain't enough," she said.

"For a show?" he said.

"For kisses," she said, "I'm sellin' kisses." When he didn't speak right up, she said: "I'm not beggin' anything, I'm sellin'."

"I see," he said, and raised his head as if someone had called his name. He looked to the corner where swarms of bugs flew in and out of the street light. Passing beneath the light were a man and woman, the man with his coat folded over his arm, and the woman a step or two away from him, as if he were hot.

"Twenty-five cents is what I try and get," she said, "but if that's all you got, it's all you got," and with her dirty brown fingers she removed the coins from his hand. One at a time, pecking at his palm like a bird. When she had them all she stepped forward, putting up her face, rising on her toes, and gave him a noisy peck on the cheek. Then she stepped back, moving out of the light, to see if he was pleased.

"That wasn't so much," she said, "but it was fourteen cents' worth. Wasn't it?"

He agreed. "Oh yes," he said, and wagged his head.

"But I can do better," she said, and lifted her arms as if she were a dancer, letting her hands, the fingers parted, droop at the wrist. From a bench in the park Will Brady had seen little girls drop their jacks, or the doll they were holding, and throw up their arms, their heads back, as if they would fly. Without warning, as if some voice had whispered to them. Sometimes it was pretty, other times it was like what he saw now. She leered at him over her left shoulder, her eyelids fluttering, and he knew he had seen it all less than an hour before. On the Orpheum billboards, where two beautiful girls were wrapped in gauze. Maybe he looked unhappy, for she said: "Did I take all your money?"

"Oh no," he said.

"I'll bet I took your carfare," she said, and looked at the

coins in her hands. The dime she removed, held out to him.

"No, no," he said, "and besides, I walk. I like to walk on nights like this."

"Me too," she said, and danced around him, swinging her braids. Still dancing, she said: "And I know what you're thinking."

"What?" he said.

"That I'm not old enough. You're thinking I'm not old enough to take care of myself." He shook his head. "Well, that's what you're thinkin', you men."

"You're quite a big girl," he said.

"I am. I make my own livin'. I make up to five dollars a week. Isn't that good?"

"That's a very good living."

"It's more than my father makes," she said.

Still facing the light, he said: "What does your father do?"

"Nothing," she said, and sang that a bridge was falling down. She danced around him twice, singing, then she stopped singing, hopped up and down, and ran toward the corner, where she suddenly stopped. Her dress was too small, and she drew it down toward her sharp knees. Then she turned to wave at him, her long braids swinging, and was gone.

2

Two, sometimes three or four times a week, she "did business with him." It was strictly a business proposition, as she said herself. The fact that he seldom had the right amount of money didn't trouble her much. Sometimes she would have newspapers under her arms, usually old papers, which she would sell him, as she was in business, she told him, for herself. But kisses were a better proposition, as they cost her nothing. All she had to do was find somebody who wanted them.

On the week ends, when she specialized in kisses, she wore a large flowered hat with a flapping brim, and in the crown of the hat there were many flowers, some of them real. But what he smelled, as she always had to tell him, was her perfume. It was sometimes so strong that as she rose toward him he closed his eyes.

Inside her dress, these nights, she wore a brassiere, the pink cups folded over very neatly, and in the one on the right she kept all the money she made. It jingled as she ran off or stood hopping up and down. Week nights she had to be home early, but Saturday nights she had time to talk, if that was what he wanted, or a marshmallow sundae, if he wanted something like that. As her shoes hurt her feet, they usually had the sundae sitting down. In the ice-cream parlor she would take off her hat, as the veil on the hat tickled her face, and sometimes fell in the marshmallow sundae when she closed her eyes. She always closed her eyes, as ice cream tasted better that way. He would have a cherry phosphate, or a root beer, and when her mouth was full, and her eyes were closed, he would sit there looking at her sticky, freckled face.

Was he in love with her? That was what she wanted to know.

He said he wasn't sure. He said he didn't know.

He ought to make up his mind, she said, because if he was in love with her, really in love, he could kiss her without paying anything.

Was she in love with him?

She didn't know. No, she didn't know, she said, a whole

lot about love. She didn't know if what she felt was what she had heard, or if what she heard was what she felt about it. She didn't know if she had ever loved anybody or not. When she had a baby she would probably love it. Then she would know. Then she would know if what she felt for him was love or not.

Eating and talking also made her sleepy, and she would let him walk her home—to the corner, that is, where she kissed him for nothing. He could see the rooming house where she lived, the cracked yellow blinds, the old men on the porch, and watch the gas jets flutter when she closed the door at the end of the hall. Then he would go home, lying awake in the hot front room across from the boy, watching the flash in the night when the street-car trolley was switched around. When the last car for the night went back into town.

During the day he had eggs in his hands, things that he could pick up, that is, and put down, and tell what they were, good or bad, by holding them to the candler. But during the night there was nothing he could grasp like that with his hands. You can't take a notion into your hand, like a Leghorn egg, and judge the grade of it. You can't hold it to the light, give it a twist, and see that it is good. Nor is there any way to tell if it is what you are missing or not.

Could a man say, for instance, that what he really needed was a woman's hat? A cheap straw hat with a wide flapping brim, a long pin through the faded paper flowers on the crown. A hat made of yellow straw, shiny with varnish, with dried marshmallow stuck to the veil, and both dark and blond hairs tangled in it. All of its long life it had been just a hat, an inexpensive straw hat no longer in fashion, and then one day, in spite of itself, it was on a new head. It became, overnight almost, something more than a hat. It became a notion—something missing, that is, from a man's life.

So that when this girl Libby took off this hat and set it on the marble-topped table beside her, the man seated across from her might put out his fingers and touch the wide brim. He might sniff at the flowers, or take between his fingers a torn piece of the veil. Just as he had once, standing idle on the corner, let his hand rest for a moment on a boy's knobby head, or let his fingers tangle for a moment in the wild hair. But when this boy got away some man would say—some stranger, that is, would step up and say—"If you want to handle the kids, you better get 'em off the street."

And what do you say to that? Why, you say thank you, thank you very much. Maybe this stranger has what he calls your own interests at heart. Thinks that he is doing you a personal favor to speak like that. But a hat, after all, is just a hat, and if you want to lean over and sniff the paper flowers, or touch a piece of the veil, why that is perfectly all right. Very likely it was something you put up your own good money for.

But near the end of the summer he found the girl in a telephone booth at the back of the drugstore, and in the booth with her, sitting there hugging her, a fat blond boy. They had been to Krug's Park, and the boy's pink face was badly sunburned. On the lapel of his coat, like a lodge button, was a live chameleon. The boy said: "Howdy, Mr. Magee," as he naturally assumed Will Brady was the girl's father, but he stayed right there in the telephone booth, with one arm around the girl. She was giggling over the phone about boys to some other girl. Will Brady looked at his watch, put it away, advised them to have a nice time that evening, then walked out into the street before he noticed what he held clasped tight in one hand. A handful of coins: five pennies, two nickels, and one shiny new dime.

That was not the last he saw of the girl, but she no longer ran toward him out of the shadows, or wore on her birdlike head a wide flappy-brimmed hat. The braids were gone, and the dirt now showed behind her large ears. He would see her in the battered front seats at the Empress, sitting there with some boy, or some middle-aged man, the pale light of the screen blinking on her powder-dirty face. The large mouth open as if to help the eyes drink it all in. And later, like a sleepwalker, she would walk into the luminous glare of the lobby, where, with one finger, she would loosen the wad of gum from her front teeth. Facing, but not seeing him, she would start chewing on it.

3

Well, that was how it was, and if it sometimes seemed strange, it was hardly any stranger than anything else, and not so strange as the fact that only in hotel lobbies was Will Brady at home. Somehow or other he felt out of place almost everywhere else. In the houses that he bought, or in the rooms that he rented, and even in the cities where he lived. But in the lobby of a good hotel he felt all right. He belonged, that is—there was something about it that appealed to him.

He liked to sit in a big armchair at the front—in a leather-covered chair if they happened to have one, and under a leafy potted palm, in case they had that. He also liked a good view of the cigar counter, and the desk. He liked the sound of the keys when they dropped on the counter, the sound of the mail dropping into the slots, and the sound of the dice—though he never gambled—in the stiff leather cup. God knows why, but there was something he liked about it. Hearing that sound he immediately felt at home.

A curious artificial place, when you think of it, glowing nightlike by day, and daylike by night, with no connection whatsoever with the busy life that went by in the street. And when a man came in through the revolving doors, it was the man that changed. The dim, shaded lights and the thick carpeted floors cast a spell over him. His walk, what you think of as his bearing, the way his arms moved or hung slack from his shoulders, all of these things were not at all what they had been in the street. He took on the air of a man who was being fitted for a new suit. A little bigger, wider, taller, and better-looking than he really was. And on his face the look of a man who sees himself in a three-way glass. In the three-way mirror he sees the smile on his face, he sees himself, you might say, both coming and going—a man, that is, who was from some place and was going somewhere. Not the man you saw, just a moment before, out there in the street.

A man comes into the world, you might say, when he steps into his first lobby, and something of this knowledge brings him there when he expects to depart. If something is missing, the lobby is where he will look for it.

And yet no two lobbies are exactly alike, there is a difference in the rugs, or the lighting, in the women at the desk, the price of the cigars, and the number of plants. There will sometimes be a difference in the men and women you find in them. There may also be a difference in the marble columns, their thickness through the middle, the height of the ceilings, and the quality of brass—if that is what it is—in the cuspidors. There will often be a difference in the service, the age of the bellhops, the location of the men's room, and the size of the carpets at the sagging side of the beds. But the figure in the carpet will be the same. Not merely in the carpet, but worn into the floor. A man seated on the bed could feel it through his socks, recognize it with his feet. All hotels are alike in this matter, and all the lobbies are more alike than they are different, in that the purpose of every lobby is the same. To be both in, that is, and out of this world.

The same things go along with lobbies that go along with dreams, great and small love affairs, and other arrangements that never seem quite real. The lobby draws a chalk line around this unreal world, so to speak. It tips you off, as the closing of the hymnbooks tips you off in church that the song is finished and that it's time to get set for the prayer. It prepares you for a short flight from one world to a better one. From the real world, where nothing much ever happens, to the unreal world where anything might happen—and sometimes does. But there is no mystery about it. It is just a matter of rules. Just as there are hard and fast rules in the street that make it impossible for some things to happen, so there are rules in the lobby that make it possible. You can sense that as you come through the door. You can breathe it in the scented air, hear it in the women's voices, the creak of leather luggage, and the coin dropped on the counter for a good cigar.

And the name that is written there in the ledger? Take a look at it. Is it Will Brady, or is it William Jennings Brady, or is it perhaps just Will Jennings, as it doesn't really matter, for the time being?—you can be whom you like. And as for that young woman there at your side—is that your wife? You hope so. That is the gist of it. For it is the purpose of hotel lobbies to take you out of the life you are living, to a better life, or a braver, more interesting one. More in line with your own real powers, so to speak. The porter cries aloud a name in the lobby and you turn, for it might be yours, and perhaps you have never met this stranger before, your better self. You can see him in the eyes of those who turn and look at you. To size you up, to compare you with their own better selves. Just as there are men who are never lovers until they meet their wives in the lobby, there are women who have never been loved any-where but in a hotel room. Only there does the lover meet the beloved. In the rented room is where men exceed themselves. Lovers and seducers, prosperous, carefree men of the world. What you find in the lobby, what you hear in the music, what you feel in the air as you saunter across it, is the other man and the other woman in your life. There in the lobby the other life is possible.

Perhaps that man at the counter, rolling the dice, is the one who made the Beautyrest mattress possible—but not the sleep. No, you can't have everything. You can't manufac-ture the good night's sleep and sell it with the bed. But, still, it is something to know that the sleep would be a good one, and that the man responsible for it is quite a bit like your-self. Middle-aged, paunchy, and often subject to lying awake.

And when you've lost something you would like to get back, the lobby is where you can look for it, sit waiting for it, or, if you know what you want, you can advertise. As you probably know, it is smart to advertise. Adam Brady did it when he wanted a wife, Will Brady did it when he wanted an egg, as the only problem is in knowing what you want. Knowing, that is, how to put it in ten or twelve words. But that can be quite a stickler. Take something like this:

> FATHER AND SON seek matronly woman
> take charge modest home in suburbs.

Was that what he wanted? Well, he thought it was. But he would have to wait and see what an ad like that turned up. If what he said, so to speak, had covered the ground. On the advice of the girl in the office, he ran that ad in the "Personal" column, as he was looking for something rather special, as she said. He gave his address, of course, as the

Paxton Hotel. The lobby would be just the place for a meeting like that. It would not be necessary for him to inquire what such a woman had in mind, as it was there in the ad, and all the woman had to do was answer it. That was what he thought, this fellow Brady, when he took his seat at the front of the lobby, wearing the look of a man who was the father of a homeless boy. That was what he was thinking when a Miss Miriam Ross asked to speak to him.

"Hello," she said to him as he came forward. "Where'll we park?"

With the hat that he held, Will Brady gestured toward the back.

"Okey-dokey," she said, and walked ahead of him with her shoulders back, her hips thrown forward, with the motion of a woman going down a flight of stairs or a steep ramp. From the back Will Brady could see the rolled tops of her stockings, the red jewel clasps, and when she sat down—dropped down—he saw them at the front. He had never seen a flapper before. Not up close, that is. He wondered if, over the years, he had fallen out of touch with the motherly type.

Miriam Ross lay in the lobby chair, her arms wide, her legs spread as if the room was too hot, and smoked cigarettes while peering at him dreamily as he talked. What did he say? Something about himself and a homeless boy. Every now and then he fanned the blue smoke away from his face. Now and then the girl sighed, as if tired, or tipped her head to blow the smoke in her lap, or make little cries, like a puppy, while dusting her cigarette. Later she leaned forward, on her sharp knees, to powder her face. On a piece of gum wrapper she wrote her name, her address, and her telephone number, then she slunk along before him, coughing softly, toward the door. "Be seeing you, daddy," she said, and patted him gently on the chest.

When you know what you want, perhaps you still have to learn how to ask for it.

> FATHER seeks large matronly
> woman to mother homeless boy.

Was that too plain? He would drop the *large*. Somehow, when he was a boy, matronly women were all large.

> FATHER seeks matronly woman
> as companion growing boy.

Perhaps it was best to keep the father out of it. He let a week pass, then he ran this ad in both the Des Moines and the Omaha papers, and in the following week he received eighteen replies. He made appointments with a Miss Lily Schumann, a Miss Vivien Throop, a Bella Hess, and a Mrs. Callie Horst. Mrs. Horst's letter to him had been very brief:

> *I sometimes get so sick and tired of all of them.*
> *How old is yours?*

Mrs. Horst also lived on a farm and didn't know whether she could get to town within the month or not. But his first appointment was with Miss Schumann, who would be wearing, as she said, white feathers, a fur muff, and a red handbag. She also described herself as stylish stout.

He found Miss Schumann seated near the phone booths, asleep. She was well dressed, her hands in a fur muff, and her corset hugged her body so that it seemed to prop her upright, like a barrel. Now and then she burped, putting out a pink tongue to lick the film from her lips. She was rather short, with small hands and feet, and from time to time her brows arched up, her face flushed, and her small white teeth would bite down on her lip. She seemed to be digesting, and enjoying it very much. Without opening her eyes she removed from her handbag a small handkerchief, with blue tatting, and wiped her full lips, both inside and out, like a baby's mouth. Later she dropped a green mint on her tongue. Her small hand, with the fat fingers, rested on her muff like a picked bird, and when she sighed, her breath was scented with wintergreen. He let her sleep. She was still there in the lobby, blowing softly, when he met Miss Throop.

Miss Throop lowered herself—she did not sit down, nor drop down, she lowered herself—as her glasses, on a cord from her throat, swung back and forth beneath her large bust. "Throoooop," she was saying, "old English," and when she was lowered, her legs crossed at the ankles, she felt about on her front where her glasses had once been. This was on the top of her bust, rather than beneath. "Throoooop," she repeated, and found her glasses in her lap.

Miss Throop had spent the best years of her life as a tutor to the Countess Moroni, companion and tutor to her three lovely children and the Countess herself. This was of course in Italy. During the morning she and the children spoke only Italian and French, during the afternoon they spoke English and American. American was the hardest—she had been away so long. It bored her to death—were they seated in a draft? She stood up, wheeling, and backed herself against the radiator. Did he mind a woman standing, she asked, and spread her full skirts to catch the heat. She simply felt *better* standing—that was what years of lecturing did. As the heat billowed her skirts, she fluffed them out, let them fall, and the sweetish sour smell hung over the lobby, the smell of soiled clothes. She was getting warm, and the bangs of her wig, a crisp amber color, stuck to her forehead when she raised her hand, patted them down.

"And now tell me," she said, with her fingers on her eyelids, "about your son."

While Will Brady talked, Miss Throop inhaled her own

rich smell. She stood with one hand at her back, the other raised to her damp forehead, with the tip of the thumb and the first finger on her lidded eyes. Her glasses had made deep blue bruises at the bridge of her nose. Under her arms the colors had run, the dress snaps had parted, and there in the open were the shiny spears of her corset stays. When he stopped talking, for a moment, she turned to look at the rain.

"Rain, rain, rain, rain, rain, rain," she said, and gave her skirts a toss, like a dancer; then as they drooped she felt around once more on the top of her bust. But it was not for her glasses. Smiling, she said:

"You mind if I smoke?"

Bella Hess said no, no thank you, she'd just as soon stand up and talk, and looked about her as if the lobby chairs were so many beds, the pillows rumpled and the covers thrown back. Bella Hess had worked for years in Cedar Rapids, and she handed him a letter, several pages long, describing the cooking, the washing, and the hundred extra things Bella Hess had done. She had along with her a small bag of hard rolls, another letter of recommendation, and a wicker case with an umbrella strapped to the side. Will Brady just stood there, holding the letter, until Bella Hess picked up her bag, took the letter from his hands, and walked through the swinging doors into the street.

The next woman he met did not even trouble to answer the ad. She just happened to be standing in the lobby when he was speaking to Bella Hess, and while he stood there, wondering, she came up and spoke to him. She had a powder-stained face, bleached hair; but there was something familiar about her—about the walk, and about the way she rolled her eyes. Like the weighted, rolling eyes of a sleeping doll.

"You lookin' for somebody, daddy?" she said, and stepped so close to him that she touched him, with her head tipped back as if there was something caught in her eye—something that he, with the corner of his hankie, would have to remove.

"I am interviewing housekeepers," he said. God knows why, but he said it, and saw that her teeth no longer looked cold in her red mouth.

"You're doin' what, daddy?" she said, and pressed so close to him that he could see the pores in her nose. They had always been large. Yes, he remembered that. "I'm not so good at keeping house, daddy," she said, "but there's other things I can tend to," and she took his coat by the lapels, drew him down toward her lips. He was unable to move, or to speak, and when he saw her tongue wagging in her mouth, like a piece of live bait, he closed his eyes and put one hand to his face. At the front of the lobby someone rattled the dice, and he saw, as if cupped in his hand, the face of the girl behind the cigar counter at the Wellington. She had rocked the leather cup and said: "Come have a game on me."

"You sick, daddy?" she said.

"No," he said, "no, I'm all right," and opened his eyes and looked at this strange missing woman, his wife.

In the Cloudland

1

After putting his wife to bed, Will Brady came downstairs and took a seat in the lobby, facing a railroad poster of
a palm-fringed island in a soft blue sea. A glass-bottomed
boat, with many bright flags flying, the deck crowded with
happy men and women, sailed from a white pier—so it
seemed to Will Brady—toward happiness. The island of
waving palms seemed to float in the blue—the pale blue of
the sky, the deep blue of the sea—and to be nothing more
than what men were inclined to call a mirage. But the name
of this place was Catalina, and it was said to be real. It could
be found, like the town of Omaha, on a map somewhere.
And according to the message on the poster, this island was
just two days away—just two days and three nights from
where he sat in the Paxton Hotel. Out of this world, and
yet said to be in it at the same time.

In Will Brady's mind what the girl needed, what this
strange woman, his wife, needed, was what he had often
heard described as a change. It was linked in his mind with
white Palm Beach suits, the shoes that Lyman Bryce wanted
him to wear, gay beach umbrellas, and a wide view of the

sea. Off there, if anywhere, the grease and paint would wash from the girl's stained face, her dyed hair would grow dark, and in time he would recognize her. And in the meantime he would go through a change himself—hard to say in advance just what it would be—but they would both begin, as he had read in books, their life over again. So he let it be known that Will Brady and his wife would be away several weeks. That seemed to be the time that it took to effect a real change. Then he stepped up and ordered, from the clerk at the desk, two round-trip tickets to California, with a passage to that island advertised on the poster—if there was such a place.

But two long days and three nights on a train can seem quite a while. He hadn't seen this girl, his wife, for some time, but after one good meal in the diner it seemed that he had run out of things to talk about. There was a good deal to see out the wide diner windows, and a good deal to eat, sitting there, but when you run out of talk the long days seem to drag. Fast as they were traveling, even the view was slow to change.

Was it twelve or fourteen telephone poles to the mile? Watching the poles file past like wickets, he thought of that. The red and white road markers were faded now, and the bleak frame houses, like bumps on the land, looked as lonely and forgotten as an abandoned caboose. It reminded him of something. He had traveled west with this woman before. At that time the painted bands on the poles were new, the winter wheat in the shimmering fields was new, and the girl and the boy, there in the seat beside him, were new as well. In a certain way, he must have been fairly new himself. A second-hand label might have looked strange on any of them. But now that new coat of paint was gone, the white band on the poles had faded, and he didn't have to look at himself to know other things had faded as well. Nor did he have to be told that the town down the tracks would be Calloway, a whistle stop now. He saw the fine City Hall was like a birthday cake without the frosting, and a strip of tattered flag was flapping from the stilts on the water tank. The word DOMINOES had been painted on the window of the Merchant's Hotel. Down the spur of weedy track he saw the lumber mill, with a few weathered boards in the yard, and beyond it the frame house with the clapboards peeling, the windows smashed. He remembered there had been a creaking flight of stairs on the east side. Now they were gone, the lantern was gone, but the rust-colored scar, like a gash, was there, with the tattered, blowing strips of a Hagenbeck & Wallace circus poster. The mouth of the rhinoceros, like a great hole in the wall, was still there.

The good will prevail, Anna Mason had said, but sometimes a man was led to wonder. Was it possible that a man died just to be dead? The answer was no—if you had to answer a question like that. Will Brady's father had died, his mother had died, and around five thousand Leghorn chickens had died, but certainly not for nothing. No, they died to give him a piece of advice. What was it? Well, it seemed to have faded a bit as well. Something or other about how, in the long run, the good would prevail.

Hadn't he, for example, found his wife? After a change and a rest wouldn't she be as good as new? If he sometimes lay awake at night just to look at her face while she was sleeping, it was merely because she looked more like her old self that way. During the day he found it better not to look at her. He didn't know the face. The woman he saw looked like somebody else.

For a while it did him good to see her eat—the rest and the food would do her good, he thought—but watching her eat, his own appetite began to fall off. He stopped eating. He settled for a cup of coffee now and then. As this meant there was food left on his plate, she would reach for the toast he didn't eat at breakfast, dip it into his egg, and then finish off his marmalade. She poured his cream into her own coffee, asked for more of it. In the last swallow or two of her coffee she liked to dip the lump sugar, suck out the coffee, then leave a heavy syrup in the cup and on her lips. Between meals she ordered sandwiches from the porter, and if the train stopped at a station she would lean out the window to buy candy bars and fruit. She couldn't seem to eat enough, sleep enough, or even see enough out the wide windows, as if every moment that passed might be her last. In the evening he read to her from some movie magazine.

In the window that he faced he could see her tongue coming and going as she washed her teeth, explored her gums, or found bits of food in her mouth that she had stored away. There were little pads of fat, like sideburns, in her puffy cheeks. Stage make-up had coarsened her skin and there was a deep-blue stain, like a bruise, that would not wash out from beneath her eyes. It was part of her face, like the distracted baby-roll of her eyes. She used the white tongue to pick her teeth, and every now and then, facing the window, she would stick it out and have a look at it.

At night she slept with her mouth open, which was normal enough in some ways, except for the change that it brought to her face. Her body, all of this time, remained the same. There seemed to be no connection between this body and the face. This may have been why she could eat all day long and half the night, feeding her face, without her body showing any signs of it. The face had gone off, was going off, that is, somewhere on its own. But the body was faithful—put it like that. The body was faithful even though the face seemed to find the world too complicated, the going too rough, and the living too sick at heart.

From the Biltmore Hotel, in Los Angeles, in the big red cars chartered for that purpose, they rode down to the sea where there were piers, crowds of people, and amusement parks. Facing the sea there were benches, and seated in the sun, wearing the dark glasses, Will Brady would read from the guidebook to her. He kept himself posted in order to point out the interesting things. From a glass-bottomed boat they peered into the sea at schools of fish, drifting like birds, and in the evening they would sit on a terrace some-where, watching young people dance. Now, however, no young man came forward and spoke to her. It seemed to be clear that the woman at his side was not his child. Out on the dark sea were the lights of boats, pleasure craft as some people called them, and across the water, sparkling like stars, were the lights of the shore. Very much as if the sky—or the world they were now in—was upside down. Which was not at all strange as that was how this world really was.

There were people who told him that the City of Angels was an unreal city, a glittering mirage, and that the people were as strange, as rootless, and as false as the city itself. That the whole thing was a show, another mammoth pro-duction soon to be featured in the movie houses, and that one fine day, like the movie itself, it would disappear. Will Brady couldn't tell you whether that talk was true or not. But he could tell you that part of the description was real enough. This unreal city, this mammoth production full of strange, wacky people like himself, was an accurate descrip-tion of a place Will Brady recognized. Here, bigger than life, was Paradise on the American Plan. A hotel lobby, that is, as big as the great out-of-doors.

Every morning they rode off to look at something de-scribed in the guidebook or pictured on the cards, or they sat in the lobby, where other people came to look at them. Or they rode out in buses to watch the great lover, John Gilbert, make love. They saw him kneel, one knee on the floor, and make love to the woman whose eyes looked bruised and whose armpits were sore where she had just been shaved. In the sun a small boy walked an aging lion about the streets. Over a cardboard sea great towers fell, and men leaped from the windows of burning buildings to fall into nets held aloft on wooden spears. Half-naked women, in skirts of straw, lay about on a floor sprinkled with sand, their bodies wet from the heat of great smoking lamps. Thick custard pies, suspended on wires, made their way around corners, and curved around poles to catch the man—the villain, that is—full in the face. Beyond, the mountains rose up to be seen from the valley, and the valley dropped down to be seen from the mountains, and so that nothing might remain unseen the dry air was clear. And one went to bed, in this unreal world, but not to sleep. The eyes were closed, it seemed, the better to look at oneself.

All that Will Brady saw he kept to himself, perhaps lacking the words for it, but what the girl saw when her eyes were closed kept her awake. Lying there in the dark, as she had years before, she would talk. Once it had been men that troubled her sleep, but now it was herself. During the day he sometimes wondered if she saw anything very clearly, but during the night she seemed to have eyes like a cat. She saw everything. Even stranger, she had the words for it.

There was a Mr. Pulaski—or so she said—who took her for long buggy rides in the country, where he would fish, with a pole, while she played at rowing the boat. In the afternoon he took naps, lying with the newspaper over his face, and she ate chocolates and shooed the flies off his big hands. They were red on the back, with knobby knuckles, and the nails of one hand were blue from how he had worked in Poland, the old country. He napped with his hands lying at his side, like a dead man. He was good with horses, and they would run without his whipping them.

Every week he gave her a five-dollar bill, saying: "Now you go and buy yourself something," but that wasn't what she wanted to do. He kept giving her money for something she didn't want to sell. He was very nice, but she stopped seeing him.

There was a Hazel Roebuck, who was head cashier at the Moon. Hazel Roebuck knew in advance when Wallace Reid or Francis X. Bushman was coming, and she would give her tickets for the mezzanine seats free. Hazel Roebuck had a nice room at the Paxton Hotel and she liked to have help while trying her clothes on, taking a bath, or doing any number of things. There wasn't anything that she liked to do alone. She liked to let down her long hair and let someone do it up, or leave it long and try on broad-brimmed summer hats. She showed her what ice would do to the nipples of her breasts. Hazel Roebuck did not give her money, but she left her with the feeling that what she got, she got for nothing, so to speak. As she didn't want it for nothing, she stopped seeing her.

There was a Mr. Marshall, who was head floorwalker for Burgess & Nash. He wore expensive clothes like an actor, a paper flower on his coat, and, under his vest, buttons that held his shirt pulled down. As he was the last man out of the building, they could use the ladies' lounge, or the men's dressing-room on the second floor. He would sit on a chair and patiently watch her take off her clothes. He liked her to undress so that all of her clothes fell in a puddle at her feet, except her black stockings, which he liked her to leave on. Then he would give her all new clothes to put back on. He never once put his hand on her, said anything nasty, or giggled, and everything that she could wear out of the store she could have. In the winter that was quite a bit. He was very shy, and the first man ever to call her Miss Long. He didn't give her money, or tickets, but when she had all of the clothes she could wear, summer and winter, she had stopped seeing him.

Did she *like* him? he had asked. He had interrupted her to ask her that.

Like him? she had said. Oh, she had liked him all right.

Did she feel any *love* for him—that was what he meant to say.

No, she had replied, she hadn't felt anything like that. It was Francis X. Bushman who had awakened her to love.

When she recognized it for what it was she sat in the movies eight hours every day, loving him and hating the women that he kissed. That was love. A woman only felt like that just once.

What about—he said—what about himself?

Whatever it was, she said, it was not love at first sight. Maybe it was not what she would call love at all. She might not have even looked at him if it hadn't been for the way he looked, and the way he didn't seem to know what to do with himself. He just sat there in the lobby. Or he got up and went for long walks. All the other men she had ever known were able to talk, to smoke, or do something, but he just sat there without doing anything. He had money, wavy brown hair, and strong white teeth like Mr. Pulaski, but the first time she saw him she simply didn't feel anything. The second time maybe she felt sorry for him. Then one day, God knows why, she saw what was wrong. She saw that Will Brady knew how to give, like Mr. Marshall and Mr. Pulaski, but what he didn't know was how to receive anything. Maybe what she felt was love the day that she saw that. Maybe she really loved him, that is, the day that she saw that he was hopeless—or maybe what she felt was something else.

Getting back—he said—getting back to other men besides himself, just what was it that she felt for them?

For *them?* she said.

The other men in her life. What did she feel for the other men in her life?

Sorry, she said, she felt sorry for them.

Just what did she mean by that, he said, what did she mean by feeling sorry?

They were moths, she said, that flew away from the flame.

And where, he had asked her, where in the world had she picked up *that?*

It was a line in one of her plays, she said. In this play she would climb out of the bed, or if she was out she would climb in it, and the man in the bed or the room would run away. She would call to him that he was a moth afraid of the flame. Everybody would laugh. Why did they laugh?

It was the way of men to laugh, he said. That was their way.

Was he different, then, she said, from other men?

Was he? Did she mean that he had been burned? Did she mean that he, Will Brady, had not run away from the flame? Did she mean that all the other men had got out of the bed or hid beneath it, or did she mean that all the other men were part of the play? She liked this play? he asked.

She liked the view from the stage.

The *what?* he said.

She liked the view. From the stage she had a good view of all of them.

Them—? he said.

The men, she said. It was like a new show for her every night. They came to see her, they paid their good money, but the light from the stage was on their faces and she didn't have to pay a cent to see all of them. And they didn't care—they all wanted her to look at them. So she made it a point, lying there in the bed, to look at each man in every row, and if the town was big and the house was full this took time. It might take her two or three weeks to see all of them. If the show had a long run, as it often did in the larger places, sooner or later she saw most of the men in town. Five or ten thousand men, some of them single, some of them married with wives and children, some of them rich, some of them poor, some of them good and some of them bad, but every living one of them there to be seen, and to look at her. She knew them all, and all of them knew her. But they were all moths, she said, that flew away from the flame.

It made him smile, lying there, to hear her talking in terms like that, and to think that of all these men she had picked him out to be burned. When she had held the flame up to him, he hadn't run. Some people would say that he hadn't even sense enough to do that.

But he didn't laugh, as he might have, or ask her if she thought he was such a fool as to believe the only men in her life had been under her bed. No, he didn't ask her. He didn't even bring it up. The longer he lived the easier he could believe wild talk like that. He didn't find it hard to believe at night, and it didn't strike him as silly in the morning when he took a seat, with the other old men, on a bench in the park. In the unreal world, talk like that seemed real enough.

On the one hand you would say that the old men in the park had either lost or given up something, like the ratty-tailed pigeons that paced up and down on the walk. They had given up the notion of being some fancier kind of bird. They were no longer ashamed to let their feathers drag on the walk. On the one hand you could see they had given it up, on the other hand there was a man called Teapot. That was the only name that he had—where had he picked it up?

Every morning, like the sun itself, he entered the park. To the casual passer-by it might appear that this fellow Teapot had some kind of trouble, bodily trouble, that forced him to walk along with one hand on his hip, the other raised in the air. But those who knew better knew that this fellow Teapot had become a new thing. No longer merely a man, he was a Teapot. He was meant to be poured.

"Brother, pour me!" Teapot would say, and the brother would take Teapot by the arm, as you would a kettle, and tip him forward till he poured. Whatever Teapot contained would flow out the long spout of his arm. "Thank you, brother," he would say, and proceed across the square. Later in the day, several times, he would need to be poured again. Now, there were people who would class Teapot as odd, or even downright wacky, but Will Brady had acquired a different feeling about such men. Put it this way: he felt right at home with them.

Every day Will Brady saw, on the bench near the fountain, an old man with brown bare feet, his soiled pants legs rolled, and three or four wiry hairs, like watch springs, on his flat, leathery chest. He passed most of the day with a newspaper spread over his face. Morning and evening he fed the pigeons, wetting the hard dry bread in his mouth, rolling it into a ball, then feeding this spittle to the birds. Some of the old men in the park sat and wagged their heads over something like that. But not Will Brady. No, he felt very much at home.

Was there any man, Will Brady asked himself, who didn't understand something like that? Who wouldn't like, that is, to be fed to the birds himself? Well, there were several men who said the old fool with the bare feet had a brain that was soft. Sitting in the sun, they said, had done that to him. The old man's hands, lying in his lap, had got to be the color of walnut stain, and if he napped sitting up, the pigeons roosted on his shoulders, dirtied his front. It soon dried in the sun and he chipped it off later, absently. The way Will Brady would chip the hen spots off a Leghorn egg. In one pocket of his coat the old man kept reading matter, in another pocket eating matter, and every hour or so he got himself up and took a long drink. He would peer through the palm trees at the clock to see how much time he had passed.

Was this an example of what the sun would do to a man? Perhaps it was, as Will Brady passed the time that way himself. The great problem in life, as any old fool could tell you, was not so much about love, or the man and the flame, nor did it have much to do, in the long run, as to who it was that was burned. No, the real problem was nothing more than how to pass the time. Every day it was there, somehow it had to be passed. The really great problem in life was merely how to get out of the bed in the morning and put in the time until you went to bed again. The girl solved this problem by lying awake at night, having breakfast in bed, and trying to sleep during the day. Will Brady got up and sat on a bench in the park.

In the early evening the girl would get up and they would go out some place for dinner, but one evening, after his walk, she was not there. Neither in the lobby nor up in the room. That usually meant she would be in the ladies' room, and he took a seat near by in the lobby, across from a tall flat girl who stood in the door chewing gum. This girl seemed to take an interest in him. On the seat beside him was a magazine open at a picture of Pola Negri, but Will Brady couldn't keep his mind on what he read. The girl in the door kept staring and smacking the gum. So he put the magazine back on the seat, took time to look at his watch, but when he walked across the lobby the girl followed him.

Before he could make a getaway she said: "You lookin' for somebody, daddy?"

"I am waiting for my wife," he replied.

"Adds up to the same thing," she said, and when he looked at her face she smacked the gum she was chewing, sucked in on it. "You got a nice long wait," she said, and when he didn't answer that, she added: "I'd just as soon sit down, daddy," and then she pushed through the swinging door and walked into the street. He followed her. She was wearing the kind of clothes that the girl liked to wear. A shabby fox fur hung from her shoulders, and the shriveled grinning head, with its glassy eyes, bounced on her hip. He walked behind her to the corner, where she turned and said: "This be all right, daddy?" and nodded her head toward the corner drugstore. As they went in she called to the waitress: "Make it a double chock-Coke, honey," and as they sat down at the back she took her gum from her mouth, stuck it to the seat.

"You have seen my wife?" Will Brady said.

"Not any too good," she said, "she was on the floor, and it was hard to see her." He stared at her, and she said: "Daddy, you want me to begin at the first?"

"Why, yes," he said, and felt his head nodding. When the girl brought the Coke he asked her for a cup of coffee, black.

"First you get a bottle, daddy," she said, "then you lock yourself up in a nice pay toilet, then you empty the bottle, and then after a while you fall off the seat. When you fall off the seat I come along and pick you up."

"Thank you," he said, "very much."

"Oh, I'm paid for it," she said, and tapped a cigarette on her thumbnail. "I'm paid," she said, "but God knows I've done it for nothin' enough." She lit the cigarette and blew the smoke in his face.

"She's all right, then?"

"Daddy," she said, and closed her eyes. With her eyes closed she let the smoke drift through her nose. "Daddy," she went on, "a nice man like you makes a bad girl like me feel better. You owe it to a girl—where'd she pick you up?"

"Miss—" Will Brady began.

"Clinton," she said, "Flora Clinton."

"Miss Clinton," he said, "if you have seen my wife—"

"You a Mr. Metaxas?"

"Brady," he said, "Will Brady."

"Next time you pick up a little girl," she said, "say you look in her handbag and see who she is. Say you find out whether you're a Mr. Metaxas or not." He looked at her, and she said: "Well, daddy, you asked for it."

He turned from Flora Clinton and looked at the palms in Pershing Square. The old man with bare feet was feeding the pigeons from a paper bag. He wet the food in his mouth, then spit it out and fed it to them. The flapping of their wings stirred the stringy hair at the back of his head.

"You mind a personal question?"

"No," he said, and wagged his head slowly.

"Where'd she ever find you?"

"Omaha."

"Where is that?"

"It's a town on the Missouri," he said, and saying that, he saw it there before him, a town on the bluffs. He saw the muddy river and the new toll bridge they had put over it.

"That must be a great place," she said, "Omaha, I'll remember that," and took from her purse a small card, wrote a number on it. She handed it to him and said: "Next time you feel like a little girl, daddy—"

"This woman is my wife," he said.

"That makes it even worse, daddy," she said, and finished

her Coke. There was ice in the glass, and she tipped her head back till it spilled into her mouth. Then she patted his arm and said: "I've got to run along now, daddy," and stood up from the table, smoothed the wrinkled front of her dress. "You say this kid was your wife?" she said.

"This woman is my wife," Will Brady replied.

"I don't get it," Flora Clinton said, "I don't see why she didn't talk." She looked at her face in the mirror, then said: "When people don't talk they think they're in love. Maybe she was so drunk she thought that she was." That made her smile, sucking in the air from the side of her mouth, where a tooth was missing. "Well, bye now, daddy," she said, and he watched her walk away.

From the corner, where he stood at the curb, Will Brady watched the old fool who was feeding the pigeons, and saw on his face the rapt gaze of a holy man. A circling flock of pigeons hovered above him, flapping their wings. On the old man's face was the look that Will Brady had seen, many years before, on one of the calendars at the foot of his mother's bed. A religious man, it was said, who fed himself to the birds. So it was not a new notion. No, it was a notion of the oldest kind. Very likely this old fool let himself think that in just such a manner he might fly himself, grow wings like an angel, and escape from the city and the world. As the spirit is said to escape from the body, when the body dies. Perhaps he thought that—or perhaps all he was doing was making love. There were many ways to make it, after all, and perhaps that was one of them.

No voice had ever spoken to Will Brady before—or even whispered to him, for that matter—but now from out of the sky, above the noise of the pigeons, one spoke to him.

"Old man," this voice said, "so you think you are a lover?"

Did Will Brady smile? No, he kept a sober face.

"Speaking of heaven," the voice went on, though of course they had not been speaking of heaven, "I suppose you know there are no lovers in heaven. I suppose you know that?"

"No lovers in heaven?" Will Brady replied, but the voice did not answer. Will Brady thought he heard it sigh, but it might have been the wind. "Then why go to heaven?" Will Brady said.

"I don't know," said the voice, "I've often wondered." Then it added: "But I suppose the small lovers like it. They like it up here."

"And the great lovers?" Will Brady said.

"There's no need," said the voice, "for great lovers in heaven. Pity is the great lover, and the great lovers are all on earth."

That was all, that was all that was said, but somehow Will Brady was left with the feeling that this creature in heaven, somehow, envied every old fool on earth. That something was missing in heaven, oddly enough. As it had never occurred to Will Brady that something might be missing in heaven, he turned to watch the pigeons wheeling over the park. They were rising, and filled the sky with the sound of their wings. On Will Brady's face, strangely enough, was the rapt, happy gaze of a holy man, like the old fool who stood barefooted in the park. Together they watched the pigeons wheeling until they were gone, the sky was void, and the old man suddenly threw into the air his flabby brown arms. Over his head, for a moment, floated the empty paper bag.

In the Wasteland

1

He had asked the porter to wake him out of Cheyenne. That was not necessary, however, as he was wide awake, his eyes were open, when the porter rattled the curtains of his berth. With his pajama sleeve he wiped a small hole in the frosted glass. A new fall of snow, like a frozen sea, covered the earth. In the spring and the fall, through the wide diner windows, a man who had felt hemmed in by the city, or who had had, as he thought, enough of people, might find relief in the vast emptiness of the plains. He might feel what some men felt when they came on the sea. In the winter, however, there was no haze to soften the sky, blur the far horizon, or lead a man to think that he might, out there, make a go of it. Everything visible had the air of being left there, dropped perhaps. Every mound or post had the look of cattle frozen upright. Will Brady, for example, had seen such things as a boy. It was strange to find them, after so many years, still vivid in his mind.

He could see the winter dawn, a clear ice color, and far out on the desolate plain, like the roof of the world, were two or three swinging lights. He could make out the dry bed of the river, and as the train was stopping for water, he could hear, down the tracks, the beat of the crossing-bell. The rapid throbbing of this bell, at such a godforsaken and empty corner, seemed to emphasize that this scene, the birthplace of Will Brady, was as remote, and as dead, as a crater on the moon.

As the train slowly braked to a stop, he could see the frame of the cattle loader, and then, suddenly, the station along the tracks. A lamp, with a green glass shade, hung inside. It threw an arc of light on the wide desk, the pads of yellow paper, and the hand of the man who sat there, a visor shading his face. The fingers of this hand were poised over the telegraph key. His head was bare, getting bald, and the green celluloid of the visor cast a shadow the color of illness on his face. He was staring, absently, into the windows of the passing cars. On the table before him lay a bamboo rod, curved at one end like a plant flowering, and a sheet of folded paper was inserted at the curved end. Will Brady saw all of this as if it were a picture on a calendar. Nothing moved, every detail was clear. He could smell the odor of stale tobacco, and the man's coat, wet with snow, gave off the stench of a wet gunny sack. He could see the wood stove, just back from the light, and he thought he could hear, out there in the silence, the iron ring of the ground where a brakeman stamped his feet. In the man's dark vest were several red-capped pencils, and as Will Brady gazed at his face he raised his head, suddenly, as if a voice had spoken to him. He gazed into the darkness where Will Brady lay on the berth. And Will Brady fell back, he held his breath, and as his hands gripped the side of the berth he heard again the mechanical throbbing of the crossing-bell. He seemed to see, out there on the horizon, the snout-like mound of the buried soddy, where he had been, even then, the last man in the world.

He closed his eyes, and when the morning light came through the window he drew the blind to keep it from his face. He did not rise on his elbow to look at Murdock, or Calloway. Nor did he get off at Omaha, although that was his destination, and the conductor came back through the car to speak to him. Where was he going? Well, he hadn't made up his mind. He was going where the train was going, and when that turned out to be Chicago, he implied that that was all right with him. All the roads seemed to lead to Chicago, so there was no reason why Will Brady, who followed the roads, shouldn't go where they led.

2

To get to Menomonee Street in Chicago you take a Clark Street car in the Loop and ride north, twenty minutes or so, to Lincoln Park. If you want to get the feel of the city, or if you like to see where it is you're going, you can stand at the front of the car with the motorman. On certain days you might find Will Brady standing there. Not that he cared where he was going, but he liked the look of the street, the clang of the bell, and the smell of the track sand that came up through the floor. He liked to stand with his hands grasping the rail at the motorman's back. At certain intersections he liked to turn and look—when the door at the front opened—down the streets to the east where the world seemed to end. It didn't, of course, but perhaps he liked to think that it might. When it did, as one day it would, he wanted to be there. On up the street he could see the park, and in the winter, when the trees were bare, he could make out the giant brooding figure of Abraham Lincoln himself.

Soft green, like the color of cheap Christmas jewelry, or the fine copper gutters on the homes of the rich.

Lincoln Park was right there where the street angled. He could see the Moody Bible Tabernacle, and at the next stop Will Brady would step forward and get off. Menomonee was the street that went off like an alley to the west. To get to 218 on this street he would follow the curb on the north side to where this number was nailed on the first door on his right. The second door was the entrance to Plinski's delicatessen store. The first door was usually kept shut, even in the summer, to make the rats from the store go around and use the stairs at the rear. But the second door was open until ten or later every night. There was a sign on the door saying as much, but anyone who lived in the room overhead, and who tried to sleep there, didn't need to be told.

Will Brady lived in the room at the front, over the screen door that slammed with a bang, in a room that was said to be suitable for Light Housekeeping. To get to this room he walked up the stairs, along the bright-green runner of roach powder, and at the top of the stairs he took the door on his left. It opened on a small room with two windows on Menomonee Street. The window on the left was cut off by the bed, but over the years and through many tenants one window on the street had proved to be more than enough. On a winter afternoon it might even be warm, as the slanting winter sun got at it, and by leaning far out one could look down the street and see the park. An ore boat might be honking, or the sounds of the ice breaking up on the lake.

Inside the room was a small gas plate on a marble-topped washstand, a cracked china bowl, a table, two chairs, a chest of drawers, an armless rocker, an imitation fireplace, and an iron frame bed. Over the fireplace was a mirror showing the head of the bed and the yellow folding doors. The bed was in the shape of a shallow pan with a pouring spout at one side, and beneath this spout, as if poured there, a frazzled hole in the rug.

To get from the stove to the sink it was better to drop the leaf on the table and then lean forward over the back of the rocking-chair. On the shelf over the sink were four plates, three cups and one saucer, a glass sugarbowl, two metal forks, and one bone-handled spoon. On the mantelpiece was a shaving mug with the word SWEETHEART in silver, blue, chipped red, and gold. In the mug were three buttons, a roller-skate key, a needle with a burned point for opening pimples, an Omaha street-car token, and a medal for buying Buster Brown shoes. At the back of the room were the folding doors that would not quite close.

To get to the bathroom, the old man who lived in this room would open these doors, greet Mrs. Plinski, then proceed to the back of the house. Mrs. Plinski was usually there in a rocker, nursing her twins. In the bathroom, seated on the stool, was her oldest boy, Manny Plinski, watching his baby turtles swim around in the tub. Manny Plinski was seventeen years old and had the long narrow face of a goat, big wet eyes, and a crown of silky, corn-yellow hair. This hair grew forward over his face and he stroked it forward, with a raking motion, as if there was something tangled in it that would not comb out. When he was displeased, Manny Plinski would make a sound like priming a pump. Mrs. Plinski would put down the twin she was nursing and wet her fingers under the tap, then sprinkle Manny Plinski as if she was dampening clothes. That would make him all right, and he would just sit there, staring at his turtles, or he could be led out in case you wanted the bathroom to yourself.

That wasn't very often, as the old man had got to be fond of the turtles, nor did he seem to mind Manny Plinski just sitting there. He would wink at the boy while the lather was thick on his face. Manny Plinski never laughed, but if he was pleased he would take one of the turtles, one that he liked, and slip it into the pocket of the old man's pants. The old man, somehow, never seemed to catch on to this. Later, of course, he would find it there and cry out for help. For a man so fond of turtles it was strange how they nearly scared him to death.

Leaving the bathroom, he would come back through the house, nod to Mrs. Plinski, then pass through the folding doors without closing them. He would let them stand open, as if his room was part of the house. He could see out, or any Plinski that cared to could see in. If a turtle was missing, this would be Manny Plinski, raking his hair in an excited manner; otherwise it might be Mrs. Plinski herself. What did she want? Well, the old man in the room had spoken to her. He had called out, perhaps, to ask if she had ever heard the likes of this. A clipping of some kind, or a passage from a letter spread out in his lap. So she would get herself up, this woman, in spite of the twin she was nursing, and brace herself, as she often seemed tired, between the folding doors. One heavy arm she would prop on the door, as if it weighed on her. The old man himself, seated at the table, would have the long sleeves of his underwear rolled, as otherwise they dragged in the food on his plate. He would be eating; that is, he had been eating, but he had stopped eating in order to examine, as the writing was fading, the letter in his lap. Two sheets of yellow paper, each sheet with widely spaced green stripes. The top sheet spotted with grease like a popcorn bag. The old man had spread the letter in his lap as his own fingers might be greasy, or in order to open, with the bent prong of a fork, the plugged hole in a milk can.

The letter was not new, it was cracked at the folds, and there were coffee stains in the margins, but it described in considerable detail an unusual event. How a snake, taken sick at the stomach, threw up a live frog. It described how the boy, the writer of the letter, picked this snake up by the tail, twirled him like a rope, and then watched him whoop up this poor frog. Not many city people would be familiar with anything like that. Mrs. Sigismund Plinski, for example, who had lived for forty-six years in Chicago, had heard the letter many times but couldn't seem to get enough of it. She would just stand there, wagging her head, as she did when the world was too much for her, and listen to the old man read parts of it aloud. Sometimes he just read the last of it, which he thought was particularly clever, and then went on to read how the boy had signed his name.

Your son—Willy Brady Jr.

that was what it said.

"You would think," the old man would say, putting the milk can down on the table, "that a boy who could write a letter like that would write a little oftener." Not that he meant it, of course, as a smart boy like that had things on his mind. It was enough for him to know that his father was sometimes one of them.

"Oh, how he must love you!" Mrs. Plinski would say. "Oh, how he must love you!" and that would be all. In some respects that was about all that she ever said. Then she would wag her big head, with the loose flesh on it, and roll the little eyes that were too small for her face. "Oh, how he must love you!" she would go on, and before Will Brady went on with the letter, or read the passage over, he would blow on the coffee that was already cold in his cup. It was never hot, but it seemed to do him good to blow on it.

"Mrs. Plinski," he would say, "now you know how boys are," and indeed Mrs. Plinski did. Both men and boys. If she knew anything, that is, this woman knew that.

"How he must love you!" she would repeat, and shift her

great weight as her feet were tired, and whichever twin it was, astride her haunch like a saddle, would be asleep.

Once a year this boy wrote to his father, and maybe ten or fifteen times a year Will Brady wrote, but somehow never mailed, a postcard to his son. It would have a picture of the park or the wide blue lake on it. But every month Will Brady expected to move into larger, more homelike quarters, and when he moved—the very day that he moved—he would mail that card. It was there in his pocket, already stamped and addressed. All he had to do was put his own new address on it. This address would be—as he told everybody—over facing the park. There would be trees and grass when the boy walked to the window and looked out. There would always be a cool summer breeze blowing off the blue lake. Every year he had to write this card many times as the writing would get smudgy from the dirt in his pocket, or even the picture on the front of the card would begin to fade. So he would buy a new one, in the hotel lobby, and seated at the table where the pens were chained, he would write on the back in such a manner that it also showed on the front. It had got so the message was more or less the same. It was always spring on this card, the same robin always caught the same worm.

DEAR SON—
    Have moved. Have nice little place of our own now, two-plate gas. Warm sun in windows every morning, nice view of park. Plan to get new Console radio soon now, let you pick it out. Plan to pick up car so we can drive out in country, get out in air. Turning over in my mind plan to send you to Harvard, send you to Yale. Saw robin in park this morning. Saw him catch worm.

Sometimes he said radio, sometimes he said coupe, every now and then he put Princeton instead of Yale, but he always held out for a place of their own, a nice view of the park. He always insisted that the robin caught the worm. Perhaps that was why, after three years, he was still in the room over the delicatessen, and why that postcard with the view of the park had not been mailed.

It might be wrong to say that Will Brady, an old man in yellow underwear with the sleeves rolled, lived in this room any more than he lived anywhere else. He slept there, or tried to sleep there, and that was enough. It gave him certain habits that he found very hard to break. All during the day the screen door slammed, strange children ran in and out of the hallway, and the old man who sold snails seemed to sell most of them right in one spot. Will Brady would lie there, listening to the strange cry that he made. He could hear the snails scooped out of the tub, hear the man put his hand in the striped popcorn bags, and then hear the shells when the little boys stepped on them with their heels. A powdered sound, like the track sand, but without the fresh flinty smell.

The room in which he lay had folding doors that would not quite close. The boy named Manny Plinski often stood there peering in. He was said to be a mute, that is to say that he couldn't speak in the usual manner, nor understand very much, nor do very well at the other boys' games. But the old man in the bed seemed to understand him pretty well. They had found there was very little that needed talking about. Once a week, in the good weather, the old man and the yellow-haired boy might be seen in the zoo, facing one of the cages of monkeys, bears, or strange exotic birds that looked and sounded like Manny Plinski himself. If there was a difference it was not in the feathers, nor in the cage. The man who came to feed them never stopped to sprinkle water on them.

In Will Brady's room was an iron bed, several chairs, and what a man might need to do a little housekeeping, but these things were not, strictly speaking, inhabitants. Like

Brady himself, they might easily be taken away. One morning Mrs. Plinski might peer in and find them gone. But while the room was there, there would always be the smell. It was there in the floor, in the plastered walls, in the draft that stirred but never departed, in the idle curtains, and in whatever clothes hung on the back of the door. Day in and day out, winter and summer, this smell was there. A stranger might refer to this smell as a stink, as some of the lodgers were loose in their habits, and another might notice the odor of the grease, and the stale coffee grounds. But only Will Brady knew this smell for what it was. It was the smell of man. And there was something that he liked about it.

This smell was in the lining of the brown coat that both the sun and sweat had faded, and everything in the pockets, old or new, had picked up the scent. The money in the wallet, and the letter even before it was read. Once opened, and read, the letter might be said to be full of it. The message might fade, but with every reading the smell increased.

"Just listen to this," Will Brady would say to Bessie Muller, the waitress at the Athens, and read her that part about the boy and the frog-sick snake. She was a farm girl herself, but she had never seen a snake carry on like that. Or get sick at his tummy just like she did.

"You would think he liked his father," Will Brady would say, "to sit down and write him a long letter like that," and Bessie Muller would agree to that, naturally. She would even point out that nobody—*no*body—was writing letters to her.

"That kid sure likes his daddy," she would say, and take one of the bobby pins from her hair, clean her nails with it, and then bend the point between her chipped front teeth.

If the night was warm Will Brady would walk past the moss-green statue of Abraham Lincoln, then on across the tennis courts with their sagging nets and the blurred chalk lines. There would be men with their shoes off padding around in the grass. There might be women with white arms in the shadows, fussing with their hair. Under the sheets of newspaper, with what was left of the food, some child would lie asleep.

If there was a moon, or a cool breeze off the lake, Will Brady would walk through the park to the water, where he would stroll along the pilings, or under the trees on the cinder bridle path. He had walked on cinders, he seemed to remember, somewhere before. As he had in the past, he would have to sit down and tap them out of his shoes. In the dusk there would be lights on the Wrigley tower, an airplane beacon would sweep the sky, and at Oak Street beach people would be lying in the warm sand. The drinking fountain would give off a strong chlorine smell. He would wet his face at the fountain, then take his seat among those people who had come to the beach but didn't care to take off their clothes; who had been hot in their rooms, and perhaps lonely in their minds. In the dark they could speak what they had on their minds without troubling about their faces, the sound of their voices, or who their neighbor was. Will Brady was their neighbor. He sat with his coat folded in his lap, his shirtsleeves rolled.

All over the wide beach he could see the white legs of the men, the white arms of the women, and the half-empty milk bottles propped up in the sand. Matches would flare, cigarettes would glow like fireflies. He could hear someone wading, and see the water foam at their feet. When the excursion boat left the North Pier there would be a lull in the beach murmur, and men would rise on their elbows, as if awakened, to watch it go by. They would crane their necks as if they feared to miss something. The red and green boat lights would swing on the water, the music blow in, then out again, and later the long white wave would draw a line on the beach. And after the wave, if there was a breeze, the music again.

"I see by the paper," Will Brady would say, and smooth the sleeve of the coat he was holding, "that it was over a hundred in western Kansas today."

To whom was he talking? Perhaps the murmuring air. It had come, one might say, from Kansas itself. Many things had. Perhaps the old man seated there on his left.

"Bygod, now that's hot!" this old man says, and rubs the balls of his eyes with his knuckles, as if he could see—could look back to Kansas and see for himself. He stares at the night, cranes his head, then makes a blowing noise and says: "Kansas—what part of Kansas you from?"

"I'm from Nebraska," Will Brady says, "I'm a Nebraska boy myself"—though God only knows why he calls himself a boy. An old man more or less at the end of his run. "Born and bred in Nebraska," he says, as if talk like that would revive him. "Got a boy out there now. He writes me that it's pretty hot."

"You don't say," the old man replies, and wets his lips. It would probably turn out that he had a boy somewhere himself. Or if he didn't, that he was small-town boy himself. Nearly everybody was. Where else was there to be coming from? It might surprise you how many men are small-town boys at heart, and how many small towns it takes to make a big one. Make it go, that is.

"The city's no place for a boy," Will Brady says, and gets to his feet as if that would end it. As if he didn't want to hear what the place for a boy was. "No, the city's no place for a boy," he would say, and then he would turn, look at the clock on the tower, and see that it was time for one old man to get back to work.

Another day he might not walk in the park at all, or even stop in at the Athens to see Bessie Muller, but he would go down Clark Street to the Gold Coast Café. He would sit at the counter and order one of their chicken-fried steaks.

"And how is your boy?" Mildred Weigall would say as she poured him a glass of water; she took it for granted that he would always order a chicken-fried steak. "Is he feeling his oats yet?" she would say, as she liked to think that he probably was, for she was young and feeling her oats herself.

"He's the outdoor type," Will Brady would reply, though it was hard to say what he meant by that. Did he mean that outdoor types didn't feel their oats? Probably not. Hard to say what he meant. It just so happened that one day Will Brady had sat there, reading a letter, when a snapshot of the boy had dropped out of the letter onto his plate. Mildred Weigall had wanted to know, naturally, who in the world it was. "Just a snap of the boy," Will Brady had said, and showed her that snapshot of the boy, without a stitch on, holding up one end of a canoe. But he was turned from the camera, so it didn't matter very much.

"Why, he's a nice-lookin' kid," Mildred Weigall had said. "Why don't you bring him around?"

"You think I'd try an' raise a boy like that back here?" Will Brady had said, and waved his hand, with the letter he was holding, toward the street. It had been snowing that day, and the street was full of slush.

"Not on your tintype," he had said; "kid's out in the country where he belongs."

"He's a nice-lookin' kid," Mildred Weigall had said, "he's got nice legs."

"Got his father's brains," Will Brady had replied, "and his mother's looks." That was pretty good. Somehow, it was always good for a laugh. "Thought I might bring him back," he had said, "just to show him what this place is like. But he wouldn't like it. He likes nature. Just take a look at this—" Then he would read her that piece about the frog and the snake. Like Mrs. Plinski, Mildred Weigall couldn't seem to get enough of it.

"He's a nice-lookin' kid," she had said. "When he comes, you bring him around."

On the left side of Clark Street, near Division, he passed a small movie house. Sometimes, just in idling by, he would see through the lobby doors, through the darkness behind, to the glowing silver screen. As if there was a crack in his world and he could see into another one. For a moment he might see, as if in a dream, men leaping from trains, trains leaping from bridges, lovers embracing, or the flash of guns in a battle scene. Or he might hear a song—hear it, that is, from the lover's lips. One night he had stopped, turning like a man who had been softly tapped on the shoulder, to hear the love song that came through the crack in the lobby door. A love song, and a pagan lover was singing it. This was something new, and, an old lover himself, he surrendered to it. He became a young man more or less without clothes, his strong tanned legs washed by South Sea water, and with the sunset behind him he sang this love song to his mate. *"Come with me,"* the pagan lover would sing, and Will Brady would, he came gladly, transporting himself to the land of White Shadows, to the land of true love. There he stood ankle-deep in the warm green water, sometimes spearing fish, sometimes singing love songs, and sometimes, on the palm-fringed islands, making pagan love. What kind of love was it? The doors usually closed before he found out. He might have bought a ticket, but perhaps he didn't want to know. It was enough for him to know that the young lover was there, still doing what he could.

Sometimes, standing there in the street, Will Brady felt that perhaps he had died, but the man in charge of him, the man this side of heaven, had not closed his eyes. So he stood there, a dead man in most ways, but with his eyes looking out. Eyes that seemed to look backwards and forwards at the same time. An old sorter of waybills and a pagan lover at the same time.

Was he—or was that just a way of putting things? Perhaps he was in his mind, the one place that was more or less his own. For instance, just a block or so up the street was a library, with a desk near the door, and a friendly gray-haired woman sat there in charge of things. He had walked up to this woman and said: "What I have in mind is something on education, something on leading colleges, institutes of learning—"

"You have something in mind?" she replied.

"I have a boy," he said.

"Well now," she said, "that makes it interesting."

"The place to raise a boy," he had said, to show her he had thought quite a little about it, "is in the West, but the place to educate him is in the East." Now, that was sharp. He had read that in a book that she had given him. "Boy is also quite a writer for his age," he told her; "think he might become a writer of books himself."

"In that case," she had said, "he will need the very best this country affords," and that statement had come to mean a good deal to him. He had never really thought about it before, in just that way.

"That's just what I figure," he had said. "Right now I'm thinking of Harvard, thinking of Yale. Boy has a mind of his own, but I guess his father can think of these things."

"Yes, indeedy," this woman had said, which was a favorite expression of hers, and a sign that maybe she ought to get back to work.

He went without dessert at the Gold Coast Café in order to stop for a bite at Thompson's, where the coffee was good and there was a wider range of pie. The chimes would ring when he pulled his check from the checking machine. Mrs. Beach, the cashier, would smile at him, and if she was not too busy counting change, she would swing her chair around so they could talk while he had a bite to eat.

"And how is *our* boy?" Mrs. Beach would say, as she was a mother with four boys of her own, so there was nothing you needed to tell her about boys. When a picture of the boy had stuck to one of his bills—he carried it in the wallet along with his money—Mrs. Beach had insisted on knowing who this fine-looking boy was. Luckily, it was not the picture of the boy without his clothes. It was just his head, showing his mother's wavy black hair.

"Boy takes after his mother," Will Brady would say, and to that Mrs. Beach always answered:

"She must have been a very lovely girl—she certainly was that."

"Out of this world," Will Brady would say, and turn to blow on his hot cup of coffee. He would sip it, then add: "Died no sooner than the boy was born."

"You don't mean to say," Mrs. Beach would reply, "that that boy of yours has never had a mother?"

"Just me and the kid," Will Brady would say, and blow on his cup.

"Why, I just think you've done wonders, Mr. Brady," and it was clear that Mrs. Beach did. She couldn't imagine a boy without a mother like herself. "I just wish," she would sometimes say, "that she could come back for just an hour, just be with us for an hour, to see what a wonderful father you have been to him."

When she got around to that, Will Brady would turn to his pie. It was hard for him to straighten out the many things he thought. Rather than get into all of that, which might require quite an explanation, he would go back to the counter for another cup of coffee, drink it standing up. There were things that a mother like Mrs. Beach might find it hard to understand.

From Thompson's he went on down to Chicago, and some nights, there at the end of the street, he found the drawbridge rising on the sky, like a wall. The guard bell would be clanging, and the red lights blinking at the top of the span. In the bridge tower room, on warm summer nights, the man in the tower might lean out the window, the visor shadow on his face, and his shirtsleeves rolled on his thin white arms. He liked to spit in the street, and use a tenpenny nail to tamp down his pipe.

If the span was up, Will Brady would stop in LaMonica's Lunch. At that time in the evening Mrs. LaMonica would be cleaning up. On a sultry summer night she might be out in front, sitting there on a chair with her little girl Sophie, or in the back of the store cooking up tomorrow's hamburgers. She left the front door open as the back of the store would get pretty hot.

When he asked for coffee, Mr. LaMonica would say: "What the hell'd we do without a hot cup of Java?" and Will Brady, for the life of him, never seemed to know. It seemed a simple question, but he never had an answer to it. Into his own cup of Java he would pour some of the cream from the milk can on the counter, a small can with two holes punched in the top, and the picture of a cow on the side. But Mrs. LaMonica, who had never seen a cow, liked her coffee black.

"When you know what I know," Mrs. LaMonica would say, rolling her eyes to think about it, "when you know what I know, you drink your coffee black." No doubt she knew a good deal, but it was never clear what she had against cows. She had never seen one. Perhaps that was it.

But she had often lain awake at night and heard the moos they made going by in the trucks, and she smelled the empty trucks the next morning, on their way back. It was enough, anyhow, to make her drink her coffee black.

"Maybe a new prideswinna?" Mrs. LaMonica would say, and all because Will Brady, having nothing else to do, happened to mention that the boy had won a prize.

"Oh, nothing much," Will Brady had said, and showed Mrs. LaMonica the picture of the boy that had appeared in the *Omaha Bee*. The name was clear, but his face didn't come out very well. "*Tech student writes prizewinning letter,*" it read. "You would think," he said to Mrs. La-Monica, "that a boy who can write prizewinning letters would find the time to write a few more of them to his dad."

"They're all of them no goddam good," Mr. LaMonica said. He stopped frying hamburgers to say: "You start out all alone, and that's how you end up. You live long enough and bygod you're right back where you start up from."

"They're a comfort at the breast," Mrs. LaMonica said.

"A lotta good that does a man," Mr. LaMonica said, and slapped himself on the chest. "A hell of a lotta good!"

"A prideswinna is a comfort!" she had said, and there was no use in arguing the matter. Mr. LaMonica had tried. It was better to fry hamburgers.

"Well, I better get to work," Will Brady would say, "or I'll never get him to college."

"Oh, Mike!" Mrs. LaMonica would say. "Collitch—you hear?"

"If you and I were college men," Will Brady would say, when Mr. LaMonica turned to admire him, "we wouldn't be here. No sir, we'd be over on the Gold Coast."

"Now bygod you're right," Mr. LaMonica would say, and look to the east, where it was said to be.

Will Brady would take a toothpick from the bowl and say: "If the kid's going to do better than his dad, he's going to need the best this country affords. He's going to need the finest education money can buy."

"You hear that, Mike?" Mrs. LaMonica would say, but before Mike would answer Will Brady would get up, drop his nickel on the counter, and walk out into the street. Talk like that always made him excited, and he would be out on the bridge, over the water, looking down at scum, wide and green as a meadow, before he knew where he was. But the sight of all of that, and the smell of it, would cool him down. Something about that smell was like a good whiff of salts, the way it cleared his mind. But like the salts, it left him a little wobbly, walking along with his head in the air, and he usually tripped as he crossed the tracks in the cinder-covered yard. It would remind him to put away the letter, or the snapshot, that he still held in his hand.

3

If the old man who sorted waybills in the freight yards felt himself more alive there than anywhere else, it had something to do with the tower room where he worked. On one side of the room was a large bay window that faced the east. A man standing at this window—like the man on the canal who let the drawbridge up and down—felt himself in charge of the flow of traffic, of the city itself. All that he saw seemed to be in his province, under his control. He stood above the sprawling freight yards, the sluggish canal, the three or four bridges that sometimes crossed it, and he could look beyond all of these things, beyond the city itself, toward the lake. He couldn't see this lake, of course, but he knew that it was there. And when the window stood open he thought he could detect the smell of it.

Between Will Brady and this lake were thousands of people, what one might call a city in itself; people lived there, that is, without the need of living anywhere else. They were born there, and sooner or later they died. Mrs. LaMonica had lived there for forty-eight years, hating all cows and loving pagan lovers, nor had she ever found it necessary to go anywhere else. It was only necessary to have the money and to pay the price.

The bay window in the tower room was a frame around this picture. It hung there on the wall. The man in the room could stand there, at his leisure, and examine it. He would come to know, after a time, just what bulbs were out in which electric signs, and how the shadow of the bridge, like a cloud, moved up and down the street. If he was more alive there than anywhere else—if he seemed to come to life when he faced this picture—it had something to do with the fact that he was cut off from it. Which was a very strange thing, since what the tower room made him feel was part of it.

During the long day there were trains in the yard, and a great coming and going over the bridges; whistles were blown, and the tower room trembled when a train went past. But at night this old man, Will Brady, was alone in it. When the drawbridge went up he was on an island, cut off from the shore. Without carrying things too far it might be said that this tower was the old man's castle, that the canal was his moat, and that at night he defended it against the world. That is to say, that he felt himself the last man in the world. He was back—sometimes he felt that he was back—where he had started from.

In the windows along the canal the blinds were usually drawn, and behind the blinds, when the lights came on, he could see the people in the rooms moving around. Nearly all of them ate at the back of the house, then moved to the front. There they would talk, or sit and play cards, or wander about from room to room until it was time, as the saying goes, to go to bed. Then the front lights would go off, other lights come on. A woman would stand facing the mirror, and a man, scratching himself, would sit on the edge of a sagging bed, holding one shoe. Peering into it as if his foot was still there. Or letting it fall so that it was heard in the room below.

In all of this there was nothing unusual—every night it happened everywhere—except that the people in these rooms were not alone. The old man in the tower, the way-bills in his hand, was there with them. He had his meals with them in the back, wandered with all of them to the front, listened to the talk, and then saw by his watch what time it was. With them all he made his way through the house to bed. He sat there on the edge, looking at his feet or the hole in the rug.

It seemed to Will Brady that he knew these people, that he had lived in these rooms behind the windows, and that he could walk about in the dark as if the house was his own. The life and habits of the house were not strange to him. No stranger, you might say, than that house down the tracks in Calloway, where a man named Schultz was said to have lived with a city girl. To have lost her, that was the gist of it. Quite a bit like what another old man, Will Brady, had done himself. As so many men seem to do—to have won, that is, and lost something—and to end up sitting at the edge of a bed, holding one shoe. Or to lie awake until the shoe upstairs has dropped.

From the tower room Will Brady could see all these people at their work, what they called their play, and the hours that they spent at what they called their sleep. Lying

sprawled on wrinkled sheets on hot summer nights. Thinking. What else was it that charged the night air? That gave
it that hum, that flinty smell like the sand crushed under the
car wheels, until he felt that the lid to the city was about to
blow off. And that the city itself, with a puff of sound,
would disappear.

And then there were times—there were times toward
morning when the city itself was as real as a picture, but the
people who had lived in the city all seemed to be gone.
Every man, woman, and child had disappeared. The lights
still burned, the curtains still moved in the draft at the
bedroom windows, and here and there, like a young cock
crowing, an alarm went off. But there was something or
other missing from the damp night air. The smell of man—
as Will Brady could tell you—was gone from it.

What had happened? It seemed that the inhabitants had
up and fled during the night. As if a new Pied Piper, or
some such wonder, had passed in the street. Hearing this
sound, they had rolled out of bed, or raised on one elbow as
if the siren, the voice of the city, had leaned in the window
and spoken to them. Beckoned, whispered to them, that the
time had come. Nor were they surprised, as every man
knew that it would. So they had risen, soundlessly, and gone
into the streets.

Still there on the floor were their socks and shoes, on the
bedpost their ties, on the chair their pants, and on the
dresser, still ticking, the watches they could do without.
Time—that kind of time—they could now do without.
They had marched off in the manner of sleepwalkers—and
perhaps they were. They had moved in a procession, with
the strong helping the weak, the old the younger, and what
they saw—or thought they saw—out on the water, cast a
spell over them. Perhaps it had been the bright lights on a
steamer, or the white flash of a sail. But whatever it was,

whether true or false, whether in their minds' eye or far out on the water, they had followed this Piper, followed him into the water, and disappeared. They had waded through the cool morning sand still littered with cigarettes, pop bottles, and rubbish, and without hesitation, like sea creatures, they disappeared. Nor was there any sound, none but the water lapping their feet.

So it was with those who had the faith; but there were others, even thousands of them, who wanted to leave, but they wanted to take the world along. They had brought along with them everything they would leave behind: magazines and newspapers, chewing gum and tobacco, radios and phonographs, small tins of aspirin, laxative chocolate, and rubber exercisers to strengthen the grip. Decks of playing cards, and devices to promote birth control. They had brought these things along, but the water would not put up with them. As they entered, it washed them back upon the sand. There it all lay, body and booty, like the wreckage of the world they had been departing, as if a great flood had washed it down to the sea ahead of them. In the pale morning light their bodies looked blue, as if they had been long dead, though living, and a child walked among them spreading sheets of newspaper over each face. As if that much, but no more, could be done for them. How live in this world? They simply hadn't figured it out. Nor how to leave it and go to live in another one.

Sunday morning Will Brady would walk through these streets, marveling at the empty houses, and gaze at the lake where the faithful had disappeared. He was not one of them, but it was a thing he could understand. He had his own way for departing one world, entering another one.

On these Sunday mornings he wore his Florsheim shoes, his Stetson hat with the sewn brim, and both the pants and coat to his Hart Schaffner & Marx suit. He did not walk in the sand, but in the grass at the edge of the bridle path. The Stetson hat, level on his head, he would tip to the ladies on the well-bred horses, their long tails braided, and a sudsy white lather between their hams. The ladies in turn would tip their heads, or lift their leather riding crops in a friendly gesture, as any man out for a walk, at that time in the morning, was one of themselves. One who preferred to walk rather than ride, but who was up like them to breathe the morning air before three million other people were breathing it. A thing reserved, by and large, for successful men. Men who hadn't the time, during the busy week, to idle and play like normal people, but who could make the time early Sunday morning, while normal people slept. Most of these men liked to ride, but there were others, like Will Brady, who were known to walk.

Both these men and women came down from the north, in the big cars with the very small seats, or they lived in the apartments overlooking the lake, along the Gold Coast. In these windows the blinds were always drawn against the morning sun. Uniformed men stood at the doors to these apartments, as they did before the fancy theater lobbies, but a man with Florsheim shoes, and the pants to go with them, could walk past. A man who knew when to à-la-carte, when to table-d'hôte. Such a man could walk into these lobbies, seat himself in a chair, examine the potted plants, or step to the desk and ask to speak to Mr. So-and-so. Will Brady usually inquired if a certain Will Jennings Brady was there. A big egg man from Texas, friendly, rather elderly. So he would take a comfy seat in the lobby while the bell-hop, or the secretary, or the manager himself would see that this matter was looked into. When he wore his Stetson hat, his soft leather gloves, and the hair combed back from his high forehead, quite a fuss might be made as to who this

Will Jennings Brady might be. He would be paged in the lobby, and his name would stop the music in the dining-room. Words would be exchanged between himself and the management. Important gray-haired men, with their young wives, or perhaps it was their lovely flaxen-haired daughters, would pass in front of him with their thoroughbred dogs on a leash. Some of these dogs would stop and sniff at Will Brady's feet. They knew, these dogs, but they said nothing. Between the old man and the dogs there was quite an understanding, and they both needed it.

Sometimes Will Brady's fine voice would be heard in the lobby, also his laugh, perhaps a little strained, and that habit he had, when laughing, of cuffing himself on the knee, as if nailing that leg to the floor. Quite a performance, when you consider who this old man was. An old fool with one suit of underwear to his name. Just one pair of pants that he could cross at the knee like that. Naturally, Will Jennings Brady was never on hand, but one day an Ivy Brady, from South Carolina, spoke to him over the house phone and asked him to come right up. Hell, a Brady is a Brady, Ivy Brady said. But Will Brady asked to be excused as he had, he said, an important engagement with a big out-of-town man in the Loop.

But all of this took time—the sitting and the waiting, the patting of other people's dogs in strange lobbies, and the reading of papers left on the bench along the walk. The morning traffic would flow toward the city from the north, white sails would appear on the lake, and in the park life would begin all over again. Candy and peanuts were sold, men would roll the sleeves on white arms, put away for the winter, and women would sit fanning the flies away from baskets of food. Games would be played, young men would run and fall, others would stand in a row behind chicken-wire fences, and others would run toward Will Brady himself, waving him away. Crying that he should look up, or down, asking if he had eyes in his head. So he would make his way north, careful to avoid the deceptive clearing, where the unseen might be falling, or the games of young men who would suddenly turn and chase him away. The papers he found here and there he carried under his arm. It gave him the feeling that along with other people there was something in the park for him to do; also, he could sit on them in some places, in others he could read. It seemed to be the thing to do while waiting for the zoo to open up.

Later he would find himself a seat facing the strange big birds, or the melancholy bears, with an elderly man, about his own age, seated on his right. Not on his left, as that side of his face didn't feel right. There was an opening there that talking wouldn't fill up. He would take this seat, sighing, then say: "Kid writes me that there's bear where he is in the woods. Hardly a day, I guess, he doesn't stumble on a bear of some kind."

"You don't say!" That was what this man at his side would say. If he didn't, Will Brady would get up, sighing again, and try another bench. Sooner or later he would find a man who knew what was what.

"Only thing that worries me," Will Brady would go on, "is how a kid like that, a boy who loves nature, is going to like it in some place like Harvard or Yale. How he's going to like it in some quiet place like that."

It might surprise you how many men knew all about Harvard and Yale. Had a definite opinion, one way or another, on a subject like that. Had a boy there themselves, or a friend, or the son of a friend, or a brother, or some member of the family who had passed through there, going somewhere else. Who had seen it anyhow and knew what it was like. Nine out of ten men, you might say, seemed to have given either Harvard or Yale, or both of them together, more thought than Will Brady managed to. Their opinions, anyhow, were stronger than his own. They were either all for Harvard, without a quibble, or all for Yale. None of these men had been to college themselves—being tied up at the time with something or other—but they seemed to have a clear idea what they were talking about. They were glad to advise a man who hadn't quite made up his mind. Who had a boy who wasn't tangled up, as yet, with some damn girl. The general consensus seemed to be, in so far as Will Brady could order the matter, that great scholars went to Harvard and great athletes went to Yale. Albie Booth, for instance, he was going to Yale right now. But what about a boy who was showing signs of being both of them, an athlete and a great letter-writer at the same time? The first in his class, if it hadn't been for five or six girls. The place for a boy like that, one man told him in a confidential manner, was neither Harvard nor was it a place like Yale. It was Princeton, a place he had seen himself. He was a big man, with a beard, reduced to selling flags on pins for a living, but who nevertheless spoke with authority. As a boy he had passed—and he remembered it well— within a few miles of the place.

But it all took time—the life of the mind seemed to take as much time as a real one—and it would be midafternoon and the air would be hot when he started for the house. He would carry his coat folded over his arm and walk in the grass. His collar would be open and the Stetson hat pushed back on his head. Wherever tennis was being played he would sometimes stop and watch it, as the boy was said to be a coming tennis man. It helped him to see with his own eyes what the boy was. If one of the white balls came his way he would stop it, pounce on it, then hurry to where he could toss it to the players underhand. He had never learned to throw anything the other way. Tossing the ball, he would say: "I've got a boy who plays for Harvard," and then he might stand, if they would let him, close to the net. Some of them played very well, but it was clear that they were no match for the boy.

Sunday afternoons snails were sold on Menomonee Street. They were sold by a man who drove a small wagon, wearing on his own head nothing at all, but with three, sometimes four straw hats on the head of his horse. This was to make, as he said himself, the children laugh. He was a sad man and never laughed himself. He kept the snails in large tubs of water, and when he counted them into the bags, they made a sound like lead coins dropped on a slab. It was hard to tell the good snails from the bad. Most of them were bought by Nino Scarlatti, a boy with wild eyes and a curling harelip, and by Manny Plinski, who stood there with his money in his mouth. He would keep it there until he held the snails in his own hand.

After eating the snails, Manny Plinski liked to put the empty shells back in the bag, twist it at the top, and then make a fool out of somebody. That was always Will Brady, who would buy it for five cents. He would make himself a fool at the foot of the stairs, where the whole world could see him, and Manny Plinski would cry like a bird for his mother to come and look. So Mrs. Plinski would come, leaning over the railing, and Will Brady would stand there, a smile on his face, and with the nickel Manny Plinski would buy himself another bag of snails. "Oh, how he will love you!" Mrs. Plinski would say, and wag her big head.

On a hot summer day a big woman like that would not have much on. She would be in her bathrobe, or maybe her slip, with a damp towel thrown around her big shoulders, and she might have to stand there with her bosom gathered in her arms. In the winter she would be in the bone corset that made her arms stand out, as if she was crowing, and made it hard for her to scratch her back, pick her teeth, or get a comb into her hair. And in the corset she would always stand up rather than risk sitting down. She would stand between the folding doors, as if propped there, with her arms half raised.

"A new letter?" she would say. "A new winner?" And the old man there in the room, with his elbows on the table, would hold up the sheet of paper that he held in one hand. New? Well, hardly—the pages were torn at the folds. The light came through where bacon grease had been dropped on it.

"I was just wondering," the old man would go on, "what a boy like that"—he would wave the letter—"what a boy like that is going to do in a place like Harvard, or Yale?"

"Oh, how he will love you!" she would say, which it was hard, offhand, to picture the boy doing. But Mrs. Plinski was like that. A big, friendly woman who knew how it was.

4

In the papers that he found in the park on Sunday mornings, Will Brady always read the want ads, as a man who wasn't quite sure what it was he wanted might find it there. Perhaps somebody, some man or woman, was looking for him. Perhaps a man like Insull had a position for him to fill. Perhaps—anyhow, Will Brady read the ads. And one Sunday morning—a cool November morning—he came on something that made him chuckle, made him put down the paper, rub his eyes with his knuckles, and wag his head. He looked around for someone to share it with, but he was

alone on the bench. "Well, well," he said aloud, as he did
with Mrs. Plinski; then he read it again.

MAN WANTED FOR SANTA CLAUS

Now, that made him smile—he could feel the tightness at
the corners of his mouth. It was enough to make him
wonder, an ad like that—but he tore it out. He slipped it in
with the letter and the photographs he had from the boy.
Having it there in his pocket, as well as on his mind, he
naturally showed it to Mrs. Plinski, asking her if she knew
where they might dig up a good Santa Claus. Where
Montgomery Ward—for that was who it was—could lay
their hands on a man like that: a man big enough, fat
enough, and of course out of this world. And then, just by
way of a joke, asking her what she thought of a man like
himself—a man like himself, that is, as Santa Claus. But this
woman would surprise you. This woman didn't think it was
a joke at all.

"How they will love you!" was all she said, as she seemed
to have the idea that something like that was all you needed
for a Santa Claus. It didn't seem to cross her mind that his
cheeks, for one thing, weren't rosy enough.

As he had that ad right there in his pocket, he also
showed it to Bessie Muller, asking her if she thought he was
jolly enough for a Santa Claus. As a joke, of course, but she
didn't take it that way.

"Why, you'd make a honey of a Santa Claus, pop." That
was what she said.

"I don't know as I'm plump enough," he said.

"Oh, they put a pillow in you," said Bessie Muller,
"you'd be all right. You'd make a honey of a Santa Claus."

Mildred Weigall thought the same thing. He didn't even

show her the ad, he just happened to say that the one thing he missed, around Christmas time, was the right kind of Santa Claus. One that was, so to speak, really fond of the kids. Mildred Weigall had interrupted to say that she had known of kids, friends of hers, who had been pinched while they were sitting on the lap of Santa Claus. By the old bastard himself. That was what she said.

"If you don't like kids—" Will Brady had begun.

"You'd make a good Santa Claus," she had said. "What they need is a man like yourself for Santa Claus."

Mrs. Beach said, holding the want ad close to her face, as she was nearsighted: "Why, Mr. Brady, all you need is just a touch of color on your cheeks." Then she looked at him as if she was the person to put it there. When Mr. Beach was alive, she went on, there was not a single Christmas that passed, in those happy days, that Mr. Beach himself wasn't Santa Claus. A big man—perhaps a little too big—he was especially good with other people's children, his own, of course, knowing him just too well.

He had been turning it over, Will Brady said, just turning it over in his mind, that he might at least stop by and look into it. He was alone pretty much, and it would give him something to do. It would at least be better than being alone at Christmas time.

"I think you'll find," Mrs. Beach said, "that they don't pay much."

"I just thought I'd ask," Will Brady said, and then put some toothpicks in his vest before going on to say that the pay wasn't what he had in mind. He had a job. The pay wasn't so important to him. "I just thought I'd inquire," he said, as, if the honest truth were known, it hadn't crossed his mind that a man would be paid for something like that. Was it possible they paid a man to be Santa Claus? Perhaps it was. It seemed that anything was possible. His first thought had been that he would have to pay for that himself.

"It just so happens," Will Brady said, "that I'm more or less alone at Christmas."

"I can understand that," Mrs. Beach replied, as her own children were gone and seldom came around, as they all had children of their own. Nor was there any chance of her, plump as she was, pretending she was Santa Claus. She was simply not the type—whatever that might be.

The retail store of Montgomery Ward & Co., where they were looking for a Santa Claus, was right where the draw-bridge crossed the sewage canal. So it was not any trouble for Will Brady to just stop by, as he said. To inquire what it was they had in mind for a Santa Claus. But as he entered the store the main aisle was obstructed by ten or twelve people, gathered in an arc, facing a corner with a well-lighted display. There was a comfortable chair, of the re-clining type, several lamps with large aluminum shades, and a young man with taffy-colored hair and a deeply tanned face. He wore a clean white jacket of the type Will Brady had seen on dentists and doctors, and held in his tanned right hand a long wand. With this wand, as he talked, he pointed at the statements on a large poster, which included a detailed, cut-away picture of one of the lamps. The name of the lamp was Nu-Vita, which meant new life.

The voice of the young man was pleasant, and he had that healthy outdoor look that city people, like Will Brady him-self, liked to gaze upon. It might be that Will Brady was reminded of his son. Not that there was any particular resemblance—this boy was older, larger, and blond—but Will Brady saw the boy whenever he saw the outdoor type. The athlete who still wore his study glasses, so to speak. As

the young man talked, in his persuasive voice, Will Brady
read the statements on the poster and discovered that the
lamp he saw on the platform was a marvelous thing, a lamp
that trapped the sun, so to speak. That gave off the same life-
giving rays of light. These rays gave plants the color of
green, and man the life-giving coat of tan. The city dweller,
the young man was saying, lived little better than the life of
a mole, but science had now discovered how to bring the
sun right into his room. Right into his attic, if that was
where he lived. With this wonderful lamp he could sit at
home—reading a book, or just resting with his clothes off—
and absorb the mysterious life-giving rays of the sun. Without the sun there would be nothing on earth—nothing but
cold rocks and fishless seas. But with the sun there was light,
plants, and creatures like themselves. And with this lamp a
man could have the sun with him anywhere.

Perhaps it was the sun-tanned face of the young man—
the very picture of life, if Will Brady had ever seen it—that
led the old man in the aisle to gaze at him in a certain way.
Perhaps it was this gaze, somehow, that attracted the young
man. Whatever it was, he suddenly stopped talking, turned
the wand he was holding from the poster, and pointed it
over the heads of those who stood at the front. Pointed it,
that is, at Will Brady himself.

"Will the gentleman," the young man said, "be so kind as
to please step forward? Will the gentleman allow me, without cost or the slightest obligation, to demonstrate?"

It would be wrong to say that Will Brady followed all of
this. He saw the pointer, he heard the young man's voice, he
felt the eyes of those assembled upon him, and when those
at the front made way, why, he stepped to the front. He
took a seat in the reclining chair that was prepared for him.
A white bib, like a barber's cloth, was placed upon his front.
Then his head was raised—through it all he heard the clear,

225

calm voice of the attendant—and a pair of dark glasses was placed over his eyes, tied at the back. For a moment he saw all before him darkly, as if submerged in muddy water; then he was tipped back, and as his head went down, his feet went up. Over his head appeared the wide shade, he watched the adjustment of the black carbons, heard the hum of the current, then the crackling as the flame leaped the arc. A burning smell, perhaps the breath of life itself, made him wrinkle his nose.

"If the gentleman will kindly lid his eyes," said the voice, and as the crackling spread into a glow, Will Brady felt himself in a warm, colorless bath of light. The odor of the carbon was strong in his nose, and the flavor in his mouth. But he felt no fear; in the words of the voice, now disembodied, that he heard above him, he felt himself "cleansed of pollutions and invigorated from head to toe." The life-giving rays, as the voice went on to say, were mingling with his blood.

He felt suspended—out of this world, as he described it to Bessie Muller—and then, just as he was reborn, the power went off. For a moment he felt that his own worldly system had come to a stop. He made as if to rise, he gasped for air, but the young man's firm hand pressed him back, removed the white cloth, and then slipped the glasses from his head. As he sat up, blinking, the young man said: "You will notice the healthy touch of color that the life-giving rays have given to the gentleman's face."

And so they did, as he saw them nodding, their eyes filled with wonder, as they gazed on what it had done to him. For himself, he could feel the tightness in his cheeks. "That was but a moment," the young man was saying. "If the gentleman could spare me more of his time—just a few moments a day—he would soon be as sun-tanned as myself." So saying, he rolled up his sleeve, showed the brown arm. He smiled, showing in his dark face the firm white teeth. Then he assisted Will Brady to his feet, putting into his right hand, as he did so, a wide selection of charts concerned with what the Nu-Vita would do for him. It could also be purchased, as he pointed out, on the easy-payment plan. His own brown hand on Will Brady's shoulder, he called everyone's attention to his fine, healthy look, and asked him, when he found the time, to drop by again. A few more treatments, as he said, and he wouldn't recognize himself.

In this rejuvenated condition Will Brady found himself in the aisle, and he wandered about, from counter to counter, for some time. He seemed to have forgotten why he had entered the store. He stopped to gaze, wherever it was reflected, at his own new face. It was different. There was no doubt about that. Around the eyes he was whiter, but the warm cheeks were pink. Rosy? Well, there was even a touch of that. His own yellow teeth seemed to look whiter when he smiled. In this condition he sought out the man at the back of the store—a Mr. Nash—and inquired of him what they had in mind for Santa Claus. Mr. Nash, looking at him soberly, begged him to have a seat.

What they had in mind, Mr. Nash said, speaking to him very frankly, was no monkey business. They had to be sure of that. While he was on the job he had to be Santa Claus, nobody else. Having said this, Mr. Nash looked at him, and what he saw in the new pink face before him seemed to be what he wanted, seemed to be a Santa Claus that he could trust. One that he could turn over, as he said, their reputation to. He had on file other applications, but if Will Brady wanted the job he would take him upstairs and show him the setup, give him the suit. All that he would have to dig up himself was a kid to blow the balloons.

"To blow what?" Will Brady said.

He would need a kid to blow the balloons. He would give

away balloons, but he would need some kid to blow them up. The kid sat under the throne, under the seat, that is, where Santa Claus would be sitting, and after blowing up the balloon he would pass it between his legs. That was how they did it. He would have to find the kid to do that himself.

Will Brady said that he would think it over—if he could find the right boy, he would surely think it over—and on his way through the store he passed a new crowd of people around the sun lamp. The young man with the pointer, seeing him pass, waved the wand at him.

"There goes a satisfied user, right there," he said, "it has made that gentleman look years younger," and everyone in the crowd, half the people in the aisle, turned to look at him. He smiled, he felt the strain of trying to throw his shoulders back. He reached the street, he crossed the bridge, he made his way through the freight yards and into the tower room, before he noticed that he still held the literature in his hand.

"Plug in at home or office," it said, and he read that the small model in question, meant to sit on a table, could be had for just four dollars a month.

On the first Monday in December, following another successful free trial, Will Brady purchased a desk-model sun lamp, carrying it along with him, in its carton, as he left the store. The warm glow of the lamp, in the crisp night air, was still there on his face. Mrs. Plinski had remarked the new look to his face, which she thought was due to the brisk fall weather, and after thinking it over he decided to let it go at that. Woman that she was, she might find it hard to understand something like the Nu-Vita, a marvel that brought the sun, so to speak, right into the house. And along with it the crackling sound, and the crisp frying smell. As he could plug it in either at home or at the office, he decided on the office as he could be alone, day or night, in the tower room. He could give himself a treatment, as it was called, any time that he got around to it, which turned out to be two or three times a night. Once when he arrived, as a rule, and then again when he left. He would clear one corner of the table of waybills, take off his vest, his tie, and his shirt, then open his underwear so that some of the rays fell on his chest. The only problem he faced was in keeping the time, as it passed very fast. Five to seven minutes were supposed to be enough. But seated there in the glow, like a warm bath, it was hard to keep from dozing off, or thinking thoughts that he could time or bring to a stop. With the dark glasses on he found it hard to read his watch. So he may have slipped over now and then, but not that it mattered, as he had only five days to prepare himself as Santa Claus.

As Santa Claus he wore a red cotton flannel suit, loose in the seat and very long in the arms, a pair of black rubber boots, and a soiled, strong-smelling beard. He sat on a throne, which in turn was on a platform, between two large cardboard reindeer, one of them with electric eyes that sparked on and off. At the back of the throne was the room where he dressed, hung up his clothes, and walked out on the fire escape, now and then, for a breath of fresh air. Under the throne was Manny Plinski, seated on a stool. In his lap he held a large bag of Christmas balloons, and at his side, in a glass jar, the baby turtles he had brought along to keep him company.

When Santa Claus wanted a balloon he would tap with his heel on the throne, and Manny Plinski would blow one up and pass it to him. Sometimes, however, he handed Santa Claus a baby turtle instead. As you can't risk passing out

live turtles to little city boys who had never seen one, Santa
Claus would have to slip these turtles into the pocket of his
coat. Toward the end of the day he might have more than
his pockets would hold. He would have to get up and take
out the sign reading:

MAKING DELIVERY
Santa Claus Back Soon

and go through the side door and speak to Manny Plinski,
personally. There were times when Manny Plinski was
ashamed and took it all right. There were other times when
he giggled, ran his hands like a rake through his yellow hair,
and passed up another turtle as soon as he laid his hands on
one. These times Santa Claus would have to rap his knuckles, or sprinkle him with some water from the empty turtle
jug on the floor. That sometimes did it; other times it didn't
work out too well. He would blow up balloons and sit there
popping them with his teeth.

Another thing that Manny Plinski liked to do was take
the brown tweed suit that belonged to Will Brady and fill
the pockets with turtles and balloons. He seemed to like the
brown suit better than he liked Santa Claus. He liked to take
the brown suit and go off alone somewhere and sit with it.
Santa Claus would have to stop and hunt him down, as he
couldn't blow balloons for himself, but this wasn't too
often, and Manny Plinski was never far. He was usually out
on the fire escape, just sitting there. He liked to watch the
trains shifting around in the freight yards, and the boats on
the canal. He would blow Christmas balloons, like bubbles,
and let them drift away.

Not that it seemed to matter, as there were plenty of
balloons, plenty of time to stop and look for him, and the
old man in the Santa Claus suit seemed to like his work. He
would have paid Montgomery Ward & Co. in order to

carry on with it. Out on the street an old man cannot hold hands with children, bounce them on his knee, or tell them lies that he will not be responsible for. Nor can he bend his head and let them whisper into his ear. Very much as if he, this old man, could do something for them. Very much as if he knew, like the children before him, that there was only one man in this world—one man still living—who was prepared to do certain things. To live in this world, so to speak, and yet somehow be out of it. To be himself without children, without friends or relations, without a woman of his own or a past or a future, and yet to be mortal, and immortal, at the same time. Only one man in the world could answer an ad worded like that. Only one man, that is, and get away with it. For in the world it is evil for an old man to act like that. There is a law against it—unless the old man is Santa Claus. But for this old man these things are all right, they are recognized to be the things that count; and the children, as they do in such cases, all believe in him. Some men will put up with a good deal, from certain quarters, for a job like that.

"Oh, how they will love you!" Mrs. Plinski said, and every day his cheeks seemed a little redder, his smile a little brighter, and the face in the mirror no longer his own. It had become, it seemed to him, the face of Santa Claus. Only the eyes, with the white circles around them, were still his own. They were there because of the goggles, and the darker his face seemed to get, the redder his cheeks, the more pale and sallow his eyes. So he began to move the goggles up and down, first to one side, then to the other, and one evening he tried it without the goggles for a little bit. It wouldn't matter, he felt sure, if he kept his eyes closed. Nothing came of that, so the next evening he tried it a little longer, and was pleased to find that the white circles were getting pink. They began to blend in, a little more, with the rest of his face. So he tried it again, this time a little longer, as it was past the middle of December, and Santa Claus had before him only one more week.

That was the morning of December 19, but it was late in the afternoon, the daylight gone, before his eyes began to smart. They watered a little, and the lids were red when he looked at them. He had to buy a handkerchief in the store and keep dabbing at his eyes when he stopped for supper, and he noticed that the boy, Manny Plinski, kept staring at him. Sometimes he would whimper as if he wasn't feeling good. In the evening the lights seemed to make it worse, and he had to stop, every half hour or so, to step back behind the curtain where it was dark and press the lids shut. When he did that, he found it hard to open them. The salty liquid that kept running seemed to make them stick. Something in the lids seemed to draw them closed, so that he had to stare to hold them open, but all the time, without letup, the tears ran down his face. Around his red, peeling nose the skin was very tender, smarting when he wiped his cheeks, and he thought he detected in the handkerchief the burned-carbon smell. As if the rays that had soaked into him were now sweating out.

Later he put up the sign; he found it hard to recognize the little boys from the girls, and to open his eyes he had to use his fingers, separate the lids. The inside of the lids was bright red, like the gills of a fish. When he removed his fingers, the lower lids would roll up, as a curtain rolls. Nothing he could do, even with his fingers, would put a stop to this. For air, for fresh cool air, as that in the room seemed to blow hot on his eyeballs, he walked to the back and opened the door to the fire escape. It was snowing a little, and the sharp, cold pricks felt good on his face. He opened the door and stepped out on the landing, facing the freight yards, the sluggish canal, and the blinking traffic that passed on Halsted Street. The water in the canal looked like pig iron poured out to cool. Rising from the water, like a dark-red planet, was the lantern on the drawbridge, and beyond the arc of the bridge he could see the tower room. The light was on. He had probably forgotten it. Beyond the bridge, and the sluggish water, were the smoke and steel of the freight yards, where a brakeman, waving his lantern, walked along the cars. Beyond this, as if a fire was raging, there was a bright glow over the street, and from these flames there arose, along with the din, a penetrating smell. The old man let his eyes close, as this was not something he needed to see. He could breathe it, like the carbon, he could taste it on his lips. It was like the grating sound of steel, a blend of the sour air and the track sound, of the gas from the traffic, and the sweetish smell of powdered Christmas balloons. All of the juices of the city were there on the fire, and brought to a boil. All the damp air of the chill rooms that were empty, the warm soiled air of the rooms that were lived in, blown to him, so it seemed, by the bellows of hell. An acrid stench, an odor so bad that it discolored paint, corroded metal, and shortened the life of every living thing that breathed it in. But the old man on the landing inhaled it deeply, like the breath of life. He leaned there on the railing, his eyes closed, but on his face the look of a man with a vision—a holy man, one might even say, as he was feeding the birds. But when the lantern dropped down, and the traffic flowed again, he did a strange thing. He went down the turning stairs toward the water, toward the great stench as if he would grasp it, make it his own, before it could blow away from him. Or as if he heard above the sound of the traffic, the trains in the yard, and the din of the city, the tune of that Piper—the same old Pied Piper—over the canal. The one that had drawn him, time and again, into the streets. So he went on down, groping a little, as he had no proper eyes for seeing, or for knowing that there was no landing over the canal. A rope swung there, the knotted end sweeping the water, heavy with ice.

There was no one on the stairs, nor any boat on the water, and only Manny Plinski, with a brown tweed coat, was there on the landing when they came to look for Santa Claus. In the pockets there were turtles and a postcard to his son that had not been mailed.

PART II

ON
THE
ROAD

MY
UNCLE
DUDLEY

From *My Uncle Dudley*

W HEN it was cold we walked around. When it was morning the pigeons came and looked but when nothing happened walked away. When it was warm we sat in the sun. Cars came down Sunset and when the light was red we could see the good-looking women inside. When it was hot the pigeons left the square. They made a great noise and spilled shadows everywhere, on my Uncle Dudley looking up at them. He looked off where they would come back just as they did. He waited till the last one came down, then he looked at me.

"You had enough milk and honey?" he said.

"I guess I've had enough," I said.

We got up and walked across the street. A boy selling papers held one out and my Uncle Dudley stopped to read. A fellow named Young had just won twenty-five thousand bucks. He'd swum all the way from Wrigley's island to a place right on the coast. There was a picture of him still covered with lard.

"You chew gum?" said Uncle Dudley.

"Sure," the boy said.

"Look what you've done," said Uncle Dudley, "look what you've done—ain't you ashamed?" We all looked at the fellow still covered with lard. Yesterday, it said, he hadn't a cent. Now he had twenty-five thousand bucks.

"Paper?" said the boy.

"No," Uncle Dudley said. We walked through the pigeons and crossed the square. We walked up Main Street past the City Hall. The hock shops were just putting out their signs—Buck Jones was at the Hippodrome. Uncle Dudley looked in a mirror on a door. When he was in shape he was like an avocado, when he wasn't he was like a pear. Now he was mostly like a pear. We walked on down to a corner in the sun. "If I could lay my own eggs—" said my Uncle Dudley very loud, "if I could lay my own eggs I'd like it here!"

"Ain't it the goddam truth," said a man. My Uncle Dudley looked at him. The man looked back and Uncle Dudley smiled and felt where he kept his cigars. Then the light changed and the man walked away.

We crossed to be on the shady side. A fellow with tattooed arms was making hot cakes in a window, a row of bacon sizzled on the side. On one arm he had a man and on the other arm a woman—where the woman was his arm was shaved. Except her head and other places women have hair. She was a red-headed woman and had two diamond rings.

A man chewing a toothpick stopped to look at her too. He took the toothpick out and pressed his face to the glass. Bubbles were showing in the dough and the smell of bacon came out in the street—the fellow turned the cakes and they were the tough kind. He stacked them on a plate and set them aside. He poured three more on the griddle and wiped his hands. Then he picked up the plate and walked to the end of the counter, unrolling his sleeves before he sat down. He buttoned the one on the red-headed woman and began to eat.

"If I could lay my own eggs—" said Uncle Dudley, and he looked at the man as if he could. But the one with the toothpick didn't seem to hear. He kept looking inside at the new cakes on the griddle. The fellow at the counter began to eat very fast.

We crossed back to the sunny side. Near the corner there was a crowd looking at a doughnut machine; a woman was working it and wearing rubber gloves. The doughnuts went by on little trays and she sugared them. When she got ahead of the machine she held up two cards—one said 2 FOR 5, the other one said GOOD FOR YOU. "A wonderful thing!" my Uncle Dudley said. The door was open and the woman looked at him. She put down the cards and leaned on the doughnut machine. "If I was a machine," went on Uncle Dudley, "if I was a doughnut or nickel machine—" He looked around and everybody looked at him. The man with the toothpick came in close and chewed on it. "If I could just lay my own—doughnuts," Uncle Dudley said.

"Ain't it the goddam truth," said the same man.

"Harry—" said Uncle Dudley, cuffing the man on the arm, "come have one on the Kid and me—a little farewell. We're leavin this wonderful land—this sunshine. We're goin home."

"Bygod," said the man, "I sure wish I was too." He was a tall man and used to wearing overalls. His thumbs kept feeling for the straps, scratching his chin.

"And now that we're leavin," said Uncle Dudley, "we never felt better in our life. We never felt better—did we, Kid?"

"Never!" I said.

"Mister—" said the man with the toothpick, "you sound like a Eastern man?"

"Right!" said Uncle Dudley. "Chicago's our home. . . ."

"Good old Chi?"

"Good old Chi!"

"I'm a Chicago man too," he said.

"My friend," said Uncle Dudley, "—that I knew."

"Not right in Chicago—more like Oak Park. Used to drive in Sundays to Lincoln Park—"

"Lincoln Park! Spring in Lincoln Park. No green in the world like Lincoln Park—boats on the lagoon—"

"Not on the lagoon—"

"Harry," said Uncle Dudley, "permit me—in my time—"

"Lived in Oak Park ten years—"

"Boats—" said Uncle Dudley, "on the old lagoon. No green in the world like the green in that park. And that's the green on the back of a bill. What I seen out here all that green's back there too."

"When you leavin, Mister?"

"Tomorrow," Uncle Dudley said. "Kid and I just now on our way to the *Times*. Put in a little ad—driving back, have big car. Too big for us, glad to share it with few friends. Share gas an oil—help us all some that way. Must be plenty men here like to get back to old Chi. Only trouble is Kid and I won't have room. How much room, Kid?" he said. "How much room we got?"

"Well—" I said.

"Not much—maybe two—three. Want it to be nice—southern route all the way. Be in New Orleans in time for Mardi Graw. Any you men been to the Mardi Graw?"

"Thought about goin," said the Oak Park man, "—one fall."

"The Mardi Graw," said Uncle Dudley, "is not in the fall."

"How much?" said a man.

"The Mardi Graw?"

"Good old Chi—"

"That—" said Uncle Dudley, "Kid and I'd like your opinion on. Kid and I think twenty-five—twenty-five do the trick. Not tryin to make any money. Just gas—gas an oil."

"What kinda car?"

"Big car—but easy on gas. Very easy on gas. What we been gettin, Kid—?"

"Eighteen and twenty," I said.

"Time I come out," said a man, "didn't get any more than ten. Goddam car was like a long leak on the road. We was 'fraid to get outa town . . ."

"Ring job—need the carbon out. When was it, Kid, we had the carbon out?"

"Last week," I said.

"Well—" said Uncle Dudley, "got to get on with that ad. Want to get out of town by noon. Since you men think twenty-five O.K.—twenty-five goes in the ad. First come first served. Too bad can't—"

"Twen-fife dolls?"

"To Chicago—all the way."

"Dee-troit?"

"Right next door. Fine town—right next door."

"Twen-fife dolls?" Uncle Dudley looked at him. He was a big man in a brand new suit. He stood very straight like it fit pretty tight.

"Detroit," said Uncle Dudley, "—maybe five dollars more."

"More?"

"More."

The big man looked at him. Then his mouth was open and his eyes half closed—he finished counting and looked out again. "Twen-fife dolls?"

"Chicago—" Uncle Dudley said. The big man smiled and reached down in his pants. It pulled the buttons open and he had to stop and button up, then reach down in his pants again. He had a small roll of brand new tens. He counted off three into Uncle Dudley's hand.

"Right negs door?" he said. Uncle Dudley nodded and smoothed the bills. They were so new they all made a frying sound.

"You can never tell," said my Uncle Dudley, "—bygod you can never tell." He was just talking to himself like no one was around. "Old as I am," he said, "I still can't tell." The big man took off his hat and grinned. Something made him blush and the color showed through his hair, it went clear back where his head started down again. "Glad to meet you, Harry," Uncle Dudley said. "My name's Osborn —Dudley Osborn."

"Hansen—" said Mr. Hansen, and put on his hat.

"You're a lucky man," said Uncle Dudley, "—a very lucky man." And he shook Mr. Hansen's hand and slapped his arm. Mr. Hansen was wearing a pin and it fell off. It said, Visit Minnesota—Land O' Lakes. Mr. Hansen had more in his pocket and he gave me one, Uncle Dudley one. The man from Oak Park wanted one but Mr. Hansen just looked back. Uncle Dudley took out his fountain pen and one of his T. Dudley Osborn cards and we all moved back so he could write on the glass. He put the card right where the woman was looking out. Under Dudley Osborn he wrote Biltmore Hotel, and on the back Mr. Hansen's receipt. "And now," said Uncle Dudley, "—twenty-five from thirty, right?"

"—negs door," Mr. Hansen said.

"Hmmm—" said Uncle Dudley, and walked in by the doughnut machine. He bought a half dozen doughnuts just plain and then three with the powdered sugar; the woman got red and put on more sugar than she should. Then he bought two White Owls and came outside with the change. Mr. Hansen took off his hat and put it on again. "Well—"

said Uncle Dudley, handing him five, "come by early—
want to get away early." Mr. Hansen gave me another
button and patted my head. "Well—" said Uncle Dudley.
Mr. Hansen grinned and walked away. Uncle Dudley didn't
wait to see where but turned, and we walked away too. We
stopped once and looked at shoes, once we looked at boys'
hats. We stopped once where a movie was showing and
looked at the signs. We crossed the street and then we
stopped and looked back. Uncle Dudley stood on the curb
and rocked at the knees. When he saw one that was really
all right he rocked at the knees. I looked up and down for
her and then I saw her on the corner; she was looking back
our way but not at me.

"Should we buy a car now—or should we eat?" said
Uncle Dudley.

"Let's eat first," I said.

"O.K.," he said. "Let's eat."

We went in where a man was frying eggs. His back was
turned and his neck very white where it came out of his
yellow underwear. He went on talking to someone sitting
behind. "Hell, Natchez—" he said, "if you can't who the
hell could?" The man sitting behind didn't say. "Slide
around here," said the cook, "so I don't have to talk so
loud," and then he put the man's plate of eggs beside me.
The man behind the stove coughed, then he stood up. He
was tall and had a coat with a real fur collar and his hair was
long and curly at the ends. He came over and sat on the
stool beside me. His nails were clean and he sat with his
hands like he was going to pray.

"Natchez," said the cook, "you like a side a ham—more
coffee?" he said.

"It's getting so, Roy," Natchez said, "a good crook can't

make an honest living—two cent poker, half a day to make a dime." He looked at Uncle Dudley.

"Pair of ham and eggs," Uncle Dudley said. Natchez drank his coffee black, leaving in the spoon. Roy took four eggs from a pan and cracked them on the edge of the griddle—he cracked two at the same time and in each hand. He spilled them clean on the griddle with just one hand.

"Man like you," said Uncle Dudley, "—chewin your own ashes around here. If you don't make money you gotta go where it is." Natchez put down his coffee and looked at him.

"What kind of man am I?" he said.

"You're tryin to be a slick basterd," Uncle Dudley said. "But you're only wearin off your finish slidin around here."

"Bygod—" said Roy, "now that's good. Bygod that's good as hell. Guess the old man sure picked you clean—huh, Natchez?" Natchez just shrugged—twisted his ring around and around. He tapped his nails and they made a hollow sound. "How you men like your eggs?"

"Up," I said.

"Nice an sunny," he said. "Real California eggs," he went on, "nice an sunny side up." Uncle Dudley took out a cigar and looked at him.

"If I could lay my own—" he began, then he stopped and looked at Natchez. "Be in New Orleans soon—just in time for the Mardi Graw." Roy slid the plates down the table and they stopped by me. I took the one with the most potatoes, smallest eggs. The ham was so thin it wouldn't lay flat without the potatoes. I left them there and began to eat the eggs.

"New Orleans?" said Natchez.

"On our way to Chicago. Nice town, New Orleans—warm, plenty of dough."

"Driving?"

"Only way we'd ever go. Only way to get the country—feel it," Uncle Dudley said. He put down his fork and squeezed a handful of air. "Western air—" said Uncle Dudley. Natchez finished off his eggs. Roy poured us all more coffee, slid down the glass of spoons. Natchez took it black but he put in too much sugar.

"Bygod—" said Roy, "su⌐e wish I had some extra dough. Heard so damn much about New Orleans—what's it they call it, Mardi—?"

"Graw." Uncle Dudley looked up at him, then looked back at the door. A red-headed sailor with a small bag was standing there. He stood with his behind off to one side and kept his mouth shut chewing gum.

"How's them ham and eggs?" said Roy, very loud. "How's them home-cooked ham and eggs?"

"Best I've ever had," said Uncle Dudley. "Eggs fried in country butter is really good." Roy stared at him and Uncle Dudley smacked his lips. He took a piece of bread and wiped the grease off his plate.

"Yeah—" said Roy, and the sailor came in and sat down. The red hair on his chest grew right up to his neck where it stopped like grass along a sidewalk would.

"New Orleans—" Uncle Dudley was saying, "there's one town a man should never miss. Kid and I go out of our way just to be drivin through—"

"Just you an the Kid?" said Natchez.

"Most the time—except on a long haul. On a long haul Kid an I like some company around. Got a big, roomy car—helps while away the time. Everybody buys a little gas, helps everybody along."

"Gas?" said Roy.

"Little gas an oil—everybody sharin expenses all the way. Kid an I furnish the car an you help furnish the gas an oil."

"Bygod—" said Roy, "now that sounds O.K. Bygod if I had some coin I'd jump at that—"

"Just on our way now to put in a little ad. Pick up a couple boys who'd really like to go east. Must be plenty in this hole like to get back in the east."

"Omaha—?" said Roy.

"Sure—all points east. Kid an I live in Chicago—Omaha right next door."

"Bygod—sure like Omaha. Was a kid in Omaha. Keep tellin my wife, 'Hell, Mabel, what good this goddam sun do me? My face paler'n my behind. When I was a kid in Omaha I was . . .'"

"Bowl of oatmeal," the sailor said.

"How much gas—" said Roy, scooping oatmeal, "—you figure to Omaha?" Uncle Dudley took out his pen. Then he took out one of his cards and wrote Biltmore under his name.

" 'bout twenty is what I figure to New Orleans—same to Omaha."

Natchez was picking his teeth. He had a little gold tooth-pick in a silver case and it slipped inside like a sword. When he faced the light he had a thin black moustache but side on you couldn't see a thing. "What car you drivin?" he said. "Twenty bucks buys a lot of gas."

"Ever buy gas—" said Uncle Dudley, "in Wagon Wheel, Socorro? Ever buy gas in Caballo, Malaga, Corona, Alamogordo?" Natchez shook his head. We hadn't either as yet but probably would in time. Uncle Dudley looked across at the sailor and the sailor looked him back.

"Sounds O.K. to me," the sailor said. Uncle Dudley looked at Natchez.

"Bygod—" said Roy, "if it wasn't for Mabel—"

"When you leavin?" said Natchez.

"Morning—" said Uncle Dudley, "try to get away early,

want to be on our way by noon." The sailor stopped eating his oatmeal and looked right straight ahead. He was adding up something and blinked his eyes when he got at the end.

"Warm, southern route all the way," said Uncle Dudley. "Back home just in time for spring. Nothin like Lincoln Park in the spring. Remember Lincoln Park in the spring, Kid?"

"Boy!" I said. I stopped eating and looked around. I looked out at the street like the park was there and the pigeons walking around. The sailor made a noise with his spoon. He had blue eyes and was the kind Uncle Dudley called a clean-lookin kid.

"You drivin east?" he said.

"Points east," said Uncle Dudley.

"You got any room?"

"Well—" said Uncle Dudley, "depends on the Kid—Kid likes room. Likes room in a long haul. How about it, Kid—we got room?"

"Well—" I said.

"Where you goin?" said Uncle Dudley.

"Pittsburgh—"

"Hmmmm—right next door."

"That is if you're goin that far—if you're not, goin as far as you go."

"We're goin to Chicago—twenty-five to Chicago. Pittsburgh right—"

"Straight ahead," said Natchez.

"Sure," said Uncle Dudley, "right—on."

Natchez dropped a quarter on the counter. He put away his gold toothpick and looked a long time at his nails. Then he said, "Say we split the difference—say, seventeen-fifty?" Uncle Dudley squinted at his card. He turned it over and wrote on the back *Received from*—then, *for sharing expenses to Chicago.*

247

"Really prefer somebody goin all the way," he said. "like to have you along—but like a man to go all the way."

"Count me in," said the sailor. "You want the dough now?"

"Pardon me—" said Natchez, "but this gentleman and I—"

"My dough's on the counter," said the sailor, and unbuttoned his pants. He had a money belt on and had to half take off his pants.

"Well—" said Natchez. "Since money talks—"

"Now, now, boys," said Uncle Dudley. "Now— Now—" he said, and reached and took the two fives from Natchez. "Got to keep peace in the family—got to share and share alike. Can we find room for 'em, Kid?"

"Well—" I said.

"Sure—that's fine. Like a nice car full myself. An now, Mr.—"

"Ahearn," said the sailor, and handed some more new tens to Roy. Roy wiped his hands before he took them, then passed them along. Mr. Ahearn put his belt back on and buttoned up his pants.

"Received—" said Uncle Dudley, and wiggled the pen around, then he wrapped the card in one of Natchez' fives and Roy passed it along. "And now—" said Uncle Dudley.

"Blake," said Natchez.

"Received—ten on account—from Mr. Blake," and he gave him a card.

"Biltmore?" said Natchez.

"Nice place—" Uncle Dudley said, "nice roomy lobby—make yourself at home."

"Where's it at?" said Mr. Ahearn.

"Funny thing—" said Uncle Dudley. "Yes *sir*, a really funny thing, but Kid an I been there a week an I still don't know where it is. Kid leads me around by the hand. If it wasn't for the Kid I'd never get there—where's it at, Kid?"

"Not far—" I said.

"Biltmore?" said Roy. "Hell, that's right up the street."

"Sure—"

"Sure," I said.

Natchez walked and stood in the door. His coat had wide padded shoulders and the bottom nearly reached the floor. He wore gray button spats and one of them was nearly new.

"Leavin in the morning?" he said, without turning.

"Want to be on the road by noon."

"I gotta lot to do," said Mr. Ahearn, and dropped a dime and walked out. Natchez watched him walk off down the street.

"Where the sailors get them nice behinds?" he said.

"It's a gift," Roy said. Natchez shrugged and looked at his hands. He took out his gold toothpick and cleaned one nail, then he put it away. He walked out and stood on the curb.

"Bygod if it wasn't for Mabel—" said Roy, and walked behind the stove. He began to wash dishes back there.

"What if there hadn't been one?" I said.

"There's always a Biltmore," said Uncle Dudley.

"A swell dump," said Roy, "Mabel likes to meet me there and stand around." He came out and stood wiping his hands. He poured us more coffee and I sat and ate doughnuts while Uncle Dudley telephoned.

We stood on the corner of Sixth and Spring sizing the women up. They were pretty good right around here. When Uncle Dudley saw something he really liked he first always looked away. I used to wonder about that. Then I saw that made the women look at him and when he looked back there they were. And they all looked better that way.

From right then on they even walked better and stopped so they stood the right way. They both sort of enjoyed it somehow. He liked them big and built high off the ground but sometimes he'd look at anything. Sometimes I thought they would too. But he had a good leg and with his hat off it was only the part in between. Which was more than I could say for some of them. Though I wasn't sure how I liked them yet. But Uncle Dudley said all of that would come in time. Like my knowing it wasn't how much a woman weighed—but where.

A man walked by with a sign on his back that said TRAVEL BY BUS AND SAVE. Uncle Dudley and I walked behind. In the middle of the block the man turned in but left his sign parked out in front. Another sign was nailed on the door. An old man with one leg leaned on his crutches and read all of the prices out loud. He wore a black derby and a black overcoat, and had black shoes with elastic sides. "Well, well—" said Uncle Dudley. "Guess we drive back after all—I thought you told me that the bus fare was cheap?"

"I guess I was wrong," I said.

"Hell—" said Uncle Dudley, "I'd take a man for twenty-five. Yes *sir*—clear to Chicago, all the way." The old man on crutches turned and looked at him. His face was like tanned leather and something smelled. "Yes *sir*, clear to Chicago—" Uncle Dudley said.

"How much for two?" said the man.

"A gentleman?"

"A gentleman."

"For two—" said Uncle Dudley, "Kid and I might make it forty-five."

"He's no bigger than the Kid," said the man, "and hell—I'm only half here!"

"Thought of that—" said Uncle Dudley.

"We're actors—we're in the Miracle Play."

"It didn't work?"

"How can I work?"

"Maybe forty-two fifty," Uncle Dudley said.

"But—" said the man. Uncle Dudley looked at me.

"Maybe you're right, Kid—" he said. "There just ain't room—no room for two."

"You just said—" said the man.

"Yes?"

"Forty-two fifty."

"Can you manage, Kid? They're willing to be crowded a little—but are you? I leave it to you."

"Well—" I said. Uncle Dudley took out a card. Under his name he wrote Biltmore, and under Biltmore Room 331.

"Mister—?"

"Demetrios," said the man.

"All now—" said Uncle Dudley, "or thirty now—the rest in the morning?" Mr. Demetrios made a sound with his teeth. His uppers hung down so I could see the rubber gums and he let them hang there, his tongue making the noise. "Well—" said Uncle Dudley. Mr. Demetrios leaned on his crutch. From under his arm he pulled a bag that snapped back on a rubber string. He pulled it out again and pried open the drawstring top. It was full of pennies and two rolls of bills. He counted off ten and then he stopped and took a very long look at me. I took a very long look at him. He counted off twenty more and Uncle Dudley gave it to me. "And now your friend's name?" said Uncle Dudley. Mr. Demetrios made the noise again.

"Pop—" he said.

"Pop?"

"Just Pop—we call him Pop." Uncle Dudley wrote down Pop. "He's no bigger than the Kid."

"Kid ain't so small."

Turning away, Mr. Demetrios spit.

Wright Morris

"Biltmore—" said Uncle Dudley. "Make yourself at home."

"In the·morning?"

"In the morning," Uncle Dudley said. Mr. Demetrios read the card over to himself out loud. The man running the bus station came outside and looked at us.

"What's goin on here?" he said.

"You gotta match?" said Uncle Dudley. He gave Uncle Dudley a match and watched him light his cigar. Uncle Dudley blew the smoke out slow and we walked away.

We had an orange drink at Fifth and Main. Uncle Dudley bought popcorn and we walked up toward the Biltmore, sat down on a bench in Pershing Square. We ate popcorn and looked at the hotel. It was a pretty smooth place with a man out in front with nothing to do but open doors. Pigeons came and ate from Uncle Dudley's hand. "How many we got?" he said.

"Five now," I said.

Uncle Dudley fed some popcorn to the squirrels. Some of the pigeons didn't have any tails at all, worn clean off like those on Halsted street. "How much that leave for a car?"

"About twenty dollars," I said.

"That enough?" said Uncle Dudley.

"That ain't enough," I said.

"Isn't—" said Uncle Dudley. I let it pass. "That's what you sold it for," went on Uncle Dudley.

"Buyin isn't sellin," I said.

"Well—I guess you're learnin," he said.

"That was a good car," I said. "Only two gallons of oil."

"Maybe he'll sell it back," Uncle Dudley said.

"It's not that good," I said. "No rubber on it—no lights—no brakes—no second gear."

"I could sit an hold it."

"Not all the way," I said. "An besides you can't hold everything." Uncle Dudley got up and walked away. He

252

listened to a man giving a speech near the fountain and he clapped very loud when the man was through. Then he came back and looked at me.

"Sometimes—" he said, "I like it here."

"How much we got?" I said.

"We'll have about a hundred."

"That's just about gas," I said. Uncle Dudley walked away. He listened to another man talking about something and when he stopped said something to him. The man called Uncle Dudley one. By the time I got there the man was gone and Uncle Dudley was on the box. When he saw me he got down again.

"Well," he said.

"We got to get going," I said. We walked across the street and into the Biltmore while the man was holding the door. We crossed the lobby and went up the stairs. There was a long hall with lights shining on pictures and people sitting around. Uncle Dudley said the pictures stank. When he was young Uncle Dudley used to paint. He said he learned how to paint so he could paint right over the pictures his Dad had on the wall. We came back down to the lobby again. Uncle Dudley stopped at the desk and asked if he had any calls. "I'm driving east," he said, "driving east with a few friends." A man buying a cigar lit it and looked at him. "Good time to drive," said Uncle Dudley. "Cool on the desert—best time of year."

"Tch," said the man. "How I enfy you."

"Ha!" said Uncle Dudley. "Nothing fancy—just going home. Sharing expenses with a few friends—easier that way."

"Fery smart," said the man. "How I enfy you."

"You're going east?" said Uncle Dudley.

"New York—I titch in New York. I am a muzic titcher in New York," he said.

"My name's Osborn," said Uncle Dudley.

"I am Mr. Liszt," said Mr. Liszt. Uncle Dudley slowly shook his hand. Mr. Liszt was a good-looking man and beside him Uncle Dudley's pants weren't pressed. Mr. Liszt had glasses that made his eyes big and a ribbon hanging down to his coat.

"Now—" said Uncle Dudley. "If we weren't full—"

"Oh—too bat," said Mr. Liszt.

"Yes—you wouldn't be comfortable. Wouldn't mind myself but you professional men—"

"Ach—" said Mr. Liszt, "I ride anywhere. I haf rode across France in a car."

"France—" said Uncle Dudley.

"I ride in front. In New York I ride all ofer three in front."

"Well—" said Uncle Dudley.

"I be frank. I plan to titch here—no titching at all. I haf but fifty dollars between us and New York. I gif you haf an we ride three in front?"

"Chicago—" said Uncle Dudley.

"Chicago! I haf already titched in Chicago."

"Well," said Uncle Dudley. Mr. Liszt reached into his coat. He walked to the window and tipped his billfold to the light. Then he turned his back to Uncle Dudley and stood awhile. "Twenty-fife?" he said.

"Twenty-five," said Uncle Dudley.

Mr. Liszt came back with the bills in a small roll. "Count it," he said, "fife fifes." Uncle Dudley counted it. He felt in his pocket for a card but this one said JOE'S DAIRY LUNCH. "Pleese—" said Mr. Liszt, "there is no neet. I count myself a fery goot chudge of men."

"That's very handy," said Uncle Dudley. Mr. Liszt smiled and wet his lips.

"Infaluble—" he said. Uncle Dudley put the bills away.

"Well—" said Uncle Dudley. "Biltmore—make yourself at home."

"Right here?"

"Oh—" said Uncle Dudley. "Yes—right here." Mr. Liszt smiled and put his hand on my back.

"Your poy?"

"My brother's kid."

"A fine lookink poy."

"He's a nice kid."

"Three of us—" said Mr. Liszt. "Riting in front—riting, riting, riting—"

"Well—" said Uncle Dudley, "Kid an I got to pick up the car."

"Ah!" said Mr. Liszt.

"Yeah—" said Uncle Dudley.

Mr. Liszt shook Uncle Dudley's hand very hard. In the lighter on the desk Uncle Dudley tried to light his cigar but it kept bouncing up and down like a rubber one. Uncle Dudley took it out and put it away. We stopped and looked at a potted plant near the door. A woman carrying a dog came in and we went out the revolving doors while they were still going and the smell of her was inside. We crossed the street and the pigeons followed us in the square. We walked around it once, then we stopped for an orange drink.

We had another orange drink on Fifth and Main. She was from North Platte and knew some people Uncle Dudley knew there. She liked it here and then again she didn't, which was about the way I felt about it too. Uncle Dudley said he'd tell her folks she was looking fine. She gave us another drink free and we gave her the doughnuts we had. Uncle Dudley left her two-bits and we both walked off very fast.

We walked out Seventh Street where we knew Agnes would be. She was still there in the lot on the corner, her front tires flat. Somebody had shined up her hood but nothing else. She still had her Michigan plates and no glass in the windshield, the cardboard I used against bugs said, MAKE OFFER—CHEAP. There was still no glass on the light where I'd cracked the steer. I crossed the street and stood alongside and nobody came out so I got in the seat, I put my hands on the steering wheel and my foot on the clutch. I made noises like little kids make and put her in high. She wouldn't stay there before but she stayed now. I felt the sawdust they'd put in her to make her shift. I could smell Uncle Dudley's cigar and feel his knee bumping mine and I knew that he couldn't hold her any longer and I'd have to shift. I could feel it down in my stomach when I did. I could feel my initial on the wheel and whether the clutch was dragging or not and if the timing gear would last until Santa Fe. I saw that they'd set her back so she read in five numbers now. I got out and let the door swing for she wouldn't close. I walked out in front and when I looked back she was still out of line—like a dog runs or a barge on the sewage canal. I crossed the street where Uncle Dudley was waiting for me.

"She was a good girl," he said, and we walked on by.

When we got to Alameda we turned right. On the side-walk in front of a garage was a big car with little wire wheels, an old Marmon but she still had class. AIRPLANE ENGINE—SWEET RUNNER, the windshield said. We walked on by—there was even a tire on the spare. All of them held some air and the one up front had tread showing, retread maybe but showing anyhow. We crossed the street for a side view and she really was some wagon, belly right on the ground and a high, smooth-lookin hood. The little wire wheels did something to me somehow. We went back and walked by again and she had seven seats—could be eight with three riding in the front. I looked inside and the dash was keen as hell. She had a rear-end transmission and somehow I liked that too. We went on by and around the corner to a stand. Uncle Dudley had root beer and I had a bar.

"What's it worth, Kid," he said.

"Maybe ninety bucks," I said. "Maybe eighty—ninety bucks."

"What'll I offer?"

"Sixty," I said, "maybe go to seventy-five."

"Twenty-five down?"

"Twenty-five down," I said. Uncle Dudley bought another White Owl and we went back. We stopped right in front and stood looking at it. The man looked at us and we didn't leave so he came out. He stood wiping his hands.

"Like a good wagon?" he said.

"Right now like a car," Uncle Dudley said.

"A three-thousand-dollar wagon—" said the man, not laughing. "Rubber up—perfect shape—fired to go."

"Blue book about seventy bucks," said Uncle Dudley.

"What?"

"Maybe less," Uncle Dudley said. "On a trade maybe eighty—cash deal fifty-five. I'm offerin fifty-five."

"Gee-*zus*-crist!" said the man.

"Make it fifty," said Uncle Dudley.

"The engine in there cost a thousand bucks to build—airplane engine—same goddam engine they used in the war. More goddam power than anything you ever seen. An you offer me—"

"Fifty bucks," said Uncle Dudley. The man wiped his hands. He threw the rag on the ground and started back into the garage. Then he turned—

"You really want that car—make me an offer—an honest offer?"

"How's she sound?" Uncle Dudley said. The man came back and got inside. He stepped on the starter and she turned right over, smooth. He raced her and she took it— no rap when she lagged.

"Pretty loose," I said.

"My god yes," said Uncle Dudley, "she'll bend both ways at the knees." The man let her idle a bit.

"Want to try it, Kid?" Uncle Dudley said.

"O.K.," I said. I got in and Uncle Dudley sat in the rear. The hood was so high I could hardly see over and when I stretched the pedals slipped away. But I horsed around until it felt all right. I tried the clutch and it felt clean. I let her out. The man gave me a hand at the corner to get her around. In high she picked up all right, no carbon ping.

"Better take it easy," said Uncle Dudley, "prob'ly get about six blocks to the gallon. If you poured it in with the engine runnin you'd never get it full."

"Listen that motor!" said the man.

"I can't help it," said Uncle Dudley. I couldn't either and she sounded all right. She had a nice throaty cough and when I gave it to her it was the nuts. When we went between sign boards she sounded like a racing car. I managed the next corner by myself, leaning on the wheel. On the next one it was easy and I had the knack. The brakes were wheezy but the pedal didn't get to the floor. When we stopped the man leaned forward and shut her off.

"Not much gas in her," he said.

"Not any more," said Uncle Dudley. "Well, Kid—is she still worth fifty bucks?"

"About," I said.

"Bygod!" said the man. "You can go to hell," and he got out.

"Not in this," said Uncle Dudley. "Cost too damn much," and he got out too. I didn't want to get out but Uncle Dudley coughed. "Well—" he said. "You're sure one damn fool if you think that freight car's money today. Who the hell wants a truck like that? Who the hell but me?"

"Listen," said the man, "seventy-five bucks cash."

Uncle Dudley shrugged and looked very sad. "I tell you what—I can use it—twenty-five down till I know it works."

"None of that," said the man, "cash—sixty bucks cash."

"If it's *cash*," said Uncle Dudley, "fifty stands." The man walked away. Uncle Dudley lit his cigar and we moseyed down the street. On the corner we stopped and Uncle Dudley lit his cigar again. Then we looked up and down the street, then back at the garage. The man was standing in the door waving at us. Uncle Dudley and me slowly moseyed back.

BOYD

From *Ceremony in Lone Tree*

IN Acapulco, where Boyd had gone to sulk, he consumed several cups of the shaved ice doused with sirup from hair-tonic bottles that he knew with reasonable assurance would make him sick. As it did. Deathly sick, but he did not die. The long night of nausea and fever merely stimulated him to remember the details he had come to Acapulco to forget. Running into the McKees at Sanborn's, herding them like goats out to the bullfight where he had acted like a fool, but somehow not quite fool enough. Everything called for talent, and that was one more talent he lacked.

The morning after, McKee had come around and honked his musical horn beneath Boyd's window, not wanting to leave his station wagon parked in front. The car was full of Mexican loot—pottery, baskets and *sarapes*—and he also feared for hubcaps valued at five and a half bucks apiece. In his slippers and soiled bathrobe Boyd had walked down the four flights to the street, to see the face of Lois McKee in the depths of a new straw hat. In the back of the car, like something new in knickknacks, sat the boy with his coon-skin hat, and the mad old Scanlon hugging a pair of mounted bull horns.

"Just wanted to tell you," McKee had bawled, "that at least on our side there's no hard feelings," and he had slapped Boyd on the shoulder with his broad hand. Boyd had agreed, then McKee had blurted, "You know you're closer to me than a brother, Gordon," which had left Boyd standing there, speechless, and Mrs. McKee said:

"Why, McKee, what a thing to say to Mr. Boyd," and put one of her gloved hands lightly on Boyd's arm. Hardly a moment, but long enough to finish what the bullfight had started. After thirty years of exile Boyd was back where his life had begun.

So he had gone to Acapulco, to a tourist *posada*, and one of the landlady's numberless offspring was a child named Quirina—Quirina Dolores Lupe Mendoza, as she said. She ran errands, she fanned his sweaty face with a palm-leaf fan. She had, from God knows where, honey-colored hair that hung below her shoulders, with a downlike frost of it along the bony ridges of her spine. Her body was sticklike, the skin along her ribs transparent as vellum, the armpits as smooth as a marble faun's. The doll-like head seemed so large he thought it might break off when she laughed. When she realized it gave him pleasure, she would sit with her hand resting like a bird in one of his own. His hair was sometimes in his eyes or plastered to the film of sweat on his forehead, and she would sit as if daydreaming, running one of her hands through it, as if he were a pet. And when not with him, sitting there on the bed, she would stand in the yard like a flower of evil, growing out of the filth and vileness just for him. Always where he could see her. Oh, she never overlooked that. And puzzling at first, then disturbing, were the large limpid eyes of a kept woman—a well-kept woman—in the face of a child. A woman, that is, who both accepted corruption and savored it.

She seemed incredibly quick to learn all the strange things that he told her, but a day or two later she seemed to have forgotten most of what he said. The same story spread wide the beautiful eyes. The same joke had her laughing again. And then he happened to notice how, hours on end, she would explore her own body like a monkey, not for lice but just as a way of passing the time. She was also very dirty—in the heat he could smell her, although a warm sea lapped the house—and thinking it would please her he gave her his scented shaving soap. The perfume she liked, but not the lather, and would rub it dry on parts of her body. Imperceptibly at first, Boyd began to get well. The pleasures he took in his illness began to wane. He bought a pair of shorts and wandered alone up and down the beach.

He collected shells, driftwood and post-card pictures of himself. In these pictures, taken by boys with antique tripod cameras, he looked for evidence of moral deterioration, but found none. Quite the contrary. He looked reasonably well. He saw himself, sitting or standing, his body several shades darker than his shadow, on the jutting rocks or the salt-white sand, looking much better than he had in years. In one of these pictures a vulture on a post at his back seemed to peer over his shoulder, the bird looking evil indeed, but not Boyd. Knowing how it would shock them, he sent one of these snapshots to the McKees. Nothing surprised him more than the letter he received by return post.

McKee wrote that he was glad to see him looking so well, and that both he and Mrs. McKee wondered if he might be passing through Nebraska toward the end of March. That happened to be the old man's birthday, and they were planning a family reunion—which included him in—at the old man's place in Lone Tree. Nothing would please the whole family more than to see him there. Especially the old man's great-grandson, little Gordon, since he never tired of talking about Boyd, but McKee was thinking in particular of himself. It wouldn't be a family reunion if Boyd wasn't there.

Lone Tree? When Boyd read the name he laughed out loud. Was there a more desolate, more inhuman outpost in the world? Treeless and bleak, home of the Dust Bowl and that eccentric old fool, Scanlon, boarded up in his dilapidated hotel. It made him grateful Acapulco was so far away. And then a week or so later he searched half the day for the letter to see if he still might get to Lone Tree in time.

At sunrise the following morning he hired the boys who spent the day diving for coins to give his '48 Plymouth a push. When it started he just kept going, up the coast route where it was balmy, but when the weather changed at Nogales so did his mind. The idea of going to Lone Tree struck him as mad. The thought of McKee and his wife, of the clan assembled at the dry water hole, led him to wonder if the Acapulco sun had softened his brain. So he went northwest, up through Phoenix to Las Vegas where he looked right at home, in his soiled resort clothes, with the week-end shipment of suckers from Hollywood. A plump matron about his own age, the eastbound side of her face sunburned, nudged his elbow at the bar to ask if he was from Anaheim. She was hopeful. There was something to be said for Anaheim. On the fingers that dunked the ice cubes in her drink were several large stones. Had he ever, she asked him, longed for the unknown? All she wanted before going home was a look at the life south of the border, since she had gone to the trouble of getting the shots, and her arm was sore. Tucking up her sleeve, she showed him her vaccination scars.

Lone Tree, so far away that morning, seemed nearer at hand. On a stool at the bar, the slot machines churning behind him, Boyd recalled that it was in Lone Tree that

Walter McKee had taken Lois Scanlon to wife. Did the place show it? Did it have the air of hallowed ground? He left town in the evening, following lights that he thought led him north into Utah, but he had got in with a stream of army-base traffic headed northwest. About midnight, at a place near Beatty, he pulled in for the night, but the motel south of town was full up. He asked the elderly woman who came to the door if the all-night gambling explained it.

"Gambling?" she said, as if it had skipped her mind. "Oh, no, it's the bomb."

The bomb? For a moment Boyd did not reply. In Mexico he had forgotten about the bomb. It seemed strange to hear about it in a wilderness of slot machines, from an elderly woman who twisted the apron tied at her waist. The radio at her back played old-time hymns. She was white-haired, motherly, and pinned to her dress like a brooch was a piece of metal about the size of a dog tag. But nothing on it. Was that why Boyd stared? "That's to check the fallout," she said when she noticed where he was staring. "Everyone who lives here wears one. After the test they come around and check it. That way they know if the place is safe to live in or not."

Did she smile? Boyd gazed at her as if he failed to grasp what she had said. It led her to feel he was not too bright, and being a motherly sort of person, she opened the screen, asked him to step in. If he didn't mind a room without a bath, she said, and no TV in it, she might put him up.

No, he said, he wouldn't mind, and she showed him the room—one used by her son, but he was making good money helping dude ranchers look for uranium. She wagged her head to indicate what fools she thought they all were. She would let it lie. It didn't poison people in the rocks where they found it or make the dust hot. As Boyd signed the register she added: Did he want to be up for the bomb?

For the bomb? He saw that it was a routine question.

Just before dawn, she replied. That was when the breeze died, and they did it. When he didn't reply she said if he hadn't seen a bomb go off, he should. He owed it to himself. Terrible as it was, it was also a wonderful sight. There was this flash, then this pillar of fire went up and up, like a rabbit's ear.

Boyd turned as if he saw it.

"You better be up for it," she said, and after his name in the register she added:

WAKE BEFORE BOMB

then added an exclamation point.

Boyd had gone to bed soon enough, but not to sleep. Neon signs at the gambling halls made a pattern of lights on the ceiling, and he could hear gusts of jukebox music when the doors opened. It seemed an odd place to be having a hell of a time. He got up, built a fire in the stove out of the shingles in the wood box, then sat there, the lights off, warming his hands. The sound of the draft in the chimney made him think of the house he was born in, he and McKee lying awake in the cold room upstairs. His mother would pound on the pipe with the poker to shut them up. Later, standing at the top of the stairs with her lamp, her shadow looming on the wall like a monster, she would hold it out before her and ask, "Gordon, you two awake or asleep?" They had to stuff the corners of their pillows in their mouths to keep from laughing out loud. Why was it so funny? Had it seemed—to kids as smart as themselves—a strange question to ask anybody? Awake or asleep? But if that voice now spoke to him from the pipe—what would he say? What would McKee? In Boyd's estimation, McKee had been asleep most of his life. He had curled up snugly in the cocoon God's Loveliest Creature had spun for him. What sort of bomb would wake him up? Back in Polk and

Lone Tree no bomb was expected, no matron stopped the stranger to put to him the question, wearing the dog tag that bore, like a headstone, his invisible number. No one cried out back there, because everybody slept. The old man in the past, the young ones in the future, McKee in his cocoon, and Lois, the ever-patient, ever-chaste Penelope, busy at her looming. WAKE BEFORE BOMB? How did one do it? Was it even advisable? The past, whether one liked it or not, was all that one actually possessed: the green stuff, the gilt-edge securities. The present was that moment of exchange—when all might be lost. Why risk it? Why not sleep on the money in the bank? To wake before the bomb was to risk losing all to gain what might be so little—a brief moment in the present, that one moment later joined the past. Nevertheless, as the lady said, it was a wonderful sight. There was this flash, then the pillar of fire went up and up as if to heaven, and the heat and the light of that moment illuminated for a fraction the flesh and bones of the present. Did these bones live? At that moment they did. The meeting point, the melting point of the past confronting the present. Where no heat was thrown off, there was no light—where it failed to ignite the present, it was dead. The phoenix, that strange bird of ashes, rose each day from the embers where the past had died and the future was at stake. To wake before bomb was tricky business. What if it scared you to sleep?

When that pillar of fire went up and up, what would be revealed? He raised the window as if he might see. Down the road where the signs were blinking a small one read BREAKFAST AT ALL HOURS. It made him hungry. He dressed and walked down the road to the restaurant. Through the window he could see the ranks of slot machines. Under a hooded lamp at the rear men with their shirt sleeves rolled, ties dangling, stood around a table like a pit exhibiting snakes. One with a rake, his eyes shaded, leaned forward to drag in the dice. The bar looked empty, the fellow behind it with a visor shading his face, one of the metal tags like a campaign button clipped to his shirt. Boyd had stepped inside before he saw the girl on the stool at the end. She faced a slot machine, her sweater sleeve pushed to the elbow on the arm she rested on the crank. Did she need the stool to reach it? She looked that small. She dipped her hand into the bag that hung from her shoulder, the mouth gaping, then used what weight she had to lean on the crank. Boyd could hear the cylinders spin, click to a stop. In the dim light she leaned forward to read them, said aloud:

"Two friggin oranges and one pineapple. Sweet Jesus, what would he make of that."

"What's he like?" said the barman, giving Boyd a wink. "Vodka or gin?"

Her hand clawed around in the bag for matches. The flame lit up a face that Boyd had seen on the sly birds in the animal fables, neither young nor old. She blew out a cloud of smoke, then turned and said, "Big Daddy, you got change for a dollar?" and held up a crumpled bill.

"She means you," said the barman. "I'm her Baby Doll."

Boyd walked down the counter and made change for the dollar. The hand into which he dropped the coins snapped shut on them like a trap. The small fist shook at him, and she said, "That's the last of his friggin money."

"You better keep a dime for carfare," said the barman.

"A friggin buffalo nickel," she said, sorting the coins, "don't that mean luck?" The skin across her nose was so tight Boyd could see the dimple in the sharp tip. Something about her eyes made him stare. Birdlike, she cocked her head to one side.

"You see something funny?" Before he replied she tipped her head to the bar, and put her fingers to one eye as if to pop it. Something dropped on the bar. One eye lidded, she looked back at him. "How you like that? Better?"

"She pullin' that eye business on you?" said the barman. "Thought I'd lose my lunch when she pulled it on me."

She tipped her head to the bar, covered one eye, then felt around till she found what she wanted. On the tip of her finger Boyd could see it. Like a tiddlywink.

"You ever see such a friggin silly thing in your life?"

His mouth a little dry, Boyd said, "Does it work?"

"Glasses got me Irwin. I'm for anything but glasses. He took me for a friggin intellectual type."

"I'd like to see this guy," said the barman.

"What type are you?" said Boyd.

Both eyes open, she looked at Boyd's face, a piece at a time. On the glassy pupil of one eye he could see the reflection of the pressed-tin ceiling.

"What type am I? Big Daddy, what type you like?"

"Say she was the shy type myself," said the barman, "wouldn't you?"

"What a friggin bore it is to get to know people. Don't you think they're nicer before you know them?"

"How you like that for an approach?" said the barman.

"At thirty-two," she said, "he'd put it all behind him. Imagine that?"

"Who?" said Boyd.

"Irwin. Sweet Jesus."

"If I was thirty-two—" said Boyd.

"You know what? You probably sounded just like him. The friggin good old days. How it was in college. How all that jazz in the old cars was so different. Sure it's different. It's gone."

"I take it you didn't like him?" said Boyd.

"How the hell you like life insurance? He was a friggin computer. He computed his love life. He had it all computed when it would be over. Sweet Jesus, that's one thing I'm not computing, are you?"

"Not at my age," said Boyd.

"I got news for you," she said. "You're just like him. The friggin brainy type." She turned on the stool to give the crank a jerk, then wheeled and said, "You think we meet the same person over and over? He's so friggin scared of everything, like you are."

"What makes you think I'm so friggin scared?" He hadn't meant to say friggin. It had just slipped out.

"Big Daddy, let's not get personal. It louses up everything when you get personal. I don't mind your bein scared. I'm no goddam Joan of Arc."

"How you like that?" said the barman. "Now I ask you."

In the bag where she had spilled the coins she clawed around for one, turned to the room. Three men and a woman sat at a green-covered table, playing cards. No one moved. Smoke rose into the hooded lamp as if the woman's hair were on fire.

"Let's get some friggin life in this joint," she said, and stepped down from the stool into her sandals, then shuffled through the sawdust to the jukebox in the corner. She wore new Levi's, and crossing the room, slipped her hands into the tight front pockets. "Big Daddy," she called, reading the labels, "what sort of music you like?" Before he answered she said, "Don't bother. Sweet Jesus, I can hear it. One of those great old tunes you used to sing in college. One of those friggin classics that went along with the good old cars, and the good old lays. I don't dig that jazz." She dropped a coin into the machine. "If you're like Irwin you met the only real friggin woman of your life back in high school. That's all, you just met her. Lucky for you she married somebody else." The music started and she came back to the bar, her arms raised as if she wanted a lift to the stool. "This is on my money, Big Daddy, let's dance."

Boyd slipped an arm around her. In the corner of the bar, like an eye, the TV screen flickered at them. Her head flat on his chest, she said, "You coming or going to Reno, Big Daddy?"

"Daughter," he said, "I'm like Irwin. The only real friggin woman of my life got away."

She stopped dancing and said, "You kidding?"

"Lucky for me, as you say, she married somebody else."

"I only said that. Sweet Jesus. I never thought it really happened."

"That's what's good about the good old days. The other fellow got the girl."

The music stopped, but she didn't seem to take note of it. At the front of her mouth, pushed back into service, was a piece of gum she had forgotten.

"You like another dime?" he said. "The music's stopped."

What little weight she had hung on him, as if she had fainted.

"She pass out on you?" the barman said.

Boyd eased her over to the counter and hoisted her, gently, to one of the stools. He hadn't noticed at the part in her dark hair the blonde roots coming in. "Give her a shot of this," the barman said, and slid a short one down the counter. When he held it to her lips, she sniffed it like a cat, turned away.

"You all right, Daughter?"

"The friggin music's stopped. You think a dime will start it?"

"First she says let's not get personal, then she faints and lets you have it."

"When Irwin's feelings were hurt, he would get out of

bed and go sleep in his Eames chair. That hurt him worse than I did. When my feelings were hurt, he would say, 'Go buy yourself something.' Sweet Jesus."

"Pretty goddam decent of him, I'd say," said the barman.

"Why didn't she marry you, Big Daddy?"

"For one thing, I didn't ask her."

Did she hear that?

"First sensible thing I've heard a man say in thirty-two years," the barman said.

She put the heels of her hands to her eyes. The stool she sat on started rocking. "You hear anything?" she said. Boyd listened. At the gaming table he could hear the rake drag in the dice. "You don't hear it?" He shook his head. "You think if I gave you a dime you could hear it? You think if you gave *her* a dime she could hear it?"

"I have it on good authority," said Boyd, "she doesn't need the dime. She makes her own music."

"Sweet Jesus, would I like to hear it."

"You would? Maybe we can arrange it."

She spread her fingers so her eyes could peer at his face.

"How you like that one," said the barman. "How you like that on a bar stool?"

She dropped her hands, and Boyd said, "She's throwing a little party, old friends of the family." He smiled. "Like me to introduce you? I'm your Daddy. You're my Daughter."

"Why you say that?"

"For a long time, Daughter, she's expected the worst. Maybe this is the time to let her have it."

She struck at him, the cigarettes in the pack fanning out on the floor and on the bar at his back. "I'd hate to be the only friggin woman in your life! You know why? I wouldn't be in it. Any more than she's been in it. You're too friggin scared to play *any* music!"

The street door swung open and a woman in slacks,

blowing on her hands, a man's hat pulled down on her head, came in and said, "Any coffee? Guess they called it off. Goddam place looks about the same."

"The bomb?" the girl yelled. "You mean they didn't do it?" She hopped off the stool and ran through the door. At the curb she looked around as if surprised to find the town was still there. Boyd left money on the bar and walked out and stood beside her. In the green light of dawn her painted toenails looked black; some chain she had stopped wearing had left its shadow on her neck.

"You going my way?" he said. "The good old days are gone, as you say, but I've still got one of the cars."

Her bag hung gaping, stuffed like a bureau drawer, and she put a hand into it as he walked away. "Sweet Jesus!" she said, just before sneezing, then blew her nose. He left her there and walked up the grade to the motel where the office door stood open.

"Mr. Boyd," said the woman, "there was no bomb, so I didn't wake you up."

"Maybe next time," he said.

"Oh, there'll be a next time all right," she replied. "Maybe tonight. Where'll you be tonight?"

"If I don't see it, maybe I'll hear it," he said.

He put his bag in the car, then spread the map out on the hood where the morning light fell on it. Where was he going? Lone Tree was not on the map. "If you're driving," McKee had written, "just ask anybody in Calloway. They all know the old man. They'll tell you where to turn off." He folded up the map, then turned to see her at the front of the drive. Her handbag was still gaping, and she had a canvas bag with a fresh flight sticker.

"A friggin Plymouth?" she said. "That's what Irwin was driving." Boyd stood there, silent, and she said, "I thought

272

you might need a push. Didn't everybody need one in the good old days?"

During the day she slept like a kid, curled in the seat. Boyd covered her with his raincoat, seeing no more of her than the green circle around her neck, one of her earrings and the hand that clutched the pack of filter-tip cigarettes. From one finger the ring was missing; on another a school ring with red stones was caked with the soap she had used in the washroom. By dark they were over in Wyoming and stopped near Evanston for the night. She didn't seem surprised to see where she was. "My brother was here in the war," she said, and looked around as if she might see other members of her family. In his raincoat, the sleeves rolled up, one side of her face patterned with the seat cover, she looked like a teen-age schoolgirl. The night cook in the diner assumed Boyd was her father. "Let me bring the kid a hot chocolate," he said. Boyd let him. She drank it, leaving her plum-colored lipstick on the rim of the cup. He took a room with two beds, stepped out for a smoke, and when he came back she was facing the wall, asleep. On the floor were her sandals. Had she gone to bed in her clothes? On the shelf in the bathroom she had left her piece of chlorophyll gum, as if she meant to chew it later, and in an aspirin tin her contact lenses. He took a shower, lit a cigarette, then dropped off to sleep before he had smoked it.

Toward morning she woke him up. She was there above him, his raincoat around her shoulders, an arm raised to twist a strand of her hair.

"What's that friggin noise?"

He sat up to listen for it. The bomb? Neon lights blinked on the diner and a trailer flicked by, the tires whining.

"What noise?" and he leaned forward to see if somebody might be fooling with the car.

"*That* noise." She pointed toward the back. Behind them in a gully a train was passing. Boyd knew the sound of it so well he hadn't heard it.

"You mean the train?"

"That friggin awful rumble."

"That's just a train, a freight train." He sat up to find a cigarette for her, light it. "If you live out here, you get used to it."

"Who the hell would live out *here?*"

"They do," he said; then: "She does," and he pushed up the blind so that the moonlight spilled into the room. A strip of snow fence, rippling like surf, lay on its side near the cut where the train passed. Reflected in the window Boyd could see her face, owl-eyed, the chapped lips slightly parted. At her side, a few inches from his head, she clicked her nails like a metal cricket.

"What do you see?"

"Me?" she said. "Moonshine."

He raised his head from the pillow to look at it with her. All moonshine, he thought. Is it all in your mind? The friggin good old songs, the good old cars, the good old bags, the whole friggin business? Where else? Through the fence the lights of the caboose flicked by, and he said, "Now you see it, now you don't, eh?"

"I didn't see it at all. What was it?"

She took one of the bobby pins from her hair and bit down on the tip in a way that made him shudder.

"Daughter, when you go home, how do you feel?"

"Third Avenue? You think I'm crazy?"

"Just supposing you did."

She thought a moment, said, "Awful. Sweet Jesus."

"Daughter, you express my own feelings."

"Then why you going back?"

"I want to know if it's there, or all in my mind."

She said nothing. In the yard at the front, like dozing pachyderms, he could hear the purr of the idling Diesels.

"I don't care if it's there or not, Big Daddy. You need me for that?"

"They take me for a clown. We're going to clown it up."

She dropped down on the bed at his side. "You scared of your own friggin kind? Is that it?"

"Daughter, I'm scared they might be real—I mean realer than I am."

She didn't seem to question it. "You think they know you as well as I do?"

"Nope. They're not friggin perfect strangers."

She got up from his side and crossed to her bed. His coat dropped in a puddle at her feet, and he could see the gold chains on her sandals. "I hurt your feelings?" he said. "If you're part of this family, you don't have them. You don't show them, that is. It's the law of the land."

After some time she said, "You ever feel you're in a friggin movie? You ever stand up in a movie and tell the friggin hero which way to run?"

"That's right, Daughter, and this is the movie."

"The friggin moonlight made me think of it," she said. And that was all.

In the morning she waited for him in the seat of the car. She wore a pair of dark glasses and a straw hat with a visor that she had bought in the gasoline station. Instead of Levi's she wore corduroy pants that fit snugly around her ankles. Her face showed a little windburn from the day before.

"I look more like your daughter?" When he nodded she said, "It's the friggin dark glasses." She didn't explain. At the highway in front of the diner she took his hand and let him lead her across it. She waited to see what he ordered for breakfast, ordered the same. The idea of being a daughter appealed to her. When he spread a map out on the counter, she leaned toward him, her head on his shoulder, her arm around his back in a daughterly way. He pointed out where they were in Wyoming, and where they were going, over in Nebraska. "Where's Duluth?" she said. "Irwin's from there." He explained it was not on this map. He saw that a map without Duluth held little interest for her. He bought her cigarettes and chlorophyll gum when he paid the bill.

Near Laramie he had a little trouble with the car. He thought it might be the head wind, but near Cheyenne, with the wind at the back, they almost stopped on a grade. The motor ran fine but seemed to be disconnected from the wheels. In Cheyenne a mechanic explained the clutch was shot. But since it was downgrade from Cheyenne he might nurse it along to where he was going. Boyd nursed it along in the wind stream of the big trucks. The girl slept, her head on his shoulder, the brown hand with the high-school ring resting on his pants leg, gripping the pack of cigarettes. In Nebraska they picked up a tail breeze and cruised along like a prairie schooner until a freight train blocked the road on a detour near Cozad. Boyd had to bring the car to a stop on an incline; it began to drift backward while still in gear. To keep from blocking the road he let it slide into the ditch. He sat there, the motor idling, the clutch spinning as if disengaged, and watched one of the brakemen go along the cars toward the caboose. Seeing Boyd in the ditch, he waved his stick, hollered, "Next time, take the train!" Down the tracks, no more than five or six cars, Boyd could see the caboose.

He gave the girl a shake to wake her. He took her bag from the rear, went around the car to pull her into the open and tugging her by the hand, went along the waist-high weeds in the ditch toward the caboose. He fell on the embankment, tearing the knee of his pants, and the girl stood and laughed at him until he brought the soft side of the bag flat against her bottom. The brakeman was there on the caboose platform, and put his hand down for the girl. As Boyd gave her a push from behind she said, "Sweet Jesus. It *is* a friggin movie!"

Before he reached the platform he felt the car jolt. The brakeman pushed the bag into the aisle, then slipped off his glove to take from his bib a silver watch with a snap-lid case. He wore one of the high-crowned striped denim hats Boyd had often seen on McKee's father, a railroad man retired to the swing on the porch.

"You stop at Lone Tree?" Boyd asked.

"Lone Tree?" he said, and took a moment to look at the girl, her face flushed from running, then at Boyd, with the knee showing through the hole in his pants. He snapped the lid on his watch, then turned to wag his head at the door of the caboose. Down the aisle, facing the door, sat a big fellow with his hat tipped over his face. One of his feet stood in the aisle, the pants leg tucked up, and Boyd could see the sock bulge where the underwear was folded. "He's getting off at Lone Tree, too," said the brakeman. "What's going on at Lone Tree?"

The cab jolted again, and the creaking of the wheels sounded like a carful of squealing pigs. The brakeman dropped down the steps to wave his flag. At the detour crossing Boyd saw the Plymouth and wondered why it was that the windshield seemed to be vibrating.

"Sweet Jesus," said the girl, "you leave the friggin motor running?" He had. In the ignition were his keys, a tab with his initials and a charm guaranteed to bring luck to the bearer. Perhaps it had. He gripped the rail, his eyes on the tracks that drew the two halves of the plain together, like a zipper, joining at the rear what it had just divided at the front. Why, he wondered, reaching toward the girl, did things coming toward him seem to break into pieces, and things that receded into the past seem to make sense?

"It makes me dizzy," she said, gripping his arm, and over her head Boyd winked at the brakeman who doubtless was also a father, and knew he had a problem on his hands.

LARKSPUR

From *One Day*

WENDELL Horlick came back from Korea with a collection of firearms that filled two footlockers to a five-year-old son he had not once set eyes on. He didn't know it, but that was something to be thankful for. When he first heard the remark, "get off my back," Wendell knew what it was that ailed him. That was it. Whether he was or not, Wendell always felt the kid was riding him.

The firearms were not much of a problem. He used them to decorate his den in the basement and made a regular museum out of the room for the kid. That was the year he didn't do so badly, but after that it was no contest. The kid had a five-lap start that he never made up. Wendell first knew he was in trouble when Irving took no interest in guns or Samurai swords. None whatsoever. No interest in guns or sports. Back in Winnemucca High Wendell had put the shot eleven inches farther than the state record. The coach gave him that shot. *To a Real Big Shot*, it said, and was signed by the coach. So he gave that shot to the kid and what did he do with it? He used it to flatten tin cans and crack rocks he thought there might be gold in. That was the tipoff. But it was Wendell who got tipped off.

Ill at ease with the sexy sort of girl he liked, Wendell had never been ill at ease with Miriam. They grew up together. He just didn't think of her as a girl. Her name being Hadley, which came before Horlick, she had the seat right in front of him all through grade school. A good thing, or he'd still be there in it. He told her that. He did learn to read and figure well enough to sort the mail at the P.O. window, and not be long or short at the end of a busy day. Winnemucca was no jerk town in some ways. People bought a lot of stamps.

But this idea that the brains were all in her family was one that Miriam took up later, when she had to. When she saw how other women looked, she took up brains. The years Wendell was away, sorting mail for the Army, Miriam took a college degree and did a little substitute teaching. She liked that. Where else would they pay her so well just to talk? He was in the Philippines, at the time, and to be nearer to him she took a job in Sacramento. The pay was pretty good. She put away enough money to mortgage a house. But by the time he got back she was used to money and making more of it than he was. They couldn't keep up the mortgage and live on the salary he made. When he pointed out a woman's place was in the home—and he meant one they could pay for—she pointed out that she was the one who bought it, and besides nobody was in it. She took the kid along with her in the morning to school. Wendell walked the five downhill blocks to the P.O.

That too should have been a tipoff, but Wendell had other problems. He didn't like Escondido. He didn't like the summer fog and the long winter rain. He missed the hot Winnemucca sunshine and the smart good-looking broads who walked around the streets or sat on the bar stools with the dude ranch cowboys. He didn't admit it, but he missed the whirring clank of the slot machines. During the war

Winnemucca had turned a new leaf and it was one that
Wendell could read. Everybody gambled. Everybody
played bingo and had a good time. He neither gambled nor
bingo'd himself but he liked to sit on a bar stool and watch
them. A woman gambling was a sight. A woman tight in her
pants cranking a slot machine.

One of the old biddies in Escondido smart enough to
know what a dice cup looked like, objected to the fact that
Wendell kept one at the stamp window. Pencils in it, but
she objected. How you like that? That had been the tipoff
of what he was in for working at the P.O. in Escondido: the
goddam old biddies hated him, and he hated them. They
had *him* behind the bars, and that was how they looked at
him. They would stand there counting their stamps, counting their change. Naturally it bugged him, and the way
they watched him got him so fuddled he sometimes made
mistakes. One of them reported he short-changed her,
deliberately. By the time they were saying he was hard of
hearing and asking him to please stop shouting at them, it
was too late to tell if he was hard of hearing, or had just
stopped listening to them. Shout he did. There was no
question about that. When his own kid came to the window
and moved his lips without making a sound, Horlick had
been too shocked to shout. He hadn't made a sound. He had
just stood there, leaning on the counter, till Miss Ames, at
the money order window, nudged him aside and took the
stamp business herself. That was the payoff: for a while he
sorted mail at the back of the room, where nobody saw
him, but his eyes went bad and he had these headaches. He
couldn't sleep. To avoid a nervous breakdown—this was
openly discussed by Miriam and the kid as if he couldn't
hear them—he was given a leave of absence. Dr. Creeley, in
cahoots with them all, recommended a change. What Wendell would have liked would have been Winnemucca, just

to go there in his Jeep and do a little hunting, with a little bingo and blackjack on quiet nights. Miriam wouldn't hear of it, of course, and turned up this relative in Pennsylvania, an uncle of Wendell's he didn't even know he had. He didn't smoke tobacco, but he raised it. That would be a change. The whole thing was an excuse to buy herself the foreign-type car she had wanted, since she refused to make a trip like that in the Jeep. She also wanted a rest from Irving, who was getting too much for her, and shipped him to that camp where Evelina sent Alec and where only French was spoken. Wendell had been all for it. Nothing else in this world would ever shut him up.

As a matter of fact he liked the trip, the Pennsylvania Turnpike in particular where Miriam, scared to death of the tunnels, let him drive. His uncle, a man named Mavis, didn't have much of a farm by western standards, but he was even crazier than Wendell about guns and dogs. He hunted all the time, not having much else to do. Miriam almost went crazy sitting in the kitchen with his wife, Arlene, who was putting up berries, the heat and smell so bad she couldn't eat. But as Wendell told her, it had been her idea. Every other day Wendell and Mavis took their guns and went off with the dogs, sometimes putting in three or four hours before they treed anything. These dogs, big hounds and small beagles, were like nothing Wendell had ever seen. To say they were smarter than people wasn't saying anything. He could talk to those dogs. They would sit or stand and listen to him. At other times they would come back and talk to him. One of the smaller hounds, named Larkspur, took a shine to Wendell that was pretty to watch. She never left him. In the morning she pawed at the latch on the door. To say that Larkspur was smarter than people was to say less than nothing. It was better to be silent. As Mavis liked to say, "A good hound bitch don't need to read your mind, she's got it." That was true of Larkspur. If Wendell had a mind, it was hers. At the table, or around the stove where they preferred the heat to the mosquitoes, Wendell didn't need to face Larkspur, or catch her eye, to get her tail to thumping. No, bygod. Her tail would begin to thump if he just thought of her. The same—if he had had a tail to thump—would have been true of him. This dog almost preferred Wendell to the coons that the pack would go after, baying, since she would be in torment seeing him lag behind. When the time came to leave—which was Miriam's idea, since Wendell still had plenty—it was not surprising that Mavis suggested that maybe he should take Larkspur. After all, *whose* dog was she? She would just pine away if he left her behind. That was the last thing Miriam wanted, but it was Wendell who was having the breakdown. He didn't throw it up to her. He just gave her a choice. Then there was the problem, in such a small car, of how to get the dog back, since Wendell wouldn't think of shipping her all that way in a box. The car had a seat, a sort of half-rumble, where they stored most of their luggage; if the luggage was shipped instead there was room for Larkspur. To keep her from scratching the car Wendell bought several war surplus blankets, so the dog could sit up, when she cared to, and look around. This was what she did. In fact she soon cared for nothing else. She would rather sit up and look out than eat and drink.

All that was now in the past, but it was not hard to reconstruct. Wendell had told the story often. Those who had not heard it were able to read it in the local papers, where it had been illustrated with Miriam's photographs. At the editor's request she had written the article. There were those who said that Miriam Horlick was laughing at Wendell, rather than with him, but Wendell had no such impression himself. He had read that piece dozens of times. The article and the photographs were framed on the wall of his den. Miriam's style, for his taste, was a little high-falutin'—as Mavis said when he received a copy—but the facts and the pictures spoke for themselves. She said that man and dog were a pair. And so they were. If that was what gave the fools their laughs, Wendell was content to let them have it. The last laugh would prove to be his, and it was. Thanks to Larkspur he was superintendent of the Escondido Pound.

It all began very simply, as important things will. That morning on the turnpike Larkspur dozed for about half an hour, ducked down in the cockpit. A stop for gas and oil woke her up. Wendell himself had a cup of coffee and bought a hotdog he shared with her. She liked the rolls better than the dog. That was typical. When they pulled out into the traffic the wind and the passing cars seemed to excite her. Instead of ducking down out of it, she put her paws on the seat back, her nose to the wind. In a low-cut foreign-type car that is quite a sight. From a bit up the road it looked like the dog was driving it.

They both liked that, Wendell and Larkspur, with people giving them a smile when they pulled around them, or giving a toot on their horns as they approached. Larkspur loved it. In the cool dark tunnels she bayed like a wolf. It went without saying Miriam *didn't* like it, but the trip was her idea; Wendell liked it, Larkspur liked it, so it was two to one.

Everything was okay until they stopped for lunch. At that point Wendell noticed that Larkspur's eyes, normally bright as marbles, were watery and bloodshot. That was the wind. The way she stuck her nose into the wind. He thought the dog would have sense to lie low for a spell, but when they started up again there she was. The afternoon sun had her long tongue lolling out of her mouth. When Wendell stopped the car to check Larkspur's eyes they were almost closed. But nothing would force her to lie low. The moment she heard the shift of the gears she was up. Somewhere near Pittsburgh Wendell left the freeway and stopped in a town where they had a dime store. He bought a sporty cap with a visor for himself, and a pair of fur-lined goggles for Larkspur, the sort that young hoodlum cyclists like to wear. The elastic band fit snug on Larkspur's ears. Miriam's comment, when she stopped laughing, was that she looked like a space-age bloodhound. Larkspur sensed how she must look, and pawed them off. Wendell stuck them back on, and before she had time to paw at them again he got the car started. That did it. She forgot all about them the moment the car started. The sight of a hound wearing motorcycle goggles led people coming toward them to turn off the road. Wendell couldn't see it, but he guessed it was quite a sight. When they slowed up to pass through a town people tooted their horns and doubled up laughing. Larkspur felt the excitement and barked quite a bit. That was how it went till they stopped for evening and the poor dog drank half a bucket of water. Then, like she was soused, she just passed out. They didn't hear a peep out of her the rest of the night. The next morning she pawed the goggles when they first went on, but once they got under way she didn't mind them. And that was the story. That was how they went west.

Before they got to Salt Lake Larkspur was so poohed she would sometimes drop off to sleep without eating. She lost weight. There was a blank, stage-struck look to her eyes. With the desert coming up Wendell bought her a hat, of the sort girls wear to the beach, with a ribbon that tied under her chin. She either didn't care, or was too far gone to notice. With a sober, bored expression she would sit and look at people laugh at her. Wendell was never closer to her than at times like that. Word about the bloodhound that wore goggles travelled west faster than they did. In Reno, waiting for them, were several newspaper reporters who took their picture. Neither Larkspur nor Wendell could have cared less. But that was the tipoff: when they got to Escondido there was something like a reception committee, with two reporters sent over from the *Chronicle*. They took one shot of the car and Wendell, but Larkspur didn't show in it. She was dead to the world in the back seat. She did nothing at all for two or three days but drink and sleep. By that time so many people had heard so many different versions of the story—one had it that Larkspur did the driving—Miriam was persuaded to write it up herself. This appeared in the *Chronicle*, with a big blowup snap of Larkspur. There she was. Everybody but Wendell thought she looked fine. Whether it was too much travel, too much excitement, too much adulation or just not enough of something, Wendell knew that things were not the same. Was it Escondido, was it the clean swept basement with the hissing, popping heater she had to sleep with? Was it Irving? Wendell caught *him* wearing Larkspur's goggles and staring into her face like a diving frogman. Was it perhaps Wendell? God knows, he had undergone a change himself. Or was it, as Dr. Cowie suggested, that Larkspur just didn't like *people*. In Escondido that's all there was. *People*. Even the dogs were like people. When they saw another dog, a real honest-to-God dog, these other mutts got excited as women at a bargain counter. They weren't dogs, in Wendell's opinion, they were pets. A big setter up the road had gallstone trouble. All the females were fixed. A dog's life was all Larkspur wanted, but not the one she had.

If he let Larkspur run she would be gone all night and people would hear her baying like a banshee, since the hills around Escondido were full of deer and coons. She almost lost her mind trailing a scent, but there was nobody there to share it with her. She missed the pack. She missed the bang, bang, bang of the guns. Everyone in Escondido sat up half the night waiting for Wendell to bang one, at which point they would have the game warden on him in about five minutes. He knew that. They just sat around waiting for him to make a slip. After a night in the bush Larkspur would come home with her coat all spattered, her ears torn, the loose flesh at the sides of her mouth sore and bloody, her paws so cut up you would think she was scratching in glass. People complained about the noise. It got the other mutts in the town riled up. Wendell had no choice but to keep her in the basement, or leashed up in the yard. He built a run for her along one of the clotheslines, which sounded like a trolley when she took after something. There's always these hoodlums who like to torment a good dog. One night they filled an oil barrel with cans and rolled it down the slope to hit the box she slept in. The racket was so terrible it frightened Wendell half to death. When he got out in the yard Larkspur was gone, the collar snapped right off by the way she took off. He spent all day in the hills looking for her. Not till the next night did she come home, but you couldn't really say it was Larkspur. A beaten, shaky hound, with a hoarse way of breathing, had Larkspur's markings, but was *not* Larkspur. She hid in the basement. All she did all day was scratch and lick herself. Her eczema didn't respond to treatment since it was obviously caused by her nervous condition. Except to do her business she would not even go into the yard. Wendell himself got careless about the basement door, since she showed so little disposition to use it, and she may have been gone as long as half a day before he missed her. Gone she was. And no collar or tag on her neck. She had the itch so bad she couldn't stand anything around her neck. Wendell went into the hills, but when he got back in the evening there was this story circulating about the bus station. A hound dog, spotted like Larkspur, was seen on and off in the station. Some swore that they saw her get on the bus. That was just the sort of crap Wendell expected to hear from the baboons in Escondido. Their idea of a really smart dog was one that acted like a dim-witted human being, got up in the morning, took the bus, and went to work. Larkspur was not dim-witted, but in one way she was every bit as crazy as most human beings. She was nuts about cars. If it had wheels, she would go off in it. In a town like Escondido, full of sports cars, or station wagons with their windows run down, what had probably happened was that Larkspur had hopped into one and gone for a ride. Where to? Almost anywhere she could get away from people. That was harder and harder to do, but she was a smart dog. Evelina Cartwright was absolutely sure she would turn up back in Pennsylvania. Maybe she did. Wendell never got his courage up to write. If that was where she was, that was where she belonged. If she wasn't, it would make him unhappy the rest of his life.

When people brought up the subject to Wendell he first said, "Hell, I guess she likes dogs better than people." That was pretty pointed, but it wasn't pointed enough. In a week or two he was adding, "I guess she don't like people any more than I do. She's a smart dog." It was just a step from that to what Wendell next found himself saying. It was nothing new. He had been saying it to himself all along. Now he didn't bother to keep it to himself. He just said it out. "People are no damn good," he would say, "but hell, that ain't news."

CHICKPEA

From *One Day*

SOMEWHERE in the Sierras—she never really knew where, not having a sense of place or a sense of direction—Alec had spent most of her summers at a camp where, it was said, only French was spoken. In the fall she came home with pimples, chronic constipation, and a good accent. With the accent she had the shrug, and when she went to Paris it proved to be enough. She lived in a room on the turn of the stairs, so narrow that she had to dress and undress in bed. A slotted window, showing nothing but the sky, let in cats and the traffic noise from St. Germain des Prés. Over dude ranch blue jeans with brass studs on the pockets, she wore a lightweight Brooks Brothers raincoat, given to her, with advice, by a young man she had met on the boat. He cautioned her about dope, sexy Arabs, and diseases easily contracted in washrooms.

As it turned out, she looked too young to attract most young men, and too old to attract most of the others. Women, however, she attracted. Those who were old, and saw at a glance what it was she needed, or those who made change in washrooms, phone booths, and sold American cigarettes. Unhappily, she was not attracted to them. From her father, perhaps, she had the low blood pressure that made her very self-sufficient. Always cold, she did not crave creature warmth. Except to light cigarettes, her hands were usually deep in her pockets. Free from the tyranny of vegetables, milk and meat, she lived on baskets of bread and coffee. She was thought to be a model, a classic version of the starving saltimbanque.

Not having slept very much in college, she spent most of her time in bed. It gave people the impression that she had been up all night. But that was seldom. She was usually asleep by ten o'clock. She came to Paris with introductions to several famous people, some of them painters, some of them poets, but after five months in the city she had not troubled to look them up. She had met one casually and thought him a fool. Another was too good a poet to be bothered. If little else, she had her standards. She knew where she stood. A twenty-three-page book of poems, one poem each to nine pages, the rest serving as an ample and tiresome introduction, had been published in an edition of one hundred and twenty-five copies, one copy to be seen in the window of a shop off the Boul Mich. Her first fear was that nobody would buy it, then that somebody might. The author's name was A. P. Cartwright, with a signature slanting upward. In two reviews the poems were assumed to be those of a man. There was not much praise, but she considered that more than enough.

Lean as she was on arrival, she still managed to lose weight. In bed her bony knees dug into her own spare flesh. Perhaps the strong cigarettes, or too much coffee, led her heart to race and often skip beats. Without too much concern she felt she might die one night in her sleep. The cemetery at Montparnasse did not depress her with its hosts of the dead so much as humiliate her with the smallness of her talent. There had been too many poets. Too many who had been good. In this world it left her with a sense of being unemployed.

One rainy afternoon, her coat pulled over her head, she ran through a gate to get out of a downpour, taking shelter with others under a row of dripping trees. Sheets of blowing rain pelted the toy boats floating on the pond. Without a child nearby, it might have been a mountain lake seen from the distance, the fragile boats suddenly caught in a mountain storm. Then it was over. Out of the very trees, it seemed to Alec, streamed the children of Paris. Shrilly they chattered like birds. Others, like unleashed pets, ran back and forth between the water and the benches. There the mamás sat on newspapers, their broad laps full of mending.

Her hair wet, her coat steaming, Alec stood where the sun would help dry her. The cries of a large family of girls filled her ears. Two were as tall as Alec, but they were still dressed like children. One did not sit down out of fear of showing her legs. How old were they? Much too old for nymphets. Out of pity for them Alec could have cried.

To spare the feelings of these poor girls Alec took pains to keep her eyes elsewhere. But it hardly mattered. They had eyes only for each other and their plump mamá. She sat under a tree with a sheet of newspaper shading her face. The five girls, shrieking like parrots, proved to have charge of one small, thin boy. He raced about with a hoop and a plastic boat crying, *me voici! me voici!* What a joke that was! They had eyes for nothing else. What else was there to see? One would have thought, listening to them, that he was the last male child in the world. Little wonder they grew up to be such primping egoists. The matron, a plain, corseted woman with a bag of wool and a cushion to sit on, now and then wagged her needles, or slapped her hands like an animal trainer. In a moment they were before her, wagging their tails. What had she to offer? Candy, money? Nothing but herself. In a clucking humorless tone she gave them advice. Then dispersal. Off toward the pond raced the boy, rolling his hoop, three of his long garter-legged sisters fencing him in, shrieking at him. But the two older girls, as in a play, seated themselves cross-legged in the gravel, and held up their hands for the winding of balls of wool. They sat so erect the ribboned tips of their braids swept the ground. And how they chattered! Had they been separated for weeks? For months? There in the park they set up a camp as if their piece of it was private. Jacks were played, rope was skipped, periodically the boy, screaming *me voici!*, appeared at the fringe of the circle for his crumb of praise. At a clap of the woman's hands, no more, this afternoon camp was broken, and in sober military order, precedence given to the male, they left the park.

Alec was amused, knowing better than to believe her own eyes. A child herself, she knew a thing or two about children. A normal child, even an abnormal child, *rebelled*. It did not go through a performance that resembled a charade on Home Sweet Home. Not the wickedly clever and adult children who tormented each other in the best French novels. In order to see what motivated their behavior, Alec came back to the park the next day, and the next. The next also. From a bench across the path she spied on them. The same stupid childish games seemed to be enough. A hoop for the boy, a skipping rope for the girls, a sort of hopscotch they played in the gravel, forever glancing up to see if the mother was watching them. The boy lost his plastic boat and did not get another. He shrieked for four minutes then clammed up. One minute later he was rolling his hoop, screaming *me voici!*

It was all so simple-minded and cliché Alec felt someone should write a book about it. When the boy wet his new button sandals in the fountain his mother grabbed him by one arm, unbuttoned his pants, and gave him ten sharp slaps with the palm of her hand. This reddened his thin little bottom and brought tears to the eyes of his sisters. His howls were horrible to hear, his face was still wet as he raced off screaming *me voici!*

The surface of this life was so transparent it left very little to be seen through. Alec sat with a volume of Valéry's poems in her lap. They went unread. What was the point of being so subtle if life was so obvious? The surface of life seemed to be more sufficient. The depths were a bore. A plump plain matron, five plain girls, one touched with something like promise, and a small male child with his unabashed, hooting, male arrogance. How explain its witless felicity? Into his hot little arrogant face something was always being pushed, to show how much they loved him. One day it was his cup of soft ice cream. An accident, she said. On another, held like a sack, his dirty face was dipped into the fountain until Alec herself, breathless, feared for his life. But after coughing and gagging for a moment he was all right. With the lap of her skirt an older sister blew his nose, wiped off his face.

What effect did all this have on Alec Cartwright? Quieting. She sat more, read less, and acquired a taste for the cheaper brandy. Idle speculations were all she had, and seemed to be enough. If people could go on *as if* nothing had happened, what, if anything, *had* happened? *Me voici* the child still shrieked, and the mother looked. So did Alec. It was very depressing to a girl who had put childish things behind her. What other things were there? The question hung in the air. Peanuts she loathed, but over that summer she learned to eat them, and feed them to pigeons. Her French also improved. When she said *me voici* the children looked.

At the Deux Magots, where the waiters liked her, she listened to the stories of strangers, smoked their cigarettes, but had little to say herself. Cars with California license plates pulled over to the curb to beckon to her. Were they so fresh? No, they merely recognized a girl from home. They didn't have to ask her if she talked the lingo, they just *knew* that she did.

Boys and girls as ill fed and ill housed as herself borrowed money from her in the washrooms, asked her about VD, and cautioned her about Algerians. She knew about Algerians. They were the ones who stopped her to ask for cigarettes.

In August the hot muggy nights led her to use the hotel lift, when it was working. The four-flight climb set her heart to pounding, and her feelings had changed about living and dying. There was a cat in her room that would die without her. Or so she hoped. He had given her the fleas that made it hard for her to sleep.

The elevator, a small iron cage with open, ornamental grillwork, was subject to stopping between floors when the power went off. This was more pleasurable than frightening, since she had a view of the stairs and hallways. It was always possible to call to somebody, or wave to someone. There was also a tarnished mirror she could look at and a menu in case she desired room service. With the night clerk, who had a blond moustache, she had a little joke about the room service, since she pretended that her room *was* the lift. She preferred it on the hot muggy nights.

On the floor below her lived an English couple, the woman several inches taller, with a hat like a lampshade, her gloved hand always hooked to her husband's arm. They walked about Paris, arm in arm, rain or shine, taking identical strides. He carried an umbrella and a camera that flapped at his side. They had begun to feed the pigeons at their window in the morning until they gathered in a cloud and it couldn't be opened. The noise of their wings woke Alec up every morning.

Directly above her, in a room like her own, lived a young man Alec took for an Algerian. He was tall, bronze-colored, and wore a small, tight-fitting beret. On a strap around his shoulder he carried a portable radio. She knew when he was passing in the elevator from the way the music rose and went by her. Like most young Frenchies he was mad for *le jazz hot*. It continued to play in his room far into the night.

A Friday night in August she got soaked with rain coming home. In the lobby, her shoes squishing, she took off the coat that soaked up the water, rung it out at the door, then came back and waited for the elevator. The way the music came along with it she knew the young man would be inside. Didn't he know it was raining? He wore his soiled seersucker coat. Up till that moment they had exchanged a few greetings in French. On seeing her he whistled, said, "Man, are you wet!"

She had done no more than look down the hall to where it was pouring. As he stepped from the elevator cage his radio suddenly boomed on louder.

"Don't you ever turn that damn thing off?" she had said.

From his height, his face tipped sidewise, he had looked at her without smiling. She had noticed the white fleck, like a reflection, on one eye. The lid blinked while the other held steady.

"You not only look wet," he said, "you smell wet. You know what you smell like?" With that she understood he was a deadpan artist. A feeder of lines.

In a shrill voice she had replied, "I'm sorry, I can't hear you!" She held his gaze, and he was the first to shift his eyes. Fumbling at the radio he lowered the volume. "What

I said was, you sure smell wet. I was just about to say what you smelled like."

"You think I don't know?"

"No, you don't know," he said. "You got no idea whatsoever what you smell *like*. What you smell like to me is the sweetest goddam smell in the world." His wide smile showed her the coral roof of his mouth. "A wet girl, a wet American girl, that's just about the finest goddam smell in the world."

That was how it began, if it had a beginning. No more and no less.

His name was Jackson, Lyle P. Jackson, from Omaha. The Omaha she didn't believe for some time. Indians perhaps, not black boys, came from Omaha. He liked to say, "Man, you know what it's like, Omaha?" and look around him as if he hadn't left it. What he saw always led him to slowly wag his head. She had been amazed to hear that he had gone to an integrated school without even knowing it. White boys and girls went to it. That seemed unheard of for Omaha. The school sat on the edge of a colored district and there was simply no other place for them to go to. The school had been an old one of red bricks with the high stairways and tall windows, a cinder-covered playground all along one side. But when they built the *new* school they didn't build it *there*. He could tell her that. They built it right at that point where no black boy could get to it. He liked to say *black boy*, although he wasn't black himself. He was more the color of the Tansu chests that her mother couldn't find a use for, a shade darker than Chavez, the dog catcher. His hair was kinky, rusty in color, but worn so short it might have been his scalp tone. He liked to stroke it when he sat talking, like a pet in his lap. He had been four months in Paris and took his big meal in a café on the Boulevard Montparnasse, where poor artists and painters were a specialty. He was a painter then? No. A writer? No. She had let the point drop since it hardly mattered. But it did to him. "Chickpea," he said, which he liked to call her, "why don't you ask me what I'm doin' in Paree?"

"What are you doing in Paree?" she asked him. The question was intended to transform him. Had he waited these four long months to be asked?

"What am I doin' in Paree, woman?" He had turned on the bench to look at her sidelong, the eye with the white fleck away from her. Concealing that eye gave his glance a certain style. She had thought the question rhetorical, but he waited for her to repeat it.

"Okay, man," she said, "what are you doing in Paree?"

"You can see me, okay. Can't you, Chickpea?" Her head had nodded. Yes, she could see him. "Well, that's what I'm doin' here, Chickpea. I'm bein' visible, that's what I'm doin'. When I was back in the un-tied states I was an invisible man!"

This pronouncement meant they had something in common. They had read the same book.

"You think this is the *other* country?" she said. But he had read just the *one* book, not all of them. "This country suits me fine, but I don't like the lingo much." They were having their brandy on the Boul Mich where half of Paris seemed to be passing. Few noticed them, or anybody. Everybody seemed to be invisible. The paradox of that thought weighed on her mind while they watched the French police, with their paddy-wagon, pick up students like corpses where they had stretched out to form a line in the street. Inside the wagon they were chanting. It had something to do with Algiers. "I'm just as visible here as anybody," he said, although it seemed to be the contrary. Here he had become as invisible as *everybody*.

When the police were gone he asked if she had ever been

in a paddy-wagon. It amazed him that she hadn't. He had assumed she had had experience of the world. For himself, he had ridden in plenty, and spent all of thirty-one nights in jails. Different jails. All over the same South. He had been put in jail for drinking coffee out of a paper cup in a lobby entrance: he had been put in jail for sitting down where he should have stood up. He had been put in his place, that is, and that place was always jail. When he ran out of money, which would be soon, he was going to go back to that same town, and they would put him in that same jail. When there wasn't any room to be had in the jail, they'd put him in the bus, in the back of the bus. In the Jim Crow section of the bus he was invisible.

This had been the longest speech he had made and left them both silent. They sat for several moments before he turned his radio up. He seemed to have the feeling she thought he was lying and took out his billfold stuffed with clippings. There they were. And there he was. Even in the black newsprint she could recognize him. In one picture he was shown being dragged by the feet, with both his shoes off. In the background the faces of the whites were like caged animals, snarling. In one piece he was listed as Lyle P. Jackson. The "P" in quotes.

"What's the P for?" she asked, being curious.

"That's what they call me," he said, "that's what the boys call me." His pride made him taller. He folded the clippings carefully.

"They call you P? P for what?"

"Little Chickpea, the P is for Protest, what else?" He laughed. "Protest Jackson. That's who *I* am."

"I like Jackson better. Just Jackson."

"It's not a question of what you like or dislike. Before you like or dislike you got to Protest. You let like or dislike come in and you get all screwed up."

It amused Alec Cartwright to think that Protest Jackson considered her less a rebel than he was. But perhaps she was. She had spent no more than four hours in jail. In Boston, with five boys from Harvard, she had picketed a bookstore that refused to sell *Lolita*, and been booked, along with two Smith girls, for disturbing the peace. It was not the sort of protest Jackson would appreciate.

Once his position was clear, however, Jackson didn't talk much about it. It led to his feeling that they had a good deal in common. The less they talked the more in common they felt. And vice-versa. The more Alec talked the sadder he got. This ran counter to Alec's experience and the sleepless nights she had spent in college, doing everything she could to explain her own and understand the opposing point of view. Jackson merely got glum and turned up the volume of his radio.

The truth was that Alec was all for Protest, but she was often ill at ease with Jackson. Why was that? The problem was simple. Did he like her for her *mind*, or because she was white? She could not free herself of the suspicion if *she* was as black and tan as *he* was, she, Alec Cartwright, would have been invisible to Protest Jackson. For all his hate of the word, there was something in the color white he liked. When he looked at her that was what he saw. He couldn't get enough of it just looking, so he liked to have pictures of them together, sitting on a bench, or on one of the bridges over the Seine. There he could see it. Because of the light she would come out whiter, he would come out blacker. He put these pictures in a wallet with his clippings. They were proof of what had happened to him in Paris, the way the clippings were proof of what had happened to him in the South. They showed how far he had carried his protest in Paris.

One day she asked him, "Are there any blind black boys?" How he laughed, showing the roof of his mouth.

"You think black boys don't go blind? You think it's only white boys who have troubles?"

"I just wondered—" she said, "what they'd do in the way of a protest. How would they know, when they met a girl, what color she was?" That disturbed him.

"Chickpea, you saying what I like about you is your pale color?"

"I'm not saying one thing or another. I'm just asking. How does a blind black boy go about making a protest? How does he know who is on his side?"

"You got a real deep race prejudice in you, Chickpea, you know that?"

"I like your color better than my own. I think your color is beautiful. Is that race prejudice?"

"You just like my suntan color, Chickpea. You don't really like black. You don't like your hair kinky."

"My hair *is* kinky," she cried, "and I hate it!" Her hair was not kinky, but it was frizzly and gave her the same kinky sort of problems. Jackson leaned toward her to put his hand on her head, give it a rub.

"You call that kinky, Chickpea? Why that's lamb's wool. That's the stuff that grows on white babies' bottoms. You like to know what kinky hair is?" He wiped his beret off, thrust his head toward her. "Say, you take a feel of this, Chickpea!" he said, but she couldn't. God strike her dead, as her mother would say, but she could not lift her hand to his rust-colored topping. Kinky indeed it was, like a worn pan cleaner. "Feel it, Chickpea! It's time a girl like you knows what kinky hair is. What good's the suntan color when you know you're black inside?"

She couldn't move. That shocked her so much she couldn't speak.

"What's the matter, Chickpea?" he said, looking up. "You buy all that jazz about white inside stuff? You sit around cryin' your eyes out about sooty black boys so lily white inside?"

"I guess I bought a lot of jazz, but I didn't buy all of it. I didn't come to Paris to have my picture taken in bed with a black boy."

His hand moved toward her slowly, the fingers close together, and she knew he would slap her. Her eyes were closed as it moved along her cheek to the back of her neck. Gently he cupped her head in his palm. Was he pondering how to crush it?

"That one we don't have yet. That one I'd sure like for my collection." Was the smile he gave her that of a lover, or a priest? How gentle he looked. On her neck and arm she could feel the gooseflesh form. "Anybody ever tell you how you look like Marlene Dietrich?" No, nobody had. "If you weren't so skinny you'd look just like her. You got her eyes."

She controlled an impulse to say how much he made her think of Gary Cooper. Perhaps he wouldn't like that. Gary Cooper was white inside and out. Who—if she wanted to praise him—would he like to look like? Willie Mays? Would he resent her thinking he looked Algerian? Strangely enough, when she thought of him with pleasure it was a black boy she thought of. The pink palms of his hands. The clear white roll of his eyes. Although from Omaha he talked like the minstrels she had heard on records. That she liked. And the coral roof of his mouth. What would he think if she said he had a voice like Al Jolson? A good voice, that is. A voice she liked. She didn't know, and she doubted that he knew himself. His *self*, after all, was the one truly invisible object, having no perceptible color, no questionable type of hair. If she liked him, *who* did she like?

If she should love him, *what* should she love? Not anything visible, or material, or it might be the source of a misunderstanding, the very thing that he was determined to protest about. Not to mention what invisible problems he saw in her.

Although he said he wanted that picture in bed for his collection, Alec didn't really believe it. Was she too skinny? He didn't have to go to bed to look at her eyes. He was friendly but respectful, his long arm often rested on her narrow shoulder, his fingers lightly toying with the curls on her neck. But his knees drew away when they bumped hers under the table. He made no advances. This was something he left up to her. The comment she heard from him the most was, "You're the boss, Chickpea. You name it," which usually referred to what was offered on the menu or the cinema. But need it stop there? She was the boss. It was up to her.

At night, rising in the lift, he would place his hand on the back of her neck, in such a manner that her skull seemed to be cupped in the palm of his hand. In this gesture there was something that pleased, something that frightened her. Was that part of desire? Her body seemed weightless as it dangled from his hand. She was the boss, she was the one who pushed the buttons for the lift to stop, and she would be the one who did not push the button the night it went on. "You're the boss, Chickpea," he would say, and laugh his musical, blackboy laughter, his brown hand rocking her head from side to side like a cup of dice.

He had sweetness and affection but there were flaws in his character. As his money began to get low he would be in the toilet when it came time to pay the bill: if *she* was in the toilet he would rifle her pack of cigarettes. Not her money. She left it purposely, hoping he would, but he drew the line at money. At *her* money, that is. He was not above accepting the money of a fat, wig-topped female painter who paid him, so he told her, to pose. Alec was pained by her age and slobby drabness: she openly suggested that he ask for more money. At the very least, she said, he should be well paid for *that*. But he was fool enough to be pleased with what he got. An invisible black boy paid to be visible. This female had an apartment in Barcelona where she was willing to take him for the winter, but he balked at being carted away, actually at living with her. It was not so much a matter of taste but his fear of the law. Spain was another country. He didn't want to get mixed up with crossing lines. There was a law he knew about that put a man in jail for that, even if he was white. A half-respectable woman, in her fashion, there were always letters for her from her children who went to school in Switzerland, where they could ski and skate. She paid his taxi fare to collect her mail at the American Express.

If Barcelona was out, as it seemed to be, Jackson had a deadline early in November, when his freighter sailed from Antwerp to New Orleans. He referred to this as a return to the barricades. He said that so often he began to believe it, and behaved like a college boy drafted to go to Korea. He talked about training, and cut back a little on her cigarettes. If talk like that struck her as amusing it gave a war-like flavor to Jackson's departure. He was not going home to Omaha. He was going to the *front*. He planned to take up his permanent residence in jail. Since all the boys she had known felt themselves threatened in one way or another, Jackson's war of protest was perhaps unusual, but not at all strange. It was, after all, just another war. It was radically different in one detail, however. *His* war made sense. A civil war: a Protest war: a war to make himself visible. It was crazy as a story by Kafka, and like that story it made sense.

In the Paris *Herald* accounts were printed that showed the tempo of this war was rising: something called Freedom Riders, white and black, were carrying it to the enemy. Photographs were printed showing these Riders being emptied from buses, like corpses, precisely in the manner Jackson had so often pointed out. Never having been south of Bethesda, Maryland, Alec did not know much about the front and rear of buses, black and white johns, black and white counters and drinking fountains, and those borderline towns where a black man never knew if they *saw* him or not. But she had read Faulkner. If that was the South she felt familiar with it.

As the day approached for his departure Jackson talked a good deal about the war he was fighting. Alec listened. She understood this was pep talk for himself. He didn't really want to go and he had to persuade himself that he should. In this persuasion he applied to himself he proved to be smarter than she had thought him. One of the phrases he had she didn't like was *think-win*. You got to think-win, Chickpea, he would say, and snap his fingers like a jazz drummer. A think-winning black boy, according to Jackson, was like a good resistance fighter in France who found his country in the hands of the enemy. To live in it he had to lie low, work underground. He didn't want to take over, or rape anybody, or make some goddam commie revolution, all he wanted to do was get a lot of white men off his back. When he first met her he liked to say, "Chickpea, I don't want to marry any white man's daughter—" but he dropped that in favor of *off my back*. Was that a small point? It wasn't lost on either of them.

On the warm October days they sat in the gardens, the gravel paths lit up with flaming leaves, the sounds of the traffic, the voices of the children, louder and sharper now the trees were bare. What Alec called her family—the one that came to the park—had been reduced to the small boy and his mother: without his sisters, his captive audience, he seemed like a child recovering from an illness. While his mother knitted, he sat dreaming with his eyes on the pond. Jackson liked to sit, but his hands were nervous and he usually had to be toying with something. He made paper airplanes from napkins, or rolled his handkerchief to resemble a puppet. One day he said, "You like a family so much why don't you have one." He had a way of blurting things out that left her with the burden of the explanation. After something like that he would roll up a newspaper and peer at her through the tube. She had answers to that, but she couldn't think of one that didn't say more than she intended. Was that his intention? She couldn't tell. They knew each other so well, and so little, they could talk like the children in French novels. But his questions were probing. Did he want her to say more than she said?

In late October she would wake up feeling that he had gone, or that something had happened, because of something she had failed to do. That was easy to trace, and should have passed since she understood the origin of it so well. A Tate boy who thought he was Holden Caulfield had asked her to spend a weekend in New York with him, which she had. But right at the last they both chickened out about his room reservation at the Wilcox, and spent most of the night drinking coffee in the Automat. His point was it would *kill* his mother if she found out. He didn't think about Alec, and *her* mother, whom Alec didn't think about much either, but wouldn't it be a kid like that who would crash in one of those boxcars flying to Alaska? All she could think of was the miserable night they had begun in the lobby, as if waiting for their parents, then had walked the streets until they found the all-night Automat.

Anything, anything was preferable to that, especially

after Alec had seen the mother who wondered if she might not have some interesting letters from her son. Would she and Jackson spend their last night together watching waiters stack the chairs at the Café Flores, even the one who liked them waiting for them to leave? That seemed to be more horrible, because it was more childish (and Lyle Jackson was *not* Holden Caulfield), than anything else that might happen; and would not, in any case, kill Alec's mother. Other things might happen, but nothing she could think of would accomplish that. She came to this decision five days before he left, a day when it had drizzled since morning and Jackson had showed signs of coming down with a cold. Having worn out his shoes, he padded around in sneakers that soaked up the water. She gave him aspirin, brandy, and advice. Early in the evening, huddled under newspapers, they slapped through the puddles to the hotel lobby, shivered in the draft that ventilated the lift. At *her* stop, without comment, they both got off.

She was spared what Jackson might have said or done, thanks to his well-developed sense of doom: wet feet, or the sniffles, showed his number was up. Like a sick pet he was docile, laid himself down so he could be covered, let her peel the wet socks from his gleaming feet, pull off his pants. His feet were like ice. Rubbing them tickled him, but did little good. She put his wet clothes in the transom where the draft might help dry them, and for warmth, pure creature comfort, curled up on the bed beside him. How they stank, but he made no comment. The overdose of brandy soon had him sleeping. She lay awake full of pity for the sons of men. In the night he pulled her under the covers and with a stubborn, nuzzling persistence, like a nursing puppy, made a moaning, groping love. Not a bit of it was like the thought she had given to it. How being leggy, they would writhe like a bed of snakes. How her passion would surprise or embarrass him. But there was no lunging, or bed creaking, but a movement as if they were being fitted to make a tight seal. A large pulse that seemed to beat the length of his body set up a response in her own, and that was it. Then they slept. In the morning she was the one to get up, put on the wet clothes, and go out for coffee, rolls and brandy. He had a fever, and his sneezes dimmed the room light. She found it wonderful to sit within the mist and let it rain the germs around her, knowing that she had whatever he had, and that it was right. That night he was almost ill with his throat sore, his head bad, but he was not so ill he turned away from her when she got in the bed. A fairly normal cold, with a touch of fever, Jackson's mood was that of a man who was willing to die if the circumstance was just about right. He felt that it was. Almost, but not quite, he said as much. He took a dim view, at night, of his life as a soldier on the barricades. He would just as soon die right there in Paris, if she didn't mind.

She did mind, but on the third morning he was worried about drowning more than dying since he could not swim a stroke, and November was a bad time for a small boat. He was not a good sailor. But he liked airplanes even less than boats. She saw to it that his pants were pressed and made him a present of a heavy wool sweater sold by an Italian who made a business of wearing them in from Milan.

Jackson's Antwerp train left at noon but there was not a chance for them to be maudlin. He had to fight with a pack of women tourists for a seat in the coach. Other heads blocked the window. He did not call to her or wave. She walked about aimlessly: a chain smoker, she forgot to smoke. Coffee cooled in her cup, she left the food untouched on her plate. In shop windows she sometimes saw the curious smile on her face. Was it that of a person who had lost something, or a terminal case? She felt nothing. No, nothing. Not even tired. In the evening a weariness like an illness made it difficult for her to move. She sat on benches. On the rock walls that supported a fence. A cab driver who had passed her several times stopped to ask if she was all right. He took her to the hotel, helped her across the lobby, and paid money to a clerk to bring her food. But in the morning it was cold on the tray, untouched. She woke up with his throat, his fever, but he was not there in the bed to help warm her. She had chills and horrible sweating fevers by turns. What she thought to be two nights and one day proved to have been two days and three nights. What happened to the others? She had dreamed of being on the barricades. She had dreamed of positive and negative people, black and white prints. She had also come to decisions she had given very little thought to. The decision was there, established, when she got up. It settled her future. All she had to do was wait. If she proved to be big with child she would fly to Protest Jackson, in New Orleans, with the answer to that question he had asked her weeks before. If she didn't, she would wait until she heard from him.

Was it Jackson or waiting that changed her life?

Waiting left upon her the greatest impression since it gave everything an importance. It seemed meaningful, of course, that Jackson was at sea in the same sense that she was, and perhaps for about the same time. She had never cared for milk in any form but she began to take it in her coffee, and use a filter holder when she smoked her cigarettes. In her freshman year she had dissected a cat and for weeks patiently put the bones back together, but of a child she knew very little. Did it breathe air? When would she know, like her own heartbeat, that she was full of its life? The plain French matron, wrapped in a shawl, her short plump legs hanging free of the gravel, sometimes glanced up with her intact, preoccupied gaze as Alec strolled by. How well Alec understood it. She was leading six lives, none of them her own. How well she grasped how her husband, poor devil, could seem a stranger to her. Those five splendid girls who had hovered about her and without question wrote her long weekly letters, were never completely out of the radar screen of her mind. Otherwise she might have had more than a glance for Alec Cartwright, on occasion the only other person in the park. Her copper-colored hair now blended well with the leaves. One of the gardeners, an old man who once showed her the kitten in his pocket, often spread a paper on the bench where she liked to sit. With a little encouragement he would have given her some advice. He went so far as to say he had grandchildren almost her size. Or if the matron had smiled at Alec, the story might have been different. But that is only a guess: it might have been the same. It was clear she did not care much for young women in pants. She brought along a coat that was perhaps her husband's that she slipped about her shoulders; in the brim of her hat and her bag of sewing a few leaves fell. The boy ran around throwing pieces of gravel at the squirrels.

In December Alec received a letter from her mother, warning her about the Asian flu, a postcard with a drawing from Luigi Boni, and a postcard with a message from Lyle Jackson. It came from an island, where the freighter had stopped, and said simply, "You're the boss, Chickpea." There was also a piece of 3rd class mail, forwarded. A bulletin from her college, it carried the announcement that Alec Cartwright was travelling in Europe, and listed classmates who had married, died, or who had babies. A classmate who had died was Ruth Horton Elyot, class of '61.

Ruth Elyot had been Alec's roommate her sophomore year. The school made a specialty of strange girls to the limits of a limited scholarship fund. A bright scholarship girl was usually assigned to one who paid. Ruth Elyot was from Virginia, north and west of Culpeper. Her specialty was Chaucer, but she read as late as Sir Thomas Browne with pleasure. To extend her appreciation forward, and lengthen that of Alec Cartwright's backward, they were put together in the crucial sophomore year. Alec Cartwright had read very little with pleasure earlier than Gerard Manley Hopkins.

They got along fine, although their tastes remained unchanged. Ruth Elyot might have worn Alec's clothes, if Alec had possessed clothes Ruth Elyot would wear. They were the same height, and both weighed less than one hundred pounds. Seen in the hall, however, or on the campus, Ruth Elyot was sometimes taken for a teacher, and parents followed her, respectfully, when she led them to their own children. Her hair was sparse but long, drawn to a tight bun at the base of her neck. Few had ever seen the freckles on her forearms, the tiny mole on her throat. She kept her limbs covered, wore cameo brooches, a jacket with a small gold watch on a chain, wool skirts, shoes with laces and sensible heels. Her walk was that of a person whose shoes hurt her feet. A fine dusting of powder evened the tone of her almost sallow face, concealing the freckles under her eyes, the thin bridge of her nose. Her mouth was lipless, showing small spaced teeth when she smiled.

In one of the few letters to her mother Alec had used the word plain, over and over, in order to avoid using less friendly terms. She had sensed the word was poor, but how else describe her? That was how she looked until one had heard her voice. From her small mouth, her tight chapped lips, came something to which speech was poorly related. As others might sing, Ruth Elyot talked balladry. Everything she said seemed to call for accompaniment. Teachers and students were inclined to fall silent when Ruth Elyot answered the dullest question. The small voice had an oracular leanness, pared of waste. There was nothing to explain. It was how the people in her family talked. It proved, on questioning, to be more like a county than a family, growing like brambles on the mountainsides. They talked a lot, she said, and *that* was how they talked.

Ruth Elyot went home over the summer as the Irish returned to Ireland or the Italians dreamed of returning to Italy. Her time seemed to pass adjusting herself to new members of the clan, and tutoring those who were not likely to go to school. In some parts of the hills Elyots were plentiful, but schools were scarce. She planned to teach in one of the prep schools that sent their charges north to college, and therefore required more than a lady-like brushing up.

For several weeks Alec Cartwright felt she was one of Ruth Elyot's students. If there was one thing she needed it was brushing up. She wore soiled blue jeans, dirty sweaters, and sneakers without socks. Ruth Elyot paid her no heed. Her only comment was that for four hundred years there had always been *rebels* in her family—in her mouth the word rebel had an authentic civil war flavor. In her family it had not been brought up to date. Alec's slovenly, ridiculous habits, her childish lingo and beat jargon, she observed with curiosity but respect. If Alec did it she was sure it was important to her family. Alec did not comment on the family she did not have. In the skull with its sparse swatch of hair, behind the small, almost colorless eyes, Ruth Elyot was never far removed from the Elyot clan in Virginia. One never knew if the one in question was alive or dead. In her mind this distinction was meaningless. If an Elyot had been of any interest so he still was. She spoke freely, even with pride, of the number of half-wits in the family who distinguished themselves as characters. She recognized the strain as important to tribal life.

From Virginia, in the fiber carton that she used to ship home her laundry, she brought back one jar of blackberry preserves and two bottles of sour mash whiskey, a sniff of which, for generations, had promoted health and well-being. These two bottles were stored in the water closet and sometimes hampered the flushing of the toilet, but the temperature was that of good whiskey cooled in a creek. A spoonful at bedtime promoted a good night's sleep.

One Christmas Ruth Elyot returned to school with a nagging cold. To help the cold she sniffed a little more than usual. A thing about the Elyots she hadn't mentioned was the funks they were inclined to get into, brought on by such weather as they were having, or a nagging cold. Alec understood it well enough. Ruth was often in bed by the time that Alec came back from the library, an eggcup, which she used for sniffing, under her bed. To avoid drafts, which she complained of, she wore one of Alec's soiled raincoats, the pockets stuffed with wads of Kleenex and lozenges. It was not unusual, of course, for a girl to have a cold that was hard to shake. Alec had one. It moved from her head to her chest. She spent two weeks in the infirmary and came out with a voice no louder than a whisper. Spring vacation she spent with a friend in New York. The two girls went down on the train together, and shared a taxicab to East 38th Street, from where Ruth, with her fiber laundry carton, went on alone to the Pennsy station. For travel she wore a small straw hat level on her head. She might have been Alec's mother. Alec had cried, "For god-sakes get well, will you," and kissed her bony forehead.

That was Friday. In the Monday morning paper, which she read in Schrafft's, Alec caught the word Holroyd in a headline. A young woman, identified only by items left in a laundry carton, had commited an all but unmentionable crime. Somewhere between Washington and Richmond, she had managed to give birth to a child but failed in her attempt to dispose of it. Born prematurely it was not known if the child was born dead, or had been murdered. The infant was found before the train had made a stop, and the young woman was taken into custody. She was identified as Ruth Elyot, a student from Holroyd.

Two days later a physician testified that the infant, without question, had been born alive, so the charge against the young woman would be murder. A small point, in the horrifying details. Ruth Elyot had attempted to dispose of the child in the train lavatory. She had failed because her strength had failed her, as she said herself. Her purpose had been to protect the father of the child from scandal, and the child from shame. That too had been in her own words.

To avoid anyone she might know Alec had taken a room in the YWCA. She did not leave it. Pretending to be ill she remained in bed. The horror of the crime seemed somehow related to her own incomprehensible unawareness—that she had lived with Ruth Elyot and suspected nothing, observed nothing, felt almost nothing. She felt more than guilt. If the police had come for her also, she might have been relieved.

This state of shock lasted several days, then gave way to something even stranger. Horror and admiration. If she could believe her own feelings, that was what she felt. The horror gave way: it was quickly absorbed in the act of heroism, such an act as she knew herself to be incapable of. Tiny little Ruth Elyot had ended her story in the same way heroes ended their ballads: the sword dripped with blood, the body lay in the cold cold ground.

It came as a relief to Alec, ten days later, to find that she was firmly implicated, and that it was understood she had known of this tragedy all the time. Much better to believe that she knew it all, than that she knew nothing. Since it also seemed clear that one could do little with or for a person like Ruth Elyot, Alec's sense of implication was considered to be punishment enough. As it was.

Strange how the horror diminished, the admiration increased. From where did such a small fragile creature get such strength? No one would have dreamed that she had a demon lover, let alone the passion to murder for him. Where did she get it? Was such passion in her mind, or in her blood? One thing certain was that Alec Cartwright did not have it. Was that why she admired it? Her mouth went dry to think of it. That such a brutal act impressed her so favorably was not a good sign. Was she perverse? Was it cruelty she loved, and not tenderness? Not until the crime and the punishment faded did she sense what enthralled her was the will that made the crime possible. In one breath it was horrifying and fine. At a given moment the Elyot clan, countless generations of them, had possessed little Ruth Elyot, like a demon, and given her the strength of Gods. It was not pretty. But it was what one meant by that culprit life.

Until this event Alec Cartwright had been on good terms with the word experience. She wanted lots of it. It was something that one went out to get. *Bad* experiences would prove, in time, to be more worthwhile than good. "It ought to be a great experience"—one of her favorite remarks— usually meant it might be hell at the time, like a venereal infection, but it would prove to enlarge one's character. Holroyd girls who formed picket lines for peace demonstrations, protested the banning of outspoken books, went to bacteria-ridden places on errands for the Peace Corps, were all girls who might find it a bore at the time but would come to look with pride on it later. A girl who got herself in trouble was the girl, of course, due to profit the most in the long run. Life might trample her a bit, but it would not have passed her by.

It was the custom at Holroyd to speak out frankly on all aspects of experience. If a girl got in trouble, Holroyd helped her get out of it. With the exception of death, the one experience where firsthand reports were lacking, the word experience was able to come to terms with the facts. But when this word was placed near the flame of Ruth Elyot it gave off an odor. In the heat of the event the word lost its temper. Whatever demon had seized her, toward whatever end, and whatever survived the heat of such a passion, the word experience as once valued by Alec did not explain it or describe it. So what did? That was just the trouble, nothing did.

Several months had to pass before Alec would admit to a curious fact: for life in this world Ruth Elyot's heroism had left her unchanged. If the standards were too high, to what did they apply? Dreaming. She had the same problem with Saint Theresa whose passion had made her a true bride of Christ, but this proved to be at too great a remove from the passion available to Holden Caulfield, a realistic prototype for Ivy League boys. A feeling that she would never again be the same was replaced by a feeling that nothing had happened. To Alec Cartwright. Ruth Elyot had simply been too far out, or too far in. Her example did not apply to the commonplace world where people lived. And where, after such a brief sojourn, Ruth Elyot did not.

What had killed her? She seemed indestructible. The bulletin carried no more information than her birth and death, vital statistics. She proved to be two years older than Alec, which helped. Given time she might be more of a person herself.

The first days of December a cold drizzle kept Alec out of the park. By the time she returned it seemed like a camp from which the army had departed. An old man with a

raincoat over his pajamas walked a small dog that was con-
stipated. Was it to fool them both the little dog kicked
around so much gravel? The less that happened, the more
he kicked. It made a dry raining sound on the old man's
coat, and fell into the gaping tops of his slippers. He stood
smoking. He did not curse the dog nor jerk on the leash.
When they got home perhaps it would be the dog's turn to
wait.

A few days before Christmas she received a letter with a
picture showing pickets in front of a courthouse, an assortment of shirt-sleeved men and boys gathered on the steps.
The placards were carried by a line of men and women,
black and white. The back of the card said simply

Jail's at the rear. Time you get this I'll be in it.

L. "P" Jackson

She had looked at the clipping for some time before she
recognized one of the figures as Jackson. He wore the
sneakers in which he had caught his cold. On the back of his
shirt was a sign—

WHY DON'T YOU WHITES

GO BACK

WHERE YOU COME FROM?

Her first feelings were mixed, since it hadn't crossed his
mind that she might be having her *own* problems, half of
which were his. On reflection she realized that was characteristic of the male, and the jail, being there in the building,
was more on his mind. It was also characteristic of Jackson
to share all of his troubles with her, without getting around
to what troubles she might be having on her own. He was
going to jail. He wanted her to admire and feel sorry for
him.

In spite of what she knew about him, she did both.

Knowing him so well she knew that he would suffer the moment his rebellion was not so attractive, and his picture was not in a paper he could clip and send to someone. He could stand on principle, but if he got a bad nose bleed he would play dead. His best reflex was sensing when to duck. Someone who didn't realize this might hurt him, and it enlarged her pity for him. Were all men soft where women were so tough? She realized she could never, without falsifying it, tell Jackson the story of Ruth Elyot, since all he would manage to feel would be the horror. Bottomless. He would think it unfair for her to even tell him something like that.

The Paris *Herald* had the news about the Freedom Riders, but they seldom mentioned names. Eighteen were jailed, forty were jailed. And details like that. After a week of this her interest flagged, then suddenly revived when she knew she was pregnant. *Enceinte*. It was her mother's favorite word. Her mother would like her better if she knew how well the word fit. Her mother's use and abuse of the word had given it an air of mystery, and that was proper. It had brought Alec to Paris, to Jackson, and finally to the condition the word described. One expecting. One expecting God knows what.

In late December she wired her mother for plane fare hinting at the cold Paris winter. While waiting she had another postcard from Jackson, showing a heel print on the front as if someone had stepped on it. On the back of the card were four or five smudged fingerprints. In pencil someone had added—

we all sents our luv from Jackson

That almost made her ill until she noticed that it was postmarked Jackson, Mississippi. Was that his idea of humor? She was not amused.

Her mother sent her no money but a tourist flight ticket from Paris to San Francisco. The bargain winter rate, good for a limited time, worked out to her advantage thanks to the bad weather. Out of New York she got a plane to take her to New Orleans. The picture of the courthouse Jackson had sent her she showed to half a dozen bus drivers. All of them smiled. Half the towns in the South, they told her, had courthouses like that. And Freedom Riders.

She had never been in the South before and it upset her to find that she liked it. The streets were full of odder-looking people than herself. As a white, she seemed as invisible as the blacks. She began to like grits in place of potatoes with her eggs. As in Paris the lower class of people didn't seem to know or care or realize they were riffraff. They impressed her as odd as the people in Paris, odder perhaps. In the cheap hotel where she rented a room a blind old Negro ran the elevator. A fleece of pure white wool fit tight on his head. The pupils of his eyes had long ago rolled around and fixed their gaze upward. Everybody was Massuh. She was Massuh. The sing-song musical chant of his voice could be heard as the lift went up and down. That too was like Paris. Was he ferrying the blacks to heaven or the whites to hell? The horrible thing was that it was not horrible. Like Ruth Elyot he had long ago crossed to some country that lay beyond. If his musical laughter seemed to rise from hell when the bell called him at night, it seemed to Alec, hearing him pass, that he was long gone to heaven.

In the bus terminal, a clearing house for Freedom Riders, she met Sarah Lawrence girls and five Ivy League boys, white and black. They had all heard of Protest Jackson, but none had set eyes on him. But the bad country was the place to look, and that was to the north. With the Sarah Lawrence girls and fourteen assorted boys she sat in the colored section of a bus making the night run from New

Orleans to Memphis. She felt close to Jackson. It was just the sort of life he had told her about.

Late at night, the stop nameless, she piled out of the bus with the others and stood in the darkness, behind the bus lights, holding a paper cup of coffee which spilled hot down her front when she was grabbed. The man was behind her, and with a deft movement he used her jacket to pin her arms down, then picked her up like a child and passed her to men seated in the back of a car. One hand went over her face—did it smell of urine? The other lifted her dress like a blind: a leg thrown over her body held her fast. She was not raped. Could she say it was something she had been spared? In the glare of a red stop light where they stopped she saw the face of a man seated at the front: he wore an officer's hat and the gleeful expression of an obscene child. His eyes were on what was happening in the rear seat. Sometime later she was pushed from the car across the road from where she had started, where some of the Freedom Riders leaned against the building, trying to sleep. How had she looked? The lights went off with the car. The doors of both washrooms had been locked. In back she found a car, with the doors unlocked, and crawled into it as into a hole. Rags smelling of grease she used to cover her head. A drug-like exhaustion put her to sleep. In the morning she was found by the Negro who came to open the store—wide-eyed he gazed at her, his mouth open. Was she invisible? He saw only what he could bear to see. "Why missy!" he said, with a smile like they were playing hide and seek. He turned away, he fumbled with his keys and opened the lavatories, a hole so filthy her first act was to be sick. In the tarnished mirror she saw her face, in fragments, and a leech-like wound on her neck. There she had been bitten. There were others at the back. About her waist, like a money belt, were the cups of her bra. Her leg showed the snail-like glass of the man's spilled lust: straps on his boots had torn her flesh.

A white man, wearing a collarless shirt and soiled pants with the tops rolled, made her coffee that was tasteless until she added the canned milk. He avoided her gaze. Through the food slot at the end he glanced at her furtively, waited for her to leave. In his fear she saw the familiar glint of lust. What had happened? He could hardly wait to hear. A morning bus took her into Jackson where she bought a sweater to cover the bites on her neck, a boy's reversible coat with pennies in the pocket, in a Salvation Army outlet. She saw none of the group she had traveled with. In the terminal a man from the central organization was preoccupied with his schedule. He was black, and *she* was invisible.

One Easter, as a child, Alec had taken the change she found on her mother's dresser and bought herself three large, chocolate-covered, coconut Easter eggs. Off by herself she had eaten two of them. The third she left where it fed ants almost up to summer. What she had felt at that time was not unlike what she felt now. Nausea. For people rather than Easter eggs. White people looked to her worse, but toward the black her vision was clouded. For what incredible folly did *he* desire to look white? For what conceivable reason did *he* want to integrate? With what? With men lower than the animals? Had the black man been invisible so long he thought this deathly white was a desirable color? He should be told to bless his luck that he was black. That the laws of the country prevented him from being something worse. Before Jackson made a fool of himself in this matter she would find him and put him straight. Run for your life! she would tell him. Thank God that you're black! Together they would go where the sun would blacken her. *He* was all right. *He* had the right color. *She* was the one who had to pass.

She went from stop to stop, idling in the streets, sitting in the squares of towns that had them, sleeping in the seats of buses or terminals at night. A song she heard in Mobile, "Been here and gone," seemed to be a song written by Jackson. She could hear him sing it. She could see the color at the roof of his mouth. In a copy of *Life* she saw him marching at the head of a picket line. He wore a tight-fitting, small-visored cap and two signs that squeezed him like a sandwich. There were holes in the sign where it had been poked or struck by rocks. The white mob, a frieze of animal faces she sometimes saw through the bus window, had no more color for her than the faces she saw in the zoo. She did not identify. She had stopped feeling shame. Was it that she was no longer *white* herself? One day a woman with a child, dragging it along beside her, the woman with the spare, gaunt face of Ruth Elyot, came right toward her as if to speak and then spat in her face. "Nigger-lover!" she hissed. And yet this did not disgust her so much as the line of boys and girls, all of them black, singing spirituals and carrying signs, who wanted to use the same filthy wash-room at the bus terminal. The horror of slavery was what it had done to their pride. A rat was a rat, a cat was a cat, and nothing would persuade it to change its nature. Did respectable black men want the freedom to be pigs? If the pig could eat and pee where he wanted, the answer seemed to be yes.

Nevertheless, through no will of her own, without the pleasure or anxiety of a decision, purely as a matter of creature comfort she was only at home where she didn't belong. A sallow white face among the black and tans, among the sooty black. Could they conceivably feel that she had some advantage that they lacked? In the mirrors on the scales she looked like an illness. Something under a rock. Was it any wonder her race had a mania for the sun? To put on, or take on as much blackness as they could stand?

As the weather warmed she spent the day like a cat,

moving from one sunny spot to another. She found she could catnap seated on benches, her head tipped back. The bridge of her nose burned and peeled: the sallow skin of her eyelids reddened. Her lips chapped. She gave off the smell of a drying sack. But slowly, like a ripening fruit, she darkened. The bulge of her forehead was the color of Jackson. Mahogany lights appeared on her cheekbones, her teeth gleamed white. Walking the streets at night she toyed with the idea of trying to pass. But it shamed her to know that it was a toy, and not a passion. The black boy who saw her naked would swear she was crazy. Perhaps he would be right.

In Columbus, Georgia, she lay on trampled dead grass reserved for the use of dark-skinned people, several of whom, she saw with pleasure, were lighter than herself. Sprawled there, the sun on her back, she heard as in a dream the voice of Jackson: he had this musical stutter as he started to speak, as if warming up. This voice came from a car, a pickup truck, where Jackson sat with three white boys eating ice cream out of Dixie cups. He wore his tight-fitting cap, and sat with his narrow shoulders hunched. He dipped the ice cream with a wooden spoon that he honed clean on his whitened tongue.

Alec didn't want to hear what he would say with the three white boys listening, so she waited. It was Jackson who talked. He didn't sound much like a black boy from Omaha. Two, three times he said, "Man, I dig trouble. Trouble's what I dig." That was for the white boys, she was sure, who wore earnest expressions and turtle-neck sweaters. They sat on sleeping bags and smoked Home Run cigarettes. Jackson had an assurance she didn't remember, slapping the white boys on their fat knees, putting out his pink hand to take a cigarette from their lips. A changed man. That was how he talked. His look was still slantwise, the chin down in an almost military manner, the eye with the white fleck partially concealed by his nose. He was the boss. He gave the orders, and when he hopped out of the pickup it was like a man who knew his picture might be snapped. He no longer wore his sneakers. He wore a pair of half-boots with stirrup heels.

He swaggered—yes, she saw that he swaggered with his long legs in her direction, coming on her so casually he made not a sound. No, not a sound. The blood drained from his face showed plainly how he would look when sick. Not a black man, but an old man with something like jaundice. Along his right cheekbone was a scar that had not quite healed.

"Goddam," he said. "Goddam, Chickpea, you want to kill a black man?"

She tried to think what was new in what he had said. He let himself drop down, scooping a tuft of grass, and it pleased her to see his eyes were blurred. "Goddam you, why you sneak up on a man like that?" He smiled, putting his hand so that it cupped her skull in his palm. "You fatter. How come?"

He meant her face, of course, not her body, but she had lowered her hand to her tummy. The gesture only made him smile. "You fillin' out?" That nothing else crossed his mind was not the reason she made no comment. She realized that in Paris he would not have said, "You fillin' out." Nor, "You fatter. How come?" He was talking black now, as he had once inclined to talk white. A professional black man, he tipped his head and laughed like the black man on the minstrel record, "Two Black Crows." He put a stem of grass in his mouth.

"This is my country, Chickpea. I don't want it, but what you doin' in it?"

"I like it."

"Don't let these white boys hear you talk like that, Chickpea. This the black man's Auschwitz. This barbed-wire country. Right over—" he wagged his finger in the direction of the river, of Alabama—"right over theah is the concentration camp." He put fingers to the scar on his face. "Trouble over theah, Chickpea. I dig trouble."

Not believing that she said, "I *don't* dig trouble. What does it get you?"

His eyes closed. On his half-smiling face the scar was like the proud wound of a Heidelberg schoolboy.

"You know what I dig?" she said. "Black faces. I dig segregation from white faces. I think white faces and filthy white cans, and lousy white food are godawful. I think white girls are evil and mawkish. I think the white boys are cruel and vicious. I believe in segregation and I want a black face so I can't be integrated. I don't want to be in. I want to be out!"

Her voice was shrill. He listened without opening his eyes. Had he lived in a white man's shadow so long he didn't know who he was when he moved out of it?

"Chickpea, you go on like that you make a great white-nik funny man. Sick-nik white-nik. Man, they pay to hear you. Man, they'll sure dig that."

"Maybe I'm a sick-nik white-nik," she had yelled, "but I'm not a goddam imitation minstrel! I'm not putting on an act. I'm telling you what I think."

With the back of his hand he struck her mouth and cheek. The slap brought tears to her eyes but she felt nothing but disbelief. He rocked to his feet with a movement that revealed much practice, slapped his seat with the same hand that had slapped her.

"Now you know what I think, eh Chickpea? Now you know what your daddy minstrel think." That idea pleased him. He slapped the puff in the knee of his pants. "We don't care what color you are, Chickpea—high yaller, copper color, stove color, sick color—it's all just no-color to us, you hear me?" He wet his finger, then put it to her forehead as if that color would rub off. "You know what, Chickpea? You're so goddam white an' you wanna be so goddam fair-minded, people like you is the first people *we* don't dig. You know that? It's people like you we *don't* want. When we get this revolution it's people like you cause all the trouble. Right away you wanna be so goddam fair-minded, ain't that right? We don't want you anymore than the white trash wants you, Chickpea. Fair-minded people is a pain in the ass, so get off my back." He laughed, pleased the way he had put it, showing the pink roof of his mouth. She knew that laugh. So he laughed when he was not sure of himself.

"A revolution? You talk about a revolution? You want to sell him used cars and use his filthy crapper and drive one of his ugly cars into the suburbs? You want a house full of shit and wall-to-wall carpets? You want some ugly white trash to clean off your windshield, check your oil, saying yes suh, Mistuh Jackson, of course, Mistuh Jackson, anything you say. Is that what you want, Mistuh Jackson? That what you want for your wife and kids, Mr. Jackson? Give a shit where the bus is going, what you want's a good seat. Well, I don't, you hear me! If that's your revolution I've had it. I'm not on your back, Mistuh Jackson. You're on mine."

He walked away, swinging his boots at the tufted grass; she waited knowing he would turn and look back. Had he lost weight? His pants fit him loose in the seat. She regretted she could not tell him that he had Gary Cooper's long legs. He stooped to take a long drink from a hose that seeped water into some bushes, then passed the cool palm of his hand over his face. With pleasure she watched him, knowing his strength as well as his weakness, and how it would be up to her to understand and forgive him, as she would. The half-boots were loose on his feet, the stirrup heels dragged. He stood at the curb like a dude ranch cowboy, hands dipped in the slits of the tight front pockets, his gaze down the sunny street toward the approaching bus. When it drew to the curb beside him, he stepped on. So casual it was, so unexpected, that her head did not lift from where it was resting. Her chapped lips were parted, but no sound emerged. When she saw his head in the window at the rear his hand covered one ear as if he thought she might call him. She didn't, of course. She felt nothing but the heat on one side of her face.

She learned that he was referred to as the "cowboy," which he seemed to like better than Protest. Cowboy Jackson. Gary Cooper Jackson in his great role as a Freedom Rider. Was this sort of humor white-nik, or sick-nik? She did not know. A Welsh poet she had known very well for one weekend talked of nothing but the humor of desperation, all other forms of humor being childish or obscene. She wondered if this was what he meant. She often had fits of laughing. She liked to laugh with a twist of rag in her mouth.

In a matter of time she would hear from him, but before that happened she was having other problems. Morning sickness kept her in bed until noon. She had spells of giddiness. A husky NYU junior, Anna Gossfield, explained to her that the problem was psychic: she was being poisoned by the segregation evil, and perhaps she was. Anna Gossfield had money from a step-father who was a big man in the Volkswagen business. Being a Jew he suffered from profound guilt feelings. He was always buying something or somebody off. This year it was her. Whenever his suffering was bad, or his business was good, she got a check from him. His favorite phrase was "have yourself a ball," which he believed she was doing. In his opinion, Anna said, they were both a big pair of CARE packages.

They lived in a cut-rate integrated motel given over to integrated love on weekends, but very quiet and respectful during the week. Alec lay for hours in the bottom of a drained swimming pool. She and Anna were admired by northern boys as barrier-breaking lesbians. In Anna Gossfield's opinion, Alec was in the grip of an hysterical pregnancy, which was certainly a nuisance but nothing to actually worry about. Nor did Alec worry, she did little more than cover herself with Anna's sun cream in the morning, and check the blackness of her tan in the evening. Anna Gossfield busied herself keeping a record of her "case." She had read all the literature on the subject but nothing that compared with Alec's innovations. She saw it as a best-seller, both timely and shattering.

In May her step-father stopped sending her money which meant something was wrong with his Volkswagen business. She thought it wise to take a few days off and investigate. She left Alec an icebox full of frozen food, her portable TV, her folk records, and a bundle of laundry with her name on her blouses. That was all. A week later when Alec looked for an address she found nothing she could write to. Was her father's name Gossfield? She was not even sure of that. Anna had hinted that he changed his name when he went into the Volkswagen business. She called him *Frankie*, he called her *Johnny*, which was certainly cute but not much to go on. Nothing came for Anna Gossfield in the mail but a letter from the NAACP beginning Dear Friend.

Alec stayed in the motel until the icebox was empty, then she took a smaller room in the city. From the hundred dollars a month her mother sent her she had saved up more than four hundred dollars: a hundred dollars a month, in her mother's opinion, was money enough to keep from starving, but not money enough to get into trouble or support someone. So she lived pretty well. She had Anna Gossfield's record player and her TV. Nor was she such a fool as you might think to see her, since she used the advice of the city clinic, once a week presenting herself at the maternity ward. They saw much that was strange in her appearance, but little that was strange in her condition. The times had changed.

She slept until about noon when the room got hot, the blind at the window like a bronze radiator. In the afternoon she dawdled in the vieux carré, eating shaved ice and feeding corn to the pigeons. She lived on cantaloupes with a scoop of ice cream they served in a nearby watermelon garden. It seemed to suit her fine.

Loitering—she always wore the soiled raincoat to drape the startling bulge in her figure—one afternoon she heard, at her back, a voice that she took to be that of Jackson. Black boys streamed from the lobby of a movie palace, but not him. The swinging lobby doors were propped open, and the voice she had heard had come from the screen. In the sour, subway exhaust of the draft she stood listening to it, as if waiting for him. Curtains on the aisle veiled off the screen. The clamor behind it made her curious, like the hawkers of a street carnival in Paris. The odor was as rich as that of something long gone to pot.

A shabbily elegant establishment, the palace featured the original decor, heavy red plush carpet, worn to the backing, velvet drapes the color of bad meat. But the best: one knew it to have been the best at one time. Curtains of the same faded material, like a cloak that has been worn forever, screened off the aisles so that riff-raff in the lobby could not enjoy the performance when the doors swung open. The performers themselves were celebrated figures Alec had never heard of. That too seemed proper, even important.

The pictures had to go with the album, the story with the binding. Several stories, in fact, since the palace featured not a common double feature, but a triple. Three full-length movies, plus the news and selected short subjects. Vaguely bemused, Alec had wandered away, then she wandered back. Popcorn was sold in the lobby: she bought a butter-dripped bag as she went in. The lobby itself was curved and spacious, with shaded boudoir lamps marking the exits. A ladies' lounge was available on the mezzanine. All of this grandeur, wrapped in velvet like an assured woman of pleasure, soaked up the light so that Alec hardly materialized in the mirrors. No, she was more of a trick, an optical illusion, with her fantastically swollen midriff, like those monsters seen in mirrors at a fair. Even that, if disturbing, seemed appropriate. The very smell of the place seemed so dense that some of the first odors were still in it, expensive perfumes, delicate sachets, talcums that left their trace on the seat cushions. Into this scenery music was piped, as if heard from afar. Marveling, munching her popcorn, Alec sensed she had stumbled on a treasure. What was this cloudland but her private *Voyage à bonheur?* Others were there for the *bonheur,* but the *voyage* was hers. With the piece of chalk statuary in the niche she exchanged glances of connivance. *They* knew. They *knew* that this was the sur-real world. Out there in the dust-flecked heat and light was a performance that had no meaning: a script without an author, sound and fury and dull to boot. In here it was all nonsense that made sense. She knew that. This was so clear it made her apprehensive about going further. What would she find behind the curtained aisles? She dared to peek. Light splashed on faces that appeared to be wearing masks. They sat in a pit, peering upward, under a gold and gem-flecked ceiling. Were they black or white? That too was difficult to tell. The light painted each face with a sublime or ridiculous expression. They resembled the frieze of plaster carvings framing the screen. All of a piece, with the screen itself wavering like a visionary fata morgana, an illusion of life painted on the air by life itself. What more could one ask? Every stupid semblance of *real* life had been shattered, this was what it professed to be, a House of Dreams. In darkness—that void on the face of the deep before light had been created—one sat in a spell and watched the divine creator at work. There on the screen the hand of God illustrated his own, private surreal lectures, and wrote his own, orphic prophecies on the wall. Let there be light, the voice said, and that was what one saw.

Strange? Strange, indeed, if one thought of Alec Cartwright. Half of her life, such as it was, had been spent in ridiculing bad movies: now it proved to be that *bad* movies were precisely those she loved. The worse the better. No, they could not be bad enough. An indescribably bad movie, with the horses shyly nuzzling one another, what was it but the waxworks museum of life *brought* to life. All crazy. All indescribably marvelous. There it all was, the loony bin of life, so desperately sad, so intolerably touching, that her eyes filmed over, she choked on her popcorn, and the godawful background music was so ghastly she tearfully, shamefully giggled. They took her for mad, those around her. A fool who laughed when she should cry, who sat tearfully weeping when the screen bounced with joy. But they were human. In the cloudland palace there was room for all kinds. So long as she was there, squirming in her seat, she was not out in the world getting into *real* trouble. That too made her giggle. She had never been so happy for so long.

Was that why it couldn't last? An educated little fool, she *knew* that it couldn't. She waited as a crime waits for its criminal. In the dim ladies' lounge, combing her hair by the fragmented reflection she saw in the mirror, she heard, piped to her from the screen, a barking dog. Yap, yap, yap, yap, he went, like a singing dog commercial. Did it seem familiar? Why did this dog seem to speak to *her?* Her mother, not Alec, had been fond of dogs, and once had several around the house. Barking. Always one who neurotically, compulsively barked. Her father had not been able to stand it, and to get rid of the dogs he had built her a Pound. That was just a joke, of course, but it happened to be true. Alec was like her father, and it was precisely what she would have done.

This dog that barked over the loudspeaker system both amused and disturbed her. Was it the bark? She had the feeling she knew just what he said. Help! help! help! he yapped. It was as plain as that. Alec had never cared for dogs, in general, but she cared for them more than she did for people. If a dog was a man's best friend, he *needed* help. And from the horn in the ladies' lounge this dog barked at her, Help! help! help! How right he was! And how well she understood just what he had said.

The movie proved to be something called *Mondo Cane,* and had to do with the theme of dog-eat-dog. Typical that man would phrase it like that. It was the man who was eating the dog. It was the man who was eating everything, and on occasion himself. This movie horrified and fascinated her at once. One moment she was leaning forward to leave, the next settling back. One creature or another was forever yapping, Help! Help! Help! Including men. Yes, God help them, including women and men. A peasant woman with a blank, drugged face held a goose by the throat, as if strangled, while another forced down his throat a machine that resembled an oiling can, cranking into its stomach food that it would not, could not, eat. On its side was a handle, which the woman cranked, making the harsh grating sound of a ratchet. The crank twirled. So was created *pâté de foie gras*.

All of that, of course, was an old, old story, not unlike the faces of the women. Good solid peasants they were, right out of Van Gogh. They had the faces of the matrons at Buchenwald, doing their oven job. Then came chow puppies, yapping in cages, at that tender age when their flesh was savory, on exhibition where the diner personally picked his meal. Then came small men, like dwarfs in a nightmare, who pounded and massaged the flesh of hump-backed cattle while another forced bottles of beer into their mouths. Then came two maidens, squatted in cages like beasts, who stuffed themselves for the bridal feast, their ravishing lover a king who resembled a withered and fleshless scarecrow. This senile old goat would bounce on their bellies, suck at their breasts.

But why was Alec Cartwright so horrified? Was not this the way one *possessed* an object, by eating it? Had she not herself, as a child, drunk the wine and tasted the wafer, representing the flesh and blood of Christ? Was it not the way one acquired supernatural powers? She remembered the children, a gored matador's children, who had acquired the testicles of the bull that had destroyed their father and in a ritual of revenge and rebirth roasted and eaten them. The fins of sharks, the eyes of fish, ants, roaches, rattlesnake meat were directed toward one end, the human mouth. Small wonder man had taken so easily to eating himself. The mystery was, what had led him to stop? It seemed to Alec Cartwright, squirming on her bed, tormented by dreams that swooped to devour her, that this small oversight was one of the most easily corrected. Supply and demand. That was the law of life. When every other living thing had been devoured, why then he would turn on his own kind. A sensible move, considering the oversupply. It would solve that number one problem of the future, the overproduction of human beings. The lamb, the ram, the dog and the ox would at long last give way to the true wine and the wafer, the blood and flesh of man himself. A certain squeamishness would trouble a few, but those who prevailed would have stronger stomachs. One only had to think of Donner Pass. One only had to think of a lover's judgment pronounced on herself. "Chickpea," he had said, "you're just too goddam fair-minded. You the decent sort of people we got no room for. You the first sort of people we can do without."

So it was hardly strange, after all, that she should have her own revelation. Many people did. Her own seemed to be more interesting. She was with child, as they said, and any day now it would take its place in the world. What world? Not, if she could help it, in the world of men. Not, if she could help it, among the cannibals. Clearly as if a moving finger wrote it on the wall she remembered a passage she had read in college, a fable of sorts, about a youth who chose to live with the animals. Naïve, the tone of it like a scene that was illustrated on drapery, with the Garden of Eden, forbidden to men, lying on a hilltop in the background, toward which the youth with the Botticelli figure slowly made his way.

> While I was a man I liked my condition well enough, and had a very low opinion of beasts, but now that I have tried their way of living I am resolved to live and die as they do.

And why not? My God, why not? Why did one have to live among the destroyers? Russians took the children away from their parents: why not take them away from their destroyers? Why not let them go, as the poets suggested, and live with the animals?

This thought was not new. No, it was old, perhaps it was one of the first thoughts Eve had had: new was the fact that such a place existed, the first time since Eden. Her mother, of all people, had erected it. A place specifically created for the prevention of cruelty to animals. All animals. Even such a strange creature as her child.

Did Alec actually believe that her child would inhabit it? In the broad cruel daylight she did not. The dream would not materialize. It was not even *crazy*. But in the cave of the palace, the screen like an opening on the technicolor world of fiction, there she almost believed it: there she was free to say why not? Not for one moment did she believe that this was an answer, but it was a *protest*. It was what Jackson dreamed of but could not imagine. An unheard-of thing, a protest to be *heard*. Who could misunderstand it? Who would not believe in his soul the child was right? It was—as nothing else in her life could be—on a level with the protest of Ruth Elyot: it would horrify people. They would want to burn the mother at the stake. Perhaps something like that might even be arranged. At such a moment, bound to bundles of faggots in the Escondido square next to the bus station, Cowboy Jackson would see her picture in *Life* and cringe with shame. And when he came crawling she would taunt him with his own claptrap jeering. "Chickpea, you know what? When we get this revolution you're the first people we don't dig. You know that? It's people like you we *don't* want." That's what she would tell him, but knowing him to be a fool she would probably forgive him. After all, why not? She didn't believe in cruelty to *any* animal.

This phantasy, her own private revolution, had one surprising characteristic. It banished time. As if in a timeless capsule, she lived in it. No time had passed, it seemed to her, before the moment was upon her. Without the pain cracking the mirror of her reflection nothing might have happened. But the pain was real. She panicked like a child. In the middle of the night, fearing for *their* lives, she had herself taxied to a hospital, where a pimpled interne with a flat-top hair-do tapped on her belly like a gourd, then advised her that she had some time to wait. A few hours? No, he meant a few weeks. She knew he was a child and lied to boot, but he proved to be right. Three weeks to the day, in a room she had the foresight and money to arrange for, she moaned so shamefully the nurse actually yelled at her to be quiet. Did she think she was bearing the world's first child? In a way she did. The first to be immortal in this preordained way. The first, if not the last, to resign from the damned human race.

The child, of a jaundiced color, the narrow small-eared skull unmistakably Jackson, had a pelt of the golden Cartwright fleece on its head. A tail it should have had, she thought, with the golden fleece all over. Black or white it would hardly matter, if it had a tail.

Not seeming to care one way or the other, it lived. It also seemed to get pleasure, if little else, from the bud-like nipple she let it suck at. In a week it looked reasonably human. The nasal cat-like howl she found reassuring. What if it proved to meow and purr like a cat? Her impulse was to put it in a box and fly on the next plane to Escondido, where she would deposit it, like a foundling kitten, in the emergency entrance labeled ARRIVALS, a special feature that was kept open day and night. As a child she had herself dropped strange things into it.

But this *Protest*, as she called him, weighed only six pounds after two weeks of feeding, and required fattening up if he was to fulfill his role. This took time. He showed as little interest in food as herself. But he grew, he was lean but *not* sickly as the matron Mrs. Apfel told her, squirming with the wiry, twisted strength of a growing pup. He was tough. He would not stop breathing if a shadow happened to fall on him. To keep him held down she bought a small harness on which he chewed. A good sign. As was his preference to go on all fours.

She picked the weekend before Thanksgiving as the proper time for her startling donation, and bought him the simple, rough sort of wear he might need in a Pound. More thought along that line led her to make one expensive purchase. A basket. A basket large enough to serve as a cage. One that might float a child, say, like Moses in the bulrushes. This basket came with a quantity of food, fruit, jellies, and imported cheeses, which partially justified the expense since she could eat it herself. It also helped to disguise, with its strapped-on lid, just what it was she was transporting, and no questions were asked when she took her seat with it on the plane. A big gift parcel for friends on arrival. That was how it looked.

The four hours she spent in the air the child slept. From the city airport a taxicab drove her through the fog that softened the lights, and blew like smoke through the cables of the Gate bridge. In Escondido this fog was so heavy the cab driver could not see the street lights. He sat at the wheel, his wipers flicking, while she delivered her gift parcel; two of the dogs whimpered when they heard her fumbling with the door of the trap. A hood of smoking light seemed to hover, symbolically, over the waiting cab.

That was all it took, just a moment, no sound from the child and just a whimper from the kennels, then she was back in the cab and he was driving her slowly up the winding ridge road. As they rose the fog thinned, she could see the pale dawn of a new day. What would it be like? One day she would never forget. In the wide shaded yard, where he turned the car, not a light was visible in the house: the place had always frightened her and she was afraid to go in alone. At the front, under her mother's window, she called and tossed pine cones to the balcony. When a light came on her mother appeared like a spirit at a séance. It suited her well. Lady Macbeth with her candle out.

"My God, hon, what are you doing? You mad?" The baying voice seemed to speak from the sky. Without Alec troubling to ask she dropped the purse full of coins usually reserved for parking meters and bridge tolls. It required all but two of the dimes to pay the fare. Inside the house, her mother loomed at the top of the stairs like the Winged Victory. Was she cold? She carried her enormous bust in her arms. Hoarsely she was greeted, described as mad, asked how she was, asked why she had returned, then told to sleep in her father's study since her room was occupied by Adele Skopje.

That was how it was, her homecoming, and how she spent the night was of small moment. Her mission was accomplished, as Jackson would say, and if her eyes were wide as those of the oracle at Delphi it was because she, too, held the future in her hands.

ON
THE
BEACH

From *Love Among the Cannibals*

THIS chick, with her sun-tan oil, her beach towel, her rubber volleyball, and her radio, came along the beach at the edge of the water where the sand was firm. Soft sand shortens the legs and reduces their charms, as you may know. This one pitched her camp where the sand was dry, slipped on one of these caps with the simulated hair, smoked her cigarette, then went in for a dip. Nothing particular, just a run-of-the-mill sort of chick. She was out beyond the surf when I noticed that the tide was dampening her towel. I got up and dragged it back alongside our own. When she came out of the water I explained what had happened and she thanked me without being coy. She dried her hair and accepted one of our cigarettes. We got to talking, the way you do, and since everyone in California is from somewhere else it gives you something, at the start, to talk about. She was from Dubuque. The one in Iowa. Married a boy from Port Chester during the war. That didn't pan out, so she had come to California on a scholarship good for fifty bucks. All she had to do was earn her own living and raise the other three hundred twenty-five. She lived with two other chicks at the school and they all worked as waitresses at the same Wilshire drive-in. They all liked California, but they thought the people were cold. Her childhood had not been too happy and her mother often complained that her father was too small for a satisfactory sexual partner. Her mother didn't use those words, of course, but that was what she meant. If her father had not been so *conventional* it might have worked out. Why were men so perverse they always had to be on *top?*

That's what she said. She said why are men so perverse. Then she asked me if I had any ideas, and I had a few ideas but what I said was that the *conventional* sort of thing, with maybe a million years behind it, had a lot to recommend it. How do you know what's conventional *now*, she said, was conventional *then?* Her shift at the drive-in began before I had an answer to that.

I'd never seen her before. I'll probably never see her again. She was twenty-two or -three, I suppose, and I'll be forty-one the ninth of September, having lived and loved more or less conventionally. Things can change in twenty years. More, I mean, than I have changed myself. When I was her age I didn't know beans. She knows too much.

I did ask her, just before she left, what she thought of that movie of the Kansas picnic where the frustrated schoolteacher tears the shirt off the visiting bum. I was born in Kansas. I went to a lot of picnics as a boy. But in my time, the big scene would have been the other way around. The lady's, not the gent's, shirt would have to be torn. I asked her what she thought of that scene and she said it was a fine job, artistically speaking. You see what I mean? Things have changed. I carried her volleyball and wet towel to the road, where she took a bus, one that went down Wilshire, then I bought two cans of beer for Mac and myself and walked back to the beach.

*

My story begins, like everything else, on the beach. Beaches
are the same the world over, you peel down, then you peel
off; they serve you up raw meat, dark meat, or flesh nicely
basted in olive oil. A strip of sun and sand where the sex is
alert, the mind is numb. The beach in question, one of the
best, is near where Sunset Boulevard meets the sea. I don't
mean to be ironic. California is that way naturally. It's hard
to do malice to California, but this particular strip might
have been in Acapulco, or down in Rio, or along the
Riviera. If it's world brotherhood you want, go to the
beach. If you like parallels, the beach is where we came in,
and where we'll go out. Having crawled from the sea, we're
now crawling back into it. That solution of salt in the blood
is calling us home. And in a mammary age, what better
place to compensate for an unsuckled childhood? Where
else, these days, does the pretty matron shyly lower her bra
straps, hugging her charms? Not to nourish the future, alas,
but to preserve, in sun oil, the present. A season in the sun
before going under. Is that what we want? My friend Mac
has a colleague who wears on her tanned thigh the white
shadow of a man's hand—his own, as it happens. A climax,
of course, to her nightclub act. A purely professional assist,
in every respect. They often pass the time at the beach
together, and one man's hand is as good as another's. She
sings his songs, so he really belongs in the act.

When people ask me where I ran into Mac, I say the war.
We have the stamp of things that came out of it. I've pieced
together that Mac was born in Brooklyn, but I've never

really heard him say so. He doesn't talk. I mean he doesn't articulate. If he's in a friendly, expressive mood he might sing his own songs, one of Cole Porter's, or variations on a number called *Dancing in the Dark*. That's Mac. If you add Noel Coward you've covered the field. If he has ever felt anything else I don't think he would recognize it. Which leaves me with a real problem. How to keep him up-to-date. I take an old cliché, soak him in it, then give it just that squeeze of the lemon that leads him to think he thought of it himself. In the flush of that sort of emotion he can speak.

"Man," he will bark, "it's great!"

In the song-and-dance business self-confidence helps.

Mac is thirty-eight, just three years my junior, but he looks a good deal younger. He has a round, bland, background-music sort of face. He tends to run a little heavy, his complexion is mottled with what I suppose was teenage smallpox, and he gives strangers the impression he's a little deaf. He isn't, but he seldom hears anything. When I'm in a rare sympathetic mood I tell the chicks that he's listening to his own music. But he's not. Nor is it what you would call a blank. The absence of any popular song to describe the vacant moods Mac passes his life in will leave most of his life a mystery. Two or three times a month he will roll over and say—he never thinks of anything unless he's lying down— "I ever tell you how I shot down that ME-109?"

In fifteen years you can shoot down a lot of 109's. But that event keeps coming back to him like the theme of one of his songs—a hit song, I suppose, he is still trying to find the music for. He looks to me for the words, but I don't have them. I never shot down an ME-109 myself.

I had lived with Irwin K. Macgregor for eight months in England without speaking to him. But that was not unusual. Nobody did. He was not the silent type, but the army had silenced him. Like a lot of silent men, he didn't have much to say, but in an inarticulate sort of way he can be fluent. This fluency consists of a theme and variation. The theme is, "Man, it's great!" The variation, "It's great, man!" If you know the army, you know what it would do to a vocabulary like that. "It's great, man!" will cover most of the verbal problems in the song business, but the army was no song, so Mac had nothing to say. Nothing at all, I mean, until he met me.

Mac was no great shakes as a pilot but we both fagged out the same cold winter, and we were sent upcountry to the same warm spa to recuperate. That's where we met. The place featured the usual lousy food, but some nice girls from Holland and a grand piano. I didn't know till he gave the stool a spin, and sat on it, that he played. I'd sit down at one end of the room, with a book, and watch this army-silenced guy dust off the stool with his knuckles, then squat on it and *talk*. A fluent keyboard lover. A real poet, of sorts, on the black keys. One day he played with a little more schmaltz than usual, and although we hadn't exchanged a word he looked up and said:

"Like that, eh?"

"It's not a bad tune," I said, since it sounded familiar.

"It's great, man!" he said. "I wrote it."

And he had. I could name you, but I won't, about a half-dozen tunes he had written before I met him. Not bad, not good. Lacking the master touch. The sort of *unheard* music you need to fill out a TV program. But his piano was good. It was the piano that gave him his start. He could have sat out the war in a Fort Dix jazz band but he got this idea that he wanted to fly. He thought the war had come along so he could pick up, without charge, the rudiments. He did, all right, and as he points out himself—that's where he met me. I couldn't do much for his talent, but I could give the lyrics a certain touch. If the lyrics were *good*—I mean if the clichés were coined before he was—he had the sort of talent that could almost live up to them. What I'm saying is, as he puts it, we make a great team.

There have been so many corny movies about jazz pianists I don't have to tell you about them. That's how he was. I mean he was like *all* of them. He believed. He even believed in his own stuff. After he met me there was some point in it—some point, that is, believing in *my* stuff—but up until then it was all a matter of faith. Until he met me all of his songs were songs without words. I took his music and pasted the right sort of labels on it. I used to do that sort of thing for nothing, what we referred to in my youth as amusement, and I found it more amusing than trying to read a book. Sitting there, day after day, I heard the same tunes over and over, and I found it entertaining to write a set of lyrics for some of them. One little tune I liked went something like this:

> *Roses are nice, violets are too,*
> *But tulips are what I share with you.*
> *Stamen, pistil and pollen connect*
> *The tulips of Kansas with old Utrecht.*

I had reference to a particular piece of light meat from Utrecht. One day Mac played this tune and from my corner of the room I chipped in with the lyrics. It made quite an effect.

"Man, it's great!" he barked, and with that modest statement the song team of Macgregor and Horter was born. It didn't help me with the maid from Holland, but it settled me with Macgregor. "You got a talent, man!" he said. "You know what I mean?" As it happened, I did. We've been inseparable, as our billing says, ever since.

It's probably fair to say, as Mac often does, that I've made him whatever he is—*is* being a man with a fat check from ASCAP every month. In the trade we are sometimes referred to as the poor man's Rodgers & Hart, since the big-time money has a way of eluding us. It might be that my lyrics, like some cough drops, dissolve very pleasantly on the tongue but have a way of coming back, like the taste of onions, during the night. I don't really know. But something like the taste of onions is at the back of my mouth right now.

In the *Who's Who in the Missouri Valley*—in it at one time, that is—you will see my picture and find me listed as the Shelley of the corn belt. The next year I was drafted. That makes me sixteen years a poet *manqué*. I understand that the war made some poets the way a man is said to make a woman, but that wasn't my war, and it had another effect on me. The only poetry I now hear is when Mac brings a chick to the apartment and plays my recording of Eliot reading *The Waste Land*. He has the record nicked so it retracks when the voice says:

> "Hurry up, please, it's time!"

Something about Eliot's Oxford accent seems to do the trick. It's never long before he gets up and turns the record off, and the lights on. Although I've stopped writing it myself, I'm responsible for spreading some pretty good lines. Trapped with a chick of the brainy type Mac will say:

> "Does the imagination dwell the most
> Upon a woman won or a woman lost?"

If she says lost, he dates her. If she doesn't, he claims he hasn't missed anything.

Before you feel sorry for either of us, let me tell you that we spend our time on the beach, where, if you had our time and money, you'd like to spend yours. We came here, instead of Bermuda, where the sun is also shining, because I had, and sold, this idea for a new musical. New? Well, something in the line of a Latin-American *Porgy and Bess*. Yankee money, Latin passion, good-neighbor policy, everything. I've been to Mexico, which takes care of *that*, and Mac has listened to a lot of Xavier Cugat. We don't want it so Latin it might alienate Uncle Sam. Three of the major studios fought for it, and we are now living in what they call a château, in one of the fire-trap canyons, with a view of all the water that is out of reach in case of fire. Mac has a piano, and I have all day at the beach. What I do, I can do anywhere, but Mac can only sound chords at night, or very early morning on the St. Regis roof. He sleeps under the beach umbrella most of the day, then we go out to eat where they have background music, with a girl in the foreground singing Macgregor & Horter's latest hit. A little after midnight we drive back up the canyon and go to work. Something Mac once read in a muscle magazine led him to feel that sex drains a man's creative energy. He means the same night. It doesn't seriously handicap a song writer. Sex is something he takes like vitamins, and it has nothing to do with immortal love, tenderness, loss of sleep, and songs like *Stardust*. As Mac says himself:

"Sex is sex. You know what I mean?"

I do. It is part of my job. The problem is to find a nice respectable chick who needs a little push along, professionally, and who doesn't mind a little do-re-mi from a respectable guy. They're not too hard to find. A little French Bikini number, who needed a very long push, had been on Mac's hands for the past three weeks, but she had this idea that you don't need a voice in the song racket. You don't. But you need more than one close friend.

That side of my colleague's nature is cut and dried, offers little in the way of complications, and leaves him fairly famished for what he calls the *real thing*. The real thing is hard to define, but roughly it's what Charlie Chaplin found, beginning with Paulette Goddard. We might call it *The Million-Dollar Baby in the Five-&-Ten Weltanschauung*. I think he got it from the song, which he ran into a little early, but he was, and is, precocious about songs. As another man stumbles on *Jean Christophe*, Kahlil Gibran, or Dale Carnegie, Mac stumbled on the Million-Dollar Baby in the five-and-ten. That did it. That's what he means by *heart*.

"It's got no heart, man!" he'll say, so I'll take whatever it is and slip in a few words about how he found her in the automat. A girl with a green stain on her finger from a piece of Christmas jewelry can name her price. Mac will double it.

Like a talent scout in Woolworth's basement, Mac likes to hang around the record department, waiting for some Million-Dollar Baby to buy one of his songs. When she does he will lean over and say, "Like that, eh?" As a rule she does, having bought it. He will then introduce himself as the author, and the next thing you know he asks the chick if she can sing. Did you ever hear of a girl in a dime store who couldn't sing? I suppose we have roughly half a million records proving that not one of them can, but the way some of them *can't* is interesting. Mac has turned up a dozen or so of them. Any one of these girls will tell you that Mac has a heart of gold, combined with the loftiest Father's Day sentiments. All of which is true. His Million-Dollar Babies are left untouched. They are all heart, having nothing in common with the chicks, of a respectable sort, who need a little practical push along. They can be found in dime stores, drugstores, hot-dog stands, orange-drink shops, and all those places Charlie Chaplin had the knack of turning them up. Nowadays they can also be flushed at the beach. Million-Dollar Babies with that spring-green Christmas jewelry look.

You never know the other side of an army man until you see him in mufti. But Mac has no mufti. He stepped out of one uniform into what I'll have to call another. If you have sometimes wondered who it is who really wears the two-tone ensembles that set the new car styling, Mac is your man. That's why I keep him down at the beach. He's quite a sight on the beach as well, in his Hawaiian shorts, made of coconut fiber, a cerise jacket with a bunny-fur texture, a sea-green beret, and something like an ascot looped at his throat. Those shops that have the latest thing for men always have something, hidden in one of the drawers, too early for anybody else but just right for Mac. On the beach I let him wear it. He still looks better with it on than off. He has one of those complexions that will never tan, so he passes the day under the beach umbrella. Having no complexion problems I lie in the sun and watch the chicks go in and out of the water. When the beach is crowded I listen for the up-and-coming clichés. That particular morning it wasn't crowded; we had a little morning fog, which is customary, but I rather like the beach in a cloud of fog. There you are; the sound of the sea is off behind the wall.

This little chick with her hair in a pony tail came up from behind us, sprinkled a little sand on me, then pitched her camp where the tide had smoothed the sand. She spread out her little towel, let down her straps, put on her gem-studded glasses with the built-in visor, daubed Noxzema on her nose, then lit up a Parliament and smoked. I thought the little leather case might have her lunch, her radio, and her sun-tan lotion, but this was no run-of-the-mill sort of chick. Not on your life. She opened it, cranked it, and put a record on the gramophone. Owing to the radio Mac was playing, we didn't hear her taste in music till he turned it off. A sultry-type songbird was crooning a number entitled "What Next?" That happened to be the last song we had written with a chance to catch on. The songbird was the not-so-little girl we call Pussy, the one with Mac's hand on her thigh, who specializes in what I call Music for Leching, without accompaniment. She sings under the name of Faith Amor. The one exception to my practice of using clichés, and not writing them, will be found in "What Next?" I had to write them. It explains the song's brand-new old look.

> *What next?*
> *The life of love I knew*
> *No longer loves*
> *The things I do.*
> *What next?*

When Mac heard those moving lines he sat up and barked, "Man, it's great! You know what I mean?"

This little chick really did.

"Ah think she is simply *wonnaful*," she said, modestly pulling up one suit strap. "If Miss Ah-moh does it, I just have to have it. Ah reahly do."

If you keep your ear to the ground for clichés, as I have to, you get these shockers. First you hear it, then you meet it in the flesh. Since Mac gives the impression of being a little deaf, she turned her blinkers on me.

"It's a nice song," I said. "What's the girl's name?"

Nothing rocks these chicks back so much as to hear they are mad about someone you never even heard of. She rocked back and said, "You nevah hurt of Miss Ah-moh?"

"You mean Pussy?" I said. "The chick on the strip?"

That cut her. You could see where she was cut.

"Pussy can do a nice piece, all right," I said, "if she's got the right material."

"Ah'm sho yoh can't mean Miss Ah-moh," she replied. "Ah nevah hurt Miss Ah-moh refurt to as Pussy."

"Her mummy calls her Pussy, her daddy calls her Pussy, her friends call her Pussy, and we call her Pussy."

"Yoh ackshilly know huh?"

"Mr. Macgregor here does," I said, giving Mac the nod. "He wrote the song foh huh." I have to watch myself with these Suthun belles, since I tend to imitate their lingo.

"Yoh ackshilly dit?" she said, looking at Mac. Mac ackshilly did, but I could sympathize with her. "Ah feel chus mortafite, Mistuh MacGraw—" she began, but if you're going to follow what it is she says I ought to stop telling you how she sounds. But if what she said really mattered, I'd translate it for you. It's all in how she sounds. What she went on to say was that if she had half the sense she was born with, a doubtful statement, she would have known it was the song, not just the ah-tist, that appealed to her. She managed to say that, then she looked at Mac as if talking to him would move him to speech.

"Pussy hams it up a little," I put in, "but it's not a bad piece."

She wiggled like a wet puppy on her towel, then she pinched herself and asked Mac if she was asleep or if she was awake. That was actually one that Mac might have answered, but he let it pass. Then she wanted to know if we thought she was crazy, a young unchaperoned little girl like herself, coming down to the beach with nothing but her record player and her Parliaments. I was about to answer that one when she sighed, then said:

"Mistuh MacGraw, ah get so sick an' tahd talkin' to mahself."

Mac generally looks so dead that any sign of life in him makes quite an impression. It made one on her. It made one on both of us. He suddenly sat up, leaning forward so far that the crucifix he wears around his neck swung free on its chain, showing the 18-carat stamp. He's not religious, but he believes in playing the odds. I could see the idea drip through his mind that there was a song here, a *great* one, and the words "so sick an' tired talkin' to myself" formed on his lips. Then it crossed his mind why he thought so. Someone had already done it. The wind of hope that had filled him seemed to leak out through his pores.

"Yoh know why ah come to the beach, Mistuh Mac-Graw? Ah come to thaw out. Ah was nevah so colt anywheah in mah life as ah am out heah."

She shivered. If I had half the brains I was born with, I would have heard the alarm right there. Mac's alarm, I mean. The buzzer that rings when one of his Million-Dollar Babies turns up.

"It's a nasty climate—" I said, edging away. "You freeze in the fog, then—"

"Honey—" she said, giving herself a little hug, "ah doan mean that climate. Ah mean the hu-man climate. Ah nevah crossed paths with so many colt shoulters in all mah life."

In a moment of excitement he can hardly bear, Mac will take off whatever hat he is wearing, run one hand through his hair, then put the hat back on, pulled down tight. He did that. Then he looked at me and said, "Crossed paths, man! Crossed paths an' cold shoulders!"

His eyes were on me, but they were actually leafing through our song-title file. If "Crossed Paths" wasn't there now, it soon would be.

"Miss—" I began, but she was telling Mac that the only friend she had was her little record player, and by that she meant it was the only friend she had of the masculine sex. Was she out of her mind to think her little gramophone was her boy friend? Well, she did. It just went to prove how lonely she was. She was one of these chicks who close or flutter their eyelids whenever their mouth is open, acting on the same principle as these dolls with the weights in their heads. I couldn't get a word in edgewise. Her pretty little cold shoulders were covered with duck bumps. I thought

Mac would take his shirt off and wrap it around her, but he was too excited, too full of the *big* one, so all he did was jam the hat down around his ears, then say:

"Baby—you sing?"

"Mistuh MacGraw!" she said, shocked with recognition. "Why, *Mis*tuh MacGraw."

"Miss—" I began.

"What in the wohld should evah make you think so, Mistuh MacGraw? Ah do sing. Ah suppose ah should say ah wanna sing."

"Miss Garland—" I said. That clicked. I mean that cut her to the quick.

"Harcum," she said. "Miss Billie Harcum. Ah'm a stootun of Marlene Mazda Joyce, although yoh-all probly know huh, an' refuh to huh as somethin' else."

"Muzzy Joyce has some nice contacts, Miss Harcum," I said. "We sometimes find a cage for her little songbirds. You dance?"

"Why, Mistuh—"

"Horter. Of Macgregor & Horter."

"Ah'm the awfullust fool, Mistuh Hortuh. Ah know yoh name as well as mah own."

"Let's focus on Mac here then," I said. "The name is Mac*gregor*, not MacGraw, but he'll probably insist that you call him Mac."

"Oh, Mistuh Macgregaw!"

"My name is Earl," I went on, "but I don't insist on it."

"Uhl? Ah chus love Uhl as a name."

"We're not casting right now, Miss Harcum, but we have a small spot for some dark-complected dancers—Mexicali roses instead of Memphis roses, if you know what I mean."

She did. I waited to see if she could take it, and she took it.

"You'll need a little more color," I said, sizing her up.

"The shade we're going to want is octoroon, or light mulatto—"

When I said mulatto she darkened to the shade I had in mind. Over the years I've noticed that a flush of indignation does more for a girl than Max Factor. There's more to flush in a woman, that is, than her face and eyes.

"You'll do if you can dance, honey," I said, and she suddenly saw right through me. I was a *card*. It had taken her all that time to catch on. I didn't really mean what I'd said about mulatto, it was just my way of pulling her pretty leg. She put it out where I could reach it, and said:

"Mistuh Hortuh, ah'm essenchuly a singah. A singah of the Continental type."

Continental-type singers, *aus* Weehawken and Memphis, are almost as rare as girls who sing in dime stores.

"What we *need* is dancers, Miss Harcum," I began, but Mac sat up suddenly and barked:

"Baby, can you take it?"

"Take it?" echoed Miss Harcum. Fearing the worst, she turned to me.

"We have a little test number, Miss Harcum," I said. "If a girl can't take it—" I rolled my eyes, shrugged my shoulders.

"Can ah try—right heah, Mistuh Hortuh?"

"Sure, baby!" barked Mac. "If you'll turn that thing off—" and he wagged his hand at her whining record player. I don't sing our stuff often, but when I do Mac knows I like it quiet. Our little cannibelle number, as a matter of fact, is a litmus test. The chick can take it or leave it, and we can take or leave the chick. Miss Harcum wiggled over to switch off her machine, then she came over like a seal with a fish at its nose, and let me have the benefit of her pretty little duckies. I wet my lips, huskily crooned:

"Baby cannibelle, once you try it,
I'm the dark meat in your diet,
You eat me while I eat you,
Since it's the economical thing to do,
Baby, baby can-ni-bellllle!"

Well, they don't do it so much any more, but she almost swooned. The Memphis type, *her* type, don't go in for playing it cool. She bit down on her lip, gasped for air, scooped little holes in the sand to hide her feet in, and gave no thought to the fact that both of her straps were down.

"Man," bellowed Mac, "she can take it! You know what I mean? She took it!"

"Oh, Mistuh Mac—"

"—gregor," I said. "The number's not particularly Latin-American, but it is *muy* Acapulco," giving the *muy* a roll that made it clear just what I meant.

"Aca-pulco?" she said. "Now did you evah— Ah'm invited to a pahty of some folks who just come from Acapulco. Theatuh people. You would know theah names. Ah'm invited but ah jus got too much self-respeck, I suppose."

"What kinda party is it, baby?" said Mac, since he loved nonrespectable parties.

"It's not the kinda pahty a respectable gurl is seen at alone."

I got the picture pretty well, and said, "Too bad all our nights are sewed up, Miss Harcum, but since Mac, here—"

"Baby—" said Mac, "when is it?"

"This particulah pahty just so happens to be tonight, Mistuh MacGraw."

"Baby—" chanted Mac, but in his excitement he forgot what he meant to say. But I hadn't. When a chick has passed the Horter test, it's always the same.

"You happen to have a girl friend, Miss Harcum?" I said.

"Mistuh Hortuh—" she said, fluttering her eyes as if the

idea of a girl friend left her nonplused. It gave me time to slip a pencil out of Mac's shirt pocket, tear off a piece of his score. When her eyes stopped fluttering it crossed her mind that she did have a girl friend, one she worked with, and being theatuh people they all more or less lived in the same house. I took the address, the telephone number, and to make sure we would find the place after dark we drove her home and dropped her off on our way to eat.

This car the studio put at our disposal was in the quiet, unassuming good taste of a hot-rod parts manufacturer on his day off. Fireman red, with green leather upholstery, it had a crush-proof steering wheel, a crush-proof dash, compartments in the doors for whisky and soda, and a record player where the glove compartment usually is. We didn't even have to buy our own records. They supplied us with them.

I'd say one of Mac's ideas of heaven is to have Eddy Duchin playing Cole Porter while we cruise along the coast highway toward Santa Barbara. You don't have to whistle at the girls in this car, just sit in it with the top down, the music going, while you drive along the strip. This little chick and her friends lived in Westwood, in one of those attractive slums for tomorrow, a cool arrangement of glass and tin sloped to catch the heat. This chick had sworn her girl friends would be dying to meet me, an actual living man who wrote song lyrics, but she came down the steps alone, and joined us in the front. I must say she looked sharp. You know how these little girls learn to walk so they make a sharp clack on the pavement, and almost whinny when they pull up alongside your fence.

She climbed in—she got in between us—then she said she just *had* to be frank with me, and that her girl friends didn't feel they should be running around with a man my age.

"Well, what age am I?" I said, since I hadn't mentioned my age. "All ah said was you certainly weren't over forty," she replied. I could see she pulled that deal just to flatter Mac, in his baby-face thirties, and at the same time have the two of us to herself. All the time she put on this little act her hand was on my knee, not Mac's, indicating that a man my age offered certain advantages.

Anyhow, I went to this party without a chick. We drove back to Sunset, I remember, into that section they call Bel Air, then we drove into the hills where the movie stars live. You can't bring the Riviera over in crates, the way Citizen Kane would have liked to, but you can name the streets Cannes, Antibes, Monaco, with an Italian wing running from Amalfi to Sorrento. We took the French wing, that night, and followed it to the summit of the hill, where we curved along the vine-covered wall of a château. So that the effect wouldn't be lost, or if you came up at night and might have missed it, the drive in went across a drawbridge over a moat. Inside the open court, about the size of a gym, there were representative sports cars of all nations, with a patriotic sprinkling of Thunderbirds. On the East Coast that would mean money, but here on the West Coast a soda jerk, willing to choose between a chick and a Thunderbird, can have the Thunderbird. He lives in a closet, gulps his sandwich at the counter, and can't afford the salve for his athlete's foot, but when you see him on Sunset he's on a par with the movie stars. Unless they get off the highways, it leaves most movie stars with no place to turn.

Surrounded with all that quiet, imported good taste, our bright fire wagon had a certain class, and I left it where we could sneak off early, since I intended to.

One of these professional catering outfits had taken over the place. They had a fellow in the yard to lead you to the right door, a man at the door to size you up and frisk you, then one in the hall to guide you to the proper facilities. One of the minor dividends of forty-one years, fifteen of them passed among the gay counterfeiters, is that you can size up a piece of scenery pretty fast. The way these caterers knew their way around they probably lived in it. This mansion full of trophies—they had a viking sled with the reindeer harnessed in the main hallway—was probably rented out, furnished, for parties of this type. This one had been given an Acapulco flavor by stringing a fish net along the stairway, and scenting the place with the smell of Mexican cigarettes. They had a Mariachi outfit from Olvera Street, featuring an old man, his shoulders snowy with dandruff, who would let out that *yip* so characteristic of carefree, childlike, passionate Mexican life. The drinks were served in those blurred Mexican glasses, by waiters in creaky huaraches, and *aficionados* were encouraged to take their tequila straight. I'm nothing if not an *aficionado*, and I attracted more than the usual attention by scoffing at the plate of sliced limes, and crying for salt. I had spent most of one summer mastering tequila and salt. You sprinkle a little salt on the back of your hand, where you can lick it off, like a tourist, or by tapping the wrist, sharply, get the salt to hop into your mouth. I did, then raised my eyes to see—the way a man meets his fate in the movies—a woman, a young woman, who had just entered the room. The directness of her gaze caught me unprepared. I returned it, that is. The word chick—the word I *rely* on—did not come to mind. This tremendous girl—the scale of this girl made me step back a pace to see her—wore one of the flowers, one of the favors for the ladies, in her hair. That's all I could tell you. I turned away at that point to collect myself. It took me more than a moment. The jigger-size glass that held my tequila was slippery on the outside from what I had spilled. You know the feeling you have that in your grasp, *within* your grasp, you have the dream that has always escaped you—followed by the feeling that your eyes, and your heart, have cheated you again. When I turned she was gone. Gone. Had she really been there? I walked back to the main hall where I could see up the curve of the stairs, where the women congregated; pretty good-looking women, in the main, thanks to the California sun. But this girl was not there. Looking up the flight of stairs it occurred to me that I wouldn't know this girl by how she looked—I didn't *know* how she looked—I would only recognize her by how I felt. How did I feel? The way I often feel in elevators.

They had a table of food in the center of the hall, one of these smorgasbord setups where you help yourself, and just to occupy myself I selected a plate of food. I have to do that for Mac, anyhow, otherwise he will eat nothing but stuffed olives, *stuffed* olives being for him what *baba au rhum* is for me. A symbol of the carefree, indulgent life lived by the rich in the Great Bad Places. I let him have some pumpernickel to settle his liquor, then I found him very chummy with the Señorita, a bugle-voiced Mariachi singer from First Avenue and 96th. Since Miss Harcum had brought him to this party, I brought him back to the main hall, where she was waiting, having sprayed herself with something irresistible. I got myself some stuffed celery hearts and a tall drink with the cidery flavor of Sidral, then stepped into a room off the main hall that was not occupied. It had some comfortable chairs, and a big window that looked toward the sea. What they call the jewel box was glittering between the foothills and the coast. It was still just light enough to make out the shore, the dark hulk of Catalina, and the blinking lights on an airliner that had just taken off. I moved a chair around so I could face it, having once, as a poet, compelled myself to sit and stare at what I considered beautiful. It's impossible. Try it sometime. If the sight really moves you, the first thing you do is turn away. That's how, I would say, we know that it's beautiful. We can't really cope with the sensation except to turn away and talk about it, but I had once made the effort, years ago, on the isle of Capri. The view across toward Naples, or south toward Sorrento, is of that sort. Something in the mind lights up, then blanks out, at the sight of it. I sat there all afternoon, staring, but when I think of Capri right now what I see are the views in my Uncle Clyde's stereopticon library. It is still intact. Vesuvius wears its immortal plume. A woman dressed like my mother gazes toward it from beneath her parasol.

I sat there thinking of that, and how I had turned from the sight of that wonderful girl the same way, having on my mind's eye nothing that I could call a picture of her. Over the loud-speaker system, which they had in every room, I could hear the ghostly rumble among the drums and the asthmatic whisper in the trombones that swung me back, just the way they did Fitzgerald, to a world that seemed obliged to get better and better in every way. Listening to the band it occurred to me that every sentiment had its own pitch, the way that every generation has its own sentiment. Good or bad. The pitch we hear today, the phony pitch, is absolutely right for the phony sex, the phony sentiment, and the phony mountain ballads poured out of the pine-scented plastic maple syrup cans. If you think that crime doesn't pay you haven't been to the movies lately, or checked the juvenile and senile delinquents on your local jukebox. The word for it is slobism. They grunt, groan, and grind, but seldom reach the level of speech. If I sound a little bitter, remember that I'm old enough to know better, but I'm paid according to how well I can forget what I know. The current crop of singers are medicine men and snake charmers. Everything is in the sales talk and nothing in what they sell. The phony pitch has to make up for what the song lacks. The pitch of Pussy Amor, singing one of our songs, is based entirely on the assumption that you have heard *better* songs, but at least this reminds you of one of them. I thought of all this because I was listening to one of the few songs I wish I had written, and I sat there, just the way Mac would have, crooning "Just One More Chance." I sang the refrain, but it had been so long since I wanted another chance, I'd forgotten the words. The way Bing used to do it, I whistled. I finished off with the refrain—

"Just one more cha-ance . . ."

like I really meant it.

My drink was on the floor, I had this plate in my lap, and I sat there facing this view through the window—but the window itself, as I gazed, obstructed the view. In it I could see, clearly reflected, the girl who stood in the doorway behind me. The girl I had looked for. The one I doubted was real. She saw my own reflection in the window—she saw that I saw her now, and said:

"Just one more chance . . . what for?"

How long had she been there? I was certain that if I turned to look at her, she would disappear. As a rule I am handy with words, glib, you might say, but I said nothing. I gazed at her face—I tried, that is, to penetrate behind the impression, the one reflected in the glass, that she was beautiful. The face oval. The hair, I hardly thought of the color, in loose ringlets. The mouth—as I looked at her lips they slowly parted, as if to speak, but instead she raised the glass she was holding and took a sip. That was all, just moistening her lips, leaving a cool film that made them shiny, and perhaps exaggerated the whiteness of her teeth. I'm a little uncertain without my glasses, but whether it was her reflection or the window that wavered, what I saw blurred in focus and rippled like the shadows that water casts.

"Yes—?" I heard her say, as if expecting an answer. Then I heard a voice in the hall calling, "Eva! Oh, Eva!" and she turned away. I rose out of my chair spilling the plate on the floor and kicking over my drink. Behind her, through the door, I could see this big fellow coming toward her with two plates.

"Look!" I heard myself say, and she wheeled around toward me, took that flower from her hair, and as she tossed it toward me said:

"—in case you want that chance."

The young fellow with her saw what she had done, and they both laughed. I let the flower lie there while I cleaned up the mess. I tossed it on the tray, with the celery, the ice cubes, and the pieces of plate I had broken, carrying them down the hall to where the dirty dishes were stacked. In the dim light of the hall my hand went out and picked off the flower. I slipped it into the pocket of my coat, then stood in the main room, with perhaps forty people, listening to an old lecher sing the usual run of dirty songs. He got a big hand. At one point I heard Mac shout, "That's great, man!"

I saw her twice. Looking for the men's room I saw her seated on one of the landings, her back toward me, two young men at her feet and her hand held by the one seated at her side. I was relieved to see their fingers were not laced. Then, an hour later, looking for Mac, I saw her reflected in a cloakroom mirror, running a comb through her hair, her strong brown arms raised above her head. That was where I recognized it. I may have said it aloud. The word *Greek*. One without the mutilations. One with all the limbs intact.

I would have gone at that point rather than see who would be holding her hand on the next landing, but I couldn't go off without Mac. You may find it hard to believe that a man of thirty-eight, who flies his own airplane, neither drives nor has the nerve to drive a car. I couldn't leave him to a cab, since I'm never sure he knows where he lives. I asked one of the caterers if they had a piano, and he replied that they did, in what he called the playroom, and, as I might have expected, Mac was there. So were fifteen or twenty other people, listening to him. He loves old upright pianos, and he has this idea they go with his music. They don't. But he loves the idea. He had been trying some of our new stuff on them, and this little Southern chick, with her big damp voice, was talking the words I had put into her mouth.

> "What next?
> The life of love I knew
> No longer loves
> The things I do.
> What next?"

If the test of a song is what it stands up under, this was a good song. She got a hand from the crowd, and she was set to run through the few little things she knew, which would have been plenty, but I stepped forward at that point and raised my hand. The answer to "What Next?" I said, was that I had to take its composer, the gent seated at the keyboard, home so he could finish the song. We had just three verses, I said, and it called for four. Then, to make this little chick feel good, I made a few remarks about our new songbird, and how much her style brought back the old days of Fanny Brice.

Nobody laughed when I said that. They gave us all a big hand. There you have the new show business in a nutshell. You tell them what they're going to like, they like it, then they all stand and applaud themselves. In the general happy hubbub I got Mac away from the piano, grabbed hold of the girl, and got them to the stairs. I kept my eye peeled for the Greek, but she was gone. Some prankster had propped up a poster of Rin Tin Tin in the back seat of our car, lifelike as hell in the moonlight, and I just left it there and drove off. We drove this little chick back to her apartment, where Mac kissed her chastely on the forehead, then let me wait five or ten minutes while she looked for her keys.

Driving west along Sunset, cruising through the blinkers and coming out above the lights, on some of the rises, kept the feeling that was building up in me from being localized. Not till I parked the car, came in through the back, and made Mac his usual nightcap of whisky—not till I had one myself, a little stiffer than usual, did it all come back. I hadn't eaten. I felt squeamish and a little sick.

"Whassamatta?" Mac said, dunking his cubes, the way he likes to, with his finger.

"Must be something I ate," I said, which he didn't question, since that often happened.

Our bedroom is at the top front of this mansion, from where you can view the sea in the morning, but I could hear Mac, after I had gone to bed, hammering the baby grand. Like everybody in the world, he likes to play Rachmaninoff. I lay there thinking, of one thing and another, and when it was clear I was not going to sleep I got out of bed and looked in my pocket for that paper flower. I stepped into the bathroom, closing the door, to examine it. I know nothing about flowers. This one had white petals you could pluck off. I plucked off several, then I noticed that one petal seemed to have a serial number. I could see very plainly the number 2-8117. I could not make out the letters that preceded it. It was slow to dawn on me that what I had was a phone number. Part of one, that is. We have about a dozen telephones in the place, but it took me half an hour to find a phone book, then another half-hour to grasp the problem. I had no exchange. Thirty-two were listed in the general Los Angeles area.

What did I know about the girl?

Her name was Eva. That was not very much.

THE
FIELD
OF
VISION

A novel

The mind is its own place, and in itself
Can make a Heav'n of Hell, a Hell of Heav'n.

—John Milton
Paradise Lost

You mustn't look in my novel for the old stable *ego* of the character. There is another ego, according to whose action the individual is unrecognizable, and passes through, as it were, allotropic states which it needs a deeper sense than any we've been used to exercise, to discover are states of the same single radically unchanged element.

—D. H. Lawrence

McKee

THE seat in the shady side of the bullring made McKee cold. *Sol* would have been better, as they called it, but McKee had wanted the best. Tell him we want the best, he had said to Boyd, but that turned out to be shade. The people over in the sun, however, looked a lot more comfortable. They were drinking cold beer, and they sat there in the sun with their shirt sleeves rolled. It just went to prove, McKee reflected, if you didn't really know what the best was, the smart thing to do was not stick out your neck and ask for it. Not in Mexico. Not if what you really wanted was a seat in the *sol*.

When they came out of the tunnel into the bullring McKee had felt a little dizzy, took a grip on the rail. Same feeling he got watching motorcycles spin in one of those wooden bowls. "We going to sit right smack down on the drain?" he had said, since that was how the bullring itself really looked. Small. Just a round hole at the bottom of a concrete bowl. And these seats they had were right on the lip of it. Cold as a street curb the moment the sun went down. Between the seats these iron bars as smooth as a pump handle, and just about as cold as a pump handle in the winter time. McKee had put his hand on one and said—turning to his grandson he had said—"Cold enough, by-golly, to freeze your tongue to a pump handle." You wouldn't believe it, but that boy didn't know what a pump handle was. Not knowing that he naturally couldn't grasp what McKee meant. To make it worse, when McKee explained it he couldn't get it through his head why anyone with any sense would stick his tongue to one. "You go ask your Uncle Boyd—" McKee had said, just to get rid of him. He didn't know what to make of a boy like that.

Not that he wanted to complain. About the weather, that is. It was on the cool side in the shade, but not cold. Whereas it was eight or ten below back where they came from. Probably colder, since the Omaha paper tended to minimize the weather. People wouldn't cross the state of Nebraska at all if they knew how cold it was. They would go through South Dakota, which was even worse, but south of North Dakota so it sounded warmer. Mexico sounded hot, but that was due to the food. McKee himself would have preferred Hawaii, but that would have meant going off without their grandson, whereas by traveling in the car they could take both the boy and his great-granddaddy. They could have gone to Florida, for that matter, where they could have seen people who talked their own language, but maybe even fewer who were willing to shut up and just listen to it. But as he often said to Mrs. McKee, you could count on the fingers of one hand the people who knew what it was they wanted, or meant what they said. And she knew who he meant. You couldn't pull the wool over Mrs. McKee.

Take what he'd said to Boyd. When he had run into Boyd in the Sanborn's lobby, Boyd had said, "How are you, McKee?" and what had he replied? That he couldn't be happier. *Mrs. McKee and me couldn't be happier.* That's what he had said. The moment he had said it he knew something about it didn't sound quite right. If he'd been asked by anybody but Gordon Boyd he would have said it and very likely believed it, but he always wondered if he meant what he said to Boyd. So did Mrs. McKee.

"These seats remind you of anything, Lois?" he said, since they reminded McKee of something. The time they went to see Boyd's play in Omaha. Had these reserved front seats since it was Boyd's play, and didn't cost him anything. Play purported to be about a walk on the water the young man in the play planned to get around to, but there was no more on the stage than there was in the bullring. Maybe less. In the bullring at least there was sand, which was what the play called for, since the water was in this sandpit east of Polk. But on the stage in Omaha there was nothing but talk. McKee had found most of it hard to follow. He was the only man alive, besides Boyd, himself, who had been there at the sandpit when it all happened, but the scenery wasn't there, and without the scenery it didn't make sense. What sort of sandpit can you have on an empty stage? The strangest thing McKee had ever set his eyes on, a lot stranger than ghosts or flying saucers, had been a person like Boyd thinking he could do something like that. Listening to a lot of talk, in an auditorium, about a boy who was *thinking* of walking on water, had nothing to do with being out at a sandpit, and seeing it done. Seeing it tried, that is. Seeing him come within an ace of drowning himself. The strange thing wasn't so much that he tried—it was what you might expect of a person with a screw loose—but that right up till he failed, till he dropped out of sight, McKee had almost believed it himself. It was that sort of thing people talking on a stage couldn't bring out. It wasn't only Boyd who was crazy, and believed it. McKee had believed it himself.

"Don't remind you of a sandpit, does it?" he said, since

the bullring struck him as quite a bit like one. A dry one. The way he'd like to see every sandpit. Without the water there no kid would feel he had to walk on it.

"No, it *does not* remind me of a sandpit," she replied.

In her opinion, especially when they traveled, McKee was always being reminded of something. That is to say, everything reminded him of something else. The outside of this bullring, for instance, reminded McKee of the Lincoln Library basement. Of the big framed pictures on the walls of the basement, Roman ruins, the Coliseum, places like that. McKee had never been to Rome himself, but he had raised a boy who had lived in that basement. The ruins that looked like the bullring were over in the corner where he usually sat. The boy's name was Gordon. Named after Gordon Boyd, that is. Grown up and married now, with four youngsters of his own, the oldest one right there in the bullring with them, sitting right beside Boyd, the man who had almost ruined his daddy's life. Back at that time his daddy, Gordon McKee, had been just about as crazy as Boyd had been, a moody stage-struck kid who would have tried to walk on air, if the play called for it. He might not have almost drowned himself, like Boyd, but he would have been up in the air all his life if they hadn't made that trip back to New York, where he saw Boyd. Where he saw, that is, what was left of him. The great man in his life looking no different than a common bum. When the boy saw what it was like to walk on water—what it was like, that is, if you failed—he at least had sense enough, which he got from his mother, to give it up. You didn't have to rub his nose in his own mess to make him see the point.

"Anybody want a cool drink?" said McKee, and leaned forward, his hands on the rail, to look down the row to the man at the end of it. Gordon Boyd. He could look right at him since the row was curved. But he wouldn't have known it, or guessed it, if he hadn't been told. Big and soft now, almost the yellow color of the Mexicans. Habit of stroking his face, one side, as though he thought he might need a shave. Next to him was the boy, McKee's grandson, wearing his coonskin hat and Davy Crockett outfit, and in a coonskin hat right there beside him was the old man. Not a real coonskin, an imitation with a stringy tail that wouldn't fool anybody, but the old man was so blind all he could do was feel it, and it felt like a tail. McKee had never openly said, nor did he like to think, that his wife's father had a screw loose somewhere, although everybody said so and he knew it himself everytime he looked at him. Now that he was eighty-seven they could blame it on his age, but the screw that was loose had been loose from the beginning. His own wife—a woman with a lot of horse sense—had been the first to point it out. He didn't really live in this world, as she put it, but he left her with a string of kids to raise in it, and one of those kids, as it turned out, was McKee's wife. She didn't look much like her father, but she had his pale blue eyes, and let her get a little riled and you could see his jaw jutting out of her face.

Next to him was Mrs. Kahler, a woman whose eyes were as good as McKee's, if not better, but due to some mental trouble she saw very little out of them. If McKee understood it, she saw only what she wanted to see. Here at the bullfight, for instance, she didn't seem to see the bulls. They just brought her along because she liked the music and the company. First thing McKee felt, when he set eyes on her, was how long it had been since he had seen George Arliss, since she had the sort of face, homely but friendly, that you like right off the bat. She liked to knit at the bullfight, and was knitting Dr. Lehmann a pair of red sox. He was right beside her. She had already knit him the mittens he was wearing, and the red wool scarf.

If there was one thing that made McKee tired, it was to hear people say that Nebraska was flat. Lehmann had said so. A foreigner to boot. McKee could show him, both around Polk and Lincoln, as lovely rolling country as he'd ever set eyes on, but it wasn't the Alps, it wasn't the Riviera, and the people weren't busy making cuckoo clocks. As he understood they were back where Lehmann came from, wherever that was. Boyd himself had once said, and McKee had never forgotten it, that Switzerland was like a national park where they let the cows run on the golf course to keep the grass short. Dr. Leopold Lehmann, like those foreign types McKee had met in Omaha and Lincoln, didn't seem to feel at home if he wasn't at the bottom or the top of something. Nebraska hardly ever went up and down like that. But if you'd take a little place like the Swiss Alps, which was all up and down, and put it through a roller, some sort of open country, like they had around Lincoln, was what you'd get. Which was just about what, if McKee understood it, that big sheet of ice did when it covered Nebraska, leaving these little sandpits where kids like Mc-Kee and Boyd could drown.

Sandpits always gave McKee the willies, which was why the empty bullring made him so uneasy, as if they were all just sitting there waiting for the water to rise. When it reached a certain level, some fool kid would try to walk on it. If you got as many people as there were present sitting around a little hole in the ground, like this ring was, it just naturally followed that something would happen. Almost anything. Where you had so many people a wild streak would turn up in one of them.

McKee looked for it where he had once seen it. The face of Gordon Boyd. He didn't look so well. On the other hand, he didn't really look sick. It was hard to judge a man who left egg on his front and drove all over Mexico in a '38

Ford coupe. McKee would like to know if he was sick upstairs, which was why he was down here with this Dr. Lehmann, or if they were doing some sort of book together, as he seemed to imply. If their seats had been closer he would have asked. He could talk to Boyd. After all, there was nobody who knew him so well, nobody who had seen him up and down the ladder, and who liked him any more than McKee—if that was the word. It probably wasn't. If he had to name it, it seldom was. Whatever the word was, when he saw this tourist in the Sanborn's lobby, with his fly unzipped, he had felt no compunction—as he ordinarily would have—about speaking to him. He didn't know this tourist from Adam—what he felt was, when he began to feel something, that it was an old feeling and he had felt it many times before. He recognized the feeling. After that he recognized the man. The feeling—which hadn't changed, and in respect to the feeling the man hadn't either—was that he'd never notice anything was wrong. McKee would have to. McKee would have to tap him on the shoulder, lean forward, and speak the word *fly*. The responsibility—*that* was the feeling—had always rested with McKee, in such matters, since Boyd had always lacked what McKee had been born with, good horse sense. He had never had it. He had even done without it—while he had McKee. The real trouble—if the truth were known, but of course it wouldn't be, and perhaps it shouldn't—the real trouble began when McKee was no longer there. When he could no longer, in the plainest sense, be responsible. Keep an eye on his wild streak, his fly, or whatever it was. When he went off to that school in the East, where he turned up, suddenly, famous— and when he turned up in Lincoln, needing McKee, it was too late. McKee had his own Gordon Boyd by then. He had to run his own life. He had a woman on his hands who would almost whoop-up if he mentioned Boyd. He did

373

what he could, both then and later; McKee gave him a son he knew he would never have, and in going that far he almost ruined all of their lives. All except Boyd's. *He* had taken care of that all by himself.

The last time they'd seen Boyd—Mrs. McKee hadn't seen him, just McKee, the boy, his Uncle Roy and Aunt Agnes —had been in '39 when they all drove to New York for the World's Fair. In one of those doughnut shops around Times Square Agnes had thought of Boyd, found his name in the phone book, and the upshot of it was they had all gone down to this loft where he lived. They found him up there with his shirt off, no furniture to speak of, nobody anywhere around to look after him, and this fool ballplayer's pocket lying on his desk. One he'd torn off Ty Cobb's pants, way back when he was a kid. McKee had been with him the time he did it—the way he'd been with him out at the sandpit—but who would have dreamed he would have hung on to a soiled rag like that? Twenty-five years. When Agnes asked him why it was he still had it, he said it was the only thing he hadn't lost his grip on. Everything else he got his hands on, he said, he'd dropped. It had been just pitiful to hear him say it, and to see the truth in it, but it had been a life-saver for the boy, Gordon, to see it for himself. He saw exactly where it was the sort of life he was leading led. Except for Boyd, and that fool pocket, he might not have married and settled down. And McKee's grandson, this little tyke in the bullring, might not have been born. A boy they also called Gordon, after his father; but the name really belonged to Boyd, and McKee often wondered if it hadn't been the name that ruined Boyd's own life.

If there had ever been anything like a real misunderstanding between McKee and his wife, it had been when he named his first-born son Gordon, after Boyd. They'd made an arrangement, the way young people do until they get older, and know better, that if it was going to be a girl, she would name it, whereas if it was a boy she would leave it to McKee. So he named him Gordon. That was not only what they named him, but who he was.

The other two *she* named, to see if she could get even, one of them Seward after an uncle, and the other one Orien since she had been hoping it might be a girl. And yet the boy who started off worst, and gave them nothing but trouble, was the first to settle down and now gave them the least. After being stage-struck for more than two years, chasing around with girls who were crazier than he was, he turned up married to a good solid girl they hadn't known he'd even met, from a part of the state they hadn't known he'd ever been in. His father-in-law, O. P. Rideout, of Chadron, settled eight thousand head of steer on them the day they were married, and it might have been the weight of all that beef that calmed the boy down. Mr. Rideout himself, who had raised five boys, said it often turned out that the first pup in the litter, meaning one like Gordon, tended to run a little wild. Lead dog, as he put it, had nothing to follow but his own scent. But Gordon did. In fact, it was the scent that threw him off. Threw them all off, just a little, since there was something about Boyd, besides the scent he gave off, that got people to acting as if they didn't know their own minds. Which they usually didn't. Mrs. McKee had said as much herself.

Take the way he acted when McKee recognized him. He hadn't set eyes on Boyd for fifteen years, but the first thing he said, without any introduction, was—

"McKee, how's the little woman?"

It wasn't till he heard *that* that McKee was sure just who he was. McKee had said she was fine, just fine, remembering in time not to ask about *his* wife, which he usually made considerable effort to do, just to be polite. As he had to say something, McKee had inquired what in the world had brought him to Mexico.

"All Gaul's divided into three parts," Boyd had replied, "Juvenile, Mobile and Senile delinquents. I'm in the Mobile division. How are things with you?"

Right there, in a nutshell, you had everything that was wrong with him. The way he'd keep you guessing. The way you couldn't be sure where the devil you stood. Mrs. McKee had pointed out, even before she met him, and long before it got to be popular, that just hearing about Boyd gave her a feeling of insecurity. The way she put it was, the ground didn't seem solid beneath her feet. Anything might happen with a person like that, and he had gone out of his way to prove her right. It had almost happened, according to her, the first time she met him. Boyd had kissed her. Up till then she'd never been kissed.

In answer to his question McKee had said that he and Mrs. McKee couldn't be happier. Reason he did, of course, was to reassure Boyd on that point. Then he mentioned Gordon, the big cattle ranch he had, and how the boy— when he heard where they were going—asked him to keep an eye peeled for a nice pair of bulls. The boy had said oxen, not bulls, since he was thinking of breeding a strain of them, but when McKee got to that point he heard himself say *nice pair of fighting bulls.* What had struck him? An example of what Boyd did to him. To all of them. Just to keep in the running with a person like Boyd they had to stretch the point, in so far as they had one, and a fighting bull was what McKee got when he stretched an ox. One thing led to another, after that, with Boyd offering to take him out to the bullring, and McKee trying to act as if he wasn't flabbergasted. What he said was, naturally, that he'd have to speak to the little woman, since the bullfight was the one thing she didn't like about Mexico. She hadn't seen one, but it just made her sick to know they took place. McKee would have bet the shirt off his back that she would refuse to set her eyes on Boyd, let alone be seen at something like a bullfight with him. That was where he was wrong. That was where he never knew about Mrs. McKee. She'd been simply horrified that he could even suggest it—just hearing Boyd was alive had sort of upset her—which was why McKee hadn't stepped to the phone and called it off. Then they went to lunch, and before lunch was over she'd changed her mind. The only reason Boyd had even brought it up, she said, was that he knew it would upset her, which naturally placed her under the obligation to go. Once she saw it in that light, of course, they went. McKee had bought the tickets, priced about the same as a Big League game back in the States, with the center of the bullring about as far away as the pitcher's mound. Right smack in the center, like a big Maypole, they had this giant Pepsi-Cola bottle, which was the way they advertised things in Mexico. It made McKee smile. It also reminded him of something else.

"Anybody like a cool *soft* drink?" he said, just in case his wife's father got any fancy ideas. Whatever the old man had, they would have to give the boy. Eight and eighty, but alike as two peas in a pod.

McKee watched the boy shoot up his hand, then aim his plastic six-shooter at the Pepsi-Cola bottle. The idea of a soft drink like that in a bullring made McKee smile. He felt it called for hard ones. He found it hard to believe they'd soon be killing a bull where a bottle like that advertised Pepsi-Cola. On the other hand, he didn't feel so bad about bringing the boy. It couldn't be too bad if people sat around drinking something like pop. Boyd had said he didn't need to worry about the boy since kids liked blood and just loved to poke an eye out. That was like Boyd. He wanted to

shock Mrs. McKee, and that was just what he did. But she'd
made up her mind she was going to sit through it if for no
other reason than Boyd thought she couldn't. He hadn't yet
learned that you couldn't scare a woman like Mrs. McKee.

"Hey you!" McKee said, and wagged his hand at one of
the boys with soft drinks in a bucket. Boyd *pssssst* at them,
which sounded like hissing, but McKee didn't want to pick
up that sort of habit. If he hissed at kids selling pop in the
States, they'd throw the bottle at him. This kid came up
with his pail, the bottles floating in water, and took the cap
from one of the Pepsi bottles. He looked to be about the
same sort of boy McKee saw around Lincoln, in the poorer
sections. He wore a striped paper hat, advertising something, and it crossed McKee's mind that it might be paint.

"Pintura mean paint, Lois?" he said, and out the corner of
his eye he saw her head nodding. Back at Thanksgiving—
when Mrs. McKee had made up her mind she had to go
somewhere, or go crazy—she had got these Spanish records,
since that was what they talked in Mexico. But a week or so
of listening to that had almost led McKee to think he'd
rather go crazy. He got so he almost hated the man on the
record—just his voice, since he never really saw him—and
he hated the woman who was Señora somebody, and her
two damn kids. The only word he really learned was *agua*,
which turned out to be worse than useless, since *agua* was
the one thing nobody even touched in Mexico. They drank
cerveza, which was beer, or anything in big bottles, like
Pepsi-Cola.

Not that McKee didn't sort of like Mexico. In the four
days they had been in Mexico City ten or twelve people had
asked him for the time, then thanked him kindly no matter
what it was he said. He liked that. He paid a little more
attention to the time himself. Having it there in his pocket
meant more down here than it did in the States.

"Here you are, son," he said, passing along the bottle, and when Boyd reached for it he added, "See that hat the kid's wearing is a paint hat. Guess old Sherwin Williams still covers the world."

"Coffers wot?" said Dr. Lehmann, and put a red mittened hand to his ear. McKee had thought the old man was crazy to wear a pair of wool mittens to a bullfight, but he could see he wasn't. Not in what they called the *sombra*. McKee would have preferred hot coffee to pop. Dr. Lehmann had a wool lap robe across his knees, and between his hands, that is, the red mittens, he held a silver flask that had a tiny cup for a cap. He took a snifter now and then, Boyd had said, for medicinal purposes. He was old. His circulation wasn't so good. "Coffers—?" Lehmann repeated, eyeing McKee, since he was a foreigner and didn't quite catch that.

"It's a house paint," said Boyd, reaching for the bottle. "Company that sold the paint used to give away hats. Had them when we were kids. Looks like the same old line down here."

Dr. Lehmann smiled as if he grasped that. McKee doubted that he did. Using the heel of his palm, his back to Mrs. McKee, McKee honed the spout to the bottle, then tried to take a swallow without tipping back his head. It didn't work, but it made him think of something.

"And now what?" said Mrs. McKee, who never missed a trick. Even at a bullfight. Back in Lincoln McKee would have the fork in his mouth, or the bottle to his lips, then he would stop as though it was poisoned. But when she asked him what in the world the trouble was, he hardly ever knew. She asked him now, and he said—

"Just thought of something."

He meant reminded, of course, but it wasn't a word he could use. But when he'd half tipped his head, when he'd got his eyes closed, he saw a whole bunch of kids wearing

379

those fool paint hats. He could see the paint hats, that is, but he couldn't see who the kids were. Like all the paint hats he'd ever seen, they were too big for a kid. These kids were snorting up and down like Indians, some of them with knives, some with pieces of bottle, which if you got it to break just right made a pretty good blade. What was going on? Aloud, McKee said—

"Gordon, you ever shoot a hog?"

Although he knew he hadn't. Just woodpeckers. As a boy he took the line they were bad for the trees.

"A *hog?*" said Boyd. "When was this?"

It pleased McKee to hear him ask it. He didn't answer right away for two reasons. He had to think again himself when it was that had happened, and once he had thought he didn't want to spoil it. He never had much to offer. He had to keep from blurting it out.

"Year you was away," said McKee, and let *him* figure out when that was. McKee had gone to Texas, and Boyd had gone to a school in the East somewhere.

"This was in Polk?" asked Boyd.

"Nope," said McKee, "this was in Texas."

"This was *where?*" said Boyd, since that was what he said if he liked what you told him. McKee held on. He took a mouthful of the pop. As if it didn't really matter where he spent the winter, he spit it out.

"This was where in Texas?" said Boyd, and McKee replied—

"Near Amarillo."

Surprised, once he said it, that he still remembered it. How long? Almost forty years. In his mind's eye, bigger than life, he could see the state of Texas. A sea without water in it. Anyhow, that was how he felt about it himself. But he knew better than say that to Boyd, so he said—

"Down there with my Uncle Dwight. Guess he invented

the dust bowl." Although he really hadn't. All that winter he had had McKee's help.

"Christ!" said Boyd. "I didn't know you had an uncle."

Shamelessly, McKee gulped down half the pop. Too fast, so that the fizz backed up. He belched.

"Tastes good both ways," he said, since that was why *they* used to do it. When they did it, that was what *they* said. Boyd's idea. McKee tried to think—turning over in his mind what he remembered about his uncle—if there was anything about him that Boyd might admire. A very strange man. McKee never knew where he got the idea of raising wheat. Down there, that is. Where nothing like wheat had been grown before. Panhandle grassland that had never been turned by a plow. But they had turned it—he and McKee had turned it—and the first swirling clouds of dust had begun to blow. When it had darkened the sun over places like New York, McKee had thought of that.

"Guess we stirred up the dust bowl between us," he said, and for all of that they might have.

"You're not kidding?" replied Boyd. Which meant that he believed it. He doubted everything, as a rule, but he was free to believe anything he wanted.

"Think we did," said McKee, soberly, and ran his tongue along his gums; up front, that is, just the way he used to when they were covered with a film of dust. Think of that. He could almost taste it after forty years. All the time he was in Texas his teeth had looked rotted because of the mud caked around the roots, the way dirt would pack hard and black around the foot of a post. Nothing would budge it.

"So you shot this hog—?" said Boyd, wanting to get on.

Bigger than life, McKee could see him. Looked as big or bigger to him then than a bull did now. He'd been in the pen with him. He could almost touch his snout with the barrel of the gun. Reason the hog had moved in so close was that he'd waddled over to where he could smell, as well as see, the ear of yellow corn McKee had in the front of his pants. Sticking out of his fly. Which was why, come to think, he had never mentioned it.

"Shot him right between the eyes," went on McKee, and put up his little finger to indicate the hole size.

"He have three eyes then?" said the boy.

"That's just what he did," said McKee.

"Two to look out, and one to look in, eh?" said Boyd.

"I do believe there is a limit," said Mrs. McKee, but before she reached it they all heard this racket. A bugle? It pulled, like the suck of a lemon, at McKee's ears. Way up behind him, up the slope that made him nearly dizzy when he turned and looked at it, way up there where they let them all sit for three pesos he could see the band. But just trying to look made him feel like he was spinning. Was it the rows of hats? There was no sun behind him, but every one of those Mexicans had a straw hat. Made the slope as shiny as a tile roof. He watched one go sailing off. The noise the band made poured down on them and McKee felt heavy, as if the music was like water. It pulled the way the tub drain did when the plug slipped out.

"Granpa!" yelled the boy. "Look, granpa!" and McKee wheeled around, his hands gripping the rail, to watch men who looked like midgets going off with the Pepsi bottle. They looked like circus dwarfs with that bottle, and confirmed McKee's feeling of some basic disorder. Some disproportion that made him feel a little unbalanced, unsure of himself. The way he'd feel if he landed on the moon, or felt drawn to it. He watched the men, all of them so many midgets, and it crossed his mind what was wrong with it. Back in the States they'd have a truck, or some machine, to take care of that. But people—pretty little ones at that—still did the work in Mexico. On the highway coming down they'd crossed an iron bridge that looked like it was crawling with hundreds of insects, but on closer inspection they turned out to be Indians. Full grown ones. What were they up to? They were chipping the rust off that fool bridge with sharp pointed rocks. Coming on them like that McKee had had the feeling that his eyes were slipping, or that liquid was in his ear drums, since the scale of the thing, like the men with the bottle, threw him off. They took it out through a gate where McKee could see, when they got the gates wide open, a bunch of young men who looked like trapeze artists in tights. All men. No pretty girl to lead off swinging her baton. Then he caught sight, just before the gates closed, of a dark horse and a black frocked rider. A somber note. Was he going to be part of the same parade? He thought he'd ask Boyd, and leaned over to do it, tapping his bottle on the rail to attract Boyd's attention, when the gates swung wide and this fellow on the horse pranced into the ring. All by himself, the horse a high fancy stepper, but as if they both forgot the parade was behind them, and they'd gone off not knowing they were out there all alone.

"See that, Lois?" said McKee, since what it made him think of was her father. Whether he had a screw loose or not, he could handle a horse. This dark horse and his rider came right at them, clear across the ring without a thing behind them, then stopped right there below them, where the rider doffed his black hat. He said a few words—McKee turned to see who it was he had his eye on—but when he turned back he could hardly believe his eyes. Both horse and rider were backing up. Anybody who had ever tried to back up a horse could appreciate that. Clear across the ring, maybe a good hundred yards, every inch of it backwards to the gate he had come in, where the young men in their tights, and the rest of the parade, were waiting for him.

"Know what happened?" said McKee, nudging his wife's

elbow. "He meant to bring 'em along, but he forgot to hitch 'em up. Got clean over here before he noticed he was alone."

Over his mouth, to indicate he was laughing, McKee cupped his hand. Mrs. McKee said nothing. She didn't even trouble to edge away from him. Which meant she felt it too, whatever it was, since when she felt something pretty strong, she froze up, whereas McKee always tried to say something good for a laugh.

And then, without really knowing why, he stood up. Got to his feet as though the national anthem was being played. "Here they come!" he said, as if she couldn't see it, and then like a fool he took off his straw hat. The one he'd bought for just two pesos outside the ring. People thought he did that—as he heard later—so the ladies could see in the row behind him, since the brim of this hat he'd bought was pretty big. Nobody in his own row, luckily, took notice of it. He watched this rider on the dark horse lead the way, which gave it an off-key flavor, but the young men in their tights, and the mules with the pom-poms, made up for it. When they spread out in the ring, so he could see them, he thought all the young men in the front row were injured, since they carried their left arms in a sort of sling. But it hardly seemed likely they'd all been bull-struck on the same arm. It was part of the parade, the curious way they did things, like having that sad looking black horse leading, and the slinky sort of way they all seemed to march, sticking out their hips. The music was sharp, but not the way they marched to it. Fairly good-looking boys in other respects, with a row of older men right behind them, some of them a little fat in the midriff and the rear for bullfighting. From the pictures he'd seen, it didn't strike McKee as the place to stick out. Right behind the men were the mules, with their pom-poms, then these fellows with outfits like street cleaners, and from what they brought along with them, maybe that was what they were. Wheelbarrows, shovels, brooms, and that sort of thing. They came along behind the mules, and McKee thought that was good. Charlie Chaplin had made a mighty funny movie out of something like that. The point was good, if McKee got it, but what interested him most were the mules, since he wondered if these were the horses everybody complained about. Had it reached the point where people couldn't tell a mule from a horse?

"Boyd—" he said, and leaned forward to ask him, when he happened to notice the rear end of the horses. Two of them, looking like upholstered furniture. A little fat-bottomed man sat on each of them. It seemed hard to believe he hadn't seen such a sight when it came right at him, but he hadn't, and it should teach him, only it wouldn't, to keep his mouth closed.

"What are the mules for?" he said, since he had to say something.

"The mules drack oaf the det bools," said Dr. Lehmann.

"*Bulls?*" said McKee, since it hadn't crossed his mind there'd be several of them. Nor had it crossed his mind what they did with any of them. It wasn't a bullfight. It was a *bulls* fight. For the first time he wondered if he was going to like it. In a cheery voice he said—

"Well, folks, what's next on the bill?"

Someone shouted right behind him, like he meant to tell him, but when McKee turned all the hands waved at him; feeling a tug on his sleeve he glanced at Mrs. McKee. She pulled him down. Right there before him, as if he'd come in with the parade but they'd gone off without him, was the bull.

McKee thought he looked small.

Mrs. McKee

DR. Lehmann's breath—he was that close—had the sweetish smell of furniture polish from the lozenge she could see, green as a horse's bit, when he opened his mouth. He was saying—his language was so garbled she hardly knew what he was saying—if she hadn't read it all, nearly every word of it, somewhere else. How the parade, this procession they had seen, was a parable of life. The heroes at the front—he had said *sheroes*, but that was due to the lozenge—and ahead of them, a portent, the horseman who wore black. A somber foreboding of what lay ahead in the hero's life. And then the riffraff—he had used the word riffraff, indicating his foreign extraction—the riffraff, the mules, and the men with brooms and shovels who cleaned up the mess. All of this he had recited as if he had thought it up himself. But the night before, in the little book McKee had smiled at her for buying, *Toros without Tears*, she had read the same thing but much better put. Not the riffraff, no, that was his own, or the idea of people cleaning up the mess, but that the procession had allegorical elements. Something that hardly needed, she would have said, pointing out.

If only her mother could have seen the man on the horse. Coming in alone like that, like her father, not caring if the parade was or wasn't behind him, making his little speech, then backing out of the picture. Just like that.

"When the century turned, darling," her mother had said, with a sour look, "your father didn't." He not only didn't turn, he backed right out of it. For almost forty years there was nothing that pleased him, nothing that he either cared to live or die for, which had a good deal to do with the fact that he was neither alive nor dead. One of those people she had read about somewhere who could sleep with their eyes wide open, and, like this Mrs. Kahler, look through them without seeing anything.

Nobody knew, for instance, if her father was as good as blind, or not. He wouldn't answer simple questions. He wouldn't look through the glasses doctors tried on him. If he had no common sense he seemed to have all the others— he could scoot around like a bug when he cared to—or he would just sit as though every muscle in his body was paralyzed. The way he sat now. Absolutely determined not to see anything. She had had to lead him in like a blind man, poking at everything with that cane he carried, looking like some sort of clown in the silly coonskin hat. He knew perfectly well the impression he was making and that she looked like a fool; that is to say, they all did, coming to a bullfight with a poor old man who was blind as a bat. "What froze him up?" McKee has said, as if it was something she had done herself. Her father had frozen up the moment the boy began to talk to Boyd. Which meant that it was now absolutely hopeless since the child ignored him completely, and acted just as if he had lived all of his life with Boyd. Nothing had changed. It made her flesh crawl just to think of it.

"You cold, Lois?" said McKee. "You got goose pimples."

Naturally, she didn't hear that. If she let on that she heard it he would take off his coat—showing his elastic garter-type arm bands—since he would take off his coat at the slightest provocation here in Mexico. Before he had it so much as draped around her shoulders, he would start sneezing himself.

Not that she was cold. Anyhow, not so cold as she looked. She looked at her hands—one of them dark brown from the sun on the side of the car she had sat on—but both of them, as she knew without her glasses, jittery. The pyramid? Let them call it the pyramid. She had gone up the pyramid: many people did, but it had been ill-advised in her case, since she had to take injections to quiet her down, then pills to pep her up. The pills made her so nervous that something in the mattress, the springs, or the straw in her pillow, made a crackling sound that kept her awake all night. On top of that she had set eyes on Boyd, something that always unnerved her, and to make matters worse here she was with him in an actual bullring. She tipped forward, as if to peer into the runway, what they called the *callejón* in that book she had read, then glanced down the row to the man at the end of it. Was that what tropical nights and Latin women had done to him? She saw it all very clearly, and remembered that she had been the *first*.

Walter McKee could see the goose flesh on her arms very easily, but he had once stood, like a wooden Indian, and watched his best friend be the first man to kiss his future bride. What McKee had felt she couldn't imagine, but she would never forget what it had done to the bride. It had affected her—now that she had made it—like the pyramid climb. Queasy in her middle. Her legs trembling when she was lying down. Just to be witty Boyd had said that the arms of girls made him think of folding chairs, the easy way they would bend backward, and for weeks she had suffered from the notion that her own arms might. This habit she had of hugging herself dated from that time. It kept her elbows bent the *right* way, and covered up how jittery she was. The crazy thing about it was that he had them both— her friend Alice Morple had been there with her—but he had kissed Alice second, so that she had a little time to prepare herself. As McKee himself would verify, Alice had stuck her neck out like a goose. But that was all beside the point, the point being that Boyd had kissed her *first*, and Alice Morple had said, "If you were so surprised, why did you kiss him back?"

She had been too shocked to speak.

"All I've got to say is," Alice Morple had said, which she always put in if it certainly wasn't, "I didn't have time to lick the candied apple off *before* he kissed me."

Then they had gone to bed—Alice Morple was visiting her for the week end—and since they couldn't sleep Alice Morple had naturally made some further remarks. "It was a good thing he went off when he did," she said, laughing as if she was being tickled, and more or less implying that it didn't seem to matter that McKee had been there. Did it? How could she ignore the terrible truth? He had been there on the porch, right there with them, when this boy she had never seen before in her life, although she had heard about him, stepped forward and kissed her smack on the lips. The point being she had known he would. Her own lips were prepared. They had been eating candied apple and she had put out her tongue and licked the sticky part off.

Then came the dream—but she wouldn't go into that. She hadn't slept a wink that night or the next one, her knees would almost knock when she stooped for something, and she felt all over like the hum the wires make in a telephone pole. If McKee or Alice Morple touched her, it would make her jump. It wasn't in her mind at all, like the books say, but a current all over her body and a feeling that if she touched something it would spark. Somewhere near her middle a buzzing sensation, as if she had swallowed a fly. For two or three weeks she was like one of the chickens who had eaten the laying mash that had soured, his head off to one side, walking around like he was on thin air. Nothing he managed to put his foot on felt right to him. What he had taken for granted as solid ground was more like air. He didn't trust his own senses, or anybody else's, and McKee had pointed out it was a fine example of what fermented spirits would do to anyone. But without fermented spirits, just a candied apple, she had been in the same condition as the chicken; she didn't trust her own senses, and the ground kept shifting beneath her feet. She had just enough wit to do what she could. She married McKee.

She also took it for granted that he understood *something*, since he had been there, and saw what had happened, but when their first child was born what did he do but name it after Boyd. So he had been there, but he hadn't seen a thing. McKee was the kindest person in the world, but he never saw more, when he looked at her, than whether she had migraine or goose pimples on her arms or not. He would never see more than he could cover up by taking off his coat. When he called her on the hotel telephone and said, "Lois, you'd never guess who I just ran into—" her body had been crawling with goose pimples before she heard. *It* knew, even before *she* did, and in that respect nothing had changed since she had licked the candied apple from her lips more than thirty years ago. Not that he would want to kiss her now, or she would let him, but the knowledge that her body knew what she didn't, and would not let her forget it, was exactly the same. Anything might happen. And once it almost did.

Until that night she hadn't set eyes on Boyd, but she had

heard about him from the morning that McKee, who had an egg route then, had stepped into her aunt's kitchen to thaw himself out. He'd made a joke about the chickens being frozen in the shell, which got them all to laughing, then he said it wasn't really his joke, but one he'd heard in Omaha. Her aunt said, had he really been to Omaha? And McKee had said he had, he had been there for Christmas, which he had spent with his old friend Gordon Boyd. She had been just fifteen at the time, which meant McKee was seventeen, since he was two years older, but it seemed strange to hear him refer to his *old friend*, Gordon Boyd. He hardly ever said Gordon. He always said Gordon Boyd. When she knew him better, and asked him why it was he never talked about himself, only about this Gordon, it hadn't crossed his mind there was anything else to talk about. When it did, he thought it over then said that Gordon Boyd, his old friend, was half an orphan. His father had died before he had really set eyes on him. It hadn't been McKee's fault, but he seemed to feel responsible for him. Other people he knew felt the same way; a family named Crete, who were very wealthy, and when their own boy died they more or less adopted Gordon Boyd. He lived with them in Omaha, where they had better schools, and long before the New York theater people knew about him Mrs. Crete put up the money and made the people she knew come to see his plays. One of them was a talent scout, from the East, and although nobody in Omaha could believe it, the crazy play he wrote about the sandpit had made a big hit in New York. Otherwise she and McKee might never have seen it. At that, it was almost twenty years; then the WPA revived it, and her own son, who was stage-struck at the time, played the leading role. Doing all of those things, that is, pretending to do them, that Gordon Boyd had done nearly twenty years before him, such as brazenly kissing the girl, the fiancée, of his own best friend. He knew just what he was doing, and from there went off and drowned himself. Not intentionally, but with the full understanding that if he failed to walk on the water, which he naturally did, it would prove that he was not truly worthy of her.

There was of course more to it, everybody talked for hours, but as McKee himself told her later, none of it was made up—Boyd had once tried to walk on water, and nearly drowned. It was certainly just like him, as Alice Morple said, to write a play where he could take full credit for drowning, but still be around, in the lobby somewhere, and able to enjoy it. The meaning of the play, so far as she could understand it, was that if he had managed to walk on the water he would have come back and run off with the girl he had just kissed. The same night. While the taste, as he said, of the candied apple was still on her lips. The point being that the girl, all of this time, was sitting up and waiting for him.

"Know what happened?" said McKee, and she almost blurted that *nothing* had happened, which was the trouble, but he wasn't directing the question to her, but to Boyd. He waved his arm at the horse and rider, said—"He meant to bring 'em along, but he forgot to hitch 'em up. Got clean over here before he noticed he was alone."

He brought his hand down hard on her knee, as if it was his own. It was something he normally wouldn't think of doing, and she knew, from the way he did it, that he was as jittery and queasy in the middle as she was herself. Was it the altitude? He had climbed no pyramid. Or was it something that Gordon Boyd did to both of them? She had always been so upset herself—the two or three times she had seen Boyd—there had hardly been a chance to see how he affected McKee. Now she could see it was the same. If you asked him, he probably couldn't tell you *where* he was.

He was acting like a clown to cover up how nervous he was. Was it all one way? Didn't Boyd ever feel very much himself? She turned her head, her lips tight to keep her tongue from misbehaving, and looked at the face of the first man to kiss her. He looked sad. It seemed strange, but that was how he looked. Had such a large sad man actually tried to walk on water at one time? How many girls, on how many other porches, had he kissed? But married none. As if he *really had* drowned himself. As if—she turned to see what the shouting was about, saw McKee standing, his hat off, facing the rows of people waving at him. She pulled him down—was he so befuddled she was going to have him, as well as the others?—she pulled him down and directed his attention toward the ring. A little bull, a calf she would have said, perplexed to be alone out there, his tail wagging, looked around for the 4-H boy or girl who belonged to him. The one who had brought him in, then forgotten him. One of the men shook a cape out, shouting at him, but that wasn't at all what he wanted, and when another ran at him, trailing the cape on the ground, he turned and trotted for the fence. Over he came, the way she knew he would, just as if McKee had a ripe apple for him, and stood there scratching his chin on the top rail. Like a little sprig of flowers, there were green and white ribbons pinned to his hump.

"That what you call a bull, Gordon?" McKee said, and she might have forgotten, if he hadn't, that it wasn't one of her son's beef cattle, but a bull. That the ribbon on his hump wasn't for a prize he had won. She turned to Boyd—he was standing, holding his Pepsi-Cola bottle like a cocktail shaker, his thumb tight across the top, but she could hear the fizz escape. She watched him lean over the rail, away over, his soft mid-section folded around it, and using his thumb like a nozzle squirt the fizzing pop into the little bull's face. Did he like it? He put out his blue tongue and licked off his snout. Boyd gave the bottle a shake, then squirted him again.

Everybody who saw that began to laugh—the child, her grandson, was almost screaming—but even people who were older, who knew better, seemed to enjoy it. Those who were farther back stood on their seats to get a better view. Boyd used up one bottle and called for another, which the man across the aisle was quick to hand him, and the bull kept his head on the rail, his tongue slapped on his snout. The bullfighters themselves, if that was what you could call them, stood around with their capes, grinning like small children, and when the bottle was drained she saw Boyd wave his hands like a prize fighter. He faced the crowd, he waved the bottle, he bowed at the waist and blew the ladies kisses, and all the time they were whistling like they did when they weren't doing anything else.

"Guess he hasn't changed much, has he?" said McKee, and they watched him take one of their grandson's toy pistols and shoot into the air. On her father's face, blind as he was, she saw that he had followed the entire performance, although his gaze remained on the little bull.

"Why, he's hardly more than a calf—" she said, as if that was all there was to see, and settled back in her seat the way she did when a fever turned out to be no more than a common cold.

Scanlon

THE old man couldn't believe his eyes—the ones he had—but his ears told him the worst. He could hear the crowd yell and the fizzing squirt of the pop. If anybody had told him he would live to see the day a grown man would stand up and squirt pop at someone—but of course, he didn't. Live to see the day, that is. He'd had sense enough to go blind before he lived to see something like that. But one thing he didn't have sense enough to do was just stay put. Where he belonged, that is. He hadn't had sense enough to live, then die, back in Lone Tree.

When they told Tom Scanlon that his wife had died—his daughter, Lois, was the one to tell him—he had taken a kitchen match from his hat band, bit down on it. He let his daughter wait, then after a while he said, "Loey, what'll the hens do?"

She replied, "Uncle Roy and Agnes are taking them."

It didn't mean that Scanlon didn't feel death any, or not care about people, or other things they said about him. What it meant was that he seldom felt *much*, so any feeling threw him off. When he thought about the chickens he

395

knew what it was he felt, and that the chickens would feel it even more than he did. But being chickens they might not grasp it. So they would need help. They would miss her. That was what he meant.

Scanlon and his wife had been married forty years, but they had not lived more than half of them together, since she had decided, as she said, to go along with the century. So she went. Tom Scanlon didn't. He stayed right on in Lone Tree. Lone Tree was where—the way Scanlon would put it—the century he didn't care for turned on its axis, looked up and down the tracks just the way he did, then went east. But Lone Tree, along with Tom Scanlon, stayed put.

For fifty years, closer now to sixty, he had worn a drayman's hat with brown cane sides, a license at the front, and a soft crown that shaped to his head. When he hung it on a nail, you could still see his head in it. But when they took a picture of him the week he nearly froze they wanted one without the hat, which he gave them, then he put it down somewhere and couldn't find it when they were gone. This coonskin hat he wore to please the boy. Not a hair of it was coon hair, as he told him, and the top got hot when the sun was on it, but still he wore it. Anything to please the boy.

This coat he was wearing—mohair they called it, from the horse hairs in it—was all he had left, all they would let him wear of the outfit he had worn since his wife had left him, dating from the fall Herbert Hoover had defeated a man named Smith. A brown derby pin, stamped I'M FOR AL, was there in the frayed lapel of the coat. Scanlon had not been for Al, or anybody else, but a traveling salesman known to be a Catholic had stuck the pin there and Scanlon had let it stick. The pin was part of the coat, and the coat was part of the man.

Tom Scanlon was a plainsman, but he had a seaman's creased eyes in his face. The view from his window—the one in Lone Tree, where he had the bed pulled over to the window—was every bit as wide and as empty as a view of the sea. In the early morning, with just the sky light, that was how it looked. The faded sky was like the sky at sea, the everlasting wind like the wind at sea, and the plain rolled and swelled quite a bit like the sea itself. Like the sea it was lonely, and there was no place to hide. Scanlon had never been to sea, of course, but that was beside the point.

He looked to be a man in the neighborhood of ninety, and his passing, as people referred to it, had been expected from year to year, for the last thirty years. His wife, in good health when she left him, had had that understanding with his children, and the necessary arrangements had all been made. An undertaker in Cozad, the nearest town that had one, would meet the members of the family in Seward, where they would have a simple service, then drive back to Lone Tree and bury him. His father, his mother, and such life as he had lived were buried there. But he did not die. His death was prepared, but he put it off. With little or nothing to live for, he continued to live. He had renounced his children the moment it was clear that they intended to face the future, or even worse, like his daughter Lois, make a success of it. Tom Scanlon lived—if that was the word—only in the past. When the century turned and faced the east, he stood his ground. He faced the west. He made an interesting case, as Boyd had once observed, being a man who found more to live for, in looking backward, than those who died all around him, looking ahead.

The last of nine children, his mother dying within the year she had borne him, Tom Scanlon grew up waiting on his father, who was mad as a coot. Timothy Scanlon might have been mad all of his life, but only his wife would have known that, since it was only in his later years that he talked. Bedridden, that is, he tried to talk himself out of it. He ran this hotel—that is, his wife did—and when he could no longer get up and downstairs, he crawled into the bed in the room at the back of it. The single window looked down the railroad tracks to the west. His son, Tom Scanlon, would go up with his meals, sit there on the bed while the old man ate, then listen to him talk while he smoked his daily cigar. He was an odd one. Even the boy knew that. He slept in his clothes, lying out on top of the bed. If it got cold he might throw a comfort over his feet. One reason for that might be the fact that he wore cavalry boots, with tinkling silver spurs, that he found it harder and harder to get off. The spurs were made of iron, and even rusty, but little silver drops were attached to the rowels, and when he tapped the boot on the foot of the bed they made a tinkling sound. He also wore a leather jerkin, so dirty on the front that it looked like a piece of greasy oilcloth, and on a cord from his neck was suspended a powder horn and a firing wire. Also an awl, with a cherry wood handle, a bottle he had carved from an antelope's horn, and a small piece of leather with nipples on it for caps. They were the clothes he had worn, and the things he had used, as a young man. He saw less and less reason, as he told the boy, for taking them off.

But he was not full of yarns, as people said, but just one long yarn, told over and over, so long and drawn out that only the boy had heard the end of it. He had heard it many times. He never seemed to tire of it. The reason was his age—as his daughter pointed out—he was going on seven or eight at the time, and that same age group were Davy Crockett crazy at the present time. But her grandchild, just as crazy as the rest, would grow out of it. Her father didn't. He had been Davy Crockett crazy all his life. Nor was it hard to see why, according to his daughter, if you knew Lone Tree, where he was born. In growing up there when he did he felt no need to get out of it. *His* father had opened the West, his brothers had closed it, and his children had gone East. Everything had been done. Everything, that is, but just stay put.

If you knew Lone Tree—if you knew it, that is, right around the turn of the century, you might get an inkling as to why Tom Scanlon stayed. What was it like? A photograph had been taken of it. From a balloon, at an estimated height of two hundred thirty feet. Dated on the back July 4th, 1901. The century had just turned. The locomotive in the picture was headed East. It had come from the East—as a matter of fact, it had *backed* in from the East since there was no local roundhouse—and the balloon was due in Omaha later that night.

The town itself, the lone cottonwood tree, the row of tin-roofed buildings and the railroad tracks, seemed to dangle like toys at the far end of a string. On the roof of the hotel were the men who had gathered to watch the balloon rise. William Jennings Bryan, the man who might have been President, was one of them. Around the cottonwood tree, in its shade, were the ladies fanning themselves, and a water sprinkler that had dripped a dark trail in the dust. Down the tracks to the west, like a headless bird with the bloody neck still bleeding, the new tublike water tank sat high on stilts. A bunch of long-stemmed grass grew where the spout dripped on the tracks. To the east, beyond the new hotel, stood the lone cottonwood tree, dead at the top but with clumps of leaves near the bottom, like a man stripped for action. Out of the clumps the dead branches curved like cattle horns. The Western Hotel, a three story structure faced with sandstone blocks and red brick, sat where the caboose of the westbound trains came to a stop. The hotel faced the plain, once called a square, where a mixture of hardy grass had been planted, and it was believed that the town would appear like the orchards in the seed catalogues. A man with time on his hands, like young Tom Scanlon, could watch it grow. The picture had been taken to impress Eastern men that there was a future in Lone Tree, and a copy of it hung in the hotel lobby, with the calendars. Tom Scanlon, his shoeless feet propped on the desk top, used to sit and look at it.

Across the street stood the bank, with its marble front, a door to go in and one to come out, but turned into a movie palace before the money arrived from Omaha. In the empty lot adjoining were the rubber-tired wheels of a fire hose cart, without the hose, and a strip of wooden sidewalk, like a fence blown over on its side. A city hall, to house the hose cart and the Sheriff, was planned, but never put up. At the back of the Feed Store, under the racks of harness, was the covered wagon that belonged to Tim Scanlon, in which he had traveled West, and in which five of his sons were born. Later known as the Dead Wagon, it had been used for funerals. Still later, it was used in parades in nearby towns. In the photograph it looked like a caterpillar put on wheels, to please the kiddies, and bore a legend that had been painted on both sides.

LONE TREE
The BIGGEST little town in the World

Timothy Scanlon's wife, an Ohio girl who had made the trip to California with him, had given the town, just a tree then, its name. In her opinion that was how it looked. A lonely tree in the midst of a lonely plain. Not much had changed—in so far as you could tell from the photograph.

Before the old man finally died (as of course he did) his son, Tom Scanlon, may have thought him immortal, his mind full of his deathless deeds. Because of the timeless life the old man had lived when young, something died in them both—as the doctor put it—leaving one you could bury, and one you couldn't, but in any sense that mattered just about as dead.

But a lifetime later, almost several of them, after being as good as dead for four generations, Tom Scanlon had suddenly turned up alive. Almost. One of the brakemen on the eastbound freight—one of the few who stopped for water—had found him in the kitchen of the Western Hotel almost frozen to death. The coal fire in the kitchen range had long burned out. He had been found sitting there, his feet in the oven, wrapped up in blankets and buffalo hides, a cold cigar in his mouth as if waiting for spring. Some of the brakemen were accustomed, summer and winter, to see the glow of his cigar in the curtainless window, since he had moved to his father's old room at the rear of the hotel. Men working on the tracks, or those hired to burn the ditch grass, might see, both morning and evening, the matches he struck on the sill of the window, or the rim of his pot. He was in bed, but he usually slept in it sitting up. He claimed that it made his wheezy breathing easier. There was some truth in that, but of course the thing that made his breathing hard in the first place was the open window, and the asthma he got from the burning grass.

But he was free—as he told his children—to do as he liked. To sleep in his clothes, or to just lie there and not sleep. He owned the bed. He slept in it alone. In the summer he liked the window open, in the winter he liked it closed, but summer and winter he liked to lie there looking out. There was nothing to see, but perhaps that was what he liked about it.

But the winter he froze—that is, almost—something had to be done about it, and his youngest daughter, Lois Mc-

Kee, had the largest house; almost empty, since her own children had grown up and moved out. Those children, naturally, had seldom seen him; he was the ghost in the family closet, and there was nothing to be gained—they understood—in bringing him out. Since he put off dying it had not been necessary to bury him. He was still there, that is, when another generation made its appearance—oddly enough, at the same time he did, and in the same house. Gordon Scanlon McKee, the old man's great-grandson, wearing a coonskin hat and sporting two six-shooters, had been the first member of the family, so to speak, to speak to him. It had been love—as the family feared—at first shot.

Tom Scanlon never cared for his own children, but he hardly knew why until they grew up and had children of their own. Then he saw it. What the world had been coming to, had arrived. What could you expect of the younger generation if they had fathers like McKee, a hog shooter? Nothing. Which was pretty much what they got.

For twenty years—no, it was more like thirty—Scanlon hadn't said more than "Clippers in the back, Eddie," which he said to the barber over in Cozad about every six weeks. When the boy came along he had to learn to talk all over again. Not so much at first, since the boy did the talking, but when they got in the back seat of the car, way back where they put them, why, then he was free to talk a little more. The country they were in, which was south of El Paso, was dry and open the way his father had described it—country where there was nothing for the wind to blow on but himself. When a man died out there, which was often, they had to bury him deep, pile some big rocks on him, then run the wagons over him if they wanted to keep him dead. Otherwise the Indians or the coyotes would dig him up. Once his father saw an Indian with a hat he'd made from a wagon lantern, like a sort of helmet, the lantern door like a visor he could wear up, or down. He told the boy. The boy liked to hear stories like that. Just the telling of it led him to think of another one. One of the old squaws with a big family used to follow the wagons and live off the garbage, but the trouble was she had more little shavers than she could get on her horse. So what'd she do? Different than most squaws, she was smart. She rigged up a sort of sled, using saplings for runners, which she could trail along behind her little pony, and back on the sled, just as pretty as you please, were all her kids. Might not have been hers at all, but she'd adopted them.

The boy couldn't hear enough stories like that, and when they both got sick, on the little wild bananas, they had to sleep in the car, which got him to remembering more of them. That place where the flowers bloomed only at night, and this girl in the wagon, whose name was Samantha, kept fireflies in a bottle so when they buzzed their lanterns she could look at them. The flowers, that is. And while she looked at the flowers, Timothy Scanlon could look at her face. Well as he could see it, he couldn't tell you what it was like. He (his father, that is) said her hair was black as it was where the harness scuffed the hair off a mule's hide, but when he looked at her eyes he looked right through them without seeing anything. He couldn't tell you, he said, what color they were. All he could tell you was they weren't like his own eyes much, since she only saw different things with them—from the seat of the wagon she would see a flower, where he only saw a track. Even when she pointed and they looked at it together, they never saw the same thing.

That was something for the boy, so Scanlon told him that; the more he talked the more he remembered, and the more he remembered the nearer all of it seemed. He couldn't see more than the light out there in the bullring, but let him close his eyes, and just remember, and he could see from the fork of the Platte to Chimney Rock. The buffalo like an island with a brown furze on it, the wind blowing, the wagons strung out in a line like so many caterpillars with their fuzz burned off.

The truth was, he didn't know he was so blind until they came for him. In Lone Tree, where nothing had changed, he saw things in their places without the need to look at them. They were there, in case he wanted to see them, in his mind's eye. All he had to do was close his eyes and look at them. That was how it was with this remembering business, and one reason he talked so much, once he got started, was that the more he talked the clearer it all became. Back around El Paso, where he began to get started, he would say, "I tell you how they shot the Mormon?" but the boy couldn't seem to get it straight through his head who he meant by *they*. He seemed to think Scanlon did it. He always said *you* when Scanlon meant *they*. Since he couldn't seem to get it straight in his head, and since it simplified the story to tell it that way, Scanlon found it easier to go along with it, and just say we. And the more he told it that way, the truer it seemed.

"I tell you how *we* put in the time?" he would say, and it seemed that he had. He had put more of it in back there than anywhere else. Anyhow, that's how it seemed. That he had put that time in, all of it, himself.

"Don't it take you back, Gordon?" he heard McKee say, a man who never once had a place to go back to, who had done nothing but try to go forward all of his life.

"I tell you how—" he began, and poked his elbow in the boy, but blind as he was he could see the the commotion, people jumping up like popcorn, and the boy hopped up like he'd sat down on a pin. But where the light was, out there in the bullring, he saw nothing, just the slope beyond it spotted with snow and scrub trees of some sort, blowing in the wind. He closed his eyes. He remembered where it was, and just how it had been.

IF you had asked Boyd who the one man was he would never live to see in Mexico, if you had wanted an answer, that is, he would have said McKee. Rather quickly, in fact, as if he had asked himself that question. Which was the case, oddly enough, since people *like* McKee, thousands of them, were crawling out of the woodwork all over Mexico. They could be found in Guanajuato, photographed in Paztcuaro, touched for a five spot in Acapulco, and observed with bowed heads in the tunnels of the bullring whooping up their lunch. Good honest corn-fed people with the hard to wrinkle suits, the new two-toned car with the *Turista* sticker, and the kid on the bumper hired to watch the hub caps and the stuff piled on the seats. Baskets from Oaxaca, blankets from Cuernavaca, gems from Querétaro and the new Sears, Roebuck, plus several of those crackling steerhide chairs that looked and sounded like musical instruments. All of them like McKee, with one exception. Only one would have Lois McKee along with him, a serene wooden Indian equally blended of fire and ice. The chaste virginal mother of three sons and nine grandchildren. All by divine compensation, miraculous birth, since husband and wife shared the ice side together. The fire side, as Boyd could tell you, had long been out. He had been the one to blow it alive, then let it go out.

"Anybody ever show you this, son?" he said, and took the boy's Pepsi bottle, gave it a shake, then let a thin spray of the liquid squirt over the rail and stain the board fence of the bullring. The boy's eyes popped. Boyd could see that nobody had showed him that one.

"How's that?" he said, shook the bottle again, and let it arch and fall on the sand in the runway. The way Boyd used to stand, after drinking pop, and pee in the soft hot dust behind the firehouse, making a sound like a quick summer shower in the road. He always drank red pop hoping he would pee red, but he never did. "How's that, boy?" he said, and arched a thin stream clear over the runway into the bullring. One of the bullfighter's *peones*, leaning on the funk hole, gazed at him with admiration.

"Let me!" said the boy, and reached for the bottle.

"Easy now," said Boyd, and kept a grip on it. He peered down the row to see if one of the McKees had been in on that. No sign. No visible sign of life, that is. Did these bones live? It hardly seemed possible. Fossils. In what was usually described as an excellent state of preservation. Where found? In the pits around a bullring. Exhibiting the usual state of high animation. What did they feel? What would they see? They would feel and see what they had brought along with them. The Passion of the Bullring as seen from the deep-freeze along the Platte. The final goring of old Bullslinger Boyd.

"Let me squirt it!" said the boy, and reached for the bottle.

Boyd took a swig of what was left and said, "It ain't what it used to be, Crockett. When I was your age we could drink it or squirt it. Think I'd just squirt it now."

That pleased the boy, but the old fool in the seat beside him said, "Hmmmmmmmphhh." Only sound he had made. What passion had forced it out of him? Jealousy. His old man's lust to possess the ears and eyes of the boy. His own fading. Deaf? No, just a little *deef*. Cloudy snot-green eyes with a cataract blur. More like a horned toad than a man, a big one, trained to grunt noises, and go around on a leash wearing an imitation coonskin hat.

"Us boys—" he said, looking the boy in the eye, the sea-born eyes in the plainsman's face, "us boys like our powder dry, and our likker straight."

"What's straight?" said the boy. In his open mouth, the flesh-pink scented wad of blowgum. At the moment sidetracked. He couldn't chew, blow *and* think.

"They tell me Davy Crockett was straight," Boyd said, and paused to wonder, rocking the Pepsi bottle. The boy aimed his plastic pistol, fired it, and sang—

> "He feared no man, he feared no beast,
> And hell itself he feared the least."

"*Hell?*" checked Boyd.

The boy nodded. He took a quick suck on the barrel of his gun, then added, "If you want to go to heaven, you got to go to hell *first*."

Mirror-like the ice-blue eyes that Boyd looked into returned his gaze. Sober.

"So you want to go to heaven?" he inquired.

"I do if I can go to hell *first*," was the reply.

Did Boyd seem to doubt that? The boy turned on his seat, poked the old man with his gun, then said, "Don't I?"

"Shortest way to heaven's right smack through hell," the old man barked.

Boyd swallowed. Over the old man's head, the plastic crown of his hat, Boyd peered down the row at the old man's daughter. Did she know *that* sort of thing was going on? That heaven, hell and God knows what else were being bandied about? She didn't seem to. Still no visible scars of life. She sat stiffly erect, laced into her corset of character. Another way to heaven, Boyd reflected, was right smack through the hell of such a woman. Had McKee made it? He sat there chewing on a match. It skipped from one corner of his mouth to the other, flicked by his tongue. A match that he had lit, then allowed to burn down so one end, as he said, was charcoal, with just enough sulphur in the head to sweeten the breath.

McKee had been doing that, believing that, for more than forty years. Picked it up as a kid and never had reason to question it. The way he picked up, the way he did not question, everything else. His life, for instance. A simple frame-house sort of life with an upstairs and a downstairs, and a kitchen where he lived, a parlor where he didn't, a stove where the children could dress on winter mornings, a porch where time could be passed summer evenings, an attic for the preservation of the past, a basement for tinkering with the future, and a bedroom for making such connections as the nature of the house would stand. In the closets principles, salted down with moth balls. In the storm-cave, sprouting like potatoes, prejudices. A good man, salt of the earth, suspicious of eggheads, but drawn to them, a practical cogitator but believer in mysteries, soberly mindless but afflicted with thinking, conscientiously unconscious, civic pillar by day, daydreamer by night.

Had such a man picked up a friend like Boyd? Had he picked such a wife? If Boyd could read and understand the signs, he had not. They had picked him. It seemed strange. What did the likes of McKee have to offer *them?* Perhaps only what they needed—if what they needed was a witness. And they did.

McKee was a believer. Having settled on something he kept the faith. The healing property of matches, the beauty of women, and the strange dreams of Boyd were all acceptable to him. He believed. He made, that is, such things possible. He also made them, alas, highly expendable. A row of ghostly light poles without lights in the grassy suburbs of his imagination, where his children, or his children's children, or their children, might live.

But not McKee. No, Walter McKee was a simple, modest man.

Mrs. McKee and me couldn't be happier.

That was what he had said. That was what he meant, so it was naturally what he had said.

"Oh, Boyd!" called McKee, catching his eye, then stopped as if he saw there what Boyd had been thinking. He turned to gaze at the bullring, the parade of matadors in their suits of light, their artificial pigtails, gliding across the sand with the slinky gait of cats that had learned to walk on their hind legs. Behind them the padded nags, with their fat-assed Sancho Panzas, the pom-pommed mules dragging their heavy chains, and then the proletariat prepared to endure it all—then clean it up. The head and tail, as Lehmann liked to say, of the bull himself. A centaur with a God emerging at the front, but all bull at the rear.

"What're the mules for?" said McKee, but Boyd had the feeling that was not the question. He let Dr. Lehmann, his lips shiny with brandy, answer it. It gave Boyd another chance to sit and stare, as if he was listening, at the woman trapped between them—the lips a skimmed milk blue, but the eyes serene as ever. *What* was on her mind? All signs and portents to the contrary, he knew a mind was there. It had, after all, once spoken to him. What had brought her to the bullfight had also brought her, thirty years before, to the edge of darkness, that twilight zone on the porch where anything might happen, and sometimes did. Invisible zones, like the circles in a bullring that were meant to stylize and limit the action, with the light above the screen door, the funk hole of the porch, the legitimate escape. But Boyd, with a little fancy cape work, had crossed the line. No more, no gorings nor bloody linen, but a foretaste, such lineaments of pleasure that what followed, if anything should follow, would be an afterthought.

What else had brought her to the bullfight? A thirty-years afterthought? The tribal memory of a man, that is, a lover, that a woman knew better than trust. What manner of man was that? The one who took *advantage* of her. If a man would be remembered, he would give and take only that.

What a crazy goddam world, Boyd was thinking—and so made room for himself. Also for Dr. Lehmann, the celebrated quack, with nothing to recommend him but his cures, and Paula Kahler, the only sort of failure he could afford. Also for old man Scanlon, the living fossil, for McKee, the co-inventor of the dust bowl, for his wife, the deep-freeze, and her grandson who would live it all over again. Here gathered at a bullfight. The sanded navel of the world. Gazing at this fleshy button each man had the eyes to see only himself. This crisp Sabbath afternoon forty thousand pairs of eyes would gaze down on forty thousand separate bullfights, seeing it all very clearly, missing only the one that was said to take place. Forty thousand latent heroes, as many gorings, so many artful dodges it beggared description, two hundred thousand bulls, horses, mules and monsters half man, half beast. In all this zoo, this bloody constellation, only two men and six bulls would be missing. Those in the bullring. Those they would see with their very own eyes. This golden eye would reflect, like a mirror, every gaze that was directed toward it—like the hub caps,

Boyd thought, displayed on their racks along the boulevards. Shining like medieval armor, available in all sizes,
taken in jousting at night, offered for sale in the morning,
this nickel-plated mirror was the modern man's escutcheon.
In it he saw, distorted to his own taste, this fantasy of
himself. A simple *Ford* man, a sporty *Jag* man, an old *Stutz*
man, a modern *Volks* man, with the Family man at the
wheel of the *Suburban,* the door monogrammed.

Any blot on these escutcheons?

Boyd stared, as he would for dents and scratches, from
face to face. Scratches and scars could be painted over,
broken parts replaced. In the face of McKee he could see a
firm believer in Authorized Service & Parts.

"Well, folks—" he said, giving Boyd a wink, "what's next
on the bill?"

Boyd put up his right hand, wagging the Pepsi bottle, to
indicate that *he* was, and he rose from the seat having in
mind a little speech. God knows what. After he had made
it, he would know. Something about old times, escutcheons,
and the strange reflections in hub caps. Take Boyd's. It
might surprise you what he saw. But nobody heard what
little he said. The horn, the shrill blast of the trumpet, spun
McKee around as though someone had twirled him, and he
stood with his back to the ring when the bull came in.

A bull? The sound of the horn itself seemed to frighten
him. Then the ring, the empty enclosure, the turtle-like
heads of the men at the funk holes. All of it strange and
unfriendly—except for the man waving at him. At the edge
of the ring, over on the shade side, a man who waved a
Pepsi-Cola bottle, then held it out before him and shot a
spray of it into the air. Was the little bull thirsty? *Something* about it appealed to him. He came toward it, he
ignored the shouts, the man who came and fanned a cape at
him, the one who moved around behind and tried to get a

grip on his tail. He reached the fence, where he dragged his chin along the rough top rail, like a mooncalf, pausing for a moment to roll his black eyes at McKee.

"You thirsty, boy?" Boyd yelled, gave the bottle a shake, felt the pressure fizz around his finger, then let a stream of the liquid arch across the runway, splash on the bull's moist snout. The swollen grape-blue tongue slipped out, slapped the froth of it off.

"You like it, eh?" Boyd cried, shook the bottle again, and shot a thin seltzer stream of it into his mouth. He loved it. The tongue lobbed out, mop-wise, and wiped it off. Boyd heard the crowd roar behind him—someone shouted *ole!*—and he turned to sweep off his hat, make a bow. He kissed the frothy tips of his fingers, blew them at the crowd. They loved it, the shouting grew louder, he gave the bottle a last frenzied shake, and then, with every eye fastened on him, he turned the bottle from the bull toward himself. Was this *la suerte suprema?* Boyd's moment of truth? Perhaps. One hand upraised, for quiet, he tipped his head back, opened his mouth, and shot the last feeble squirt of the liquid down his own throat. In the thunder of applause that followed he bowed, took his seat. Just in time, since his head was whirling, he felt the clubbing thump of his heart, and as Lehmann had told him it might now, any day, he waited for it to stop.

But it didn't. Like everything else, *that* too slipped out of his grasp.

N<small>O</small>, it didn't.

Knowing that it wouldn't, not here and now—when Boyd died it would be anticlimactic—Lehmann settled back and watched the long-horned cows come in. The friendly bull, wet and sticky with pop, shooed like a stray chicken by men with capes, made a wide-eyed tour of the ring, then followed the cows. The crowd roared—as well they might, being full of friendly bulls with a weakness for cows, and cows with a weakness for such a curious bull as Boyd. A charmer. One who mastered the bull with a sharp squirt of pop.

If you began in the morning—as Lehmann once had—and followed Gordon Boyd from bar to bar, from bench to bench, from corner to corner, you would reach the conclusion that he was a lonely man. He seemed to have no friends. That was how it looked. But Lehmann had sensed something was wrong. With that picture. With that tableau of loneliness. Boyd was alone, but seldom lonely, since the empty stool was in a crowded bar, the corner at a busy intersection, and the vacant bench was along the walk in a thronging park. He sat alone amidst gossip, pigeons, children, and photogenic squirrels. He liked to be alone surrounded by others, solitary, that is, rather than lonely, since the smell of something living, rotting, or dying seemed important to him. All that he had. He had been dying for years, himself. Only his fear of muffing that, also, kept him alive.

Where had it begun? In the beginning, like everything else. One had to take the ends of a frazzled string, or the soiled threads of a flannel pocket, and follow them back, back to the heart of the labyrinth. As Lehmann had done. He had gazed into the sightless eyes of the Minotaur. Half man, half myth, the emerging God, dream-haunted, gazed toward the light with eyes in which the pupils had not been drilled. If only the impossible seemed worth doing, Boyd would end up doing nothing. Which had occurred. But he had failed at even that. The clichés of success, from which he rebelled, had taken their revenge in his passion for failure. Too late—almost too late—Boyd had discovered that the one cliché, stamped Success on one side, Failure on the other, rang hollow at both extremities.

Lehmann had watched the performance, one of his best, with fear, trembling and admiration, but he could have told you the aging charmer would survive. At the wrong time and place he always did. When Boyd dropped dead, as one day he would, and it might be there in the bullring, whoever found him would seriously question it. The blue lids of his eyes would be turned back, a pocket mirror held to his mouth. Though he was stone cold, they would go on looking in him for life. Finger the pulse, put an ear to his chest, apply injections, prayers, and artificial respiration, since it wouldn't seem right that a young man of such *promise* should die. Not this one. Whose promise was now fifty-some years old.

Dr. Leopold Lehmann resembled those shaggy men seen in

the glass cages of the world's museums, depicting early man at some new milestone of his career. Building a fire, shaping a rock, scratching symbols on the walls of a cave, or making guttural sounds with some vague resemblance to human speech. This last he did, by common agreement, with appalling credibility. The sounds he made—a blend of Brooklynese, German, and grunts, in proportions entirely his own—seldom resembled anything else. He specialized in openings that dissolved into thin air. "Wot I min iss—" he would say, and then trace on the air, with a hairy finger, a few cloudy symbols that his older patients claimed to understand. Born in Goethe's town of Weimar, the fourth son of a cheese importer, he had early mastered English, only to learn that it did not pay. Broken, rather than proper, English spoke to the soul. A battered language, like an armless statue, had more value on the market, and Dr. Lehmann had broken, battered and glued together a language all his own.

"Thod iss olter"—he would say, to everyone's joy—"than Atom und efenink."

It was hardly necessary to go into his background. It was all there at the front. Vienna he knew like the palm of the hand that was melon colored, the fingers bent backwards, with Kärntnerstrasse, where he had lived, rising from the pink hollow to the knuckle. Freud he remembered: a small military man with a dark beard, money problems, and a walk that made Lehmann want to sneak up behind and stick a cane between his legs.

So much for background. Foreground reflected his varied life in America. A period of adjustment (thirty-eight years in Brooklyn), several years of travel (from Avenue J, via the Bridge, to Manhattan) and professional achievement (four hundred dollars in night school awards from a package deal involving magazine subscriptions). Dr. Lehmann

was so plainly the old world type, with pronounced Neanderthal connections, that the only question was how long he
had been in the States. "Nod lonk enuff!" he would reply,
which was true in many practical matters, and gave the
impression he was one of the well-adjusted refugee types.
This impression was correct. He had other people's problems, but few of his own.

Professionally speaking, Dr. Lehmann specialized in mental cases, usually female, that his more successful colleagues
had given up. The transfer type, looking for an object that
would come down with the same infection, found Dr.
Lehmann sympathetic but baffling. Talent, of Dr. Lehmann's sort, was highly unorthodox. At a point in the
treatment, usually without warning, he would clamp on his
huge head a pair of earphones, which transformed him, in a
twinkling, into a Flying Saucer pilot, or a Space Cadet. A
psychological trick? A sort of Rorschach test? No, Dr.
Lehmann was a lover of music, the quartets of Haydn and
Mozart in particular. If a female patient, at the sight of Dr.
Lehmann, remote as early man behind his earphones—if this
patient, say, should raise her voice, do anything unduly to
crack through the barrier, Dr. Lehmann would raise a hairy
finger, wag it, then hiss softly, "Moww-Tzzzzzzarrrrt isss
spikink." That left up to the patient the question of pri-
ority. Few felt up to the challenge. Those who did soon
went somewhere else. Dr. Lehmann took pains to make it
clear, at the outset, that he knew nothing of the body, little
of the mind, but that he had an arrangement of sorts with
the soul. The odd thing was that he seemed to. No, the odd
thing was that he did.

His *im*patients—as he called those who interrupted
Mozart—were seldom around long enough to take the acid
test. A little fable, hardly more, told by Dr. Lehmann those
summer evenings when nothing at all seemed to be seriously

wrong with the world. During his *drainink*, as he called it, he had lived in Vienna with a Frau Klinger, a woman from Buda-Pest, who had one son. A frail, pasty-faced young man named Karl, he would bring Dr. Lehmann his *schoko-lade* in the morning, along with a machine that made something Karl Klinger called a cigarette. It stuffed something like moss into paper tubes that could be smoked. That was of no importance to the story—just an aside of the sort that Dr. Lehmann, when he talked about *anything*, was more or less inclined to make. He and young Klinger often smoked a paper tube together, that is. The days were gray in Vienna, a city of old people, and for Christmas Dr. Lehmann went to Venice, which was no place to go, but that was what he did. No more than four or five days. But on his return Karl Klinger was gone. In less than a week he had taken sick and died. Frau Klinger passed on to Dr. Lehmann his cigarette machine.

One day in the spring—Dr. Lehmann remembered it had been very balmy, and the windows were open—he had been at work, as usual, in the dissecting room. Although the windows were open, the air was strong with formaldehyde. From the basket on the floor, full of hands and feet—they were not at all squeamish in Vienna—he had selected the pale, blue-veined hand of a child. Or a young girl. That was how it looked. Not until he had placed it on the table did he notice the nicotine stain on the fingers, and the way all of the nails were chewed. Karl Klinger, as he meant to say, chewed on his nails all the time.

That was the story. Dr. Leopold Lehmann would tell it casually. In the silence that followed he would sip his brandy, a stimulant to his poor circulation, and the shiny valspar film would remain on his lips.

What did it mean? What did *he* mean, that is? On the slightest pretext he would bring up the story—but always *up*, never down to something like brass tacks, concrete statements, or simple answers to direct questions.

Such as—was it fiction, this fable, or was it fact? Was Karl Klinger real—God forbid—or the front for somebody else, a necessary fiction that professional ethics—or was it esthetics—made imperative? There were those who intimated that the case of Paula Kahler—if she was a *case*—would throw the missing light on Karl Klinger's remains. But just try and pin the storyteller down. On his head would go the earphones, on his face the stone-age smile of early man.

Some patients, understandably, found it too much of a strain. Others, for various reasons, found it somewhat gruesome but interesting. So Lehmann had two kinds of clients. Those who left. And those who stayed. If the patient could put up with that sort of thing, Dr. Lehmann could put up with the patient. Gordon Boyd was one—he had been a Lehmann man from the word no, as he put it—and Paula Kahler was another, a Lehmann man, as it turned out, in spite of herself. She was not so much his patient, as he often hinted, as his practice.

Gordon Boyd had come to Lehmann—he had not made an appointment, or appeared with the usual recommendation, but came in with the trash man and rang the service bell in the hall. Lehmann had recognized the type. The professional soldier of failure, waging the cold war within himself. A man in his forties, theatrically shabby, the boyish face still resisting what his will encouraged, a deterioration that was meant to be total and picturesque. In the pocket of his raincoat—dropping to the floor when he fumbled for some matches—he had a piece of flannel cloth, soiled and grass stained, that Lehmann took to be a sort of shoe rag. He did not inquire about it. Boyd, without comment, had returned it to his coat. But later, as he was leaving, Boyd slipped the rag from his pocket and held it up as if the pattern would show in the light.

"For apful polishink?" Lehmann had suggested.

"Ty Cobb's pocket," Boyd had said, matter-of-factly, then added, "little Gordon Boyd's piece of the Cross," and smiled his untouched boyish smile. Likable. Lehmann himself had suggested that he should come back. Bringing with him his pocket, the portable raft on which he floated, anchored to his childhood, on the glassy surface of the sandpit where he had failed to walk. Something of a hero, something of a madman, something of an ass.

And so he had come back—not with the pocket, that did not reappear until later—but with a photograph he had torn from some camera magazine. The photograph showed a bum, seated on a park bench, sharing his last crust of bread with a squirrel. Lehmann had smiled. He smiled at all pictures of cats, dogs, birds and squirrels. But Boyd had not smiled, which led Lehmann to feel that perhaps he had overlooked something—which he had. The bum on the bench was Boyd himself. But one wouldn't have guessed it. It seemed immaterial that the bum was Boyd.

A dedicated no-man, one who had turned to failure as a field that offered real opportunity for success, Boyd had come to Lehmann when it was clear that he had failed to fail. That he had failed to touch the floating bottom within himself. Having run the full gamut of success-clichés—including the quick rise and fall from favor—he had found Failure a nut that refused to crack. Not that he hadn't worked at it. He had given it the best years of his life. At one point he had achieved—he had believed he had achieved —the recognition he had worked for, since charitable tourists would tip him generously when they snapped his photograph. Then one day he had found, stumbled on it, as he said, in a magazine left in a trash bin, this shot of a bum feeding the squirrel in Washington Square. That had done it. His bottom had been the reverse of his top.

The camera had caught every memorable cliché: the coat fastened with a pin, the cut suggesting better days, the sock there to call attention to the calloused heel, in one soiled hand a paper bag, now empty, and in the other a crust. This crust he shared—the autumn sun shining on it—with his sole companion, a moth-eaten squirrel who had plainly suffered the same misfortunes at the hands of *life*. The clichés told the story. The face of the bum bore witness to it. But of the man behind the face, the failure behind the man, there was no evidence. Every piece of his Fall had been borrowed from the wings, from the costume rack. Of Boyd the walker-on-water, the pocket snatcher, the man who had set out to master his failure—of this man there was no inkling. For that, one had to look at the squirrel. Having been cheated by Boyd, on occasion looted, having been baited, petted and deliberately tortured, he fastened on the hand that fed him a cynical, skeptical eye. But that was not in the picture. He posed with his back to the camera.

Something of a wonder-boy in the theater, Boyd had begun with a sponsor, an empty stage, and the conviction that it should be emptier. Characters—the few he had at the beginning—became a cast of disembodied voices, speaking with the hollow accents of train loudspeakers, or apartment speaking tubes. This observation was his own. He had made a career of observing himself. But even there he had failed, as Lehmann had ironically pointed out. It was the top, not the bottom, to which he had stuck. His boyish walk on the water had not been a failure, but his first success.

In a prologue to a play that was never produced, Boyd advised his public that he *hoped* to fail, since there was no longer anything of interest to be gained in success. He went on to speak of culture as a series of acceptable clichés. A photographer's salon where ready-made frames, hung on the walls of rustically historical gardens, lacked only the faces of succeeding generations in the ready-made holes. This hand-me-down world defined the realm of the possible. The impossible—become a cliché itself—had been ruled out. This left the artist—Boyd himself, that is—with only one suitable subject, and life itself with only one ironic result. This was Failure. Such as Boyd, from the beginning, had practiced himself.

Lehmann had seen, without being told, that Boyd had thrown himself into his subject. In his failure, at least, he would be a success. He had worked at being down and out in Paris, combed the beaches and the tourists of the Riviera, and in the palmy days of fascism earned his bed and board as a rabble rouser. All of it apprentice work, an author's slumming, a Bernarr Macfadden tour to end of the night, in preparation for the pay-off, the real McCoy, when the native returned to New York and the Automat. These were the years he had sounded for the bottom off Bleecker Street. His standards had been high. Too high, perhaps. The cliché of failure, like that of success, hung on the walls of the room he decayed in, and through the hole in the ready-made frame he popped his own head. The man that McKee —Boyd had described the scene for Lehmann—had found in his B.V.D.'s in a loft in New York. Squirrel-feeder and hoarder of crusty clichés. Neither going to pot, throwing in the sponge, or even working at it had brought him failure. How achieve it? It had to be imagined, like everything else. It had to undergo a sea change, a transformation, that would indicate that failure had *happened*—as the squirrel knew— to the man behind the front. The armor of clichés kept him from touching bottom, or from being touched.

And as for *the* bottom—when Boyd had brought it up Lehmann had left the room, returned with Paula Kahler.

She had been there. She had succeeded where Gordon Boyd had failed. The bottom was a long way down—as it was also a long way up. He had let Boyd, a good observer, judge the facts for himself. In time—it had taken time, since Paula Kahler had exhausted the subject—Boyd began to see there might be something in it for himself. Not in the realm of failure, this time, but success. The words that Paula Kahler had made into flesh—the words, that is, and the music—called for a further transformation, back into words again. Lehmann had made the suggestion. Boyd had taken it up. To make a beginning he had come with them to Mexico. It would make quite a story. One that Paula Kahler would never tell herself.

Could he be sure of that? Lehmann felt sure enough. Paula Kahler had learned, among other things, to do without speech. Birdlike, so fragile she looked brittle, Paula Kahler had the large sad eyes of a goat, the feet of a man, and hands unrelated to the other parts. The hands for instance, seemed to lead a life of their own. They knitted, or lay quiet in her lap like birds with their heads concealed. She had an aura, an air of peace about her, usually associated with genius or the simple-minded. The observation had been made by Dr. Lehmann, and he let it stand. There had been no need to expand upon it. Paula Kahler was enough.

For the music, shortly after the war, Dr. Lehmann would spend the summer in Salzburg, but that was before he discovered Mexico. In a newsreel theater on Fulton Street he saw a man fight a bull. The bull won. He stayed in his seat and saw it happen many times. The image of the man as part of the bull—a trick, you might say, of the camera—became fixed, like a poster, in his mind. He looked into the subject. Found where it was that men still fought bulls. It was done many places, if he could believe it, but nearest at hand was Mexico, where his friend Gordon Boyd could drive them in his car. It had been a revelation. One day he hoped to know of what.

An old man's witless passion for the life of action and romance? No, the passion was elsewhere. A passion to generalize. Never had Lehmann seen, in such small compass, so much basis for inexhaustible generalization. Man and bull. Man into bull. Bull into man. Sometimes he sat up high, for a God's perspective, up from where the huge bull looked like a BB, the object being to tip the ring and roll it into one of the funk holes. But as a rule he sat close, repelled and attracted, like the early man he so closely resembled, crouched on a rocky slope to watch a colleague battle with dinosaurs. He wore no hat, his sun-tanned pate (the only hairless patch of his body) shining above the tree line from the nervous swipes he made with his mittened hand. In his pocket was an oilskin *Regenhut* in case it rained. In the *Hut*, the chin straps dangling, his natural jaundice color a shade sun darkened, he proved beyond a shadow of a doubt the great antiquity of Mexico. At his side, for professional reasons, the white-haired old lady with the lap of knitting, and the big American who often sat there reading the newspapers.

"Varm enuff?" asked Lehmann, and took the knobby hands of Paula Kahler, the knuckles bluish, and rubbed the fingers between his mittens like so many clothespins. Whose hands were they? The question naturally came to mind. Such hands on such a fragile creature, that is. Close companions to the feet, with the large corns, laced into shoes of kid leather—the shoes dating from an era when nothing above the tops was seen.

Over her lap, tucked about her sharp knees, Lehmann spread the blanket that they shared between them, the label of a Brooklyn hotel still attached to one corner of it. The Regent Arms. Dating, that is, from Lehmann's early life and interesting times. Times that had brought him, along with his language, the strange case of Paula Kahler, the chambermaid who had strangled the amorous bellhop in the servants' lift. The bellhop, an old hand at the practice, had stopped the lift between the fourth and fifth floors, and there it had stayed until the next morning, when it was missed. Paula Kahler had been found, in her aura of peace, seated on the pile of sheets she had meant to deliver, the body of the bellhop neatly covered with one of them. She had been a little bruised, physically, but psychologically undisturbed. Using nothing but the hands that did not go with the body, she had protected herself, strangled her assailant, then respectfully covered his remains with a clean sheet. When she was turned over to Dr. Lehmann, the house physician, for a routine checkup and examination, it was found that Mrs. Kahler, as she was known, was not a *Mrs.* at all. She was a man, physically normal in every respect. Nor did she at all resist the examination—in her own eyes, and what eyes they were, there was no disparity between the body she had and the clothes she took off. She was, and she remained, Paula Kahler, chambermaid. Neither mirrors, questions, nor obvious facts seemed to trouble her. Rather than make matters worse, she had been allowed to put the wrong clothes back on.

For observation—as they put it—Paula Kahler was turned over to Dr. Lehmann, since he showed more than the usual interest in her case. She moved to the spare room at the back of his apartment, made his bed, kept the place in order, and tolerated such observations as he felt obliged to make. For several months, for a year or two, Lehmann had kept a file of notes, analyzed her few comments, and waited, patiently, for the clue to out. It would be the making of Leopold Lehmann, professionally. It would be of service to the troubled world, generally.

Didn't it out? Yes, one day it slipped out. The tumblers fell into place and the door swung open—just like that. So he went in? Better to say he just looked, rather than went in. One of those views—they use them in the movies—showing a narrow corridor, then a door, and as that door slowly opens you—well, you can do one of two things. You can look, you can go in, or you can turn away. Like the blind monkey? That was very much how Lehmann looked. But no—or rather yes and no—since it was not that he refused to see, but that these doors, these echoing corridors, would go on endlessly. What there was to see, he had seen. He came back to that. A man who believed he was a woman. What did he make of it? What he made of it, put very simply, was what he saw everywhere he looked, but he saw it clearer in the bullring than anywhere else. What did he see? A transformation. He saw it take place. Before his eyes, the commonplace miracle of everyday life. You can begin with a will, a way, and you end up with something else. The human thing to do was to transform something, especially yourself.

To Mrs. McKee, one of those women whose arms seemed too long from the shoulder to the elbow, Lehmann leaned forward to explain about the cows. A law of nature? He smiled. The male coming to heel when the female came in sight. Something that Mrs. McKee, according to Boyd, really knew something about. He watched her eyes: the focus set, as it was in Lehmann's box camera, so that all the objects in the picture were relatively sharp. Or blurred. The selection was the work of another department. A hopper into which everything was thrown, but little came out.

The horn—Lehmann did not hear it where he heard Mozart, or even voices, but rather he *felt* it, like the scrape of a nail file or eggshell between his teeth. He prepared to say as much—it was the sort of remark that made sense to a woman—when he saw her eyes, the pleated curtain of the iris, open and close in the manner of a flytrap, as if that was where *she* felt such a trumpet blast. Then he turned—Paula Kahler's hand, lying on his sleeve, had lifted—and he saw the bull, fawn colored, his hump dark as the ring sand where it was shaded—he saw him come in at full gallop and where a cape hung on the fence, he went over it. The rail along the seats behind it, on the far side of the runway, splintered with the sound of ice cracking, and the big bull seemed to hang, weightless as a cave drawing, in the echo of the sound. Then he dropped from sight, noiselessly, wind-borne on the gasp of the crowd.

McKee

D ON'T it take you back, Gordon?" he said, since it sure took McKee back, that sort of ruckus, to the crazy ball game where Boyd had torn the pocket off that big fellow's pants. Moment he saw them all hopping the fence like kids, he thought of that. The bull cleaning out that runway like a snowplow, going all the way around it before they caught him, then when they got him in the ring, they all had to leap-frog out again. Funny as hell. But all of it over too soon. The crazy business at the ball game was different in that respect. Game ended right there. Nothing for people to do but get up and go home.

Which they did. In spite of the fact that Gordon, right at that point, wasn't with them, since he was one of about five or six hundred kids milling around on the field. But Mr. Crete had said if he was old enough to start a ruckus like that, in a League ball game, he was very likely old enough to find his way home. Which he was. If Mr. Crete had known him better he wouldn't have brought up the point.

"Don't take you back, does it?" said McKee, but either he was getting hard of hearing, or he didn't want to be taken back. That was probably it. If McKee had been fool enough to have done it he probably wouldn't want to remember it either, since nothing any good at all had come out of it. He got himself all banged up in the commotion, dropped the foul ball he'd run out with, and come off with nothing better than the smelly pocket of this ball-player's pants which he hung onto. Every single other thing in his life he'd dropped. But he still had that fool pocket—McKee could hardly believe it, and it had been just pitiful to see him—the last time McKee had seen him in New York. A grown man. Nearly forty at the time, and slipping fast.

"Remind you of anything, Lois?" he asked, although she hadn't been there, not at the ball game, but at one time or another he had told her everything that had happened to Boyd. Except the New York business. He hadn't told her that. He and the boy, his son, Gordon, that is, had gone back to see the Fair with Roy and Agnes, the summer Mrs. McKee took the younger children to Estes Park. In one of those doughnut shops around Times Square Agnes had snooped around and found Boyd's name in the phone book, since she had never got over that case she had on Boyd. Like a regular hick from the country she stepped in and called him up. It was one of those dial phones, new to her at the time, so she got her nickel back when she tried to work it, but she stuck her gum behind her ear and the second time around it worked. They all heard it ring, since she had left the door open, and when he answered she said, "Gordon, this is Agnes," which naturally took a little while to penetrate. He was never good on names, and he hadn't seen her in fifteen years. But it was him, the Boyd they knew, since whatever he answered it made her blush, and then she opened the door and said, "He says we should all come up."

"Where's up?" Roy had said, and Boyd told her it was

hardly anything by taxi. What he didn't tell her was there were hardly any taxis at that time of night. They were either full, or they didn't know how to make them stop. It took them fifteen, twenty minutes to find one, then another ten or twenty minutes to get there, but McKee had no idea where it was. The street was dark as a tunnel where the driver let them out. It wasn't at all what Agnes had expected and they had to scratch matches to find the right number, since the hallway of the building he was in was dark. Then they looked high and low for an elevator, since he was up on the fifth, but they didn't find it either, so Roy suggested they walk. Up on the second floor, like a firefly in a bottle, was a light pointing out the fire escape, then no lights at all, just nothing, till they got to the top. He was standing there without his shirt in his pants and B.V.D.'s, just waiting for them. It had crossed McKee's mind it would have been just like him to have turned the lights out. What little he had on wasn't any too clean and he was changed so much McKee hardly knew him, stooped at the top, with one of those little pots that stick out in front. Agnes had been so shocked she just stood there, the way a woman will. McKee had been dumbfounded, but you could bank on Roy, who had looked all around him then said—"This is a nice little place you got here, Gordon," and it broke the ice. Not that they died laughing at it, but it broke the ice.

McKee had taken the boy by the arm and said, "You probably don't remember this little fella—" since the boy, right at that point, was taller than Boyd. A big strapping youngster the way Boyd had once been himself. Boyd had shaken his hand, then they had stepped inside into what was like a barn on top of a building. Just a big barn without hay in it. Just an empty loft. He had a bed in it, one of those cots he could cover with something and sit on later, then he had this stool, the seat cracked, that he'd been sitting on. No back to it. One it once had was broken off. Then he had this basin back in one corner, and way back, out of the light, was this toilet that McKee couldn't see, but he could hear it drip. They got to know about that since Roy had first asked him if he had the facilities handy, and McKee and Roy had gone back to use them, pulled on the light. There had been hairpins on the floor and a pair of silk stockings around the doorknob. It had been such a shock that McKee had acted as if he hadn't seen it, Roy had done the same, and that was how they both felt. Then they'd walked back into the light where he had these card tables, side by side, with a type-writer on one, and on the other one a coffee pot. Beside the coffee pot was this dirty piece of cloth, like a pot holder. While they'd been out in back Agnes must have noticed that piece of cloth, and kidded him about it, since the first thing she did was hold it up for them all to see.

"Walter—" she said, to McKee, "you know what this is?"

"Looks like a pot holder to me," he had said, to get around the fact he thought it pretty dirty.

She held it closer to the light as if she thought that might help him.

"He says you're the one person in the world who could vouch for it. What it is."

McKee had tried to think. Boyd had pulled his leg so many different ways, over the years, he couldn't think how he meant to pull it with this dirty rag.

"Guess I could vouch it's pretty dirty, all right," he had said, but nobody laughed. That was not the answer. His own boy stared at him like he knew very well he was holding something back.

"You give up then?" she said. He nodded that he gave up.

"He says it's Ty Cobb's pocket," she went on. "He says you were there and saw him snatch it."

"Holy smoke!" McKee had said, something he hadn't said in years. He looked around at them all, Boyd included, then he looked back at the pocket. It had about the right shape. He could make out the grass stains on one corner of it. He had never before set eyes on that pocket—once it had been torn from the pants—since the ruckus on the ball field had kept him from seeing what had happened to it.

"McKee—" Agnes had said—she always called him Mc-Kee when she knew she had him, and wanted an answer—"McKee, would you say this was it?"

He hadn't answered for a moment. Not that he doubted that it was, but he had his doubts about what it was she wanted. She was looking at him like a good deal more than just the pocket was in question. So was the boy.

"I would say it had the markings," McKee had said, which seemed to be about all she wanted, since she put the pocket back on the table with the coffee pot. All this time Boyd himself hadn't said anything. He had just stood there, the way they all did, and the way the dirty light bulb had been hanging McKee could see the rumpled hair on his head, but not his face. He'd let his hair grow out long, but it was thin on the top. He wore it that way, McKee could see, to cover up the thin spot.

"Ask him what he's doing with it," Agnes said, when she saw that McKee lacked the nerve to.

"I'm putting it in a book," said Boyd. "Something new in books. Small limited edition. Each book will have a piece of Ty Cobb's pocket—and Gordon Boyd's ass."

McKee had not flinched. He had expected the worst, and that was it. As Mrs. McKee had said from the beginning, he might do anything, and now he had done it. McKee had glanced at the boy, who was staring at his feet, and to show the boy how it was he should take that—

"Gordon, what you going to call this book?" he had said.

"*Touch Bottom*," Boyd had said. ."The long-awaited sequel to *The Walk on the Water*."

Then they all just stood there, as though the lights had flickered, until the boy turned and bolted through the door like a kid. They could hear him on the stairs, going down two, three steps at a time. Agnes ran out in the hall and called him, but of course he didn't answer. The whole building shook a little when he got to the bottom and slammed the door.

"Well—" Boyd had said, "I guess *that* does it." But not to McKee or Roy. Nor did he say it to Agnes. He just said it, as if in passing, to himself. But women being the way they are Agnes had said—

"You guess it does *what?* You mean he won't walk on water?"

McKee had turned to look at him. The yellow light was on his hair, then down on his paunch, where his pants were unbuttoned, and he had this old clamp-style silver buckle on his belt. It wasn't even his own buckle. McKee could see it had an O, instead of a B, for the initial. They all watched him shake his head to indicate that wasn't what he meant.

"Then what do you mean?" Agnes had said, since she was a regular bulldog once she got worked up. But Boyd just stood there as if he was wondering what he meant himself. Then he seemed to remember and said—

"I guess I mean that when he touches—he won't stick."

The shooting pain—she always managed to grip him where he got this shooting pain, like something had bit him—made McKee jump as if he'd been tapped at that spot on his knee. He looked up and saw this boy—tall for a boy, but like

Boyd at that age, awkward and gangly—he saw this boy walking along the back of the seats. Not with anything to sell, just walking, with people making way for him, till he got down to the rail where he swung his long legs over, then dropped. Before McKee could think what he might be up to, there he was again, climbing the ring fence, as if he didn't know what side of it the bull was on. And then, as McKee knew he would, he caught his heel on the top and sprawled on his face, making such a commotion that even the bull turned to look at him. It wasn't until then, because he dropped it, McKee noticed this stick he was holding, with a red rag about the size of a handkerchief tied to it. He scrambled for that rag like it was worth a lot of money, got his hands on it, shook the sand off, but instead of scramming for the fence he just stood there, like he was froze stiff. As well he might, since the bull had his eye on him. The bull was clean across the ring, where it was shady, but he could see the boy's white shirt in the sun, the little rag on the stick, and the way the boy's wobbly knees were locked. Otherwise his legs would have run away with him. McKee could see that, then he saw this bull, his head down so low just his horns stuck out, make a beeline for that boy, who just stood there. He didn't make a sound. He didn't move so much as a hair. He was froze in every part of his body, and when the bull hit him, right between the horns, he went up like a scarecrow that had been pitchforked into the air. Down he came, landing a little sidewise, then he crawled around like a fool bug, one with its head off, as if he had dropped something. What did that boy want? That fool stick with the rag on the end. Moment he found it he just lay flat, like he'd died on the spot.

In the meantime that bull—he'd gone by so fast it took him two, three seconds to wheel around—came back and nuzzled the boy like a hog. He tried to hook him, but it wasn't easy with him flat like that. All McKee could see was the rear of the bull, his tail like a piece of rope that was twisted, and in his own mind that boy was good as dead. He had to make up his mind if he was going to sit there and look on at it. If the boy was dead he wouldn't feel it so much, and that would be that. Then one of these men got the bull by the tail—he had this big wad at the end to hang on to—and when he swung around two of the others got in and picked the boy up. Like *they* thought he was dead, the way they dragged him—one had an arm with that stick he was holding—but what did that boy do, the moment they raised him, but stand up and walk. Not too well, a little off to one side like he thought the ring was tipped on him, and no bend at the knees at all as if he was on stilts. But walk he did, and people just moaned to see him alive, after what had happened, and in the next breath were so mad they would have liked to have seen him dead. They brought him in through the funk hole, right there below them, where McKee could see the sand stuck to his face, and a little froth of bubbles, like beer foam, around his mouth. In a way he looked more dead than alive—as if he *knew* he was dead, and had to unlearn it—but there was not a hole in him except for this tiny red spot on his shirt. Seeing nothing more than that scratch on him almost made McKee mad. The palms of his own hands were so wet he had to wipe them on his knees to dry them, and aloud he said "Too damn bad it didn't kill him," but not really meaning it. Then he waited for Mrs. McKee to ask him what in heaven's name he meant by *that*—but she didn't. Nor did her hand lift from his arm. He put his own on it—that is, he just touched to indicate he *knew* what she was thinking—but when she didn't draw the hand to her lap, he glanced at her.

"The boor chile!" Dr. Lehmann said, and there was Mrs. McKee's head lolling on his shoulder, her mouth open, and the gold caps of her teeth catching the light. "The boor chile!" Dr. Lehmann repeated, and into her mouth, from the flask he was holding, he let the drops of the brandy, honey colored, drip on her teeth and lips.

McKee sat there. It was something new in his life.

"She hass pass oud!" Dr. Lehmann said and smiled like a man christening a baby.

Wetting his lips, McKee recovered the power of speech.

"She's sure passed out, all right," he said, "or you'd never get away with something like that."

He turned to smile at the smiling, good-humored, sympathetic row of Mexicans. Two were already standing, fanning her face with their big straw hats.

Mrs. McKee

LOIS," he said, "you all right?" Cool air stirred the hair on her forehead, and feeling the chill on her face and throat she opened her eyes to face the flutter of fanning straw hats. Behind the hats, beaming with humor and concern, their heads like mops scented with hair oil, four or five Indians hovered over her like strange birds. As he waved his hat, absently, one of them ate a banana, fanning her with the sweet odor.

Had he been yelling? Was he faint himself? She wouldn't have recognized him by his voice, but only McKee, at such a time, would have called her *Lois*. Not honey, hardly ever dear, in more than forty years she had once been darling, but that was on a postcard he had mailed to her from New York. He was not a man to show his emotions, if that was what he felt.

"Tell them to stop it, will you?" she said, since she was almost freezing in some places, but felt damp all over beneath her clothes.

"Boys—" McKee began, as if they understood that, but Dr. Lehmann said something in Spanish, wagged his hand back and forth, and they stopped. But they went on staring. Did they come here for the bull, or to see a woman faint?

"Tell them—" she began, then she stopped, tasting for the first time the flavor on her lips, the coolness in her mouth as if she had swallowed some Vaporub.

"A cup of coffee," said McKee, "and you'll never know what hit you."

But she did. If she never knew anything else, she knew that. After what had happened to her on the pyramid she not only knew, she had the words for it. Oxygen hunger. Due to the altitude? "Well, I've been higher in my time," she said, when the Mexican doctor asked her, and being one of those Latins he had just stood there and looked at her.

The highest point in her life, as Alice Morple could have told him, was on the front porch of her home in Lincoln, where the altitude was nil, but the symptoms were the same. Queasiness, duck bumps, and that folding chair feeling in her elbows and knees. She knew *exactly* what had hit her, and it *wasn't* the bull that had hit that poor boy. She knew not only what had hit her, but where, and when that crazy boy went over the fence, she hadn't fainted at all, strictly speaking, she had *swooned*. Hadn't Alice Morple warned her that one day her dream would come true? "*That* type of boy," she had said, moistening her lips, "just loves to go over your fence."

"Let's go get you that cup of Java," said McKee, which was the way he talked when he needed it himself, and the only way to keep from hearing more of it was to go along. She thanked Dr. Lehmann—she could also thank the Lord that *he* had been in that seat, and not Boyd—then she got to her feet. She could *leave* anything, what killed her was to *go*. In that hoarse whisper that attracted more attention than if he had shouted, McKee said, "I'll put her in the car.

Got a heater in it. You wanna keep an eye on this seat for me?"

His *seat*. Not his grandson. He would leave the child in the strangest places, and ask a perfect stranger to keep an eye on him. She had found him in the supermarket with a woman who had four of her own. McKee had left the boy to watch the market cart, and then asked the woman to watch the boy. Around the aisle, the only surface anywhere that didn't slope up or down, or seem to, she headed for the tunnel where she had come in. She did not glance back. Like a cat, if she had got in, she knew her way out. Coming up behind her, never beside her, always that tag-along step behind her, she could hear McKee walking on the cuffs of his new pants.

"Makes you think of old times, don't it?" he said, and she actually turned, thinking she would see Boyd waving at them, squirting pop or something, since what other old times were there? But that wasn't what he meant. He stood with his eyes closed, inhaling deeply, the old times that he meant being the smell of manure blowing toward them on the tunnel draft. "Guess that's one thing about bulls," he said, "that doesn't change much."

Did anything really? Take McKee. Did he ever make her think of anything but *old* times. And Boyd, standing up in that seat to squirt Pepsi-Cola into the bull's face—the same look on his face, if she could believe her eyes, that he had had on the porch. Not the same face, no, that did change, but not the look behind it, the eyes shining from the porch light where the big June bugs were trapped. *That* made her think of old times, it made her wonder, that is, if anything in the world had really happened since McKee's best friend had kissed the girl he hadn't kissed himself. McKee looking on with that silly absent-minded smile on his face. Being *reminded*, as it turned out later, of something else at the very moment an absolute stranger had pressed his lips to *her* lips. And the girl who was kissed? She hadn't changed much either now that she knew what had hit her. Knowing what had hit her, and where, she had swooned.

Was she—as Alice Morple had said—drunk on Jove's nectar like the girl in the play, and were they still, all of them, back on the porch with the creaking swing? Her Aunt Agnes, a woman in her thirties, acting skittish as a girl the moment she saw him, giggling into her apron, then excusing herself to go powder her face, put on black silk stockings, and rinse off the very plates she had asked the boys to help them do. She had also scrounged around and found one of those aprons she gave people for Christmas, and never thought of wearing, and slipped the bib over Gordon's head herself. Standing right before him, her heels out of her shoes since she had to stretch to do it, putting the loop around his neck the way only his mother should. Alice Morple herself, who just hated the kitchen, and had worn her best dress for no other reason, had been perfectly happy with a rag around her middle, washing anything. Five of them, that is, in this narrow kitchen where Agnes complained if there were more than two people, and they took three hours to do dishes she could do herself in twenty minutes. Just four really, since Agnes laughed so hard at everything he said she wasn't really useful, and spent most of the time lying on the sofa showing her pretty legs. Agnes hardly knew—as she kept saying—if she would have the strength to play pinochle, but when the dishes were done her strength suddenly returned. Instead of going to a movie, as she had first planned, she came back with popcorn balls and candied apples, and persuaded them all to play with her new Ouija board. The board didn't spell out anything useful, but pointed at *her* whenever Boyd's fingers touched it, and Alice Morple hadn't been so distracted she hadn't noticed *that*. Eating the apple, Alice Morple pretended it would turn on the stick unless Boyd was there to hold it, which he could only do, sticky and slippery as it was, by using his teeth. Then she would take such a gulp that their noses just had to touch. When they had run out of apples and marshmallows they went into the kitchen and made divinity fudge, but after all they had eaten nobody could touch any of it. *That* was what did it—when she had time to think she could see that perhaps more dishes, or even candied applies—but after candied applies you can't eat something like divinity fudge. They didn't, and the next thing she knew they were out on the porch. Alone out there, since her Aunt Agnes had excused herself, at that point, and run upstairs to the room at the front of the house. If there was a moment Alice Morple *wasn't* giggling, she would know about it. But there wasn't, so far as she knew, until he was there, smiling right above her, and the next thing she knew was the taste of candied apples on her lips. And then Alice Morple—her neck out like a goose, the pigeon bust she was so proud of out like a bumper—kissed him such a smack that her Aunt Agnes turned the bathroom water on. Strange to say, she could *not* believe her eyes, but she could believe her ears. Then he went off—it didn't cross her mind that *they* went off, both Boyd and Walter, and that Walter McKee, her fiancé, had not kissed her himself. *That* would have shocked her. Which was naturally why he had never thought of doing it.

"See here, Lois?" he said, wagging his hand at her, then pointing with it at something behind the fence. "Here in the pen they look friendly. Friendlier than that hog I was telling you about."

What it meant was they were still all out on that porch. Alice Morple had sent her clippings, for years, every time she saw him mentioned in an Omaha paper, and when he stopped being mentioned she would write and ask if there was any *news*. They both knew, without her saying so, just what she meant. It wasn't only her father who was trapped in the past, who didn't turn with the century as her mother described it, but also all of the people who had once been young, with dishes to wipe. And after wiping the dishes had stepped, for just a moment, out on the porch. Trapped. If she could believe her eyes, Boyd was trapped there himself.

For what other reason had he asked them to a bullfight except to put on that clowning performance, pulling the wool over the eyes of all of them again, including himself. Until he acted the fool, clowning and squirting the pop, she hadn't known it. There was nothing so silly and hopeless in the world as a person bewitched. But until he acted such a fool she hadn't known it had been true of him, and it had been Lois Scanlon herself who caused it. She had held him responsible, never dreaming that something had happened to *him* on the porch—even worse, it would seem, than what had happened to the rest of them. In the play he had said that *he* was God's handyman, and *she* was God's handiwork.

"McKee—" she called, and when he came over she put her hand on his arm, feeling him thick and solid, and wondered again what in the world she might have done if he hadn't been there. To marry, that is. To help her get her feet back on solid ground.

"A cup of coffee and you'll never know what hit you," he said, and of course he was right.

"Bang! Bang!" the boy yelled, and fired his gun. "He's dead."

"Dead?" Scanlon said. "You sure he's dead?" He stared as if he might see, then for the hundredth time said, "If you want to keep him dead you got to pile on the rocks. You got to run the wheels over him. Now why you suppose we did that?"

"Because he was a Mormon," replied the boy, and shot him again.

The old man let it pass. Sometimes he wondered himself if that wasn't at the root of it. That fellow was a Mormon. He'd had too many wives. He probably knew from the first one that he'd come to no good end.

On the sky above him, a clean sheet of glass that looked a little rippled and smoky at the edges, he saw the speck. He nudged the boy and said, "There he is." The boy looked up, saw him, and shot him, but he didn't yell out he was dead. He knew better. At least he'd got around to knowing that. You could shoot your fool head off but you'd never bring down a bird like that.

A bird? It was a bird if a bird could croak like a frog. If a bird could smell like the dead, then it was a bird.

"I tell you—" he began, and of course he had, just that morning—and so many other mornings—he had told the boy about the wind. How it blew the words right out of your mouth. Since there was nothing out there for that wind to blow on, no sails, no windmills, nothing like that, nothing but yourself, you took it personally. Then that river they'd looked forward to, that was there on the map, hadn't a drop of water in it, just a sand so fine it was like powder in an hourglass. They couldn't see the wagons ahead or behind them because of the dust. It hung around the fires like clouds of smoke, since there were always wagons that kept going, and they could hear them coming up with their wheels bone dry, then hear the whips when they went off. Long after they had banked the fires at night the sky would be light, up where they could see it, but down in the canyon the morning and the evening were not so far apart. The wagons were like ants in the neck of a bottle, and all along the trail, wherever you looked, they were busy putting something down, or picking something up. Everybody seemed to have a lot more than they needed, and right beside the trail, where you could reach out and touch them, were sacks of beans and sugar, and slabs of bacon stacked like cords of wood. Back on the plains people would trouble to hide it, thinking they would come back for it later, but there in the canyon they just dumped it beside the trail. Anything that was heavy, that would lighten the wagon, they dumped out first. Some had brought along every fool thing they owned, rocking chairs, tables, and barrels of dishes, and others had big framed pictures they would like for setting up house. Some had brought along books, trunks of fine linen, all the tools they might need for building a home, and you could see what a man valued most in his life from where he put it down. Towards the last you began to see people, friends who had sworn they would never part, or relations who had got too old, or too weak, left to shift for themselves. They weighed too much. So they were just dumped like everything else.

No matter where it was that people had been, or where it was they thought they were going, they wanted it to be the same as wherever they were from. They brought along whatever they needed to make it that way. Cages for birds, furniture and fine clothes, bolts of calico and dressmaker's dummies, and a man who had lived near the sea brought with him a diving bell. When he saw he wouldn't need it and put it down—another man picked it up. And in that man's wagon, except for his family, he had none of the things with which he had started, since he seemed to like better anything that belonged to somebody else. Certain other people felt the same way, which was why they would see, ahead on the trail, what they had put down themselves a day's ride back. That was why things traveled faster than people, some of them a lot farther than the people who had owned them, since none of the wagons ever stopped to pick people up.

When he was asked about that, Reverend Tennant said that all of these things were possessed by the Devil, and all they were doing was delivering them to him, free of charge. The Devil himself was that fly speck they saw on the sky. A bird? If a bird could croak at you like a frog. A bird, if a living thing could smell like the dead. They could see him wheel-drawing this circle like a kid would do with a stick on water, but without any ripples, just this speck at the center of it. All around them the mountains, not so much blue as black, the valley like a dead sea in between them, and overhead was this bird—if that was what it was.

Not a blade of grass, just this brush that was white as a bone, without leaves on it, the branches like so many dead and dried roots sticking up in the air. Reverend Tennant went so far as to say that was what it was. In the Devil's country wouldn't everything naturally be upside down? He pulled up one of the plants to show them, and sure enough, just as he said, there was more of the plant beneath the ground than there was above. He said if they could turn it over, the whole valley would look like that. The Lord and the Devil had just switched places, with the Devil upstairs and the Lord in the basement, the Devil naturally being top man in his own house. That was what he said, that was how it looked, but every night he went on praying for rain, although the Devil was the man to pray to in country like that. If the Lord made it rain, it was the Devil who dried it up. He was the one who turned the rivers into sand, and the lakes into salt.

The more the Reverend prayed the drier it got, and one member of the party, a Mr. Criley, spoke up and said that he'd lost all faith in Mr. Wesley's map. He had a map of his own, which he'd bought from an Indian, and this map looked older than the one they had, being torn at the seams, and with a bullet hole in one corner of it. All of the places where there was water were marked with a well. Otherwise they were marked with a skull and crossbones, which led some to believe it must be honest, since a liar wouldn't trouble to point out to them what they didn't want to know. Scanlon knew a liar wouldn't, but it seemed to him the Devil would. It was just the sort of thing a clever sort of Devil would do. That map was just a piece of his handiwork, like the lakes some of them saw, with the shady trees around them, the water cool and shimmering in the high noon light. People wanted to believe in what they saw, so they did. They wanted to believe in Criley's map, so they left the trail, the one made by the wagons, and cut across country on the one that was just on the map.

And that fool bird? What did he do but tag along.

"Why you suppose, boy—" Scanlon barked out, as if he had been talking out loud from the start, "why you suppose that fool bird went along?"

No answer. Hadn't he told the boy that part of it? The Devil went along because he was human—lonely, that is. It put him at a certain disadvantage since he couldn't seem to either take it or leave it, but he had to tag along, like a kid, and see how it worked out.

"I tell you he was human, boy?" he said, but that fool horn, blowing from somewhere, made him crook around and stare up the slope. Like a wall. The canyon had been like that. The cooling sky was pretty much as he remembered it. The wind had not come up—it had just blown away from where they were sitting, sucking the fire out, and rain as hard and dry as pebbles fell from the sky.

"I tell you—" he began, but the boy cried—

"Granpa! Look, granpa!" and stuck the barrel of that gun he had in his ribs. So he did. He got himself turned around and looked. Out on the luminous sand he could see what had fooled him. One of them shimmering lakes.

Boyd

WHEN the boy yelled *look*, Boyd had turned from the bullring—where a new bull had just entered—to watch McKee going down the aisle behind his wife. The trouble with McKee—one of the troubles—was that you couldn't tell the normal run of his talk from his high dry flights of humor. *Don't it take you back, Boyd?* He knew sure as hell it did. But to where? And when? And for chrissakes why? Taken back. Always taken back. Never ahead.

Boyd had not lost his touch—in his bloodless fashion he had just cut two ears, with a fizzing pop bottle—but that too took him back, away back. That too had an antique charm. The derring-do of the nonprofessional touch. The high wax-winged flights of Icarus Boyd, audacious amateur. The big touch was beyond him. As a touching example, he was still alive. He should have died, fizzing bottle in hand, as he turned to receive the *oles*, as he should have drowned in that sandpit west of Polk. As something in him had. Dr. Leopold Lehmann had pointed that out.

Thanks to the curve of the ring Boyd could watch the McKees, cruising in tandem, head for the exit, good-provider McKee straining a bit at the invisible leash. Refugees from the dust bowl, Sears, Roebuck gothic, wearing the dacron they could wash if they had to, and the expression that might wrinkle a little, but would never wear off. The *little woman*, in this case, an inch or two taller, her lips set as if coated with alum, her elbows tucked in close to keep McKee from latching on. Leaving to the dogs—to worse than the dogs—the apple of her eye, the infant Davy Crockett, along with her father, the mummified effigy of the real thing. Two carnival attractions, two allegorical figures advertising the latest frontier victories, the last celluloid effort to turn time back in its flight. Away back. Where time itself seemed to stop. The Origin of the Species, Adam & Eve McKee in the Dustbowl Garden, full of park benches, with Boyd the subtle serpent hanging by his knees from the apple tree. Born to be the upstart, the naughty cupid, the pocket snatcher, the walker on water, the gray-haired youth who slew the Minotaur with a squirt of pop.

Profession? Hero.

Situation? Unemployed.

In the runway right beneath, the rag still clutched in his hand, his hair up wild and his pale forehead sanded, stood the young man with nothing more than the horn prick on his shirt. The hero. In the orphic spell of his charmed life. Little or nothing but wonder on his face. That he was alive? He seemed unaware of it. His bloodless lip bleeding where he had bitten down on it himself. The policeman who held him shook the arm in his grasp as though it was detached, perhaps a clock that had stopped—the other crooked a finger to point at the horn prick on his shirt. Smiling. To indicate he would live. To comment on the irony of it. Beginner's luck? It was clear he was alive *because* he was a fool—not in spite of it. If he had been less a fool he would have come prepared, with a cloth like a sail, and he would now be dead. Not having seen the cloth at all the bull had hit him square, *between* the horns. As they led him away the crowd rose from their seats, some cheered.

"There's nothing—" said the man across the aisle, winding the shutter of his camera, "there's nothing the world loves so much as a goddam fool."

Was that right? Did it explain the current shortage of love? If so, the world loved the hero as himself, without his beard and disguises. Without his armor, but not without his dragon. Just the plain damn fool. In his heroics a potential bungler, and in his bungling a potential hero. In him every man loved the hero in himself. There was no head on which the helmet of Mambrino would not fit. If the world loved such a fool, it could be said of Boyd, one of the goddamdest, that few men in his time had been so well loved.

"That's Ty Cobb's pocket," he would say, when the Lord asked him what it was he was wearing. In place of the leaf. In place of the hero, Eagle Scout Boyd.

The origin of this species? A log cabin, preferably. But that took trees, and there were no trees on the plains. Only heroes, sheroes, villains, and lumberyards. Around the lumberyard, like so many shavings, the clapboard house. On the ground, but not in it, with an air of having been brought out on a freight car, from somewhere better, in order to prove that life could be worse. Protestant. The ornamental ball on the lightning rod an act of protest, a finger shaken at the way the heavens were run. Temporary. A nomad's refuge where nothing like a tent would anchor, the permanent shelter being the storm cave out in back. A hole in which to hide, like a ground hog, from the elements.

In spite of that one lived there? No, one lived there *because* of it. Only where fools rushed in were such things as heroes bred. In front of this clapboard house the long-stemmed grass grew higher than the porch, where the rain dripped, and at the corner of the porch a barrel to catch the rain and raise garter snakes. Three white hairs from a mare's tail, dropped into the barrel, would give you three snakes. A miracle? Heavens no. The commonplace way to make snakes. The natural power of rain in a barrel. The power to transform went along with this barrel and the clapboard house. At the front it had a door, a slamming screen at the back, and at the side a grassy ditch where the Jewel Tea Wagon would park in the shade while the Jewel Tea mare would fertilize the grass. Across the road were the tracks, beyond the tracks the lumberyard where John Crete, Lord of Creation, doled out houses, miracles, and ice in the summertime. A red fence went all the way around it, with the CRETE in white, but the letter R missing where the boards were removed to put in a metal gate. Down the spur to the west, wobbly as buggy lanes, the tracks that led to the bottomless sandpit, circus wagons on flatcars, and the buggy seats in the trampled spring grass. Was that all? The budding hero found it more than enough. Enough, but not too much. With world enough and time to get on with it.

On the clapboard house, nailed over the scars from the quarantine signs for measles and scarlet fever, a bronze plaque that would read—

Birthplace of
THE HERO
Widely Loved and Known As
A GODDAM FOOL

Down the road from this house, up like a caboose on concrete blocks, so one could hide *beneath* it, the home of Walter McKee—

Birthplace of
THE WITNESS
Without whom there would not have been
A HERO

Boyd watched the matador Da Silva, a young man said to wear false calves, but otherwise fearless, gaze from the funk hole with beads of sweat on his face. He followed, with unblinking eyes, the fawn-colored bull. Too much bull, perhaps? As the first one had been too little. Backing away, barking at him, one of the *peones* fanned his face with the cape. Da Silva watched the sweep of the head, the hooking movement of the horns. A preview of the bull's boxing style, the way he would fight. Any tendency he had to lead with the left, hook with the right. The object? Not to kill the bull—that could be done very neatly from the funk hole—but to kill him, strictly speaking, with the cloth. According to the rules. That is to say, according to the risks. It was not a sport, it was even less a gamble, the bull would get it no matter how he gave it, and when he left the ring he would be dead. To what end then? The textbook manual said *Art*. The face of Da Silva—not a very good one, isolated from its body by the boards of the funk hole—the boyish face of Da Silva made Boyd think of something else. The origin of a species. A thatched roof, preferably. Inhabited by heroes, sheroes, villains, and matadors. And the rain barrel? It would give you more than garter snakes. The ears and tail of a bull, freshly cut, would give you a hero. A miracle? Heavens no, an everyday fact. It came perfectly natural to ears and a tail when they were cut like that. The power to transform went along with the funk hole, the face, and the cloth.

Birthplace of
THE HERO
Widely Loved and Known As
A GODDAM FOOL

On his way to Mexico Boyd had driven back to see if the town was still there, if the house was still there, and if the barrel was still there. They were. Only one detail was missing. The word CRETE was no longer stamped on everything. All five letters were now gone from the lumberyard fence. They were no longer in gold on the window of the bank, or blown up in shadow on the library blind. And the House of the Lord himself? A funeral home. For the convenience of the heroes who had not panned out, who were still unemployed.

He had parked his car where the Jewel Tea Wagon horse had cropped and fertilized the grass. A light glowed in the second floor window of the clapboard house. He could see, on the drawn yellow blind, the shadow of the stovepipe with its goiter-like bulge. Above this bulge, the damper. It was now turned up. That, too, had changed, since in his mind it was always turned down. That stovepipe came up through the floor from the coke burner in the room below, and where it bulged like a goiter it would get hot when the damper was down. He could hear the coke crackle and settle when he turned it up. But he liked it down. Not that he wanted it hot. Not that he intended—as it turned out—to fill the house with smoke. All he wanted to do by turning the damper was to bring up the woman who lived below, the way the genie in the picture would rise out of Aladdin's lamp. She would come up with her lamp, the wick swimming in oil, and cross the room like the figures in his dreams, without noises, without so much as taking steps. Holding the lamp to his face she would see that he was asleep. He would feel the heat of the chimney on his forehead, catch a whiff of the oil. She would first open the damper, then turn with the lamp so that the room darkened behind her, but her snow white hair seemed to trap the light. During the day it would be piled on her head, but when she came up with the lamp it would be in braids. With a silver-handled comb that rattled when she used it, facing the mirror that no longer had a handle, she would comb out the tangled ends of her braids. Out would come, like the burrs in a dog's tail, the knotted hairs. When all the hairs stood up, like a brush, she would pass the ends slowly over the chimney, where they would curl at the tips and crackle with a frying sound. Then the smell, as when she singed a chicken over a hole in the kitchen range, or turned the bird, slowly, in the flame of a cob dipped in kerosene.

What did it do?

Something for the hair. That was what she claimed. But it did more than that, certainly, for the boy in the bed. What did he see? More than met the eye. But in this strange transformation, what was transformed? The ceremony of the flame, the crackling and the smell, the hand that passed the taper over the chimney, made this woman something more than an aging Sarah, who had miraculously conceived this Isaac. No wonder the Lord had deprived her of Abraham. A pollen bearer. There had been no further need of him. A load of timber had providentially rolled off a flatcar, crushing him. This timber belonged to John Crete, the Lord's representative, and he saw to it that the child, the young hero, should not want. The word Crete, the Lord's seal of approval, had been stamped on him. Behind the cage at the bank, behind the grain on the scales, behind the corn in the cribs, the beef on the hoof, behind the sun when it set, setting it aright, was the word CRETE. In the beginning was the word. The education of the hero had begun with it.

From where Boyd sat in the car, the motor idling, he could see down the tracks to the grain elevator where the last coat of paint—a fading yellow—was peeling off. Under this coat, shadowy but re-emerging, was the word CRETE. Very much as it emerged, as he sat there staring, on Boyd's mind.

Boyd had begun to wear, before he could walk, the

clothes of the Crete boy, who was one year older, and later
he was sometimes mistaken for that boy in the street. His
name was Ashley. But Boyd seldom set eyes on him. Only
his clothes. Ashley Crete was always away somewhere
where he grew so fast his clothes were a problem; old
clothes were too small, and new things were never worn
out. That was left to Boyd. But he never quite grew into, or
out of them. A larger size, at that point, would replace the
suit he had almost grown into, or the shoes he had not yet
broken in. He knew the clothes, but not the boy who had
stepped out of them. That boy was in the pictures on the
piano or the table in his mother's bedroom, wearing the
clothes, shoes, stockings and cap that he would soon send
back to Boyd.

Patent leather oxfords, short velvet pants that showed the
garter hooks when he was seated, and underwear that
proved that Ashley Crete never wet his pants. These clothes
were never shortened, since Mrs. Boyd, a believer in true
breeding, was sure that Boyd would grow faster if he knew
that he was short of the mark. If the shoes had not been
larger, the sleeves longer, Boyd might have stopped growing in his fifth or sixth year, but he *had* to grow, knowing
the larger size was waiting for him. One might even say that
he went on growing—until it was not. That would be
wrong, an oversimplification, but when Ashley Crete
stopped walking on the water—of Boyd's imagination—
Boyd stopped walking on it himself. But not his mother.
No, she had kept the faith. So long as she was alive Boyd
had been supported on a raft of newspaper clippings, which
kept him in touch with the Gods in her pantheon.

The only God that had failed had been Boyd himself.

Although he had started well. Like a house afire, in some
respects.

The day he went over the fence and got himself a pocket

he had been armed with nothing but his intentions, and wearing the first pair of pants worn only by himself. A test case. To see if he could run this show by himself. On a Sabbath day like this one, in seats along the rail such as these were, with a bullring featuring Tyrus Raymond Cobb, the Georgia Peach.

What had been his object? To get a foul ball autographed. One that had been hit by the master hitter, one that Boyd had caught. To get it signed. That was the gist of it. But in the riot that followed, the ball field swarming with hundreds of small fry, each with a mission, Boyd had forgotten the foul ball he set off with, hooked on the hero's pants. He had taken a goring, but he had cut one ear, nevertheless. It was there in the form of a pocket to the great man's pants.

What he had had in mind—or below his mind, so that it occurred without complications—was not to get the ball signed, which might have been done in the hotel lobby, or the shade of the dugout, but to get it signed according to the rules. To get it transformed. And this had occurred. A stranger transformation than he had thought. Not merely a foul ball into a pocket, but a pocket into a winding sheet where the hero lay, cocoon-like, for the next twenty years. Out of this world, in the deep-freeze of his adolescent dreams. The object was transformation, but it had stopped where it should have begun. There was not one bull, but many, each transformation called for another, or the hero remained like the music in Baron Munchausen's horn. Like Boyd, that is. Snug in his flannel winding sheet.

He watched the matador, the young magician Da Silva, step from the wings of his imagination, erect but abstract in his pearl gray suit of light. On the column of his spine, like a mourning capitol, the funereal hat. He did not look up to see, nor seem to care about, the bull. The beast stood, a little winded and perplexed, with his rear end to the fence, the non-existent corner. Like so many brushes in the palette on his hump, were the ribboned darts. Two of them sticking up. But Da Silva? He stood alone with himself. He came to face them, doffing his hat, bending back from his hips like a floating diver, and with a fine carelessness tossed the hat over his shoulder, like a pinch of salt.

Did the bull feel that? He pawed the sand where he stood. Da Silva let him wait, working like a painter with the folds of the cloth, the way it draped, then he drew on the sand, with his eyes, the line that the bull would take. He took it, fanning out the cloth, then wheeling as if his master had whistled.

Ole!

The noise that Boyd had made himself left him deaf. He had its flavor in his mouth.

The bull charged from the left, then the right, then again from the left, with each charge shorter, each turn sharper, until he stood twisted on his own spine. Screwed around until he faced the direction he had come from, brought to a standstill, unable to go two directions at once.

And the matador? At this point he had turned away. As from a still life, an arrangement that would remain as he had left it, the scene transformed into a frieze of permanence. The matador a magician, holding the wand to which was attached the magic cloth, behind which the double transformation had taken place. Word into flesh, and the flesh itself into myth. He came toward them, his body buoyant, the head straining at the leash that held it, the face tipped to catch the shower of praise that came down like light. The praise making a roar, a siphoning sound that swirled about him, creating a vortex, a still point where he stood alone with himself. Not unlike Paula Kahler in that he saw, in the swirl of faces, his own reflection, and in the roar heard only what he wanted to hear. He stood before them in a trance, his hand upraised to catch the charge of their admiration, to mark the spot where the next transformation would take place.

The bull, coming up behind him, put it into effect.

Lehmann

IN Guanajuato, on the way down, Lehmann had taken sick. During the long night it had occurred to him, with the clarity of a hallucination, that he was not sick with a bug, or from food, or anything that he could *catch*. He was sick from Mother Mexico herself. From her exhausting extremes, her legerdemain, in which the limbs perform tricks without the body, from her excessive beauty as well as from her poverty and decay. It was simply too much for a pasteurized stranger from the north. Not merely what he had seen, but what he had seen and repressed. *Why order your thoughts?* Mussolini had asked, and Lehmann had always found it a disturbing question. Why indeed? But he had learned why that night, thanks to Mexico. If he could not order his thoughts, he was sick. It had been his failure to order his thoughts that made him ill. The nausea had come as a form of analysis. Intestinal Freud. Followed by relief, if not a cure. What his mind could not stomach, for very long, had to come up.

Mrs. McKee had reminded him of that—Mrs. McKee, with her head lolling on his shoulder, having fainted, Lehmann was sure, of the same sort of thing. Not bulls, not pyramids and altitude, but Mexico.

Which was certainly why—Lehmann reflected, hearing the click of her knitting needles—Paula Kahler was always in the best of health. Everywhere. Since all places were the same. The same reflection gazed at her from all of the mirrors. She had been sick to the death—she had died, that is—and passed over to the other side. From there all things looked the same. They were small as a rule, thought to be helpless, and of one sex. There were no males in Paula Kahler's brave new world.

Baby lambs, kittens, collie pups, cows in the manger, birds in the trees, but no bulls, no roosters, and no rams. Better yet, *little* things. *Anything* that was small enough. Ants, for instance. My God, what a time he had with ants. Couldn't get her past them if she saw them crossing a walk. They were not like bulls. There was no easy way to tell about the boy ants.

This roar that swelled up around her, the build up of the *ole's*, like a cheering section, she did not hear any more than her cats heard the noise in the street. But the faintest scratch, the soundless fall of seed from the cage of her canary, any sound that *meant* something, like water dripping, she never missed. Did she hear him *thinking?* Her gaze seemed to focus on something insubstantial over the ring. He looked himself, saw the young man with his hand upraised, as if in blessing, and it led him to wonder, he almost turned to *look* for the bull. He didn't have to, since right at that moment man and bull were one. The youth seemed to grow out of the bull's neck and shoulders, as Lehmann had so often dreamed it, a living centaur, the archetypal man growing out of the beast. For a moment he seemed to soar, his arms spread wide, the cloth unfurling in the wind beside him, his eyes wide with the wine of

459

astonishment. Would he fly? Would he go winging off like
the flying horse?

Lehmann himself had stood up—a man of little faith, he
had thrown up his own arms—to catch him when he
toppled like Nike from her pedestal. The bull, as if stunned
and witless, stood to one side. He did not follow up his
advantage. Did he consider it one? Having been, at that
moment, more than a bull, he was at a loss what to do next.
Man *and* Bull had both been shot down—Lehmann would
tell you—at the moment of flight. Resolving and not resolving the anguished dilemma of human life. Man, his arms
spread wide, could only take wing on the thrust of his past,
and at the risk of toppling forward on his face. Bull into
Man was followed, too often, by Man into Ghost. The horn
of the dilemma—like the one at his side—was that it led to
flight.

He placed his hand on her arm, since Paula Kahler, the
true bird that never was, having taken flight once might see
fit to take it again. He watched them lift the young man—
the stain spreading on the inside of the thigh, where one
hand gripped him—but the shock on the faces of the men
supporting him. On his own face sweat, a patch of sand as if
he had been down at the beach, napping, and they were
carting him down to the water to rinse him off.

A row or two behind him a man's voice said, "Well, you
asked for it, baby. How does it feel?"

How did it? Dr. Leopold Lehmann, the male Blavatsky,
as Boyd affectionately called him, sometimes thought he
knew, although he had never been gored himself. He had
the touch. He had been there, so to speak. If Paula Kahler
had been able to vouch for anything, she would have
vouched for that.

According to his income tax, a dependent, classified as his
housekeeper, Paula Kahler was the woman—strange to say

—in Dr. Lehmann's life. A case—he had once noted down—
of arrested development. A simpleminded wonder and
affection for childish things. A nature that refused to ac-
knowledge the aggressive elements. Maleness, that is. Maleness being at the heart of it.

Her possessions—an old wicker bag to which she had
strapped a ribless umbrella—contained nothing of interest
but her large collection of miniature animals. Hundreds of
them, a regular zoo, with one unusual feature. They were
all females. The males, and their aggressive ways, had been
weeded out. Beginning with herself.

At one point a toy Ark, sold to children at Christmas, had
been added to the wildlife haven in her room. Didn't that
make it clear? Could it have been a mere accident? Having
rounded up the female of the species she was prepared, like
Noah, to sail off after the flood and start a new world.
Lehmann had been apprehensive for months. He locked her
in when he left the apartment, trailed her around when she
shopped. Then the answer had crossed his mind one summer night. He, Leopold Lehmann, was the brave new world
himself. She had already sailed off, and arrived in it. The
female-haunted rooms of his apartment, forever burbling
with the voice of the female turtle, the male shored up in
her dreams and in other responsibilities. At that point the
case of Paula Kahler—as a case—officially closed.

A month later it reopened. Unofficially.

In the wicker bag he had stored in the closet—he had to
take it down when mice were found in it—he had come
upon a postcard, slipped into the lining, addressed to Paul
Kahler, Camp Hastings, Illinois. It was signed by Warren
Shults, of Chicago, Illinois. He had written the card from
the Larrabee Y.M.C.A.

Lehmann had walked down the street to the St. George
Hotel, where they kept a rack of phone books in the lobby,

and looked in the Chicago directory for the name of Shults. He found it. He was still at the Larrabee Y.M.C.A. On the pad in the booth Lehmann noted down the number—not quite clear in his mind what he meant to do with it—then turned back to the phone book and glanced at the K's. There were many Kahlers, but only one Paul Kahler, and, strange to relate, the address was the same. Paul Kahler and Warren Shults were listed at the same number. The same Y.M.C.A.

Lehmann had walked to the bar, where he had himself a stiff one, then he had come back to the booth, put through the call.

The voice replying said, "Good evening, Larrabee Y.M.C.A."

"I woot lak to spik to Paul Kahler," Lehmann had said. At tense moments his speech—it was no language—got considerably worse.

"Kahler?" came the reply. "We have no Kahler listed."

"Ware coot I get in tudge?" Lehmann had inquired.

"Anybody know of a Kahler—a Paul Kahler?" He had turned and asked the question of someone. Lehmann heard the answer.

"Paul *who?*"

"Kahler," the voice repeated.

"Connect the line to my office," came the reply, and Lehmann heard the plug switch him over. He waited a moment, then the voice cried, "Paul? Is that you Paul?"

"I am werry zorry," Lehmann replied. "I am nod Paul. I was callink to fine him."

There was no reply. Lehmann thought the connection had been broken and said, "Operador. Oh, operador!"

"Shults, speaking," said the voice. "Paul Kahler is missing."

Lehmann thought a moment, then took the plunge.

"Thod is wot I understand, Mr. Shoolts," he said. "Maybe he iss no lonker so missink?"

"Hermann!" said Mr. Shults. "Is that you, Hermann?"

"My name iss Lehmann," he replied, "and I may haf some noose aboud Paul Kahler."

"You knew him? You have seen him?"

"Thod iss the gueschun," said Lehmann.

"Slight and frail," said Mr. Shults, "blond hair, blue eyes. Last seen with his brother Hermann."

"Woot there be any phodographs?" Lehmann asked.

"Here on my desk—" said Mr. Shults, then stopped. Lehmann waited while he thought it over.

"If I coot zee zom pig-chur," Lehmann put in.

"I'm afraid I can't let you have it," said Shults. "Group picture. Several of them in it. But you're welcome to come and look at it." Lehmann did not speak up, and Shults said, "He is alive then. You have seen him?"

"If it iss the zame person, he iss fery mudge alife," Lehmann said.

"If you could come—" Shults interrupted, then said, "Where are you? If you could come by this evening?"

"Led us mag it tomorrow efenink," he replied, and while the voice of Shults was still talking, telling him about the street cars, and the El, Lehmann had hung up. He had to hurry in order to catch the night train.

He hadn't slept. He had sat up in the coach, since there were no berths available, staring out the window at the places his clients came from. Small towns, most of them, where the lights burned over empty corners, the houses dark with the dreams they would ask Lehmann to analyze. As Boyd had cracked, they were all great places to be *from*. But that, of course, was the dilemma. They left, but they never got away. Trailing along behind them, like clouds of glory, were the umbilical cords. On his mind's eye Lehmann saw them like the road lines on a map. Thousands stretched to reach Chicago. Millions stretched to reach New York.

The train had let him off in the heart of the labyrinth. He had taken a cab to the near north side, a neon jungle with a gold coast trimming, and rented a hotel room within a block of the Y.M.C.A. The bellhop, an elderly man, with the yolk of an egg drying in his mustache, led him down a creaking uncarpeted hall to the room at the front. As they entered the room a warning bell on a drawbridge began to clang. Lehmann watched the shadow of the bridge, like a hand, move on the yellow blinds. Because the air in the room seemed stale he lowered the transom, then tried to raise a window, a cloud of sparkling dust puffing out from the curtain when he brushed it with his hand. He had leaned there a moment, gazing at the street, the barge he could see drifting on the river, and the honking lines of traffic blocked by the bridge. He could feel the building tremble, as if with rage, when a street car passed.

Had something stopped? Were they waiting for the heart of the city to start? Above the warning bell, the idling motors, Lehmann thought he could hear the lapping of the river, just as he could smell, above the stench of the city, the sewage in the canal. As the shadow of the bridge moved on the blind the honking increased, reached a point of frenzy, and then like a pack of unleashed hounds, the traffic began to flow.

He lay out on the bed just to rest for a bit, not to sleep. Did he doze off? Perhaps; something woke him up. He was aware of the vibration in the bed that never left the room. The springs on which he lay gave off a sound like wind in a harp. Over his head, like a clouded eye, a frosted bulb suspended from the ceiling, with a knot looped in the cord to shorten it. He was able to see that the cord was lumpy with flies. That the bulb sustained an even, somewhat elliptical, swing. This movement did not trouble the flies, however, any more than the movement of the earth, tipped on its axis, seemed to trouble the man on the bed. He felt, at the moment, suspended in space himself. That might have been the heat, which was bad, the droning of the traffic in his ears, or the calendar on the wall at the foot of the bed. The date? It was May, 1931. A red-cheeked child tirelessly licked by a long-haired dog. On the sky an airplane, symbol of his future, in the background a mother, symbol of his past, but in the eternal present he would go on being licked by his faithful dog.

It struck Lehmann—it struck the person, that is, that he seemed to be at that particular moment—as if he had rented this room in a time capsule. Time—of the other variety—seemed to have stopped. Lehmann had been stored away, forever, with this small piece of it. A cord lumpy with flies, a bed that sang like a harp, a basin in the corner that smelled of urine, and a calendar dated May, 1931. These things, that is to say, were the eternal ones. They would not change. They would grow neither down nor up. They were immortal, and they represented the everlasting things in nature, as well as the everlasting nature of things. The eternal moment in the shifting tides of life. The eternal personality of sweet and sour, pleasure and pain. The changeless dreams of love and affection, licked forever the changeless face of the young, in which the changing past and future were always the same. In the dream, that is, began the irresponsibility. The sleeper awake, the shadow on the blind, the fly-clotted cord, and the drip in the basin that signified life, death and erosion in the mind. What one would find, that is, at the heart of the labyrinth. A hotel room, a guest for the night, the gift Bible with the red-stained leaves, and the figure in the carpet long ago worn into the cracks in the floor. The bed itself lipped with a spout, as if to pour out the sleeper, and the door with hooks on which to hang the empty days, the sleepless nights. And at the heart of this capsule was Leopold Lehmann, timeless man.

The way a fruit would drop, with no wind blowing, one of the flies on the lumpy cord lost his grip, fell, and bounced on Lehmann's chest. Through one cocked eye he saw the creature on its back, the legs in the air. Dead? Lehmann put out his hand, a finger cocked to snap it—then paused, and returned the hand to his side. Something he remembered. Something he had seen Paula Kahler do. A fly presumed dead, given up for lost, found by her floating in the flower water, had been revived by her with the sun and a sprinkling of salt. Lehmann had observed it with his own eyes. The fly sprinkled with salt, then placed in the sun, and after a moment one leg had wiggled, then another, pushing the salt to one side. With a toothpick, she had helped him to his feet. He had groomed a bit, before leaving, stroking his wings with his feather dusters, then buzzing his motor in an experimental flight. Paula Kahler had then opened the screen and the fly flew out.

Lehmann had thought it a fine example of the saintly and simple-minded, saving the fly so that *he* would have to swat it again. Man had to choose. He couldn't go on kidding himself. If it was man or fly—Lehmann had once more raised his hand, cocked the finger—when he saw it move. To check on that he held his breath. Squinting, he saw a twitch. No more, but a twitch. He took a quick breath and waited. Another twitch. Two legs, now working together. Had the dead come to life? Or was it a question of altitude? The heat, or the poisonous air that prevailed up near the ceiling, had been too much—so he had fallen to his proper sphere. He twitched again, as if sprinkled with salt. Easily, as well as painlessly, Lehmann could have finished him off.

Enlightened self-interest? That was the term for it. And if it was a matter of choice, that was the time. But he held off, he reduced his breathing lest the fly rock off the platform, and drop into less favorable circumstances.

Why? With the fly in *that* condition he had no choice. Lehmann, that is. He had killed, in his time, thousands of flies, and he would swat any fly with the strength to attack him, but he could not swat this fly on its back. As helpless, there on his shirt front, as man himself. Groggy with the heat, poisoned with the air, a nervous wreck from the noise and the vibration, what he needed, speaking fly to man, was help. As a man, Lehmann felt obliged to give it to him. The fly's proper business was to lump light cords, ping on screens, contaminate food, and whenever the opportunity offered, make men miserable. And the man's proper business?

Lehmann had closed his eyes. In a book he had read having to do with some brothers, all of them typical half-mad Russians, one of them had had a dream that Lehmann could never forget. This one had dozed off for just a moment—the way Lehmann had just dozed off himself—and he had this dream that hardly seemed connected with anything else. He was off somewhere, on the steppes, as Lehmann had a feeling of great bleakness, when this sleigh he was in went by these people standing near the road. Just about the saddest collection of people anyone had ever seen. All of them thin and dirty, their faces off-color, and one of the women of the party had this child which she held to her dried-up breasts. The man in the sleigh asked the driver what the devil was wrong with them. Then this driver answered, *"It's the babe weeping,"* and the man in the sleigh, along with Lehmann, was struck by the driver using the word *babe*. There was more pity in it. As there was between Lehmann and this fly on his chest. In the room he felt the presence of a strange personality. One that was part of the room, the enduring personality of life itself. It joined him, sad as it seemed, in the pity life seemed to feel in the presence of such a fugitive thing as life. Not just pity for Lehmann, nor for flies, but for pity itself.

He lay there till he heard, pinging the blind, the fly that was no longer on his chest, and to avoid a showdown he got up and left the room. He walked the few blocks to the Y.M.C.A., where the lights had been broken out of the sign, and he had to choose between a Men's and a Boys' entrance. He chose the Boys', opened the door, and stepped into the draft of chlorinated water blowing down the hall from the swimming pool. A tall thin man stood in the lobby, twirling a chain of keys. He held a small numbered ball in one hand, and spoke to a tough-looking boy.

"The ball is not *my* ball, Vito," he was saying, "the floor is not *my* floor, or you could bounce and roll the ball all that you liked." He paused there, then added, "If it *was* my ball, you could have it, if it *was* my floor, you could bounce it, but it isn't *my* ball, it's *your* ball to have and to keep."

Seeing Lehmann in the door he said, "Next door is the Men's Section."

"I'm Dr. Lehmann—" Lehmann had said. "I called you in regart—" but that had been enough. Mr. Shults had stopped swinging the keys, stepped over and gripped his hand.

"If you'll step back to my office, Dr. Lehmann," he said, and led him by the elbow, as he would have the boy, down the hall to where the smell of the chlorinated water was very strong. With one of the keys on the long chain he opened the door.

That horn—hearing the blast on the horn Lehmann glanced up as if to see a bull enter—but the entrance gates were closed. The bull he saw was dead. The mules were dragging the fawn-colored body on a tour of the ring. There was applause, and Lehmann joined it, slapping his bright-red mittens together, in spite of the fact that Boyd had snickered at such a thing. The bull was dead. What good did it do the bull?

"It iss nod for the bool, which iss det," Lehmann had said, "but for Lehmann, who muss go on lifink."

There was more pity in it. There was now that he had thought of it.

McKee

THE trouble with the bullfight, McKee was thinking, was that where other things ended, it didn't. You saw one accident, then you had to sit back and see another one. But the truth was, he liked it. More the way they came in, than the way they went out. If they had a suggestion box at the gate he'd suggest that they throw a tarp over the dead one. He always had the feeling, dead or not, that they didn't like the flies.

Take that hog he'd shot—it made his own eyes itchy just to see the flies. Like a swarm of bees around the pail full of his blood. Settled on it like they'd drowned. Like a bucket of dead flies more than anything else.

"Hot cup of coffee," he said, giving her elbow a pinch, "and you'll never know what hit you."

A lot of truth in that. They'd given him coffee when he shot that hog. It was the coffee that made his stomach quiet. If it hadn't been for that he would have whooped his breakfast up. Ham in it from the last hog his uncle had shot. It wasn't till he'd shot the hog that eating ham began to give him the hives.

Hearing the shouts—it sounded to McKee like the word for "oleomargarine," the short one—he turned to see what it was he had missed. The bull had run at the fellow but missed him. There he still was. The bull had two of these darts in his hump like someone had shot arrows at him. *That* he had missed. When he came back he would watch for that. The arrows had got him pretty bloody and some of it had rubbed off on the bullfighter's tights. When McKee shot the hog there had not been a drop till they cut him all up, which was later, but he didn't bleed a drop of blood through that hole in his head. It had stayed just as round and black as his eyes had been. Not a drop of it till his uncle, with the dishpans to catch the blood in, sliced his throat so his heart would help pump his own blood out.

This was where? Boyd had asked him. As well he might. McKee doubted it himself. Texas. The panhandle part of it. McKee had gone down in a day coach with some devil's food cake wrapped in wax bread paper for this Uncle Dwight of his he had never seen. He'd waked up in Amarillo where the sky was supported on these giant posts. Oil derricks. Highest things he'd ever seen. With the land floating on the oil beneath them, which helped McKee to explain it. The way the country seemed to roll like the floors in amusement parks. McKee had gone down there a boy, fifteen, and come back a man.

The train he came in on blocked off the crossing, so that his uncle, who had come in to meet him, wasn't there to meet him until the train pulled out. He didn't climb from the buggy, or say *Hello, Walter*, but just put down his brown hand, as though they'd already met, and McKee had come home after a day or two somewhere else. But he did say one thing. "Kid—" he said, "you ever shoot a hog?" Then he grinned, showing the caps of his teeth, and McKee could see the dirt packed around the roots and the dust like talcum powder in the creases near his eyes. The man who invented the dust bowl had been up that morning, working on it.

Nor had his uncle's place been a farm in any sense McKee understood it; just a two-room shack, with a low row of sheds, but no trees or barns. No cows, pigs, horses, or anything like that. There were a few chickens, but they were seldom in the yard since the wind down there would blow them away. The only sign that anybody lived there was the lamp in the window at night, and the clothes flapping on the line during the day. The noise the tractor made seemed to blow over from somewhere else.

It had rained down there one winter. Nobody knew why. But his uncle, the winter it rained, had made forty thousand dollars off the land he had rented, which he had plowed up and planted with winter wheat. The next winter he had added a room to the shack. The hired man had lived and slept in it; but it didn't rain that winter, nor the next, and when the hired man left, McKee had taken his place. If it rained he would make enough money to be a farmer himself.

His window looked out on a yard as clean and hard as the floor boards in the kitchen, with the outhouse standing at the edge of the first plowed strip. Fencing in the outhouse was the row of milk cans used to fuel the tractor, which was always left running since the nights were cold and it was hard to start. It struck McKee as alive, the way it would cough, snort and backfire like it was dying of something, and the way it would shake like a dog that was tired and wet. Like the wind, the coughing never stopped. A perpetual thing, like day and night, and if it dropped down, or the wind lulled it, McKee would wake out of a sound sleep knowing something was wrong. He would lie there awake, hardly breathing, till he heard it coughing again.

There was always this wind but hardly any whine since there was nothing for it to blow on, no trees overhead, or dead leaves to sweep the ground. It was when the wind stopped that he heard it, like a quick intake of breath, and the house would ease back like a sleeper turning in bed. There was nothing to blow on, but he had seen the cats, on the moonlight nights when they went about their business, cross the yard on their bellies as if stalking invisible game. The wind he couldn't see would blow them like kites if they stood up. Full grown hens would sail like bonnets till they caught, like tumbleweed, on the stretch of chicken wire that was put up just to keep them from blowing away. The nights there was a moon it seemed to rise right there in the yard, between the house and the privy, and light up the winter plain with the glow from its backside. The land seemed to fall away like the sea from a swell, rippling where the grass still grew on it, or the white-faced cattle stood in rows along the wire fence. Over this moon one night, right out of the blue, drifted a strange cloud. Where did it come from? McKee had made it himself. It was born in the plume of dust that rose from the plows.

On the tractor at night he could see the lights, thirty miles away, where oil had been found, and in the dawn light the rabbits, as if blinded by it, would get caught in the discs. Smart ones would hop from the furrows, just ahead of the noise, and then crouch to watch him pass, big-eyed as mounted trophies, their ears smoothed flat. The far lights looked as near as the rabbits, but when he threw a clod at something it seemed to rise, hang still for a moment, then drop at his feet. What was wrong? Space. He had no way of measuring it. Things were not at all, out there, as they seemed. The mud caked to his gums became part of his teeth, and a film of dust, soft as face powder, sifted through his clothes and made his body soft to touch. He learned, the hard way, not to wash it off. Water left him chapped and sore, the dust left him soft. He learned to sleep in his socks, his flannel underwear, the shirt that was pinned and hard to unbutton, and to dress in the dark that he knew to be morning. How did he know that? The sun rose, like he did, when the tractor coughed in the yard. Dawn came when the lamp glowed at the cracks in the kitchen door.

Those clouds he saw, drifting like smoke, would one day cover Nebraska, like a smog, and make the sun as red as a bolt hole over New York. Not that McKee knew that. He never knew anything. Not unless Boyd told him, or he read it in something like the *Reader's Digest*. He had to come to a bullfight to remember he had shot a hog. Anything having to do with Boyd he seemed to remember as if it had just happened, but he forgot it if it just had to do with McKee.

"Here's where they keep 'em penned, Lois," he said, and leaned over the fence to look at the bulls. He counted five. That meant they kept on hand some extra ones. In case one turned up like the one Boyd had squirted with the pop. McKee would say the beef steers on his son's ranch ran half again as big as the bulls he was seeing—but they had no fight in them. How did you explain that? What was it about a bull that made him want to fight? Some of the bulls he had seen were so fat they couldn't mount a cow, if they had to, and some of them didn't even seem to want to, which was worse. If it wasn't for artificial insemination, bulls like that would go out of business. The only fun they got out of it was eating, but it seemed to be enough.

"Little dark one here—" he said, when she didn't come over, "is not much bigger than that hog I mentioned."

He had never told her about that hog. She had never asked. He gave her a chance to ask about him now—she knew very well that a bull was bigger—but she wasn't up to snuff or she would have pinned him down about that. One sure way to tell if she was off her feed was when she let things pass.

You ever shoot a hog, kid? his uncle had said, and the day it drizzled they went over to do it. The hog belonged to his uncle but had been rented out to a family named Gudger, who had the corn to feed him. Also quite a bit of garbage, since there were eleven of them. The drizzly day had made it seem as though they went over under water, since nothing changed, the wheels turned, and the matted grass flowed under the buggy like a muddy stream. When he looked up and around they always seemed to be standing still. Sometimes the white-faced cattle were there at the fence as if they had been painted on it, other times they weren't, but it was always the same cattle, and the same fence. They saw the Gudger tree, sticking up like a sail, long before they got to it. The bleak gabled house, with the boarded windows, was like a caboose left somewhere on a siding, and behind this house the sky went up like a wall. The world seemed to end. The house itself looked vacant, but when they got in the yard a swarm of small kids, hooting like Indians, ran out like they'd been waiting to ambush them. They had old knives without handles, and the kids without knives had jagged pieces of glass. McKee was bigger and stronger, with the gun there in his lap, but it gave him a turn.

They had the hog out in back of the house, in a pen, and beneath this old tree in the yard, which was dead at the top, they had a pit of steaming water in an old bathtub. The kids needed the bath, but the water was there for the hog. Once McKee had got around to shooting him, that was where he would be dipped. With their glass blades and knives the kids would scrape all the hair off him. McKee had seen big pigs, and he had seen fat hogs, but this one, propped up like a barrel, struck him as bigger and fatter than any hog he had ever seen. They hadn't fed him any corn that day since it would only be lost in his stomach, not having had the time to turn itself into pork or fat. When his Uncle Dwight had held up a yellow ear, a big one with the tassel waving, the hog had grunted and waddled a step or two toward the fence.

"You let him move in close," his uncle said, "then shoot him between the eyes."

That was all right with McKee—he stood fingering the trigger and waiting for the hog to move in close, when this uncle of his, without aye, yes or no, took this ear of yellow corn and stuck it right in his pants. In his fly, that is, since he had a button off right at that point. The big yellow ear of corn stuck out in the air like something else. All the little Gudgers hooted and roared, the little girls as well as the boys, and McKee had stood there with the tassel of the thing tickling him.

"Here you are, kid," his uncle said, then lowered one of the poles in the fence for him, so he could climb in without dropping the ear of corn. "Stand there till he spots it, kid," he said, "and when he moves in close, you shoot him. You hear me, boy?"

Had McKee nodded his head? He didn't remember. All he remembered was hearing it. He just stood there in the pen until the hog, sniffing the air, waddled over toward him, moving in so close McKee could almost touch him with the barrel of the gun. Who had fired it? McKee himself had no memory of it. He saw the hole, the eye that was like the center of the target, but he had no memory of putting it there himself. The hog did not move, he stood like McKee, his legs spread as if waiting for something, and one of the flies on his snout crawled back and sniffed at the hole. Did he crawl in? McKee was inclined to think that he did.

They strung him up to this tree, dipped him in the

bathtub, shaved him down till he was pink and white all over, then cut off his head and propped it in a bucket with the snout sticking up. Over a fire they built in the yard they cooked down the soft parts, the pork shoulders, and stored the pieces in the fat that drained off into heavy lard pails. The light from the fire lit up the yard, the house with the windows boarded, and the swarm of hungry little Gudgers, every one of them shiny with fat. McKee had eaten no pork, his face was clean, but the smell of the fat was thick in his head, like the drone the flies made when they rose up, like hornets, from the pail of blood. He felt that he too was being cooked down, like parts of the hog. He was taking the cure when the wind blew the wood smoke over him. At his back, when he turned to look, the rimless plain lay under the moon, and the grass was the leaden color of a dead sea. The house was an ark, adrift upon it, and here and there, in the hollow of a wave, lights would sparkle as if a handful of stars had dropped. In front of him was the fire, the swarm of Gudgers, and strung up as if lynched was the body of the hog. But not all of him. There was some in the fat, and his head was in the pail. The snout up, the lip curled as if grinning, the third eye he had still open, which led McKee to feel that something in the hog hadn't really died. His head. His head was an onlooker, like McKee. Both McKee and the hog seemed to share the same feelings. That it was a joke. But it was not on the hog. Who then? It was on McKee. McKee with his gun and that fool ear of corn sticking out of his fly. He hadn't killed the hog, the hog had laughed himself to death. The sight of a youngster like McKee with that big ear of corn in his fly had called for one more eye than he had, and that he had got. Thanks to McKee. The better, that is, to die laughing at him.

In the cool of the night the Gudgers had all curled up like dogs, and slept together, but McKee and the hog had kept the vigil—the joke, that is. The lip of the hog, McKee could tell you, curled up till all of his teeth were showing, and there were times when McKee heard him laugh with a snort. Toward morning some honking geese flew over, some of them so low he could see the fire on them, but until a rooster crowed he wasn't sure at all but what he'd dreamed it all up. Was it any wonder he'd kept that story to himself? McKee with the corn in his fly, that hog with his curled lip grinning, and the night itself, as Mrs. McKee would have put it, more or less bewitched. Quite a bit like that summer night on the Scanlon porch. As much or more was going on, McKee could tell you, as the night Gordon Boyd, McKee's best friend, kissed the lips of the girl McKee himself had never kissed. And the girl? McKee could tell you something else. She'd married McKee, but she hadn't really kissed another man in her life.

"McKee," she said.

When it was flat, like that, he knew he must have been rude. He doffed his hat, tipped his face back, smiling. He didn't recognize the man in the transparent raincoat till he heard his voice.

"Today is the tomorrow you worried about yesterday," said Mr. Cole. That referred to the fact that McKee had spoken to him yesterday. About the bullfight. He hadn't been too sure about Mrs. McKee. They single filed through the gate to where Mrs. Cole was holding up a porch lamp she thought of buying.

"*Zinko—?*" said Mrs. Cole. "Harry, does he mean his money or ours?"

"You buy everything here," said Mr. Cole, "what you going to do in Acapulco?"

They left them to decide and walked down the street to where he'd parked the car. McKee was able to see they still had hubcaps on one side of it. Man from Abilene was saying that he had all four wheels taken off his car.

"Well, here we are, Lois," he said, opened the door, then just stood there, a smile on his face, waiting for what he knew she would say.

Mrs. McKee

IF anything should happen to that *boy*—" she said, and saw his mouth pucker, like a hen's bottom. Into it, like a cork, he put the wet end of his cigar. Before she heard what she knew he was about to say, she pressed the automatic button that rolled up the window. A goldfish, his lips still puckered, he stood there a moment staring at her, then he made a face to indicate he would be right back.

From the rear—the rear of McKee, from the beginning, had been a problem—the way his hands hung down as if his legs, or something, were too short. No hat he ever wore, including this straw one, covered the back of his head as well as the front, but she had never noticed *that* spot before, the way she did down here. Hair—everybody seemed to have it, nobody ever lived long enough to lose it, and when he had his hat off McKee looked like a person who had just got well. Only nurses, or people who were still sick, ever looked at him. What had Alice Morple said? *Honey, anyhow you haven't had that worry*. And she certainly hadn't. Not once. Not a suspicion in more than thirty years.

But had it ever crossed the ninny's mind to have a suspicion himself? Boyd? No, he called *that* something else. He left her alone in such places as Sanborn's. He let her sit in the parks. And here in the very shadow of the bullring, he let her wait in the car. Alone—if she brought it up he would say it had a heater and radio in it—when she had had *young* men, in the Sanborn's lobby, take her arm like a tomato they were feeling to see if it was ripe. McKee smiling. The way he did that night on the porch.

When Mr. Arnold Clokey, the science teacher from Red Wing, Minnesota, took a liking to her, McKee had actually egged the poor man on. A giant of a man—with whatever it is that made such big men have smooth, baby faces—Mr. Clokey liked the same sort of things in Mexico she liked herself. Pottery, baskets, and those strawberries with the thick sweet cream. McKee seemed to think that any man his own age would feel the same way he did, or at least feel that way about his own wife.

"You two go ahead and fool around—" he said, when they met at that place in Cuernavaca, and just sat there in the square while they went off to fool around. Mr. Clokey had colored to the roots of his hair, which he at least had, and which made him quite attractive, and they had actually fooled around in some of those side streets until nearly dark. Mr. Clokey knew a little more Spanish than she did, having been down once before, in the '30's, and in the course of their walk she got to know him fairly well. He confided in her—as he put it himself—what it was that had brought him down there, although it was a foolish thing for him to indulge in at the time. He had *flown* down, his object being to make a photographic record of the types of people, in Kodacolor, that he could use in his science class. That was why he seemed to be so cluttered up with cameras, tripods and such things. The camera club of Red Wing had loaned him the equipment, and he had gone into debt to acquire some lenses, since he wanted to make sure his trip was a success. To save money he was living with Earl Hornick, a member of the art department, who wanted to do nothing but paint water colors for three weeks. Mr. Clokey had known Earl Hornick for years, had seen him every day in the school cafeteria, without somehow noticing a very small thing. Earl Hornick whistled under his breath all the time. More or less a hiss, like a tire leaking, without much tune or rhythm to it, and he began in the morning and went on hissing like that all day. It had brought Mr. Clokey to the point where he had to do something. In a joshing manner, so as not to hurt his feelings, Mr. Clokey had said, "Earl, you like to sell that whistle?" merely to draw his attention to the fact that it was always going on. Mr. Hornick, however, had taken offense. "There must be something eating you—" he said to Mr. Clokey, "if you let a little friendly whistling upset you."

Mr. Clokey, in fairness, had been obliged to admit he must be right. He felt extremely guilty about it, but on the other hand, try as he might, he couldn't sit or lie around in the room and be indifferent to it. Earl Hornick even whistled when his mouth was full of food. It had brought Mr. Clokey to the nervous point at which Mrs. McKee had found him—more or less compelled, that is, to find somebody like herself and get it off his chest. It revealed him to be a very weak man—as Earl Hornick had suggested—but to keep from going crazy he just had to discuss it with someone. If he hadn't found her to confide in, he said, he would have gone plain nuts.

Since he wasn't married, Mrs. McKee had pointed out that if he were it might have been different, as he would have been living with somebody who whistled, clicked their fingernails, or even worse. If he thought a little whistling was a problem, she said, he should pass almost a lifetime with a man, or a woman, who couldn't pass a living moment without something in his mouth. A cigar, a match, or something he would pick right off the street. He was like a child who didn't seem to know what he was doing, until you told him about it, or like Earl Hornick, the way he made a whistling sound sucking air through his teeth. There had been a time, she confided, when he almost picked her whisk brooms to pieces, after she had asked him never again to chew on a match. She had been as distracted as Mr. Clokey, not for three weeks but for several years running, until one day, hardly knowing why, she just didn't seem to care. He had gone back to matches, when he sensed that, and there he had stayed. All she could say now was that she still preferred matches to cigars.

Mr. Clokey had confessed that he himself had never married—although the opportunity had offered—due to a gastric disturbance he had as a young man, that followed all of his meals. Burping. Nothing he took seemed to quiet it. Rather than plague another person with something like that he had lived alone, when he might have married, and when the burping stopped he had other annoying habits, like peanut butter on fruit. If he had a fresh peach, or cantaloupe in the morning, he would eat peanut butter with it. Earl Hornick had complained of that their first morning in Mexico.

It had been a very strange conversation—they had eaten strawberries on a patio with a view of the mountains—and Mr. Clokey had permitted four different boys to shine his shoes. He couldn't bear to say no, and he didn't want to make little beggars out of them. In a perfectly casual and natural way he had suggested, if she could spare the time, that they motor to Oaxaca where he had reserved a pleasant suite of rooms. Earl Hornick, in spite of his art background, was so prudish he refused to travel with a lady, and Mr.

Clokey was sure she would never forget Mitla or the world's oldest tree. He hoped he didn't have to tell her that his affection was Platonic, and stopped at that.

The strange thing was she had not been taken aback, shocked to hear it, or anything whatsoever. It seemed a perfectly normal thing for him to proposition her like that. She was sure she would simply *love* Mitla, she had said, just from the little she had seen of it at Sanborn's, but with her grandson and her father to take care of, her hands were full. She had been tactful enough to leave it at just that. It had not been necessary—nor had it crossed her mind until she saw him, an hour later—that she had not referred to McKee as a problem, or anything else. She had felt precisely as Mr. Clokey had felt himself: that she was not attached to him in any serious way. That she was free to fool around—as he had said himself. They had parted on the best of terms—she had since had strawberries with him at Sanborn's—and spent some time in the lobby looking at the pictures he had taken.

What would Walter McKee, her husband, think of something like that? She was terribly afraid—no, she was more than afraid, she was absolutely sure, if he had been there, it would have been about the same as that incredible night on the porch. Not that Mr. Clokey was a Gordon Boyd, but if McKee had been there, and heard the question, he would have said "Lois, you know you can do about as you like."

Why hadn't she?

"Lois—" he had said to her, just before they had left, "you can count on the fingers of one hand"—and he held it up—"the people who know what it is they want."

As Mr. Clokey liked to say, *she would buy that.* What did she want? Anything she had ever had? In the windshield of the car she saw her face, expectant, the lips parted. What might have happened if Boyd had walked on the water?

Would she have, that is? From her purse, the miniature bed warmer that contained her pills, her saccharin, and her aspirin, she took the pill that would help to quiet her down. Coming toward her with a paper cup of cold coffee, was McKee.

Scanlon

WHAT the devil were they yelling? *Agua. Frijoles* was beans. *Agua* was water. But where the devil was the water? In the pit before him, glowing like it was hot, there wasn't any water at all. It was sand. What sort of fool would look for water in a place like that? Well, he could tell you. An eastern sort of fool like this man Boyd, or an even bigger fool like Scanlon himself. His father, that is. His father, Timothy Scanlon, had come from the East. The East was where a man went down to look for water. In the West, he went up.

"I tell you where we looked for water?" he said, but the boy, fizzing pop, didn't hear him. As if he didn't know better he was squirting that pop into his mouth. Another thing that eastern fellow, Boyd, had done to him.

"*Agua!*" he heard them holler, and he would like to tell them that if what they wanted was water, and not this Pepsi-Cola, the place they had to look for it was up. They wouldn't find it, but that was where they would have to look. If they went up a canyon far enough they might see where it had been. See where it had coursed, when the canyon flooded, and then see where it came to an end. Where the sun had sucked it up, or the sand had sucked it underground. In that valley they crossed there were round-topped buttes, spread around like so many Indian baskets, but there was never any Indian or any living thing to shoot. The only thing in creation he could have shot with his gun would have been himself.

All he did, day and night, was scout for water, and he might be gone two, three days at a time. He'd carry that fool gun, a cup or two of water, a small slab of dried meat in his pocket, and after dark, up on one of them buttes, he'd build himself a fire. He'd eat what little he had, then he'd roll up his blanket, put his canteen at the head or foot, then go back and hide in the dark until the fire died down. But nothing ever happened. No Indian ever came to see who he was. No animal or bird ever snooped around for something to eat. It made him kind of careless, that sort of country, and if there had been any Indians in it, or anything that was hungry, he might have gone off and never come back. But the only living thing to hunt and eat in that country was himself.

From the high places he could see the wagons and the teams away back where he'd left them, crawling along so slow they always looked to be in about the same place. He found it hard to believe that the wagons he saw were full of live people, real men, women and children, who had left a home with food and water on the table, grass in the yard, trees for shade, rain in the morning if you prayed for it at night, just to come to a godforsaken hole like that. All these people really wanted, if he troubled to ask them, was exactly what it was they left behind them, even less than they had left if you could believe what they said. Every night Mr. Samuels liked to explain how much he liked to make the chips for his own shingles, and how they would stick, almost forever, once he nailed them down. Every night Reverend Tennant would read to his kids how they should sit and eat with the knife and fork, while they were scrounging around like coyotes for what bones there were left. This little Orville of his would pick in the manure the cattle had dropped.

From the butte tops he could see almost forever, but that was all he saw. It looked just about as empty, everywhere, except that to the west it looked even worse. He could see the slopes and hollows where even greasewood didn't grow. Way off to the south, round and shiny as eggs, he could see the bright shimmer that looked like water, and once, far on the side of a mountain, he had seen smoke. Maybe a week's walk away. All he could do was sit and look at it.

At night, if he could see the campfires, he'd try and figure out the Samuels' wagon, since in that wagon, wrapped up in burlap, was the water keg. When he got back to camp there would be even less in it. One night it would be gone. He didn't believe everything he'd heard, but he had seen Mr. Baumann sit and look at Mrs. Criley, a woman with water on her knee, like he was sizing up a good hog. There would be fat all over, marrow in her bones, and water on her knee. There was no water on his own knee, but he had heard Mrs. Norton complain that he wouldn't be so stringy if he didn't scout around so much. Stringy was the word Mrs. Norton used every time she put a bite of jerked meat in her mouth, and he knew that what she had in mind was him. He was too stringy already. She didn't want what little was left of him to get too tough.

He'd seen a flat-topped butte about a day's hike south, higher than most since it had juniper on it, and he headed for this peak so he could get a good look to the west. Along about noon, when he stopped to rest, he lay down with his head beneath a little greasewood, and on the branch right over his head he hung his hat. In the shadow that his hat made, he put his head. He'd seen the Indians do that with their arrows when they were in a country without any shadows, sticking the points of their arrows in the sand and their heads in the shadows the feathers cast. He took a bite of his food, a little sip of his water, then he took a little nap till the *thing* woke him up.

It wasn't the noise he made, for he didn't make any noise. He didn't fan the air, or flap his wings, but he came over so close, and it was so hot, that lying there on his back like he was, he caught the smell. Like a whiff of garbage, that was what it was. He probably didn't smell any too well himself, not ripe, anyhow, since the bird went off, and when Scanlon rolled over he noticed right beside him this small hole. All around it, like a string of beads, were these little pointed rocks, like they'd crawled out of it. They were alike in that they each had six smooth sides, and sharp points at each end. One was nearly as thick as his little finger, and one was so small he could hardly pick it up. They were all smooth and shiny as gems. He couldn't eat little rocks, or drink them, but it seemed to him they signified something, as if the Devil, down there in his hole, had got a little bored. He liked to tinker. He had all that space, and all that time on his hands. It was just another sign that he must be human, and evil as he was, with that awful smell, Scanlon couldn't help feeling a sort of shameful liking for him. Some streak in him was human. He did his best to hide it, but the rocks showed it up. If he crawled out of his hole he might even need food and water himself. Scanlon put the little rocks into his canteen, where they didn't turn to water or increase it any, but they raised the level so that it looked like he had more water than he did. Then he headed for this mountain peak to the south, and climbed to the top.

Hell itself, from the top of that mountain, lay at his feet.

The sand was like ashes, and not even greasewood grew out of it. North and south he could see to doomsday, but to the west, where they were headed, he could see a mountain shaped like an anvil, glowing like it was hot. It looked like the pit where the Devil himself had hammered Hell out. All around it were clinkers, black as coal, but going off to the south, like a crack in a stove lid, he could see a canyon where water had once been. Clean white sand gleamed at the bottom of it. It seemed hard to believe that in such a dry place there had ever been that much water, cutting a canyon right through Hell to let itself out. The only way out, once they were in, was to follow it.

When he got back to camp he fired off his gun to indicate that he had found something, but nobody ran forward to ask him what or greet him. One member of their party, Mr. Samuels, had shot himself. There was so little water left he couldn't bear to drink more of it. Reverend Tennant, as usual, had prayed for rain, but Mr. Criley had asked him right to his face why it was that the Lord, the one he prayed to, put a canteen on the back of a camel, but all he gave to a man out there in the desert was his thirst. Hearing that Mr. Samuels had crawled beneath his wagon and shot himself.

But he'd killed off more than just himself, and when they broke up camp, and headed for the canyon, the creak of the wagons made a mournful funereal sound. With that one shot he had killed off something in all of them. When Scanlon looked back and saw their little party strung out in the moonlight, the wagons ghostly, it crossed his mind they were already dead and entering Hell. And that the Devil had supplied them with just what they needed to get them there.

When they got to the canyon Scanlon went along the bottom, where there was nothing but the light, the heat, and rocks bigger than the wagons tossed around in crazy patterns as though some giant had been playing with them. The only tracks in the sand were his own, but when he came to a stop he could see his own shadow, smoking at the edges where the heat nibbled at it, and every now and then he saw this other shadow, the one with wings. It went around and around him, but when he looked up at the sky he didn't see anything. There was no croak, there wasn't any sort of smell, but every time he stopped this circle went around him like the web of a spider, or ripples on a pool.

So he didn't stop often till he found this place where the canyon opened out a little, with slopes they could get the wagons down all right, but they would never get them out. They would have to go along wherever it was the canyon went. He had a pretty good idea where that was but there was nothing he could do about it, and if it was Hell they were going to, he wanted a look at it. When he got back to the camp he told them what he had seen, without saying where he thought it led to, and during the night they spliced all their rope to let the wagons down.

They made a winch around a boulder, greasing it with fat where the rope would smoke a little, and they began with Mr. Samuels' empty wagon, and his two weak mules. Mr. Wesley handled his team, since he was young enough to jump if he had to, and the rest of them handled the rope at the top. The rope burned a little but even the mules got down all right. The men couldn't see Mr. Wesley but they could hear him hallooing to pull on the rope, which he had untied, and they pulled him up on the end of it. While it was still in good shape they put on the best wagon, with the women, the children and the water barrel in it, except for Miss Samantha who claimed she was strong enough to walk. They figured if they got that wagon down why then the worst of it would be over, but they went down the slope so easy there wasn't even a cloud of dust. The women waved from the back of the wagon, and except for the smell of the rope, smoking like a fat burn, it looked easy once they got the hang of it. So in the next wagon they put Mr. Fisher and what food they had left.

About half way down, with no more warning than the crack of a rifle somewhere behind you, the rope snapped right where it was smoking on the rock. They saw the wagon, as if the slope had kicked it, go up in the air and turn clean over, the canvas puffing out like a balloon, then fall on the team. Then they rolled along together, and they waited for the wind to blow off the dust. There hadn't been any noise, and it looked as far away as the wagon train from the top of a mountain, the canvas like a brown package all bound up with rope. Wagon, man, and mules all wrapped up together in one winding sheet. Nobody yelled, and the only thing that moved was the cloud of dust, like a ghost in the canyon, with the ring around the package that was no darker than the ring around the moon. A shadowy circle, but it kept getting smaller like a marksman drawing a bead on the target, till there was no ring at all, just this bull's-eye on the winding sheet. And right when they all had this bead on it, a shot rang out. Scanlon could see that Miss Samantha had fired it, since she stood right there beside him, and when the bird dropped on the target he could see what she had hit. He didn't let out a croak, or flap a wing, and it was Mrs. Criley who picked him up, by his long red neck, and stood there picking the feathers off him.

It had been Mrs. Criley who used to complain when they ran the wagon wheels over a grave, but she held that bird by the neck like she'd lynched him, and the awful stink he had seemed to please her. Mrs. Baumann helped her pick him, and they both cleaned the skin off the quills with their teeth.

That night they built a fire, cooked the stinking bird on it but nobody troubled to thank the Lord for it, and a wind, as though a door had opened out, sucked out the fire. It didn't blow, it just began where they were camped and went off like a noise. Then a crazy-looking cloud went over so low they could see it scrape on the rim of the canyon, and a drop or two of rain, as wide apart as a wagon, fell on the sand. It left a dent you could walk up and see, but it wasn't wet. It scared him worse than no rain at all, and then a mule, without any reason, just up and went out like the fire, with Mrs. Baumann saying she could hear the spirit of him whooshing off. Mr. Wesley pointed out that it proved mules were smart. He had sense enough to die while he still felt as good as he did.

Scanlon wasn't scared to die—what scared him was that he wouldn't die soon enough. Off by himself where Mr. Baumann, for instance, couldn't dig him up. Where Mrs. Norton wouldn't suck out of his bones what little marrow he had. So he lied to them, saying that he would go on ahead, scouting for water, and when he got off by himself he just ran around like crazy, hooting like a kid. Just to be off where he could die by himself made him feel that good. And then—as if he'd come to that place where the door had opened, and the wind had rushed out—the canyon spread out the way a river does at the sea. And it looked like the sea, one of those dead ones, not shining white like the others, but black as a pit of coal when it was wet. But hot as it was, that place looked cold, like a chill when he had a bad fever, and it gave off a light the color of water that went up to the sky. It was as though he stood at the bottom of the sea and looked up through ice. There was no trail that led in or out, no stinky greasewood, no whiff of sage, no speck on the sky, and nothing in the air that he would call light. When he looked down there was no shadow at his feet. The sun came through a hole like you would burn with a poker, and the heat came in through the hole, and went out it, but this hole didn't rise like the sun, nor set. It just came and went, but he couldn't tell you how often it did it, or where it came from, or if you could say that it was up or down, or early or late. He couldn't tell you if he walked backwards or forwards, or to the right or the left. He couldn't tell you if he thought that was right or wrong. As a matter of fact, he didn't care, but the one thing he could tell you, if you asked him, was exactly where he was. He was in Hell. Knowing that, he didn't seem to mind it so much.

"*Agua! Agua!*" one of them hollered, and ran along the pit right there below him.

"In Hell there is no *agua*," he said. Soberly.

"*Agua! Agua!*" another one hollered.

"Shut your fool trap!" he croaked, but nobody had heard him. They went on yelling. Nobody cared. He leaned on the rail—he leaned forward far enough to see the crack in the fence boards, see it blur into focus—and where they were stained with the Pepsi-Cola he directed his spit. A bull's-eye. *Hmmmmmphhh*, he said, and spit again. Then he drew a brown finger along the edge of his lips, as if wiping the blade of a knife, rubbed the juice between his fingers, held the moist tips to his nose. The smell revived him; lifting his eyes he gazed across the pit of Hell, smoking with light, to the canyon where the downdraft, so cool he could taste it, made his edges uncurl. Dimly, on the burning sand, he saw the body of a man dead for some time.

"*Agua!*" he hollered, but of course it was too late. It was the wind that made the ghostly music that came from his mouth.

Boyd

H OW did they put it?

The brave blood was the blood a man spilled first. Boyd could see it. Rose red, opening like a flower at the tear in his thigh. On the sober face neither pain nor shock, no indication that he knew, or feared to know, that this might be his last exit from the ring. All of that was on the faces of the two who bore him, one fat, one thin, like a sack between them. A torn, battered sack, splitting at the seams. Hero and meal ticket, the word made flesh, and the flesh made weak. Gored. The crumpled end of the hero's life.

"Imagine me being here," said a voice. "I've seen a man gored."

Another way should be found, Boyd was thinking, to bear him from the ring. It should be understood that he might not enter it again. Or if he did, it would not be as the same man. He would never spill the same red blood in the sand. They could do wonders, off where they would take him, the sulfa would do this, the knife would do that, and there would even be blood to replace the stuff that he'd spilled. Red, life-giving blood, but not the same. Brave blood could be spilled, but not transfused. One could see clearly how it was lost, but not how it was made. The brave ingredient did not show up in the blood-count smear. It escaped, like his breath, into thin air. It did not darken the sand, like the bull's, but like a dusty pollen, wind-borne from the wound, reappeared as a spot in the lung of some youth, a point of infection that would prove to be incurable. Nothing for him but to take the cure of fighting bulls himself. Sooner or later infecting, with his own spilled blood, the lungs of someone else.

They passed below: the youth's eyes were closed and on his forehead and cheek the golden sand of the bullring. Relaxed now. A beardless youth masquerading as a man. One who had put on the suit that called for the sword, and stabbed himself behind the arras. One who had dressed as young Washington, and saw the tree cut him down to size. Or one who—with that blood smear on his thigh—had cut through the line and hit one of the goal posts. A touchdown? No, he had dropped the ball. Very much the way a kid named Boyd had once dropped one in Omaha. The bull was now just a bull, and the hero was a youth named Da Silva, matador second class.

What had taken place?

"Well, it only serves him right," the voice replied. "If he didn't expect it, why in the world does he do it?"

A good question. To be answered affirmatively. In the expectation of the goring the hero was made. As well as broken. A crumpled top hat with the rabbit bleeding inside.

A matador named Salcedo, with the air of a man cleaning up after an operation, attracted the bull's attention, faced him like a camera, then went in with the sword cleanly over the horns. The bull *dispatched*. But had he *killed* this bull? No, he was already dead. He had merely added the finishing touch to the beef on the hoof.

The headlines would read DA SILVA GORED, the photograph show him froglike, as if leaping the horns, or crumpled like a broken toy as they carted him off. The camera did not lie. A pity, since the lie mirrored the truth. The camera would report what no pair of eyes present had seen. Not two, of the thirty thousand present, had seen the same thing.

Boyd glanced at the face of the child beside him, the pistol barrel in his mouth, his nose running, in his eyes the faint suggestion of the small fry who had overheard *something*. What had *he* seen? How long would it take him to puzzle it out? He was now a jigsaw loose in its box, the bullfight one of the scarlet pieces, but he would not know its meaning until the pattern itself appeared. And that he would not *find*. No, not anywhere, since it did not exist. The pattern—what pattern it had—he would have to create. Make it out of something that looked for all the world like something else.

Did he know that? Was there anywhere he might go to learn?

First, he would have to sense that parts were missing, and then, somewhere along the way, that the curious pattern he saw emerging was himself. Everything else he had been given, in abundance, but that he lacked. It called for transformation. Out of so many given things, one thing that hadn't been given. His own life. An endless sequence of changes, a tireless shifting of the pieces, selecting some, discarding others, until the pattern—the imagined thing— began to emerge. Death would fix the outlines. Frame the picture as no man would ever see it himself.

The problem? In an age of How-to-do-it, the problem was how not. How *not* to be embalmed in a flannel pocket, how *not* to be frozen in a coonskin hat. How to live in spite of, not because of, something called character. To keep it

497

open, to keep the puzzle puzzling, the pattern changing and alive.

The lineaments of *Paula* Kahler—Lehmann liked to say— had always been among the pieces in *Paul* Kahler's mind. One day, like the fission of matter, they would out.

But wasn't that precisely *character?* Boyd had asked.

The old man had blinked. He hadn't said yes or no. In his face the wide mouth had moved as if his tongue were cleaning his gums.

"Wot I min iss—" he had said, held up his hand as if to show the healing wound in his palm, then committed himself. "Each accordink to hiss nachur," he had said. "I min sudge nachur ass he shoult haf."

"Then you mean ripeness is all," Boyd had said.

"Thod iss wot I min," he had replied.

Boyd turned to look at him, an over-ripe old man with shiny lips, poor circulation, and a silver hip flask clasped in his mittened hands. On his mouth, however, a ridiculous smile, like the one on the face of the tiger, the flavor of the canary still moist on his lips. Was he getting senile? He had the simple-minded look. Not unlike—Boyd was thinking— the trancelike face beside him, and in that face he saw the reason for it. They had grown to look alike. An impossible thing, but they were *working* at it. A transformation, a blending of natures often observed in dogs and masters, in lovers, and in the dual nature of a man himself.

Did Lehmann feel it himself? He put up his red hands, knowing what a sight they made in a bullring, and clapped with a frenzy that brought beads of sweat to his face. His eyes closed, the Neanderthal forehead contour wrinkled to prevent erosion, and clapping like a fool. For what? A dead bull. Something he did knowing what a pain it gave to Boyd.

Boyd turned to watch the mules, their pom-poms wagging, drag the carcass of the bull on a tour of the ring while the crowd applauded, some near the exit rose to their feet. Music, wind-borne on the draft that sailed paper airplanes over the bullring, suddenly stopped—leaving a void that nothing filled. In the quiet Boyd could hear the drag of the carcass, the rattle of the chains. The left horn of the bull— the tip that had gored Da Silva—dipped into the ring sand and plowed a shallow furrow, the wave of sand rolling smoothly over the tip. Washing away what little trace of blood it had picked up.

"Can we go squirt pop now?" said the boy, and Boyd watched the whitewing, with his broom and shovel, sprinkle clean sand over the spot where the bull had died.

Lehmann

HE watched the boy with the gait of a dancer, weightless as if he walked on water, the hips arrogantly forward, flick the cape as if to rid it of a few moths. He gazed, as if along a track of ants, to where the bull stood waiting, then he offered the cape like a towel to a bather who had lost her suit. The head and eyes cast down, an attitude of dignified respect. In the pause a voice that knew cried—

"*Agua! Agua!*" and the wind, cool on Lehmann's bald head, fanned out the cape the young man was holding, exposing his bowed legs. "*Agua! Agua!*"

As if rising from the dead, the old man named Scanlon tipped his head back, croaked, "*Agua?*" He looked around as if to see it, then said, "That's water? He thirsty?"

"Dey use vater to holt the cloth town," Lehmann said, and showed how with his hands.

"*Agua's* water, *frijoles* is beans," the old man said.

"*Agua! Agua!*" and the young man followed the advice. He walked, turning his back to the bull, to where one of his assistants, just a head and arm showing, reached over the fence to spill water from a jug on the cloth fanned out on the sand. Leaving spots, staining it dark the way Lehmann's mother, when he was a boy, would spit water from her mouth on the clothes she was ironing.

He closed his eyes, as if he might hear the hissing sound as the iron steamed it, or catch the smell, on the draft from the kitchen, of freshly scorched clothes. From where he slept in the front room on the day bed Lehmann could hear the creak of the board, when she leaned on the iron, and see her strong legs through the transparent slip. His mother loved to iron in her slip if the weather was hot. She would fasten it up with pins at the back, so the cool draft would blow on her legs, and his father would slap her smartly on the bottom as he passed. A sad woman, wife and helpmate to Saul Lehmann, a sad provider, mother of Leopold Lehmann, a sad character.

"*Agua!*" they yelled, "*Agua! Agua!*" and Lehmann remembered, he could smell, that is, the strong odor of chlorine blowing through the door of the Larrabee Y. The sound of the keys Mr. Shults stood swinging on his chain.

"My wife—" Shults had said, raising the blind at his window, "my wife, she thinks I'm crazy."

Lehmann had said nothing. He had felt a little mad himself.

"That name in the phone book," Shults had continued, by way of explanation, "but ' keep telling her, Gladys, that's just where he might look."

"You min for himself?" Lehmann had asked, and watched Mr. Shults pop a mint into his mouth. He stood at the window of his office gazing at the street.

"If you're looking for someone—" Shults replied, "if you've lost track, if you're just looking—"

"I zee—" said Lehmann, and nodded his head.

"Does it matter," Shults asked, "if you're looking for yourself?" He had not put that question to Lehmann, but himself. "He was the kind that might," he went on; "you'd have to know him. He was different. He didn't just think of himself, like we do. He might not know he was lost."

"Strancher thinks haf happent," Lehmann had said.

"Dr. Lehmann—" Shults had said, paused to grope for words, then drew the blind half way as if the light disturbed him. Beneath it Lehmann could see the ice wagon that had pulled to the curb. Under the wagon the sparrows had gathered, in the cool dripping shade, to scratch and pick over the fresh manure. Lehmann could see the steam rise, like waves of heat. Shults seemed to have forgotten what he meant to say, so Lehmann had primed him—

"You were zayink?"

"Stranger things have happened," Mr. Shults said, soberly. "Stranger things did." He continued to gaze out the window as if stranger things were happening before his eyes. He sighed, then said, "What it was, I suppose, was the personal loss. For me. He grew up in the work. I had him slated for something here."

The word slated had jarred on Lehmann's ears.

"Thees wass Paul Kahler?" he asked, since he had lost the thread, if there had been one.

"He was my right-hand man," Shults replied, and held up his right hand, the fist clenched. "You should have seen him in the lobby. With the tough ones. Had them eating right out of his hands. He was so small, you know, and so helpless—"

"Wot do you think wass his proplem?" Lehmann asked.

"Problem?" Shults had replied. "*What* problem?"

Lehmann gathered he had stumbled on the wrong word. He tried to think of the right one. None better came to mind. "Wot I min iss—" he had begun.

"Nobody has told you?" said Mr. Shults.

Lehmann had been on the fence. How much, or how

little, should he have heard? "I know that he wass fery vrail—" he said, playing it safe, but Mr. Shults wagged his head like a tired man. He gazed at the palms of his hands, then raised them to his face. "Wot I min iss—" Lehmann had continued, "in a psycholotchical zense."

On Mr. Shults' round face appeared a curious mocking smile. He left it there, as if unaware of it, and then, stranger still, a sound burped from his lips. A kind of sad raspberry. A soft, vulgar, despairing sound. Something he had heard behind his back in the lobby many times. Through the window they could see the waves of heat that rose from the top of a parked sedan and made the street ripple as if it were reflected in a stream. The awning over the delicatessen window seemed to blow in a draft. As if he were feeling the heat himself, Mr. Shults had leaned over and switched on his fan, placing a weight on the loose papers on his desk. Although it stirred the air in the room, it seemed to leave a gap of silence between them, but Lehmann felt strangely at ease in it, as if there by himself. He was amused, in such a curious situation, by his own peace of mind. As if he had been drinking. What explained it? He had gone for some time without food. He had passed that curious hour or two in the hotel room. His mind seemed to be both at peace and alert, as if it were disembodied from the man who had come along with it, a valet of sorts. Shults seemed to feel some of that himself, as he opened a drawer in his desk, fumbled at the back, and took out a collapsible tin cup. He walked with it to a water cooler in the back of the room.

"Dr. Lehmann," he said, "can I bring you a drink?"

Lehmann had shaken his head, and Shults had taken a long drink himself. It seemed to revive him, he smiled and said, "He was the nicest boy we've ever had," then came back to the desk and put the tin cup away.

"Thees wass Paul?" Lehmann inquired.

"When Mrs. Kahler died, following the trouble—" he paused there, then added, "there was just Paul and his brothers."

"No girls in thees vamily?" Lehmann had asked.

"Just Paul and his brothers," Shults had replied, and they had waited till a streetcar passed, the bell clanging.

"If I coot zee a pichur—" Lehmann had said, and Shults had sorted the keys on his chain, with one of them opened the bottom drawer on his desk. He took out a small photograph that was framed. He gazed at it himself, then handed it to Lehmann. It showed a group of eight or ten boys in the woods at a summer camp. Some were dark skinned, some were light, but the boy who stood in the center was like a strange bug—Lehmann had reflected—in a pair of shorts. His legs were so thin he seemed to be suspended above the ground. The long narrow face, cocked to one side, wore a pair of shell-rimmed glasses in which the eyes, large to begin with, were like those of a fish. A simple-minded smile of brotherly love glowed on his face.

"His first summer at camp," Shults said, abstractedly, his eyes blinking as he thought of it. "The next year we made him a Counselor."

Behind the row of faces Lehmann could see the word VIKINGS painted above the door of one of the cabins, and beyond the cabins a small, weedy pond. Two boys, in a flat-bottomed boat, were out on it.

"Reading from left to right—" said Shults, who seemed to have memorized the picture, "you have Domiano, Deutsch, Guagliardo, then Paul—Paul was unusually thin that summer."

"I see him," said Lehmann; then, "How did he get alonk?"

The boy beside him, a dark-skinned number, was using his fingers to make an evil face.

"You'd have to know him," said Shults. "You'd just have to know him. Everybody wondered." He leaned over for another glimpse of the picture. "I suppose they just took him for granted. He was never any different. They just took him for queer."

"He looks a little on the simple side," Lehmann had said.

"I think most Saints do," Shults had replied, so matter-of-factly that Lehmann let it pass, then realized what he had heard. He raised his eyes to where Shults stood pointing, with a pencil he had found on his desk, at the picture of a simple-minded Saint on his wall. His hands were spread out before him, and around his head hovered many small birds. Gathered at his feet were many small creatures, some known to be friendly, others unfriendly, but for the moment at peace among themselves.

"If he *had* a problem," said Shults, "I suppose it was to get them to see him as *normal*. But he grew up around here, so they finally got used to it." That reminded him of something, for he added, "That first summer at camp was quite a problem. Bedbugs, you know, and we couldn't get him to kill anything."

Lehmann nodded, then said, "How did you handle it?"

"Handle?" Shults queried. "He taught them the teachings of Jesus Christ."

The flatness of the statement presented no openings. They both reflected on it.

"And the udder poys?" Lehmann inquired.

"They came back different," Shults replied, "than they went away."

Lehmann had glanced up to see if Shults was smiling, but he had turned away. Facing the window he had said, "Dr. Lehmann, what do you do with boys who think that Christ is a curse, and Lincoln the name of a park?"

Lehmann had not replied, wanting to know what Mr.

Shults did with such boys, and he had watched him take a sheet of paper from the drawer of his desk. A yellow sheet with the faint green stripes like popcorn bags, covered with a large scrawl that showed through on both sides. "Listen to this—" Shults said, cleared his throat and began—

"—the ringworm is worse among the Friendly Indians—"

then paused to explain, "The Friendly Indians were not in Paul's cabin. Ten cabins at camp. But the Friendly Indians were one of ours." He continued—

"—worse among the Friendly Indians where Frankie Scire has it on his hands and face and Emanuel Guagliardo has it over one eye. After prayers Emanuel asked me if the salve I put on didn't kill the ringworm, and if it did kill the ringworm wasn't that killing something? I said yes, it did kill the ringworm, but that it was each according to his nature, and it was the nature of ringworm salve to kill ringworms. What was *his* nature? Emanuel asked. And I said it was *his* nature to ask questions, and it was my nature to put salve on ringworms and answer them. Then I said it was the nature of the bird to get the worm, the nature of the cat to get the bird, of the dog to get the cat, and the dogcatcher to get the dog, just as it was my nature not to get anything. He replied he never heard of a nature as silly as that. He said a nature like that would not last long enough to get the worm. I replied it wasn't any of my business how long my nature lasted, but to be what it was my nature wanted me to be. Then I slept all night, as that is also my nature, but it was his nature to lie awake and think about it, as it is the nature of little La Monica to wet his bed. I expect to have ringworm any day now myself."

When he had finished Shults returned the letter to his desk. The fan rattled the papers, and outside, somewhere, a boy with a hoarse voice called another one a bastard. There was the sound of a scuffle. Their feet could be heard in the cinder yard.

"Let me tell you a story," Shults had said, as if the noise

in the yard had led him to think of it. "One of our big problems is slot machines. The boys rob them. They make off with the money, the peanuts, and the gum. When Paul was here we had a boy named Guagliardo—the one he mentions in the letter—who headed the gang that specialized in slot machines. The first summer Paul was here they came into the lobby with a shirt full of coins. Ran to around forty or fifty dollars in pennies, I think. They came back here and got hold of Paul, took him down to the towel room with them, and there they asked him to divvy the money up. Twelve of them, and they wanted an equal cut of it. He did as they wanted, but he refused to take a cut himself. This boy Guagliardo never got over that. I don't think he cared about the principle of it, but he'd never seen a human being turn down money. He recognized it as a superior quality. He couldn't do it himself. Anyhow, he never got over it."

"They did nod laff at him?" Lehmann had asked.

"We all laughed at him," Shults replied. "Let God strike me dead, but I laughed at him myself. When you simply can't believe something, you laugh at it. Nobody believes in goodness. Goodness without recompense."

"Iss that nod the bower of efil?" Lehmann had put in. "That it iss nod so hart in wich to b'lief?"

Shults had paused to think about it.

"Dr. Lehmann—" he replied, soberly, "I used to think that evil was the great mystery. But I don't any more. Evil is not mysterious. The great mystery is goodness. It cannot be explained."

"But efil can destroy," Lehmann had replied, "efen if it iss nod so mysterious."

"But only goodness," Shults had answered, "can create."

"That iss somethink you know?" Lehmann had asked.

"It is something I believe," Shults had replied.

And then Lehmann had said, "Wot woot you gif to zee it with your own eyes?"

"I *have* seen it, Dr. Lehmann," he said, then saw that that was not the answer. He waited, and Lehmann had said,

"Wot I do nod know iss the gootness. Wot I wonder iss if efil can make it too, no?"

"What are you saying?" Shults had said.

"Iss it nod somethink?" Lehmann had said, "to make a man into a voman?"

Mr. Shults had been standing. He let himself down in the chair at his desk.

"Wot I min iss—" Lehmann went on, "wass it gootness, or wass it efil?"

Mr. Shults had raised his hands to his face as if he might weep. Cupped in the palms of his hands, when he took them away, he seemed to see the mask of his face. With one of the keys on his chain he opened a file behind his desk. He removed a large envelope, said aloud—

"Kahler, Otto—case of," in the voice of a man who no longer felt much of anything. From the folder he took a clipping, glanced at the headline, then turned from Lehmann to face the window. "Just before Christmas we had this blizzard. Snow piled up in the streets. One night Otto Kahler, who worked in the freight yards, didn't get home. He drank, sometimes, and I suspected he had got drunk. But he didn't get home for Christmas, or New Year's. Paul spoke to me, and we got in touch with the police. Sometimes a drunk would be lost till the snow started to melt. He never came home, showed up at his work, and the police knew nothing about him. In April, that year, the drifts of snow began to melt." Shults returned the clipping to the folder, then said, matter-of-factly, "I suppose, Dr. Lehmann, you know how these things are done?"

Lehmann was not sure. "Done?" he had said.

"When you find a man dead in the street," said Shults. "Or almost dead, anyhow, someone has to pick him up. If he's dead, he has to be buried—if he is not . . ."

Lehmann felt his head nodding. "One muss wade till the man hass died. Yes?" he said.

Shults agreed. As if his mouth felt dry, he carefully moistened his lips. "Dead bodies are a problem, Dr. Lehmann, since it costs money to bury them. But they are also worth money. There are people looking for them."

"Wot iss a goot pody worth?" Lehmann asked, to show his detachment.

Shults didn't seem to hear that. "There is the record of a sale," he continued, "of a body with the first joint missing, first finger, of the left hand. In the Kahler family this missing joint was quite a joke. When Otto Kahler put that finger to his ear it appeared to have entered his head." Shults paused to place his own hands, the palms up, on his desk. He did not speak for a moment, then said, "In May a medical student, who made such things a hobby, recognized the hand that he was dissecting. He put formaldehyde in his lunch pail and brought the hand to Mrs. Kahler for identification. Paul was there at the time. He left the house in the evening and was never seen again."

Lehmann had started to speak, but Mr. Shults, as if he saw in his face Lehmann's question, slowly shook his head, a smile forming on his dry lips. They would speak the words, Lehmann knew, that he usually reserved for himself.

"The faith that moves mountains, Dr. Lehmann—" he said, then remembered the twist that this faith had taken. "Such a faith finds it simple to change the nature of man."

As if that statement had changed his own, reviving him, restoring his purpose, he rose from the desk and took long, springy strides toward the door. His hand on the knob he turned and said, "I can't tell you what this means to me, Dr. Lehmann. I have kept the faith for fifteen years, and now I find it confirmed."

He had kept the faith, and with Lehmann's elbow cupped in his palm, as if he thought he might falter, he walked him down the hall to the door where he had come in. As they crossed the lobby a billiard ball shot across the floor. Mr. Shults let it roll, a warm smile on his face. He beamed at the little thug who had thrown it, his eyes sightless with Paula Kahler's luminous gaze.

Lehmann did not wait, he made for the stairs, but before the door had swung shut behind him he heard the voice, disembodied, repeating the formula. *The ball is not my ball, Vito*—it was saying—*the floor is not my floor*, but at that point the creaking door mercifully closed. Lehmann looked up to see the lights coming on in the neon wilderness.

"*Agua! Agua!*" they were yelling, and over the ring, buoyant on the draft that twirled it slowly, like a dancer, a burning newspaper dipped and soared, like a ship afire at sea. Matadors, *peones*, cameramen and policemen, the thirty thousand who had paid as well as those who hadn't, turned their eyes from the bull to watch the sparks fly upward, skittish on the draft. His own face tipped upward, Lehmann felt the prick of blowing sand on his face.

"*Agua! Agua!*" they yelled, and then the voice of Boyd, as if closing the invocation—

"*Agua, agua*, everywhere, but not a drop to drink."

Lehmann turned to see him take the Pepsi bottle he was holding, give it a violent shake.

"So you want to squirt pop, eh?" he said to the boy, and as it hissed on his thumb, blowing a froth of bubbles, the boy pumped his small head up and down. Wagging the white-tipped tail, said to be a real one, of his coonskin hat.

McKee

SHE pressed the button to run the window down, and he passed her the coffee.

"It's what they gave me when I asked for coffee," he said, and smiled, to indicate it was a joke. She didn't smile, and he said, "If you want the heater on, what you do is start up the motor. Knob right there alongside the heater is the radio." She didn't bite at that, so he said, "Lois, that boy's safer in there with the old man than he is in the bathroom of your own house." The window she had run down for the coffee, she now ran up.

McKee couldn't understand a woman—women, that is—who couldn't bear to let a child out of their sight, but who had a bathroom with enough pills to put half the state to sleep. Or like the Cronins, these friends of theirs, scared to death of this polio business, but wouldn't blink an eye when the youngster drank the water in a cocktail glass. McKee had watched the little devil, time and again, scoot around the room like a vacuum cleaner, finishing off whatever he happened to find in any glass on the floor. "Probably do him good," Mr. Cronin had said, when McKee pointed it out.

"If they don't want to come," McKee said through the window, "I may have to sit there till the business is over."

If she didn't like that, she could always say she hadn't heard what he'd said. With the palm of his hand—a Mexican boy in Monterey had showed him that one—McKee rubbed the finger marks off the glass. Inside the car it was dark. He hadn't yet puzzled out where the light switch was. Reflected in the windshield were the lights from the fires in the shadow of the bullring. *Barbecue.* It smelled good, but he didn't dare offer her any of it. Never tell what piece of it she'd get, or what animal it was. Might be that little bull Boyd had squirted with the Pepsi-Cola, or the big one that had tossed that boy like a sack. Made him think of Boyd. The way he had the beginner's sort of luck.

Anything in a circle, like a ball park, or those motorcycle bowls at the Fair, McKee liked to walk around since they always brought him back where he started from. He would walk a lot more if there were more ways of doing that. But back in Lincoln, if he walked around the block the neighbors thought he was sick and just getting up, but if he walked in one direction he ended up clear to hell and gone.

He stopped to watch a dog, a cur with hatpin eyes, put his head down in a hole for a drink of water. He'd seen a little bantam rooster, in a place called San something, chase a dog like that. And yet the same fool dog would have the nerve to stick his head into a hole. Led McKee to think of the time he had done just that himself. Stuck his head into a hole and all but had it chopped right off.

Naming his firstborn Gordon—when McKee thought of that he wondered how he could have been so crazy, so soft in the head, as to have done a thing like that. Came within an inch, God knows, of ruining his life. His mother wouldn't call him by that name, or very much else. That worked out all right for her, but the boy grew up with the idea that he was one thing to his daddy, and another to his Mom. What trouble they had with the boy, which was plenty, could probably be laid to the fact that right from the first he didn't really know *who* he was. It took him a little better than eighteen years to find out.

One reason it took so long, in McKee's opinion, was due to what happened while the boy was still a youngster. It wasn't only women who could have their intuitions, and McKee realized, when he saw Boyd that Christmas, that he would probably never turn up with a family of his own. The fact was, he never did. Much as women fell for him, there he was all by himself. The name of Gordon on other people's kids, instead of his own.

He'd always had that crazy wild streak in him—taking that ballplayer's pocket was typical of him—and it had been just like him to turn up out of nowhere at Christmas time. They hadn't seen or heard of him for eight or nine years. Gordon had been eleven, going on twelve, they had this big tree lit up in the house, although it might have been toward New Year's since most of the needles had fallen off. Right out of the blue—McKee had been down at the office—Boyd called him up. McKee could have said he was awfully busy, since he was, and it was around Christmas, but he wanted Boyd to see how far he'd come along, especially his new house. Things were really looking up; he'd bought that little Maxwell with the California top, and he wanted Boyd to see how much the kids had grown. Then too, Mrs. McKee was looking better herself, with the kids over the worst part, and the time he had seen her while she was still carrying Seward had stuck in her craw. So McKee had picked him up and driven him out to the house. Along the way he stopped to pick up a pie, since it would catch Mrs.

McKee on short notice, and he and Boyd had sat out in front of the bakery and talked a bit. That is, McKee had talked, and Boyd had just listened, which showed from which direction the wind was then blowing, since McKee, as a rule, never said a word. Anyhow, they'd just sat there, the motor running, and McKee had got the feeling, hard to say why, that Boyd had lost a lot of his bounce. He'd been taken down a notch. A rug of some sort, as they say, had been yanked from under him. McKee had guessed it was probably some woman, but he felt so good about the turn things had taken in his own life that he wanted Boyd to feel more like that himself. Which was why he said, just in passing, that the family would be so glad to see him. Especially Gordon—he had said, then waited to see the effect.

"Who?" Boyd had said, since McKee had never told him he had named his son Gordon.

"Gordon," McKee had repeated, and sometimes he wondered if he would have mentioned it at all if they'd been anywhere but sitting there in the car, with the motor running. Just the two of them, sealed off from everybody else. McKee's eyes had watered, from the way he felt, and Boyd had put out a hand and gripped his shoulder, the way he had so often done when they were kids. Then they drove over to the house, and since it was Christmas there were red and green lights over the streets in streamers, and the big evergreen in the high school yard was all lit up. McKee had never felt the spirit of Christmas, before or since, as he did at that moment, and he sometimes wondered, until that happened, if he'd known what it was.

When he pulled into the yard the kids were there in the car lights, and Gordon had run ahead to open up the garage. He was a big oversize kid like Boyd himself had been. When McKee saw him there in the lights—after what he had just been saying—he had the damdest sort of feeling that maybe he had been right. That the boy was *really* Gordon's after all. He was only McKee's boy in the sense that he fed and clothed him, kept an eye on him, but the time would come when Gordon would bring him up. So he knew it. He sensed that even before the evening began.

All the boy really knew about Gordon was that they were having a guest for supper, since he didn't know his name, or that he had been named after him. And Boyd didn't give him any special favor, he treated them all like they were his kids, and had them laughing so hard Orien couldn't finish his pie à la mode. They just couldn't help it. Mrs. McKee had nearly died laughing herself.

After supper they all moved into the parlor where he let little Orien crawl all over him, the way kids of that age do when they like someone. Mrs. McKee had been proud of her parlor, but without her having to hint or say so, Boyd pointed out how much he liked everything. When they built the new house, to go along with it Alice Morple had given them this oil painting, which showed a lone wolf standing in the snow on a winter's night. The scene was Christmas, more than likely, as there were bright lights in the farmhouse windows, which gave you the feeling of how warm it was inside, and how cold it was out. They had that framed over the fireplace with a sheet of glass to protect it, and Boyd pointed out how much her own house was warm and cozy like that. It wasn't lost on her that he probably felt like the wolf himself.

Later they put Orien to bed, but as a special dispensation, since they saw Boyd so seldom, Mrs. McKee let Seward and Gordon stay up. Boyd had been almost everywhere since they had seen him, and McKee led the talk around to that, it being the sort of thing boys like to hear. He made it seem as though the Leaning Tower was right there in the room, about to fall on you. He didn't talk just to Gordon, but

since Gordon was older, and in certain ways smarter, it was
natural that he absorbed a little more of it. He got so
wrapped up listening he didn't even notice his leg had gone
to sleep. McKee did, since he could see his toes wiggling, as
if they were wet inside of his shoes, but that boy was so
smart he didn't want to let on that anything was wrong. In
particular, that any part of him had fallen asleep.

They had traveled all over the world that night, and
about ten thirty, when Seward got a little sleepy, Mrs.
McKee had to tell them both that it was time for bed. McKee
had felt sure that they would have trouble with Gordon,
but he didn't make a peep. He seemed to be off in some of
those far places where Boyd had been. Seward came forward, like a little man, and shook Boyd's hand, telling him
good night, then Gordon had got up, and before they could
stop him had thrown his arms around Boyd's neck. He had
hugged him like crazy, kissed him two, three times, then
turned and run off.

Right up till then there hadn't been a misfire. It had been
out of this world. But when he hugged and kissed Boyd like
that—something he had never done to his mother and
father—Mrs. McKee had got as red as if Boyd had kissed
her himself. As red, if not redder, than the time he did.
After what McKee had been saying and thinking, it was
such a strange thing that he felt a little spooky, as if he was
a stranger of some sort in his own house. The boy had done
it, McKee was sure, just the way that Boyd had once kissed
his mother, because right at that point he simply couldn't
help it, she had been so beautiful. He couldn't either. And
he was just like Boyd in that respect.

But the damage was done. They all just sat there until
Mrs. McKee put down her sewing, as if she suddenly felt
sick, and got up and left the room. Then Boyd had hopped
up, reached for his coat, and before he had it on was out on

the porch, although he had come out with the intention of staying for the night. McKee had helped him get his other arm in the sleeve, where he could see the lining was torn out, then he went off without either of them having said anything. McKee had just stood there, the sky so bright and cold it was hard for him to look at it, and for four or five minutes he could hear the iron creak of Boyd's shoes in the snow. Like that wolf in the picture he had moved in close, then he had turned and run off.

Music—if that was what it was—led McKee to wheel around and look behind him. A whirring sound. At the front of a café called *La Casa de Usted*. On a raised platform near the entrance there were ten or twelve people, maybe more, some of them sitting, some standing, but all of them making this whirring noise. Mostly violins. But he could also see a row of boys with guitars. Two little girls, their long hair in braids, sat with something like zithers in their laps, plucking the strings with what looked like long steel finger nails. The noise was considerable. McKee listened, but seemed to miss the gist of it. He counted fourteen, all of them working away like so many little beavers, but without a living soul in the restaurant. Was it practice? All of them seemed to know their parts. But the only person who was listening was McKee himself. It sort of gave him the willies, like a movie he had seen years and years ago, when he was a boy, featuring an orchestra that was going down with a sinking ship. They had gone on playing to cheer up the dancers, but the dancers had all left, and then the orchestra had gone on playing just for themselves. That was how they looked, not scared at all, but resigned for what was in store, the little girls at the front aware of this as much as the rest. They looked, McKee thought, as if they had never been young. They were sad and resigned in the same way as the old. The noise they made was meant to be gay, full of string plucking and all kinds of whirring, but behind it all McKee could hear the life boats being lowered. They were going down, without a whimper, with the ship.

So was McKee. He stood rooted to the spot as if waiting for the floor to tip, the water to rise, when the noise, as suddenly as it began, whirred to a stop. There they sat as if the boat had sunk, and they had sunk with it. Would all be found in their places when the men with the diving helmets came along? It gave McKee the willies—he turned and went off not caring what direction, just to be going, and when he heard the roar in the air above him he began to run. They roared again. He caught the *ole*, which meant that he was missing something, but it had nothing to do with why he kept going, or the music he went on hearing, or the fact that he came within an ace of killing himself. Hit one of those cables they used to prop a pole up, went over on his face. Didn't kill him though, he got up the way that boy did in the bullring, thinking he was dead but surprised to find he wasn't, just light on his feet. He leaned there on the cable, catching his wind, and saw that he was almost back to where he'd started, and there across the street he could see the Terre Haute people talking to his wife. Funny what the sight of his own kind of people did to him. Cleared his head like seltzer; he calmed right down, and except for the sweat all over his body, and that bruise on his leg, he felt about as good as new. He lit the second of those two cigars he had bought, and without further mishap went around to the gate.

Mrs. McKee

SHE thought it must be planes—those you have to look ahead of the noise for—but just as she looked ahead, her forehead pressed to the windshield, she saw the lights come on. Up on the rim of the bullring, where the roar came from; but when she ran down the window to listen, the roar stopped.

Were the lights what they wanted? Had it got so dark in there they were yelling for lights? She could believe it—like people everywhere, they tried to get what they wanted by yelling for it. McKee among them. If she wasn't there with him he would yell himself hoarse.

It simply hadn't crossed her mind she would be leaving the boy where it might get dark. McKee would be there, but what good was McKee? He had been there—right there on the porch—the night everything had happened. That silly smile on his face. Bewitched even more than she had been herself. She *did* have a reason, after all. If Boyd had been to her what she was to McKee, and if he had then kissed Alice Morple, it would have been the last time he ever set foot on the Scanlon porch. Bewitched or not. She had said as much to Alice Morple who had smiled smugly, then said that she didn't see a person like Gordon Boyd wasting his time on a *porch*.

"What in the world do you mean?" she had replied. She knew perfectly well, but wanted to hear her say so. They were sleeping together on the screened-in porch at the back of the house.

"If you think you're *still* bewitched," Alice Morple had said, "I wouldn't sleep out here alone on this screened porch."

That had done it. In many ways it had done it more than the kiss. They were sleeping on that porch at the back of the house where Alice Morple, in her tomboy phase, had once shinnied up, and out in back was the lawn swing, painted white, and her sister's rabbit hutch full of big white rabbits she could see in the moonlight, and hear thumping the hutch. After that last remark she had pretended to sleep, but her mind had been in such a whirl that she couldn't. And yet she *had* dreamed. That much was certain, if nothing else. They were lying on this bed—the one they folded up and put in the basement over the winter—Alice Morple on the inside, she on the outside where the screens were hooked. When she was just a little girl she would unhook the screens and feed the squirrels that came to the roof.

So there they were—the sky so light it might have been almost dawn, but probably wasn't, because of the feeling she had that she had never before been up for so long. Then she had dozed off—there was no other explanation—and according to Alice Morple, who hadn't, she sat up in bed as though someone had called her name—and unhooked the screen. Alice Morple said she sat up and did it in a way that left *her* covered with duck bumps. She would have sworn there was someone on the roof, just waiting, that she couldn't see herself. That was Alice Morple, of course, prone as she was to exaggeration, but the fact was that somebody did unhook the screen. It wasn't likely Alice Morple, since the hook was far out of her reach. A disturbance like that, besides, would have waked them both. It had not been Alice Morple for the simple reason that Lois Scanlon knew she had done it herself. She had dreamed of doing just that, and that was what she did. She had done it when a man climbed to the roof—the roof of her dream, that is—said "Open up, sweetheart," and she had opened up. A moment later—just long enough later for the man who had spoken to have crawled through the window—the bed on which they were both sleeping collapsed. A simple statement of fact.

Fold-away beds do that all the time if they are put up badly, or have some extra weight on them, but they had already slept on that bed for two nights. Why then did it collapse? More weight had been added to it.

She couldn't say another body—there was no real proof that another body had been on the bed—but this weight had been there, and that had been enough. Did it seriously matter if all of that was described as a dream? In this dream the bed had broken down under the weight of what had come through the window—it did not break down, that is, *then* give birth to the dream. The dream began farther back, *away* back, but happily it ended when the bed collapsed. Otherwise—but never mind about *that*. Alice Morple had been lying right there beside her, and observed her sit up, as if she had heard a voice, and open the screen—and then the bed, mercifully, had collapsed.

Alice Morple had cried out—and both Roy and Agnes had come running down the hall, her Uncle Roy with a flashlight, but she did not speak when they called out her name, or flashed the light in her face. She seemed to be, they all said, in another world. Well, she was. She would have sworn it was Boyd, and not Alice Morple, there at her side. The foot of the bed had collapsed—where the screen flapped open—and her Uncle Roy had flashed his light on it, then leaned over and hooked it shut again. Alice Morple had been kind enough not to bring the matter up. The weight of the dream had collapsed that bed just the way it could be said that dreams weighed on people, bending them over till they broke under the weight—like the bed.

That much was known and witnessed. The rest she kept to herself. Alice Morple had been too flighty and jealous to be trusted with it.

When she read of those people at spiritualist meetings who weighed half again as much as or less than they should have, she knew in her mind that the scales were right, and the skeptics were wrong. She had once undergone such a change herself. Under the weight of a dream she had once collapsed a bed.

Was it any wonder that her feet, at the time, hadn't been on the ground? Where *was* the ground? What were the plain facts? One fact was, the plainest of all, that a girl could be swept off her feet, and in the plainest sort of way never be quite the same again. If McKee hadn't been there—"Honey," Alice had said, "no bed is going to collapse with *him* in it"—if McKee hadn't been there she might have settled for anything. Any Tom, Dick or Harry before she did something queerer than unhook the screen. Or before something more substantial than a dream collapsed her bed. Somewhere she had once read in the *Reader's Digest* of girls who thought that a kiss might give them a baby—but it was not at all as silly or as strange as some people seemed to think. Not if one of them had been kissed by a man like Boyd. And this kiss followed up by a dream that would collapse a bed.

If they pooh-poohed that, and some people surely would, take the boy that McKee himself had fathered, but was no more like him than if he had been the son of the moon. If he was like any human on earth, it was Gordon Boyd. Being his mother she was not free to say if the effect he produced on other women was like that, but the moment his eyes were there on *her* level, it seemed the same. When he acted in that play Boyd himself had written, and tried to walk on the water, there were girls in the audience who *swooned* when they heard he had drowned. Nobody needed to tell her what the dreams of some of those girls were like. Or of the beds that collapsed. Wasn't it possible that the bed was right? That it knew, just the way she did, and just the way that McKee himself did; otherwise would he have acted like a madman and given the child *his* name. *Gordon*. The name of his first-born son. Anybody would think that he had been having stranger dreams than her own.

And then when they had—according to McKee—finally straightened out their boy, Gordon—what did he do when his own son came along? Make an end of it? Not on your life. The first child had been born within the year, and Gordon was his name.

There would never be an end of it—there would be this new Gordon, he would have others, and they would have Gordons, all of them like him, all of them the same in the sense that you would never put an end to it. She hadn't. McKee hadn't. And now their own son had come up with this new one. The Scanlon jaw—she could speak for that, and the eyes wide apart in his face—but it was neither Scanlon nor McKee who looked out of them. It was Boyd. They would never put an end to a look like that.

One day—and it would not be too long, not the way he was growing and customs were changing—one day he would kiss a girl and the props in her life would collapse.

Jittery and bewitched, she might even marry him. Not that it mattered. The crazy dream would weigh her down. She would unhook the screen, or if she didn't she would marry McKee, a pollen-bearer, and the first-born son wouldn't look like one of his own. No reason it should. Gordon would be his name. The tapping—she almost made a face, McKee *always* tapped at her; but there at the window was Mrs. Leon Ordway, of Terre Haute. She ran the window down and Mrs. Ordway said—

"Now if that wasn't smart. To come here and just *sit*. Now if that wasn't smart."

"If we hadn't done that climbing, yesterday—" she replied, as Mrs. Ordway had taken the pyramid excursion with her. But she hadn't climbed. *When I get up like that,* she had said, *it makes me want to jump.*

"Well, you've seen it, anyhow," said Mr. Ordway.

"Is it nearly over?" she asked.

"They go on till they kill everything and everybody," said Mrs. Ordway. Mr. Ordway turned, his head cocked, to hear the swelling roar.

"Sounds like another touchdown, Irene," he said, just the way McKee would have said it.

"I thought you came down here to get away from that?" Mrs. Ordway replied.

The roar came again.

"Kicked the goal, too," Mr. Ordway said.

Scanlon

W HAT did they want now? He could hear them yelling for it. On the sand before him, cold but looking hot, was the light that cast no shadow, and up on the rim burned the sun that never set. He felt right at home. It was Hell, and they all might as well shut up.

It was Hell, all right, since he didn't leave a track, just a greasy spot. When he put out his hand he could see the water in him drying out. But he didn't really care about that so much, or whether there was or wasn't any water, so much as he cared about what time it was. Had he been lost in Hell for a long time, or was it short? Since he couldn't tell the time, he had no way of knowing when he ought to give up. Where there was no time, how was he to know when he had done what he could? So he just wandered around—he couldn't say if he did it for a short time, or a long one—until he stumbled on this body lying in the sand. The body of a man. One who had been dead for some time. But dead as he was, a ghostly music came out of his mouth. It was the wind that made it, he didn't, and it was a wild hollow sound, like a shell, as if it curled around and around in his head before it came out. When Scanlon tapped on his shoulder he could hear him rattle like peas in a gourd. There was just enough wind to give him this voice, make a faraway music in his mouth, and stir the crisp yellow hairs on his head. Scanlon had the feeling he had seen him somewhere, and he had. The crisp yellow beard was his own. The dead man was himself.

Was it possible? To tell the truth, he had suspected it. There were two men within him, and he knew for sure that one of them had died. The better man? The one who had survived would agree to that. The dead man had died because he knew where he was, and had died of it. There was no grease in him now, nor water on his knee, nor lean stringy meat for Mrs. Norton, but Scanlon could see that the dead man had left his mark. The tracks he had made in Hell were not just grease spots. They had come in and stopped where he did. They didn't go out. But it was not the same sort of Hell, with tracks in it, anymore than Scanlon was the same sort of man, now that he knew who had died, and what time it was.

Was he crazy with the heat? It didn't seem to really matter, in case he was. He took a good look at the dead man, his better self, who not only knew where he was, but died from it, then he went off in the tracks the dead man had left in the sand. These tracks went up the canyon Scanlon had come down to where he found the wagons, right where he had left them, with the men still asleep around the dead fire. Until he woke them and said so, none of them had known that he had been away. Nor would any of them believe him, when he told them he had been to Hell. They said that he was worse than crazy. They said that what he meant to do was lead them into a trap. Mr. Baumann said he'd feared that from the first, since he was so young, and so much stronger than they were, and what he had in mind was to have Mrs. Norton all to himself. Mr. Criley said he knew that to be the truth, but that Mrs. Norton had nothing to fear since he and Mr. Baumann would protect her from a fate worse than death. They told her to put on what she wanted to save, and they would see that she got where she was going.

At one time Mrs. Norton had been so plump her diamond rings were tight on her fingers, but she had got so skinny they rattled on her fingers when she ate. Her hands were so thin she managed to pull on five pairs of gloves. In the fingers of the gloves, as though her knuckles were broken, they could see all of her rings, the way her bony knees and shoulders stuck out in the dresses she wore. On her head were all her hats, piled up so high that her face, like everything else, looked like something that had been stored away in her trunk. All she could wear was one pair of shoes, but on her spindly legs she got all of her stockings, with the garters hanging down like fancy boot tops to her shoes. She didn't look real—there was so little but clothes that Mr. Baumann could lift her, weak as he was, like a little girl and set her on the back of the ox. Then they went off, with Mr. Baumann on one side, Mr. Criley on the other; but Scanlon had the feeling such a sight would freeze Hell over—if they got to it. They went off toward Hell, but seeing how it looked from the bottom of the canyon, they skirted around it, since the Devil didn't want them any more than the Lord. And the thing about Hell was that you had to go in, if what you wanted was out.

But he didn't talk about Heaven or Hell, except to himself. They had to be seen to be believed, and even after what he'd seen he still had his doubts. So all he said was that they had to go in, if what they wanted was out. They had gone off and left him with the women and children, an old ox named Brigham, and Reverend Tennant who was so weak he couldn't walk. He put the Reverend on the donkey, the older women and the kids on the ox, and he and Miss Samantha walked up front. He wasn't any too sure when they started they would reach Hell, but they did.

They got about half way—that is, they got to where that dead man should have been, but he wasn't—just a hole in the sand with the bottom of another man sticking out. That man was Mr. Criley, what was left of him since he had dug this hole in the sand, crawled into it, then tried to pull the hole in after him. He didn't answer when they called him, and they couldn't budge him since he fit it like a cork. He made his own wind, but the faraway music didn't come from his mouth.

A little further on they found Mr. Baumann, who had started a hole for himself, but he was still too fat, thinned out though he was, to squeeze into it. He had his snout into it, as if he smelled water, and the skin had been worn from the ends of his fingers. In a pile behind him were the rocks and sand that he'd thrown up between his legs, like a dog.

A little further on they found what was left of the ox. It wasn't much, since what little meat he had on him had been chewed off. It didn't need to be cooked, since the sun that never set had baked it right on his bones, and he had been done to a turn while he was alive, and just walking along.

A little further on they thought they could see the big sleek cat that had eaten the ox, but it turned out to be Mrs. Norton in her party dress. The velvet looked as shiny and sleek as a panther in the sun. One of her bony hands, with a glove still on it, had stringy bits of ox meat stuck to it, and some of the hair, like a mustache, had dried to her upper lip. No one had taken the rings from her fingers, the money from the purse at her throat, or the gold from the extra teeth she had brought along.

A lot farther on—but not so far they didn't make it—they found water cupped in a rock, and one of those little six sided stones at the bottom of it. And that evening, for the first time, it got cool and dark. The bolt hole of a sun that wouldn't go down, went down, and went out. But he said they had better go on, while it was cool, and they kept moving through a night that was longer, or maybe the word was shorter, than the day had been. When it grew light it wasn't off behind them, where they thought the sun should come up, but far up ahead, like a beacon, and they went toward it. They came out right smack on the trail they had once left. Then they got to Mountain Meadow, where there was food and water, and Reverend Tennant recovered enough to give thanks to the Lord for bringing them alive through the jaws of Hell.

That was how he described it, and Scanlon didn't feel like arguing with him. He had to be a little tactful, at that point, since he had to ask him for the hand of Samantha, and then turn right around and ask him to marry them. Which he did. He declared them man and wife. A little crazy with the heat, Scanlon may have got one or two things wrong, and not remembered others, but there was never any doubt in his mind about one thing.

"Boy—" he said, nudging the kid in the ribs, "what's the shortest way to where you're goin'?"

"To squirt pop, or to heaven?" replied the boy.

Scanlon didn't answer. He did not wag his head, nor blink his eyes.

"If you mean heaven," said the boy, seeing that he did, "the shortest way to it is straight through hell."

Scanlon said nothing. After a moment he said, "Hmmmmmphh."

"I tell you—" said the boy, "about Davy Crockett?" Scanlon waited, and the boy sang—

> *"He feared no man, he feared no beast,*
> *And hell itself he feared the least."*

"And see you don't forget it," Scanlon croaked.

"Okay," said the boy.

Boyd

SLOW it up," he said aloud, and closed his eyes.

A succession of *oles,* each one higher, like an object tossed in a blanket. But how slow it up? He opened his eyes and watched the bull make his charge. The man erect as a post, heels and calves together, his entire body exposed to the horns since he held the cloth in his left hand, the bull charging from the right. A pass called the *natural.* The most dangerous and beautiful. No ass wiggling, no fancy footwork, no sleight of hand with the cloth or cunning. A moment of grace when both man and bull were sure of themselves. The illusion of an irresistible force wheeling around an immovable object. A mere nothing. A man armed with a cloth.

What did it? What charm, craft or cunning dominated the bull? In his mind's eye—if he turned the flow backward, bull and cloth flowing away from one another—Boyd could see the still point where the dance was. The man rooted to it. From this point hung the cloth that blew in the draft, or quivered like flesh. The bull could understand movement, but not its absence, the man could understand both movement and its absence, and in controlling this impulse to move, the still point, he dominated the bull. Except for the still point there would be no dance. The cloth, not the sword, brought the bull to heel. The moment of truth was at that moment, and not at the kill.

Boyd glanced at Lehmann, the old man's forehead damp with the praise of perspiration. Fear and trembling, nervous indigestion, the attraction and repulsion of anticipation that a false movement would turn to boredom and fatigue. After the elevation, the drop. The orphic sense of premonition, of transformation, suddenly botched. The fever in the blood, the mood of excitement like the charged air in a jet's slip, suddenly stale as the fly-droning air at the back of a slaughterhouse. The letdown. The sour prospect of murder in cold blood.

Ask the young man Da Silva, recently gored, or the bull Traguito, recently killed. So many words. But words had brought them together, and words indicated what had happened. Words wheeling around the still point, the dance, the way the bull wheeled around the bullfighter, the way the mind wheeled around the still point on the sand. Each man his own bullfighter, with his own center, a circle overlapped by countless other circles, like the pattern of expanding rings rain made on the surface of a pond. How many had been traced on the sand of the bullring that afternoon? Two at least. He turned to look at the non-still point at his side.

"Can we go now?" said the boy, and sniffled. Across his nose, from left to right, he dragged the sleeve of his Davy Crockett jerkin, leaving the mica-like trail of a snail on his cuff.

Back. That took Boyd back to the raw chapped smear under his own nose, the mackinaw with the crust of ice on the right-hand sleeve. *That* boy didn't sleep too well, when he sniffled, and in the room with the goiter oven he would gaze at the plain, white and rimless as a polar sea. Corn, in shocks like tepees, stood in the neighbor's field. The climate and the soil out there favored corn. So it was said. But the big crop, as the boy could tell you, was an easier one to harvest. The bumper crop was fiction and romance. That was where the dance was. From that still point the mind rippled out.

"So you've had enough, eh?" Boyd said, and placed his hand on the coonskin hat. What sort of dance stirred beneath it? What sort of fizz was trying to squirt out? At the moment a miniature frontier hero, one of Disney's rubber-stamp midgets, chewing on the non-poisonous paint on the barrel of his gun. Any danger? No, the dangerous elements had been removed. From both the paint and the gun. It was safe, now, to chew on both of them. The way the coon had been removed from the coonskin hat, the way the Crockett had been removed from the frontier pants, the way Ty Cobb had been removed from the autographed baseballs, gloves and bats. These things were safe now. They wouldn't poison you, bite you, or fight back. The strangest transformation of all, that is, had taken place. The ends were all there—hats, pants, and baseballs—but deprived of their proper function. They did not transform the head they found beneath, they did not enlarge the heart. They were there, but they were no longer *possessed*. What had happened? The neatest trick of the week. All that one had to do to tame the bull was remove the risks. Along with the means, that is, the meaning dropped away from it. Instead of bulls, prime rib on the hoof; instead of Crockett, nurseries full of records; instead of frontiers, a national shortage of coonskin hats. The transformation to end all transformations had taken place. One had the object. One wondered what the hell to do with it.

"Kid—" said Boyd, giving a twist to the head, "how about me and you taking a walk on the water?"

"You don't walk on water," said the boy, soberly. "You *swim* in it."

Naturally. And if you don't swim, you stay clear of it. To eliminate the risks, you simply didn't run them. You *were* something. You stopped this goddam hazardous business of *becoming* anything. Such as a failure. Or a bad example. Or something worse. You *were* rich, or you *were* famous, you were John D. Rockefeller without the oil empire, Davy Crockett without the Indians, and the movie starlet without the suicide. You eliminated, that is, the amateur. He ran the risks, he made all the errors, he forgot his lines and got the girls in trouble, and in every instance he lacked the professional touch. The object was to *be* the champ, not to *meet* him. That entailed risk.

Saliva—a flow of saliva the flavor of the gun barrel the boy was chewing—led Boyd to shake the pop bottle he was holding, take a swallow of it. Dead as well. The life had gone out of it.

"Don't it squirt?" the boy asked.

"It's deader—" Boyd said, and ruled out one comparison, sought for another. Looking at the boy's hat he said, "It's deader right now than that coonskin hat."

The boy wiped it from his head to look at it. Had he thought it was alive?

"It's a *real* one," he said. "It's not a phony."

"Is that so?" said Boyd. "How do you know?"

The boy stroked the real tail on it, and said, "It cost more. It cost four dollars."

"That's how you can tell?" said Boyd.

The boy did not answer. He didn't like the change of tone. He gazed at Boyd wondering in what way he was being used.

"When I buy your scalp for my belt," said Boyd, "will I know it's real by the wampum it costs me?"

He followed that. He combed his hand through his own thick patch of hair. Did it feel like *real* hair? Uh-huh. He looked it.

"How will I *know*," said Boyd, holding his advantage, "if it's *your* scalp, or your granpa's?"

The boy lowered his hand with a jerk, stroked the tail of the hat. Did he detect some change? He seemed to. In the small head Boyd could hear the wheels at work. Had the word *scalp* he had used been a little too strong? Did it bring up some picture, some comic-book scene of men without scalps swapping them for coonskins? He looked worried.

"That was just a way of putting it," Boyd said, and gave his head a shake to break up the picture. But it stayed. He did not change the intensity of his gaze. The eyes did not question Boyd, or focus on him, but looked into his own as if to see behind them. Turning away, Boyd detected a change in himself. A big one. The real change-over in his life.

In New York he had often watched children, spied on them, that is, since it seemed to him that children, and only children, led passionate lives. The life, that is, that Boyd— once a prodigy of action—no longer lived himself. They struck out blindly, they laughed and cried, they cheated, hooted, looted and lied to one another, were cruel and loving, heartless and generous, at the same time. They represented the forces he felt submerged in life. All the powers that convention concealed, the way the paving concealed the wires in the street, the sewage and the waste, were made visible. The flow of current that kept the city going, the wheels turning, the lights burning, and the desires that made peace impossible in the world.

But what had troubled Boyd was not what he saw, but

that what he felt struck him as beautiful. Was it possible? Like the bullfight, he kept coming back to it. What he saw might be vulgar or cruel, botched like the amateur's kill in the bullring, but the passion behind it, the force in the blow, the absurd risks, the belief in lost causes, had in it something that struck him as beautiful. What was it? Until he saw a bullfight, he didn't know. There he saw that the running of the small fry was the first running of the bulls. Every day a fresh collection of gorings, heroes, and the burial of the dead. The kindly matron who would faint at the mention of a bullfight, would sit at Boyd's side, beaming like Paula Kahler, and watch the small fry strew gore on the battlefield.

Had that been all? No, he might have made his peace with that. But one day, on a bench near the playground, he dozed off. When he awoke the bullring was empty, the swings and teeter-totters idle, but a small child leaned against the heavy wire fence, her eyes to one of the holes. So absorbed with what she saw, or what she thought she saw, she gazed into Boyd's face as if he were blind. As if she could see into his eyes, but he could not see out of them. He felt himself—some self—in the midst of a wakeful dream. Had he dozed off with his own eyes wide open, seeing nothing? Had this child stood there for some time, gazing in? This child—for that was all she was, a soiled-faced, staring little monkey—seemed to have seen in him what Boyd could not see himself. What she saw moved her to pity. Pity seemed to be all she felt. But what *Boyd* saw, and what *he* felt, was something else. He could not seem to close the eyes that she stood gazing in. He could not speak to her, smile or wink, or indicate to her that *he* was now present. He could do nothing. If the child had run up the blind on his true *self*, he could not run it down. He seemed to be fixed, with his eyes wide open, a freshly mounted trophy with the pupils of the eyes frozen open so the passer-by could look in.

Had he been mad? For the length of that moment he might have been. Or had he been—as he had come to think—for once in his life sane. Able to see, at that moment, from the other side. Behind appearances, such as the one he made himself. Eagle Scout Boyd, the pocket snatcher, turned inside out like a stocking, so that the underside of the stitching showed. The wing of madness had passed over Boyd so closely he had felt the cool fan of it on his forehead.

"Son—" Boyd said, but the boy had turned his gaze, if not his mind, to the pair in the bullring. The bull, drained of his purpose, the head low now, the tongue hanging like a clapper, stood like a man with his hands tied behind him, waiting for the *coup de grâce*. The matador stepped back, cocked his right knee like a trigger, sighted down the curved sword as down the barrel of a squirrel gun, holding at arm's length before him, so low it grazed the sand, the red cloth. He held the sword in his right, but it would be the left hand that killed the bull. If his eye followed the cloth, that is, the bull would kill himself. Which he did; man and bull flowing together, the curved sword disappeared into the bloody hump, and on that peak the youth pivoted out of the curve of the horns.

The bull? Boyd thought he looked astonished. He had the air of a man who did not know what had hit him. He looked around, now that it was gone, for the cloth. Where was it now? A water-stained rag over the arm of the youth. Whatever life or magic it had, gone from it. And so it was, even as he stood wondering, with the bull. Cloth and bull, now that their work was done, empty of the power that had transformed them, at the moment that power had reached its highest pitch.

They watched the bull take one step forward, then drop. The matador stepped back, his right hand raised as in an attitude of benediction, and the bull, as if resting in the manger, his fore-legs folded catlike beneath him, looked pastoral. With the dagger used for the *coup de grâce* the peon sliced off one ear, then the other, and holding them like a torch the young hero began his tour of the ring.

W INESKINS, flowers, coats, hats and cigars were tossed
into the bullring, like so many golden apples, the young man
pausing to throw back a hat or a coat, keep a cigar. One of
the wineskins he caught, held it over his head, and let the
blood-red wine spill into his mouth. Bull's blood. White
wine at such a moment unthinkable. He passed below, and
on his beardless face, blood-smeared where his hand had
swiped it, Lehmann saw the expression of a youth who had
kicked the winning goal. Behind him, on the luminous sand,
the body of the bull cast no shadow, and where he had bled
one of the ring attendants tidied up. Shovel and broom. The
enduring nature of the aftermath.

Once more the mules, once more the music, once more
the slaughtered bull and feted hero, once more the horn and
as the gates swung open, once more the bull. Dark as if he
wore the cloak of a villain. Almost black. In the fading light
one could hardly be sure whether it was man or beast. One
could not be too careful. Dusk in the windy labyrinth.

One of the *peones* offered the cape and Lehmann
watched the white horns, as if disembodied, make a scythe-

like cut through the air, a broomlike swish. He heard the scrape of sand when the bull skidded, dropped to his knees. Then the wind-born whoosh of the cape as it rose into the air again. Not unlike the drapes—were they yellow?—at the back of Lehmann's apartment, blowing in the draft when Paula Kahler opened the door. Blowing in, always in, from the breeze off the East River, over Paula Kahler who liked to sleep in a draft. Over her body, that is, asleep and snoring, but not touching Paula Kahler. Where was she? She slept with wide-open eyes. It was only what she saw in her sleep that troubled her. Those luminous eyes, so serene in the light, flickered wildly at night as if the river draft fanned them, the whites showing like the moist knuckle of a bone. What did they see? They seemed to see the far country she had left. The lobby where the billiard balls rolled across the floor of her mind.

One moonlit night, awakened by her snoring, Lehmann had gone in to turn her on her side, but he had stopped in the doorway when he saw that her eyes were wide. She lay out like a corpse, her body wrapped in its winding sheet. The staring, sightless eyes had made him uneasy—he had the sensation that they must be drying, a film forming, like the isinglass film on the eyes of market fish. But he was still in the doorway when she suddenly cried out *help!*

There had been no mistaking the word, or the fact that she needed it. Gulped it out, as if choking, a last cry before going under, and he had felt that the corpse had spoken of the life beyond the grave. Needing *help.* So that both sides of life were the same. HELP WANTED was the big need in both of them. There was no trap door, no escape through a hole in the floor, or a door in the ceiling, on earth as it was in heaven and hell, a man needed help. This was his human condition. This was the basis of his brotherhood.

Lehmann had gone back to bed, but not to sleep, troubled

with the need for help himself, wondering how many times, in his sleep, he had cried for it. It was a need shared by all men. No one was spared, no one was saved, none had a corner or a concrete shelter where the need of HELP would not one day raise its head. Each according to his nature—no matter what his nature—needed help. Saint Paula Kahler, who had changed one world, still burned with need in the world she had changed, and needed even more help in the new world, rather than less.

To the question, *Where was Paula Kahler?* a simple answer. Everywhere. Everywhere that any living thing needed help. Among those who knew it, like Lehmann and Shults, among those who feared it, like Boyd and the McKees, and among those who knew as little as the fly that had dropped on Lehmann's chest. Few would need it so badly they would change their nature for it, but all of them would one day advertise for it. Under HELP WANTED. Both the fly and Paula Kahler. One world they shared was that. One groggy fly was not much, he himself could be held lightly, but his need for help made him heavy. When he fell, as he had on Lehmann, it was with that added weight. An ounce added to the world's sum total of helplessness. But the creature adding to it the most was not the fly, but Man himself.

The night that Lehmann and Boyd had come over from Toluca, driving late, through fog and rain in the mountains, they had come around a curve to see the lights of Mexico. Boyd had pulled the car to one side of the road. After two weeks of darkness, of lightless cities, the spectacle was not like those back where they had come from. It looked like magic. A bowl of light not made by man.

"You ever see a sight like that?" Boyd had asked, and Lehmann had said no, he hadn't, although, in a way of speaking, he once had. Not spread out in a valley like that, but trapped in his own head. The spectacle of the goings-on in his own mind. A labyrinth of lights, perhaps millions of them, so that it beggared any description, flickering with the current of every sensation, the pulse of every thought. A milky way in a rhythmic, cosmic dance, evolving and dissolving, assembling and dissembling, a loom of light where each impulse left its mark, each thought its ornament, each sentiment its motif in the design. A simple human mind, not really his own since he had inherited most of it, like luggage, and had possibly worn out more of the linen than he had acquired. A mind that went back, that is, to the beginning, that in order to think had to begin at the beginning, since every living cell did what it had once done, and nothing more. It was *there*, then the word came, and it multiplied. In this manner the juices percolating in Lehmann, in the mind loaned to him that he tried to look after, had the same bit of froth on it that flecked the primordial ooze. So long as he lived and breathed he was connected, in a jeweled chain of being, with that first cell, and the inscrutable impulse it seemed to feel to multiply. On orders. Always on orders from below, or from above. The final cause erected the scaffold, ran the tubing up through the framework, then called a halt when something like Lehmann finally emerged. And in the bubble at the top, flickering with smog lights, this spectacle that taxed the imagination, that is, the luminous jelly that spread like a salve over the spectacle itself. Lights. Untold millions of flashing lights. In the suburbs of the mind, the roof brain, this activity was the greatest, a switchboard where countless connections were established, with or without calls.

The *thinking* organ? So one would suppose. But if that pipe line to the lower quarters was broken, if the cables with the wiring were severed, *all* thinking ceased. Everything was there as before, but nothing came out of it. Some connection with the *first* cell had been destroyed, the cable that carried the protozoic orders, the word from the past, and without this word there was no mind. It seemed to be that simple. There was no mind if the lines to the past were destroyed. If the mind, that is, was nothing but itself. A cybernetic marvel in which the current could not be turned on. There had to be connections, the impulse had to ooze its way through light years of wiring, *against* the current, since the current determined the direction. It established the odds. It was why Leopold Lehmann had emerged at all. Why he was as he was, criminal by nature, altruistic and egocentric by nature, merciless and pitiful by nature, but up there at the front of the bull, forked on his horns, as well as wagging his tail. In Leopold Lehmann the inscrutable impulse was reaching for the light. As it was in Paula Kahler. As it was in the species with the bubble at the top. But the thrust, even in reaching for the light, must come from behind. Out of the shoulders of the bull, on the horns of this dilemma, against the current that must always determine his direction, in reaching for more light man would have to risk such light as he had. It was why he needed help. It was why he had emerged as man. It was according to his nature that he was obliged to exceed himself.

"Why the hell *aren't* things as they seem?" Boyd had asked, and waved his hand at the valley of lights. Beneath them, as they knew, they would find a spectacle of a different sort. It seemed a good question. Lehmann had been slow to answer it. The flickering lights in his mind, once he closed his eyes, seemed to increase. Some of the darker corners of the world's sorrows appeared to light up. A rhythmic volley of questions and answers left tracers of light. The mind of Leopold Lehmann, the human switchboard, the man who re-established the broken connections

—was he the one to throw light on why things were so seldom what they seemed?

And why weren't they?

They were not *meant* to be. They were meant to seem different—each according to the nature that was capable of seeing, behind the spectacle of lights, the constellation in his own roof brain. The universe in the process of being made. Each man his own, each universe unique, the darker reaches opaque with clouds of cosmic dust, or spectral in the light of old suns growing cold, new suns growing hot. Here and there in the mind's sky, without warning, exploding nova like Paula Kahler, lighting up the far reaches, the space curve ahead, the spine curve behind. Emerging and dissolving patterns of meaning, seeding the world's body with cosmic rays that each according to his nature would absorb, resist, or lightly dust off. Each according to his lights, such as they were, if and when they came on.

"*Luz!*" they were yelling. "Light! More light!" and when it came, high on the rim of the bowl, they stood and cheered for themselves, as if their yelling had brought it about.

"*Mehr licht*," Lehmann said, softly, and let his arm rest on the back of Paula Kahler. Not till then did he notice that her head was on his shoulder, her eyes wide with troubled sleep. As was her custom at the bullfight, Paula Kahler had returned to Larrabee Street.

McKee

MᴄKEE had to bribe the man at the gate to let him back in. So many of these tourists were coming out, squeezing through this one little gate they had open, the man let him stand there till he waved this ten peso bill at him. Moment McKee did it, he knew he should have tried him first with a five. Paying to go back in after the best of it was over didn't make any sense.

The people coming out were mostly tourists McKee had seen in the *Reforma* lobby, respectable sort of people you wouldn't see at a bullfight more than once. The men with the women who knew they wouldn't like it, but had to see for themselves what they didn't like about it. A big fellow who looked to McKee like Boyd, one of the sloppier type of tourist, came up the ramp with a woman on his arm of about the same sort. McKee didn't often do it, but he turned to gawk at her. She wore high rocky heels, and her stockings had a black line all the way up. Made McKee think of that loft in New York where he and Roy had found the stockings looped around the doorknob. Same sort of man they'd found in it, same sort of woman who had left them there.

That kind of streak, call it wild if you want to, Boyd had had right from the beginning. He didn't learn it. As McKee could tell you, he was born with it.

Clear back when they were kids Boyd had found that hole beneath the Crete front porch, one big enough to crawl through, and they would sneak off there and sit in the soft hot dust, squirting pop. More than McKee, Boyd seemed to get quite a bang out of that. The reason was, as it turned out, Boyd had swiped the money for it from Mr. Crete's pants, since he could do as he pleased and had the run of the Crete house. Mr. Crete slept late on Sunday mornings, and Boyd would sneak into his room, while he was sleeping, and take some of the small change out of his pants. That took nerve. God knows what it was that made him think of it. He could have all the pop and Hershey bars he could eat just by asking Mrs. Crete for them, but it wasn't the same, the money she would give him and the money he could swipe. The pop tasted different to him than it did to McKee. He really didn't like pop unless he could drink it under the porch. All he liked to do was shake it till it fizzed, then squirt it in his mouth.

He had that streak, which was why they sent him off to school. The town of Polk, as Mrs. Crete liked to say, was too small for him. But Omaha didn't really suit him either, if you took into account the trouble he caused them, running wild at that ball game and tearing the pocket off the ballplayer's pants. And then a year or two later—in the summer, since he spent his summers in Polk—he had this crazy idea of walking on water, and made a stab at it.

They had always had this sandpit out west of town, but sandpits gave McKee the willies, both then and later, so he wouldn't have gone near it except for Boyd. But they had both been at loose ends that summer—it was in the fall that McKee had gone to Texas—and they had walked down the Burlington tracks to the sandpit to smoke some cubebs. They'd smoked, loafed around a bit, then Boyd had stood up and taken off his clothes, showing how much faster he'd grown up in most places than McKee.

"Going to take a little dip?" McKee had asked, since he just took it for granted Boyd could swim.

"Nope," Boyd had replied, "just a walk on the water"; then he had walked around the pit to a sort of platform, where they scooped out the sand. McKee had thought nothing of it—it was just the sort of talk he had picked up in Omaha, where kids were smarter, and since he didn't want to sound like a hick himself he hadn't replied. Boyd had stood there at the edge of the platform, taking deep breaths and then blowing them out, as if he expected to dive to the bottom and swim all the way across. Then he stopped, he just stood there, his eyes as straight ahead as a wooden Indian, and McKee had been so sure he could walk on water—or on air if he cared to—that he just waited for it.

Boyd had put out one foot—the day was so quiet the water had a smooth glassy surface—but it seemed a long time before his foot got to it, touched, and he dropped. No splash at all to speak of, he just dropped out of sight. His hands were flat at his side, like he was walking, and it seemed so long before he reappeared, before anything happened, McKee thought he must be just walking along on the bottom of it. That he would next see him walking up the beach on the opposite side. But he didn't—he popped right up at the hole he'd dropped into, as if he'd been down to the bottom of it and then pushed off. He couldn't swim a stroke, but there was not a peep out of him. He thrashed all around, like a wild man, and it was just pure luck he didn't drown before McKee, or help of some sort, got to him. But it wasn't McKee. What help he got was from providence. McKee knew that he would sooner drown than admit he had tried to walk on water and failed. If McKee had gone toward him he would have sunk and never come up. But he didn't drown, one way or another, but managed to get his hand on the platform, hang there awhile, then drag himself out more dead than alive. He just lay there sprawled out in the sun until he showed pink on parts of his body, and the sun brought him around the way it would a drowned fly. After a while he got up, put on his clothes, and back near Polk McKee asked him, like he meant it, where it was that he'd learned to swim. He could see it was the only way out. It was plain as day Boyd couldn't walk on water, but it was not so plain that he couldn't swim. Without batting an eye Boyd told him he'd learned to swim in Omaha.

One thing McKee didn't get around to ask him—since he figured it out for himself—was why, if he planned to walk on water, he'd taken off his clothes. But it wasn't that he knew in advance that he wouldn't, as you might think. That summer he was still wearing some of Ashley Crete's clothes, just to rough around in, and if he was going to walk on water, he wanted to do it all by himself. He didn't want some of the credit to go to Ashley, just in case he did.

That crazy wild streak in him—McKee went down the ramp to where they kept the bulls, leaned on the fence to look at them. Only two of them left. That meant he had missed three or four. That crazy wild streak in Boyd sometimes made him think the Cretes had done it, spoiling him with money. Or was it the crazy pattern of the town itself, which he'd often thought about but had never figured out until the time he spent all day up in the switch tower.

Not that he was up high—the top of the grain elevator was higher, and he could have seen even farther—but he had never sat all day in such a high place. Any number of

times as a kid he had wondered why the streets in Polk
seemed to run every which way, whereas down in Aurora,
where his aunt lived, they were long and straight. From the
tower, that day, he had puzzled it out.

Offhand that didn't seem to relate to Boyd, or to how he
was feeling in general, but for the first time in his life he
finally understood one thing: why in a town with so many
fool kids he and Boyd seemed alone. You would think in a
town of twelve hundred people what kids there were would
all know each other, but they didn't, and that was the thing
about Polk. There were hardly more than eleven hundred
people, but there were two towns. There were four, that is,
instead of two, sides to the tracks. There was the Burlington
town, where McKee lived, and where the trains had bells
and cowcatchers, then there was the Union Pacific town for
people like Boyd and the Cretes. Over there trains had a
long whistle and a caboose. If a train happened to stop, the
engine was half a mile down the tracks. The caboose, or the
people in the diner, was all you saw. But McKee lived on a
railroad where the butterflies rode free to Marquette. The
time McKee and his mother had gone to Aurora a big
butterfly had gone right along with them, up and down the
aisle, but when they stopped at Marquette he got off. Like
he lived there. McKee still remembered that. When McKee
used the word *railroad* that was what he meant. But over on
the U.P., if the train did stop, the people who got on it had
one-way tickets, and the people who got off usually got
back on it again. On the Burlington the faraway places were
an hour or so, like Norfolk and Aurora, but people only
went if somebody died, then hurried right back. But Boyd
often talked about Omaha and Cheyenne, Mrs. Crete spent
all of her winters in Chicago, and Ashley Crete did nothing
on a train but eat and sleep. It made a difference. But it took
a long time to see what it was.

Forty years. McKee turned from the bull pen as if he might see, down the ramp, back to his boyhood. It was only now, more than forty years later, that he saw why the bell on the Burlington engine went on clanging the way it did when the train had stopped. The crossing on the Burlington had no gates. The train came into town like a wagon, right on the flat, so slow that a boy could run along beside it and feel the hiss from the piston blowing hot on his legs. When the engine stopped the piston left a large wet place on the walk. The bell went on clanging even when it took water, the black-faced fireman scrambling over the tender, holding down the noisy chute, and sometimes taking a drink himself. Where the water dripped on the coal it was shiny black. In the winter it looked like a load of snow, and up front, around the hissing piston, icicles with the flavor of coal oil could be broken off.

Why weren't there any gates? Nobody crossed those tracks but Boyd and McKee. On their way, as McKee remembered, down the Burlington tracks to the switch tower, where the gypsy wagons, in the spring and summer, camped night after night. They unhitched their skinny horses and let their cattle crop the ditch grass. No matter which railroad you lived on, if you looked down the tracks you could see their fires at night. They didn't sing or dance to speak of, but they burned a lot of railroad ties. Boyd had told him that gypsies would kidnap white boys, drive off with them, and hold them for ransom, which was why they walked down to see them as often as they did. In the shade of the switch tower, where the tracks crossed, they would chew licorice and wait to be kidnapped. Not McKee, but he knew very well that Boyd did. He took McKee along so there would be proof of it.

That wild streak in his nature went on turning up the way weeds would, when you plowed them under, till you honestly couldn't tell the weeds from the corn. But that was years back. That was back when he was full of corn. When he could make a woman like Agnes Scanlon, who'd been married ten years, just as skittish as a kitten, then turn and kiss a girl who had never been kissed before. Mrs. McKee liked to say that he would never in the world do that again. McKee wasn't so sure. He didn't say so, naturally, but he would bet you dollars to doughnuts that if Boyd had gone back he'd have kissed both girls again. If he'd gone right back, while it was still dark, he would have kissed her all right. McKee knew all about what her intuition told her, but there were times when that was not much help. That was one of those times. If McKee had been a girl, he would have kissed him himself.

McKee wheeled around, hearing the roar, and took a look up one of the tunnels. Was it paper they were throwing? No, they were waving handkerchiefs. He almost ran, not wanting to miss it, whatever it was. Then the way it all fell away, like a funnel with that hole at the bottom, made him so dizzy he had to stop and close his eyes. Instead of letting up, the yelling seemed to get worse. He opened his eyes and saw that everybody, almost everybody was standing up, waving whatever they had, or throwing it into the ring. McKee could see the bull over near a funk hole, dead now, looking as sorry and helpless as cows did when he saw them lying down. But right there below, so close to the fence McKee had to stretch a little to see him, was the starry-eyed boy that everybody seemed to be yelling for. He went along at a trot, holding in one hand a bouquet of flowers somebody had thrown him, and in the other, like it meant more to him, something that looked like a purse. Had they thrown him money? They wouldn't do it that way back in the States. The youngsters got the money, too much of it, but you'd never catch people throwing it at them. On the other hand they didn't run the risks this boy had just run. All along his front, and down one pants leg, you could see the bull's blood. McKee felt in himself a surge of the emotion they were all feeling, that had got them to yelling, which he couldn't do himself but he could blink his eyes and let his nose run. It crossed his mind that that boy probably felt the way Boyd might have felt if he had walked on the water, really done it, instead of almost drowning. He had never before seen it in just that light. It helped explain the bullfight a little, and Boyd's interest in it. He looked around for Boyd—all this excitement would mean more to Boyd than it did to the others—but in the general commotion, with everybody standing, it was like that crazy afternoon at the ball park when Boyd, with that dang foul ball, had gone over the fence. But it was different in the sense that he had dropped it. The bull had got him.

The boy went around twice, as though the applause had gone to his head and made him a little silly, but everybody seemed to understand that and make allowance for it. Just to see a youngster as tickled as that did all of them good. The second time around he ducked into the funk hole, where he went along the runway, waving to people, to where one of them stopped him and offered him a hat. The young man put it on his head, then passed it back. Everybody who was close enough to see that laughed, but McKee, dark as it was getting, couldn't see who it was until they had settled back in their seats. That left Boyd standing. On his head was the little fellow's coonskin hat.

Mrs. McKee

LOOKING for aspirin, she went through her purse, then the pockets of the coat McKee had left in the seat, where she found one of the questionable post cards he mailed back to old friends. A drawing of two shabby horses, one of them plainly a male, with this wretched little colt shivering between them. It was captioned MAMA'S SLIP IS SHOWING, although nothing whatsoever was showing on the female. Nothing. She turned on the dashboard light to study it. She could hardly complain about his cards if the questionable point they made escaped her, but on the other hand nothing proved so well that they were questionable. It was addressed to Emil Cory, his barber, so she put it in her purse for further study, since all of the cards he received from his clients were posted on his mirror. It would not be through any slip of *hers* showing if this one was.

Looking—she went through the basket where they kept sunburn lotion, soda mint tablets, flint for the boy's sparkler guns, and McKee's box of kitchen matches—before she remembered that aspirin was out. She had been advised to go easy on aspirin. Looking for Bufferin she found the road maps and part of an Omaha paper in the glove drawer. Months old. Why had McKee hung on to it? She read the headlines, history at the time, of unforgettable events she had already forgotten, then she opened it and saw this picture of her father looking frozen to death, his feet in the oven, wrapped up in buffalo robes and wearing his cane-sided drayman's hat. The caption read—

MAN WHO KNEW BUFFALO BILL SPENDS LONELY XMAS

She remembered McKee's hoarse voice on the phone asking her if she had seen the Omaha paper, although he knew she never saw it unless he brought it home. Which he did, with that picture of her father and the piece about the frontiersmen, now forgotten, although their very own children were living well and happy in the same state. Some brakeman, one who had known her father, had found him in the kitchen with his fire out, his feet in the oven of the range where he insisted on keeping them. He had been too cold and too feeble to get up and start the fire. He had just sat there, hibernating, until this brakeman had found him, and a story as pitiful as that just naturally made news.

There had been nothing to say. Nothing.

Everybody in Lincoln knew her maiden name was Scanlon, and that this old man out in Lone Tree was her father, but they were ready to forget that they had always known he was mad as an owl. Then overnight was an old frontiersman. He knew Buffalo Bill. She had known Buffalo Bill herself, having been lifted from the ground to his saddle, and he was every bit as silly, as smelly, and as hopeless, as her father himself.

McKee had brought the paper home, and that very evening, even though they had their grandson, Gordon, there with them, they got into the car and drove the hundred eighty miles to Lone Tree. It proved to be a turning point in their lives—all of their lives, in some ways—that little Gordon just happened to be wearing his coonskin hat. McKee had bought the Davy Crockett outfit for him for Christmas, and he had just put it on.

Not that they knew that at the time; they knew *nothing*, and by the time they got to Lone Tree, a four-hour drive, she was sure that dozens of curious sightseers would be there. Hadn't the article pointed out how old and lonely he was? But there had not been a soul, not a car in the town nor anybody who cared in the Highway Diner, where they stopped for coffee and in order to ask how things seemed to be. The old man in the diner had not read the paper, or heard anything. He said that so far as he knew Tom—that was her father—was about the same as usual, which was all right. So they had not said a word about the Omaha paper, and drove the half mile into town, if that was what you could call it, where her father had been born in the covered wagon that could still be seen behind the livery stable. The Lone Tree too was still there, what was left of it, almost the color of ice in the winter moonlight, but no light at all could be seen in the hotel, until they waded through the drifts to the back, where McKee had seen a lamp. He had it on the floor beside him, with a tin cup of coffee balanced on the top of the chimney, to warm it, and around the rim of one of the stove lids they could see the banked fire. McKee had knocked, but when he got no answer he had stepped in. Her father had been asleep. When they stepped in he turned up the lamp and held it out before him, and it just so happened, thanks be to God, that the light fell on the boy. Her father asked him who *he* was, he replied Davy Crockett, and that was that.

They could have driven home with him that night—he would have done anything the boy suggested—but McKee wanted to wait until it was light. He didn't want to drive him clear to Lincoln, then bring him back again. He wanted to see if the boy still had the upper hand after he'd seen him in the light. So they spent that night in her father's hotel, where no one but her father had spent a night for years, and everything had been left as if the people had thought the place was on fire. There were hats on the rack that were not her father's, and rubbers in the hall. In the lobby all the chairs faced the window where the town would have been, if there had been one, the snow deep in the holes for the basements of the houses that had never been built. On the seat of a chair she found a Kansas City paper dated February, 1918, announcing that an armistice might be reached almost any day. The wall clock had stopped, perhaps the same year, and the safe with the painting of the mountain waterfall on the door still had the combination for the lock written in pencil on the floor. In the keyholes just above it were two or three keys, since the guests carried them in their pockets, and a letter for a man named Lyman Young-blood, mailed from Terre Haute. It had been postmarked in May, 1926.

Her father slept in the chair where they had found him, but she had gone upstairs to make up their own beds, and found them all, the twelve beds in the hotel, as if the guests had got out of them that morning, leaving the pillows rumpled, the sheets and covers thrown back.

Had her father, as the sheets got dirty, moved from room to room? Beginning up at the top where she had once left him, sick with something called erysipelas, propped in the bed with all of his clothes on, the hat on his shaved head, a night pot full of cigar butts on the floor at his side. That had been *his* room—the one on the west, looking down the stretch of track toward Ogallala and the crossing where the downgrade freights hit so many buggies and teams. In such an empty country, how was it possible? Where there had been so few teams, so few trains, why did they meet so often at that crossing, in plain daylight, where nothing blocked the view? It had made her doubt her own life. Doubt that she knew what she knew. That trains, coming down those tracks, had killed full grown men who preferred to walk there, their backs turned to the whistle, rather than walk in the cinders just to one side.

Why was that? It was one of the things her mother knew. If I'd stayed there, she had said, I'd have walked down the tracks myself. But her father had stayed. Some would have said that he killed himself without the trains.

But from his window, where there was nothing to see, he had seen many things. There had been Emil Bickel, a bearded man with a lovely wife, and everything to live for, swinging like a scarecrow from the telephone wires, the buttons gone from his vest. Popped, her father had said, by the force of it. He had been dressed for church, all of his bills were paid, and the gold watch in his pocket, the crystal unbroken, had stopped at exactly eleven seventeen. The fast eastbound mail train, rolling down the grade, had been two minutes late.

Her grandfather had built the hotel at a time when men were saying *Go west, young man, go west*—but the town itself, and the people who were born there, all went east. No house or store, no building of any kind, lay to the west. Her father's window looked out on a short spur of tracks, an abandoned cattle loader, a pile of tarred railroad ties, and then mile after mile, or so it seemed to her, of burned ditch grass. Smoke from this grass often darkened the sky. In the winter and spring this grass might be green, a fresh, winter-wheat color, but all she seemed to remember was the smell of burning yellow grass in her nose. It seemed to be trapped in the sky overhead, and in the rooms of the hotel. In the middle of the winter, stronger than the smell of food, it was there in the hall. Eastern women would complain to her mother that they feared it was a fire, and throw open the windows, but the fresh air never cleared it out. In the summer and fall more of it would just blow in.

By the time she had been old enough to wait on him, and run up the stairs with his food, her father had been known as *the man in the room*. In the bed, as a rule, fully clothed, propped up on a pillow so he could see out the window, or see in the mirror the body of the man stretched out on the bed. That was where she looked for him, herself. On his head this silly hat, with the drayman's license, the soft crown of the hat shaped to his skull, and the row of soiled matches in the strap at the front. Then his coat—her father was made up of parts, like the hotel, of what the guests had left in the rooms—a coat of black material, scratchy-looking, left to him by a desk clerk named Riddlemosher. Part of a patchwork quilt was usually drawn over his legs. He had complained, even way back then, of the cold in his feet and hands. But he had no face—no, this man, her father, who was alive and had a face for others—seemed to have nothing, for her, between his drayman's license and his coat. Just one of those blanks, spotted with little numbers, that she used to trace in with her pencil, the likeness always turning out to be different than she had thought.

When she thought of her father—and she often did—she saw *things*. The oil lamp, with its wick floating like something that would one day bite him, and the flour-sack towels with the design that would show up when he wiped his hands. Always speechless—when she saw dioramas, the old man in them was her father—dying in the bed, feathering the arrow, or standing at the screen to judge the weather. But never comment on it. Just judge it, as her mother said, and let it be damned.

She hadn't slept a wink all that night, the stale smell of

the grass smoke was there in the room, and she remembered
how the fire hose cart, when it came, had come without the
hose. They had been scared to death the new hotel would
burn down before the hose arrived. It had been a dry
summer, bad for fires, and all the traveling salesmen smoked
cigars in their rooms. The hotel didn't burn, but at the end
of that summer her mother took all of her children and
moved to Lincoln. She had sworn before she left him that
the hose would never come, and it never did. Neither did
the speculators who would build the town, the Zion that
would bloom in the desert, nor the grass fire that would
mercifully burn it all to the ground. Nothing had *ever*
happened: exactly as her mother had said.

She remembered her mother, her skirts whipping around
her, ringed in by a blowing line of wash, her jaw set on the
clothespins in her mouth. All the clothespins had the deep
marks of her teeth. They weren't chewed. Just marked
where her teeth clamped down on them. She didn't like it
outside; she liked it better in her kitchen, a slave to the sink,
the mop and the stove, but where she could draw the one
curtain at the window and not have to look out. She knew,
without troubling to look, what she would see.

But in the evening she might sit in one of the rockers at
the front of the lobby, facing the window, and look out at
the town she knew would never go up. Rows of maples and
elms, lights that would swing over the corners and trap the
June bugs, and concrete sidewalks down which she would
never walk. Down the tracks a crossing with a crossing bell,
or the gates that dropped when a train came to keep men
who didn't know better from killing themselves. Across the
tracks big houses, spacious lawns, young women to bear and
wash the children, old women to watch and love them, and
a man to shovel snow from the walk, mow the lawns. Out in
back would be grapes, growing over an arbor, a lawn swing

stained with mulberries, and a woman like herself cutting flowers with a pair of shears.

That was what she saw, sitting in the rocker, but the view from the kitchen window showed a road where the tracks were tangled like mop strings, and never went anywhere. A picture of her husband, Thomas Scanlon, more dead than alive even before she had left him, but he had gone on to survive her by sixteen years. To see his picture in the paper, to find himself an old frontiersman, a friend of Buffalo Bill, and to spend the winter of his eighty-eighth year in Mexico. Reunited with his family, attending a bullfight with his great-grandson.

If there had been one reason she had to get away from home *this* Christmas, get away somewhere, it was that all of their friends, some of them wiseacres, would be around to ask her father if he liked *this* Christmas better than the last. And if she knew him at all, and she did, she knew what he would say. He would say no. So they were spending this Christmas somewhere else. She wouldn't care—when they asked him—if he liked Mexico or not.

She leaned forward, her face near the windshield, to peer at the dark curve of the bullring, where the lights made a soft glow on the sky. A cardboard cloud, small and unreal, like those puffs shells made in the silent movies, led her to stiffen a bit and sit waiting for the noise. It came, but it was made by the roar from the crowd. When it had passed she noticed the duck bumps on her arms.

If they should ask her how *she* liked it—it would depend who asked her, wouldn't it? If Alice Morple should ask her, and she would, she would first of all mention the oxygen hunger, the vertigo and the goose flesh, as well as what she had observed the Latin countries did to certain types of women, as well as men. No more. Let her guess what types she had in mind. Let her guess if it was all a dream, as it had once been, or if this time the bed had broken down under something else. Let her guess. The thing about Mexico was—and she would say so—that it had her guessing herself.

Boyd

HOWLING like an Indian, the boy cried, "My hat! My hat!"

"Okay, kiddo—" said Boyd, and took a good grip on him, as if he was a bottle, then clamped the coonskin on his head and screwed it on with a twist. The boy let out a yell, and Boyd said—

"There's your goddam hat. Now shut up."

Oddly enough, he did. His lower lip trembling. Unaccustomed as he was to that sort of treatment, language like that. Something he would remember? Boyd smiled. Had he given his namesake something to remember? The old fool at the bullfight who had cussed him and screwed his hat on his head.

"That hat feels better now," he said, "doesn't it?"

The boy felt it with his hand, then bit down on his lip.

"It's a real hat now," went on Boyd, "because it's been on the head of a hero. That makes it real."

Did it? He felt highly unreal himself. This time the clowning had let him down, rather than picked him up. He should have left before the hero. He should have kept his

562

big mouth shut. He felt as listless and stale as the ex-bull-fighter, the winded old man in the funk hole, whose arms seemed to hang from the padded shoulders of his coat. An ex-hero. Once something of a youth and hero himself. One could see that in his smile, stale as it was, and in the eyes now too big for the sockets, as his bottom was now too big for the pants. But once the praise had showered down on himself. More than once, perhaps, the red wine from the skin had spilled on his face. Flowers, cigars, and the lips of young women had been his. One could see it, staled as it was by the blackened teeth, the popping eyes, and the arms that hung like the sleeves of an empty coat. Once a hero, the undulant fever remained in the blood. The hot moments of the funk hole followed by the chills of polar nights. Followed by nothing. Neither melancholy, madness, nor the consolations of despair.

"Touch bottom—" Boyd whispered, with just his lips, as a man crosses himself in the presence of the disaster, then turned to see the sorrowful eyes of Lehmann pitying him. Eyes that knew. Boyd was always calling on a bottom—like a lover—to come up and be touched.

"So you haf tudge boddom?" Lehmann had asked, the day that Boyd had gone over to see him, and beamed on him with his remote, early-man smile. Then he had added, "Wich boddom?"

"The bottom of the bottom," Boyd had replied. It had seemed so at the time. Lehmann had gazed at him sadly, stroking the lobes of his ears.

"Mister Boyt," he had said, "woot you like to meed a boddom?"

"A which?" Boyd had replied, not sure that he had caught it.

"A man who hass tudge boddom," Lehmann had answered, and left the room. Boyd had thought the idea original with himself. He had sat there waiting—Lehmann had spoken to someone as an adult would speak to a child, then he returned with Paula Kahler and her knitting, her luminous gaze. No comment had been necessary. She had stood before them, smiling in her usual trance of blessedness.

"Mister Boyt—" Lehmann had said, "the boddom of the boddom iss a lonk way down."

"Facts are stranger than fiction," Boyd had replied.

"*Fax?*" the old man had cried, "*wot* fax? If you haf tudge boddom there are no fax. It iss all viction. Only viction iss a fack!"

Boyd had said nothing. Across his mind—as once he had felt the wing of madness—he felt the imprint of a fact, one blown to him directly from the horse's mouth. With it the knowledge that he might, one day, both touch bottom and push off from it.

"What's he want his *ears* for?" the boy asked.

Boyd leaned forward to see what ears, and saw them. The hero was there in the runway below them, holding, like flowers, the bull's two bloody ears.

"What do you want a coonskin hat for?" said Boyd, although a coonskin hat was a covering for the head, needed no explaining, and had nothing in common with a pair of bull's ears. The boy's gaze showed it.

"Now you're being silly," he said.

The words, the words and the music, by his grandmother. What would he think, this sensible lad, in his sensible frontier suit with sparkler pistols, of a man who had once torn the smelly pocket from a ballplayer's pants. Not his hat, nor his shoes, not even his ears. Just the pocket to his pants. What would this practical little monster think of that?

"You want to know how silly I am?" Boyd asked.

He did. Very much so.

"Whose ears you got?" he probed. "A rabbit's?"

"I don't have any ears," said Boyd, "nor even hats. What I've got is a dirty, smelly pocket."

"Where?" said the boy.

"Not here with me," Boyd replied, and slapped his raincoat pockets. "I've got it at home. It's a big, stinky flannel pocket."

Did he believe that? He took a suck on his gun barrel, reflected, then said, "You don't have the pants to go with it?"

Boyd shook his head. "No, no pants," he said. He thought about that himself, then added, "Instead of cutting off his ears, what I did was snatch the pocket of his pants."

"Why was it stinky?" said the boy.

"This man was a baseball player," said Boyd, "and his pants got stinky in hot summer weather. When he slid into base he slid in on the seat of his pants." That impressed him. "His name was Tyrus Raymond Cobb," Boyd continued, "but they called him the Georgia Peach because he was so good."

He followed that. He glanced up quickly to see if Boyd was pulling his leg. "How'd you get it?" he asked.

"Oh—" said Boyd, shrugging, "I just tore it off." They watched the bull. He was as big as Ty, but he didn't run the bases at all as gracefully. Ty could pivot. He had had to, at least, that once. "You like to hear—" Boyd said, "how I snatched Ty Cobb's pocket?"

Up and down, like the handle of a pump, the boy wagged his head.

"Well—" Boyd said, feeling his way, "it's quite a little story. He was playing for the Tigers, I was going to Farnam School at the time. He came out to play in Omaha, that fall, on a barnstorming tour."

"Omaha has the stockyards," said the boy.

"That's right," said Boyd. "Used to smell them all summer. Noticed the smell was still there on our way down here. But the old school—" he paused there a moment, "the old school was gone."

"The one where you went?"

"On the corner of 29th and Farnam," said Boyd. "Gone now. Big used-car lot in its place. School was one of those square, red brick buildings with a brick walk around it, yard covered with cinders. We played pom-pom-pullaway during recess, and before school. On one side of the yard we had these trees we swung around until we wore the bark off them. All the first floor windows usually had pictures on them, paper pumpkins, Santa Clauses, witches riding on brooms. One of the second floor windows had this landing on the fire escape."

He stopped there, glanced to see how the boy was taking it.

"We got a chute," said the boy. "We got a shoot-the-chute," and made a noise with his lips to indicate the way they shot it.

"We didn't—" Boyd continued, "we had this fire escape. To get out on it you crawled through the window. One of the jobs I had was to crawl through the window twice a day."

"What for?"

"My job was to clean the erasers. The place to clean them was out on the fire escape. I'd go out with the erasers and slap them on the bricks till they were clean. All around the window, where I slapped them, the red bricks were almost white with the chalk dust. So were my hands. Then I'd get it on my pants trying to rub them clean." He paused, but the boy sat listening. "Inside the room we had these desks, facing the blackboard, and over near the door a walnut

Victrola. Another thing I did was to wind the Victrola. I played the Victrola every morning, when we did exercises to the Clock Store record, the volume turned up high but the clocks turned down a little slow. When the motor ran down I would stop exercising and go wind it up."

"Were you the teacher's pet?"

"I guess I was. When we all pledged the flag I was the one who held it. When anything important happened, I read it out loud from the *Current Events*."

They faced the ring, the huge bull-ox with his horns hooked in the mattress on the side of the horse, the rider out of the saddle, poised like a mosquito with his spear shaft into the bull's hump, but all three without movement, as if waiting for the shutter to snap.

"And now it's gone?" asked the boy.

"Gone—" Boyd replied, and spread out his hands, as if it had all disappeared at that moment. "The real thing never lasts, you know," he added, before he realized what he had said. Was that true? Strangely enough, it seemed to be. It was the unreal thing that lasted, the red-brick phantasm in Boyd's mind, complete with fire escape, erasers, and the listening dog in the Victrola horn. "Where was I?" said Boyd, wanting confirmation.

"Pledging the flag," said the boy.

"Oh, yes—" said Boyd. "Well, let's get out to the ball park—it was over near the stockyards—where we had seats right along the rail, the way we do here. A lot of other people were behind the chicken wire, where they wouldn't get hit. They'd all come out to watch Cobb play, and maybe hit a home run."

"Did he hit one?"

"He did—and he didn't," Boyd replied. "Due to what happened, it's pretty hard to say. He hit it, that is, but he never got as far as home with it."

The boy moved in closer. He let the gun he was holding rest on Boyd's knee.

"Reason he didn't—" Boyd went on, clearing his throat, "was that when he rounded third, they headed him off. I mean, I did. It just so happened that it happened to be me."

Was it possible? Boyd sometimes wondered himself. He did once more, then said, "Your granddaddy was there and saw it. You can ask him." The boy wheeled around in the seat to ask him, but McKee was not there. "If what you want is proof," Boyd said, "I guess the proof is in the pocket." Before the question was asked he continued, "You probably wonder, why his pocket? Why not something useful like his hat, say—?"

He stopped there. The proof was not in the pocket. Had it ever been? The proof from now on was in the telling.

"It's quite a story, son—" he said, and watched the big bull, the darts waving in his hump, go along the fence looking for what no bullring offered. A corner. There was no place to hide. Trailing him, like Mack Sennett detectives, were the matador and his assistants. Impersonal as fate. Goya-like harpies in the fading light. "—Although I don't remember the start of the game. Somewhere about the middle he hit this foul ball—Ty Cobb did, that is—and I got my hands on it. A little later he hit what should have been a home run. The fielders lost track of the ball and stood around the flagpole out in center, and I don't really know if it ever came down or not. While it was still up there, somewhere, I went over the fence. I had this foul ball that he'd hit, and I wanted it autographed. I crossed the foul line between first base and home plate, and by the time Ty was rounding third, I was on the line with this ball in my hand. I had him blocked off. It just might be he thought the ball I had was the one he had hit. We'll never know. All I know is that he came around third base, saw me with the ball, and headed for the dugout. Turns out he also saw, coming up behind me, about five hundred kids who had the same idea, half of them with new balls they had bought and wanted autographed. As I say, he headed for the dugout, but before he made it we had closed in on him. Coming up behind him, I got my hands on his pants. On his pocket, that is. When he kept on going, the pocket came off. I didn't notice till later—quite a bit later, since they had to call the game off— that I'd dropped the ball I went out to get autographed. So all I had was his pocket. Piece of flannel with grass stains on one corner of it. I put my name on one side of it, and used it to kneel on when I played marbles. So long as I stuck to marbles, I guess it brought me luck."

"Why didn't you just stick to marbles?" asked the boy, and in his eyes, the ice-blue eyes of the Scanlons, Boyd saw a child's pity for the man who had turned to squirting pop. He had no answer. If he had stuck to marbles, would he have been *champeen?* Would he have slain the wild bull, walked on the water, and carried off the girl with the ice-blue eyes to live happily ever after, eating candied apples and divinity fudge? He would never know. Like that home run the Georgia Peach had hit, the ball would never come down. It would remain, forever suspended, high in the cloudland out in center, where the fielders, with their eyes on the heavens, circled the flagpole.

Firmly, feeling the round head beneath it, he placed his hand on the coonskin hat, and let it slide back to where he could grip the coonskin by the tail. Gently, as if it might be alive, he raised it from the boy's head, then said—

"Your Uncle Gordon will now bring a dead coon back to life."

The boy did not grab for it, nor cry out, but watched his Uncle Gordon, as though that hat was a lasso, twirl it by the tail above his head, faster and faster, then let it fly. They both watched it, a headless bird with a long fur tail, and strange plumage, soar out over the ring, lift a moment on the draft, then drop to the sand. The bullfighter did not see it, nor did his *peones*, since they stood as if in mourning, watching the bull die, and the roar from the crowd they took as a sign of a deed well done.

"Go get it, kid—" said Boyd, softly, and took him by the arms, held him over the rail, then let him drop on the sand in the runway. He reappeared, like a spring-wind toy in the costume of a frontier doll, through the slit in the funk hole and scooted like a BB across the ring. A troop of small fry, all of them authentic Indians, who had come in with the mules when the gates had opened, also headed for the coonskin, but Davy Crockett got there first. He had recovered his hat, but in the process lost his senses. He ran around wildly, pursued by Indians, wheeling to shoot one dead, scalp another, then ride off in all directions firing volleys of sparks into the air. Some little Indians watched him, others straddled the bull while his body was still warm and the mules had him moving, or they hung like water skiers to his frazzled tail. High on the slopes of the bullring, burning like flares, sheets of flaming newspaper soared skyward, suddenly cooled, powdered, and fell like a rain of ash.

"The bool iss det!" he heard Lehmann croak, "lonk lif the bool!" and they had come to the end—or was it the beginning—of the rites of spring? On the cooling sand the coonskin hat trailed showers of sparks.

"Touch bottom," Boyd said, softly, and feeling it beneath him, he inhaled, pushed off.

McKee

SOMEONE behind him shouted *Sit down*.

McKee sat down. That still left people standing, but the voice had shouted in English, and McKee had the feeling it was meant for him. He wasn't where he belonged at all, but since the seat was empty he sat down in it. Just in time. Right down there below him the bull came in. The sand seemed to glow like the paint on a road sign, but McKee couldn't tell you what color the bull was. His horns looked white, like they'd been painted, and he wondered if it worked out like night baseball, nothing much showing but the diamond, the ball and the bat. Problem for the bull was to figure what the pitcher had on the ball.

What McKee couldn't figure was why the bull, after fanning the air for five or ten minutes, didn't catch on sooner there was nothing behind that fool red cloth. The man stood there just like a post, but the bull went for the cloth. What tricked him? Or were bulls just naturally that dumb? By the time he began to wise up a little, it was too late. They had a rule that wouldn't let him come back for another chance.

What did Boyd say?

Before you pity the bull, McKee, don't forget he's had a chance you haven't.

That's okay by me, McKee had said. Before he thought about it. After thinking he wondered what the devil it meant. Did he mean to say McKee had wanted to gore someone? But who the devil ever knew just what it was Boyd meant. Including Boyd. He was a great one to bamboozle himself.

Take that fool pocket. If you asked Boyd he would tell you something fancy as to why it was he hung on to it—if you asked McKee it was just a fancy way of covering up. Covering up what? The fact that he'd dropped the ball. It took a sharp sort of person to hear him tell it and keep track of that.

Another instance, one McKee had forgotten, were those so-called letters he got from his mother, which weren't really letters at all since she could mail them second-class. She just turned the flap in, she didn't seal it, or care if people read what was inside or not, since they were just clippings she had snipped from the local paper. The line Boyd took, when McKee discovered that, was that his mother was smarter than Uncle Sam, and saved all sorts of money by writing to him second-class. The way he told it you could overlook the fact that his mother never sent him any real letters. Just these clippings he could have read in the paper himself.

The ones McKee had seen were all about the Cretes, Ashley Crete in particular, since he was nearly always off somewhere, doing something interesting. Mrs. Boyd would underline in ink the important points. McKee got the feeling that the printed word meant a lot to her. She could write a letter, if she had to, but it was usually just a line or two from some clipping she didn't want to send because she thought it might get lost. But they were letters, in a way, since Gordon only read the underlined parts. It gave him the kernel of what she had to say. It kept him on his toes, since every time Ashley won anything, or went anywhere, Boyd would get a letter by second-class mail.

Mrs. Boyd had the kind of horse sense Boyd could have used, but hadn't been born with, since she never lost sight of the forest for the trees. When McKee had come back from Omaha he had gone over to tell her about the ball game, and how Boyd had snatched the pocket from the ballplayer's pants. McKee had sat on the porch, which was so close to the ground grass grew through the cracks in it, and Mrs. Boyd had sat in her rocker and rocked. She was a white-haired woman, more like a grandmother, and McKee had felt silly talking about baseball, but when he had finished she said—

"Did Gordon drop that ball?"

McKee had lost track of that ball himself. After all that had happened it hardly seemed important that he'd dropped the ball. But his mother had seen right through it, which was why, in McKee's opinion, Boyd left home so early and never got along too well with her. You couldn't pull the wool over the eyes of a woman like that.

Nor any other woman, for that matter, which was maybe why Boyd was ending up alone with just some stockings on his doorknob, and that fool pocket in his grip. Boyd had pointed out himself, when they saw him in New York, that the pocket was the only thing he'd ever kept hold of—but even that was just a way of making you forget he'd dropped all the balls. Right up till his dying day he would probably keep it handy, or wave it at you, the way the bullfighter played around with that cloth. Pulling the wool over the bull's eyes with it, or using it to cover up, when you got him cornered, the wild streak in his nature that had ruined him. He was every bit as stubborn, if you asked McKee, as old man Scanlon. He just refused to believe what he didn't want to believe.

What did it lead to?

McKee had just read about it somewhere. Stubborn old man you couldn't tell anything. Mad as a coot. McKee had thought of Boyd all the time he sat reading it. This old fool had the Bible Flood on the brain, so that when he saw water that was all he could think of. Next thing you know, he would try to walk on it.

Out in the West somewhere, in Utah or Nevada, they put in this big dam to hold up the water, and in time it backed up and covered the town where this old man lived. He'd been out of town at the time, prospecting somewhere. When he'd come out of the mountains and seen what had happened he thought it was the Flood. The water had backed up, just the way it was supposed to, clean up the valley to where he'd been living, and the town was said to be forty feet under water at the time. Everybody in the town knew what was going to happen but this old man. When he came out of the mountains he saw this lake where the desert had been. Right where he had his shack, since the water was rising, just the top of his windmill was sticking out, the wheel still spinning, as he said, like a big water bug. Something about it made quite an impression on him. Did on McKee too, the way the old man told it, like he was Noah up there on the mountain, with the whole world flooded instead of just that desert valley of his. Quite a bit the way, if McKee understood it, the Biblical fathers got the same idea when the Nile, or whatever river it was, flooded the place. They thought the world was flooded, since that was how it looked to them. It looked about the same, or even worse, to that old man. He didn't have the Lord to fall back on, the way Noah did. He didn't have any animals to save, or any trees to build him an ark. And while he stood there looking, the top of that windmill was covered up.

The article didn't go on to say if he had grasped the facts of the case or not, but McKee would say he hadn't. The facts wouldn't have meant a thing to him. The engineers could talk till they were blue in the face about the dam down below, backing up the water, but what the old man saw from the mountain would always be the Flood. There were people like that. His wife's father was one of them. If he saw a bunch of cows with horns he would swear they were buffalo. If they ever backed water up around Lone Tree he probably just wouldn't believe it, since he hadn't read the Bible, and he'd drown any day rather than admit to anything he didn't believe. Boyd was every bit as crazy, but in a different way. He'd believe in almost anything, if it was just unlikely enough. Other people standing up, McKee stood up. What had he missed? The big bull, with these boys around him, was there along the fence. The one with the sword spread his cloth on the sand like he expected the bull to walk on it. The bull put his head down, as if to sniff it, and then the one with the sword, as if he meant to club him, leaned away over and poked him with it at the back of his head. Just that little poke did it. He dropped all in a heap, and the band began to play.

The man below McKee turned around at that point and looked up the aisle, like he expected somebody, and in his eyes, as in farmhouse windows, McKee could see the reflection of something burning. He turned to look at the bonfire, a good-sized one, high up in the ring. Kids old enough to know better were throwing on it anything that would burn. That explained why it was they made the ring out of concrete, with the seats that would freeze you, since anything that was soft, or made of wood, they would burn to the ground. He watched the fire, the way the sparks shot upward, and remembered the time when he and Boyd—it had been mostly Boyd—had burned the Kaiser Devil in effigy. They made him out of a scarecrow, with a big tin funnel for a hat. Any bonfire at all, with kids running around it, made McKee think of that.

When he looked back at the bullring it was swarming with kids. Maybe thirty of them, the way they'd swarm out on a diamond after a ball game, hooting like Indians and raising hell generally. Made him think of Boyd, and that fool pocket, and against the sand, bright as it was, he could see four or five of the little rascals astraddle the bull. The one they didn't have room for rode out in back, hanging on to his tail. That was just about the wildest sort of thing McKee had ever seen. The body of that bull still warm, more than likely, and those kids straddling it.

The ring was full of them, all shapes and sizes, but one little tyke struck McKee as familiar. He ran around wild, like they all did, but he never stopped shooting off sparks. It was so dark in the ring that the sparks made it easy to keep track of him. He was like a bug, the way he scooted, and McKee had to wait till he got a little closer, right there below him, before he saw the tail on the coonskin hat.

"*Gordon!*" he yelled, so loud he almost lost his voice. When he yelled again he could hardly hear it above the band. The boy heard nothing. Off he scooted trailing a shower of sparks. Just yelling like that made McKee dizzy, he dropped down in the seat, but he no sooner felt the cold than he thought of Mrs. McKee, popped up.

But he didn't holler. Bygod—he said to himself—let Boyd get him. If something happened to that boy, let Boyd explain it. He went around the curving aisle, not even running—let Boyd, this time, do the running—he was so damn crazy to climb over a fence, well, now he could climb. For the first time in his life there would be some excuse for his doing it. That wild streak in him. For the first time in his life it would be of some use.

McKee reached the aisle, but there was Boyd, if he could believe his eyes, down there smiling at him. Was he crazy?

"For Pete's sake, Gordon!" said McKee.

"What's the trouble?" he replied.

"If something should happen to that boy—" said McKee, but it left him speechless, just to think of it. "Gordon—" he said, waving his arm, "you get in there and get that boy."

"You know how kids are—" said Boyd, "when they see a fence."

"I know how that boy is," said McKee, "and I know who it was that put him over. I'm going to ask you to go in and get him, and to do it quick."

Boyd stopped smiling. McKee didn't like the look on his face.

"If he was your boy—" said McKee, "you could do as you like. Could if he was mine. But this boy—"

"If—?" said Boyd.

It crossed McKee's mind that he was really crazy. The wild streak had got the best of him.

"If this boy's name is Gordon—" said Boyd.

"This is no time for horseplay," said McKee, and cupped his hands to his mouth, shouted, "Oh, Gordon!"

"If you want him to come," said Boyd, "you've got to call him by his name."

If McKee had had the strength he would have turned and run. He didn't want to hear. "Boyd—" he said, to shut him up, "if you don't get that boy—" and Boyd turned to face the ring, cupped his hands to his face, and like the clown he was, sang out the Davy Crockett business.

> *"Davy, Da-vy, Da-vyyyy Crockett,*
> *King of the Wild Frontier!"*

McKee saw the boy wheel around as if someone had grabbed his arm. He raised his gun and fired some sparks at Boyd, shouted "You're dead!"

"Come over here, Davy Crockett!" Boyd said.

The boy just stood there with the gun in his hand. He was not going to come, and McKee could see it—he had as stubborn a streak in him as Boyd—but he slipped that gun back into the holster, and came. He just walked, he didn't run, he just walked clean across the ring to the funk hole, slipped in through it, then came along the alley to where Boyd stood.

"Am I Davy Crockett now?" he said.

"Sure you are," said Boyd, "you're the old frontiersman," and leaned over the rail at the front and got hold of him. He pulled him up and stood him in the seat, brushed the sand off his front. "Here's your man," Boyd said, slapped him across the bottom, but the boy just stood there.

"I got his hat now, too," said the boy.

"Sure you have," said Boyd, "go show it to your grandma—" and set him down in the aisle, gave him a shove.

"Son," said McKee, trying an old tack, "you want to bring your great-granddaddy along with you?"

Putting the boy in charge of something, especially the old man, usually brought him to heel. But this time it didn't. The old man popped up, like he'd heard that, and went along the rail by himself. It wasn't like him to move a foot without the boy, and McKee wondered if that was more of Boyd's doing.

"Now you come here—" he said, raising his voice, but the boy just stood there, doing nothing. McKee needed help, that is he could use it, but where could he turn with his wife gone and just this foreigner with his mental patient there in their seats? In spite of all the racket the woman,

Mrs. Kahler, looked like she was asleep. Her head lolled on his shoulder, and he didn't look too wide awake himself.

"Gordon," said McKee, "you come *here*—" but the boy neither moved nor sassed him back. McKee would have liked it better if he'd hollered *no*, or fired off his gun.

"You better go along, kid," Boyd said, and as you might expect, he came right along. McKee gave his hand a shake when he got a grip on it, but the boy didn't seem to notice that, or fight it. McKee could feel the ring sand on it that stuck to his own sweaty palm. It made him feel a little silly, since nothing much had happened. Nothing at all.

"His grandmother thinks a lot of this boy," he said aloud, to help explain how he had acted, and nine times out of ten the boy would have said how much *he* thought of his grandmother. But this time he didn't. It wasn't like him. McKee wondered if running around like that hadn't made him pretty tired.

"I guess I better get this boy where he belongs," he said, meaning in bed. Even the boy understood it.

"And where is that?" said Boyd.

Did McKee see him smile? Just the top of his head was lighted—the way it had been in that New York attic—the light in such a way that McKee couldn't see his face. Something about it, the way McKee felt about it, was the same. That anything might happen. The way Mrs. McKee had felt about Boyd most of her life. McKee too, but he usually didn't seem to mind. But the way he felt about it now troubled him. The swarm of kids on the sand, the bonfires high in the bullring, and the way Boyd just stood there, smiling at him, gave McKee the eerie feeling he had in Texas when they butchered that hog. What had it been? That there was more going on than met the eye. More to the shooting of the hog, the clotted pail of flies, the shaved body of the hog like a corpse in the moonlight, with the head gazing at him, through its third eye, from the pail. Didn't he see on Boyd, as on the face of that hog, the same amused smile?

"You know as well as I do, Boyd—" he began, but he could sense the trouble coming. That wild streak in him. He took a fresh grip on the boy's hand and said, "This boy belongs to his grandma."

"You're too late," Boyd replied. Did McKee see him shrug?

"Too late for *what?*" said McKee. Not that he wanted to know, God knows, but he just stood there. How did Mrs. McKee always put it? That Boyd had them bewitched.

"The kid's changed," said Boyd, as if the kid wasn't there. As if this change struck him as a sad one. "He's got a new pitch. He's just torn the pocket off Ty Cobb's pants."

"Don't you go putting ideas into this boy's head," said McKee and gave the boy's hand a tug.

"You're too late," replied Boyd. "Whose boy you think he is?"

"You watch what you're saying, Boyd," said McKee, and dragged the boy up the aisle to get him out of earshot.

"Right now," Boyd yelled, "he's the son of Davy Crockett. But any day now he may swap it for a pocket!"

"When he does!—" McKee hollered, shouting like an old fool, "I hope it doesn't do to him what it did to you!"

Then he wheeled and almost ran along the aisle, dragging the boy. Near the exit he suddenly remembered, looked around wildly, and said, "You see your great-granddaddy?"

They didn't. When the old man wanted to he could scoot off at quite a clip. He couldn't see, but he could smell his way around like a dog.

"We got to find your great-granddaddy, son," he said, since he knew they would never be lucky enough to lose him. If they did, somebody from Omaha or Lincoln would

run into him. There would be another article to the effect
that his children had taken him clean down to Mexico and
ditched him.

"You got better eyes than your grandpa," he said. "You
look for him."

He wiped the palm of his own sweaty hand on his pants,
then wiped the boy's hand with a piece of wadded Kleenex.
The boy let him do it. It wasn't like him to stand there and
not complain.

"I'll bet you're hungry as a wolf, aren't you?" said
McKee.

The boy did not reply. Usually he was full of talk and
tugging on McKee like a dog on a leash. Now he just stood
there like a little man. Was he shivering? There were more
of those bonfires high in the ring, and McKee could see,
now, why they had lit them. It was crisp. It got pretty cold
when the sun went down.

"It's a wonder those kids don't burn the place down," he
said, but the boy didn't bite at it. He didn't fire off his gun.
Maybe he had caught a bug, or something. He stood there
with his mouth hanging open, like he had adenoids.

"Son—" said McKee, "I tell you what we do. What do
you say me and you have a little secret?" Was he listening?
McKee gave his hand a tug. "Suppose just you and me
know you were down in the bullring, nobody else?"

"Uncle Gordon," said the boy.

"All right, him too. But just me, you and Uncle Gordon.
Not grandma. Not great-granddaddy. Just him, me and
you."

Did the boy follow that? No answer.

"It would just make your grandma nervous," said McKee,
"and she wouldn't let us go to any more bullfights."

"Ty Cobb too," said the boy.

"*Who?*" said McKee. He just blurted it out, then to

cover up he said, "All right, *him* too. But let's not say where you saw him. Let's not say—" His mouth a little dry, McKee paused to moisten his lips. It wasn't only women who could have intuitions. Did women know that? He had had one, a good one, years ago when he had known that Boyd would never have his own family, and now he had another. A good intuition, but a bad effect. He knew better than the boy knew it himself, what was on his mind. He knew it was a pocket, he knew all about it since McKee had seen it, and the boy hadn't, but he had to keep the boy from so much as mentioning it. If he could do that he might not even know that he had it on his mind—not as well as McKee did—and it might pass off like most of the things on a boy's mind.

"Let grandpa buy you something," said McKee, "what do you want grandpa to buy you?" and led him into the tunnel, where it was getting dark. Up ahead there was light, a little of it, and making the turn on the ramp McKee could see the lean forked legs of the old man. Almost trotting. Doing his damdest to get himself lost. Bygod, let him, thought McKee. Just let him. If that's what he wanted, why, let him. So he stopped right there, in the tunnel, took out that cigar he hadn't finished, and took all the time in the world lighting it up. He gave the boy the band on it, for his collection, and slipped it down on his trigger finger.

"There you are," he said. "Now how you like that?"

He didn't say anything.

"Let's take it a little easy now," he said, "your grandma might wonder why you got so sweaty."

Running around in the ring like a yahoo had got him worked up. As often as McKee wiped his hand off, it got sticky again. They went easy up the ramp, letting people go by them, giving the old fool time enough to lose himself forever, if that's what he had in mind. Right outside the gate a man was selling bulls, little black paper bulls with white horns on them.

"You can have a bull," said McKee to the boy. "You want a bull?"

"It's not a bull if you buy it," said the boy.

Who told him that? No need for McKee to guess. He was fond of the boy, but he had a strong impulse to take the paper bull and crown him with it.

"Okay—" said McKee, "since you're so smart I'll just buy a little bull for myself. And while I'm at it I think I'll buy myself a pair of these real horns."

Which he did. Just as if he was out of his mind. One of those fool toy bulls, and mounted on a big board, a pair of real bull horns. Two hundred pesos. That was almost twenty dollars for a pair of damn horns. He had to carry the bull, since it seemed a little fragile, and to take the horns he had to drop the boy's hand. Off he scooted.

"Now you come back here!" called McKee.

But of course he didn't. He ran like he was crazy, but he seemed to know where he was going. Right down the road to their own station wagon, where the lights were on. Mc-Kee saw the door open, then he saw his grandma hug him like she already knew all about it, even before he told her, but she could hardly wait to hear it again. 'Way at the back of the car, since the lights were on, he could see old Scanlon sitting up spruce as a fiddle, proud of the fact that he'd ducked McKee and made it back by himself. Very likely he had told her that McKee had walked off and left him somewhere. The way he did in Laredo. Scooting back across the bridge like McKee was trying to kidnap him.

McKee walked up slow, but when he reached the door nobody seemed to care, or open it for him. They let him stand there with this bull, with these horns he was holding, while they sat smug inside, like they were in a phone booth, and he would have to wait until they had put through their call. All the windows were up, and only the button on the dashboard would run them down. But he could hear the boy yelling like his heart was broke. McKee could tell you, even though he couldn't hear it, just what it was that boy was yelling, and that it wasn't for a bull, a bull's horns, or anything like that. Not any longer. No, he was yelling for something else. He was yelling for something, McKee could tell you, that he couldn't buy even if he had the money, and gazing at McKee were the serene blue eyes of his wife. Ice-blue, Boyd called them. In matters like that he usually proved to be right.

PART III

IN
THE
SUBURBS

THE
RAM
IN
THE
THICKET

A short story

IN this dream Mr. Ormsby stood in the yard—at the edge of the yard where the weeds began—and stared at a figure that appeared to be on a rise. This figure had the head of a bird with a crown of bright, exotic plumage—visible, somehow, in spite of the helmet he wore. Wisps of it appeared at the side, or shot through the top of it like a pillow leaking long sharp spears of yellow straw. Beneath the helmet was the face of a bird, a long face indescribably solemn, with eyes so pale they were like openings on the sky. The figure was clothed in a uniform, a fatigue suit that was dry at the top but wet and dripping about the waist and knees. Slung over the left arm, very casually, was a gun. The right arm was extended and above it hovered a procession of birds, an endless coming and going of all the birds he had ever seen. The figure did not speak—nor did the pale eyes turn to look at him—although it was for this, this alone, that Mr. Ormsby was there. The only sounds he heard were those his lips made for the birds, a wooing call of irresistible charm. As he stared Mr. Ormsby realized that he was pinned to something, a specimen pinned to a wall that had quietly moved up

587

behind. His hands were fastened over his head and from the weight he felt in his wrists he knew he must be suspended there. He knew he had been brought there to be judged, sentenced, or whatever—and this would happen when the figure looked at him. He waited, but the sky-blue eyes seemed only to focus on the birds, and his lips continued to speak to them wooingly. They came and went, thousands of them, and there were so many, and all so friendly, that Mr. Ormsby, also, extended his hand. He did this although he knew that up to that moment his hands were tied—but strange to relate, in that gesture, he seemed to be free. Without effort he broke the bonds and his hand was free. No birds came—but in his palm he felt the dull drip of the alarm clock and he held it tenderly, like a living thing, until it ran down.

In the morning light the photograph at the foot of his bed was a little startling—for the boy stood alone on a rise, and he held, very casually, a gun. The face beneath the helmet had no features, but Mr. Ormsby would have known it just by the—well, just by the stance. He would have known it just by the way the boy held the gun. He held the gun like some women held their arms when their hands were idle, like parts of their body that for the moment were not much use. Without the gun it was as if some part of the boy had been amputated; the way he stood, even the way he walked was not quite right. But with the gun—what seemed out, fell into place.

He had given the boy a gun because he had never had a gun himself and not because he wanted him to kill anything. The boy didn't want to kill anything either—he couldn't very well with his first gun because of the awful racket the bee-bees made in the barrel. He had given him a thousand-shot gun—but the rattle the bee-bees made in the barrel made it impossible for the boy to get close to anything. And *that* was what had made a hunter out of him. He had to stalk everything in order to get close enough to hit it, and after you stalk it you naturally want to hit something. When he got a gun that would really shoot, and only made a racket after he shot it, it was only natural that he shot it better than anyone else. He said shoot, because the boy never seemed to realize that when he shot and hit something the something was dead. He simply didn't realize this side of things at all. But when he brought a rabbit home and fried it—by himself, for Mother wouldn't let *him* touch it—he never kidded them about the meat they ate themselves. He never really knew whether the boy did that out of kindness for Mother, or simply because he never thought about such things. He never seemed to feel like talking much about anything. He would sit and listen to Mother—he had never once been disrespectful—nor had he ever once heeded anything she said. He would listen, respectfully, and that was all. It was a known fact that Mother knew more about birds and bird migration than anyone in the state of Pennsylvania—except the boy. It was clear to him that the boy knew more, but for years it had been Mother's business and it meant more to her—the business did—than to the boy. But it was only natural that a woman who founded the League for Wild Life Conservation would be upset by a boy who lived with a gun. It was only natural—he was upset himself by the *idea* of it—but the boy and his gun somehow never bothered him. He had never seen a boy and a dog, or a boy and anything, any closer—and if the truth were known both the boy's dogs knew it, nearly died of it. Not that he wasn't friendly, or as nice to them as any boy, but they knew they simply didn't rate in a class with his gun. Without that gun the boy himself really looked funny, didn't know how to stand, and nearly fell over if you talked to him. It was only natural that he enlisted, and there was nothing he ever heard that surprised him less than their making a hero out of him. Nothing more natural than that they should name something after him. If the boy had had his choice it would have been a gun rather than a boat, a thousand-shot non-rattle bee-bee gun named Ormsby. But it would kill Mother if she knew—maybe it would kill nearly anybody—what he thought was the most natural thing of all. Let God strike him dead if he had known anything righter, anything more natural, than that the boy should be killed. That was something he could not explain, and would certainly never mention to Mother unless he slipped up some night and talked in his sleep.

He turned slowly on the bed, careful to keep the springs quiet, and as he lowered his feet he scooped his socks from the floor. As a precaution Mother had slept the first few months of their marriage in her corset—as a precaution and as an aid to self-control. In the fall they had ordered twin beds. Carrying his shoes—today, of all days, would be a trial for Mother—he tiptoed to the closet and picked up his shirt and pants. There was simply no reason, as he had explained to her twenty years ago, why she should get up when he could just as well get a bite for himself. He had made that suggestion when the boy was just a baby and she needed her strength. Even as it was she didn't come out of it any too well. The truth was, Mother was so thorough about everything she did that her breakfasts usually took an hour or more. When he did it himself he was out of the kitchen in ten, twelve minutes and without leaving any pile of dishes around. By himself he could quick-rinse them in a little hot water, but with Mother there was the dish pan and all of the suds. Mother had the idea that a meal simply wasn't a meal without setting the table and using half the dishes in the place. It was easier to do it himself, and except for Sunday, when they had brunch, he was out of the house an hour before she got up. He had a bite of lunch at the store and at four o'clock he did the day's shopping since he was right downtown anyway. There was a time he called her up and inquired as to what she thought she wanted, but since he did all the buying he knew that better himself. As secretary for the League of Women Voters she had enough on her mind in times like these without cluttering it up with food. Now that he left the store an hour early he usually got home in the midst of her nap or while she was taking her bath. As he had nothing else to do he prepared the vegetables, and dressed the meat, as Mother had never shown much of a flair for meat. There had been a year—when the boy was small and before he had taken up that gun—when she had made several marvelous lemon meringue pies. But feeling as she did about the gun—and she told them both how she felt about it—she didn't see why she should slave in the kitchen for people like that. She always spoke to them as *they*—or as *you* plural—from the time he had given the boy the gun. Whether this was because they were both men, both culprits, or both something else, they were never entirely separate things again. When she called *they* would both answer, and though the boy had been gone two years he still felt him *there*, right beside him, when Mother said *you*.

For some reason he could not understand—although the rest of the house was as neat as a pin, too neat—the room they *lived* in was always a mess. Mother refused to let the cleaning woman set her foot in it. Whenever she left the house she locked the door. Long, long ago he had said something, and she had said something, and she had said she had wanted one room in the house where she could relax and just let her hair down. That had sounded so wonderfully human, so unusual for Mother, that he had been completely taken with it. As a matter of fact he still didn't

know what to say. It was the only room in the house—
except for the screened-in porch in the summer—where he
could take off his shoes and open his shirt on his underwear.
If the room was *clean*, it would be clean like all of the
others, and that would leave him nothing but the basement
and the porch. The way the boy took to the out-of-doors—
he stopped looking for his cuff links, began to look for
pins—was partially because he couldn't find a place in the
house to sit down. They had just redecorated the house—
the boy at that time was just a little shaver—and Mother
had spread newspapers over everything. There hadn't been
a chair in the place—except the straight-backed ones at the
table—that hadn't been, that *wasn't* covered with a piece of
newspaper. Anyone who had ever scrunched around on a
paper knew what that was like. It was at that time that he
had got the idea of having his pipe in the basement, reading
in the bedroom, and the boy had taken to the out-of-doors.
Because he had always wanted a gun himself, and because
the boy was alone, with no kids around to play with, he had
brought him home that damn gun. A thousand-shot gun by
the name of Daisy—funny that he should remember the
name—and five thousand bee-bees in a drawstring canvas
bag.

That gun had been a mistake—he began to shave himself
in tepid, lukewarm water rather than let it run hot, which
would bang the pipes and wake Mother up. That gun had
been a mistake—when the telegram came that the boy had
been killed Mother hadn't said a word, but she made it clear
whose fault it was. There was never any doubt, *any* doubt,
as to just whose fault it was.

He stopped thinking while he shaved, attentive to the
mole at the edge of his mustache, and leaned to the mirror
to avoid dropping suds on the rug. There had been a time
when he had wondered about an oriental throw rug in the

bathroom, but over twenty years he had become accustomed to it. As a matter of fact he sort of missed it whenever they had guests with children and Mother remembered to take it up. Without the rug he always felt just a little uneasy, a little naked, in the bathroom, and this made him whistle or turn on the water and let it run. If it hadn't been for that he might not have noticed as soon as he did that Mother did the same thing whenever anybody was in the house. She turned on the water and let it run until she was through with the toilet, then she would flush it before she turned the water off. If you happen to have old-fashioned plumbing, and have lived with a person for twenty years, you can't help noticing little things like that. He had got to be a little like that himself: since the boy had gone he used the one in the basement or waited until he got down to the store. As a matter of fact it was more convenient, didn't wake Mother up, and he could have his pipe while he was sitting there.

With his pants on, but carrying his shirt—for he might get it soiled preparing breakfast—he left the bathroom and tiptoed down the stairs.

Although the boy had gone, was gone, that is, Mother still liked to preserve her slip covers and the kitchen linoleum. It was a good piece, well worth preserving, but unless there were guests in the house he never saw it—he nearly forgot that it was there. The truth was he had to look at it once a week, every time he put down the papers—but right now he couldn't tell you what color that linoleum was! He couldn't do it, and wondering what in the world color it was he bent over and peeked at it—blue. Blue and white, Mother's favorite colors of course.

Suddenly he felt the stirring in his bowels. Usually this occurred while he was rinsing the dishes after his second cup of coffee or after the first long draw on his pipe. He was not supposed to smoke in the morning, but it was more important to be regular that way than irregular with his pipe. Mother had been the first to realize this—not in so many words—but she would rather he did anything than not be able to do *that*.

He measured out a pint and a half of water, put it over a medium fire, and added just a pinch of salt. Then he walked to the top of the basement stairs, turned on the light, and at the bottom turned it off. He dipped his head to pass beneath a sagging line of wash, the sleeves dripping, and with his hands out, for the corner was dark, he entered the cell.

The basement toilet had been put in to accommodate the help, who had to use something, and Mother would not have them on her oriental rug. Until the day he dropped some money out of his pants and had to strike a match to look for it, he had never noticed what kind of a stool it was. Mother had picked it up secondhand—she had never told him where—because she couldn't see buying something new for a place always in the dark. It was very old, with a chain pull, and operated on a principle that invariably produced quite a splash. But in spite of that, he preferred it to the one at the store and very much more than the one upstairs. This was rather hard to explain since the seat was pretty cold in the winter and the water sometimes nearly froze. But it was private like no other room in the house. Considering that the house was as good as empty, that was a strange thing to say, but it was the only way to say how he felt. If he went off for a walk like the boy, Mother would miss him, somebody would see him, and he wouldn't feel right about it anyhow. All he wanted was a dark quiet place and the feeling that for five minutes, just five minutes, nobody would be looking for him. Who would ever believe five minutes like that were so hard to come by? The closest he had ever been to the boy—after he had given him the

gun—was the morning he had found him here on the stool.
It was then that the boy had said, *et tu, Brutus,* and they
had both laughed so hard they had had to hold their sides.
The boy had put his head in a basket of wash so Mother
wouldn't hear. Like everything the boy said there were two
or three ways to take it, and in the dark Mr. Ormsby could
not see his face. When he stopped laughing the boy said,
Well, Pop, I suppose one flush ought to do, but Mr.
Ormsby had not been able to say anything. To be called
Pop made him so weak that he had to sit right down on the
stool, just like he was, and support his head in his hands.
Just as he had never had a name for the boy, the boy had
never had a name for him—none, that is, that Mother would
permit him to use. Of all the names Mother couldn't stand,
Pop was the worst, and he agreed with her, it was vulgar,
common, and used by strangers to intimidate old men. He
agreed with her, completely—until he heard the word in
the boy's mouth. It was only natural that the boy would use
it if he ever had the chance—but he never dreamed that any
word, especially *that* word, could mean what it did. It made
him weak, he had to sit down and pretend he was going
about his business, and what a blessing it was that the place
was dark. Nothing more was said, ever, but it remained
their most important conversation—so important they were
afraid to try and improve on it. Days later he remembered
the rest of the boy's sentence, and how shocking it was but
without any *sense* of shock. A blow so sharp that he had no
sense of pain, only a knowing, as he had under gas, that he
had been worked on. For two, maybe three minutes, there
in the dark they had been what Mother called them, they
were *they*—and they were there in the basement because
they were so much alike. When the telegram came, and
when he knew what he would find, he had brought it there,
had struck a match, and read what it said. The match filled

the cell with light and he saw—he couldn't help seeing—
piles of tin goods in the space beneath the stairs. Several
dozen cans of tuna fish and salmon, and since *he* was the one
that had the points, bought the groceries, there was only
one place Mother could have got such things. It had been a
greater shock than the telegram—that was the honest-to-
God's truth and anyone who knew Mother as well as he did
would have felt the same. It was unthinkable, but there it
was—and there were more on top of the water closet,
where he peered while precariously balanced on the stool.
Cans of pineapple, crabmeat, and tins of Argentine beef. He
had been stunned, the match had burned down and actually
scorched his fingers, and he nearly killed himself when he
forgot and stepped off the seat. Only later in the morning—
after he had sent the flowers to ease the blow for Mother—
did he realize how such a thing *must* have occurred. Mother
knew so many influential people, and before the war they
gave her so much, that they had very likely given her all of
this stuff as well. Rather than turn it down and needlessly
alienate people, influential people, Mother had done the next
best thing. While the war was on she refused to serve it, or
profiteer in any way—and at the same time not alienate
people foolishly. It had been an odd thing, certainly, that he
should discover all of that by the same match that he read
the telegram. Naturally, he never breathed a word of it to
Mother, as something like that, even though she was not
superstitious, would really upset her. It was one of those
things that he and the boy would keep to themselves.

It would be like Mother to think of putting it in here, the
very last place that the cleaning woman would look for it.
The new cleaning woman would neither go upstairs nor
down, and did whatever she did somewhere else. Mr.
Ormsby lit a match to see if everything was all right—
hastily blew it out when he saw that the can pile had

increased. He stood up—then hurried up the stairs without buttoning his pants as he could hear the water boiling. He added half a cup, then measured three heaping tablespoons of coffee into the bottom of the double boiler, buttoned his pants. Looking at his watch he saw that it was seven-thirty-five. As it would be a hard day—sponsoring a boat was a man-size job—he would give Mother another ten minutes or so. He took two bowls from the cupboard, sat them on blue pottery saucers, and with the grapefruit knife in his hand walked to the icebox.

As he put his head in the icebox door—in order to see he had to—Mr. Ormsby stopped breathing and closed his eyes. What had been dying for some time was now dead. He leaned back, inhaled, leaned in again. The floor of the icebox was covered with a fine assortment of jars full of leftovers Mother simply could not throw away. Some of the jars were covered with little oilskin hoods, some with saucers, and some with paper snapped on with a rubber band. It was impossible to tell, from the outside, which one it was. Seating himself on the floor he removed them one at a time, starting at the front and working toward the back. As he had done this many times before, he got well into the problem, near the middle, before troubling to sniff anything. A jar which might have been carrots—it was hard to tell without probing—was now a furry marvel of green mold. It smelled only mildly, however, and Mr. Ormsby remembered that this was penicillin, the life-giver. A spoonful of cabbage—it had been three months since they had had cabbage—had a powerful stench but was still not the one he had in mind. There were two more jars of mold, the one screwed tight he left alone as it had a frosted look and the top of the lid bulged. The culprit, however, was not that at all, but in an open saucer on the next shelf—part of an egg—Mr. Ormsby had beaten the white himself. He placed the saucer on the sink and returned all but two of the jars to the icebox; the cabbage and the explosive looking one. If it smelled he took it out, otherwise Mother had to see for herself as she refused to take *their* word for these things. When he was just a little shaver the boy had walked into the living room full of Mother's guests and showed them something in a jar. Mother had been horrified—but she naturally thought it a frog or something and not a bottle out of her own icebox. When one of the ladies asked the boy where in the world he had found it, he naturally said, *In the icebox.* Mother had never forgiven him. After that she forbade him to look in the box without permission, and the boy had not so much as peeked in it since. He would eat only what he found on the table, or ready to eat in the kitchen—or what he found at the end of those walks he took everywhere.

With the jar of cabbage and furry mold Mr. Ormsby made a trip to the garage, picked up the garden spade, walked around behind. At one time he had emptied the jars and merely buried the contents, but recently, since the war that is, he had buried it all. Part of it was a question of time—he had more work to do at the store—but the bigger part of it was to put an end to the jars. Not that it worked out that way—all Mother had to do was open a new one— but it gave him a real satisfaction to bury them. Now that the boy and his dogs were gone there was simply no one around the house to eat up all the food Mother saved.

There were worms in the fork of earth he had turned and he stood looking at them—*they* both had loved worms— when he remembered the water boiling on the stove. He dropped everything and ran, ran right into Emil Ludlow, the milkman, before he noticed him. Still on the run he went up the steps and through the screen door into the kitchen—he was clear to the stove before he remembered the door would slam. He started back, but too late, and in the silence that followed the *bang* he stood with his eyes tightly closed, his fists clenched. Usually he remained in this condition until a sign from Mother—a thump on the floor or her voice at the top of the stairs. None came, however, only the sound of the milk bottles that Emil Ludlow was leaving on the porch. Mr. Ormsby gave him time to get away, waited until he heard the horse walking, then he went out and brought the milk in. At the icebox he remembered the water—why it was he had come running in the first place—and he left the door open and hurried to the stove. It was down to half a cup but not, thank heavens, dry. He added a full pint, then returned and put the milk in the icebox; took out the butter, four eggs, and a Flori-gold grapefruit. Before he cut the grapefruit he looked at his watch and seeing that it was ten minutes to eight, an hour before train time, he opened the stairway door.

"Ohhh Mother!" he called, and then he returned to the grapefruit.

Ad astra per aspera, she said, and rose from the bed. In the darkness she felt about for her corset then let herself go completely for the thirty-five seconds it required to get it on. This done, she pulled the cord to the light that hung in the attic, and as it snapped on, in a firm voice she said, *Fiat lux*. Light having been made, Mother opened her eyes.

As the bulb hung in the attic, thirty feet away and out of sight, the closet remained in an afterglow, a twilight zone. It was not light, strictly speaking, but it was all Mother wanted to see. Seated on the attic stairs she trimmed her toenails with a pearl handled knife that Mr. Ormsby had been missing for several years. The blade was not so good any longer and using it too freely had resulted in ingrown nails on both of her big toes. But Mother preferred it to scissors which were proven, along with bathtubs, to be one of the most dangerous things in the home. *Even more than the battlefield, the most dangerous place in the world. Dry feet and hands before turning on lights, dry between toes.*

Without stooping she slipped into her sabots and left the closet, the light burning, and with her eyes dimmed, but not closed, went down the hall. Locking the bathroom door she stepped to the basin and turned on the cold water, then she removed several feet of paper from the toilet paper roll. This took time, as in order to keep the roller from squeaking, it had to be removed from its socket in the wall, then returned. One piece she put in the pocket of her kimono, the other she folded into a wad and used as a blotter to dab up spots on the floor. Turning up the water she sat down on the stool—then she got up to get a pencil and pad from the table near the window. On the first sheet she wrote—

> Ars longa, vita brevis
> Wildflower club, Sun. 4 pm.

She tore this off and filed it, tip showing, right at the front of her corset. On the next page—

> ROGER—
> Ivory Snow
> Sani-Flush on Thurs.

As she placed this on top of the toilet paper roll she heard him call "First for breakfast." She waited until he closed the stairway door, then she stood up and turned on the shower. As it rained into the tub and splashed behind her in the basin, she lowered the lid, flushed the toilet. Until the water closet had filled, stopped gurgling, she stood at the window watching a squirrel cross the yard from tree to tree. Then she turned the shower off and noisily dragged the shower curtain, on its metal rings, back to the wall. She dampened her shower cap in the basin and hung it on the towel rack to dry, dropping the towel that was there down the laundry chute. This done, she returned to the basin and held her hands under the running water, now cold, until she was awake. With her index finger she massaged her gums—*there is no pyorrhea among the Indians*—and then, with the tips of her fingers, she dampened her eyes.

She drew the blind, and in the half light the room seemed to be full of lukewarm water, greenish in color. With a piece of Kleenex, she dried her eyes, then turned it to gently blow her nose, first the left side, then with a little more blow on the right. There was nothing to speak of, nothing, so she folded the tissue, slipped it into her pocket. Raising the blind, she faced the morning with her eyes softly closed, letting the light come in as prescribed— gradually. Eyes wide, she then stared for a full minute at the yard full of grackles, covered with grackles, before she *discovered* them. Running to the door, her head in the hall, her arm in the bathroom wildly pointing, she tried to whisper, loud-whisper to him, but her voice cracked.

"Roger," she called, a little hoarsely. "The window— run!"

She heard him turn from the stove and skid on the newspapers, bump into the sink, curse, then get up and on again.

"Blackbirds?" he whispered.

"Grackles!" she said, for the thousandth time she said *Grackles*.

"They're pretty!" he said.

"Family—" she said, ignoring him, "family *icteridae* American."

"Well—" he said.

"Roger!" she said, "something's burning."

She heard him leave the window and on his way back to the stove, on the same turn, skid on the papers again. She left him there and went down the hall to the bedroom, closed the door, and passed between the mirrors once more to the closet. From five dresses—*any woman with more than five dresses, at this time, should have the vote taken away from her*—she selected the navy blue sheer with pink lace yoke and kerchief, short bolero. At the back of the closet—but in order to see she had to return to the bathroom, look for the flashlight in the drawer full of rags and old tins of shoe polish—were three shelves, each supporting ten to twelve pairs of shoes, and a large selection of slippers were piled on the floor. On the second shelf were the navy blue pumps—*we all have one weakness, but between men and shoes you can give me shoes*—navy blue pumps with a cuban heel and a small bow. She hung the dress from the neck of the floor lamp, placed the shoes on the bed. From beneath the bed she pulled a hat box—the hat was new. Navy straw with shasta daisies, pink geraniums and a navy blue veil with pink and white fuzzy dots. She held it out where it could be seen in the mirror, front and side, without seeing herself—*it's not every day that one sponsors a boat*. Not every day, and she turned to the calendar on her night table, a bird calendar featuring the natural-color male goldfinch for the month of June. Under the date of June 23rd she printed the words, *family icteridae—yardful*, and beneath it—

Met Captain Sudcliffe and gave him U.S.S. *Ormsby*

When he heard Mother's feet on the stairs Mr. Ormsby cracked her soft-boiled eggs and spooned them carefully into her heated cup. He had spilled his own on the floor when he had run to look at the black—or whatever color they were—birds. As they were very, very soft he had merely wiped them up. As he buttered the toast—the four burned slices were on the back porch airing—Mother entered the kitchen and said, "Roger—*more* toast?"

"I was watching blackbirds," he said.

"Grack-les," she said. "Any bird is a *black*bird if the males are largely or entirely black."

Talk about male and female birds really bothered Mr. Ormsby. Although she was a girl of the old school Mother never hesitated, *anywhere*, to speak right out about male and female birds. A cow was a cow, a bull was a bull, but to Mr. Ormsby a bird was a bird.

"Among the birdfolk," said Mother, "the menfolk, so to speak, wear the feathers. The female has more serious work to do."

"How does that fit the blackbirds?" said Mr. Ormsby.

"Every rule," said Mother, "has an exception."

There was no denying the fact that the older Mother got the more distinguished she appeared. As for himself, what he saw in the mirror looked very much like the Roger Ormsby that had married Violet Ames twenty years ago. As the top of his head got hard the bottom tended to get a little soft, but otherwise there wasn't much change. But it was hard to believe that Mother was the pretty little pop-eyed girl—he had thought it was her corset that popped them—whose nipples had been like buttons on her dress. Any other girl would have looked like a you-know—but there wasn't a man in Media county, or anywhere else, who ever mentioned it. A man could think what he would think, but he was the only man who really knew what Mother was like. And how little she was like *that*.

"Three-seven-four east one-one-six," said Mother.

That was the way her mind worked, all over the place in one cup of coffee—birds one moment, Mrs. Dinardo the next.

He got up from the table and went after Mrs. Dinardo's letter—Mother seldom had time to read them unless he read them to her. Returning, he divided the rest of the coffee between them, unequally: three quarters for Mother, a swallow of grounds for himself. He waited a moment, wiping his glasses, while Mother looked through the window at another black bird. "Cowbird," she said, *"Molothrus ater."*

"Dear Mrs. Ormsby," Mr. Ormsby began. Then he stopped to scan the page, as Mrs. Dinardo had a strange style and was not much given to writing letters. "Dear Mrs. Ormsby," he repeated, "I received your letter and I Sure was glad to know that you are both well and I know you often think of me I often think of you too—" He paused to get his breath—Mrs. Dinardo's style was not much for pauses—and to look at Mother. But Mother was still with the cowbird. "Well, Mrs. Ormsby," he continued, "I haven't a thing in a room that I know of the people that will be away from the room will be only a week next month. But come to See me I may have Something if you don't get Something." Mrs. Dinardo, for some reason, always capitalized the letter S which along with everything else didn't make it easier to read. "We are both well and he is Still in the Navy Yard. My I do wish the war was over it is So long. We are So tired of it do come and See us when you give them your boat. Wouldn't a Street be better than a boat? If you are going to name Something why not a Street? Here in my hand is news of a boat Sunk what is wrong with Ormsby on a Street? Well 116 is about the Same we have the river and its nice. If you don't find Something See me I may have Something. Best love, Mrs. Myrtle Dinardo."

It was quite a letter to get from a woman that Mother had known, known Mother, that is, for nearly eighteen years. Brought in to nurse the boy—he could never understand why a woman like Mother, with her figure—but anyhow, Mrs. Dinardo was brought in. Something in her milk, Dr. Paige said, when it was as plain as the nose on your face it was nothing in the milk, but something in the boy. He just refused, plain refused, to nurse with Mother. The way the little rascal would look at her, but not a sound out of him but gurgling when Mrs. Dinardo would scoop him up and go upstairs to their room—the only woman—other woman, that is, that Mother ever let step inside of it. She had answered an ad that Mother had run, on Dr. Paige's suggestion, and they had been like *that* from the first time he saw them.

"I'll telephone," said Mother.

On the slightest provocation Mother would call Mrs. Dinardo by long distance—she had to come down four flights of stairs to answer—and tell her she was going to broadcast over the radio or something. Although Mrs. Dinardo hardly knew one kind of bird from another, Mother sent her printed copies of every single one of her bird-lore lectures. She also sent her hand-pressed flowers from the garden.

"I'll telephone," repeated Mother.

"My own opinion—" began Mr. Ormsby, but stopped when Mother picked up her eggcup, made a pile of her plates, and started toward the sink. "I'll take care of that," he said. "Now you run along and telephone." But Mother walked right by him and took her stand at the sink. With one hand—with the other she held her kimono close about her—she let the water run into the large dish pan. Mr. Ormsby had hoped to avoid this; now he would have to first rinse, then dry, every piece of silver and every dish they had used. As Mother could only use one hand it would be even slower than usual.

"We don't want to miss our local," he said. "You better run along and let me do it."

"Cold water," she said, "for the eggs." He had long ago learned not to argue with Mother about the fine points of washing pots, pans, or dishes with bits of egg. He stood at the sink with the towel while she went about trying to make suds with a piece of stale soap in a little wire cage. As Mother refused to use a fresh piece of soap, nothing remotely like suds ever appeared. For this purpose, he kept a box of Gold Dust Twins concealed beneath the sink, and when Mother turned her back he slipped some in.

"There now," Mother said, and placed the rest of the dishes in the water, rinsed her fingers under the tap, paused to sniff at them.

"My own opinion—" Mr. Ormsby began, but stopped when Mother raised her finger, the index finger with the scar from the wart she once had. They stood quiet, and Mr. Ormsby listened to the water drip in the sink—the night before he had come down in his bare feet to shut it off. All of the taps dripped now and there was just nothing to do about it but put a rag or something beneath it to break the ping.

"Thrush!" said Mother. "Next to the nightingale the most popular of European songbirds."

"Very pretty," he said, although he simply couldn't hear a thing. Mother walked to the window, folding the collar of her kimono over her bosom and drawing the tails into a hammock beneath her behind. Mr. Ormsby modestly turned away. He quick-dipped one hand into the Gold Dust—drawing it out he slipped it into the dish pan and worked up a suds.

As he finished wiping the dishes she came in with a bouquet for Mrs. Dinardo and arranged it, for the moment, in a tall glass.

"According to her letter," Mrs. Ormsby said, "she isn't too sure of having something—"

"Roger!" she said. "You're dripping."

Mr. Ormsby put his hands over the sink and said, "If

we're going to be met right at the station I don't see where you're going to see Mrs. Dinardo. You're going to be met at the station and then you're going to sponsor the boat. My own opinion is that after the boat we come on home."

"I know that street of hers," said Mother. "There isn't a wildflower on it!"

On the wall above the icebox was a pad of paper and a blue pencil hanging by a string. As Mother started to write the point broke off, fell behind the icebox.

"Mother," he said, "you ever see my knife?"

"Milkman," said Mother. "If we're staying overnight we won't need milk in the morning."

In jovial tones Mr. Ormsby said, "I'll bet we're right back here before dark." That was all, that was *all* that he said. He had merely meant to call her attention to the fact that Mrs. Dinardo said—all but said—that she didn't have a room for them. But when Mother turned he saw that her mustache was showing, a sure sign that she was mad.

"Well—now," Mother said, and lifting the skirt of her kimono, swished around the cabinet and then he heard her on the stairs. From the landing at the top of the stairs she said, "In that case I'm sure there's no need for *my* going. I'm sure the Navy would just as soon have you. After all," she said, "it's *your* name on the boat!"

"Now, Mother," he said, just as she closed the door, *not* slammed it, just closed it as quiet and nice as you'd please. Although he had been through this a thousand times it seemed he was never ready for it, never knew when it would happen, never felt anything but nearly sick. He went into the front room and sat down on the chair near the piano—then got up to arrange the doily at the back of his head. Ordinarily he could leave the house and after three or four days it would blow over, but in all his life—their life—there had been nothing like this. The Government of the

United States—he got up again and called, "OHHhhh Mother!"

No answer.

He could hear her moving around upstairs, but as she often went back to bed after a spat, just moving around didn't mean much of anything. He came back into the front room and sat down on the milk stool near the fireplace. It was the only seat in the room not protected with newspapers. The only thing the boy ever sat on when he had to sit on something. Somehow, thinking about that made him stand up. He could sit in the lawn swing, in the front yard, if Mother hadn't told everybody in town why it was that he, Roger Ormsby, would have to take the day off—not to sit in the lawn swing, not by a long shot. Everybody knew—Captain Sudcliffe's nice letter had appeared on the first page of the *Graphic*, under a picture of Mother leading a bird-lore hike in the Poconos. This picture bore the title LOCAL WOMAN HEADS DAWN BUSTERS, and marked Mother's appearance on the national bird-lore scene. But it was not one of her best pictures—it dated from way back in the twenties and those hipless dresses and round bucket hats were not Mother's type. Until they saw that picture, and the letter beneath it, some people had forgotten that Virgil was missing, and most of them seemed to think it was a good idea to swap him for a boat. The U.S.S. *Ormsby* was a permanent sort of thing. Although he was born and raised in the town hardly anybody knew very much about Virgil, but they all were pretty familiar with his boat. "How's that boat of yours coming along?" they would say, but in more than twenty years nobody had ever asked him about *his* boy. Whose boy? Well, that was just the point. Everyone agreed Ormsby was a fine name for a boat.

It would be impossible to explain to Mother, maybe to anybody for that matter, what this U.S.S. *Ormsby* business meant to him. "The" boy and "The" *Ormsby*—it was a pretty strange thing that they both had the definite article, and gave him the feeling he was facing a monument.

"Oh Rog-gerrr!" Mother called.

"Coming," he said, and made for the stairs.

From the bedroom Mother said, "However I might feel personally, I do have my *own* name to think of. I am not one of these people who can do as they please—Roger, are you listening?"

"Yes, Mother," he said.

"—with their life."

As he went around the corner he found a note pinned to the door.

> Bathroom window up
> Cellar door down
> Is it blue or brown for Navy?

He stopped on the landing and looked up the stairs.

"Did you say something?" she said.

"No, Mother—" he said, then he added, "It's blue. For the Navy, Mother, it's blue."

KATHERINE

From *The Deep Sleep*

HER mother closed the screen, hooked it, and said, "If she thought I would give it to her, she would take it."

"Well, if you're not going to wear it, Mother."

"She is a shrewd customer," her mother said. "If *she* looks at a hat, the hat is coming back." Crossing the room her mother stopped to pick up a piece of Kleenex, but she stayed down there. "Chocolate," she said, "who's been eating chocolate?"

"Did this Muriel get her divorce, Mother?"

"I'm afraid I don't keep track of such things."

"Well, I've never seen a woman work on a married man any harder. If we had a place for her upstairs I think she'd have fainted just to let him carry her somewhere. *Doct-tah Bahhh*—honestly, do they talk like that at Smith?"

Her mother picked up two glasses and said, "I suppose you noticed Mrs. Crowell didn't finish."

"She probably wasn't thirsty, Mother. I didn't finish mine either."

"I don't think she approved of the color of the glasses," her mother said. "If a Crowell approves, they never fail to mention it."

"Right now I don't care whether she approves or not," Katherine said.

Holding the glasses in her hand, her mother stood there listening.

"That ticking—" she said, then, "Who do you suppose has been eating chocolate?"

"Mother, it's after midnight. I'm going to bed."

"If you would listen to her talk," her mother said, "you would suppose she never touched chocolate. But mention Toll House cookies and watch her eyes roll." Her mother put the two glasses on the tray, and then carried the tray into the kitchen. Katherine put the chairs back in place, turned off the lights under the shades, then turned to hear the water running into the sink.

"Mother!" she said.

No answer.

"Mother, we are going to do that tomorrow morning. We are not going to stay up and do it now."

Didn't she hear? Katherine could hear the silver rattling in the pan. She went out into the kitchen where her mother stood leaning on the sink, her hands in the water, working up a suds with a piece of Fels Naptha soap. Behind her the day's plates were stacked, and in a tray at her side was the silver.

"Those new suds are not for me," her mother said.

"Mother, I am not going to argue. I am going to bed."

When the suds appeared her mother said, "Your Grandmother washed and rinsed her dishes. It won't hurt you to listen to what your Grandmother says."

"I am going to be perfectly selfish," said Katherine, "and say that I am the one who is tired. I am the one who wants to go to bed. I've just got to get some sleep for tomorrow. I'm completely worn out."

"I suppose that's where he went," her mother said.

"I don't know or care where he went, Mother, but I know where I am going. But it will do no good if you're going to stay up and wash. You can't sleep in a house where somebody is rattling dishes around."

"Your father and I," her mother replied, "cannot sleep in a house where the dishes are dirty. There has not been a dirty dish in this house in thirty-seven years."

Katherine did not reply. She placed her hands on the sink board, and her knuckles turned white from the way she tried to grasp it, but neither the sink, nor her mother, said anything. At the top of the stairs, in the room where the Grandmother now lay sleeping, Katherine had spent most of her childhood lying awake. Lying awake in the morning listening to her father squeeze the orange juice and make the coffee, and lying awake at night listening to them wash the day's dishes. After the guests had gone, and the children had been put to bed. Then the dishpans that had been hung up the night before would be taken from the hooks and refilled with water, and the dishes that had been rinsed and stacked would be washed again. The silver that had been rinsed, scalded again. Every dish soaked in the soapy water, scrubbed down with the small raddled mop, then dropped into a dishpan of warm water, from where her father picked it up. Every dish, every piece of silver, every piece of glassware, every pot and every pan, passed through this treatment, passed through her hands, then through his. Every faded pink plate with the Willow pattern was carried into the front room and put in its place, and every piece of silver was returned to the silver drawer. Every pot was hung under the sink, or put in the lower shelf of the oven, or placed over the pilot light so it would dry out. And every single piece of it had its own sound, every piece of glassware had its own tinkle, in and out of the water, and every pot had its own rocking motion on the shelf or the wall. Without ever being there, Katherine lived through it all. And all of it without a word, without a *human* sound, as talk or speech was thought to wake them, and the ten thousand noises were supposed to put them to sleep. She never missed a one. She hung on to the last sleepy squeeze of the rag. She could hear the slushy whisper as it made a final pass over everything. Over the top of the stove, over the bread board, over the sink board, over the table, and then the wet flap as her mother hung it up to dry. Spread it out, like a fishnet, between the handles of the faucets, where it gave off an odor like a clogged drain. Then her father would come up the stairs first, carrying his shoes so as not to wake them, and some time later her mother would pad around the house. Trying all the doors, checking all the windows, opening or closing the radiators, and then, but not till then, turning off the lights. And then, but not till then, Katherine would hear the sound of her brother's breathing and the dragging of the weights in the clock that once stood at the foot of the stairs. With her father's snoring, with her mother's silence, she would go to sleep.

"Thirty-seven years and twelve days to be exact," her mother said.

If she went to bed she would lie there awake, just as she had thirty years ago, feeling sorry for her parents, and feeling ashamed of herself. She would lie there awake, curled up in the hole she had lived in most of her childhood, listening to the sounds that came to her from the mouth of the cave. She would sift every sound, every fumbling movement, through her mind. She would sort it all out, like the stuff in a drawer, looking for the key. She would live all of it over, she would bring it up to date for the last twenty years, and then she would be right back again where she started from. There was no key, there was no explanation, there was no solution to the game in the kitchen, to the rules of the house, or to the laws of her mother's world. But they were there. The laws and the rules had not changed. While in the house the only solution was to follow them.

"Where are the dish towels, Mother?" she said.

"Right where they always were," her mother replied.

Why had she asked? To make conversation. To break the spell. Something might be said, just *might* be said, that might explain something. She walked around the table to where the morning dish towel was spread on the radiator, and the lunch towel was fanned out on the rack. It was dry, as today there had been no lunch. Her mother took her hands from the pan of suds, placed her knuckles on her hips and said, "Why, over in Hershey—" she pointed "the entire plumbing system was endangered by the use of detergents in one day's wash." She paused there, then said, "Pedlars left it on the porches, I suppose."

Hershey, Katherine knew, had not suffered from detergents, from some new soap or some new gadget, but from the collapse of moral fibre from within. An un-American shrinking from an honest Fels Naptha wash. A bombing attack that they were unable to resist. Her mother returned her hands to the suds, giving them a stir that made them fizzle, then carefully, as if for a baptism, she dipped the first glass. When Katherine picked it up her mother said—

"Does that have the stamp on the bottom?"

"Yes, Mother—"

"Your Grandmother's jelly glass," she said.

That glass went into the cupboard across the kitchen, where there were five other such glasses, and Katherine and her brother had drunk their milk and orange juice from them. They were cheap brittle glasses, water too hot or too cold might break them, but after seventy years six of them were still there.

"I won't have her thinking we don't take care of her things," her mother said.

In the glass door of the cupboard Katherine could see the light over the sink, and her mother's gray head, her rounded shoulders, bent over the pan. She was worn out. There were dark circles under her eyes. But there was no indication whatsoever that what she was doing was a tiresome chore, or that she merely did it to get it done. There was every indication—if Katherine could believe her eyes—that her mother's hands, elbow deep in the suds, were where they belonged. That every washing motion had a meaning, and accomplished something. After a long day of nothing done, nothing *really* done, just a day that slipped beneath her, she could come to grips with something solid every night. What had been dirtied during the day could be cleaned up. Another day, if and when it came, could be started afresh. One cup at a time, one glass at a time, one spoon, one fork, and one knife at a time, were just so many necessary worthwhile accomplishments. Had it been possible, Katherine wondered, that for more than thirty years her mother had *enjoyed* what Katherine had believed to be the bane of her life? The ten o'clock till midnight daily wash? A time when everything in the house that had been sullied—including the lives of the inhabitants—could be put through three cleansing waters and made pure again. Had she pitied her mother for one of the real joys of her life? Running the water, stirring up the suds, dipping and rinsing the assorted objects, each one of which had some special meaning for her. The Grandmother's jelly glasses, the Willow Ware from the shop in Surrey, the bone-handled knives from the store in Munich, operated by a man named Rautzen, and the family silver that would always lack the bouillon spoons.

"Your father and I," her mother said, washing the can the ripe olives had come in, "always found the time to run our own house."

Her mother, God knows, understood nothing, neither her husband, her son, nor her daughter, but perhaps it was not beyond reason to understand her. Perhaps *that* was just what her husband had done. Perhaps that explained what could not be explained about him.

"What do you do with your extra fat these days?" her mother said.

"We just throw it out, Mother. Nobody seems to want it."

"Well, I will *not* throw it out," she said. She turned to gaze at the Crisco can on the stove, the lid tipped back so the fat could be poured into it. "The people who are pouring it out will be crying for it next," she said.

"That's human nature, Mother."

"It is not *my* nature," her mother replied, and Katherine, a tumbler in her hand, felt it slide down the towel, then strike the radiator. The pieces dropped and scattered on the floor.

"One of the amber?" her mother asked.

"I'm awfully sorry, Mother—"

Her mother turned from the sink, stooped to reach beneath it, and came up with a brush and a dustpan. "I am almost positive," she said, "that Mrs. Crowell didn't care much for them."

"Let me, Mother."

"No, I *know* that radiator." She let her mother slip by, and watched her sweep up the glass. "It gets around the leg. It chews up the linoleum." Her mother swept it up, carefully, then seeing other spots of dirt around her, she went over the general area with her brush. "You see that corner?" she said, and Katherine bent over to look at it. "He comes in and just stands there. He's worse than your father on a piece of rug."

"Mr. Parsons—?" she said.

"If I ask him to sit down, why, then he'll just sit till I ask him to leave."

"I don't know what we would have done without him," Katherine said.

"Your mother would have done whatever she was able," she replied. With the dustpan and the brush, she pushed through the screen to the rear porch. She emptied the broken glass into the waste can, firmly put on the lid, then stood there looking across the yard at the summer night. Katherine could hear her deeply breathing the cool night air. Absently, as if fingering her hair, she removed the sheet of towel paper from the clothesline, and slipped the plastic pin into the pocket of her dress. The summer night was very lovely, and her mother, while her hands were busy, seemed to be listening to the music of the spheres.

"I don't know what I'd do," her mother said, "if other people didn't go to bed."

Katherine waited a moment, then said, "Is it all right if I go now, Mother?"

"Your father would go to bed, but he never slept until I was there."

"Good night, Mother," Katherine said, and when her mother didn't answer she started for the stairs.

"Which one is Orion?" her mother said.

"I'm afraid I've forgotten it all, Mother."

"I'm going to miss your father," her mother said, and Katherine turned, her hand on the stair rail, as if another person, not her mother, had spoken. A voice, perhaps, from one of the letters she never mailed. Katherine wanted to speak, but now that this voice had spoken to her, broken the long silence, she could hardly believe what she heard. She went on up the stairs, entered her room, then closed the door before she remembered, before she noticed, that Paul wasn't there. Still, she would have called to him except for the fact that she had no voice, her throat ached, and he had been the one who had cried that this was a house without tears.

AND
ELSEWHERE

THE
SAFE
PLACE

A short story

IN his fifty-third year a chemical blast burned the beard from the Colonel's face, and gave to his eyes their characteristic powdery blue. Some time later his bushy eyebrows came in white. Silvery streaks of the same color appeared in his hair. To his habitually bored expression these touches gave a certain distinction, a man-of-the-world air, that his barber turned to the advantage of his face. The thinning hair was parted, the lock of silver was deftly curled. The Colonel had an absent-minded way of stroking it back. As he was self-conscious, rather than vain, there was something attractive about this gesture, and a great pity that women didn't seem to interest him. He had married one to reassure himself on that point.

When not away at war the Colonel lived with his wife in an apartment on the Heights, in Brooklyn. She lived at the front with her canary, Jenny Lind, and he lived at the back with his two cats. His wife did not care for cats, particularly, but she had learned to accept the situation, just as the cats had learned, when the Colonel was absent, to shift for themselves. The cleaning women, as a rule, were tipped liberally to be attentive to them. The Colonel supplied the cats with an artificial tree, which they could climb, claw, or puzzle over, and a weekly supply of fresh catnip mice. The mice were given to the cats every Thursday, as on Friday the cleaning woman, with a broom and the vacuum, would try to get the shredded catnip out of the rug. They would then settle back and wait patiently for Thursday again.

The blast improved the Colonel's looks, but it had not been so good for his eyes. They watered a good deal, the pupils were apt to dilate in a strange manner, and he became extremely sensitive to light. In the sun he didn't see any too well. To protect his eyes from the light he wore a large pair of military glasses, with dark lenses, and something like blinders at the sides. He was wearing these glasses when he stepped from the curbing, in uptown Manhattan, and was hit by a pie truck headed south. He was put in the back, with the pies, and carted to a hospital.

He hovered between life and death for several weeks. Nor was there any explanation as to why he pulled through. He had nothing to live for, and his health was not good. In the metal locker at the foot of the bed was the uniform in which he had been delivered, broken up, as the doctor remarked, like a sack of crushed ice. The uniform, however, had come through rather well. There were a few stains, but no bad tears or rips. It had been carefully cleaned, and now hung in the locker waiting for him.

The Colonel, however, showed very little interest in getting up. He seemed to like it, as his wife remarked, well enough in bed. When he coughed, a blue vein would crawl from his hair and divide his forehead, and the salty tears brimming in his weak eyes would stream down his face. He had aged, he was not really alive, but he refused to die. After several weeks he was therefore removed from the ward of hopeless cases, and put among those who were said to have a fifty-fifty chance. Visitors came to this room, and there were radios. From his bed there was a fine view of the city including the East River, the Brooklyn Bridge, part of lower Manhattan, and the harbor from which the Colonel had never sailed. With his military glasses he could see the apartment where his wife and cats lived. On the roofs of the tenements that sprawled below there daily appeared, like a plague of Martian insects, the television aerials that brought to the poor the empty lives of the rich. The Colonel ordered a set, but was told that his failing eyes were too weak.

On the table at his side was a glass of water, boxes of vitamin capsules and pills, an expensive silver lighter, and a blurred photograph of his cats. A bedpan and a carton of cigarettes were on the shelf beneath. The Colonel had a taste for expensive cigarettes, in tins of fifty, or small cedar boxes, but his pleasure seemed to be in the lighter, which required no flint. The small gas cartridge would light, it was said, many thousand cigarettes. As it made no sound, the Colonel played with it at night. During the day he lit many cigarettes and let them smoke in the room, like incense, but during the night he experimented with the small wiry hairs on his chest. Several twisted together, and ignited, would give off a crackling sound. It pleased him to singe the blonde hairs on his fingers, hold them to his nose. When not playing with the lighter the Colonel slept, or sat for hours with an air of brooding, or used his army glasses to examine the teeming life in the streets. What he saw, however, was no surprise to him. To an old army man it was just another bloody battlefield.

In his fifty-third year, having time on his hands, the Colonel was able to see through the glasses what he had known, so to speak, all his life. Life, to put it simply, was a battleground. Every living thing, great or small, spilled its blood on it. Every day he read the uproar made in the press about the horrors of war, the fear of the draft, and what it would do to the life of the fresh eighteen-year-olds. Every moment he could see a life more horrible in the streets. Dangers more unjust, risks more uncalculated, and barracks that were more intolerable. Children fell from windows, were struck by cars in the street, were waylaid and corrupted by evil old men, or through some private evil crawled off to corrupt themselves. Loose boards rose up and struck idle women, knives cut their fingers, fire burned their clothes, or in some useless quarrel they suffered a heart attack. The ambulance appeared after every holiday. The sirens moaned through the streets, like spectres, every night. Doors closed on small fingers, windows fell, small dogs bit bigger dogs, or friends and neighbors, and in the full light of day a man would tumble, head first, down the steps to the street. If this man was a neighbor they might pick him up, but if a stranger they would pass him by, walking in an arc around him the way children swing wide of a haunted house. Or they would stand in a circle, blocking the walk, until the man who was paid to touch a dead man felt the wrist for the pulse, or held the pocket mirror to the face. As if the dead man, poor devil, wanted a final look at himself.

All of this struck the Colonel, an old soldier, as a new kind of battleground. "That's life for you," the Doctor would say, when the Colonel would trouble to point out that the only safe place for a man, or a soldier, was in bed. Trapped there, so to speak, and unable to get up and put on his pants. For it was with his pants that a man put on the world. He became a part of it, he accepted the risks and the foolishness. The Colonel could see this very clearly in the casualties brought to the ward, the men who had fallen on this nameless battlefield. They lay staring at the same world that seemed to terrify the Colonel, but not one of these men was at all disturbed by it. Everything they saw seemed to appeal to them. Every woman reminded them of their wives, and every child of their own children, and the happy times, the wonderful life they seemed to think they had lived. When another victim appeared in the ward they would cry out to ask him "How are things going?" although it was clear things were still going murderously. That it was worth a man's life to put on his pants and appear in the streets. But not one of these men, broken and battered as they were, by the world they had left, had any other thought but a craving to get back to it. To be broken, battered, and bruised all over again. The Colonel found it hard to believe his eyes—both inside and outside of the window—as the world of men seemed to be incomprehensible. It affected, as he knew it would, his feeble will to live. He did not die, but neither did he live, as if the world both inside and outside of the window was a kind of purgatory, a foretaste of hell but with no possibility of heaven. Once a week his wife, a small attractive woman who referred to him as Mr. Army, brought him cookies made with blackstrap molasses, pure brewer's yeast, and wheat germ flour. The recipe was her own, but they were made by the cleaning woman. As Mrs. Porter was several years older than the Colonel, and looked from eight to ten years younger, there was no need to argue the importance of blackstrap and brewer's yeast. The Colonel would ask how the cats were doing, read the mail she had brought him, and when she had left he would distribute the cookies in the ward. A young man named Hyman Kopfman was fond of them.

Hyman Kopfman was a small, rabbit-faced little man who belonged in the hopeless ward, but it had been overcrowded and he couldn't afford a room of his own. When he appeared in the ward he had one leg and two arms, but before the first month had ended they had balanced him up, as he put it himself. He stored the cookies away in the sleeve of the arm that he wore pinned up. Something in Hyman Kopfman's blood couldn't live with the rest of Hyman Kopfman, and he referred to this thing as America. Raising the stump of his leg he would say, "Now you're seeing America first!" Then he would laugh. He seemed to get a great kick out of it. Largely because of Hyman Kopfman, there were men in the ward, some of them pretty battered, who looked on the world outside as a happy place. Only the Colonel seemed to see the connection, so to speak. He didn't know what Hyman Kopfman had in his blood, or where it would show up next, but he knew that he had picked it up, like they all did, there in the streets. What Hyman Kopfman knew was that the world was killing him.

Hyman Kopfman was in pain a good deal of the time and sat leaning forward, his small head in his hand, like a man who was contemplating a crystal globe. During the night he often rocked back and forth, creaking the springs. While the Colonel sat playing with his lighter, Hyman Kopfman would talk, as if to himself, but he seemed to be aware that the Colonel was listening. Hyman Kopfman's way of passing the time was not to look at the world through a pair of field glasses, but to turn his gaze, so to speak, upon himself. Then to describe in considerable detail what he saw. As the Colonel was a reserved, reticent man who considered his life and experience private, Hyman Kopfman was something of a novelty. He spoke of himself as if he were somebody else. There were even times when the Colonel thought he was. At the start Hyman Kopfman gave the impression that he would describe everything that had happened; which he did, perhaps, but all that had happened had not added up to much. He was apt to repeat certain things time and time again. There were nights when the Colonel had the impression that he went over the same material the way a wine press went over the pulp of grapes. But there was always something that refused to squeeze out. That, anyhow, was the Colonel's impression, since it was otherwise hard to explain why he went over the same material time and again; here and there adding a touch, or taking one away.

Hyman Kopfman had been born in Vienna—that was what he said. That should have been of some interest in itself, and as the Colonel had never been to Vienna, he always listened in the hope that he might learn something. But Hyman Kopfman merely talked about himself. He might as well have been born in the Bronx, or anywhere else. He had been a frail boy with girlish wrists and pale blue hands, as he said himself, but with something hard to explain that made him likable. His father had it, but only his mother knew what it was. Hopelessness. It was this, he said, that made him lovable.

The Colonel got awfully tired of this part of the story since Hyman Kopfman was hopeless enough. Too hopeless, in fact. There was nothing about him that was lovable. It was one of the curious conceits he had. His skin was a pale doughy color, and his general health was so poor that when he smiled his waxy gums began to bleed. Thin streaks of red, like veins in marble, showed on his chalky teeth. His eyes were very large, nearly goat-like, with curiously transparent lids, as if the skin had been stretched very thin to cover them. There were times when the eyes, with their large wet whites and peculiarly dilated pupils, gazed upon the Colonel with a somewhat luminous quality. It was disturbing, and had to do, very likely, with his poor health. It was because of his eyes, the Colonel decided, that Hyman Kopfman had picked up the notion that there was something appealing about his hopelessness. Some woman, perhaps his mother, had told him that.

627

At a very early age Hyman Kopfman had been brought to America. With him came his three brothers, his mother, Frau Tabori-Kopfman, and the room full of furniture and clothes that his father had left to them. They went to live in Chicago, where his Uncle Tabori, his mother's brother, had rented an apartment. This apartment was four flights up from the street with a room at the back for Uncle Tabori, a room at the front, called a parlor, and a room in which they lived. In the parlor there were large bay windows but the curtains were kept closed as the light and the circulating air would fade the furniture. It would belong to Paul, the elder brother, when he married someone. In the room were chests full of clothes that his mother had stopped wearing, and his father, a gentleman, had never worn out. They were still as good as new. So it was up to the children to wear them out. It so happened that Mandel Kopfman, the father, had been comparatively small in stature, and his fine clothes would fit Hyman Kopfman, but nobody else. So it was that Hyman Kopfman was accustomed to wear, as he walked between the bedroom and the bathroom, pants of very good cloth, and on his small feet the best grade of spats. French braces held up his pants, and there was also a silver-headed cane, with a sword in the handle, that he sometimes carried as he swaggered down the hall. He didn't trouble, of course, to go down the four flights to the street. Different clothes were being worn down there, small tough boys cursed and shouted, and once down, Hyman Kopfman would have to walk back up. He simply couldn't. He never had the strength.

His older brother, Otto, went down all the time as he worked down there, in a grocery, and returned to tell them what it was all about. He also went to movies, and told them about that. At that time his brother Paul had been too young to go down to the street and work there, so he made the beds and helped his mother around the house. He cooked, he learned to sew, and as he couldn't wear the clothes of Mandel Kopfman, he wore some of the skirts and blouses of his mother, as they fit him all right. It didn't matter, as he never left the rooms. No one but Uncle Tabori ever sat down and talked with them. He worked in the railroad yards that could be seen, on certain clear days, from the roof of the building, where Frau Kopfman went to dry her hair and hang out their clothes. From this roof Hyman Kopfman could see a great park, such as they had at home in Vienna, and in the winter he could hear the ore boats honking on the lake. In spring he could hear the ice cracking up.

Was that Hyman Kopfman's story? If it was, it didn't add up to much. Nor did it seem to gain in the lengthy retelling, night after night. The facts were always the same: Hyman Kopfman had been born, without much reason, in Vienna, and in Chicago he had taken to wearing his father's fancy clothes. As his father had been something of a dandy Hyman Kopfman wore jackets with black satin lapels, shirts with celluloid cuffs and collars, pearl gray spats, French braces, and patent leather shoes. Not that it mattered, since he never went down to the street. He spent day and night in the apartment where he walked from room to room, or with the silver-headed cane he might step into the hall. Concealed in the shaft of the cane was a sword, and when he stepped into the dim gaslit hallway, Hyman Kopfman would draw out the sword and fence with the dancing shadow of himself.

Ha! the Colonel would say, being an old swordsman, but Hyman Kopfman had shot his bolt. He could do no more than wag his feeble wrist in the air. His gums would bleed, his goat-like eyes would glow in a disturbing manner, but it was clear that even fencing with his shadow had been too much for him. Nothing had really happened. The Colonel doubted that anything ever would.

And then one day—one day just in passing—Hyman Kopfman raised his small head from his hand and said that the one thing he missed, really missed, that is, was the daily walk in the blind garden.

In the what? the Colonel said, as he thought he had missed the word.

In the blind garden, Hyman Kopfman replied. Had he somehow overlooked that? Hadn't he told the Colonel about the blind garden?

The Colonel, a cigarette in his mouth, had wagged his head.

At the back of the building there had been a small walled garden, Hyman Kopfman went on, a garden with gravel paths, shady trees, and places to sit. Men and women who were blind came there to walk. There were also flowers to smell, but they couldn't see them of course.

Well, well—the Colonel had replied, as he thought he now had the key to the story. One of the Kopfmans was blind, and Hyman Kopfman was ashamed to mention it. What difference did it make what Hyman Kopfman wore if his brother Paul, for instance, couldn't see him, and if Paul was blind he would hardly care how he looked himself. What difference did it make if he wore his mother's skirts around the house?

Your brother Paul was blind then—? the Colonel said.

Blind? said Hyman Kopfman, and blinked his own big eyes. Who said Paul was blind?

You were just saying— the Colonel replied.

From the window—interrupted Hyman Kopfman—what he saw below was like a tiny private park. There were trees along the paths, benches in the shade where the blind could sit. The only thing you might notice was how quiet and peaceful it was. Nobody laughed. The loud voices of children were never heard. It was the absence of children that struck Hyman Kopfman, as he was then very young himself, and liked to think of a park like that as a place for children to play. But the one below the window was not for bouncing balls, nor rolling hoops. No one came to this park to fly a kite, or to skip rope at the edge of the gravel, or to play a game of hide and seek around the trees. In fact there was no need, in a park like that, to hide from anyone. You could be there, right out in the open, and remain unseen. It was Paul Kopfman who pointed out that they might as well go down and sit there, as nobody would know whether they were blind or not. Nobody would notice that Hyman Kopfman was wearing celluloid cuffs and pearl gray spats, or that Paul Kopfman was wearing a skirt and a peasant blouse. Nobody would care, down there, if their clothes were out of date, or that when Hyman Kopfman talked his wax-colored gums were inclined to bleed. It was the talking that made him excited, and the excitement that made his gums bleed, but down there in the garden he was not excited, and nobody cared. There were always flowers, because nobody picked them. There were birds and butterflies, because nobody killed them. There were no small boys with rocks and sticks, nor big boys with guns. There was only peace, and his brother Paul sat on the wooden benches talking with the women, as he didn't seem to care how old, and strange, and ugly they were. In some respects, he might as well have been blind himself.

How long did this go on—? the Colonel said, as he knew it couldn't go on forever. Nothing out of this world, nothing pleasant like that, ever did.

Well, one day his brother Otto—Hyman Kopfman said—his brother Otto put his head out the window and . . .

Never mind—! said the Colonel, and leaned forward as if

to shut him up. He wagged his hand at the wrist, and the blue vein on his forehead crawled from his hair.

A man like you, Hyman Kopfman said, an old soldier, a Colonel, a man with gold medals—

Never mind! the Colonel had said, and took from the table his silver lighter, holding it like a weapon, his arm half cocked, as if ready to throw.

Was Hyman Kopfman impressed? Well, he just sat there: he didn't go on. He smiled, but he didn't repeat what Otto had said. No, he just smiled with his bleeding gums, then raised the pale blue stump of his leg, sighted down the shinbone, pulled the trigger, and said *Bang!* He was like that. He didn't seem to know how hopeless he was.

For example, this Kopfman had only one foot but he sent out both of his shoes to be polished: he had only one arm, but he paid to have both sleeves carefully pressed. In the metal locker at the foot of his bed hung the pin-stripe suit with the two pair of pants, one pair with left leg neatly folded, and pinned to the hip. Some people might ask if a man like that needed two pair of pants. It was strange behaviour for a person who was dying day by day. Not that he wanted very much, really—no, hardly more than most people had—all he really seemed to want was the useless sort of life that the Colonel had lived. To have slept with a woman, to have fought in a war, to have won or lost a large or small fortune, and to have memories, before he died, to look back to. Somehow, Hyman Kopfman had picked up the notion that life was hardly worth living, but it was no consolation, since he had lived so little of it. He had picked up the facts, so to speak, without having had the fun. He always used the word "fun" as he seemed to think that was what the Colonel had had.

Night after night the Colonel listened to this as he played with his lighter, or smoked too much, but he said very little as he felt that Hyman Kopfman was very young. Not in years, perhaps, but in terms of the experience he should have had. His idea of fun was not very complicated. His idea of life being what it was, the Colonel found it hard to understand why he hadn't reached out and put his hands on it. But he hadn't. Perhaps this thing had always been in his blood. Or perhaps life in America had not panned out as he had thought. At the first mention of Chicago, Hyman Kopfman would wave his stubby arm toward the window, roll his eyes, and make a dry rattle in his throat. That was what he felt, what he seemed to think, about America. But there was nothing that he wanted so much as to be out there living in it.

The case of Hyman Kopfman was indeed strange, but not so strange, in some respects, as the case of the old man in the bed on his right. The Colonel had been failing; now for no apparent reason he began to improve. Now that Hyman Kopfman was there beside him—a hopeless case if there ever was one—the Colonel's pulse grew stronger, he began to eat his food. He sat propped up in bed in the manner of a man who would soon be up. He even gazed through the window like a man who would soon be out. Here you had the Colonel, who had nothing to live for, but nevertheless was getting better, while Hyman Kopfman, who hungered for life, was getting worse. It didn't make sense, but that was how it was. Not wanting to live, apparently, was still not wanting to die. So the Colonel, day by day, seemed to get better in spite of himself.

The very week that Hyman Kopfman took a turn for the worse, the Colonel took that turn for the better that led the Doctor to suggest that he ought to get up and walk around. Adjust himself, like a new-born babe, to his wobbly legs. So he was pushed out of the bed, and the terry cloth robe that hung for months, unused, in the locker, was draped around his sloping shoulders and a pair of slippers were put on his feet. In this manner he walked the floor from bed to bed. That is to say he toddled, from rail to rail, and the effort made the sweat stand on his forehead and the blue vein crawl like a slug from his thinning hair. But everybody in the ward stared at him enviously. He could feel in their gaze the hope that he would trip, or have a relapse. But at least they were courteous on the surface, they remarked how much stronger he was looking, and made flattering comments on how well he carried himself. They spoke of how fine he would soon look in his uniform. All this from perfect strangers; but Hyman Kopfman, the one who had spoken to him intimately, snickered openly and never tired of making slurring remarks. He referred to the Colonel's soft arms as chicken wings. He called attention to the unusual length of the Colonel's neck. Naturally, the accident that had nearly killed the Colonel had not widened his shoulders any, and there was some truth in the statement that he was neck from the waist up. Nor had the Colonel's wide bottom, like that of a pear, which seemed to hold his figure upright, escaped Hyman Kopfman's critical eye. Nor his feet, which were certainly flat for an army man. A less disillusioned man than the Colonel would have made an official complaint, or brought up the subject of Hyman Kopfman's two-pants suit. But he said nothing. He preferred to take it in his stride. One might even say that he seemed to wax stronger on it. It was this observation, among others, that upset Hyman Kopfman the most, and led him to say things of which he was later ashamed. It was simply too much, for a dying man, to see one getting well who had nothing to live for, and this spectacle always put him into a rage. It also considerably hastened his end. It became a contest, of sorts, as to whether the Colonel would get back on his feet before Hyman Kopfman lost another limb, or managed to die. In this curious battle, however, Hyman Kopfman's will power showed to a great advantage, and he deteriorated faster than the Colonel managed to improve. He managed to die, quite decently in fact, during the night. A Saturday night, as it happened, and the Colonel was able to call his wife and ask her to bring a suitable floral offering when she came.

FOREWORD

FROM Hawthorne to Faulkner the mythic past has generated what is memorable in our literature—but what is not so memorable, what is often crippling, we have conspired to overlook. This is the tendency, long prevailing, to start well, then peter out. For the contemporary, both the writer and the reader, this pattern of failure may be more instructive than the singular achievements of the past. The writer's genius, as a rule, is unique, but in his tendency to fail he shares a common tradition. This blight has been the subject of many inquiries, and the prevailing opinion has been that an unresponsive and Philistine culture has, as a rule, corrupted the writer's promise. Such an exception as Henry James, the exile, would merely seem to prove the rule. He succeeded or he failed—depending on the point of view—by becoming a non-American.

"Mr. Henry James, great artist and faithful historian," Joseph Conrad observes, "never attempts the impossible." This would seem to be the opposite, however, of accepted American practice. Failure, not success, is the measure of an artist's achievement. Mr. Faulkner has given this notion fresh currency in a recent statement concerning Thomas Wolfe: Wolfe was the greatest of them all, Faulkner said, because he tried to do the impossible. This is tantamount to saying that the dilettante is superior to the master craftsman, since the master craftsman achieves what he sets out to do. Failure, not achievement, is the hallmark of success. The romantic origins of this statement are less pertinent to this discussion than the prevailing tendency to find in such a statement a profound truth. The great writer *must* fail. In this way we shall know that he is great. In such a writer's failure the public sees a moral victory: what does his failure prove but how sublime and grand the country is? This point of view has so much to recommend it that to call it into question smacks of un-Americanism. It calls, that is, for a shrinking of the national consciousness.

It is the purpose of this book to inquire if this climate of failure is not linked, in a logical fashion, with the prevailing tendency of the American mind to take to the woods. Literally, like Thoreau, or figuratively, like Faulkner, our writers of genius face backward while their countrymen resolutely march forward. It is little wonder, faced with this fact, that we lead such notably schizoid lives.

Reappraisal is repossession, and this book is an act of reappraisal. In such a fashion I seek to make my own what I have inherited as clichés. To make new we must reconstruct, as well as resurrect. The destructive element in this reconstruction is to remove from the object the encrusted cliché. Time itself, in architecture and sculpture, does this in terms of what it leaves us. The fragment means more to us—since it demands more of us—than the whole. The mutilations are what we find the most provocative and beautiful. Since we cannot, in any case, possess the original—which exists in one time and serves one purpose—our reappraisal is an act of re-creation in which the work of art is the raw material. Short of this we are dealing with the bones of a fossil, the remains of a form that has served its purpose.

Such an attitude questions, of course, one of the sentiments most congenial to our nature—the uniqueness and inviolability of art. Art is indeed unique and inviolable—but its uniqueness may lie where we do not choose to look: in the creative response it generates in the participant; in the need he feels to repossess it in his own terms. The creative act itself is self-sufficient, having served the artist's purpose, but it lives on only in those minds with the audacity to transform it. The classic, from such a point of view, is that characteristic statement that finds in each age an echoing response—echoing, but not the same. Hemingway's Huck Finn is not Mark Twain's, nor is my Huck Finn Hemingway's. Nor do I mean to suggest that art itself is atomized in an infinite series of personal impressions—but that it survives, archetypally, in and through an endless series of transformations. Through Huck Finns, that is—through each age's reappraisal—the young heart is reassured and the consciousness expands.

TECHNIQUE
AND
RAW
MATERIAL

THE history of fiction, its pursuit of that chimera we describe as reality, is a series of imaginative triumphs made possible through technique. In *Mimesis*, Erich Auerbach has charted this course from Homer to Joyce. In aesthetic terms, *facts* are those sensations that have been convincingly processed by the imagination. They are the materials, the artifacts, so to speak, that we actually possess.

At the summit of technique we have such a craftsman as Joyce. There is so little craft in fiction on this scale that so much craft seems forbidding. Is the end result—we are inclined to ask ourselves—still alive? Is life, real or imaginary, meant to be processed as much as that? In Joyce the dominance of technique over raw material reflects one crisis of the modern imagination. Raw material has literally dissolved into technique.

In *Finnegans Wake* the world of Dublin happens to be the raw material that Joyce puts through his process—but the process, not Dublin, is the thing. It is the process that will give the raw material its enduring form. A parallel transformation is still taking place in what we call modern art. In Manet's portrait of Clemenceau the subject has vanished into the method—the method has become painting itself. Both Dublin and Clemenceau are processed into means, rather than ends, since the artist's problem is not to reconstruct the old, but to construct the new. It is characteristic of the mind of Joyce that the city of Dublin, shaped by his ironic craft, should not merely disappear but prove hard to find.

The brave new world has had its share of able craftsmen, but with the exception of Hawthorne and James, both closely linked to the old, they usually lacked what we would call the master touch. Raw material, usually the rawer the better, seemed to be their forte. On certain rare and unpredictable occasions craft might break through this devotion to raw material, but the resulting masterpiece had about it the air of an accident; not so much a crafty man-made thing, as a gift from above. The author usually took pains not to repeat it, or to learn from his experience. *Walden, Leaves of Grass, Moby Dick,* and the *Adventures of Huckleberry Finn* have in common this sense of isolation. Something of a mystery to both the author and the public, they resemble some aspect of a natural force—a pond, a river, a demonic whale—rather than something cleverly contrived by man. They seem to have more in common with Niagara Falls, Mammoth Cave, or Old Faithful than with a particular author, or anything so artificial as art. They are wonders, but *natural* wonders, like the Great Stone Face.

This notion of the natural, the unschooled genius who leaps, like a trout, from some mountain stream, seems to be central to our national egotism. It reappears every day in the child—or the backward, untutored adult—who draws, writes, strums a saw or plays a piano without *ever* having taken a lesson. That lessons might corrupt his talent, and ruin his promise, goes without saying. We believe in doing only what comes naturally.

But those natural moments in which we take so much pride—*Walden, Leaves of Grass, Moby Dick,* and *Huckleberry Finn*—are, without exception, moments of grace under pressure, triumphs of craft. The men who produced them are artists, innovators, of the first magnitude. Each of these statements is a contemporary statement, and each is unique. They represent new levels where, in the words of D. H. Lawrence, the work of art can ". . . inform and lead into new places the flow of our sympathetic consciousness, and it can lead our sympathy away in recoil from things that are dead."

If we now ask ourselves under what pressure these moments of grace are achieved, I believe it is the pressure of the raw material itself. Each of these men felt the need to domesticate a continent. In his essay on Hawthorne, Melville observed: "It is not so much paucity as superabundance of material that seems to incapacitate modern authors."

He had reason to know. It was not lack of material that silenced Herman Melville. The metaphysical woods that he found mirrored in the sea, and which drew him to it, of all aspects of the brave new world were the least inhabited.

*

With the passing of the last natural frontier—that series of horizons dissolving westward—the raw-material myth, based, as it is, on the myth of inexhaustible resources, no longer supplies the artisan with lumps of raw life. All of it has been handled. He now inhabits a world of raw-material clichés. His homemade provincial wares no longer startle and amaze the world. As a writer he must meet, and beat, the old world masters at their own game. In his "Monologue to the Maestro," Hemingway states the problem in his characteristic manner:

> There is no use writing anything that has been written better before unless you can beat it. What a writer in our time has to do is write what hasn't been written before or beat dead men at what they have done. The only way he can tell how he is going is to compete with dead men . . . the only people for a serious writer to compete with are the dead that he knows are good. . . .

With this credo the Portrait of the Artist as a Young American is permanently revised. The provincial is out. The dyed-in-the-wool professional is in. Not only do we have to meet the champ, we have to beat him. That calls, among other things, for knowing who he is. Such a statement could only come from a writer who knows you have to beat the masters with style and technique, and it is on these terms that he has won his place in the pantheon.

If raw material is so bad, if it is the pitfall and handicap to the artist that I am suggesting, why is it that American writers, through, rather than in spite of, this handicap, are one of the germinal forces wherever books are read. Here, I think, we have an instructive paradox. It involves us in the problem of good and bad taste. Not the good or bad taste of the artist, but the good or bad taste we find in his raw material. Good taste—*good* in the sense that it is fashionable and decorative—usually indicates an absence of the stuff of life that the artist finds most congenial. Both the Parthenon and the urban apartment decorated with Mondrian and Van Gogh resist more than a passing reference, usually ironic in tone. The over-processed material, what we sense as overrefinement, is an almost fatal handicap to the artist: we feel this handicap in James—not in his mind, but in his material—and it is at a final extremity in Proust. Only a formidable genius, only a formidable technique, can find in such material fresh and vital elements.

Bad taste, on the other hand, is invariably an ornament of vitality, and it is the badness that cries out with meaning, and calls for processing. Raw material and bad taste—the feeling we have that bad taste indicates *raw* material—is part of our persuasion that bad grammar, in both life and literature, reflects *real* life. But bad taste of this sort is hard to find. Bad "good taste" is the world in which we now live.

In reference to Joyce, Harry Levin has said: "The best writing of our contemporaries is not an act of creation, but an act of evocation peculiarly saturated with reminiscences." This observation pertains to Joyce and Proust as it does to Fitzgerald and his dream of Gatsby, or to Hemingway's Nick in "The Big Two-Hearted River." In our time, that is, nostalgia is not peculiarly American.

But the uses to which the past is put allow us to distinguish between the minor and the major craftsman. The minor artist is usually content to indulge in it. But the labyrinthine reminiscence of Proust is conceptual, *consciously* conceptual, in contrast to the highly unconscious reminiscence in *Huckleberry Finn*. Not *knowing* what he was doing, Mark Twain was under no compulsion to do it again.

Twain's preference for *real* life—*Life on the Mississippi* —is the preference Thoreau felt for facts, the facts of Nature, and Whitman's preference for the man-made artifact. Something *real*. Something the hand, as well as the mind, could grasp. Carried to its conclusion this preference begins and ends right where we find it—in autobiography.

On this plane raw material and art appear to be identical. *I was there, I saw, and I suffered,* said Whitman, sounding the note, and the preference is still dear to the readers of the *Saturday Evening Post.* Wanting no nonsense, only facts, we make a curious discovery. Facts are like faces. There are millions of them. They are disturbingly alike. It is the imagination that looks behind the face, as well as looks out of it.

Letting the evidence speak for itself, the facts, that is, of the raw-material myth, the indications are that it destroys more than it creates. It has become a dream of abuse rather than use. We are no longer a raw-material reservoir, the marvel and despair of less fortunate cultures, since our only inexhaustible resource at the moment is the cliché. An endless flow of clichés, tirelessly processed for mass-media consumption, now give a sheen of vitality to what is either stillborn or secondhand. The hallmark of these clichés is a processed sentimentality. The extremes of our life, what its contours should be, blur at their point of origin, then disappear into the arms of the Smiling Christ at Forest Lawn. The secretary with the diaphragm in her purse, prepared to meet any emergency, will prove to be a reader of Norman Vincent Peale or Kahlil Gibran. Ten minutes of her luncheon will be turned over to *The Mature Mind.* The raw-material world of facts, of *real* personal life, comes full circle in the unreal phantom who spends real time seeking for his or her self in the how-to-do-it books—How to Live, How to Love, and, sooner or later, How to Read Books.

What was once raw about American life has now been dealt with so many times that the material we begin with is itself a fiction, one created by Twain, Eliot, or Fitzgerald. *From Here to Eternity* reminds us that young men are still fighting Hemingway's war. After all, it is the one they know best: it was made real and coherent by his imagination.

Many writers of the twenties, that huge season, would appear to be exceptions to the ravages of raw material, and they are. But it is the nature of this exception to prove the rule. In inspiration, the twenties were singularly un-American. An exile named Pound established the standards, and the left bank of Paris dictated the fashions. This lucid moment of grace was Continental in origin. With the exiles' return, however, it came to an end. The craftsmen who shaped and were shaped by this experience—Eliot, Fitzgerald, Crane, Hemingway, and so on—maintained their own devotion to the new standards, but they had little effect on the resurgent raw-material school. Whitman's barbaric yawp, which Pound had hoped to educate, reappeared in the gargantuan bellow of Wolfe and a decade of wrath largely concerned with the seamy side of life.

Once again that gratifying hallucination—the great BIG American novel—appeared in cartons too large for the publisher's desk. Once again the author needed help—could one man, singlehanded, tame such a torrent of life? If the writer caged the monster, shouldn't the editor teach him to speak? The point was frequently debated; the editor-collaborator became a part of the creative project, the mastering of the material as exhausting as mastering life itself. In a letter to Fitzgerald, who had suggested that there might be room for a little more selection, Thomas Wolfe replied: "I may be wrong but all I can get out of it is that you think I'd be a better writer if I were an altogether different writer from the writer I am."

Time and the river—was Fitzgerald suggesting they reverse themselves? That a writer swim against the very current of American life? He was, but the suggestion has never been popular. Tom Wolfe didn't take it, and the writer who does take it may find himself, however homegrown, an exile. He swims against the current; and the farther he swims, the more he swims alone. The best American fiction is still *escape* fiction—down the river on a raft, into the hills on a horse, or out of this world on a ship—the territory ahead lies behind us, safe as the gold at Fort Knox.

*

Raw material, an excess of both material and comparatively raw experience, has been the dominant factor in my own role as a novelist. The thesis I put forward grows out of my experience, and applies to it. Too much crude ore. The hopper of my green and untrained imagination was both nourished and handicapped by it.

Before coming of age—the formative years when the reservoir of raw material was filling—I had led, or rather been led by, half a dozen separate lives. Each life had its own scene, its own milieu; it frequently appeared to have its own beginning and ending, the only connecting tissue being the narrow thread of my *self*. I had been *there*, but that, indeed, explained nothing. In an effort to come to terms with the experience, I processed it in fragments, collecting pieces of the puzzle. In time, a certain over-all pattern *appeared* to be there. But this appearance was essentially a process—an imaginative act of apprehension—rather than a research into the artifacts of my life.

The realization that I had to create coherence, conjure up my synthesis, rather than find it, came to me, as it does to most Americans, disturbingly late. Having sawed out the pieces of my jigsaw puzzle, I was faced with a problem of fitting them together. There is a powerful inclination to leave this chore to someone else. In the work of Malcolm Cowley on William Faulkner, we may have the rudiments of a new procedure. Let the critic do what the author fails to do for himself. As flattering as this concept might be—to both the author and the critic—it must be clear that the concept is not tenable. The final act of coherence is an imaginative act—not a sympathetic disposal of parts—and the man who created the parts must create the whole into which they fit. It is amusing to think what the mind of Henry James would make of this salvage operation, a surgical redistribution of the parts of a patient who is still alive. Mr. Cowley's service to the reader is important—what I want to put in question is his service to the writer. This is implicit, if unstated, in any piece of reconstruction that attempts to implement what the writer failed to do himself.

This act of piety toward the groping artist—a desire to help him with his raw-material burden—is one with our sentiment that he labors to express the inexpressible. Like a fond parent, we supply the words to his stuttering lips. We share with him, as he shares with us, an instinct that our common burden of experience, given a friendly nudging, will speak for itself. At such a moment the mind generates those evocations peculiar to the American scene: life, raw life of such grace that nature seems to be something brought back alive. Out on his raft Huck Finn muses:

> Two or three days and nights went by: I reckon I might say they swum by, they slid along so quiet and smooth and lovely. Here is the way we put in the time.

In what follows we are putting in our own time. We are there. Memory is processed by emotion in such a way that life itself seems to be preserved in amber. But we know better; we know that it is more than life, and it is this knowledge that makes it so moving—life has been imagined, immortal life, out of thin air. Not merely that boy out on the river, but the nature of the world's imagination, there on the raft with him, will never again be the same. But at the end of his adventures, at the point where the fiction—like the reader—merges into fact, Huck Finn sums it all up in these pregnant words:

> But I reckon I got to light out for the Territory ahead of the rest, because Aunt Sally she's going to adopt me and civilize me, and I can't stand it. I been there before.

So has the reader. Aunt Sally has his number, but his heart belongs to the territory ahead.